ROCCO AND BLOSSOM
A LOVE STORY

Rocco and Blossom
A Love Story

---

*
*
*
*
*
*
*

Margie Lockwood

There are many forms of abuse—physical, verbal, mental,
emotional. Whether inflicted in anger or perceived
love, the effects go on forever.

*
*

A couple use the sexual intimacy of their
marriage to work through their
childhood abuse.

To order additional copies of this book, contact:
Xlibris Corporation
1-888-795-4274
www.Xlibris.com
Orders@Xlibris.com
119017

For Michaela,
wise beyond her years.

Special thanks to Susan for her help and encouragement and to Jessie for her tireless work and patience with her computer-illiterate sister.

*

*

*

And of course, Phil . . . I love you everywhere I look.

Music Acknowledgments

Room to Breathe CD 2002, produced by Delbert McClinton and Gary Nicholson: "Ain't Lost Nothing" McClinton, Nicholson, Kim Wilson—"Don't Want to Love You" McClinton, Billy Lawson—"Same Kind of Crazy" McClinton, Nicholson—"Won't Be Me" McClinton, Nicholson, Al Anderson.

Acquired Taste CD 2009, produced by Don Was with Gary Nicholson, Delbert McClinton: "Mama's Little Baby" McClinton, Nicholson, Kevin McKendree—"Willie" McClinton, Nicholson

"Any Man of Mine" 1995 Shania Twain and Robert "Mutt" Lange
"Blue Christmas" 1948 Jay W. Johnson and Billy Hayes
"Boot Scootin' Boogie" 1990 Ronnie Dunn
"If I Were a Carpenter" 1966 Tim Hardin
"If You've Got the Money, I've Got the Time" 1950 Lefty Frizzell and Jim Beck
"I'm a Cowboy" 1994 Rick Russell
"Innamorata" 1955 Harry Warren and Jack Brooks
"Loving You" 1957 Jerry Leiber and Mike Stoller
"Me and Bobby Magee" 1969 Kris Kristofferson and Fred Foster
"Nothing On but the Radio" 2010 Byron Hill, Odie Blackmon, and Brice Long
"Oh You Beautiful Doll" 1911 Nat Ayers, Seymour Brown
"One for My Baby/One More for the Road" 1943 Harold Arlen and Johnny Mercer
"Sway" 1953 Pablo Beltran Ruiz, English lyrics Norman Gimbel
"Till There Was You" 1957 Meredith Wilson

"The First Time Ever I Saw Your Face" 1962 Ewan McColl

"Theme from the Stripper" 1958 David Rose

"Then" 2009 Chris Dubois and Ashley Gorley

"Through the Years" 1981 Steve Dorss and Marty Panzer

"Why Don't We Just Dance" 2009 Jim Beavers, Jonathan Singleton, and Darrell Brown

"With You I'm Born Again" 1979 Carol Connors

"You Gave Me a Mountain This Time" 1960s Marty Robbins

PROLOGUE

"Dr. Carnavale? We have him all comfortable now if you'd like to come with me."

She looked up, the dazed and bruised expression still there after an hour of fear and confusion, hands clenched tightly on her lap.

Linda, the head ICU nurse, had seen her over the years; but she looked smaller now, dignified even in her flounced denim skirt and peasant blouse, her gray shoulder-length hair pinned back with barrettes centered with turquoise stones.

She stood carefully. Linda lightly held her arm and guided her down the hall. They turned into the room, and even though she knew what she would see, despair settled on her at the sight of the tubes and monitors. There he lay, his beautiful white hair still thick with waves, his eyelashes surprisingly black.

"As the doctor told you, he's comfortable, and nothing will happen until you say so. If you'd like, you could go home until your children arrive," pushing a chair closer for her even as she said it and moving a table closer so she could reach the tissues and ice water. "There's a blanket here, and feel free to lay on the other bed if you like. We'll be right down the hall if you need us."

She found his left hand with both of hers and laid her forehead against them. "I'm so sorry, my darling. I know I promised. It's just until the children get here. I didn't want you all stiff and cold when they came. Don't be mad. I love you."

Oh how she wished it was a dream, that she'd wake up and hear him, "Baby girl, I'm here. Where are you?" Fifty-five years—how could it be, how could it possibly be—since the day she first saw him.

Book One

BOOK ONE

ONE

They Meet

"Blossom! Blos-sum-m!" her dad hollered from the bottom of the stairs. She came out of her room to the top of the stairs, her arms folded across her chest, a petite and unusually pretty seventeen-year-old with that universal teenage what-now look about her.

"I saw Dr. Royce last night and enrolled you for an advanced class. Just don't come into the office this week, and you'll have plenty of time to finish before you leave. Here's his Web info," laying a paper on the foyer table. "Just send him your work as you go." She nodded and went back to her room.

She heard her mother say, "Cal, why do that? We just got back, and there are things she needs to get ready before we go."

"Oh, she'll be fine. She needs to keep her mind active. We've been in a relaxed mode all summer. Time to get into practice before college."

It annoyed her when they talked about her as if she wasn't there, but the class didn't bother her. Any type of math came easy, and she liked Dr. Royce. It was something to do.

By Thursday she had finished up, and it seemed rude not to see Dr. Royce at all, so she decided to drop her last assignment off in person and then go to her dad's office and say good-bye to the girls. She slipped on a white peasant blouse, a flounced denim skirt, and added the wide leather cinch belt she bought in Santa Fe and her buckskin moccasins.

She opened the door to the classroom quietly, suddenly conscious she didn't even know the hours, and they may be in the middle of something. She slipped in, hoping to go unnoticed, but Dr. Royce called out, "Blossom, come in, come in. I got all your assignments, great work."

"Thank you, Doctor, I just wanted to drop these final things off. I enjoyed the course."

"Tell your parents I said hello, and good luck at Penn. I know you'll excel there. Drop in any time."

She turned to walk between the desks back to the door, her eyes down. A pair of work boots pulled back to let her pass. She glanced up to nod thanks to the owner and looked into impossibly crystal blue eyes. The air crackled, the floor moved, there was a roaring in her ears, she couldn't breathe. She knew she bumped into a couple of desks; then she was outside blinking and gulping in air. What happened? What just happened? She saw a bench and was making her way hand over hand around to the front when a voice said softly, "Blossom?"

She knew who it was, couldn't turn, and tried to arrange herself on the bench. "Yes," she croaked; she knew she did, and he said, "That's an interesting name. I'm Rocco Carnavale, you were looking at me? Have we met before?"

She busied herself with her eyes down, placing her purse just so on the bench. "No, no, I'm sorry, I was just dizzy there for a minute."

"You haven't been in class before."

"No, no." *Oh, my heart is pounding so hard; I can hardly hear him.* "I've been sending my work to him, I mean I just got back to town, I've never been to class," wringing her hands then clutching her purse, breathing hard. "I mean I have to get to my dad's office."

"Hey, no problem, it's okay, I just wondered if you'd like to get a cup of coffee."

"Ohh." Practically gasping now, she looked at him and wobbled again, bumping into the bench. "Why, yes, yes, that would be very nice." *Oh my god, he's so beautiful.* "I'll just clear that with my mother and get back to you."

Now seeming to enjoy her panic, he sat on the bench, stretching out his legs and crossing his ankles. He grinned. "Do you always ask your mother's permission to go out for coffee?"

"Well, no"—looking around, anywhere but at his face, squeezing her purse—"it's just that it's, well, it's never come up. I just haven't done that. I mean I don't have to ask permission, I just wanted to mention it to her, I mean."

Quietly, "How old are you, Blossom?"

"Well, seventeen, I'm seventeen, but I'll be eighteen in a couple months, even sooner actually, I'll be eighteen," taking big breaths.

"Would you like to give me your number so I can see if you've got this permission? I mean, you know, after you mention it to her," grinning again, teasing her.

"Yes, I have my phone," but she dropped her purse, and her eyes filled with tears.

"Whoa, whoa"—gently now, a different voice—"it's okay, I'll put it in my phone, can you tell me?"

Staring into his eyes with a stricken look, she shook her head no, tears overflowing.

"It's okay, it's okay, give me your phone. See I'm doing it, no problem. It's all fine now, everything's okay. Right? It's okay for me to call?"

"Yes, yes. I have to go. I'm having a little trouble breathing," keeping her eyes down.

"Are you all right to drive? Can I walk you to your car?"

"No!" too loudly. Quieter, "No. I'm fine. If you'll just wait until tomorrow. I'm, I'm having a little trouble breathing. I'm going now, I have to go to work."

He smiled as she hurried to her car, trying not to run, her dark hair moving in time with her skirt. *A pretty girl, a very pretty girl.* He felt a little sleazy making her uncomfortable, and why was his heart working overtime?

For almost three years, he had told himself, "Just work, no girls, no girls." Before, he had dealt with girls in a drunken haze, couldn't remember any faces. Using them for what he wanted. Now what was this? His mind wouldn't let him think of her chest. It seemed disrespectful. All he could see were her eyelashes wet with tears lying against her cheeks and her hands flitting around, so small. A sweet scent lingered around him. No, better not call. Things were simple now, didn't need anything to think about. But it would be rude not to call after he said he would. He'd just call to be polite. Tomorrow, the next day, no hurry. Her eyes were pretty.

He lasted until eight o'clock. He told himself he should call in case she did want to go for coffee. She might want to go in the morning. It was the sensible thing to do. People usually had coffee in the morning, didn't they?

She was in her room trying to read, trying not to think about whether he would call in the morning. Her phone chimed. She didn't get many calls, and her heart stopped when she saw "Rocco" on the screen. *Oh god, I'm not ready; I'm not ready.* "Hello," softly.

"Blossom, it's Rocco. I thought I'd better call tonight. Did you check with your mother? About going out for coffee?"

"Yes, yes," nervous and breathing hard, but better since he was not near. "She did wonder how old you are. That was my fault, I didn't want to call you a boy, so I said I met a man in class who asked me to go for coffee, and I said, 'Well, he's not a man, but he's not a boy,' and she said, 'Blossom, you're blathering,' that's what she says sometimes," finally taking a breath and slowing down. "So she just wanted to know how old you are, that's all," big sigh.

"I'm twenty. Do you think that's a deal breaker?"

"Oh, no, no, she said three or four years older probably wouldn't be appropriate."

"So twenty puts us under the wire, right?"

"Oh, yes, yes, twenty is fine."

"Would you like to go for coffee then?"

"Yes, I'd like that." He could hear her taking big breaths and suddenly cared a lot that she had said yes.

"Would ten be good for you?"

"Yes, ten would be fine," the commitment making her breathe faster.

"Where would you like to go?"

"I like the chocolate one at McDonald's."

"Blossom, we don't have to go to McDonald's."

"But I like their chocolate one. I don't like to waste money, my father doesn't like us to waste money."

Sensing she was getting nervous again, he said, "McDonald's is fine, McDonald's it is. So we'll meet in the parking lot at ten? I have a silver truck, I'll watch for you." Reluctant to hang up, he said, "We're doing a little better on the phone, don't you think?"

"It was hard this morning, I didn't know what was happening and then the proximity, I was having trouble breathing, but I'm fine now," determinedly. "I'm fine now."

"Do you have to go? Can we talk awhile?"

"Why, yes," a little nervously. "That would be nice."

"You said you had just come back to town?"

"We spend a couple months in New Mexico when school's out. We just got back last week."

"So you were on vacation?"

"Oh no"—laughing a little—"we're working. My parents have a clinic on an Indian reservation there, and we all help."

"That's interesting. What kind of clinic?"

"It's a medical clinic, my father is a doctor. It's a free clinic he's been running for years. Ever since I was seven, we go there."

"You didn't work when you were seven, did you," chuckling.

"Well, actually, yes. We're all expected to work. My father says we should help other people a couple months out of the year when we have a comfortable life the rest of the year."

"Well, that's something. You said *we*, do you have brothers and sisters?" Lying back, he suddenly realized his bed was comfortable, and a nice breeze was coming in the window, and he was not angry for the first time he could remember. He loved her voice.

"I have a brother, Phoenix, he's fifteen. I call him Nixie, but he doesn't like it anymore. We're supposed to call him Nix now," giggling a little, the sound making him smile.

"You have interesting names—Blossom and Phoenix."

"I know. I don't mind. I always thought my parents were closet hippies or something. My brother doesn't like his name, but I tell him just be happy they weren't in Albuquerque," giggling again.

He was smiling again, loving it. "Where did your name come from?"

"It's from a flower in the southwest, the squash blossom. The Indians use the image on things they make, jewelry and belts. You'd probably recognize it if you saw it." Shyly, "I could wear a belt of squash blossoms tomorrow."

"I'd like that. I guess I'd better let you go now."

"Oh, but I didn't ask you about your name or family or anything. I'm sorry. I was blathering like my mother says."

"You weren't blathering at all. It was interesting. We'll pick up there tomorrow, okay? Ten o'clock. You'll be there, right?"

"Oh yes, yes," happily. "I'll be there." Quietly, "I'm so glad you called tonight, Rocco. It was very nice talking to you. I was afraid you would call, and then I was afraid you wouldn't," nervous giggle.

"I'm glad I did too, Blossom. I'll see you in the morning at ten. Good night."

"Good night, Rocco," softly.

He forced himself to hang up the phone. He would have liked to go on, but it seemed too good to be true, and he didn't want to push it. He already knew he wanted to see her again, so he hoped what he had to tell her tomorrow wouldn't make a difference. He lay there for a while, smiling, remembering her voice. He had just seen her that morning, and somehow the world seemed better.

She drove into McDonald's parking lot, and he was leaning against the back of his truck, ankles crossed. Blue jeans, denim shirt, black dress boots. *Oh god, he's beautiful.* She couldn't look at him close yesterday, black wavy hair, those eyes—she could see them from here. Oh god, her heart was pounding in her ears again. She couldn't do this. She stepped on the brake and stared, forgetting what to do next. He waved his hand slightly, reminding her to pull into a spot. Her cheeks flamed. Tears came into her eyes. She managed to stop the car and take the key out but then covered her face with her hands. *I can't do this. I can't.*

A tap on the window, his finger motioning her out. She bit her lip, breathing hard, shaking her head no. He tapped again, nodding yes, and motioning her out with his finger. She opened the door.

"Good morning, I'm glad you came."

"I don't know, I don't think I can stay," looking down and breathing hard.

"Sure you can. We did fine on the phone last night, didn't we? We'll just go have a cup of coffee like normal people," grinning. He put his hand on her back, guiding her to the entrance. She shivered as it burned through her blouse.

"We're fine," he whispered. "We're doing fine," guiding her to a booth by a window.

"You can look up occasionally," he chided as she kept her eyes lowered, clutching her hands.

"Yes, yes," she said. "I'm just having a little trouble breathing."

"Oh, the breathing thing. Well, you get that under control, and I'll get the coffee. There's a couple ones with chocolate, shall I just pick one?" She just managed a little nod, and he could see she was fighting tears again. He reached across to pat her hands and reassure her, and a spark startled them both. They looked into each other's eyes to see if they both felt it. They had—her look frightened, his confused.

She tried to breathe steadily while he was gone, fighting the urge to run. As he slid into his seat and set the cups down, he smiled, "Okay, I felt that. I'm man enough to admit it."

"Thank you," she said quietly. "It's nice not to be alone in a strange land."

He lifted his eyebrows, then a gentle smile. "You're right, Blossom, you're right."

He waited a few seconds, a couple of sips of coffee. "Well, I might as well get right into it. I'd like to see you again, so I need to talk to you about something. We got past the age thing, but this might be the deal breaker."

She looked up and said quietly, "There are no deal breakers."

"Well, I want to tell you some things, Blossom. They may not matter to you, but they might to your parents. You're their little girl, and all of a sudden, some guy is hanging around they've never seen before. Just in case they're the type who would google me, I want you to hear it from me so you can say you already know, okay?"

Shaking her head slightly, her eyes still down, she smiled and said, "My parents wouldn't do that. They're not like that."

"Well, that's fine. I just want you to know then. Before I start, though, I realized after we hung up last night that I don't know your name."

"You know my name, it's Blossom."

"I mean your last name."

"Oh, oh my, I'm sorry, it's Richards. Blossom Richards." Speaking confidently now, in known territory, "I live at 530 Shadow Oaks, and my parents are Calvin and Elaine Richards. My father is a doctor, an internist on Liberty Street, and my mother runs his office. She's actually a physician's assistant, but the government and insurance companies require so much paperwork anymore that she has to oversee things." Leaning forward a little and whispering, "She's not too happy about it either."

He reached across the table and shook her hand. She glanced up fearfully but then smiled a little. "Well, how do you do, Blossom Richards. I'm Rocco Carnavale. I live at seventeen eight-fifteen Cussewago Road. My parents are Anthony and Marie Carnavale, and he owns Carnavale Construction."

"There, we are all official. Now I can get on with why I wanted to talk to you in person."

She shook her head and surprised him by looking directly at him for a second before looking down again and saying to her hands, "There are no deal breakers."

"That's very nice, Blossom, I appreciate that, but let's stay on point here so I can get this out." A big breath, "I quit school a couple weeks before I was sixteen."

"Oh, I'm so sorry. Didn't your parents talk to your guidance counselor? You were . . ."

"Blossom, all parents aren't like yours. Let me finish."

"I'm sorry, go on. But you know, you can't quit school before sixteen, and even then your parents have to sign . . ."

"Blossom," pointedly.

"I'm sorry. I won't interrupt again."

"Nobody signed anything, and no one came after me. I'm sure they were relieved to get rid of me."

"Ohh."

"Blossom . . ."

Nodding to go on, putting her hand out, her sympathy for him overriding her nervousness. He held her hand lightly, afraid to scare her. "So I was a wise guy who thought he knew everything. Things went from bad to worse. If your parents checked, they'd see a couple years of drunk and disorderly charges, a DUI, fights, a couple overnights in jail, one time three nights. It wouldn't look good, Blossom."

"Oh, I'm so sorry, that's too bad."

"You don't have to be sorry, it's over now. A cop finally got through to me when I was seventeen, and I've been getting myself back on track. I got my GED, quit drinking, and stopped hanging out with the same crowd."

"Your GED, that's a wonderful accomplishment. I've heard that's very hard to do," smiling sincerely.

He just looked at her a few seconds. He could see she was genuinely interested, and his eyes stung, further confusing him. "You're very sweet, but this isn't about patting me on the back. Do you have any questions? Is there anything there that's a deal breaker for you? Be honest, now."

"No," she said confidently, "no deal breakers."

"Blossom, I just told you I've been in jail. Don't you have any questions?"

"But that was a long time ago, you were a child."

He shook his head in amazement. "Okay, so if they should say anything, don't make excuses for me and don't be defensive. Just say I told you, and I'll answer any questions they have." He sat back. "Whew, let's relax for a minute and drink our coffee."

She could feel he was studying her, and she began to blush even before he said, "You're very beautiful, you know."

As if by rote, she said, "My mother says appearances are an accident of birth and nothing we can take credit for. Our job is to keep ourselves neat and clean and put the proper foods in our bodies," sitting back relieved as if she had answered a question correctly.

He wriggled his eyebrows like Groucho Marx. "Well, you certainly have done a good job at that."

She blushed furiously, her hands flying around touching her cup, her lips, finally grasping each other.

"I'm sorry about that. That was rude. Men are scum."

She glanced up a tiny second before looking down again. "You're not scum," softly.

"You're being way too easy on me today. Your clothes are interesting. Is that the belt you told me about?"

"Yes," softly. Suddenly a belt was too personal to be talking about. She put her head down even further.

"Do you buy your clothes around here?" worried she might bolt at any minute.

She picked at her skirt nervously. Her dress was a fawn-colored lightweight chamois with brown ribbon around the peasant neck and edging the flounces that started below her belt. In a rush of words, "No. No, the school year is usually so busy, we usually shop in Santa Fe. My aunt Mim is there, she loves to shop. She's my father's sister. Her name is Mimosa. She's lots of fun, you'll like her," then blushed again, her hands flying when she realized what she had said.

"I'm sure I will," softly.

Her tears overflowed. "I'm sorry. Oh, is everyone looking? I'm so sorry. I'm embarrassing you."

"You can't embarrass me, Blossom. People have come and gone, there are different ones here now. Would you like something to eat? Do you have to be any place?"

"I don't eat too much here. I hate to have you wait for a special order. I'll get it."

"No, you won't. What would you like?"

"Well"—nervously—"I usually get a grilled chicken sandwich with nothing on it."

"Nothing?"

"Yes, just the chicken on the bun. Nothing else." He raised his eyebrows but went for the order. While he was gone, she rinsed her coffee cup and got some ice water, wondering if she'd be able to eat at all. She wanted to hear his voice. He was so beautiful, so nice. She put her hands over her face to compose herself, and just then he returned.

"Take a couple deep breaths, we're doing good." She smiled and breathed deep but teared up. Quietly, "We're okay, we're fine, Blossom, big breaths." Lightly, "You can see I'm not worried about their food," automatically putting hers on a napkin, opening it for her, setting her water to her right. Arranging his mushroom swiss burger and medium fries, he watched her pick at the corner of her sandwich and said, "I'm getting a Coke, I'll be right back." He detoured to the counter for a knife and fork and cut a couple of pieces of her sandwich for her. Biting into his burger, "This is really good, would you like a bite?"

"I know. Nixie had that once. It is good."

He cut off a little bite and handed it to her on the fork.

"Mmm." That is good.

"I can get you one."

"No, that's too much beef for me. A bite is fine."

"Is there any place you have to be today? Maybe we could take a drive."

The mention of being alone with him started her hands flitting around again—to her lips, her cup, her lap.

He smiled. "You're like a little hummingbird. It's just a drive."

Breathing hard, "That would be very nice, but I have to teach a class at two."

He checked his watch, saw that it was twelve forty-five, and said "We'll just chat a while longer then. What kind of class, you don't seem old enough to teach classes."

"I wish I didn't have to go, but my dad volunteered me. It's a computer class. I've been teaching computer classes of one kind or another since junior high. I have some kind of affinity for them. Do you have somewhere you should be?" She seemed anxious to change the subject.

"I should be working, but if I carry books around with me, no one asks questions. They're so relieved I'm shaping up." He winked at her, and her heart flipped.

"You haven't told me where you work."

"Actually, there's another reason I wanted to meet today, so since time's short, let's talk about that tonight. May I call you tonight?"

"Yes, yes, please," smiling so happily; *his* heart flipped.

"Well," he said, sitting up straight and talking formally, "the reason I called this meeting today"—and was rewarded with a lilting laugh—"today we're having coffee, so now I wondered if you'd like to go on a date?"

"A date, a-a date?" worried look, her voice breaking, her hands flying around.

"Yes, Blossom, a date. You know, where I come to your house and pick you up, meet your parents—like that."

"But, but, what do you mean? You mean in your truck?" Breathing hard, tearing up, shaking her head, "I don't know if I could do that. I mean, where would we go?"

"Whoa, whoa." Quietly, "Do you want to go outside and get some air?"

She shook her head yes and covered her face with her hands. "Ohh, I'm embarrassing you. I'm so sorry."

"Blossom, I told you, you can't embarrass me. Let me clean up here—you've hardly eaten anything—you take big breaths, and we'll go outside." He took a step toward the garbage can, and she covered her face and whimpered. "I'm right here, I'm right here." He didn't care who heard him. He took her arm gently and led her outside.

They leaned against the side of his truck. "I'm so sorry, I'm so sorry. I better go. I can't breathe, I'm dizzy, I better go."

"No," sternly. "No," softly. "We've had a nice time. I don't want you to go like this. It's just a date, Blossom."

"I want to go on a date. I do, I do, but I can't breathe. I don't know what's happening."

"Blossom"—turning her chin toward him, her eyes full of tears, a strange feeling in his chest—"look at me just a second. We're attracted to each other. That's all it is. It's nothing to get upset about. Are we okay? May I still call you tonight? Can I see a smile—something? You're killing me here."

Eyes down, but a tremulous smile.

"Okay, go teach your class. Get ready, though, I'm going to ask you again." He could tell she was taking deep breaths as she walked to her car. So beautiful, so fragile. She gave him a weak little wave as she drove by, and he was already counting the hours until he could call her.

She got through her class, fixed dinner for her family, saw her mother watching her, but couldn't mention him—afraid he wouldn't call if she did. *She probably embarrassed him. He probably wouldn't call. Who would call a girl who cried all the time. Oh, please let him call.*

Her mother asked casually, "So you had coffee with your friend today? What was his name again?"

"Rocco. Rocco is his name. Yes, we had coffee at McDonald's. Lunch too, actually. It was very nice."

Just hearing the last part, her dad said, "You ate at McDonald's? That's a bad habit, honey, that food's not good for you. Don't be eating at those places at Penn. You're carrying a heavy load, you need nutritious food."

"Cal, she knows how to eat."

And from Nixie, "Rocco? Rocco who? Why didn't I hear about this?"

Blossom smiled at Nixie, already knowing how much she would miss him and worry about him. "I met a fellow at Dr. Royce's class. His name is Rocco Carnavale, and we had coffee this morning."

"And lunch, you just said."

"Yes, and lunch. He's very nice."

"Why would you have coffee with anyone? You never did before."

"Nixie, I'm almost eighteen. I'm going to have coffee occasionally."

"Well, you're having coffee, you're going to college, I don't like any of this."

She got up and started gathering dishes, kissing him on his head as she passed his chair. "You're just going to have to take over for me, then you'll be off to college yourself before you know it. Come help me with dessert."

In the kitchen, "Seriously, Blossom, it's going to be tough here."

"You'll be fine, just speak up for yourself when you need to. Really, they'll listen."

"All I hear about now is your grades, it's going to be worse when you're gone."

"You're a good student, Nixie, do your best. I'll be right at the end of the phone."

"They don't want good, Blossom, they want genius like you."

"Don't say that word, Nixie, you know I don't like it. I do good at a couple things. You're good at so many more things. Here, you take these two, I'll get these," handing him two bowls of the quick dessert she had made of lemon pudding, raspberries, and Cool Whip.

Her dad said, "Nix, you're going to have to learn to cook, huh, with Blossom gone."

Speaking up for him as she had slipped into the last few years, "Dad, let him enjoy the rest of the summer. He can think about that after school starts, and if he's in track or swimming, he won't have time." She reached over and ruffled his hair. "He worked hard this summer, didn't he? All those plants and then the office work."

"Yeah, good work, Nix, good work. So you all set, Blossom, you have everything you need?"

"Mom and I are going to check the list again Saturday to be sure. It's not like they don't have stores there, and I have my card. We'll see when we set my room up."

"Well, you be careful. Stay close to your area, use your head."

She usually enjoyed the after-dinner small talk. Knowing she was leaving had made it more melancholy, but she couldn't help hurrying through clearing up and stacking the dishwasher to get to her room, hoping he would call.

She could have kissed the phone when it vibrated and she saw his name. "I was afraid you wouldn't call."

"Why wouldn't I call?"

"Well, who wants to call a girl who cries all the time."

"We'll work through that, Blossom, it's not important. Are you okay now?"

"Yes, I'm fine, I'm fine. I just don't understand, and then I'm afraid I'll embarrass you, and then it gets worse."

"Blossom, I told you, you can't embarrass me. Remember when I said your parents would see 'drunk and disorderly' if they checked. That's just a nice phrase for disgusting. You couldn't possibly embarrass me more than I've embarrassed myself, so don't ever worry about it."

"I'm so sorry you were unhappy, Rocco—so young and so unhappy. It's sad, my heart hurts for you."

"The past is the past, Blossom, let's not get into it now. Where were we today?"

"You were going to tell me where you work," she said, wiggling into her pillow and smiling at how happy she was.

"Well, I work for my father at the construction company, and a couple nights a week, I cook at Mangia's."

"Really! I cook too. I mean I can put a meal on the table, not like at a restaurant. You must be really good. Did you go to school for that?"

"Not hardly," laughing a little. "Remember I said a cop finally got through to me? He's a friend of the owners. I think he twisted their arms. And once it was obvious I was staying home at night, my father said come back to the shop again. I've worked there off and on since I was a kid, but it never worked out. We fought all the time. Things have eased up lately since he's seen me carrying books around."

"But he must be very proud of you, getting your GED."

"Blossom, maybe I better get this in up front instead of dancing around it. My parents and I don't talk."

"What do you mean you don't talk?"

"I mean I don't talk to them, and they don't talk to me."

"Ohh, I'm so sorry."

"No big deal, Blossom. I work, I get something to eat, I go home to my room, I study, I watch TV or listen to music, it's been that way for the last couple years."

"But they must see how wonderful you're doing?"

"Like I said before, all parents aren't like yours, Blossom. My father has always been an angry man, it's best just to stay away from him. I've been deciding whether to continue courses for the construction business, like blueprint reading or something, or go to culinary school in Pittsburgh like the guys at Mangia's think I should." In a different voice, "Now I'm wondering if I'd want to be in Pittsburgh all week."

With a tentative, nervous laugh, "You'd be in Pittsburgh, and I'd be in Philadelphia."

"What do you mean, you'd be in Philadelphia?" an icy feeling forming in his stomach.

"At Penn, Rocco, that's where Penn is. Remember when Dr. Royce said, 'Good luck at Penn'? I'm going to college there a week from Sunday."

Long pause, voice gravelly, "Aren't you too young for college?"

"No, maybe a little, but seventeen isn't too unusual. Rocco, is it okay?" Breathing hard, "I thought you knew." Whimpering now, "It's not a deal breaker, is it? Is it, Rocco?" Desperately, "Rocco?"

"No, never"—but with a catch in his voice—"we'll work around it. It's okay, Blossom, we'll work around it."

"It's not okay, is it? Oh god, it's not okay," sobbing openly.

"Blossom, Blossom, it took me by surprise that's all. It's okay, it's okay, we'll work around it." Trying to put a smile in his voice, "A week from Sunday, huh. Wow, I have to work fast."

"Work fast?"

"Yeah, you know, to get you to like me . . . and she says, wait for it . . ."

Smiling, she filled in, "I already like you."

"And she reads her lines just right!"

Laughing, the danger past, "So what are you taking in college?"

"Computer sciences mostly, maybe some premed. My mom wants me to be a doctor, but I'm not going to be unhappy like they are. I mean, they're not unhappy, unhappy, but they don't like the profession now, so why would I want to do that. I just want to help people, I'll figure a way later."

"Those sound like tough courses, you must be really smart."

She overlooked it and said, "You must be really smart, taking Dr. Royce's class."

"I almost didn't go, and I wasn't sure I'd make it. I'm sure glad I did, Blossom."

"I don't know what made me take those last papers in either. It makes me shiver thinking what if I didn't. Oh, what if I didn't?" She teared up again.

"Don't get upset, we met that's all that's important. You know what I'm going to ask you now, don't you?"

A tiny, "Yes."

"So would you like to go out tomorrow night?"

"I do, I do, I just don't know, I don't know. How long do dates last?"

Laughing, "Well, say we went to a movie—there's a couple hours, and then maybe we stop for ice cream or something like that. Do you think you could manage that? Or I'd like to take you to dinner so we could talk now that I know you're leaving, that's a couple hours too."

"I think I could do that, I just like to know things ahead. If I know what to expect, I mean, like an outline, I mean."

He laughed. "I can make you an outline. At six thirty, I pick you up."

"Are you making fun of me?"

"No, I'm not, Blossom, I'll do anything you like. Do you have to ask your mother?"

"Of course not, I'm almost eighteen. Well, I'll just mention it to her since I haven't done it before, but I don't have to ask permission, for goodness sake."

Laughing softly, "So what do you think, dinner or a movie? I'm not sure what's on, but I'll check. Dinner, we'll be sitting across from each other, in case that's too much 'proximity' as you say. A movie, we'd be looking straight ahead if that would be easier."

"What would you like to do?"

"I'll check the movies and see what's on. I see a lot of movies, and I think I'd know if something good is on."

"I see a lot of movies too," happy to have another thing in common. "My family has movie night every Wednesday. We critique them, and we play games about famous lines. We've seen all kinds of movies."

"Well, let's do this. I'll pick you up at six thirty either way, and we'll check them out in the meantime. You know, we have a week, we can do movies and dinners all week. Do you have a lot planned for next week?"

She was so relieved he was thinking ahead. "No, I'm pretty sure my parents haven't planned anything. It might be a little touchy with Nixie. He thinks I'm abandoning him, but I'll spend time with him during the day. Tomorrow during the day, my mother wants to check over my list for college, but I'll tell her I have to be done by six thirty."

"What kind of list?"

"They list suggestions about linens, towels, laundry, things like that. I have my computer and everything. You can't have a car the first year, so shopping might not be easy."

"I've seen college dorms in movies, they seem pretty wild," trying to sound casual.

Sensing what he was thinking, she said in an adult tone he hadn't heard yet, "They are what you make them, Rocco. My father made sure I'm in an all-girl dorm. I'm going there because he wants me to study with a particular professor, and I owe it to my parents to do well. I have a scholarship, but it is still a very expensive proposition, and my parents expect a lot from me. I'm going to treat it like a job and immerse myself from eight to five, eat something, and get ready for the next day." Quietly, sighing deeply, "I was looking forward to it until yesterday."

"You keep looking forward to it, Blossom. I don't want your parents to think I'm interfering at all. Your family is important, we'll work around anything, okay? Do you want to?"

"I want to so much, Rocco, so, so much."

"Whatever it takes, then, whatever it takes." Hearing her start to cry, "I'll call you tomorrow, little one. Sleep tight, don't cry."

Sobbing now, inexplicably exhausted, "Good night, Rocco."

He sat on the edge of his bed, his head in his hands, breathing heavily. Finally, slapping his hands on his knees, he got up, went to his desk to start studying, and looked up—"If this is your idea of a joke, it's not funny. Throw anything you want at me, I'm not slipping," turned on his computer, and went to work.

She enjoyed her clothes, loved to shop for them, loved to wear them, but usually put on the first thing she saw when she opened the closet. Saturday she selected, then discarded, three or four before settling on the white crinkly flounced skirt and peasant blouse set. The red and blue embroidered flowers around the neck and flounces matched her favorite blue high-top moccasins. They were kid glove soft, comfortable, and familiar. She pinned back the sides of her hair with silver barrettes centered with squash blossoms and touched her lips with gloss. She occasionally used a touch of mascara, but she didn't have any waterproof, and crying was bad enough without having mascara running down her face. Her chest was already fluttering and her heart beating in her ears.

He pulled into the driveway through the open gate at six twenty-five, wanting to be early, but not too early. Blossom and her mother were on matching porch swings built on each side of the entrance door. He knew construction. The house was extremely well done and obviously expensive. As he got out of the truck, they took a couple of steps, Blossom a step behind her mother, biting on her clenched hands, looking worried.

"Good evening, Mrs. Richards, I'm Rocco Carnavale."

"Hello, Rocco, Dr. Richards is late this evening. I'm sure he will want to meet you another time. Where will you be going tonight?"

His mind had registered her "another time." Thank goodness she knows there will be another time. "Well, there are no appropriate movies on, so I thought dinner at Mangia's. Is that okay, Blossom?" He could see that she was close to falling apart, so he casually touched her elbow to guide her to the truck and said, "I'm sure we'll be back by ten, if that's all right?"

"That will be fine. Have a nice time, dear." Blossom raised her hand and waved without looking back, her eyes swimming with tears.

Taking his time putting on his seatbelt, pretending to check his visor and mirror to kill a couple of seconds, he grabbed some tissues from the center section and said, "Quick, dry your eyes and turn and wave. I don't want her to think you don't want to go." She did it quickly and gave her mother a happy smile as they pulled away. He got out of sight and pulled over.

"You okay?"

"I'm sorry, I'm sorry, I was okay until you stepped down from the truck," taking big breaths. "I don't . . ."

"We're doing fine, we're okay. Now let's have a nice time, this is our first date. See, we're in my truck driving down the street, you didn't think you could do that yesterday, right?"

She kept her eyes down but nodded yes.

"Is Mangia's okay? I didn't want her to think we didn't have a plan."

"It's fine. Is it expensive?"

"Blossom, I have money. I only spend money on food and my truck anymore. I have plenty of money."

"No, I didn't mean that. I don't eat that much, and I don't want you to waste your money."

"Don't worry, we'll find you something you like. They have a nice variety. I usually just grab fast food, so I'm looking forward to something good. You know, this is my first date too."

As before, when she was thinking of him, she forgot her nervousness. "But you're so handsome, you must have been on dates."

"The kind of girls I was around weren't the kind you ask out on dates, Blossom." She startled him by reaching over and putting her hand over his mouth and shaking her head no.

"You don't want me to talk about my crazy times?" She shook her head no, and he said, "Okay, if you want to know anything, you ask. I was young and stupid, that's all you really need to know."

She walked ahead of him to the door of the restaurant, and he thought, *My god, she's beautiful.* She turned at the door, looking frightened, biting her lip, and started to say, "I don't . . ."

"Yes, you can, we're going to have a nice evening like normal people. You look beautiful," touching her hair. She shivered but smiled. "That's my girl, let's do this."

The girls at the front desk looked startled, "Well, hello, Rocco, you working tonight?"

"No, I'm a customer tonight. This is Blossom. Blossom, Jean and Tammy."

"Hello," shyly, her eyes down.

"Any place you'd like to sit, Rocco?"

"Anything for two in section 4?"

"Sure, right this way." She sat them and then almost ran to the bar where most of the girls gathered at the service area. "Rocco's here with a girl in section 4." The available ones had virtually thrown themselves at him since he'd arrived to work, and nothing. They were dying of curiosity, and one by one made excuses to check the tables in section 4. "She's darling, but what is she, an Indian? Look at her clothes, did you see her shoes?"

She sat with her hands in her lap, looking down. He asked, "Would you like a shirley temple or something like that?"

"Water is fine."

"Come on now, this is a special occasion."

"I'm afraid the ginger ale will fill me up, and I won't be able to eat." Just then the waitress arrived, and she surprised him when she spoke right up and said, "I'll have water with lemon in a pretty glass, please," smiling at him. His smile was so beautiful; her heart jumped to her throat.

He said to the waitress, "A Bud Light with a frozen mug."

She whispered after the waitress left, "You're not twenty-one."

He whispered back, "I have a driver's license that says I am."

"But I don't want to be the reason you drink," looking concerned.

"I don't think I was an alcoholic, Blossom. I drank to get drunk so I would think I was having a good time. Now I set a one drink limit on myself just to live by some rules, and that's all I'll ever have."

When the waitress returned, she ordered a house salad with grilled chicken. He, a New York strip, baked potato with sour cream, and a vegetable gratin. "Wouldn't you like a little filet mignon, something like that?"

She smiled. "I'll have a bite of yours, I don't want to order it and waste any."

"You look beautiful, am I allowed to say that, and your hair is remarkable." When she looked uncomfortable, he said, "Oh, that's right, an accident of birth." She smiled and looked down at her hands.

"Did you go over your list today for your dorm?" Her look changed, and she started to breathe fast, so he said, "You know what, let's don't talk about college tonight. Tell me some more about New Mexico. Do you have a home there?"

"Oh, goodness, no. It's a very, very poor area, Rocco. It's not like there are homes to rent or anything. We used to have an RV the first few years, and then when Nixie got bigger, one of the families moved in with relatives, and we rent their home. It's more comfortable for us and gives them three months' rent. It's very basic though."

"Is that a nice way of saying it's a dump?"

She laughed a little. "Yes, I guess it's a dump. But when you're tired at night, a shower and a bed are all you need."

"That's really kind of amazing. What made your parents want to do that?"

"Well, my aunt in Santa Fe was a nurse too, so she and my mother went to help a friend, and my mom told my dad the doctor needed help, and it just went from there. Going there in the summer just became our normal way of life. My dad and mom are really happiest there. They're the team they wanted to be, and there's no paperwork. We keep files on the patients, of course, to know their medical histories, but since it's free, there are no insurance forms or any of that annoying paperwork. The last few years, I've been in the office, but I set up computers in their school for my senior project, and Nixie did the office. He did great."

"You mean your senior project for Meadville High?"

"Umm." She nodded. "I raised money to buy a dozen computers and then convinced the Bureau of Indian Affairs to let me put them in and teach. That's another government agency on my dad's list. He thinks they are the reason most reservations are so poor. I know people think they're all fine now because of casinos, but that's just a few tribes.

"A young girl like you did that? That's amazing. How do you know what to do?"

"Oh, I have a knack for computers, it's nothing unusual. You could have done something in construction for your senior project. I'm really mad at your guidance counselor for not encouraging you."

"Blossom, you're getting yourself upset over something you can't change. I'm fine now." Winking, "Even better the last couple days. So let's get back to you. I know I said we wouldn't talk about college, but I'm interested. What will you be doing there?"

She sighed and looked distressed. "Well, the short story is my dad wanted me to work with a particular professor, Dr. Ng. I had an interview to see if I was qualified. I was, so I'll be taking his class and working for his business. So that will be my main focus, along with my other classes, of course." She took a big breath and sat back.

"What will you be doing for him?"

"Companies want him to break into their computer systems to see if it can be done. We'll do that and then build a firewall so no one else can do it."

"Get out, you can't do that!"

"Umm, I can."

"Blossom, you're a tiny girl. You're a hacker?"

"It's not hacking if they want you to do it." She smiled.

"So say you wanted to break into the computers here. Could you do it?"

"Well, this is just a little business using their computers for intracompany information, but sure I could."

He looked stunned, pointed at her, and said, "*You* could do that."

"Sure. Just like that," lifting her hand and snapping her fingers.

The combination of her smile and the finger snap made him laugh out loud, so loud the waitress and patrons in the area looked startled. "You are unbelievable. Un-be-liev-able!"

She smiled happily, for the first time ever enjoying her knowledge because it tickled him.

The waitress came by and said, "Rocco, I believe that's the first time I've ever heard you laugh."

He smiled and said, "I think I'll be laughing a lot more from now on," looking at Blossom and giving her a slow wink.

She blushed bright red; and her hands started flitting around, to her lips, her glass, the table. He casually reached over with his left hand, caught one, then the other, and put them on the table under his, telling the waitress, "Bring us one cup of chocolate mousse, two decaf coffees, and the bill. Then we'll pop into the kitchen and say hi so they don't have to strain their necks, and tell them I said that."

They ate the mousse—he, two bites; she, licking the spoon with every bite. "Umm, I love chocolate," scraping the sides and examining the cup for any residue, not seeing him staring at her intensely. They said hello to the fellows in the kitchen, good-bye to the girls at the desk, and Rocco said "Let's stop at the restrooms on the way out."

"I'm fine."

"Blossom, don't be silly, we've been here three hours, and you've been drinking water. Stay inside the door until I call your name, okay, I don't want you to be out here alone."

She went, put a touch of lip gloss on, and looked in the mirror to see if she looked as different as she felt. Then the door opened an inch and a soft "Blossom?" She smiled at how wonderful it sounded.

On the way to the truck, "Your family has never come here?"

"No, maybe my parents have, and I didn't know it. We eat out a lot in New Mexico, but I usually cook here in town because they are tired at night. What do you do in the kitchen?"

"Saturday, I help the chef, I'm called a sous chef, and if it's quiet on Sundays, they let me do the entrees. I started as a dishwasher, and I've done about everything." They were settled in the truck, and he said, "I hate the evening to end, but I told your mother ten o'clock."

Shyly, "We could sit on the swings at my house. We'd technically be home."

He pointed at her and said, "That's a plan, baby girl. I don't want to get on their bad side. So how did you like our first date?"

Looking at her folded hands, she said quietly, "It was the most wonderful night of my life."

He squeezed her hands and said, "Mine too, Blossom, mine too."

As they walked to her swings, she pointed him to one and sat in the other. "We're doing so well, can't I sit beside you?"

"Please. It's been so nice, I don't want to fall apart. It's too close on one swing."

"Okay, okay. May I ask you a personal question?" She nodded yes, and he said, "Do you have a bra on?"

She jerked back, her eyes big, startled, put her hands to her mouth, but seemed to change her mind, and said, "Why, Mr. Carnavale, how you talk."

He laughed. "Scarlett O'Hara, *Gone With the Wind*."

She clapped her hands and said, "That's what we do in our family!" Then pretending to be serious, "That was very inappropriate, Rocco, but yes, I do. It's built into my blouse, but that's all of that discussion."

"I'm sorry, it was inappropriate," but grinned and said, "We have rules here."

She giggled and clapped again. "George Kennedy, *Cool Hand Luke*." They smiled at each other, happy they had found another thing in common. Just then the porch light flashed, and they both laughed out loud. He said, "Our first date and I'm already getting the flashing light. I better get out of here," standing up. "This was really nice, Blossom, may I kiss you good night?"

Her hands flew to her mouth. "I can't, too close, too close," tears welling up, breathing hard.

"It's okay, don't get upset. May I call you tomorrow?"

"Yes, please, please, yes." She watched as he got in his truck—so beautiful, so beautiful—and waved shakily as he drove away. She backed up to the swing as tears ran down her cheeks. Just then her mother opened the door. "Blossom! Did he say something to you?"

"No, not at all, it's just that he's-he's just so wonderful." She almost wished her mother would ask more questions, but instead she brushed aside the comment and said, "He seems very nice, but let's remember our priorities, you leave for Penn in a week."

"I know, Mom, I know," wishing she had asked him to call when he got home. She started upstairs, and Nixie came from the family room and walked up with her. "So how was your date, what'd you do?" She smiled happily at him. At least someone cared. "We had dinner at Mangia's, it was unbelievably wonderful." He wrinkled his brow and looked at her curiously, then turned and went to his room.

Rocco called at nine in the morning. "Is this too early to call? I didn't know if you went to church."

"No, I haven't been going to church for a while, but we're going to the country club to have brunch with friends. I didn't want to go, but Dad said they wanted to wish me luck at Penn. I don't know when we'll be back, probably two-ish."

"Darn, I have to work at four. It will probably be eight before I'm free. Maybe I better just call tonight. They wouldn't want me coming over at nine at night."

"Oh, Rocco, I'm sorry. Maybe I should tell them I'm not going."

"No, no, it's okay. I don't want to get on their bad side already. We have next week, we'll work around things."

Just then her mother called out from the hall, "Blossom, are you ready? This tardiness isn't like you."

"I have to go, she seems testy lately. Please call, no matter how late."

"I will, little one, I will."

Tears in her eyes, she hugged the phone to her heart and put it in her skirt pocket, patting it as she walked.

He didn't take time to shower after work, called at eight thirty, and heard her crying as she picked up. "Roccooo!"

"What, what"—his heart thudding—"are you all right? Blossom, what?"

"They want to go to Penn Thursday morning, Thursday morning!"

"Okay, take some breaths, I'm here. Why Thursday?"

"They said they want to make it a family trip, go to New York City and see a play and a ball game and shopping. Oh my god, a ball game? I can't do it, I can't! Let's run away."

"Blossom, your age is showing. You can't even look at me, how are you going to run away with me? We knew this was coming, and it's coming a little sooner than we thought, but we'll deal with it."

"I can't, I just can't. I'll tell them I can't go to that school. I hate that school."

"Blossom"—sternly—"we've known each other four days, they're not going to let you rearrange your life for someone you've just met. Look at it from their point of view."

"But I've known you all my life, I was just waiting for you to find me," plaintively.

He hadn't cried his whole miserable life, but tears spilled over as he tried to keep his voice normal. "I don't know why we met now, but we did, and we have to go from here, baby girl. Now I'm the mature and responsible one, and here's what you're going to do. You're going to go on your family trip, you're going to be pleasant and enjoy it, and if you can't call me, I'll call you Sunday night when you're all settled in your room. That's our plan, okay?"

Softly, "I don't like the plan."

Gently, "I know what it's like not to have a family who cares for you, Blossom. They just want what they think is best." Trying to change the conversation, he said, "Have you ever been to New York City before?"

Reluctant to let go of her indignation but resigned now, "Yes, a few years ago."

"Did you see a show before?"

"Yes, we saw *Lion King* and the museums and like that. Rocco, I don't want to talk about *Lion King*."

"I know you don't, but you need to get settled down, so let's just talk. What other shows have you seen?"

"Well, that's all I've seen in New York, but we've seen things in Pittsburgh."

"Good, maybe we can do that sometime. Tell you what, be real observant on your trip so you can tell me everything, and we'll decide what we want to do there if we just have a couple days."

"I know what you're doing, and you're so nice. Oh, Rocco"—shuddering back sobs—"I'm so exhausted, when they brought it up at the table, everybody said, 'What a nice idea to celebrate Blossom's next step.' I wanted to scream, and you were working, and I couldn't call, and the day was so long . . ."

"Shh, take a breath. We have a plan, remember. You like plans, right? I'll call right after work, and if we can't eat together, we'll go for ice cream and come back and sit on the swings again, how about that? If you want me to skip work, I will."

"Oh, no, no, I don't want you to get into trouble. I have to teach a class anyway."

"Okay, then, you go to sleep now. I'll call you on my lunch break."

"Oh thank you, five o'clock seems so far away. I love your voice. I just needed to hear your voice."

"Okay, until tomorrow about noon then. Everything is okay now, Blossom, we'll be strong and deal with whatever comes up, right?"

"Right, strong," very sleepy now, her voice fading.

"Good night, baby girl." He hung up, exhausted himself from trying to hold it together. Four days, four days, and she was his every thought.

He called at noon and knew someone was with her. "Can you talk?"

"A little. Mom just called Nixie and said she and Dad would be late and he and I should go for hot dogs before I leave. I just told him I'd like you to come too, could you?" Under her breath, "Please, please, please."

"Sure I can. I'll pick you both up at, when, five?"

"Oh yes, five would be fine. We'll see you then." Softly, "Call me about four if you can, I'll be in my room."

Nixie said, "Blossom, I don't want to meet that guy, and I don't want to go for hot dogs. Slim is coming over to swim."

"Nixie, please do this for me. This way, you can tell Mom we went for hot dogs, and we'll have you back quick as can be for swimming. Or I know what we could do," excitedly. "I'll ask Rocco to pick up the hot dogs and bring them here. Then if they come home, we'll be having a picnic out back."

"No, that sounds like disobeying, and she'll have a cow. Is there room in his truck for Slim?"

"I think it is one of those trucks with a second seat, and if it isn't, we'll just take my car."

"Okay, I'll call Slim and tell him to be here at five for supper, but things just seem funny, Blossom. It's bad enough you going away, then that dumb trip out of the blue."

"Oh, Nixie, I'm sorry. I think she's just trying to keep me away from Rocco. I know it's new for her, and I'm trying to understand, but he's really important to me. Please?"

"Okay, you owe me though, and don't forget, I'm Nix."

"I'll always owe you"—hugging him—"Nix, Nix, Nix."

He called at 3:45 p.m., "Everything okay?"

"Yes, the final plan is we take Nixie, I mean Nix, and his friend, Slim, with us at five. Is that okay?"

"All good to me, I don't care how I see you as long as I see you."

"Maybe we can sit alone there, I know Nixie wouldn't mind. Maybe we should talk about all these appointments my mother has been making for me, I see a pattern here, and I don't want you to think it's you."

"That's funny you said that, I was going to talk to you about it. You're going to be okay in front of Nix, aren't you? You know, crying and everything? You did good most of the time at Mangia's, so you try hard, okay?"

"I'll be fine. Oh, Rocco, you're so wonderful."

"That's my job, baby girl. I'll see you at five."

"Rocco, this is my brother, Nix, and his friend, Slim Cousins."

Rocco put his hand out to Nix quickly. "Rocco Carnavale, Nix, glad to meet you."

"Nice to meet you, Mr. Carnavale," warily.

"My father's Mr. Carnavale, I'm just Rocco," he said, shaking hands with Slim. "You fellows game for squeezing into the crew seat?"

The ride to the hot dog stand was quiet. Rocco squeezed Blossom's hand. She smiled shyly and kept her eyes down. His throat constricted looking at her. Her hair was back from her face more with barrettes, and she had a summer-type dress with bows on the shoulders. The middle was tight and brown, the skirt the same Indian print as the bows. So fragile, so beautiful.

They found a table at the busy and popular outdoor stand, and Rocco took their orders. There were two lines with four or five ahead of them. "I don't want you to pay, Rocco."

"I have money, Blossom," putting his arm around her.

"Isn't this fun," she said. "We're just like normal people." He smiled down at her and winked, and the tears started. "What, what?"

"I can't go, I can't."

He guided her out of the line and through the other line out of Nix's sight. "Blossom, we'll talk about it later. Try to hold it together, Nix is here."

"Oh, I've embarrassed you, I'm so sorry. I just can't go, I can't."

"Big breaths now," breathing with her and wiping her tears, already knowing which tears would pass quickly and which would get worse. "You go sit with Nix and keep your mind off things. I'll bring the order over." He started to the end of the line, but the fellow he'd been in front of motioned him back to his spot. "Women, huh."

"Yeah," Rocco said, looking over at her talking to the boys, his heart overflowing, "women."

They got the boys set up, and Rocco knew they would be occupied as a car full of girls had just arrived. He and Blossom went to a table at the other side of the lot. "So what about the trip you wanted to tell me."

Her eyes down, but voice strong, "It didn't register bringing up the trip at the brunch, even though I thought she was putting me on the spot so I couldn't make a scene in front of the others. But calling Nixie about going for hot dogs instead of me, it's like she's trying to give us as little time as possible."

"I thought that too, but we'll have to live with it, Blossom. She's worried, and I told you she would be—someone you didn't go to school with, two years older. She's thinking if she can just keep us apart, you'll be gone in a couple days. She doesn't know it's too late."

He paused and looked at her. "Is it too late, Blossom?"

"It's way too late, Rocco," looking directly into his eyes, smiling, melting his heart. "It's way too late."

He was the first to look away this time, his eyes wet. He busied himself cutting her hot dog in thirds, giving her seven french fries from his order, opening her water. He glanced at the boys, and they were only half done, making fools of themselves with the girls. "Do you think I offended her somehow when I picked you up on Saturday?"

"Oh no, you did everything right. No one would have known it was your first date. You were very sophisticated."

"Good thing I watch so many movies. Actually I was scared to death. Eat a little more."

"I only eat these a couple times a summer . . .

"Hold that thought, sweetheart, I have a situation here."

She watched as he went over to the boys. She didn't know if she was shivering because he had called her sweetheart or from the way he walked. She wondered what he had seen that she hadn't.

"You fellows need anything else?" he asked, his foot on the picnic bench. "No, we're good," Nix said a little nervously. "We're going across the road for ice cream."

"You need any money?"

"No, I have some, thanks."

Rocco leaned down and said quietly in Slim's ear, "You'll earn points if you apologize to her for being rude," and walked back to Blossom.

Slim colored but glanced at one of the girls and said quietly, "Sorry 'bout that." He was really surprised when she smiled at him and said, "Why thank you, Slim." He elbowed Nix on the way over to the ice cream stand.

"What happened?" Blossom asked.

"Oh, Slim was just being fifteen, making obscene gestures at the girls."

"Oh my goodness, it wasn't Nixie, was it?"

"No, but he's fifteen, Blossom, they're walking hormones at that age."

"Oh, don't say that, I'm worried enough about leaving him."

"Why?"

"They expect too much of him, and I'm worried with me gone it will be worse."

"What do you mean, they expect too much of him?"

"Can we talk about it later? We better check on the boys. May I have some chocolate ice cream?"

"Of course. You can have the moon if you want it, but you hardly ate a thing, you shouldn't be allowed to have dessert," he chided.

"That food's so bad for you, I had plenty."

"Oh sure, half of a third and two sips of water, that's plenty," trying to be stern, but she was swinging his hand and half skipping across the road, and he was too happy to keep it up.

The boys were done, so he got Blossom a small dish of chocolate to take with her and again watched her utter concentration using tiny spoonsful to clean every morsel.

Her parents weren't home, and she said, "Would you like to sit in the gazebo out back while they swim?"

"Do they need babysitting?"

"No, but I'm sure my parents expect me to be there just in case."

The gazebo had swings facing, and again she pointed to one for him and sat in the other.

"This is a really nice lot, wonderful backyard."

"It's all Nixie, really. I mean he doesn't do the work, but he tells the gardeners what he wants. He's been doing it for a couple years. It's really a gift."

"What did you mean back at supper, then, about them expecting too much from him?"

"Well, it's not like this is a course they have in high school, and all he gets are comparisons to me. It's not fair, he's a good student," she said indignantly then sighed. "I'm going to look for colleges with landscaping majors. Penn State has a good one. He's so good in New Mexico too, maybe something in the park ranger field," sighing again.

"He has a couple years to decide, doesn't he? Should this be your burden to carry, Blossom? You're the sister, not the parent."

She looked around nervously. "Being my brother isn't easy, Rocco, imagine hearing only about my accomplishments since you were five or six."

Looking around again, biting her lip, he knew she had something she wanted to say.

"Go ahead, Blossom."

"I've never said this out loud, and I don't know if I should, but you said I was my parent's little girl. I'm not their little girl." And then at the questioning look on his face, "No, I don't mean I'm adopted or anything like that, but to my parents, I'm a trophy."

"Go on," quietly.

"Since I was six, they entered me in competitions. Whatever they found—math or computers mostly. I would always win, and they would get a trophy. I mean, I would get it, and they would take it. After a while, they accumulated, and thank goodness they didn't put them in the family room, and I certainly didn't want them in my room, so they built a display case in their bedroom," hurrying, looking around. "I wasn't very old before I felt they were more important than I was. I hated it, and when I was thirteen, I could see it was starting to affect Nixie, so I said, no more. It was a rough time, but they really couldn't force me because I could just not do well, and that would humiliate them."

"I'm sorry, Blossom."

"No, no," she said, raising her chin and straightening her back. "My parents are really wonderful people, Rocco, and I'm very fortunate to have such a nice lifestyle."

"Are you trying to convince me or you," he said softly and smiled.

She looked down for a few seconds and then up, her eyes swimming with tears. "Thank you for listening, I know I'm lucky. It wasn't long after I said no more that the college talk started then the advanced courses and extra classes. That's why I enjoy New Mexico so much, they're busy and happier. Thank God he signed me up for one more class. Oh, thank you, God." She covered her face with her hands, breathing deeply. "I can't go, I can't."

"Blossom, you're going to go, and you have to go for yourself, not because you owe it to your parents. You said you wanted to help people, right, so do it for you."

"I can help people with what I know now," petulantly.

"Blossom, your age is showing again. You're seventeen, aren't you curious about what this professor can teach you?"

Softly, "A little, and I'm almost eighteen."

"So do it for you. It will put a different slant on it. You have a gift, see where it takes you."

"But just give me two more weeks. I've never been so happy. Please, one more week."

"They didn't call me when they set up the schedule, baby girl."

Her voice strangled, "I just looked up to thank you for moving your feet. Why, why?"

"Blossom, I don't know why we met just now when you have to leave. Maybe it's a test to see if we really want this. I've been trying to think, and you know, I told myself one more fight with my dad and I'm joining the army."

She turned white, her fists to her mouth, "No, no—"

"I'm not, I'm not, not now. I just wanted to tell you maybe God was telling me, you're on the right track, let me show you how good things can be."

"Oh, Rocco, that's beautiful, you're so poetic," giving him a teary but sweet smile.

He laughed. "I wonder if a couple years ago, anyone would have connected *Rocco Carnavale* and *poetic* in the same sentence.

They noticed the boys had left at some point. He said, "I better go, there's something I need to talk to you about, and I don't want you to be crying when your parents come home. I'll call when you're in your room for the night, and you can cry as much as you want to," smiling.

"*What,*" looking terrified.

"Nothing bad, nothing bad. Get all ready to sleep, and I'll call later. How about ten?"

"Are you sure it's nothing?"

"Don't worry about it. It's just something we need to discuss."

She wrinkled her brow and pouted.

He laughed. "You're so adorable, Blossom, I can't imagine not knowing you now." He wanted to say more, but Nix called out, "Blos-som, Mom's on the phone."

"Go, go, I'll call at ten."

"Blossom, is Rocco still there? I really intended for you and Nixie to spend some time together alone."

"Mom, don't be silly, Nixie and I are together all the time, and he took Slim anyway." Changing the subject, "So what were you and Dad doing?"

"We were just rescheduling some things to be gone a couple days and then went to dinner," not realizing her comment reaffirmed Blossom's impression that the trip was a last-minute idea.

"So is Rocco still there?"

Casually, "No, he left, I'm going up for a bubble bath after I check on Nixie and Slim. See you later."

She opened her door after her bath to hear her parents come in and ask Nixie, "What did you think of Blossom's friend?"

"Rocco? He's a nice guy. I'll see you in the morning. Night, Dad."

When he was at the top of the stairs, Blossom motioned him into her room. "I heard that, thanks."

"He is nice, Blossom, but isn't he a little old for you?"

"He's twenty, hon, and I'll be eighteen. Two years isn't very much."

"Twenty, huh, he seems older. Tall too."

"I don't know what twenty is supposed to look like, but I like him just the way he is."

Shaking his head but smiling, "Night, Blossom."

She had an hour, looked over her packing, and reminded Nixie to do his. She had been ready for weeks so just needed her daily things.

She had the phone on vibrate so her parents wouldn't hear it when he called at ten. "Hello, Rocco," softly, her heart pounding in her ears and her throat constricting.

"You know, I never liked my name until I heard you say it."

"But it's a beautiful name."

"A little too ethnic for me, and I don't think I'm all Italian either."

"Isn't your mother Italian?"

"I don't really know. I don't have any grandparents that I know of. We weren't the kind of family who had get-togethers. People talk about great Italian family dinners, but I don't remember any."

"We have to check into it, Rocco. People need to know their history. It makes them feel grounded."

"I told you, Blossom, every family isn't like yours. Let's talk about it another time. Remember, I wanted to discuss something with you."

"No, I don't want to talk about that yet. What is your middle name?"

"Well, I'm Italian, what do you think it is?"

"Umm, I have to think what sounds nice. How about Anthony?"

"You're good, right on the nose."

"Rocco Anthony Carnavale, it's beautiful. I love it."

"So what's your middle name, as long as you want to stall for time."

"I'm not stalling, really, I just wanted to know. You'll never guess mine though, it's another strange one, so I'll give you a hint—it's a bird."

"Umm, New Mexico, a bird, how about Eagle?"

"Oh, that's not it, but I would have liked that. It's Dove, Blossom Dove Richards. Do you mind it?"

"I wouldn't care what your name is, little one, it's beautiful though. It's funny it's a bird because when you get nervous, you act like a little bird."

"Well, I get upset when things are unexpected. I like things to be orderly and predictable."

"Hey, there's my opening. We need a plan and a schedule for when you're away."

"Rocco, I don't—"

"We're going to talk about it, Blossom. It's not going away. I'll call you Sunday night to hear about your trip, and I'll call Monday night to see how your first day went, and then I'm not going to call until Friday, baby."

"Noo"—sobbing already—"noo."

Softly but sternly, "Blossom, remember when you said you had to immerse yourself in your work. Now that you've told me more about it, I can see that."

"Noo, noo."

"Shh, listen now. You can't start thinking at three o'clock that I'll be calling. It will be a daily distraction and interrupt your concentration. Let's both look forward to Friday nights. We'll talk as long as we want. I'm going to take that blueprint course so that will take up some weeknights, I'll cook on the weekends, and you work really hard. There's no sense going down there and not working hard. You know I'm right, baby girl."

"Oh, Rocco, I hate this, I really, really hate this. You don't understand, my heart is breaking."

"Mine is too, Blossom, mine is too. I know what, I'll give you half of mine if you give me half of yours," he said it lightly to amuse her, but it just started another wave of sobbing.

"How about tomorrow," trying to distract her. "Will we be able to get together?"

"Oh definitely. I don't care what happens."

"Should I call about three thirty and double-check?"

"Uh-huh"—yawning—"but don't go yet, tell me about when you were a little boy." A long pause, "Rocco?"

"Let's save that for another time. How about you, what do you remember?"

"I don't remember fun until Nixie came. I never cared for dolls, but he was like my baby doll. I know I didn't want to go to preschool and leave him. I vaguely remember everyone whispering when I went to preschool. Of course I know what it was about now, but it upset me until I started doing little puzzles and my mother would clap. I liked to see her happy, so I didn't care when they did it over and over. Then my dad came, and there was more whispering."

Her voice was getting strained, so he said, "No, honey, not about that. How about little girlfriends, like that?"

"I don't remember that. I remember a couple birthday parties, I think I had fun. And before we sold it to fund the New Mexico work, we had a house by the ocean. I remember loving the ocean. I must have been four because Nixie was on a blanket once"—a smile in her voice—"and I got to him just before he put a handful of sand in his mouth. He had sand all over him, he looked like a teddy bear. It's so wonderful to talk to you, Rocco. I know I'm very fortunate to have material things"—her voice got very quiet—"but I never had anyone to talk to."

He wanted to say something profound. He wanted to say talking to her made the world wonderful, but all that came out was a hoarse "Me either."

He knew she was crying. "Tomorrow is our last day. We have to keep talking, we have to keep talking," her voice fading.

"Tomorrow isn't our last day, Blossom. It's just our last day for a while. Just remember that, okay?" No response. "Close your phone, sweetie, good night."

Blossom took a breath and called her mother at four on Wednesday. "Hi, Mom, Rocco and I are going to dinner. I have all the side dishes ready, do you want me to do the chicken in the oven or marinate it for grilling?"

"Why, Blossom, I assumed our family would eat together your last night home. You really shouldn't have made other plans."

"We'll be together all weekend, Mom. So baked or grilled for the chicken?"

"Well, Dad will be tired, so baked I guess. But really . . ."

"Okay, baked it is, ready for six thirty. I want to get my cosmetics to pop right in tomorrow morning, so say good-bye to the girls for me. Rocco said to tell you we'd be home by ten. See you later." She hung up and backed onto a kitchen chair, exhausted from the tension. But at least it hadn't turned into *words*. Nothing had been important enough to take a stand on since she had quit competitions, but they had both walked on eggs many times. She finished dinner and set the oven timer. *Now, what to wear, what to wear*—trying to think of that instead of it being their last night. The summer cashmere halter dress caught her eye. It matched the cream-colored doeskin high moccasins. Add the squash blossom belt and barrettes. How could her life have changed so much in six days. *Don't cry, don't cry. Breathe, breathe.*

"Wow. Now I'm having a little trouble breathing," as he twirled her around with one hand above her head, walking her to the truck.

"Thank you," shyly, her eyes down.

"Another Aunt Mim dress? It's beautiful and soft," settling her into the truck. "Can I afford these clothes?"

She blushed at his implication. "I don't need expensive clothes. Aunt Mim just likes to buy me pretty things, and I wanted to look pretty tonight," smiling.

"You were successful. You look *very* pretty tonight." Looking at her clenched hands, "Blossom, do we have to start over every time? We do so well on the phone."

"It's, it's"—her hand fluttered between them—"the proximity," they both said. He laughed. She smiled.

They had decided on Mangia's again. Tammy was the only one at reception since Wednesdays were quieter. "Well, hi again, Rocco and Blossom, the same table?"

He didn't question her when she ordered water, nor she him when he ordered beer. More comfortable, little by little.

The girls were in a tizzy when Tammy came back to reception, asking if she had found out who she was. "I haven't been working when he is, so I haven't had a chance to ask. Someone who can afford a whole dress of cashmere, though. I just want a scarf. Now, back to work and no staring."

"You look unusually beautiful tonight."

"And you look unusually handsome. Your blue shirt matches your eyes."

"How can you tell? You never look in my eyes."

"I do. I sneak a peek now and then," smiling and glancing up shyly.

"Are you flirting with me, Blossom Dove?"

She blushed furiously but said, "I think so."

"Do you like being a girl, then?"

"I've really liked it these past six days"—looking down and wringing her hands—"but sometimes it gets in the way."

"How so?"

"Well, I told you about working with the Bureau of Indian Affairs. I didn't think they took me seriously. Actually, they were very condescending and infuriating, and I lost my temper more than once. But at least I learned that wasn't productive, and I learned not to put myself in situations where my dad had to step in."

"Was that this past year?"

"No, the year before, when I was sixteen."

"Maybe it was your age, then. Were you dressed like that?"

He was amazed when she looked right at him with narrowed eyes and spoke up firmly, "I was dressed the way I always dress, and it shouldn't matter what I dress like. I know what I'm talking about when it comes to computer programs."

"Wow," he said, holding up his hands in surrender, "a strong woman, I like that."

"I'm sorry. That was impertinent."

"No, it wasn't, you were right, and you spoke up for yourself. I really like that. I love everything I'm learning about you. But men are fools, baby girl, and you're beautiful. You're always going to have that problem. No offense, I'm just telling it like it is."

33

She was ready to get huffy again; then their food arrived—his, a steak with all the trimmings; hers, a shrimp cocktail and a side salad. "Would you like a bite," putting a piece of steak to her lips with his fingers.

"Umm, that is so good," her lips touching his fingers. He didn't move them, and they looked at each other until she reached up to take his hand away, slowly moving his fingers across her lips as she did. She closed her eyes and shuddered. "I'm not going to lose it tonight, I'm not. I'll leave, and you'll think, 'Thank goodness she's gone.'"

"Blossom, you know that is never going to happen. You could be thinking the same thing, you know, 'I'm glad I'm rid of him.'"

"Don't say that," tears starting.

"Okay, then, let's don't play those high school games. We know we're serious about this, we'll go from there, right?"

She shook her head up and down, biting her hands.

"Eat some more. Do you want another bite of steak?"

"You have a shrimp, and I'll have another bite."

"You going to bite my finger if I feed it to you?" winking and making her laugh.

"I love it when you wink at me. Are you flirting with me?"

"Absolutely!"

"Let's talk about you tonight. Every time I bring it up, you say later."

"I told you all about me the first time we had coffee."

"No, that was fifteen to seventeen. What about when you were five to fifteen or seventeen to twenty."

"Remember, I said I work, I eat, I go to my room, I study, I watch movies, and I start all over again."

"But that sounds so lonely. Didn't you have any fun times?"

"I thought I was having fun times from fifteen to seventeen and it didn't get me anywhere, so I figured I'd try it another way for a while."

"What about the fellows you were with?"

"One's in jail, one's in the service, and I think the other one is okay, but I just decided to keep away. Maybe I'll contact him someday and see how he's doing."

She smiled at him so sweetly; it hurt his heart. "What you did was so admirable, Rocco, I took a stand once, and it was like one bad week. You are so strong, you did it all at once. I could have never done that. Was it very hard?"

"There were a few bad nights, but look where it brought me," winking at her. "It was all worth it."

"I'm so glad you think that. Now let's cover five to fifteen."

"Enough about me, what about your friends?"

"I had acquaintances. Girls are more cliquish than boys I think. When I was little, I could come back from New Mexico and join right in. When I was ten or so, it changed. Everyone had their friends, and I didn't belong anymore. Then in middle school, I was taking high school courses, and in high school, I was taking college courses, and I worked at my dad's office after school, so I really didn't develop any friendship. I didn't mind, really. But I don't want to talk about that. I want to talk about our plan. I don't like the plan."

"I know you don't like the plan, Blossom, but let's see how it works out before we change it." Trying to distract her, "Do you think your parents are planning on being back for work on Monday?"

"I think so because she said they were arranging things for a couple days off, and that would be Thursday and Friday."

"Okay, so I'm thinking they wouldn't leave for home much later than five, so how about I call at six on Sunday?"

She cupped her chin in her hands and stared directly into his eyes. "I don't like the plan."

He closed his eyes and sighed deeply. "You look at me like that, and I'll do anything you want, but I can't take college away, Blossom, and you need to do well—for yourself, and me too. I'm sure I'm not their favorite person right now. Let's don't give them any reason to give you a hard time. Please try it for a while."

She was trying hard, but tears were trickling down.

"How about this? We last as long as we can, and I come down for your birthday. It's in October, right?"

Delighted disbelief came over her face. "It's the twenty-sixth, but I couldn't ask you to do that, it's too far, and gas is so much."

"You're not asking me to do it. I'm saying I'm going to do it." He got out his phone and checked the calendar. "Maybe they'll come on your birthday, so I'll come the second Saturday. How about that?"

She put her forehead in her left hand and reached for him with her right. "Oh, you're so wonderful. I thought it would be Thanksgiving. Maybe I can do it now. Six weeks instead of twelve, maybe I can do it."

"Sure we can. Thanksgiving, pb-b-pbbth, the semester's practically over," snapping his fingers. They both laughed as she said, "*Seinfeld*, Miami episode."

Swirling a pretend mustache, "You want some chocolate mousse, little girl? I've got your number, you know," winking.

"I know," softly.

"We better not stay in the truck, or she'll start flashing the light." They got out, and he was astounded when she put her arms around his waist and her head on his chest. She had never been so close. He was dizzy and didn't know what to do with his hands, sure her mother was watching, finally gave up and did what came naturally, putting his arms around her.

Her ear against him, she said, "I can hear your heart beating."

"Like a drum right now, huh?"

"Umm." She looked up at him, inches away. "I just want you to know this has been the most wonderful six days of my life." Talking quickly and breathlessly, "Really, I'm not a person who cries. I've cried more than I have in my whole life. And I'm practical, Rocco, I'm a very practical person, and I'm organized, and I'm intelligent, and . . ."

"Blossom, Blossom, I don't need your resume, baby. I didn't know any of that when I followed you out of class. I followed you because I had to, I couldn't help myself. Let's walk toward the door and get out of sight. May I kiss you tonight?"

"Oh I can't, I just can't," wringing her hands. "It's too close, I won't be able to leave. In the future, in the future."

"It's okay, it's okay, don't get upset," hugging her. "I'm going to go now."

"No, no," clinging to him.

"I'm going now," kissing the top of her head. "Six o'clock Sunday, baby girl."

She backed up to a swing, one hand covering her eyes, the other clutching her stomach, trying to rub away the sick feeling. Her mother opened the door. Seeing her stricken look, "Well, really, Blossom, there's no reason to get upset about a boy you've just met. You'll meet lots of new people at Penn."

"Yes, Mother," as she walked past. Nixie was in the foyer, his look saying he was hurting for her. "You want to watch TV, Blossom?"

"Both of you should be going up, we want to get an early start."

Two

They Part

The days of fear and anxiety fell away as soon as she opened the phone and he heard her tears. "You okay?"

"This is the first I've cried, honest. It's just when I saw your name on the screen, the distance got to me."

"How was it?"

"It went okay. The shopping was difficult, but the show was good. It was *Jersey Boys*, the one about Frankie Valli and the Four Seasons. The music was fun. Even Nixie liked it, but he didn't want to admit he liked a musical."

"What are you doing now?"

"I'm just deciding what my morning routine will be for getting dressed. There's not much privacy here."

"I'm working, so could you keep doing that and get ready for bed, and I'll call again about eight?"

"That will be fine, just hearing your voice makes everything better."

"Same here, baby girl, same here. Call later."

She decided to use one of her stackable boxes for her next day's clothes. She had never worn jeans and T-shirts, so she needed room for a skirt, petticoat, top, boots and underthings plus her cosmetic bag. As she organized things, she realized they had both sounded tired, resigned, what, she wasn't sure. She'd have to be stronger. It wasn't fair to put all the pressure on him. Oh well, she'd try the box for a couple days and see how it worked. She was pretty sure she'd be up before her roommate, Megan, and didn't want to wake her. She seemed nice but went out after they said hello and hadn't come back yet.

She took her shower and got on her smurfies, as she liked to call her old blue flannel pajamas with Smurfs on them. They were pretty worn, but she liked wearing familiar things when she was tense.

"You all comfy?"

"Umm, are you?"

"I'm lying on my bed, but I haven't showered yet. Blossom, I had a panicky feeling when I pressed the button, what if she doesn't answer? We're so far apart, and we never talked about a plan for that."

"I'll always answer, Rocco."

"No, seriously, what if you get hit by a car or something. They'd contact your parents, right—maybe I should have their number. You don't know anyone there yet. Maybe in a couple weeks you'll know your roommate well enough, but I'd just feel better if we had a plan."

"Okay, I'll give you Nixie and Mom's numbers. You'd probably be more comfortable with Dad, but his cell is seldom on. How can I reach someone for you?"

"I'll give you the company number for daytimes. Helen is on the phone, so if a woman answers, it's her, and she knows where everyone is. The foreman is Bob, and he sometimes answers, and he always says 'Bob speaking.' If any other man answers, just hang up."

Now getting worried herself, she said, "What about nights, honey, what if you say you're going to call and you don't?"

"I'll give you Mangia's number and Bob's cell, but there's really no one who would know where I am. But I'll always call at eight on Fridays, or I'll call to tell you if I'll be late."

"The distance is starting to scare me, Rocco."

"I know, sweetie, but we'll learn to work with it. Now that we have a kind of plan, let's don't think about it. Tell me more about the trip. What did you mean the shopping was difficult?"

"I didn't realize it was Dad and Nixie going to the ball game and Mom and I were going shopping."

"Is that a bad thing?"

"I love to shop with Aunt Mim, but Mom and I have different ideas of what I should wear."

"Uh-oh."

"Right. She wants me to wear black like she dressed me for competitions, and I've hated black ever since. But she headed right for black dresses and said, 'You're doing serious work, Blossom, you should dress seriously.' I'm being bad, aren't I?"

"No, you're not. But Christ, wasn't that what I said to you the other night?"

"Don't swear, Rocco, no, it wasn't. You said I shouldn't be surprised if men don't take me seriously. You didn't say I should dress differently."

"Whew, you're being too easy on me. Did you buy anything?"

"No. I don't know why she planned a whole day of shopping. But we had a nice lunch and a nap before the guys came back." She giggled. "I kept drifting into the men's departments and holding things up and saying, 'Rocco, would look so good in this.'"

"Isn't that just making things worse?"

"She had a look, but I was just letting her know the distance isn't going to change things."

"What else do you two talk about?"

"Well, at home we're usually both working, so we talk about office things. When everyone's home, I stay in my room unless it's movie night or Nixie and I are doing something. And when we're shopping and trying to get along, we talk about shopping, you know, 'Look at these darling shoes,' like that."

"But you generally get along, right?"

"We get along because we both know life would be very unpleasant if we didn't. As soon as I said I wouldn't go to any more competitions, things changed. Before, she was totally in charge, and I did as I was told. When I said no more, they didn't believe me until they started talking about the next one and I said I wasn't going. They said, 'Of course you're going,' and I said, 'No, I'm not, and if you put me out on that floor, I'm not saying anything!'"

"Wow, what happened?"

"Well, Daddy just thought I hadn't cared for that one, so he said for a while, 'How about this one, Blossom, it looks interesting,' and I said, 'They serve no purpose, Daddy, I'm not going anymore.' He said it was a shame I wasn't using my brain and eventually started signing me up for online courses, and I didn't care as long as it didn't affect Nixie."

"How about your mom?"

"She's really a good person, Rocco."

"I know that, little girl, but you've come this far, go ahead and say it."

Conversational before but crying now, "Well, she said I was selfish and inconsiderate and spoiled and didn't deserve the nice lifestyle Dad worked so hard to give us. And I'm not like that, Rocco, really, I'm not. I'm not spoiled, I don't want anything, I don't. And I'm not selfish—well, maybe I wasn't thinking of them, but I was thinking of Nixie and all that traveling," sobbing now.

"It's okay, baby, it's okay. I know you're not spoiled, I know you're not selfish."

"And, and"—trying to get air—"one time Aunt Mim came to a competition and when she saw me in that black dress, she said, 'My god, Elaine, she looks like she's in mourning,' and she sent me a pretty flowered sundress, all ruffles, and Mom said it was ostentatious and wouldn't let me wear it, and I was nine, and I loved it so much, and . . ."

"Okay, okay, big breaths now, you're getting yourself all worked up."

"But it's so nice to talk to you, I've never told anyone. I know it doesn't sound like a big problem, I know it sounds petty, and I know I'm lucky, but it's all I've ever heard, and . . . and, I'm so glad you don't like my brain, Rocco."

"Baby girl, I love your brain, I just don't love it more than you. It's nice you're smarter than the average bear, but I don't care. You're adorable and funny and sweet, and I love you, Blossom."

"Oh, Rocco, I love you so much." So tired, she hardly took note of what they had said and never knew tears were running down his face. He'd never known love, never felt love. He whispered, "Close you're phone, baby, it's one o'clock. Work hard, I'll call Friday." He put his head in his hands. *I don't deserve her, I don't deserve her, help me.*

They had known each other eleven days.

Friday, she raced back to her room, thinking she'd shower and get comfortable before he called.

The guard said, "An overnight Fedex came for you today, Blossom. I gave it to Marcy at the desk."

"A Fedex? I'm not expecting anything."

"Carnavale Construction."

She smiled but still felt a little uneasy. He hadn't said anything. A blue velvet box and a little card. "Thank you for the three most beautiful words I've ever heard. I love you, Blossom Dove."

Her knees buckled. She sat on a step and opened the box. "Ohhh," and clutched it to her heart. A necklace with a heart-shaped deep blue cameo of two white doves on a tiny branch. It was only five o'clock, but her phone vibrated, his name showing. "Oh, Rocco, I just got it. It's so beautiful, you musn't buy me things, I don't deserve gifts."

"You deserve the moon, baby girl. Do you like it? I was looking for diamonds, but I saw the doves."

"It's the most beautiful, precious gift I've ever had. I love it, I love it. You're so wonderful."

"That's my job, baby girl. I have to get back to work. Get comfy, I'll call back at eight."

"I love you, Rocco, I love you so much."

"I love you, Blossom Dove, eight o'clock."

She was crying when she got to her room, and Megan's look said "What?"

"My boyfriend just sent me the most beautiful thing," as she showed her. "My middle name is Dove."

"Wow, does he have a brother?"

She got the strangest feeling—she had no idea if he had any brothers or sisters.

"Rocco, my roommate saw my gift and asked if you had a brother, and I didn't even know. Honey, I'm so ashamed, all we talk about is me. Let's talk about you."

"I told you everything about me, Blossom," his voice a little strained.

"No, you haven't, honey, do you have a brother?"

"I don't have any brothers, but I have a sister, Lindsay. She's married and lives in Ohio."

"And . . ."

"And . . . what?"

"Well, are you close, is she older, younger, does she visit, does she have a family, like that."

"She's two years older, she doesn't visit, she has two girls, we don't talk."

"Rocco Carnavale, you are purposely being difficult. You know all about me and my family. We're just having a conversation here."

"Blossom Richards"—trying to laugh a little—"I told you all families aren't like yours. I have a father, mother, and sister. We don't talk. You're only seventeen, you don't need to carry my baggage."

"I'm almost eighteen, and my aunt says I have an old soul. I gave you my baggage to carry, now give me yours."

"Blossom, really"—voice tight and stern—"I don't want to get into this now, let's drop it."

A long pause, a big breath, "Rocco, did your father ever hit you?"

Really angry now, "Blossom, I said drop it, I mean it."

Softly, lovingly, "I'm not going to drop it, Rocco, and don't you dare close that phone. You need to tell me. Did your father ever hit you? Just tell me, honey."

Seconds went by, and she heard him breathing deeply. "Okay. This is the first and last time we ever talk about this, Blossom, and I'm telling you right now this is not a good idea." Big, raspy breath, "My father beat me every day of my life," he heard her gasp and a strangled scream but kept going. "When I was fourteen, I told him if he ever did it again, I would kill him." She was openly sobbing now. "I hated my mother because she didn't stop him until I realized he would have gone after her. I hated my sister because she left. I couldn't leave my mother with him, so I stayed and quit talking to her. That's all."

"Oh, I can't bear it, I can't bear it," sobbing uncontrollably. "Oh god, not when you were little, not when you were little."

He let her go on for a while longer then said softly, "Are we done now?" As he heard her shuddering sobs slowing, "That's all in the past, baby girl, the miracle is I met you. I'm happier than I have a right to be, and I'll spend the rest of my life making you happy. I mean that with all my heart, Blossom."

"Oh, Rocco, I need to be with you right now. I can't stand it, I can't stand it," whimpering.

"Hug me in your mind, baby. Remember your last night home, and you hugged me and heard my heart? Let's think of that for a minute, and then you tell me about your week. This is our Friday night call, we don't want to waste it on the past. We have one week under our belt, five to go before I come. Isn't that good?"

Shuddering still, "Yes, yes," sounding exhausted.

"Do you think your work with that professor will be interesting? How are your other classes?"

In a monotone but gaining strength, "Yes, I think it will be interesting. I-I thought I knew everything, but I can see I can learn more. That's progress, right?"

"There you go, when you know you don't know is the first step they say," just filling space.

"And I dropped one class when I showed them I took it at Allegheny, and I think there are one or two others I can test out of," with a little more strength.

"What's that mean, test out of?"

"I take the final as though I took the class, and then I go on to the next one."

"Can you do that?"

"Well, you need your advisor's help. I think I have him convinced on one, and on another one, he said maybe next semester."

"Sweetie, is this something your parents would approve of?"

"Oh sure, it's something Mom can brag about. People waste so much time here. I wasn't going to say anything yet, but I have a plan in my mind to get out of here in three years instead of four."

"Blossom?"

"I can do it, Rocco, I don't think it will even be hard."

"You've only been there a week, baby girl, don't do anything too quick."

"I won't. Tell me about your week."

"I checked out that class. It's Monday to Thursday from seven until ten for three weeks, so that works out."

And on they talked, both worn-out but not willing to hang up. Finally, "It's midnight, sweetie, you'd better go to sleep."

"Rocco."

"Yes, baby girl."

"I won't be able to sleep tonight."

"I knew it was a mistake, Blossom."

"No, no, it wasn't. We can't have a whole part of your life we can't talk about."

"We're not talking about it, Blossom, no more."

"I know, I know, I just meant that I don't know about and you avoiding it, you know."

"Let's close that door then. Just remember hugging me and that I love you every time it creeps into your mind. It's over. Try to stick to the plan but call me if you need to. Good night, precious girl, I love you."

"Rocco, I can't . . ."

"Shh, go to sleep."

She clutched the phone to her heart and cried herself to sleep, waking twice when she thought she heard Nixie crying then crying herself to sleep again when she realized it wasn't Nixie.

Saturday morning when she thought he'd be up, she called Nixie, hoping he was okay. "How's it going, you?"

"It's okay, Blossom, how about you?"

"I'm settling in—classes are okay. My roommate is nice so far. She doesn't take college very seriously. She lives in Scranton and went home for the weekend."

"Do you talk to Rocco?"

"We talked after the trip, but we're only going to talk on Fridays."

"Why only Fridays?"

"He thinks I should concentrate on my work, and him calling every night at eight would distract me. I know he's right, but it's tough. How are things there?"

"It's kinda strange, they never talk about you—like you're dead or something."

"That's nothing, honey, it's called empty nest syndrome. I left, and it just makes them realize soon you will and their lives will change—get it, 'empty nest.' It's an actual thing parents go through. If you want to talk about me, go ahead, don't let them intimidate you. Have you started any practices yet?"

"Yeah, I've been out already this morning for cross country. It's not bad, I'm still in pretty good shape from New Mexico. Hey, Slim's here. I'll call you later."

"Okay, hon, anytime this weekend. Mom is going to call Sundays at four. Love you."

"Love you too, Blossom."

She sighed but felt better for talking to him. Nothing, not even close to Rocco, but she knew she had protected him in some small way and was glad.

Ponderously the week went by; and she was showered, in her smurfies, and propped up in bed when her phone vibrated. "Hey, baby girl."

"Oh, Rocco, oh it's so good to hear your voice. I didn't realize how tense I was, and the minute I heard you, my whole body relaxed."

"Umm, I like the sound of that. How was your week?"

"Honey, your voice sounds funny, are you all right?"

"Sure, sure, it's been a funny week."

"Tell me about it."

And he, who had never trusted anyone, trusted her completely and told her about it.

"Well, I started that class like I told you. Things were going good, I put an Elvis CD in Tuesday to study, and the last song was 'Lord This Time You Gave Me a Mountain,' and"—he cleared his throat—"and I don't know if I realized how far away you were or what, but I just lost it. Nothing like that has ever happened to me before. I was crying so loud, I had to go in and run the shower to cover the noise. Funny, huh?"

"Oh, Rocco, do you want me to come, I will. I'll get on a plane and come."

"No, you can't do that. I got through the rest of the week kind of in a daze."

Softly, "Rocco?"

"Yes, sweetie."

"Do you think maybe it was a reaction to talking about something you've held inside sixteen or seventeen years?"

Seconds passed, but he didn't yell. "No, I think I just miss you, baby."

"Okay, okay, I just wanted to mention that. Do you have more you want to tell me?"

"No, it was strange, that's all."

"I can come if you need me. I was thinking about it the other day. I know I'm too young to rent a car, but I can take a cab to the airport and fly to Pittsburgh. Wouldn't that be wonderful if we could meet in Pittsburgh?"

"It'd be great, Blossom, but we can't be thinking like that, or that's all we'll think about. It's a good plan, though, if we ever need it. Do you want me to send you money just in case?"

"No, I have a credit card."

"Do you get a bill for it, or is it one of those tied to your Dad's?"

"Oh, I guess it is. I never get a bill."

"It would show up on his bill then. Not that we'd do it without them knowing, right?"

"I guess I was just daydreaming."

"It was a good daydream. Check and see where's a safe place to keep cash, and I'll bring you some."

Giggling a little, making him smile, "Now it's sounding deceitful, and I didn't mean it that way at all. I just wanted to hug you."

"Okay, naughty girl, tell me about your week," the world better now or as good as it could be with her so far away.

They settled into a routine of work and study, waiting for Fridays when they talked and laughed and cried, learning about each other.

"What about our politics?"

He laughed. "Does my history sound like I gave a thought to politics?"

"So you're not registered to vote?"

"I don't even know what that means."

"Well, we go to the courthouse and get a voter registration card, then we vote somewhere near where we live. We can go register the next time I'm home because I'll be eighteen."

"Sure, when do we vote."

"The Primaries are in May—that's when you decide who's running, then in November you vote for who you want."

"So who do we want?"

Giggling, "We don't know until we check them out."

"This is starting to sound like homework, but I'll do anything you want."

Another time . . .

He said, "You said you hadn't been going to church. Should we go together?"

"Well, I was raised Catholic, but the scandal totally turned me off. You know about the abuse thing?"

"Yeah, I heard a lot of gross jokes and stuff, but it wasn't something I thought about."

"But you must be Catholic. Most Italians are."

"I don't know, sweetie, church never came up."

"Well, Nixie was eight, and it actually made me ill, so I quit going. Dad and Mom weren't happy, I'm sure just because it didn't look good to their friends. And it was about the time I was questioning the competitions, so it was just another thing to argue about. I do a lot of spiritual reading, though, and I'd like to study more, but I don't know where."

"So as soon as we're together on Sundays, we can decide, okay?"

Another time . . .

"Rocco, I wanted to mail you something, and I didn't know where to address it."

"I used to get my truck payment at the shop. Helen would keep it for me, then I started paying online."

"You could get a post office box."

"What is that anyway?"

"You have a drawer at the post office and get a key. I think it's about $15 a year for a regular size."

"That's fine. I'll check it out tomorrow. What are you going to send me?"

"I read a little prayer book every morning, and I wanted to send you one. It's online too, but I like something to hold. And maybe I'd like to send you a love note," she said coyly.

"All right! I'm getting one tomorrow."

Another time . . .

"I ruined a shirt at the Laundromat last night. I haven't done that since I started doing my own things at fifteen."

"Doesn't your moth . . . oh, I mean you do everything yourself, towels and sheets too?"

"Sure, you do too, right?"

"I do now. Most of my clothes I send out, and I do my unmentionables in the bathroom sink."

"Unmentionables?"

"Yes, you know"—whispering—"underthings. It's just a colloquial expression."

Laughing, "The things I learn from you. What did you mean you do your own laundry now?"

"All my life Rosalita has done our laundry. You didn't get a chance to meet her before I left. Her name is Rosalita Penna. She came when I was born and was full-time for a long time, and since we got bigger, she comes three times a week from eight until noon to clean and do laundry. She used to cook, but I started doing that, so we do, I mean, did, the shopping list together on Mondays. I forgot to ask what's going on now. I'll ask Nixie."

"Wow, that's eighteen years."

"I know. 'Course she's off all summer. I'm sure she has other clients now. She and Mom are pretty close. They have coffee together when she comes. She was about my age when she started, now she has a family of her own."

"Are you friends?"

"Well, when I was in school all day, we hardly saw each other. Then when the tension started about the competitions"—her voice getting shaky—"she looked like she felt sorry for me or like 'you can talk to me,' but she does work for my mother. She has to be loyal to her."

"So you had no one to talk to?"

Fighting tears, "I could have called Aunt Mim, but I knew if she called my dad, it would just cause them to feud. I just stayed in my room. I was exhausted from all the tension. I don't want to talk about it right now, honey."

"I'm sorry, baby girl, it's okay."

Until finally . . .

"Are you ready for me tomorrow? You never talk about it."

"Oh, Rocco, I don't know if my heart can take it, and it's so far for twenty-four hours, and I feel so selfish asking you to do it, and . . ."

"I told you, you didn't ask me, it was my idea. Now I have to check in at the shop at seven, but I should be on the road by seven thirty. Even if it takes me six and a half hours the first time, I should be there by one thirty. The GPS should bring me right to you, but I'll check in as I get closer."

"Oh, I'm so happy, I can hardly stand it."

"Did you find out if Megan is going home?"

"Not yet, she stays out so late, and I'm up so early, we hardly see each other. I'm practically positive she will because she didn't last weekend, but you can stay in the common room if she doesn't act like she wants you in here. There were a couple fellows in there last Saturday night."

"Remember, baby, if you're the least little bit nervous, I can stay in a motel."

"No, no, I couldn't stand it if you were in town and not with me. That's like eight hours out of our twenty-four. Rocco?"

"What sweetie?"

"I'm scared."

"I know you are, Blossom. We'll be fine. We've been talking for six weeks. We know each other—it doesn't matter if we haven't seen each other."

"But you'll be so close, sometimes I can't breathe just thinking about it."

"You know what, I can't breathe either, but we'll be fine, baby girl, we'll be fine."

"Does your GPS say Route 80 or 76?"

"I'm not sure. I've never been on a road trip before, so I'll just do what it says this time. I've been using it around town just to get used to it. Did you tell your mother I'm coming?"

"No, and not for any particular reason, honey. It's my gift, and I just don't want to share it or have her discuss it. I can't explain it, is that okay?"

"It's okay, but you tell her on Sunday, Blossom. I don't want it to come up later and sound sneaky. Tell her, and tell her where I stayed, whatever we decide. That's going to be the first thing in her mind. Promise me."

"I promise, I just didn't want to tell her before, after is fine."

"I think I'm ten or fifteen minutes away, baby girl, go to the corner."

Whimpering, "I'm here, I'm here," desperate excitement in her voice.

"What's the trouble?"

"Oh, Rocco, I've had a very bad morning, very bad."

"We'll take care of it, baby, I'll be right there, hang on."

There she was, Thirty-fourth and Walnut. *Thank you, GPS. Oh god, so adorable, jumping up and down, can knees turn to jelly when you're sitting down? Denim skirt and jacket and boots, something pink. I don't deserve her. Oh, God, thank you.*

Instinctively grabbing the tissues as he got out, he ran to her; and she threw herself against him, hugging him around his waist, sobbing. "I'm here, I'm here," kissing the top of her head.

"Six weeks is too long, Rocco, six weeks is too long, I can't do it."

"I know, baby, I know. We'll think of something else. I love you, I love you." They hugged and whispered until she stopped sobbing. He dabbed at her eyes and wiped her nose. "Can you tell me about your bad morning yet?"

"Oh, Rocco, I have to talk to you about some things. It wasn't fair not to talk to you about them before I left. I just couldn't, and now you've come all this way, and I'm so selfish, and . . ."

"Okay, okay, calm down. I want to talk to you about something important too, but let's save that for later and have a nice day."

"But Megan was so mean, and I couldn't believe it, and . . ."—she shook both hands as if shaking something dirty off—"and . . ."

"Shh, tell me about it from the beginning."

"I-I said to her Rocco is bringing his sleeping bag"—catching her breath and shuddering—"but if he uses your bed, I'll have everything washed when you get back. And she said, and she said"—the tears starting again—"'Oh get real, Blossom, he's not driving for six hours to sleep in a sleeping bag, he's coming here to . . .' oh"—her voice rising and her hands shaking—"I've never heard that word out loud, and I just stood there with my mouth open, and she walked out before I had a chance to defend you, and . . ."

"Okay, okay, I get the picture, baby girl, I get the picture. First, I'm a big boy, and you don't have to defend me. Second, look in my eyes for a minute, Blossom, just for a minute." He looked into her eyes, staring seriously. "Your roommate is wrong, Blossom, she is wrong. I did not come down here to make any moves on you. I came because I love you, and I miss you beyond words. I want to see where you live and eat and do your laundry. Then when you say I had dinner, I can picture you there, and you won't seem so far away. You know that, don't you?"

Her eyes wide, she slowly nodded yes.

"Then let's have our nice twenty-four hours and not let Megan spoil them, okay? Now show me where to park, and we'll have some lunch, I'm starved." She got in the truck and showed him the lot at Thirty-fourth and Walnut; then they walked toward her dorm, his sleeping bag over his shoulder.

She slipped her hand into his; the smallness and softness gave him chills. She smiled up at him. "I can't believe you're really here."

He winked at her and held her hand tightly; her jacket fell open—*don't look at her chest, don't look at her chest*—and managed to get out "I like your necklace."

She touched the doves. "I love it so much, Rocco." As they neared her dorm, "We have to check you in. You'll need your driver's license, and she'll say you can only stay one night. The other day, Megan checked off that she doesn't mind if you stay in our room, otherwise you'd have to stay in the common room. Then she'll give you a Visitor's Pass to wear."

"You don't see this in the movies."

"I think this is the only dorm on campus it applies to, for people like my dad." She smiled.

"So this is your home away from home, huh? It's not bad." They had checked in, and he had his pass.

"This is my side, and that's Megan's. Some of the girls complain about the size, but it's so much nicer than our place in New Mexico, I don't mind it at all. The bathroom is a nice size too. Where are your things?"

"There's a pocket in the sleeping bag. I'm all set. Baby, did you find a secure spot for money? I brought you some just in case."

"I got one downstairs. The system seems secure, and I can get to it anytime, night and day."

He took a bank envelope from his sleeping bag. "Here's $500. Two hundred is in twenties for cabs and stuff."

Her mouth agape, "Oh, Rocco, I couldn't possibly take that much, honey. Oh my goodness, that's your money."

"No, it's our 'just in case' money, and I'll feel better if you have it. Let's put it away and get some lunch."

She fussed about it a little more until they got to the Moravian Cafe. He wanted to try the philly cheesesteak. "Is this like the one I saw on the Food

Channel, those two places downtown?" She smiled at him as she nibbled at a piece of spinach pie, taking huge bites of his sandwich and fries with cheese on them. "I didn't want to stop, so I'm starved."

They sat and chatted for an hour, so happy not to have a time limit. Her back was to the room, and she noticed him looking around but just thought it was an interest in the college atmosphere. "Would you like to take a tour now of the area I cover? This is a huge campus. It goes way down to at least Forty-second Street, but my classes are at this end."

"There are a lot of guys here," he said, trying to be casual.

"It's a college, Rocco, there are a lot of young people at colleges." She smiled.

"Yeah, and most of them seem to be guys."

"Rocco, remember when you said we weren't going to play high school games? It doesn't matter who's here, and it doesn't matter who's in Meadville, right?"

His eyes down, "Right."

"Okay, first I want to show you ENIAC. It was the world's first electronic digital computer and was developed right here at Penn. It's right by my dorm, then we can make a circle and end up at my favorite spot to read or eat if it's nice."

She showed him all her classes, the gym, where she ate breakfast; and they ended up at Biology Pond. "Isn't this nice? It's usually peaceful and quiet. I come here a lot. The Green is closer to my dorm, but it's hectic there." The golden mums were still blooming. They found a bench and smiled at each other, holding hands.

"This is just what I hoped to do, baby girl. See where you go and what you do." He pulled his old CD player out of his jacket pocket and set it on the bench. Elvis started singing. She gave him a glorious smile, thinking of how wonderful the day had been when he put his arm around her shoulder and started singing along in a beautiful voice. Her eyes were wide with awe and wonder when he got up and held his hands out to her to dance.

"Oh my, no. I don't know how to dance," she said nervously.

"I do. I'll show you how," pulling her to her feet, singing, holding her fingers lightly, gently touching her waist, her shoulder, turning her here, there, holding her hand over her head twirling her . . . she was dancing.

"I danced, I danced. I never did in my whole life!" Her delighted smile clutched at his heart. "You never said you could sing and dance. You are wonderful!"

"I just sing along with anything that's on, and the dancing was the one good thing I learned during my misspent youth." He grinned.

"But you're so wonderful. I don't know how to dance, and you made me feel like I can."

"Sure you can. I haven't been back to the bar in Edinboro where I learned for a couple years, but we'll go sometime. It kept me sane when I was really bad, and the owner was nice enough not to call the police when I was at my worst."

They listened to Elvis and danced until dark, other couples doing a step or two as they walked by. Once when she was overcome with emotion, holding her head in her hands, a girl misinterpreted it and said, "If you don't want him, I'll take him." Blossom looked up at him with a joyous smile. "Oh, I want him."

When it became too dark, he said "Would you like to go up and watch a movie and order pizza, or go to dinner?"

"I'd like to order pizza. I never have, but all the delivery places are listed right by the entrance door." They walked back to her dorm in comfortable silence, both a little nervous about the night ahead. "Would you mind asking for a quarter of it to be artichokes, sliced tomatoes, and mushrooms, then the rest for you? I don't want to be difficult, but the other kinds bother me."

"Sweetie, I've learned at Mangia's the customer is always right. You can have anything you want. Which place is the closest?" She pointed to the one she'd seen the most boxes from, and he ordered a quarter what she wanted and three quarters cheese and pepperoni with a two-liter Coke for himself.

They went to her room, and her eyes got big when he said, "Do you shower in the morning or at night?"

Shy again, her hands flitting around, "Usually at night."

"Why don't you give me your keycard, and I'll get the pizza while you shower. I'm going to shower in the morning so I can shave for work." Seeing her growing nervousness, "It's okay, Blossom, we're fine, we're doing fine."

"It's just strange, talking about showers," wringing her hands.

"I know—and wear something old and unattractive so you can tell your mother. I bet you she'll ask." He grinned.

He got the order, pulled her nightstand over for a table, and figured out the remote. "Blossom, *Witness* is on, have you seen it?"

"Oh, I've wanted to see that"—she opened the bathroom door an inch—"but Mom said there was an inappropriate scene for Nixie."

"I'll warn you when it's coming, I'm pretty sure I know which one she means, then you can decide."

She came out in her smurfies with a blue headband, unaware of how she looked or affected him. They pushed the two chairs together in front of the TV. "These are nice chairs for a dorm."

She lifted her shoulders. "My mom. She didn't want me to watch TV in a desk chair, and Megan didn't have one, so she got two. She's so funny sometimes. She said I should bring my old bedspread to save money then bought two chairs."

"I'm sure she wasn't thinking of me being here, but we'll take advantage. Eat your pizza now, you've hardly eaten today."

"This is so nice, Rocco, the day started out so bad, and you made it so good. Thank you, thank you, it's just been magical, my bestest day ever."

He lifted his Coke up and said, "So far, baby girl, so far."

They watched the movie. She covered her eyes when he told her to, and she actually ate two pieces of pizza, the most she had ever had. "That's my favorite kind of movie"—she yawned—"a mystery with a good back story."

"I'm going to clean up and brush my teeth, baby. Do you want to go first so you can lay down?"

"No, no, I don't want the day to end, you go first." She folded down her covers while he was in the bathroom and opened his sleeping bag onto Megan's bed. When he came out in a sleeveless T-shirt and navy lounge pants, she blushed and averted her eyes.

"We're doing fine, Blossom, everything's fine. Go brush your teeth." He took the sleeping bag from Megan's bed and put it on the floor next to hers and called to her, "I'm going to lay on the floor next to you, baby—no ulterior motive," when he saw her frightened look.

When she came out of the bathroom, he held out his arms from a chair and said, "Come sit on my lap, and we'll watch TV for a while."

"That's too close," biting her hands.

"Blossom, get Megan out of your mind. Here," he said, taking the quilt from her bed and wrapping it around her. "Now I don't even know you're in there," picking her up and sitting in the chair holding her like a baby. "See, no big ulterior motive, I just want to hold you before I go back. You don't have to look at me, you can fall asleep if you want to."

"No, I don't want to sleep at all." He shivered as she wiggled close to him, getting comfortable. "Umm, you smell good, and I've never seen your arms, they're very muscular."

He flexed, making her smile. "I swing sledgehammers all day, I should have muscles."

"Rocco, may I ask you a question?"

He knew immediately where she was going. His body stiffened, his eyes darkened, his jaw clenched. "Blossom, I told you we were done with that discussion."

She patted his cheek. "One quick question, please?"

He inhaled almost angrily. "Go ahead, just one."

"Why do you work for your father?"

Talking quickly, "He said to come back to work or get out of the house. I couldn't leave my mother there, so I went back. The money's good, I don't see him too much, and I like the other people. That's it."

She hugged him tight and whispered, "That's all, I just wondered. I love you, Rocco."

She could feel him breathe out and relax. Then he said, "You know what, we're all comfy and relaxed, we should both talk about what we wanted to say to each other."

Her arms tightened around him. She put her forehead against his chest, "Nooo, it's been such a beautiful day. Tomorrow."

"Baby girl, why do it in a restaurant? Something's bothering you. In a couple minutes, it will be over. Just dive right in."

"But what if you leave," anguished.

"I will never leave, Blossom," kissing her head. "Just go ahead, baby."

"And you won't interrupt so I can get it out?"

"I won't interrupt."

"I have to say some words I don't like to say," tears starting.

"You're just giving me information, use whatever words you need to."

Taking in air, talking quickly, "A little bit in tenth grade and more in eleventh, girls started talking about things, you know"—hiding her head in his chest—"sexual things." He nodded but did not interrupt. "Then in twelfth, like, 'Oh I got drunk' and . . . and . . . and"—squeezing his chest and talking low—"'did it with Ryan,' and they would laugh. Or 'we were in his car and the gearshift was in my back,' and, oh, I just can't repeat it. And I just thought that can't be what God had in mind, it just can't be . . . grappling in a truck? Being with someone because you're drunk? And now here, it's like a pastime or something. And then"—talking faster, digging into his back—"I was reading this spiritual book, I mean I'm not a kook or anything, but I do read spiritual books, and there was this passage that said, that said, I'm paraphrasing it, when two people join together in sexual intimacy, their ultimate closeness brings them closer to God. And I thought, that's it, oh thank you, God, that's it. And . . . and, Rocco, that's what I have to have, I just can't have that other, I can't." Burying her face in her hands, "And you're young, and maybe you just want to have fun and not wait for me to be ready, and"—sobbing now—"I'll really try to understand, I really will," shaking.

Reaching for tissue, patting her eyes, wiping her nose, "Sh-sh, I'm not going any place, Blossom. I have a past, I told you that, but I haven't been with girls a couple years now. I don't read spiritual books, but even I knew there had to be something more. We're on the same page, baby girl, we're on the same page. And we do everything at your speed, okay?" A new wave of tears came, and he waited until her breathing was even and said, "I guess it's my turn, huh?"

Softly, "It's your turn. I'm glad we didn't wait until tomorrow. Thank you, Rocco."

"We'll see, sweetie. This is way too soon, I know, and Megan didn't help matters, but I don't want to talk about it on the phone, and we have to talk about it sooner or later. I'm supposed to be the mature and responsible one, so here goes. We both know we're serious, right?" She nodded up and down, solemnly. "So I think we need to talk about birth control."

"Oh, oh, no, no." She jumped back.

"Don't pull away, hug me, we're just talking like adults, baby."

"Oh, no, no, I don't want to talk like adults. I don't like this conversation."

"Sh, sh, we're doing good, let's keep going. Did you talk about pills in school, or has your mother talked to you about them?"

"No, no, never, and I tried not to listen in school."

"Okay, okay, I don't know anything myself, just what I heard around. In the movies, though, they say they have clinics in colleges. Do you think you can check into that when you get your courage up?" She was whimpering, but he went on, "I'm just assuming you don't take them one day, and they work the next, you know. We have all the time in the world, baby, I'm not pushing you. I just wanted to get this part out of the way, and we don't have to talk about it again."

"I read about the clinic in our information, so I know it's here, but Rocco"—covering her face with her hands—"I don't want to talk about this."

"I know, sweetie, I know," rubbing her back. "Let's just get it settled, and it will be behind us. Didn't your parents say anything before college, they're doctors for heaven's sake."

"They just don't think of me that way. I'm like an object. Maybe they didn't think they had to, and then you came along so suddenly, they didn't have time to reevaluate."

"Or maybe they sent you here because you're old enough to make your own decisions. How about that?"

She looked up at him with a quizzical expression, tipped her head, and furrowed her brow. He could almost see the wheels turning. Then she gave him an angelic smile. "You're right, I can make my own decisions, I can make my own rules," she said with wonder as it dawned on her.

"So let's make a plan. You check into it when you want to, and you know what, I'll check into it too, and we'll compare notes." A few seconds went by, and he whispered against her hair, "There is something I can do, baby, do you know what I mean. Did you talk about that in school?"

She buried her face in his chest. "I don't like that, it doesn't seem like love."

"Okay then, I just wanted to mention it so you don't think it's all up to you."

"Rocco, I can't believe we're talking about this. I don't like it, I just don't like it."

"We're done, baby girl, all done," holding her close. He found some music on TV, humming and rocking until she was asleep. Putting her in bed, he arranged the quilt, pulled another blanket over her and just looked. Overcome with such emotion, tears ran down his face. Some of the worst things he'd endured crept in; but he shook his head, looked at her again, and smiled. Miracles happen.

He was up, showered, dressed, and watching her, and could tell from her breathing when she woke. She turned quickly with big eyes and a worried look then smiled radiantly when she saw him. "I thought it was a dream."

"No dream, pretty girl, good morning."

Words running together, "Oh, you're all dressed, I wanted to watch you shave, what time is it, am I holding you up, I never heard anything."

"Slow down, we have plenty of time. I get up early, and I'm used to being quiet. It's nine fifteen."

"Nine fifteen! My goodness, I usually wake at six."

He took a couple steps, picked her up, and put her on his lap. "Did you sleep okay? I was thinking maybe we covered too much territory last night." As her softness and warmth reached him, he realized how thin her pajamas were. "On second thought, why don't you get dressed, and then we'll talk."

She bounced up and opened her closet, taking out a cream-colored chamois skirt and a blue angora wraparound sweater set to match her doves, stepped to her dresser for underthings and went into the bathroom.

"You look like an angel, baby girl." He sat beside her on her bed as she pulled on her cream-colored high moccasins. "What was that pink thing under your skirt I saw when we were dancing?"

She smiled. "That is a petticoat, it makes the skirt fuller. Aunt Mim sent them in pink and red."

"I liked it. I like your clothes. They're more interesting than T-shirts and jeans. Are you okay? Did I say too much last night? I don't want to scare you."

"I'm so glad I said what I needed to, Rocco, I've been so scared you'd leave. Your part upset me, but I do like to have a plan." She cupped her hand around his ear and whispered, "Can we say 'the pill' and not the other part?"

He smiled and whispered in her ear, "Okay."

"Baby, I need a real breakfast, where can we go?"

"We'll go over on Sansom Street. There will be a place where you can get eggs." They dropped his sleeping bag off at his truck, and he slipped something into his pocket. He ordered enough to make her shake her head, and she got a multigrain bagel and hot chocolate.

"I have something for you," he said, handing her a jewelry box.

"Oh, honey, I told you not to buy me things. I don't deserve anything."

"Happy birthday, Blossom, you can't object to a birthday present." He got excited as she opened it and said, "It's called Add-a-Pearl. Whenever we have a special occasion, we add another one, and in about ten years, it's all full. See the little diamonds on each side," he said excitedly. "Every few pearls we put another one. The lady said start with a big pearl, and then we'll remember we started with your eighteenth birthday. Do you like it, baby girl?"

She looked at him with such adoration; it stunned him. "Rocco, it's breathtaking," as she held it to her cheek. "You musn't spend your money on me."

"Your birthday is coming, Blossom, let me put it on."

She turned the doves around to hang down her back under her sweater and lifted her hair so he could close the clasp behind her neck. The pearl lay between her breasts, the diamonds twinkling. "I'll love it forever, Rocco." She tried not to cry as she looked down at it through breakfast. Quietly, "It's very humbling that you went into a store to find something for me, I mean, to take time from your day. I don't feel worthy."

"Blossom, you are a very wonderful, special girl. Why would you think that? Have you told me everything about when you were little?"

"I think so. It was just the competitions, nothing like you."

He had a worried look. "I wonder, baby, such a pretty and smart girl, you shouldn't be feeling unworthy."

She lifted the pearl to admire it again and dropped it back. "I love it, Rocco, thank you so much."

He lifted his eyebrows like Groucho Marx and said, "I wish I were that pearl."

"Rocco! Why are you talking like that?"

"I'm sorry, that was inappropriate. I just don't want to go back."

"Oh, honey, you have to be strong. One of us has to be, and you know I'm not."

"I know, I know. I'm okay." He paused. "Are you going to kiss me good-bye this time?"

When she closed her eyes and bit her hands, they were shaking.

"Forget I said that, Blossom, everything's been wonderful, I don't want to rush you."

Looking down, very softly, "Would it be a little kiss?"

His heart flipped. "It can be any kind of kiss you want."

"Not like on TV—that scares me."

"Okay," quietly. "Not like on TV. I promise. We better go now, I have to work tonight."

As they went to the truck, she said, "Don't drive fast, honey, call them if you can't make it. Please don't take any chances."

"I won't. Remember now, tell your mother everything. And I'll tell you Friday what I find out about," he whispered in her ear, "the pill, and you check when you really want to. Are you ready for a kiss?"

"Oh, Rocco, it's just too close, I can't," breathing hard, the tears starting.

"Sweetie, we were just as close last night, and you were fine. Look at me a second." She tipped her head up, and he kissed her quickly on her lips. Her eyes opened wide. "See, nothing to it." He grinned and kissed her again.

"That's so nice." She let out her breath. "Your lips are so soft."

"Once more?" He lingered three seconds this time, and she clutched his jacket. "Ummm."

He hugged her tight and kissed the top of her head. "I have to go. Work hard this week, I love you."

"I love you, Rocco, it was the most wonderful twenty-four hours ever. Thank you for teaching me to dance, thank you for the beautiful gift, tha . . ."

"I'm going, Blossom, I love you."

Holding her fist to her mouth, she backed up to the bench on the corner, trying not to cry. The truck pulled away, he waved into the rearview mirror, and she blew him a kiss.

She gasped when the truck stopped so suddenly; the rear seemed to lift up. He hopped down, staring at her. She stood, hands clasped at her mouth, but couldn't move. He seemed to be coming in slow motion, moving steadily but not running. Her heart was beating out of control. He was so beautiful in his jeans, a curl falling unto his forehead, his shirt and his eyes so blue, those eyes never leaving hers. When he was two steps away, she threw herself forward to circle his waist, her head on his chest.

He whispered into her hair, "Don't blow me kisses, little lady." She smiled and squeezed harder, listening to his heart pound. "It wasn't right to leave you here. I'll stay here while you run to your dorm. Go quick."

She looked up and nodded. Her lips were so close, her sweater so soft; he could drown in her eyes . . . he broke his promise.

She moaned and went limp. He picked her up and carried her to the bench. "You promised, not like on TV, you promised," weakly pounding his chest.

"I'm sorry, I'm sorry, baby, I couldn't help it. I'm sorry."

"Oh, I embarrassed you, I screamed. Oh god, I think I fainted. You promised," pounding again. "Is everyone looking?"

"No one's here, sweetie, no one's here. You can't embarrass me. I didn't mean to, it's just you were close and soft and warm," kissing her head. "I love you, Blossom. Go now, I'll call you from the road. Go, baby girl, don't look back."

She was still crying as she ran. He watched until she turned a corner and was out of sight. Resting his elbows on his knees, he put his head in his hands. *Get in the truck, she's seventeen, get in the truck.* And he did, knowing he had to.

He drove for two hours and called, "Are you okay?"

"No, no, I'm not okay," she said indignantly. "You're supposed to be mature and responsible. You said a little kiss. It wasn't little, it wasn't little at all," her voice rising, sobbing.

"Baby, I said I was sorry—Jesus, the traffic's crazy all of a sudden, I've got to pull over, I shouldn't be on the phone. Oh, good, a rest area—okay, baby, I'm sorry, are you all right?"

"No! And my mother is going to be calling in an hour, and I can't breathe. That wasn't fair, Rocco. You should have told me, I like to be prepared. I know I embarrassed you, you know I like to be prepared," crying loudly.

"Okay, baby girl, calm down now, calm down. Take some big breaths, big breaths. We good now?"

She said softly, her voice still catching, "You could come back."

"Blossom"—quietly—"you know I can't come back."

"You could," she said hurriedly. "You could call people and tell them you're staying another day, and Megan would be here, but we could go somewhere else, and—"

"Blossom, stop, you know we can't do that."

"I want you to," she wailed.

"Dammit, Blossom, I'm trying to be a stand-up guy here. We have to stick with the plan."

"Now you're swearing at me," she sobbed.

"I'm not swearing at you, sweetie, I'm swearing at the situation. Now take a nap or do something to settle down so you'll be ready to talk to your mother. Do you want me to call you at eight? Will you be ready for bed by then?"

"I'll talk to Mom until four thirty"—her voice catching—"then get something to eat and get my things ready for tomorrow. Yes, eight will be good." Then she added sarcastically, "But aren't we messing up the plan by talking on a Sunday?"

"Blossom, behave yourself, your age is showing. I'll just call to check in and see how you are. I love you, baby girl, I'm sorry."

"Rocco," she said softly.

"What?"

"It was a wonderful kiss," she breathed and closed her phone.

He put his head on the steering wheel and pounded the dash, finally slid out of the truck to get some coffee, and an elderly man walking by with his dog said, "Lady love leaving?"

"No, sir, just the opposite."

"Well then, you're a lucky man, son, a lucky man."

It brought him up abruptly—a lucky man. Who would have thought. Rocco Carnavale is a lucky man. Smiling, he wanted to call her back, but she might be napping before her mother called.

She decided to go the upbeat route instead of being defensive with her mother. It hadn't been just since she met Rocco that any exchanges were strained. The last five years, since her outburst at thirteen, had been tenuous. She regretted it but had never backed down and definitely wouldn't now. She wished her mother could be happy she had met someone, but she knew she would just see it as a deterrent to what she had in mind for her. "Whatever that is," she sighed out loud.

"Hello, dear, how are you?"

"Hi, Mom, I've had the most wonderful weekend, well, twenty-four hours, really," laughing. "Rocco came down."

"Rocco came down?" stunned. "You mean he came down there?"

"Yes, he came yesterday at one and left today at one. We had such a good time, it was wonderful."

"Why didn't you tell me he was coming. Where did he stay?"

"Well, I didn't mention it because I couldn't believe he'd actually do it. I mean driving six hours down and then back. Oh, we had the best time. Mom, he taught me to dance, can you imagine, and I showed him all my classes so he can picture where I am, and we watched *Witness*, and he told me when to cover my eyes—remember you didn't think it was appropriate, and—"

"Blossom, where did he stay?"

"Oh yes, well, he stayed right here. Megan didn't care, and he brought his sleeping bag. He said he'd go to a motel if I was uncomfortable, but that seemed silly. It worked out just fine. Oh, and Mom, he brought me a birthday present, the most wonderful gift. It's called Add-a-Pearl," talking faster and faster. "You start out with one, and every special occasion you add another, and in about ten years you have a whole strand. It's so beautiful, I can't wait to show you," breathlessly.

"Ten years?" her disbelief growing.

"Isn't that wonderful, and there are diamonds on each side of the first one. I love it so much."

"Well, that sounds very nice. Are you still talking only on Fridays? You really should devote your time to your work."

"Yes," deflated from her lack of interest. "Yes, Rocco thinks it's important. How's Nixie doing?"

And they continued on with the usual family and college talk, ending at four thirty right on schedule. She always felt her mother figured a half-hour obligatory call into "daughter at college" on her calendar and ended it right at four thirty as if watching a clock.

She stared at the phone at 7:58 p.m. willing it to ring and at eight opened it at the first hint of sound. "And you quit saying my age is showing, Mr. I'm-only-twenty!"

"Oh oh, phone call with your mother didn't go well, baby girl?" He was smiling to himself. She was fine.

"Oh, Rocco, I want you here, I miss you so much. It's worse than ever."

"We'll be fine, baby, it was wonderful, wasn't it."

"Oh, I can't even tell you. You were right, she said where did he sleep the first thing," giggling.

And on they talked until nine o'clock, then ten o'clock. "My goodness, aren't you supposed to be working?"

"I called from the road and canceled. Sundays are slow, and I didn't want to rush. I'm probably going to have to quit so I can come down more often."

"Really"—breathlessly—"but you like it there."

"I do, but six weeks is too long, and taking one weekend a month off isn't fair to them. I'll wait and see what your parents do about your birthday. If you don't come here, I'll come again in November. Maybe I can switch my hours to weeknights after this class is done."

"Oh, honey, you're making so many adjustments for me, it's not right."

"No, I'm making adjustments for me, and it's what I want to do. It's late, you better go to sleep. Think of dancing to put yourself to sleep."

"Rocco, you know what I'm thinking about, and it's your fault."

"Sorry, baby, sorry. I know it's my fault. Try to think of dancing then."

"Are you thinking of dancing to go to sleep?"

"No, but I'm a dirty old man." He laughed.

"It's not funny, Rocco."

"I know, baby girl. Do you want to talk about it?"

"No," pouting.

"Can you tell me why?"

Softly, "Because, because—no, I can't."

"Honey"—instinctively knowing what it was about—"feelings are fine. I don't know anything about anything, but I think you've been burying your feelings so long, now that you have them, you just cry. Why didn't you tell your parents you thought they liked the trophies more than you?"

"Rocco, how did we get on this subject? We were talking about going to sleep."

"Okay, sweetie, we'll set that aside for now, but we shouldn't sweep things under the rug. It's not good. I love to think of the dancing, but when I'm going to sleep tonight, I'm going to think of holding you in my lap and you fell asleep. I loved that."

"Oh, me too. I felt so safe. I love you, Rocco," sleepily.

"Good night, little one. We're back on the plan now, so I'll call you Friday. I love you."

"I hate the plan," as she closed her phone.

He made the call Monday morning during his break at ten o'clock. He had planned it, but something he saw on TV before he fell asleep made it more urgent. Scared him to death, actually.

"Good morning. This is Rocco Carnavale. I have some questions about birth control pills I'd like to see the doctor about. Could you fit me in this week—about fifteen minutes at the end of the day? It's important."

Ordinarily she would have said this week is full, but his young voice and directness intrigued her. "Would Wednesday at five-thirty work?"

"That's fine."

"Please spell your name. Phone. Insurance company."

"I'll pay cash. Be there Wednesday at five thirty."

"Please come fifteen minutes early for some paperwork. We'll see you Wednesday."

"Rocco Carnavale for five thirty." He filled out those parts of the paperwork he felt appropriate and handed them back. The only other client was just in for a seventh month weigh-in, and the receptionist noticed he wasn't intimidated by the surroundings but did have a worried look.

As instructed when she had told the doctor about the day's appointments, she showed him into the doctor's office instead of an exam room.

"Mr. Carnavale, I'm Dr. Kreinson. How can I help you?"

The only sign of nervousness was a slight clearing of his throat as he began. "My girlfriend and I are discussing birth control pills. I thought it was a pretty cut-and-dried thing, but I just happened to see a commercial on TV Sunday night that they might cause heart injury and something called pulmonary embolism. It was pretty scary." He started twisting his hands. "I can't be responsible for hurting this girl, I can't let her do this if there's any danger." She saw his eyes were moist.

"Well, first, Rocco. May I call you Rocco?" He nodded yes, still twisting his hands. "Birth control pills have been around since the sixties, and really, any complications are extremely rare. The TV spot I've seen lately is with a product called YAZ. Is that what you saw?"

"I'm not sure, all I heard was pulmonary embolism, and then I started listening."

"Of course, I can't prescribe anything for her without seeing her, but let me give you some information, and you and she can go from there. If she'd like to come in to ask questions, it's completely confidential."

"She's in college six hours away," a little more relaxed.

"Well, if she's in college, I'm sure they have a clinic where she can get information, or she can come in when she's in town. Without getting into how birth control pills work at this point, just stay with the tried and true, and if you have any questions, call me anytime. I'm sure everything will be fine," she said as she patted his shoulder and opened the door.

After he paid his account and left, Dr. Kreinson came by, putting her coat on, and said to Laura, "Well, that's not something you see every day," smiling.

"Hi, baby girl, how was your week? Did you get some mail from me?"

"Yes," softly. "I haven't done anything yet. It's so nice to hear your voice."

"Whatever you do, you do at your own speed, baby, I just wanted to send what I got, and you can compare it with what you find out and then decide. Remember, you have all the power."

"I don't want the power, Rocco, can't we both have the power?"

"Sure we can, sweetie, but in the end, it's up to you, okay?"

"Weren't you embarrassed to go to the doctor. I think she's in Dad's building. Oh, you didn't mention my name, did you?"

"Of course not, baby, and no, I wasn't embarrassed. I needed information, so I went where the information was. Besides, doctors can't say anything about their patients. And she said if you wanted to come in, it would be confidential. I know you don't like this conversation, Blossom, but just let me say one more thing, and we'll drop it. If you do see a doctor, they might say something, or you're a smart girl, and it might enter your mind." Big breath, "When I decided not to have any more contact with girls, I . . ."

"Rocco, I don't—"

"Sweetie, just let me finish. I got tested for diseases . . ."

"No, Rocco, I don't want to hear this."

"Baby, just let me say it. I got tested, I was fine. That's it. Okay?"

Crying, "I don't want to think of that time. You said we wouldn't talk about it. You're spoiling our Friday night call."

"We're done, we're done. I love you. Now I'll tell you something funny."

"Something funny? Your voice doesn't sound like it was funny."

"Well, it was funny-strange. I worked Tuesday to make up for Sunday, and Tammy came in the kitchen and said Dr. and Mrs. Richards would like to say hello."

He heard a big intake of breath. "No!"

"Oh yes, and I was scared, but your mom said, 'Rocco, you haven't met Dr. Richards yet.' We shook hands, and he asked me if I cooked their dinners, which I hadn't, and then your mother said, 'We understand you went to see Blossom last weekend?' I just said I wanted to see where you were and looked at your dad and said it appeared to be very safe. Then your mom said, 'Of course we want Blossom to concentrate on her studies, she's a very special girl.' So I said, 'I understand completely, she is a very special girl.' Then she stared at me and said, '*Girl* being the operative word here, Rocco.' I just nodded and said, 'Understood, Mrs. Richards.' Told your dad it was nice to meet him and got out of there."

Indignantly, "Why did she say '*girl* being the operative word' what's that supposed to mean?"

"I think she's just reminding me I'm older and should let you enjoy college. She probably wished she had talked to me before I came down to remind me you're not legal yet."

"What do you mean I'm not legal yet?"

Regretting he had started the conversation, "Ah, you're not eighteen yet. But it's beside the point because you'll be eighteen this weekend."

"But what difference does it make if I'm seventeen or eighteen?"

Trying to get out of too much detail, he said, "Well, legally seventeen you're a girl, and eighteen you're a woman."

"Oh, that's nice," happily. "So now I'll be a woman?"

"Yes, sweetie, now you're a woman," smiling, relieved. "Now tell me about your week."

"I know you said I didn't have to defend you, but I just had to say something to Megan. She was so mean before. It was hard, and I raised my voice, but it cleared the air. I showed her my pearl. Oh, I love it so much, Rocco, then I put it in with the just-in-case money. I'll get it out every time you come."

And on they talked—she cried, she laughed, she cried again. He soothed, he scolded, he sang. When she yawned every few minutes, he said, "Ask your mom Sunday about coming home for your birthday, baby, but don't panic if she says no. You can say if they'll come and get you, I'll bring you back, but I'm thinking she won't go for it. I hope they at least come down, but don't worry, if they don't bring you home, I'll be down the second week of November."

"Oh, that seems so far away, Rocco."

"I know, baby girl, but it's only three weeks from now. We did six weeks before, we can do it. Now you better go to bed. Try to stick to the plan but call me if you need me. Better yet, I'll call on Thursday to see if they're coming."

"Good, that doesn't seem so long. I love you, Rocco Carnavale."

"I love you, little one, sleep tight."

When he called Thursday night, she said they were coming Friday at dinnertime and leaving Sunday after brunch. "I'm so glad you called tonight. I asked if they were coming to get me, and she said it would be foolish to drive another twelve hours. When I said you could bring me back, she said that was too much to ask of a friend. I don't know what to do when she says things like that, Rocco. Should I say, he's not a friend, I love him? I don't know what to do," crying.

"Blossom, it's not important. If you don't know what to do, it just means you don't want to get into it yet. It's okay, it's okay. Why make a family feud when you don't have to. She's just trying to give you the impression this is a passing thing. We know it isn't, so just brush it off."

He had kept talking to give her time to settle down, and her tears were under control. "Oh, Rocco, I love you so. Everything is better when I can talk to you. They can't say anything—my grades are perfect, they know I could walk away if I decided to. It's like competitions all over again. I hate this, it never goes away. At least they're bringing Nixie. It will be fun to see him."

"There you go. Have a nice time with your family, baby. I don't like it that I might be causing trouble."

"Honey, I told you, there was trouble way before I met you. Can we talk about something else for a while? How was your week?"

"Well, something strange happened. My dad said my name for the first time I can ever remember."

"What do you mean?"

"I mean he has never said my name. Yesterday, Bob and I were checking blueprints, and I was showing him on my laptop where I thought they were wrong, and we should change them. My dad came over to see what we were talking about. Usually I walk away, but I just took a couple steps back, and Bob showed him, and he said 'Do it Rocco's way' and walked away. Bob looked at me and lifted his eyebrows. It was strange."

"Oh, honey, should I be glad? Are you glad? Could things change? I just don't know what to feel."

"Sweetie, don't read anything into it. I just said it was strange, that's all."

Sunday, 8:00 p.m., "Hi, baby girl, how was your birthday?"

"It was nice to see everyone, I guess. It seems like Nixie has grown."

"You seem a little down, baby, not like someone who just turned eighteen."

"Well, while we were having dinner Saturday night, everyone was talking, and I thought it's nice to see these people, but every few months would be okay. When you came, all I could think of was I need to see you every day. It's like an ache that I can't."

"I love you, baby girl."

"I love you so, Rocco."

"What else did you do?"

"We went into the city to show Nixie the Liberty Bell. He couldn't have cared less," giggling. "But he said things aren't too bad. He had As and Bs the first marking period, and they didn't make too much of it."

"Something else happened, I can tell. What was it?"

Getting teary, "At brunch, Mom said, 'Well, you're eighteen now, Blossom, what do you want from life?' And I just wanted to say I want Rocco, but as usual I didn't want a scene, so I said I'd like to help people just like I always say. Then Mom said, 'I think medicine is the way to go, Blossom.' They wear me out 'til I'm not sure what I'm doing."

"Baby, I know it seems long to us, and maybe it seems long to them, but you've only been there two months. Give yourself time. No matter what path you take, it's not going to be done your first year, right? Just keep working hard, and things will start to gel."

"Thank you, honey, everything seems clearer when I talk to you. How about you, what do you want from life?"

"That's easy, baby, I want you and a couple kids to love and protect and keep safe. And a house I can go into every room and feel comfortable."

"Oh, I wish I had said that. What about work?"

"I can always make a living, Blossom. I'm good at both things I do, and they're things I can do any place. Being with you is the only important thing. Everything else is incidental, baby girl."

Crying softly, "Oh, Rocco, what am I doing here? I have no feeling for this work."

"Give it a chance, baby. You're doing some premed things now, didn't you say? Next year, put more emphasis on that if you want to. Let's put this to bed for now, it's getting you upset."

"I love you, Rocco, I can't wait until you come. Oh my goodness, are you working? I hear some noises."

"I'm just finishing up, it's okay."

"No, no, I better go, honey, I'm so selfish. We always talk about me. On Friday, we're only going to talk about your week, I promise."

"You better get some sleep, baby girl, you sound tired. I love you, sleep tight." He stepped outside to get some air, pacing for a minute to calm down. Should he be mad at them? Should he be mad at himself? She's hurting. Who can he blame? Where's a wall he can put a fist through? Guess he was getting older. He would have just done it before. Would she be better off without him? Pacing, literally stamping back and forth, fists pounding into each other. No. He wasn't giving her up. They met for a reason. It was too right. He was sure of it. If he had to go every other week to keep her happy, he would.

Steve came out. "Have words with Blossom?"

"No, just the opposite. I guess I'm going to have to quit, Steve. Weekends are when you need help, and I think I'll be going down more often. I can help out when I'm around, but maybe you should find someone. No hurry."

"I hate to lose you, Rocco."

"Thanks. I appreciate everything you've done for me. I know it wasn't easy. I really like it, but I can't quit my other job."

Was she excited to tell him or nervous? She wasn't sure, but she had butterflies waiting for eight on Friday, biting her lips, willing the phone to ring.

"How's my baby girl tonight?"

"I'm good, honey. I felt strong after we talked Sunday night."

He smiled at her upbeat voice, relieved. "I told Steve I had to quit after we talked."

"Oh, honey, I'll be all right. You like that job."

"It's okay, baby, I can't quit the other one, and I have to be able to come down more often. Tell me about your week."

"I know I said we'd only talk about you tonight, but guess what I've been doing the last four mornings," a smile in her voice.

"What have you been doing, little one?"

"I've been taking birth control pills!"

She heard his intake of breath; then he breathed out, "Blossom?"

"I have, I have. You said when I got the courage, and I got the courage, and I did it!"

Hoarsely, "Blossom?"

"Rocco, are you crying? Why are you crying, honey? I told you I'm determined when I put my mind to it. I know I'm always emotional around you, but I can be strong, I really can. Are you all right?"

"You went all by yourself? I thought you'd want me to go with you. You floored me, that's all, baby."

"I'll show you when you come. They are in the paper you sent me. Rocco"—softly—"remember when we were talking about your dad and you said 'don't read anything into it.' Don't read anything into this, please, honey. You said let's get it out of the way, so I did, that's all. Is that all right?"

"It's totally all right, baby, you're amazing, and you're completely in charge. I love you, Blossom."

She settled into her pillow, content and happy. Ten o'clock came, eleven, nearing midnight; and yawning, she said, "I don't know why I had butterflies, honey, I thought there would be an elephant in the room. We're fine, aren't we?"

"We're more than fine, sweetie. Will you let me kiss you when I come? I would have asked you anyway, you know."

"The little kiss, not the other one?"

"You said you liked the other one right before you closed the phone. Wouldn't you like to try again?"

"Rocco, it's too much. I don't like what happens."

"What happens, baby? It's okay, just tell me."

"I tingle all over. It's scary."

"That's what's supposed to happen, baby. You don't have to be afraid. How about we start with the little one, then you decide. Would that be okay?"

"Okay," she breathed. "Next trip."

"Next trip," precious girl. "Next trip," his heart thudding.

Only the next trip was a long time coming.

"Blossom?" She loved it when he called during the week, but four o'clock? And his voice was funny.

"What's wrong, honey?"

"I wanted to call in case your mother heard something." Ice started to circle her heart. "My father died today."

"Oh my god, oh, Rocco, my darling, I'll come right away."

"No, no, I mean he died, he's gone, but they're keeping him on a machine until my sister gets here. I don't want you to miss too much school, so I'll tell you when to come."

"Honey, I should be with you. I don't care about school."

"No, baby, it's okay. I'll be tied up most of the time, so wait until I tell you. My sister had to get her kids and house ready to be gone a week or two, so I'll let you know."

"Honey, are you okay. How did it happen, how old was he?"

"He was fifty-two, it was in his office this morning, a massive heart attack, they said. Helen found him. It's been a hellish day, but Bob's been with me all day, and we're meeting tomorrow at the office to talk about work. I'm at home now, and my mother is just sitting and staring. She doesn't answer me or anything, I mean, I haven't talked to her in years."

"Rocco, call Helen and ask her about Home Health Care people to come and help you with her. If she can't help, ask at the nurses' station where they have him. They have people at the hospital to help families in crisis. It's only four o'clock, so do that now, and someone will come and get her to eat and change for bed, and they'll see if she needs something to help her sleep. Can you do that, or do you want me to?"

"I can do it. Thank you, sweetheart, I think I'll go right back to the hospital now. I'll call you tonight. I love you, Blossom."

"I love you, Rocco. I'm so sorry I'm not there to help you, honey. Call me."

She called her mother, and although she was sympathetic, she was cool. Blossom was glad she hadn't told Rocco to call her. She agreed that the hospital could help and that Blossom could fly to Pittsburgh when the funeral was set, cautioning her not to miss too much school.

He called her that night to tell her the hospital set him up with someone. Talking into the night, gaining strength from her, he shared his innermost thoughts. Should he be sad? He was too busy thinking about the business and what to do about his sister and his mother. He wasn't sad; was he wrong? It was funny Helen knew more than he did. He would see the lawyer on Monday that she told him would know something about the business.

He hadn't been in the kitchen in years but had coffee made when his mother came down. He asked her if she was all right, and she smiled weakly.

He remembered she took cream and sugar in her coffee so put it on the table. He made toast and just set it in front of her, and when he ate his, she took a few bites.

"I'm meeting Bob at the office. Do you know him at all?" She shook her head no. "Do you want to go to the hospital today?"

She surprised him by saying, "I'll wait for Lindsay. We talk sometimes on Gloria's phone."

He knew they had been in touch somehow because she had met him at the door once and showed him a picture she took from her pocket of two little girls. He had just nodded and went to his room but felt bad now that she might have wanted to talk and he brushed her off. Gloria was a neighbor and had been for years. Maybe his mother got mail there too. Christ, what a life.

"Okay, I'm going to meet Bob now. The company is pretty good sized, we can't just do nothing." She nodded. "The same lady who came last night is coming about noon. You tell her if you need anything. I'll be stopping at the hospital just to check things out." He cleared his throat. "You understand he's gone, right?" She looked disconnected but nodded yes.

It was Saturday, so he waited to call Blossom until he was in the parking lot of the shop in case she slept in a little. "Hi, baby, the same lady is coming back today. Mom and I had coffee and toast this morning. She said a few words."

"Oh thank goodness. You sound a little better. You're young, honey, but I know you can do this. I wish I were right there to help, but I'm praying for you every second. I love you, Rocco."

"Thank you, baby girl. I'm at the shop to meet Bob. I'll call again tonight, if not sooner. I love you, Blossom."

Talking with Bob brought up more problems. Bob knew Helen could do payroll but didn't think anyone could legally sign other checks. They decided to have the men finish the jobs they were on that already had all the materials and find out more when Rocco saw the lawyer. A call to Helen found that Tony didn't believe in modern technology, so all payments were made by check, and there was an astounding $480,000 in the checking account. She was pretty sure there also was savings but didn't know the account or the amount. She did know he had seen the lawyer lately, and they would learn more then. A check through his desk didn't reveal anything, but there was a locked safe, and they'd check and see if Helen knew anything about that on Monday instead of calling her back. They agreed to report in on Monday as usual, and Rocco would see the lawyer at nine.

He waited until his mother was in bed, thanked the Home Health lady and asked her to come one more day until his sister came on Monday, and then he called Blossom.

Her old soul kicked in; and as they talked, she uplifted him, encouraged him, cheered him, and soothed him. Talking for two hours, short for them, she heard the exhaustion in his voice and was the one to say time for bed as he had always done for her. They both cried themselves to sleep—she, in frustration that she couldn't be there; he, in gratitude for her.

Sunday, his mother seemed different. It had been a day and a half without him in the house, and she still had a tentative attitude, but something was different. He said, "We better plan sleeping arrangements. I can go someplace if you need my room."

"No, there are two beds in our, my, room and two in Lindsay's," her voice a little stronger than yesterday.

"Do you need help making up the beds?"

"No."

"Would you like to go to the store with me for some groceries? I just wanted to get some basics, and then Lindsay can tell you what she wants."

"No. Probably peanut butter and jelly. And I haven't had eggs in the house for a while. Oh, and milk and cereal, and maybe chips and cookies. I'll go with Lindsay."

"It will be nice for you to see her and the girls."

A big sigh, "Yes, it will be very nice." A faraway look, "Very nice. On second thought, I need to wash some sheets."

"Your room?" he said softly. She shook her head yes. "I'll do that right now. You drink your coffee. The lady will be coming again, you watch for her."

"She's nice."

"Have you talked to Gloria yet?"

"No, I wanted to wait for Lindsay," twisting her hands.

He went upstairs, felt funny going into his parents' room, didn't think he'd ever been there. He stripped both beds and picked up the towels in the bathroom, looked into his sister's room and saw it still looked like a teenage girl's. It was clean and dusted.

He put a load in the washer and looked into the garage. He hadn't been in any rooms but his since he was fifteen. It reminded him his dad's truck was still at the shop. Might as well leave it there and rent Lindsay a car. He didn't even know if his mother could drive. He'd ask later. He checked the refrigerator and cupboards, made a few mental notes, and went to the living room where his mother was with the aide. "I'm going out for a while. I'll finish the beds when I get back. Does anyone need anything?"

The aide walked with him to the door, saying quietly, "She seems better. A little in denial, but that's normal when the situation is, umm, up in the air. Could you tell me anything about their relationship?" Not wanting to say too much, unsure of her job classification, he said, "He was a hard man to live with."

She nodded kindly. "I just wondered. She shows certain signs. At some point, it would be good if she talked to someone. The office can refer you."

He bit his lip and nodded. "You'll be here until I get back?"

"As long as you like. You talked about charges when you first called?"

"Yeah, that's taken care of. I'll be back in a couple hours."

He stopped into Enterprise Car Rentals to make sure they had a couple to choose from and then got groceries from Walmart. Did his dad get the groceries? Did they go together? He had no idea. He kept a few things in his room but had never bought much of anything. He wished Blossom was here, glanced into the Subway area to see if it had a private corner where he could call her, but decided against it, got what they had discussed, and checked out.

The aide said his mother was napping and a neighbor, Gloria, had come to the door to say Lindsay had decided to drive. He asked her to stay in case he had to leave, put the groceries away and the wash in the dryer, and called Enterprise to say he wouldn't be needing a car after all.

He thought it only polite to fill Gloria in, just in case Lindsay hadn't. He hadn't seen or talked to her since he was little, but it would probably be easier on his mother if she didn't have to tell her. It was a little awkward, both thinking, but not saying, she'd be better off. Gloria told him Lindsay had decided to drive in case her mom would like to come home with her for a while.

That brought up a whole new area of thought. What was his relationship with his mother now? Do they wipe away the years he thought she should have protected him? Should he live here? Oh well, Blossom had said one day at a time, so he'd do that for now. Bad time to call her, checking his watch, her mother would be calling.

He told the aide he was going out and there were cold cuts, bread, and soup. He felt compelled to stop at the hospital. He told the nurses' station his sister would be arriving Monday night and sat in his father's room for a few minutes. Since he'd met Blossom, the hate had abated, but nothing had replaced it. He felt nothing.

He stopped at McDonald's drive-thru, taking comfort in the familiar, and went to the shop—he didn't know why. He walked around for a while, sitting at Helen's desk and gingerly at his father's. He felt his lack of education, not knowing what happens in cases like this. Maybe he had told Steve he was leaving the kitchen too soon. Oh well, he had told Blossom if you need information, go where the information is. So see the lawyer tomorrow and get some information. One day at a time.

He called her at eight, and as soon as he heard her "Hi, darling, how are you feeling tonight?" all the edges softened.

"Hi, baby girl, I'm good."

"Have you heard from your sister?"

"Not directly, but the neighbor says she's driving. That's another thing I have to do—get my mother a phone. But you know what, sweetie, I don't want to talk about it tonight. Let's just put it aside until I see the lawyer. This whole thing is like a puzzle, and I don't have all the pieces. Thank goodness Helen knew about the lawyer, or I wouldn't know where to begin. Let's pretend I just called. You all comfy?"

"Uh-huh. All washed and brushed and in my smurfies."

"Umm, I wish I was there. So what's your name?"

Laughing at his game, she said, "Blossom. What's yours?"

"I'm Rocco. What do you look like?"

"I'm pretty ordinary looking. I have brown eyes and brown hair."

"Ordinary. Are you kidding? Your eyes are like liquid chocolate with gold specks in them, and your hair is heavy and shiny and swings when you walk."

"Oh, Rocco, you're so sweet."

"So how tall are you?"

"I think I'm almost five feet."

"Umm, and what are your measurements?" A grin in his voice.

"Rocco!"

"That's a perfectly legitimate question. I've heard it on TV lots of times."

"Well, I don't know my measurements. I wear a size zero or two if that helps."

"No, miss. I mean what is your bra size?"

"Rocco! What is the matter with you tonight? Every time you've ever said anything inappropriate, it's been about bras," laughing.

"Well, as they say on TV, you are unusually well endowed for a girl your size. It's hard not to notice."

"This is a totally inappropriate discussion, but I think I'm a 30C, which probably doesn't mean a thing to you anyway."

"So what's it mean?"

"The 30 is the measurement around the back, and the C is the," she whispered, "cup size. And that's enough of that."

He forged on anyway, "So how does it go, then? A, B, C? Oh, wait, I get it. There's a strip club called the Double D, so that's what it means. I get it now."

"You are just bad tonight. What's going on?"

"We were supposed to be together kissing right about now, remember?"

"I know, I know," she sighed. "We'll be together soon. You have things to do. We don't know when you'll be done, but you'll be done eventually. You call me tomorrow, and I'll make my reservations."

"I love you, Blossom."

"I love you, Rocco. So much. Call me no matter what time. I'll get away."

The call came at ten fifteen in the morning. She saw his name and, even though she was an integral part of the class discussion, started walking toward the door saying "I have to leave for a while" to the surprised looks. She opened the phone before she was out of the room, and they all heard the shouting even if they couldn't understand the words.

"He left me the business for Christ's sake! What the hell is that supposed to mean?" Screaming now, "That son of a bitch. He kicks a little kid all over the house and thinks he makes it right by leaving me his goddamned business?"

From far away, "Rocco, Rocco," in a soft voice. He finally heard it but still couldn't lower his "WHAT?"

"Rocco, I can hear you're upset, but please don't swear. It's very offensive to me. Take some breaths and tell me about it."

He took in some air, shuddering, still pounding the dash.

"What's that noise, honey?"

"Nothing, nothing, I hit the dash," breathing hard.

"Big breaths, honey, remember how you tell me, big breaths." She waited a minute while he breathed deep. "Can you tell me about it now?"

Still breathing hard, "He left me the business and left Lindsay the house. If she doesn't want it, I'm supposed to buy it for $200,000. The son of, I mean, he didn't leave my mother anything."

"Okay. Take some more breaths. The funeral director usually helps apply for the husband's social security. If he doesn't, you can take her right down to that office in the Plaza. She's not old enough, but there may be a way around that. If not, you can give her something every month. You said she's had a hard life. It would have been too much for her to leave her the business, and even the pressure of owning the house all of a sudden wouldn't be wise. Can you tell me any more?"

"I'm the executive or something."

"That's executor. Go on."

"How do you know this stuff?"

"I must have read it sometime."

"Well, anyway, it has to go through the court, and that will take time, but I have a power of attorney to run the business. Christ, I don't even know if I want the damn business."

"Don't swear, honey. You don't have to decide that yet. I remember you said you got a good feeling when a job went well. Maybe you would like it. Just take your time. People's jobs depend on you, so don't do anything in a hurry. Things will settle down in a few months, and it will be clearer to you."

"Blossom, baby, I need you here."

"I have something I have to finish today and tomorrow, but I'll be there by Wednesday night at the latest. I'm pretty sure there are several flights to Pittsburgh a day."

"I can come to get you."

"No, honey, I'd love that, but you'll be busy. One of my parents will come. Are you okay now?"

"I'm sorry I swore so much. I can't tell you how furious I was. I thought I was going to explode in there. I almost lost it."

"Keep taking deep breaths, honey. You'll feel better if you're doing things. Check on your mother. Tell Bob to carry on. He'll probably be relieved. Find out what jobs are coming up, get his advice about them. I know you can do this, Rocco. You're wonderful, and I love you to the moon and back."

Suddenly exhausted from his tirade, "Blossom, Blossom, you're such a miracle. I love you beyond words."

Her mother wasn't too pleased she was coming before the funeral was set but agreed to pick her up on Wednesday at four in the Pittsburgh airport.

He called Monday at eight, quickly said "I'm tied up, call later, I love you," and hung up. It had never happened before, and she just stared at the phone. Scenarios passed through her mind, all bad. Her common sense told her his sister had come. It was as simple as that. They had a lot to discuss. Her heart started to thud. Her breath was short. *Get ahold of yourself. Rocco's right, my age is showing.* She looked at her work, couldn't concentrate, decided to wash some unmentionables, tried to smile because he didn't know what they were, put them back in the mesh bag, couldn't do it, ended up sitting on her bed looking at a TV she didn't see.

She grabbed up the phone when it sounded at nine fifteen. "Are you okay?"

"I'm okay, how about you?" sensing something was wrong.

"You'll say my age is showing and be mad at me."

"Baby, you helped me so much this morning, I'll never say your age is showing again. Tell me."

"You hung up so fast, and I didn't know why, and I couldn't find my common sense, and I couldn't concentrate, and I was so scared, and . . ."

"Baby, baby, we're way past you worrying like that. I should have said more, I just saw it was eight and wanted you to know I saw it was eight. I was in the middle of something weird at the hospital."

"What was weird?"

"It's like they want to keep him on that machine to get back at him or something."

"Oh my goodness."

"Yeah. Lindsay came. She was cool to me, she's always been that way, but the little girls are great. Gloria came over to watch them, and we went to the hospital. The nurse explained they like to have a consultation, but my mom could decide then and there if she wanted to. I'm low man on the totem pole, so I just left and sat in the waiting room. Lindsay came out and sat for a while then said, 'We should let the SOB rot there.'"

"Oh, Rocco, what you all must have been through."

"So anyway, I had a chance to tell her he left her the house or if she didn't want it, I'm supposed to buy it. Then she wanted to get things moving. But Mom has the final word, so I'm in my room, and they're talking downstairs."

"One day at a time, darling, one day at a time."

"I know, I'll call the lawyer in the morning. Bob's got things covered at work for the rest of the week. If things move along, maybe the funeral will be Friday or Saturday. Are you coming soon?"

"Wednesday sometime, honey. You do everything you have to do and then call me, and we can be together for a while. I don't care how late it is."

"Your mother might not be too happy if it's nine or ten, baby girl."

"Rocco, this is an unusual situation. She'll just have to adapt. I'll tell her on the way back from the airport. It will be fine."

"Okay, I'll call tomorrow night. You won't be worried, will you?"

"I'm sorry, honey, you have enough to think about right now. You were so wise about our Friday calls. When I know you'll be calling, it's all I can think about."

"Blossom, baby, I'm going to see you every day for five days, and that's all I can think about. I don't care what time and for how long. I love you, baby. Good night. I have to go downstairs and see what's going on."

He was able to call Tuesday at eight. Things had been arranged for Wednesday morning. He wasn't sure how he felt. "Blossom, don't ever let that happen to me, okay. No machines, okay," desperation in his voice.

"Honey, there are papers you can have on file. I've been wondering if he'd been ill. Something made him do the will, but maybe he couldn't bring himself to do the end-of-life papers. I know people have feelings about them from my dad's office. We'll make some out together if it will make you feel better."

"Just don't put me on a machine, baby, please. It's worse, it's bad for you. Promise me."

"Of course, I promise, Rocco. You're way too young to think about it. I'm almost there, honey, take some breaths and tell me about the little girls," trying to calm him down.

"They like me. Madison is seven, and Marlee is five. Lindsay brought some schoolwork, and she can check online so Maddy won't get behind. She and I haven't had a chance to talk, and I haven't heard anything about her husband, so I don't know what's going on there."

"How's your mother seem?"

"Quiet, but she smiles a lot when the girls are around. Maybe when the funeral is over, she'll be better. This whole thing doesn't seem real. Let's put it aside for a while. Did you get the things done you needed to so you can come?"

"I'm at a good stopping point. I can pick it up Monday. I can't believe I'll see you tomorrow night. I'm glad I'm flying. It's kind of a dry run if we want to use our just-in-case money."

She heard a muffled "Uncle Rocco, Uncle Rocco." "Just a second, baby." She heard him open his door. "Hi, Maddy, why aren't you in bed?"

"Will you read me a story? Marlee's asleep."

She said, "Rocco, go ahead, honey, it's so nice you have someone at the house. I'll see you tomorrow."

"I love you, Blossom, see you tomorrow."

"It seemed to bother her mother that she had traveled so lightly. She had on her flounced denim skirt with matching jacket and boots, a light blue cashmere turtleneck, and only carried her Coach shoulder bag.

"Where is your computer, Blossom? You should really try to get some work done."

"I can work from the one in my room, Mom. It would be just my luck someone would want to check it, and it would hold me up trying to explain what's on it."

Without talking about Rocco's situation, she told her mom that his father had left him the business. Discussing that and all the attendant problems pretty much filled up the hour-and-a-half ride. She laughed to herself when her mother said, "That should keep him very busy."

It was nice to see her dad and Nixie. Her dad seemed genuinely concerned about the responsibilities Rocco had to take on and agreed with her that he should not make any decisions right away. It made her feel good that he was talking about him like he was a close friend, maybe not a member of the family yet, but not someone to be dismissed as a temporary interest like her mother tried to get across.

He called at nine, and she asked, "Honey, could I come out and sit in the truck?"

"Sure, baby girl, why?"

"If you come in, I know Mom will sit in the room the whole time. I'm just going to tell her you're coming over to bring me a gift. I've never shown them my doves, so I'll pretend you just gave it to me."

"I wouldn't care if she stayed in the room, sweetie. Maybe we should know each other better."

"Maybe tomorrow night, Rocco, I don't want to share you tonight."

"Okay, baby, I'm almost there."

She tucked her doves inside her sweater, went downstairs and casually called into the family room, "Rocco's coming over for a few minutes. He wants to give me something. We'll be in the driveway," and didn't wait for any reply.

He jumped out and ran to her, picking her up and swinging her around. "You should have a jacket on, but the truck's warmed up. Let's sit on this side so I can hold you in my lap."

"But I was wrapped in a quilt before. This is so close."

He winked at her. "I know, that's why I like it," grinning.

"Rocco?" worried.

"Don't think about it. Tell me about your trip."

She settled against his chest, taking a big breath, closing her eyes.

He said, "Nice, huh. Let's just sit here a minute. You're here. This whole thing doesn't seem real. Holding you does," kissing her hair. "I love you, Blossom Dove. Where are your doves, if I'm supposed to be giving them to you?"

She reached down in her turtleneck to pull the chain out.

"Can I do that for you," winking.

"Don't be bad, I can't handle it in person." She arranged the chain and patted the heart against her chest. "I love it so much." She surprised him by lifting up and kissing his cheek.

"Does that mean I might get a kiss tonight?"

"Honey, we should be talking about what happened to you today."

"We have our whole life to go over it. Right now you only have five days, and hugging you is more important. The visitation is Friday night six to eight at Mitchell's, by the way, and the funeral there at eleven on Saturday. But let's talk about that tomorrow. Now, about that kiss?"

"Rocco"—against his chest—"you're so close, my heart is pounding in my ears, it's hard to breathe." Swinging her left hand around in the air, "You consume this whole space. Please try to understand why I can't."

He smiled at her tiny hand flailing around, took it in his right, and kissed her fingers, whispering, "For all those same reasons, I want to kiss you, baby. Can you understand that?

She went very still. "You mean I'm selfish, like my mother says?"

"No, no, no, Blossom, get that out of your mind. You're the least selfish person in the world. What I mean is maybe you're reading the signs wrong. Maybe all those things mean you want me to kiss you."

Still talking into his chest, her eyes closed, "What if I cry and when I go in the house, they'll know? Wouldn't it be better at school?"

"You're stalling, little one. If you cry, we'll stay here until you're done. Why wait for school, we're inches apart. The little kiss?"

She nodded yes, and he turned her chin and kissed her gently, making sure it was only three seconds long. Still she whimpered and hugged him tight and breathed hard. He touched her chin again. She said, "No, no, no," but found his lips with hers and put her hand behind his neck, holding him tight, moving her lips with his, whimpering, "Rocco, Rocco," breathing hard.

"I'm here, baby girl, I'm here. That's enough for tonight. Are you all right?"

"It's too much, too much."

"You're allowed to feel, sweetie, it's supposed to feel good. Did you like it?"

"Oh yes, yes, yes"—breathing fast—"but it's too much."

Breathing fast himself, desperately wanting to go on, but controlling himself, "Blossom, I love you so much." He kissed the tears at the corners of her eyes.

"Did I do it right?"

"Oh, baby, you did it so right!"

She leaned back and looked at him, smiling coyly. "I like kissing."

He shook his head, grinning. "I should spank your bottom, I swear to God. You keep me hanging for three months, and now you like kissing?"

She clapped her hands. "Want to kiss some more?"

"Rocco can't kiss any more. You're too good at it, and he might do something he shouldn't. You better go in. Let me put my jacket around you until we get to the door."

She skipped ahead of him happily, hugging him tightly when they were hidden under the portico. "Do you want to talk about your day? I don't want to be selfish."

"You couldn't be selfish, baby girl. May I call you anytime tomorrow and see when we can get together?"

"Anytime. I think they're going to work, but you never know. Kisses?"

"Little kisses or I won't want to go."

"I love you so much, Rocco. Do everything you need to do and then call me. I'll tell them about Friday and Saturday. Good night. Thank you for the delicious kisses."

He pushed her in the door, taking his jacket as he did so, shaking his head, and winking. She stood inside the door blowing him kisses. He drove away thanking God for the miracle she was.

The next morning he went to McDonald's drive-thru, still not comfortable enough in the house to have breakfast. At noon he called his sister to ask what she had planned for dinner. Gloria had asked them over. She and her mother were taking clothes to the funeral parlor, and she would ask them if there was anything else they should be doing.

He said, "As long as you have a plan, I'm going to take my girl to dinner. She's in town for the funeral, and I'd like to spend some time with her."

"Your girl? What bar did you pick her up in," she said snappishly, laughing to ease the sting, but not really caring.

"Actually, I picked her up in college," he said, unaffected. "You'll meet her tomorrow night."

"College! What were you doing in college?"

"I've been taking some classes trying to clean up my act. I'll tell you about it later. Maybe you and I can get away alone Sunday night or Monday to catch up."

"Yeah, I guess we better."

He called Blossom to see if she could get away at five-thirty for dinner and was tickled when she breathed "Oh, yes" but sensed something reserved. She was at the door and came right out when he pulled in. He jumped out and hugged her. "I wanted to come to the door and ask for you like a gentleman, baby."

"No one's here. Can we go right away before they come? I just left a note."

"Sure. Are you okay? Did they give you any trouble last night about the gift?"

"No, no. Actually it went really well. Of course, Mom said I don't deserve gifts, but Dad made a fuss over it and said you were lucky to find doves. Then when I was going up the stairs, she said something I couldn't hear, but he said, 'He's in the picture, Elaine, there's no point pretending he isn't.' I really liked that."

But she was sitting stiffly, looking straight ahead, and clutching her hands in her lap. "So what's bothering you then, Blossom, you were so happy last night."

She moved her left hand around in circles. "Blossom, don't say proximity again. Haven't we moved beyond that?"

"But you're filling up this whole truck, my heart is pounding in my ears."

"Baby girl, every time we take another step, you get worried. It's okay, we're fine."

"I just don't know, honey. I don't know if it was a good idea to kiss, I just don't know," tears starting.

He pulled into Mangia's parking lot, couldn't see anyplace secluded, so went to the far end. "Can you talk about it inside, or do you want to stay here a minute?"

She put her hands to her mouth, tears flowing now. "I couldn't sleep very well, I was uncomfortable. I always fall to sleep easy. I think of you dancing or when I was sitting on your lap in my dorm, and I fall right to sleep, and I couldn't sleep," she wailed.

"Okay, I'm coming over there, sit tight a second." He picked her up and got in her side.

"No, no, not in a truck."

"Sweetie, relax, we're just talking. Now tell me why you couldn't sleep."

"All I could think of was our kiss."

"But you said you liked it, baby girl."

"I had feelings, and then I thought of the kiss, and I had feelings again. I didn't know what to do."

"Baby, I told you it's okay to have feelings. You've buried yours so long, you don't know what they are. It's okay, I had feelings too. I loved having feelings about you."

"Rocco, you don't understand," whimpering.

"Tell me, then. I told you, you can tell me anything."

"I could tell you on the phone. It's easier."

"Blossom, I love talking to you on the phone, but we have to be able to talk in person too, so just say it, it's okay."

Cupping her hand around his ear, she whispered, "I have feelings in private places," burying her face in his jacket.

Hugging her tight, his heart filled with so much love; it hurt. "Baby girl, it's okay. You're a woman, you're going to have feelings like a woman. It's just building up to when we make love—in the future, in the future," he added hurriedly when she stiffened and cried "No!" "Remember, you have all the power," wiping her tears, kissing her nose. "We'll kiss when you want to. Now let's go have a nice dinner. This is such a gift that you're here."

Her voice still catching, "D-Do you think we should be going out to dinner when your father just died?"

"People have to eat, Blossom, and as far as anyone knows, it's almost been a week."

"Oh my goodness, I was just thinking of you, and I wore red. Do you think that's inappropriate?"

"Sweetie, we're two people having dinner. Don't worry about it. We're going in through the kitchen, so I'll have to make some small talk."

They said their hellos, Rocco acknowledging sympathies for his loss. He said he would help out until they found someone, and they were seated at their table. Blossom said, "I really like it here, it's comfortable, and everyone is so nice."

As he helped her out of her jacket, he whispered "Wow" at her red angora halter top, lightly kissing her shoulder as she shivered. "So that's what matches the red petticoat I saw in the truck. Very, very nice," making her laugh as he did a Groucho Marx leer. They ordered comfortably, fed each other, settled into the easy conversations they had on the phone, flirted, and had a wonderful time.

"Are you ready to meet my mother and sister tomorrow night?"

"Yes, I'm looking forward to it regardless of the circumstances."

"Well, Lindsay's a little rough around the edges. We haven't talked much, but I'm sure things haven't been easy. I think the girls will stay home. I don't know how many people might be there. He didn't have friends, I'm sure, maybe business acquaintances. I'm not sure what happens after, but can you stay and I'll take you home?"

"Yes, they said we'll all come tomorrow, and I'll come by myself Saturday morning."

"I'll come and get you Saturday, then, and you won't have your car."

"Are you sure I won't be intruding? You don't know what will be happening."

"Blossom, as long as this has happened, let's stay together so everyone can see we're a couple."

"I like that. Whatever goes on, we'll do it together. The funeral director will tell us step by step, I'm pretty sure."

They settled back, and he said, "So you're in charge, can we kiss tonight?"

She smiled and tilted her head. "Can it be somewhere between the little kiss and the big kiss?"

Her eyes widened as he grinned and said, "Lady, we haven't even had a big kiss yet."

She looked worried and then wrinkled her forehead and squinted. "What you talkin' 'bout, Willis?"

His laugh rang out. "Gary Coleman, *Different Strokes*," and she clapped.

Their waitress came over. "Nice to see you're still laughing, Rocco."

"I'm a happy man, Jean, a very happy man," winking at Blossom as she blushed furiously. "We'll have a cup of chocolate mousse, two decaf coffees, and the check."

"Now she thinks there's something going on between us. I've embarrassed you."

"You can't embarrass me, I told you, and there's definitely something going on between us," lifting his eyebrows.

As before, she gave total concentration to the mousse, so comfortable now she licked the spoon and caught him watching her intently. "I love chocolate." She smiled.

"I see that. Weren't you allowed to have chocolate when you were little?"

A shadow crossed her face, the smile gone. "Only after competitions and then not at all until I could buy my own." She pushed the cup away, the pleasure gone. "It's not important, I don't care."

"I care, can I have a bite?" She fed him a bite, the bad moment gone, eating again and then cleaning the residue with her finger and offering it to him. He held her hand and sucked her finger, making her shiver. She bravely stared at him and sucked her finger to be sure it was gone while he shook his head. "What am I going to do with you?"

"It tastes better when you're here."

"I love you, Blossom."

Softly, "Thank you."

"We better get back. I'm not sure what's going on tomorrow, but if I'm not helping my sister, I'll be at the shop. I'll see you when you come, and then we'll take it from there."

She looked at her clenched hands. "I wish we had someplace to go where we could be alone. I never thought I'd miss the privacy at school."

"We don't have a place right now, baby girl, and I don't think you really want one yet."

"I don't mean that! I just want to kiss you, and I don't think my mother will leave us alone in the driveway another night."

"Maybe she won't bother us on the porch for a little while, and that's enough for now."

He doused the lights on the truck before they pulled in, shutting the doors quietly, hoping to buy a few more minutes. He touched his lips 'sh,' winking at her conspiratorially, making her smile. On the porch, her eyes widened as he unbuttoned her jacket, pulling her closer, his hands on her back. He whispered against her neck, "Reach behind my neck and see if I need a haircut for tomorrow," and as she did, pulling her closer still. "Little kiss?"

She shivered in anticipation. "Yes."

"You sure?" moving and nibbling against her lips as her breath came harder and she started whimpering. "You see why we can't be alone," he whispered. "This is serious business." He leaned back and looked in her eyes, rubbing the tears away with his thumbs. "Serious business." He smiled. She smiled weakly and nodded. "I'll see you tomorrow night. Will you sleep better tonight?"

Still breathing hard, she nodded yes, her eyes wide.

"I love you so much, Blossom."

Barely able to get the words out, she breathed, "I love you, Rocco."

A quick kiss on her nose and he ran to the truck.

He let himself enjoy thinking of the kiss for a minute but then chastised himself for what he had thought during the night—that he could push the issue, they could go to a motel. She thought she wanted to go further. He could talk her into it. But he felt like scum he had even thought it. He didn't want to be that kind of man. She was too important to him. Precious, precious girl, she had told him her private thoughts. He was so lucky to have her. He could not hurt this girl, this woman-child, so smart but so innocent. God, he loved her so much. What a miracle he had found her, an out-and-out miracle.

His phone vibrated at eleven-fifteen. He had half expected it. "Hi, baby girl."

"I can't sleep."

"Blossom," accusingly.

"You know what would be fun," she said. "You could come over and stay in the street, and I could sneak out and meet you!"

"Is this one of your daydreams?"

"Well, yes, but we could really do it. Right now even."

"And then what, Blossom?"

"Then we could go someplace and kiss," whispering.

"And then?"

"And kiss some more," she said happily.

"Baby girl, remember when we had our serious talk, and you told me you wanted things to be right and not in a truck?"

"Yes"—deflated—"but I didn't mean that."

"Well, what do you think all that kissing in the truck would lead to? What were you feeling when we kissed? Remember what you told me?"

"But I just want to be with you. I can't sleep."

"Blossom, for a while longer, we'll have the little kiss hello and the big kiss good-bye. You were sure about what you wanted, let's don't take any shortcuts." He knew she was crying. "Lay down and cover up, and I'll sing you an old song I heard from *The Music Man* the other day." And he sang "Till There Was You" until he heard her breathing evenly. "Good night, baby girl. Close your phone, I love you." Then he sat with his head in his hands, wondering how long he could last.

She came in with her family at seven and hurried to him and held his hand. "I tried to get them to hurry so you wouldn't be alone."

"It's okay. I wanted you to meet the guys from the shop, but we can do that another time."

Her family came over, and he said, "This is my sister, Lindsay Cunningham. Lindsay, this is Blossom, her parents, Dr. and Mrs. Richards, and her brother, Nix. My mother is up front, it's been difficult for her," he said diplomatically. As her parents moved toward the front, he guided Blossom to another room.

"You look so handsome." She smiled. He was in a navy sport coat, a navy turtleneck, and gray slacks.

"You're breathtaking. Another Aunt Mim outfit?" She nodded yes, in a dark gray princess style wool coat with a shawl collar showing the neckline of a matching ribbed knit dress. Her black leather headband matched her Gert McGraw high-button shoes.

"Will you walk down with me? Maybe you can introduce me to your mother."

"I wasn't going to go down there. I don't want to."

"I'll hold your hand. Close your eyes if you have to."

When she started to kneel, he jerked her lightly, indicating he didn't want to. She saw him looking downward. "I think it's good to take a tiny look. I read that someplace," she whispered.

She looked into the casket, briefly, and then looked again, her brow furrowed. When she met Lindsay, she had seen a slight resemblance to

Rocco around her chin and eyes, but Lindsay's eyes were hazel and her hair a reddish-brown. He tugged at her hand, and they took a couple steps to his mother. Her coloring resembled Lindsay, but she was painfully thin with a gauntness about her features. She must be about my mother's age, she thought, but looks decades older.

"Mother, this is Blossom Richards. Blossom, my mother, Marie Carnavale."

"It's nice to meet you, Mrs. Carnavale, I'm so very sorry." His mother looked up for a second and smiled tentatively.

"Blossom will come back to the house with me, so we can talk more there."

They chatted with her parents, Rocco talking comfortably with her father about the cause of death and business, breaking away now and then to greet others with Lindsay. As they started discussing leaving, he bravely said, "I'll be free Sunday, so I can take Blossom to the airport. Thank you so much for letting her come, I really appreciate it," squeezing her hand and holding his breath. He saw her mother begin to speak and was relieved when her dad said, "Well, thanks, Rocco, we appreciate that. Are you sure you'll have the time?"

"Yes, sir, after the funeral tomorrow, we'll take a day to regroup, so I'll enjoy the ride."

They said their good-byes, and Blossom said, "Oh thank you, thank you, honey. I'm so glad I didn't have to do that."

Lindsay was listening with a questioning look but didn't say anything. While Rocco and she talked with the funeral director about the Saturday schedule, Blossom went down to sit with his mother, and Lindsay took the opportunity to say, "That outfit cost a thousand dollars if it cost a dime. What does she see in you?"

"I don't know, but I'm sure glad she sees something."

They all got into Lindsay's van, and he whispered, "Thank you for staying with me, baby. We'll be at the house a little while. Maybe there will be something chocolate there. The neighbors have been bringing things."

It seemed surreal seeing Blossom in the house, rooms he had just started going in again. He had never seen her with children. Madison and Marlee took to her immediately, and she listened intently to everything they said, helped them with their snacks; and when Marlee picked up her pearl, he heard her say, "This is a birthday present from your uncle Rocco, isn't it beautiful?"

"Uncle Rocco, will you get me a birthday present?"

"I surely will, Marlee, do you want a necklace too?" Blossom smiled at him over her head, achingly beautiful in her knit dress. *This is what families do*, he thought, *eating together, talking about birthdays*. Nothing he had ever done. Things he was determined to have with Blossom.

When Lindsay said the girls should get ready for bed, he said, "I better take you home," but once in the truck, "Would you like to see the shop. You've never been."

She saw the outside was basically a metal building with some brick trim, paved parking area, nicely cared for, the rear extending for quite a ways to a fenced lot.

He showed her around but seemed distracted. There was a small entrance before the window where Helen greeted any walk-in customers. Behind the window, Helen's work area, more space with a counter, an aging table with six chairs, coffee machine, lockers, and a restroom.

She asked about Helen's safety, whether she was often alone, and was happy to see a ceiling camera. He was surprised she mentioned it and told her 911 was on speed dial and Helen could slide out of sight quickly. She smiled at his questioning look. "Doctor's office. We always have to think of break-ins and safety."

The other room was his dad's, now his, office—large, but only one desk and two dining room type chairs, restroom off to the side. "You could fix this up easily. A couple nice chairs in front of the desk for customers. Maybe a big table and chairs for morning meetings. That helped in our office, people like to feel their opinions count."

He was looking at her funny, so she smiled and said, "Have I overstepped my bounds?"

"No, Blossom, not at all. You're my baby girl, and sometimes I forget how smart you are."

"I'm only smart in one area, honey. But the morning meetings helped in our place. Maybe here you could do one on Monday to say what you'd like to accomplish and then on Fridays to see how you've done. Mom won't let us have donuts, just fruit or vegetables, but donuts on Friday would ease the mood if you're not happy with how things are going."

All of a sudden, he sat heavily into one of the chairs, so she took the other. "What, Rocco?"

A big sigh, "It's just that the world shifted . . . again," his head in his hands.

Softly, "Tell me about it."

"I felt the world shift when we met. I thought it was a new beginning, and then this . . ." Her heart ached when he came over, got on his knees, and put his head in her lap. She started caressing his hair and neck. "I made it through the days 'cause I always knew I could walk away." He raised his head; his eyes were wet. "I was this close to telling you I was coming down there to work, this close," putting his thumb and finger together. His head fell back in her lap.

She tried to be casual. "Oh, honey, that's so funny. I was going to ask you if you could find someone to look in on your mother, so you could come down to work too. We have to believe it's divine order, Rocco, you know how it says in that prayer book I sent you?"

"But now I have this place, plus the house. I feel cornered. Who knows when I can even get down for a weekend."

"Honey, remember, you only have to give it a try." She was rubbing his back with both hands now and could feel him relax, his breathing steadier. "We met three months ago, and see how the world changed. Give this three months and then see how you feel. I know you can do it. Thanksgiving and Christmas are coming up, we'll be together as much as we can. I love you so much, Rocco. I know you can do this."

He sat back on his heels, took her hands, and kissed them, pulling them both to their feet. "I'm supposed to be the mature and responsible one," he said grinning. "I'm sorry, baby girl."

She smiled sweetly. "I can be strong when you can't be, honey, you help me all the time," putting her arms around his neck.

Just then her phone rang in her pocket. She rolled her eyes. "Yes, Mom? We left Rocco's house, and I'm giving a cursory look at the computers in his office. No, there's not too much I can do yet, it's a pretty dated setup. Maybe in time. We'll be along soon. Yes, go ahead and go up. I can set the alarm. Bye, bye."

"I worry myself, I can lie so easily to her." She looked chagrined. "I guess I thought I should say we were doing something definite."

"Sweetie, don't lie to your mother. We're not doing anything wrong. And what about the computers here?"

"I'm sorry I was late and didn't meet Helen. Was she there earlier?" He nodded yes. "Well, you have to gauge the person you're working with. You don't want to offend her, and she might be worried about all the changes ahead. The business has been doing well, so after a while, I'll check your books and see what you need. You'll want a setup in here for you. It will be an easy transition. Is Helen a flexible person?"

"I've always gotten along with her. She had to be strong working for my father. I don't think there have been too many changes or anything modern for quite a while."

"Don't let it overwhelm you, honey, one day at a time." She smiled.

"Enough about business." He grinned. "How about kisses?"

She moved tight to him, her arms around his neck. "Remember, one kiss hello and one kiss good-bye."

He said against her lips, "What fool made that rule?" gently at first, then more insistent, moving, nibbling, opening her lips, brushing the inside of her lower lip with his tongue.

She pulled back, breathing hard. "No, no, no more."

He pulled her back to him, kissing her ear. "It's okay, it's okay, it's just a kiss."

"It seems like more than a kiss," her face in his chest. "I can't, I can't."

"You can't what, baby girl? You can't love me? You can't have feelings? What, Blossom?"

"I don't deserve you, Rocco. I don't deserve to feel good. I'm not a good person. I ruined my family," crying.

"God, baby, what have they done to you? You deserve the world, Blossom, you're a wonderful person. I'll spend my life showing you how wonderful you are. God gave you those feelings, sweetheart. They're your gift, they're our gift to share." He had backed onto a chair and held her, caressing her hair, kissing her head. "You need to tell them how they've made you feel, baby, you won't get past it until you do. How could they not love you, Blossom?"

"It's all the next accomplishment, Rocco, and it's never enough. I don't want to talk about it, it's so trivial compared to what you went through."

"It's hurting you, Blossom, so it's not trivial, and it's affecting us. I want you to love me with no shadows in the background. Soon I want to kiss you and not stop, baby, and I don't want another thing on your mind except how much we love each other."

"I can do that, I can do that," she breathed. "In the future, I can."

He laughed a little and set her down, kissing her forehead. "I see you got 'in the future' in there. That's okay, baby girl, no shortcuts, right? We better get going, it's late."

"I love you, Rocco."

When they got to her house, he walked her to the door, put his arms around her, and smiled as she looked worried. "Just a little kiss, baby girl, then you go in and blink the light when you have the alarm set." He kissed her lightly. "I'll pick you up at ten fifteen. Sleep tight, Blossom Dove, I love you."

If nothing else, she had plenty of black dresses to choose from for the funeral. She picked one her mother had bought for a Mathcounts group competition in high school. She took off the white collar, wore her pearl and the black Gert McGraw boots. She hated black, and the only jacket she had in black was a Tommy Hilfiger hip-length trench coat in quilted black satin. It would have to do.

Rocco looked indescribably gorgeous in the same outfit as last night, except a gray turtleneck. She closed her eyes and shook her head. "You are so handsome. So, so handsome."

"I had the pants from GED graduation, but I had to buy the sport coat at Peebles. Maybe next time you're home, we can go to Erie, and I'll get a suit. What?" as she looked at him smiling delightedly.

"I just love it when we talk about doing ordinary things like ordinary people. Won't it be wonderful to go to work, come home, cook dinner, and watch TV like normal people?"

"Can't wait, baby, can't wait," as he pulled into the funeral home.

Lindsay met them at the door looking determined. "What is it," Rocco asked.

"I want to talk to the funeral director about going to the cemetery."

"Linds, do you think that's too much for Mom?"

"I think it would be good for her, and I know it would be good for me," startling Blossom when she said, "I want to see the son of a bitch go in the ground."

Rocco made a face. "Blossom, would you go sit with Mom for a minute. We'll be right along."

He came back in a few minutes, his jaw tense. "We had to see if he could schedule the extra hour. Do you mind going, or would you like me to take you home?"

She touched his cheek and took his hand. "I'm with you all day," and his shoulders relaxed a little.

They were the only ones there until Bob arrived at ten fifty-five. "Blossom, this is Bob Petillo, our foreman. Bob, Blossom Richards."

The service went quickly. As far as they knew, he hadn't been to a church in at least twenty years, so they had asked the funeral director to say a few words—none about family, a mention of the successful business okay. Blossom had been to some beautiful ceremonies and felt bad for Rocco. She fought tears for that reason, but neither his mother nor sister shed a tear, so she just held Rocco's hand tightly.

The trip to the cemetery was equally grim. After a few verses from the Bible, he asked if they would like to toss roses on the casket. Lindsay humphed and said, "I've seen people put a shovel of dirt on. Can I do that?"

"Of course," he said and motioned a grave worker over to help her. Rocco did likewise, and they both supported their mother as her knees buckled.

As they turned to go, Lindsay asked the worker, "Will that be done today? The casket in the ground and covered, I mean. I'd like to come back." They assured her they would be done and gone in a couple hours. Rocco shook hands with the funeral director, looked in his eyes, and said, "Thank you for everything. Any paperwork send to that business address I gave you." The director patted his shoulder and nodded.

He and Blossom got in the truck. "Well, that was rough, but it's over. I can't see how that did Mom any good."

"Maybe she and Lindsay have been talking, and Lindsay felt it was something she needed."

"I think it was more for her than Mom. I tried to take the worst of things, and I can't remember him ever hitting her, but she has some things she hasn't worked through yet even though she has been gone seven years. We're going to talk alone after you go back, so I'll see."

She squeezed his hand tightly. "I can't even imagine what you've been through."

"Hey, I'm fine. I faced my demons and moved on," he said with his jaw clenched.

She didn't say what she was thinking, just rubbed his arm and patted his cheek.

As with other services she had been to, Blossom felt sorry there was no after-service luncheon or family gathering. Lindsay continued her mood when they returned to the house, and Rocco suggested they all go out for a late lunch. "What, to celebrate his transition to heaven, Rocco," she snapped. The tension was lightened when Maddy said, "We want to go with Uncle Rocco, can we, can we?"

"Why don't you and Mom rest then, and the girls can come with us. We'll take your car since their seats are in it. Here are my keys in case you need a ride."

"Okay, but no MacDonald's and no soft drinks."

As they started out, Blossom said, "How would you like to go someplace where they serve a donut with every meal?"

"Tim Horton's," she mouthed to Rocco.

"Shouldn't they have a real meal at Mangia's or Perkins," he whispered.

"They've been cooped up all day. They need to be able to move around a little."

He nodded, and as they got out of the van, Blossom said, "Now, of course, they only give you the donut if you eat your soup or sandwich, everybody understand?"

"Yes, yes," in unison.

Blossom and the girls picked out soup and a roll; Rocco, the large BLT. Blossom said, "Your mom wants you to have milk, which is good because we can dunk!" Picking out the donuts was a major decision. "What are you getting, Aunt Blossom?" She smiled gloriously at Rocco to be considered their aunt. "I like to get the little chocolate balls, then I can get three of them."

"Me too, me too," said Marlee, but Maddy went for the big one with sprinkles.

Finally, "We have to take Aunt Blossom home so she can get into some comfortable clothes." To her, "I want to take you someplace casual, so wear that jean skirt or something like that. I'll say eight so you can spend some time with your parents, but if you can get away earlier, call me. Aunt Blossom has to go back to college tomorrow, girls, so say good-bye."

"Nooo," they whined.

"We aren't saying good-bye, we're just saying see you the next time." She stepped between the seats and gave them a kiss and blew kisses as they drove away. All she had hoped from the time home was to help him through it; so meeting his family had been sometimes uncomfortable, a little unsettling, but somehow comforting.

Her mother was testy that she was going out again, but she didn't care. She wore a gored denim skirt he hadn't seen with a high-fitted waist, a squash blossom belt around the hips, and a long-sleeved white blouse with denim collar and cuffs. She put on her dove necklace, denim boots, and jacket and went out to wait for him.

"You okay?" She could feel tension when he settled her into the truck.

"I'm fine. Let's stop into the shop for a few minutes."

There he looked around, sighing deeply. "I have to come in here Monday and run this place. I don't know step 1."

"Well, I'd see what Bob is making, and if it's feasible, give him a raise and tell him you'll be depending on him a lot and what does he think step 1 should be." She lifted her eyebrows. "Just a thought."

"You know what, I don't want to think about it tonight. I want to take you dancing," with a big smile.

"Dancing? Do you think it's appropriate to go dancing the day of your father's funeral?"

His eyes narrowed; his jaw stiffened. "Blossom, do you think there's something wrong with me because I don't care that my father died?"

Softly, "I don't think there's anything wrong with you, but I'm wondering if you do." She moved close to him and put her arms around his neck.

He stared at her for seconds and then kissed her gently before hugging her tightly to his chest. She felt his breathing quicken as he said hoarsely, "Let's make love, right here, right now."

She pulled back to see if he was smiling, but he looked at her with need, his eyes dark with desire. She backed up to a chair, her hand on her stomach, blood draining from her face, chills through her body. "You're serious?"

"Right here, right now," his breath ragged.

"Our plan. We were on the same page. Remember?"

"Blossom, you have to go back tomorrow. I need you," almost panting, desperate.

"On the floor, Rocco, on the floor? Is that what you're asking of me?" She looked at him in agony, tears starting. As his eyes raced around the room, she saw them stop at the desk. "On the desk, Rocco, on the desk?" She sobbed, "Or are you going to say the truck? My nightmare, the truck?" Covering her face with both hands, "Rocco, Rocco?"

Suddenly he swayed and took a step to catch himself. "No, no," as he rushed to her, picking her up and setting her on his lap, almost crushing her as he clutched her to his chest. "Oh my god, no, no, Blossom. I'm sorry, baby, I didn't mean it. Forgive me, I didn't mean it. I lost it for a minute, don't let me ruin this, Blossom, Blossom, please, baby, forgive me. Blossom," louder, "Blossom!"

She gasped as if coming up from too long underwater. "You can't ruin us, Rocco, I'm here, I'm here. I couldn't breathe," as she dug into his back. "I was scared, I was scared."

"Oh my god, Blossom, I swear to you I'll never bring it up again. I'm worse than your parents. Oh, Jesus, God, putting more on your tiny shoulders. I'm so sorry, my baby girl, I'm so sorry."

Standing up and swinging her around, covering her face with kisses, "This never happened, we're going dancing," carrying her to the truck, kissing her hands as he buckled her in. "We are on the same page, Blossom, forever." He got in on his side and looked at her with agony on his face. "Don't let me mess this up."

She smiled weakly. "You can't, you can't. I love you, Rocco."

He breathed hard for a few miles, gradually becoming himself. "I'm taking you to the place I learned to dance. I wanted to get up there and check it out 'cause I haven't been for a couple years, but I didn't have time. It's a bar, baby, and people drink, so if I say let's go, just get up and go, okay. It's not too late, and people shouldn't have been drinking too long, so I'm thinking it will be okay. The regulars are nice people. They put up with a lot from me, and if it hasn't changed, it's good for dancing."

He pulled into the parking lot. It was about half full, mostly trucks. Before he turned the truck off, he turned to her. "See, right there I just got a knife in my heart."

"What, why?"

"When I leaned toward you, you backed up."

"No, honey, it wasn't that. I'm not afraid of you. I just thought you were going to say something again after you said you wouldn't. I just wasn't ready to handle it again."

"Oh, Blossom, God, don't let me mess this up. You're the only thing good in my life, you're the only thing that's gone right."

"Rocco, it's okay, it's okay."

"No, it's not okay, Blossom. When I was drinking, I had an awful temper. Nothing's happened in a couple years, but something happened then. Slap me if you ever see it again."

"Rocco," she said gently, "the slapping and hitting are over. That is not the solution to anything. I could never slap you. I love you, and that's what I'll tell you if I see it again. You've had a very strange week. It's been a lot to handle."

"Don't make excuses for me, Blossom. I scared you. That's unforgivable."

"Honey, we've talked about it enough for tonight. Let's go inside. I would love to dance with you again."

He came around to her side, lifted her out, and kissed her lightly. "Do you remember some steps?"

"Every single one." She smiled. "I go to sleep thinking about it."

He sighed deeply, "I love you so much, baby girl."

She patted his face. "I know you do, I know you do."

They walked up to the bar, he looking quickly everywhere as they went. "Hey, Charlie."

"Rocco, as I live and breathe. It's been a long time. I hope you haven't been in jail."

"No, thanks to you looking the other way a lotta times. I've been trying to clean up my act. This is Blossom, I wanted to show her where I learned to dance. How are Saturday nights now? Safe to have her here?"

"Friday nights are still the regulars. Saturdays usually college kids and date night. The band doesn't start until ten. Did you bring Delbert with you?"

"No, not this time. Maybe next time she's home."

"Well, use the jukebox for a while and watch your back. She's a pretty little lady, don't leave her alone."

"Not a chance. Give us a Coke and a ginger ale. I'm on the wagon. Great to see you."

"That was a funny conversation. I've never been in a bar before. Is it like that?"

"Like I said, baby, people are funny when they drink. Nobody knows better than me."

"Who's Delbert?"

"A CD I used to bring of Delbert McClinton songs. Great to dance to."

He found some Elvis on the jukebox; and as before, he touched her lightly here, turned her by the waist there, twirled her with one hand above her head, and they were dancing. They had been on a small brick area at Penn. Here they had a whole floor, and he took her breath away. She was not even aware she did the same to him.

The live music started. It was different to dance to, louder, pulsating. Her eyes never left his face, watching for directions, in his eyes, by his touch. Even though it was hard to hear, he whispered directions, slowly walked her through new steps; and they danced almost every dance. When he put her hands on his shoulders and wiggled her hips to the beat with a hand on each side, catcalls and whistles started from a table of college boys. "Time to go." He laughed. "I can't fight all of them."

Once in the truck, she said, "That was so much fun. I'm so glad we came. You're wonderful, Rocco."

Still worried, "So we're okay, right?"

"Honey, of course we're okay. Things are going to happen in our life, and we're always going to be okay."

A big sigh escaped him as if he had been holding his breath, "God I love you, Blossom. Do you want to stop for anything—coffee, McDonald's?"

"We better not. It's after midnight, I don't think I've ever been out this late. I'm surprised my mother didn't call."

He didn't even try to coast into the driveway without lights. She was probably watching, and he didn't want to appear sneaky. He was apprehensive about a kiss as he walked her to the door. Would she be afraid? Oh god, how could he have been such an idiot.

He needn't have worried. She hugged him tight and nibbled his chin, looking in his eyes and lifting her eyebrows suggestively. "Thank you," he whispered. He kissed her softly and gently and didn't press for more. "I'll pick you up at nine. I hope you get enough sleep. I'm sure glad I'm taking you."

"Oh, so am I. I'll try not to make a scene and embarrass you."

"You can make all the scenes you want. I love you, Blossom Dove."

"I love you, Rocco Anthony," whispering in his ear, "forever and ever."

Her mother met him at the door in the morning. "This really isn't necessary, Rocco, we can take her. You should spend time with your sister."

"It's a pleasure, Mrs. Richards. Lindsay will be in town for a while. Don't you have a suitcase, Blossom?"

"No, this is it," swinging her large bag onto her shoulder, wearing the same outfit she had arrived in adding both her doves and the pearl. Nixie wasn't up, but she kissed her dad as he came to the foyer, hugged her mother. "See you at Thanksgiving. Bye, bye."

As he pulled onto the street, she heaved a big sigh. "Oh, I'm so glad you're taking me."

He pulled over to the berm, taking her chin in his hand, and kissed her lightly. "Good morning, sunshine, did you have a good sleep? Did you enjoy dancing?"

As he pulled back into traffic, she smiled. "It was so much fun, honey, I can't remember having fun when I was growing up. Can you?" looking concerned.

"No, I can't, baby, but this is now, and I'm definitely having fun," winking at her.

"I rode a pony once in New Mexico. I remember thinking this is *fun*. The wind was blowing my hair. My friend and I rode all day. I felt like an Indian princess. Then Dad said, 'We're not here to have fun, Blossom, we're here to work.' It's not really the same, but I feel like that dancing with you. Like I'm reading your mind and feeling what your muscles want me to do. I feel free like I did then. It's so wonderful."

"Wow, now I feel humble, baby girl." Then he smiled hesitantly. "Blossom, I need to ask you something. It's about the thing we're not talking about."

She took a breath and looked at her hands. "Okay," quietly.

"If this has anything to do with why you want to wait, I just want to tell you I'll go to your parents and tell them we want to get married. If you want that or need that, I can do it, and I will do it."

"Rocco, I love you so much. They would never agree to that. It would just make things worse, I'm sure of it. She's trying to keep us apart now. She would try even harder if we brought that up. It's just a big step, and I'm scared." She smiled, looking down. "It's as simple as that. I need more time."

"Can I fix something or do anything? I'm not talking about it, I promised you I wouldn't, but I can't fix something if I don't know what's wrong."

She kissed his hand. "There's nothing you need to fix. You're perfect, and I love you. No more talking about it."

They were quiet for a while but soon settled into easy conversation, and the airport signs came much too soon. "I've never been to an airport before. Will the GPS take me where I should be?"

"You know, honey, you could just drop me at Departures. You can't come very far anyway."

"That's never going to happen. Where do I park?"

"Just follow the signs for Short-Term Parking then. I hate to have you spend more money." They made their way to US Air. She had everything she needed for her return flight at 12:20 p.m.

"Why can't I go sit with you until the plane leaves?"

"You have to have a ticket and a boarding pass to go any further."

"Well, I'll buy a ticket then, I don't like you sitting alone."

"Rocco, don't you dare do that. I'll stay here until quarter to, I only have my purse."

They found a chair, and she sat on his lap, a little uncomfortable drawing attention to herself but soon oblivious to the crowd. "Just set the GPS for home, honey. If it's confusing, follow the sign for 60 North, and then the GPS can take it from there."

"I couldn't have gotten through this without you, Blossom. I hope I can do the next step."

She put her hands on each side of his face, looking into his eyes, "You can do it, Rocco, I know you can. Remember what you told me when I left for school, 'Do it for yourself'? You did so much when you were seventeen, honey, starting all over all alone," her eyes tearing up. "I know you can do this."

They hugged tightly, silently, he caressing her hair. He said, "The reason you came aside, did you have a good time?"

"It was wonderful. The girls were adorable. Your mother was nice, but I don't know if Lindsay liked me."

"Baby girl, who couldn't like you. I think she's going through some stuff herself. It's been seven years. I don't really know her anymore, if I ever did. I'll find out more in the next couple days. What did you like most about the trip?" lifting his eyebrows.

"You know," she whispered in his ear, "kissing."

He found her lips and kissed her a little too long, making her whimper. "Are people looking, am I embarrassing you?" She covered her face with his jacket lapel.

"Everybody's saying good-bye to someone, baby, nobody's paying attention to us. You know what I'm going to say now, don't you?"

"Yes, we're back on Friday night calls. I just hate it, but I know you're right. Last week when you called every day, I couldn't think straight."

"So we're going to be strong, no matter what your mother comes up with, right?"

Her voice rising, worried, "What do you mean? What will she come up with?"

"Little one, it's probably going to be like your birthday. She might say you only have a couple days, so there's no point in coming home for Thanksgiving."

"But I want to come home. She has to let me."

"Blossom, it hasn't happened yet. I'm just saying let's be prepared and be strong. Christmas is coming too."

She jumped up, her voice rising, for once not caring who heard. "Christmas is six weeks away. I can't do six weeks."

"Come here, baby. Blossom, *come here*." She settled on his lap again, her arms crossed, pouting, staring at him with narrowed eyes. "Look at you"—nuzzling her ear—"getting upset about something that hasn't happened. We've done six weeks before, we may have to do it again. I'll do what I can after I see what I'm getting into at the shop." He stood up, putting her on the floor. "You better go, baby girl, I love you beyond words. Good-bye kiss?"

She sighed sadly. "I really hate this, Rocco, I really do." She put her hands behind his neck and smiled weakly. He hugged her tightly against his chest then kissed her gently, then more insistently, nibbling, biting, softly touching her lips with his tongue until she moaned and went limp against him. He sat her back on the chair and knelt in front of her. She looked at him, her eyes big, awed.

"You're going to be a good girl and go quickly."

Her eyes big, biting on her fist, nodding silently.

"You're going to work hard and be ready for our Friday night call."

Eyes still big, nodding yes.

Then smiling and winking, "And you're going to love me forever?"

Smiling now, through tears, nodding yes.

"Okay, go. Go. Don't look back. I'll wait until you're gone. I love you, baby girl."

She got up and ran; and he collapsed unto the chair, heaving a sigh, finally, at twelve thirty, dragging himself to his truck. A twenty-year-old boy getting ready to run a construction company on the shoulders of an eighteen-year-old girl.

She stared at the phone, willing it to make a sound, any sound, please, please. When it did, she opened it and heard "Hi, baby girl" and burst into tears. Sobbing, "S-s-sorry, sorry."

He said, "It's okay, it's okay. Go ahead and cry. If I wasn't the mature one, I'd be crying too." He let her go on for a minute, then "Did you have a good week? Did you work hard?"

Catching her breath, shuddering, "Yes, I got a lot done."

"Would I understand what you were doing?"

"No"—laughing a little—"probably not. It's not important. How did you do?"

"One day at a time, sweetie. I got a table for my office like you said, and we had donuts and coffee there this morning. Bob and I measured a garage to make into a family room. I put it on the computer okay, but now we have to make folders of different suggestions for walls and floors and windows. That kind of stuff was already done when I went on the job. There must be computer programs where all the choices are there and you can show the customer how it will look different ways like Home Depot does. He did it the old-fashioned way, and there was work, but I'd like to update things. The scary part is going to come when all the jobs are done that were scheduled and I have to keep the crew busy."

"I know you can do it, honey. Ask your suppliers if they have programs already. If you came to my house to measure, I'd give you the job just to keep you around." She laughed.

On they talked, comfortable again. He told her about having dinner with Lindsay. She was going to take his mother with her, at least for a few months, but she was waiting until she got her money and after Thanksgiving.

"My mother will probably tell me Sunday what they're going to do," her voice catching.

"Whatever it is, we'll handle it, baby. I volunteered to cook, but Linds said she'd rather go out. Mom hasn't been out since the funeral. I thought she'd be a little more lively as time went on, but she seems quieter."

"It's only been a couple weeks, honey, and it's such a life change for her. What did you and Lindsay talk about?"

"I think she always blamed me somehow. Maybe she remembers a time when things weren't bad, I don't know," his voiced getting strained. "I told her I didn't do anything, and I didn't. Sure, maybe about ten I started mouthing off, but it didn't matter, it was going to happen anyway."

"Oh, Rocco, I'm so sorry. I love you, honey, I'm so sorry."

"It's in the past, sweetie, in the past. You're here, that's all that matters now. I did ask her about Randy. They're separated, but he's been coming around, and she hopes the money will make her more relaxed and easier to get along with. With Mom there, she'd like to go to work, even part-time. Mom would only have to watch the girls a couple hours after school, and Linds thinks she could handle that."

He didn't tell her their exchange about her when Lindsay said, *"I still don't know what she sees in you. You banging her?"*

"Jesus, Lindsay. If you were a guy, I'd smash you in the mouth for that. She's the girl I'm going to spend my life with. Let's change the subject. You've done a great job with the girls and not much to go on."

"Thanks. You try to do things the way you wish they had been for you, I guess. Hey, if Mom does want to stay, can you throw in some extra money every month?"

"Sure, what do you think? A hundred a week?"

"That sounds okay. I'll see how it goes and call you. It'll be funny to have a number for you. Listen, I'm sorry what I said about Blossom. She seems really sweet, and I hope everything works out for you."

"Back to us, now. Last Saturday we were dancing. Do you remember?"

"Of course I remember. That's how I put myself to sleep, thinking of every dance. I usually fall asleep before the second one is over. Is that what you think of to get to sleep?"

"You know I don't, I—"

"Don't say it, Rocco, I can't handle it right now."

"I'm going to say it anyway, baby girl. I think of our kiss at the airport. It made me weak in the knees. Tell me you didn't like it."

"You know I did, but I can't handle it, it's too much," starting to cry. "I don't know what to do."

"Don't cry, Blossom, I'm sorry. I just want to be with you so bad. Do you want to be with me? I mean really with me?"

"Rocco, you said you wouldn't talk about this. You're so far away, and I'm not a good person."

"Baby, you're the best person. Don't you talk like that."

"But my mother says I'm a disappointment," crying fully now. "Oh, Rocco"—in a small voice—"what if I disappoint you?"

"Blossom!" He blurted it out as if kicked in the stomach. "Blossom, baby," and then he was crying uncontrollably. "Oh god, this distance is killing me, I can't," unable to speak.

Her control came back first. She knew he needed to talk about other things. "Should I be worried about who taught you how to dance?"

He knew what she was trying to do so took some breaths and tried to laugh. "Not hardly, baby. When I started, line dancing was popular, and you don't dance with anyone, only a group in a line. Then one of the regulars at the bar taught me the details. She's older, her name is Big Sallie, and that doesn't begin to tell the story. Worrying about me is the last thing you need to do now or ever. I'm sorry I lost it back there, baby girl, you can't think like that. I can't even respond to something like that."

"I don't want to talk about it anymore, Rocco. Can you sing something so I can go to sleep?"

So with his head in his hand, wanting to strangle her mother, he went through three Elvis songs before he heard her breathing evenly. He didn't want to wake her so never told her to close her phone.

He broke the rules and called her in the morning, pretending it was to make sure she charged her phone. "You okay, baby girl? What are you doing today?"

"I'm working on a paper, and I might use a treadmill later. I have to be in shape for dancing," she said with a smile in her voice. "Thank you for singing me to sleep. You have the most wonderful voice."

"It was my pleasure, little one. I'll sing to you our whole life. I have to go, I'm at the shop. I love you."

He broke the rules again and called at five on Sunday, holding his breath. He knew as soon as she said a weak "Hi, I was hoping you'd call." Then a big sigh, "They're coming here for Thanksgiving. I'm not coming home," dejectedly.

"Okay, okay, we expected it, baby, don't let it get you down," trying to be upbeat, but in his mind, *Damn, damn, damn.*

They talked until eight, both deflated but trying hard, covering anything and everything. "I looked for some classes to take, but nothing is offered this time of year. After Lindsay leaves, I think I'll put a door from her room into the bathroom off Mom's room. It's an old house, so it's unusual to have two bathrooms, but it's strange that room never had access to one."

"You're so talented, Rocco, I don't have any talents."

The kick in the gut, "Blossom, baby, quit putting yourself down. You're nothing but talent."

"I love you, Rocco."

Thanksgiving came and went. December started, raising their hopes but afraid of the other shoe falling. Sure enough, when he called the second Friday, "I'm coming home Sunday, honey," weakly.

"Thank God, baby, but what's wrong?"

She burst into tears. "I'm riding home with someone from Erie that Mom found out goes here. Why didn't she call you?" But then quickly added, "That's not even the worst," her voice catching, unable to go on.

"What, baby, what," fear knotting his stomach.

"I'm coming home for one day, Rocco, *one day,*" wailing. "We're leaving for Aunt Mim's on Tuesday and not coming home until after New Year's. Oh, honey, I can't do this, I can't. I have to transfer to Allegheny, I do," sobbing.

"Okay, baby girl, breathe, breathe. Now we know the worst. We'll deal with it. Can I see you Sunday night and Monday?"

"Oh, yes. When I cried and cried, she said we can have our Christmas on Monday. They're going to put up one tree and have an Open House because we'll be gone the whole holiday time."

"So I'll see you Sunday no matter how late? Who is this person bringing you anyway?"

"Ann something." He breathed a sigh of relief at the female name. At least her mother wasn't trying to set her up with somebody. "I was so upset I didn't listen. She's older, and she's already called me. We're meeting here at ten. Can I call you as soon as we get there, and you come and get me?"

"For sure, baby, I'll be right there. Blossom, we know what's going on. We can do this. Work will straighten out soon, and I'll get a schedule going to come down. It will get better, baby, it will. You know what I said to myself when I was trying to shape up and it got tough and I couldn't see anything good ahead?"

She was calming down as he talked. "What?"

"I'd say over and over, don't give in, and don't give up. So when she throws something like this at us, what do we say?"

Softly, "Don't give in, and don't give up."

"That's my girl. And look what happened to me, the miracle of you."

"Oh, Rocco, I love you so."

"I love you, Blossom Dove. I love you beyond words."

So they faced it, wrestled with it, and put it aside, settling into their Friday night talk. In encouraging her, he could feel himself gaining strength and determination and knew he'd have to be strong enough for both of them.

He came to the door Sunday night at seven and wasn't surprised her mother was standing with her. "Good evening, Rocco, how have you been?"

"Fine, Mrs. Richards, and yourself?"

"We're fine. I'm assuming your mother and sister have left? Blossom thought so."

"Yes, Mother did go with her. They may be back over the holidays for a short while if the roads aren't too bad."

"I see. Well, as I was just telling Blossom, I don't think it's appropriate for you to take her to your house with no one there, so please remember that. And don't be too late, dear, people will be in and out all day, and Rosalita will need our help. A perfunctory, "You're welcome to come tomorrow as well, Rocco," as she walked away.

She bit her lip as they got outside. "I'm sorry, honey, that sounded so juvenile."

"It's okay, I wanted to show you the door I put in upstairs, but we'll do it another time. Have you eaten? Where would you like to go?"

"Rosalita had dinner ready, so I had to eat. I've been thinking about the wildberry pie at Perkins. Would you like to go there so you can get something to eat?"

"Perkins, it is." They had pulled out of her development onto the street, and he pulled into the first secluded area. She looked questioning. "Sit tight, I'm coming over."

He came around to her side, pulled her out as he shut her door. "Rocco, Rocco," worried.

"Baby, it's been a month. I need a kiss."

"But there are cars going by."

"It's just a kiss, Blossom."

"Not too big, not too big," she said against his lips then whimpered and melted into him.

He pulled back first. "I love you, Blossom, I love you, baby girl."

"I can't go, Rocco, tell them I can't go."

"I think this is a critical time, sweetie, her last chance to keep us apart. There's no more holiday breaks. She can't come up with too much more. Let's be strong and get through it. She'll see it doesn't matter what she does, we'll still be together. What do we say?"

Shuddering, trying not to cry, "D-D-Don't give in, and don't give up."

"There you go. We're strong, right?" He raised his arm and flexed his muscles and got a smile. "Let's go eat, I'm starving. What took you so long to get here?"

"Oh, she had to be the slowest driver ever. I mean she was nice and everything. I don't know how our mothers met, but I tried to get across this was a one-time thing, and she shouldn't feel bad saying it wasn't convenient if they asked her again. I hope she sticks to it."

They both sat on the same side of the booth at the restaurant. He ordered pork chops, eggs, and pancakes while she shook her head lovingly. "I'm sorry I was late. You're so hungry, aren't you?" She asked for water with her pie, with hot chocolate to come later. She ate her pie then played in the whipped cream on her hot chocolate while he finished. She mouthed "I love you" every time he looked at her, almost overcome with love and emotion.

He finished his dinner, had more coffee, and ordered her another hot chocolate, put his arm around her; and they talked inches apart for a couple hours. Unable to change the next three weeks, they settled into their phone call discussions, talking about the minutiae of their lives. "You don't eat enough."

"Honey, I eat plenty. I'm not very big, my stomach is small."

"Okay, tell me everything you ate today."

"Well, I had a hot chocolate before she picked me up. I was a little agitated, and it always settles my stomach. Then she wanted to stop for lunch at Wendy's, and I had a baked potato. I thought she'd never quit talking, and I know it was rude, but I got up in the middle of a sentence and took my tray to the garbage just to get her moving. Then Rosalita had meatloaf for dinner, and I had a piece of that."

"How big a piece?"

"You're only supposed to eat meat the size of your palm or a playing card, so I guess mine was the size of my palm."

"Baby girl, you're palm is tiny," holding his hand against hers, her whole hand barely covering his palm.

"Well, you have big hands. You should be using the playing card for your guide."

"Yeah, right."

"Well, you could have a small strip. That would be a start."

"We're not talking about me. What else did you have at dinner?"

"Uh, let's see, five stalks of asparagus and some potatoes."

"What's *some*?"

"Two chunks. And I had the pie and a bite of your pork chop and a bite of pancake and two hot chocolates, don't forget.

"Actually, that's not bad, although it was one hot chocolate and some whipped cream off the second one."

"I like food, honey, I eat a little bit of everything. I don't have an eating disorder if that's what you're implying."

"I'm not, I was just checking. Would you like your Christmas present now?"

"No, I didn't bring yours. I'll find us a quiet corner when you come, or maybe we can get away."

"What's the schedule tomorrow?"

"The invitation says noon until three, so there will be lunch-type finger food. It's not sit-down or anything, but there will be plenty of food. I'd love you to come at noon if you can. I'll be helping before then, so we can't have breakfast together, but after we clean up, I'll be able to get away. I'm sure she'll come up with something, but we can definitely have the evening. I don't care what I have to do."

"Let's do this, then. We'll wing it from three o'clock on. If it bothers her, I won't stay, but I'll be back to take you to supper, or how about we go dancing?"

"Oh, that would be so wonderful." She clapped. Oh, so wonderful, Rocco!" Then she looked around, worried. "Am I embarrassing you?"

"Never, baby girl, never. I better get you home. I'll go into the shop in the morning and come around noon then."

They walked to the truck, and he turned her into him before opening the door, kissing her intently. "We might not get a chance at your house."

"Oh, Rocco, just this morning we were so far apart. I'm weak in the knees just knowing we're in the same town," nibbling on his neck.

"Blossom, baby, you can't do that. I won't be able to take you home."

"Rocco"—urgently, biting his lips—"I can't go away, I can't. Please don't let them take me."

"Sweetie"—pushing her against the truck—"you're killing me here," breathing hard. "We have to go now. Right now, baby," his eyes stinging. He lifted her into the truck, clicking her seatbelt and looking into her dark, questioning eyes, shaking his head no.

As he drove out of the parking lot, she whispered, "Your house is close, Rocco."

He heaved a sigh, watching the traffic, not her. "Blossom, you wouldn't let us make love when I was scared to take over the business. I won't let us make love because you're mad at your parents."

She was staring at her clenched hands, blushing, tears escaping. He squeezed her hands. "No shortcuts, baby, remember? We'll know when it's right, and it's not right when your mother said don't go to my house, and we have a time limit."

"You're so smart."

"Oh, yeah, just me. Quitting school at fifteen, real smart."

"I mean, smart about life, smart about me."

"I'm a better man since I met you, Blossom. I'm different. I listen more. I think ahead more. I'm not thinking of reasons to punch anyone," smiling at her.

"You're so good, Rocco. I have to work so hard at it. You're just good."

"I'm going to work at it, baby girl, because of you."

At her house, he took her to the door and hugged her tight. "I love you, Blossom Dove, beyond words. I'll see you at noon," kissing the top of her head.

He had forgotten to ask her if jeans would be okay but figured Nix would have them on if no one else. He pressed them as a precaution, polished his black boots, and put on a white dress shirt, rolling up the sleeves a couple of turns. He had gotten Nix a landscaping book, put Blossom's pearls in his pocket, and headed to the liquor store for some champagne. This literally was his first Christmas. He had never received a gift as far back as he could remember, never given a gift, but knew from movies what was expected. The best bottle of champagne the store had was a Dom Pérignon for one hundred forty dollars. He figured that would be safe.

She took his breath away when she opened the door in a white knit dress, formfitting on top and flaring out below her waist to her calves. She had on high button white shoes with a heel, giving her a different posture. The sides of her hair were gathered on top with a pearl barrette, and she was wearing her pearl. "Wow," he mouthed, "you look older, taller." She smiled delightedly.

"Let's pretend it's Christmas," she said, kissing his cheek. He was about to kiss her back when her family came into the foyer. He handed the champagne to her mother. "Thank you for inviting me, Mrs. Richards. Merry Christmas, Doctor. I thought you might like this, Nix," handing him the package with his book.

"Come in, come in, Rocco," her dad said. "Elaine, do we have something for Rocco?"

"Well, I'm sure Blossom does. Let's go into the living room," turning away, walking toward the kitchen.

Blossom took his leather jacket and hung it in the closet, rolling her eyes. She took his hand and led him to the tree, sitting on the floor. "I hope you like this," she said shyly, handing him a package. He opened it and looked at her in quizzical wonder. "This is the nicest gift ever, baby girl," blinking rapidly, trying to remember her family was there.

"I thought you'd like it." She smiled.

"What do you have there, Rocco?"

He held up Mel Simons's *The Movie Trivia Book.* "Movie trivia, sir, it's a hobby of mine."

"Well, I'll be. We all enjoy that too."

Just then the doorbell rang, and the afternoon started. She loved introducing him to everyone and kept him close, pointing out the rooms to the house as they went through replenishing trays. He met Rosalita and felt her giving him the once-over, making him wonder if Blossom's mother had discussed him. She softened when he complimented her hors d'oeuvres and chatted about a couple of cooking methods.

The day went well, and nearing three o'clock, Blossom said, "Maybe I can show you my room when they all leave."

Just then her mother called, "Blossom, Nixie, come here, please." She looked slightly annoyed when Rocco came too. "Mary Ann and Jim would like you both to come over this evening. The girls haven't seen you in a long time and are having a little get-together."

Blossom didn't miss a beat. "Oh, I'm sorry. We're leaving tomorrow for the holidays, and Rocco and I are going out this evening. Maybe another time. You all have a nice Christmas," turning to say good-bye to another guest.

Her mother looked momentarily stunned but recovered quickly and said, "How about you, Nixie?"

"Sure," he said, looking at the Balmers. "Can I bring Slim along?"

"Of course," Mrs. Balmer said, "the girls will be delighted. About seven then, Nixie?"

"Sure," he said, "and it's Nix."

Rocco got the black velvet box from his jacket before they went back into the living room. Her parents were in the dining room giving Rosalita instructions about the remaining food.

"Your gift was so thoughtful, baby. I feel bad you'll always know what I'm getting you." But she was squirming with anticipation and gasped and clapped when she saw a dual box holding two pearls.

"Thanksgiving and Christmas." He smiled.

"Oh, Rocco, you shouldn't spend so much money on me, I-I . . ." He put a finger over her lips before she could say she didn't deserve it.

"Let me put them on, they showed me how," lifting the chain over her hair, kissing her cheek as he did so. He unscrewed the clasp, slipped a pearl on, and then got a diamond separator from under the velvet, and slipped it on.

"Honey, you can't get diamonds for between every one, it will cost a fortune."

"I have money, baby girl," as he finished the other side. The three pearls were glowing in the Christmas tree lights, the diamonds sparkling. She leaned forward and kissed him lightly on the lips as her parents came in the room.

"Look, Daddy, Rocco got me pearls for Thanksgiving and Christmas to add to my necklace."

"That's beautiful, kitten, a lovely gift."

"I'm going to show Rocco my room and get into something more casual."

Her mother chimed in, "You go up too, Nixie, and show Rocco your room."

Blossom and Nix laughed as they went up the stairs while Rocco raised his eyebrows. Blossom's room was in cream and sand colors. He could tell the bedcovers and drapes were very expensive and thought of Lindsay's room back at his house—pretty sure the things there were from Walmart. Blossom's room was very calm, no girly things, the only decoration a painting of two young Indian girls over the fireplace. It almost looked like an empty room, never used, except for the elaborate computer setup in an alcove.

Nix had not come in, and Blossom put her arms around his neck. "I didn't care if you saw my room, I just wanted to thank you for my pearls," kissing him suggestively on the lips.

"I don't want to get kicked out of here, baby girl, point me to Nix's room."

He could tell Nix also had New Mexico on his mind from his decorations. Whereas Blossom's room had an unlived-in look, Nix's was comfortably messy. They chatted a bit and headed downstairs, Blossom calling out that she'd be down in a minute.

She came down in a long-sleeved denim dress with a tan suede vest and matching high-top moccasins. She looked expectantly at him, and he winked his approval, making her blush.

"Don't be too late," her mother said. "We leave for the airport at ten, and there are always those last-minute things to do."

"Where you kids off to," her dad said.

"I don't think I told you, Daddy, but Rocco taught me to dance. We'll get a bite to eat and go to a place in Edinboro to dance. It's the most fun ever." She beamed.

"Well, that is surprising, kitten, you'll have to show us sometime."

She knew they were watching but felt comfortable enough to hold Rocco's hand as they walked to the truck.

"Think we made any progress today, baby girl?"

"I think Dad's coming around, don't you?"

"I hope so, Blossom, and oh, remind me not to get on your bad side," pretending he was concentrating on the traffic.

"What do you mean?"

"Tell me refusing to go to those people's house wasn't payback for last summer when she put you on the spot at the country club. You could have stopped in for a half hour to keep the peace."

"Rocco, please understand. I can't let her push me into things. She will never stop. I had to let her know if she tries to make me do things thinking I won't speak up in front of a group, she's wrong. Don't think I'm bad, honey, I have to keep control, I have to," wringing her hands.

"Okay, okay, don't get upset. You don't have to keep control now. I love you. Is Applebees okay? All that finger food was good, but now I need a meal."

She lifted his hand and kissed it. "Applebees is fine, honey."

Back at the house, her dad said, "You know, I can't ever remember Blossom talking about having fun."

"Don't be silly, Cal. She's always enjoyed a job well done. Fun is relative. She's playing you like a violin."

"I don't care, Elaine, she hasn't called me Daddy in five years. I didn't realize how much I've missed it. She needs to have fun just like anyone else."

"Cal, I'm telling you. This whole thing can fall apart with Rocco in the picture."

"What do you mean 'this whole thing.' We can't orchestrate her whole life, Elaine, she's already shown us that. She's found someone she care for, she's doing well in school, what more can we ask. She's only eighteen."

"Doing *well* in school, doing *well*? Cal, that's just not enough."

"Hon, I keep in contact with Dr. Ng. He says she's amazing, but for heaven's sake, she's only been there four months. You act like she should be world famous already."

"Well, she never will be world famous if she doesn't devote herself to her work."

"And would that be so bad, Elaine?"

She threw her hands up and stamped away.

They pulled into the parking lot, surprisingly full for early on a Monday. "I think Big Sallie's truck is here, baby. She's loud and a little rough, but nice. Don't let her scare you." He reached down and pulled a CD out of the holder. "This is Delbert McClinton, for dancing."

Looking the room over as they crossed the floor, he handed the CD to the bartender. "Here's Delbert, Charlie. Was that Big Sallie's truck in the lot? You remember Blossom?" Just as they got settled at a table and ordered a Coke and a ginger ale, a voice boomed out, "Is that Rocco, for Chrissakes?"

Blossom looked in the direction of the sound. The largest woman she had ever seen was coming toward them with surprisingly light steps. Tall, huge, broad, wide, every adjective went through her mind, as well as 'I didn't know they made jeans that size.' Rocco stood up with a genuine smile of welcome, and Blossom realized why he had chosen a table with a picnic bench.

"Don't worry, honey, I'm not going to bother you," she bellowed, slapping him on the back. "I can see you're in love. You haven't been in jail, have you?"

"No, I haven't been in jail. Just keeping my nose clean. And yes, I'm in love. This is Blossom. Blossom, Sallie."

"I'm Big Sallie, Blossom, always have been. He's trying to put on airs. Are you responsible for straightening him out?"

Blossom smiled. "No, he had straightened himself out before we met."

Big Sallie hit the table with her palm, shaking the area. "Damn, I'm glad. You were one I worried about. I'm sitting with Fred over there, you two have a good time. Let me see how you're dancing nowdays, Rocco."

The opening of Delbert's *Room to Breathe* CD started. Blossom looked worried. "Honey, that sounds awfully fast. Can I dance to that?"

"Sure you can, baby girl. Listen to the beat in the background. We'll start slow." He smiled at her encouragingly, whispered some directions, and soon they were in a groove. She could feel his light touches, watched his eyes, and they moved around the floor as if they had been dancing for years. During one up-tempo number, Rocco moved away, came back, moved away again, taunting her. Big Sallie boomed out, "Don't let him intimidate you girl, give it right back to him." Blossom sashayed back then shimmied her shoulders as she danced toward him, laughing when his mouth dropped open in surprise.

Although she dwarfed who she danced with, Blossom was dumbfounded when Big Sallie danced. Her size disappeared. "Would you like to dance with her, honey, someone who really know what they're doing?"

"Blossom, in the first place, I would never leave you alone, and in the second place, you know what you're doing. You're really good, baby girl."

They continued to dance every dance. He knew every word to every song, thrilling her when he sang in her ear. After a couple of lines of one called "Don't Want to Love You," she said "Honey, I don't like this song." It was a slow tempo, and they were moving slowly pressed together.

"Don't listen to the words, baby, just feel the beat, it's great."

She stopped. "Rocco, I can't, I can't. You're going to sing those words, I don't want to hear you say them. Please," plaintively.

He caught the waitress's eye—"We'll be right back"—lifted her jacket off the back of the chair, and hurried her out the door.

"I'm sorry, honey, I just couldn't hear those words."

"It's okay, my baby," holding her against his chest, swaying with her. "It only lasts a couple minutes. Are you having a good time?"

"I'm having such a good time, Rocco, you're so amazing."

Smiling into her eyes, "You're the amazing one, Blossom Dove. I think you can go back in, you ready?"

They finished the CD, played the jukebox, and after a restroom break, "I'm afraid we'd better go, baby, it's ten thirty, and your mother might be calling." She looked sad, and he said, "I'm the mature, responsible one, remember. Let's say good night to everyone."

As he tucked her into the truck, she said, caressing his cheek, "That was so wonderful, Rocco, I really like your friends. Big Sallie is so funny. I think she feels dancing is a competitive sport. If I saw her on the street, I would never, ever think she could dance," a genuine laugh ringing out. But then a shadow crossed her face, and the tears started.

"Oh, Blossom, what? You were just laughing, and it was beautiful."

"I'm sorry, Rocco, I forgot for a minute that I have to go. You have to tell them I can't, you have to," really sobbing now.

He came around to her side and put her on his lap. "Remember last August when we said we could do this, baby girl? We can do this."

"I loved you last summer, but I had no idea how much I would love you by now," crying, trying to catch her breath.

So he said everything he had said before, the same words, different words, soothing, encouraging, because in helping her, he could get through it himself. "You'll have fun with your aunt Mim, the time will go fast. Do you want me to call every Friday?"

"No! I want you to call every night. You have to call every night."

"Baby, I don't think your mother would like it every night. How about every other night?"

"No, Rocco"—her voice rising in desperation—"I can't do it if you don't call. Please. Please."

"Okay, baby, okay."

She sighed against him. "I just want to be normal."

"I hear you, baby girl, I hear you." He knew she wasn't just talking about their situation.

They were forehead to forehead whispering, didn't notice the bar door had opened and let out a group, when Big Sallie hit the side of the truck bed, shaking the whole thing. "Get a room, you two," laughing uproariously. They jumped and laughed, the somber mood broken.

Christmas had always just come and gone for him. His early teens, it just meant alcohol was easier to come by. The last couple years he had enjoyed the music, the return of the holiday movie classics, but he had hoped for more this year, and he missed her more than he even imagined he would. It was twice as hard as he tried to be strong for her, but inevitably it came through in their phone conversations, and few were satisfactory.

On the twenty-third, she asked him to call early on Christmas Eve as they were going to midnight mass. She was weepy and melancholy, and in a lapse of judgment, he sang Elvis's "Blue Christmas" to her. She started crying in earnest and choked out, "Honey, I have to do something. Can I call you back after a while?"

"Sure, baby, no matter how late." He vowed to give himself a pep talk before she called to quit transferring his sadness to her.

At her end, the damage was done. Even before the song, she had lost her appetite, she wasn't sleeping, and it just pushed her past her resolve to hold it together. Down the stairs she ran, bursting into the room where her parents, Nix, and Aunt Mim were watching television. "I'm going home. I'll wait until the day after Christmas, but that's all!"

———

111

They sat with their mouths open for a second. Her mother spoke first. "Blossom, don't be silly. We have our return tickets for the second. We'll all go home together."

"I have my own money, I'll buy another ticket," clenching her fists at her side. "I'm not staying here, Rocco is all alone. I'm not staying here!"

Her mother started again. "Don't be ridiculous, Blossom," but her dad interrupted,

"Elaine," shaking his head. "Blossom"—quietly—"did Rocco ask you to come home?"

"No, I want to surprise him. He's all alone. You can understand, can't you, Daddy?" Plaintively, "Please, Daddy."

"Cal," her mother warned.

He held his hand up to stop her. "Well, honey, Rocco seems like a very practical young man. I don't think he would feel it was wise to buy another ticket at a high holiday price when you already have one. And I couldn't cash yours in, so that's like throwing hundreds of dollars away, kitten. I know it's hard, but it's only another week."

"But, Daddy, we only had a day and a half before we left, and we'll only have a day and a half when I get back. It's not fair," her voice rising, looking around for affirmation. "It's not fair, is it, Nixie?"

"Hey, I don't know why we came in the first place," Nix said throwing up his hands. "No offense, Aunt Mim."

She looked around, her agitation rising. Mim bit her lip and shrugged her shoulders. Blossom pressed her arms tight to her sides and screamed, "It's not fair!" and ran upstairs sobbing.

"Calvin Richards, you simply must speak to her. Her behavior was rude and childish. I told you this was getting out of hand."

Mim interjected, "Elaine, she's never been childish. For god's sake, she's never been a child! Look at her, she has dark circles under her eyes, she's just been pushing food around her plate, and she's been holding on to that phone like it's a lifeline or something. Let's all give her a little slack. She's sensitive, she's probably already sorry she made a scene. I'll check on her."

"Don't coddle her, Mim, you've always spoiled her," her mother said.

"What are aunts for?" She smiled. She called out, "Lourdes, bring a couple hot chocolates up to Blossom's room, and see what everyone else wants to snack on."

She tapped on the door and went in. Blossom was in her smurfies, lying on her side clutching a pillow and sobbing. She looked up ready for a fight but softened when she saw her aunt.

Mim said, "I'm sorry I couldn't help you down there, honey. It would have started a family feud, and I'm usually on your mother's list for one reason or another already."

"I'm sorry too, Aunt Mim. I really missed you, and I'm happy to be here, but they're just doing it on purpose."

"What are they doing on purpose, honey?"

"They're, well, Mom really, is just trying to keep me away from Rocco," blowing her nose. "We've never been on so many trips. It's so obvious."

"Well, I'm the benefit of one of those trips. It's been a great Christmas having you here, and the clinic has sure appreciated the unexpected help. But I'm sorry it's been so hard on you, and we've been so busy you and I haven't had a chance to shop and chat. Why don't you tell me all about Rocco."

Just then Lourdes knocked and brought in hot chocolate and cookies. They put the tray between them, and Aunt Mim said, "Start at the beginning and tell me everything. First"—raising her eyebrows—"is he good-looking?"

Blossom closed her eyes and shivered. "Oh, Aunt Mim, I know looks are an accident of birth like Mom says, but he is sooo beautiful. He has black wavy hair and crystal blue eyes. He's tall and has so many muscles, and the way he walks . . . oh, I just can't tell you. And he taught me to dance, and he sings me to sleep . . ." On and on she talked, smiling, laughing, the color coming back to her cheeks, eating cookies without realizing it. She hadn't brought her pearls, but she showed her aunt the doves pendant and the note he wrote that she kept tucked beneath the velvet in the box.

"I just panic thinking what if I told Daddy no when he signed me up for that class," tears spilling over. "I don't know when to take a stand and when not to. Oh god, what if I hadn't gone? And then I cried so much, what if he hadn't called?"

Mim hugged her. "What did he say about the crying?"

"He said it would pass, and it has almost, but look at me now. Anything can set it off. It's a wonder he likes me. Really, Aunt Mim, I think I should have been told what might happen. I can handle things if I'm prepared. I like to be prepared," she said with distress. "I looked in his eyes, and the room tipped"—and seeing her aunt's smile—"I'm serious, I couldn't breathe, there was a roaring in my ears. I think it's only right that I should have been told," indignant now.

"Sweetie, I'm sure you heard in health class or gathered from movies or books that there is an attraction . . ."

"An attraction!" she interrupted, "an attraction! That just doesn't explain what happened, Aunt Mim. I can still barely look at him sometimes. Oh god, he's so beautiful, so wonderful." She closed her eyes and took a breath and tried to talk normally again. "What about you and your husbands?"

Aunt Mim chuckled. "Your dad and I had a privileged childhood, honey. The older I got, the less inclined I was to give anything up, so being fond of someone was enough as long as they had money. And here I am, lucky to see you and Nixie a couple times a year. Lourdes and I, two old ladies rattling around in this house." She laughed. "At least she had a family. Along with you and Nixie, I've seen them grow up too. The clinics are my children, really. You know, honey, since Rocco is a carpenter, you should ask him to schedule a week or ten days here in the summer. We could use the help, and it will make it more fun for you."

Blossom's eyes got big. "Oh what a wonderful idea! Oh, thank you, Aunt Mim. I have to call him right now and ask him."

Mim gathered up their tray and was at the door when she heard the love in her voice as she said softly, "I'm sorry I've been so bad. Were you sleeping?"

"No, just laying here waiting for you to call. I'm the one who's been bad, baby girl. I'm supposed to be the mature and responsible one, and I've been feeling sorry for myself when I should have been thinking of you. You sound a little better."

"Aunt Mim just had the best idea ever. Can you tell Helen not to schedule any jobs for ten days when we come after school is out so you can come too? Would that be possible? Oh, please, honey, please."

"Slow down. Tell me again."

She said more slowly, "After Nixie's out of school, we'll be coming to Albuquerque for most of the summer like last year. So you could fly with us and help at the clinic for ten days or as long as you could. Please, please. I can't think of not seeing you all summer, oh I just can't."

"Of course I'll do it, baby, but what can I do at the clinic?"

"Aunt Mim says there always so much a carpenter can do."

"Now we're talking. I thought you meant in the actual clinic. Too bad I won't have my truck and tools."

"We'll find tools, honey. Oh this could be so wonderful. Won't it be fun when we can drive out in your truck?" Her voice was completely upbeat now, making him smile for the first time in days. "Oh, Rocco, I can't wait until we can do things together. Living from break to break is awful. I just hate it." And she was back to crying again.

"Blossom, you were happy just a second ago. Now don't cry about something we can't change right now. Take some breaths, sweetie, we're going to be fine."

It was the best evening they had since she got there. Christmas was poignant but upbeat. Her aunt tucked her in at night and listened to her stories about Rocco. She, in turn, was happier all day, and the final week was night-and-day different from the first two.

The night before they left, her aunt said, "You should tell your mom more about Rocco, sweetie, it might ease the tension."

"I've tried a couple times, I really have. She feels he's distracting me from my work. But he's the one who said we'll just talk on Friday nights so I can concentrate. I'm there because they want me to be there, Aunt Mim, but he's my life," tears flowing but smiling through them. "He's my life," she whispered.

Mim hugged her. "I can see that, honey, but I have the luxury of not being your parent. I know they want the best for you."

"Aunt Mim, you know that's not true," wiping her nose and looking into her aunt's eyes. "You were there all along. I heard you all arguing. They don't want what's best for me, they want what's best for whatever is in their minds. They say things like 'your work' and 'fulfill your potential.' What do those things mean? Dad got me involved with Professor Ng. I'm doing what he asks. I'm good at it. But what am I doing there?"

"Oh, sweetie, give it time."

"That's just what Rocco says. Well, I'm doing what they want, and I'm sure I can get out of there in three years. But that's my main focus—get out of there in three years. Should that be why I'm there?"

She waved her hand dismissively. "Let's don't talk about it anymore. It wears me out. Thank you for listening to me, it has helped so much to talk about Rocco." She closed her eyes and sighed, her whole body softening. "He's so wonderful."

Mim said, "May I ask the $64,000 question? Just tell me if I'm out of line." She raised her eyebrows and asked, "Are you intimate with him?"

Blossom blushed and looked down shyly but smiled. "No, we're not ready yet, but we know it's coming, so I'm taking birth control pills." Her aunt leaned back in surprise. "Well, we figured they don't work right away, so we wanted to just start and not worry about it anymore. Rocco went to a doctor to be sure they were safe. He's so sweet and brave."

"Kitten, your parents are doctors. Don't forget you have them to ask questions."

"I know, Aunt Mim, but at that time, Mom was being particularly nasty. It wasn't a good time, and I couldn't deal with it. She really would have worked hard to keep us apart, and it's bad enough now. I could probably ask Dad things, but I don't want to ask him not to say anything. That wouldn't be fair to him."

"Well, I don't want to get between you and your mother, but you can call me if you want to."

"Thank you, Auntie. The pills were scary, but we got through it. I think we can handle anything that comes up together."

"You're a precious girl, Blossom," kissing her forehead. "I hope he knows that."

THREE

They Love

By the time he drove in, she was in her coat, jumping and squeaking with excitement even as her mother came into the foyer. He had told her he wanted to come in the house like a gentleman; but she was out of the door as soon as he came around the truck, threw herself into his arms, her legs around his waist, her face in his neck.

Her dad came into the foyer. "Oh, she's gone? I wanted to say hello to Rocco."

"Look at this, Cal. I was hoping it would wear itself out." They were laughing and spinning around, Blossom crying openly, and it looked like Rocco was too. He put her down and twirled her around, evidently admiring the cream-colored swing coat and Ugg boots Mim had given her for Christmas.

"Elaine, they're in love. Remember what it's like to be young."

"Cal, you know what Professor Ng said—she is destined for greatness. He's too much of a distraction."

"Elaine, he didn't say that. He said she's unusually gifted."

"Whatever," swinging her hand as if swatting a fly. "She should be concentrating on her work."

"She's doing fine, hon."

"That's just it. She's doing fine. She's doing the work, there's no passion, nothing extra. I just don't like it." He put his arm around her, but she shook it off. "He's nothing but trouble, Cal, mark my words."

"Elaine, for god's sake, he's a hardworking kid, he's been nothing but polite and considerate. She's got all the brains in the world. She can't work all the time."

"You used to be with me on this, Cal," she said with exasperation. "She needs guidance in the right direction."

"Elaine, we gave her guidance. She's in a good school getting perfect grades. Let it be now." She stamped away in a huff.

Outside, Rocco settled Blossom into the truck, adjusting the seatbelt around her coat. "Is this the coat you told me about? You look like a little doll." She smiled a little nervously. "It's a beautiful day. Since we can't go to my house, do you want to get some coffee and take a walk on Ernst Trail?"

They went through McDonald's drive-thru for coffee and parked at the trail. He took the lid off her coffee so she could put her finger in the froth, and she did, and he smiled, but she was suddenly shy and keeping her eyes down. He didn't give her the "do we have to start over" lecture but said, "Before we get out, can I just say something?"

She kept her eyes down, nodding yes. "I love to talk to you on the phone, Blossom, but Christ, three weeks? Your whole break! I never ever had a Christmas, and that was the worst Christmas ever."

She realized she was starting to squeeze the cardboard cup too tightly so with clenched jaw and precise motions, set it in the cup holder. "And you're blaming me, aren't you?"

"No, baby girl. I'm just making a statement."

"No, you're not. In your heart, you're blaming me, and you're mad at me. My parents are mad at me because I was a bad girl the whole time we were gone, and"—biting her lip and her shoulders starting to shiver—"and you sang 'Blue Christmas,' and I made a scene and said I was coming home, and . . . and everyone's mad at me, and I didn't want to go in the first place, and . . ."

"Okay, sweetie, okay. I'm sorry I even brought it up. It was selfish of me to bring it up. You couldn't help it. I was frustrated I didn't have time to come there. Your mother is trying to keep us apart. We know it, and we shouldn't fall into this trap of blaming each other. It's probably just what she wants, so let's don't play that game."

He took her hand and kissed it, first her fist and then her palm. She closed her eyes and shivered. He swallowed hard. "I'll come over and lift you down and kiss you hello properly, okay?" At the look on her face, "Don't you dare say no."

He carefully lifted her down, closed the door; and before he could step close, she crossed her arms in front of her chest. "No, we're past that, Blossom," taking her hands and putting them behind his neck. "See if I need a haircut," winking when she looked up smiling tentatively at his line. He kissed her gently, then a little more insistently, murmuring, "Welcome home, baby girl," into her ear, moving down to her neck.

"Rocco, Rocco! I can't breathe"—panting—"I can't breathe."

He pulled back, aching. "I love you, Blossom, baby girl."

"Oh, I love you, Rocco. I missed you so much," laying her head on his chest. "I just can't go back already, I just can't."

"I'm so sorry, Blossom. It was all my fault. I couldn't think straight from missing you so bad. I'm sorry I couldn't come, I'm sorry I couldn't make you laugh. I was awful, baby, I'm so sorry." He buried his face in her hair and cried.

"Darling, darling, no, no. It was me, it wasn't you. It was me. I'm spoiled, I wanted . . ."

"No, no. Don't go there, baby." They clung to each other. It seemed unreal they were together. He sucked in some air. "Come on, we'll walk and talk and forget about Christmas. It will be better next year, I promise. Are you cold?"

"No, it's nice today," skipping ahead, suddenly happy, twirling, and clapping her hands. "I have my pearls on, I love them so much," unbuttoning her coat to show him the strand with the two new ones.

He bit his lip at the formfitting cream turtleneck sweater and brown suede skirt. "You look beautiful," dropping on to a bench along the way. "Come sit on my lap and tell me about Santa Fe."

"I told you almost every night about Santa Fe," wrapping her arms around his waist. "It was awful. I was awful. I'm ashamed about how I behaved, but I couldn't help it."

"You're here now"—his lips in her hair—"and you smell so good. So are you taking your pills?" He tried to say it casually and hoped she couldn't hear his heart.

"Yes, every morning," she said proudly. "I put them with my toothbrush so I won't forget. I hide them, but I really don't care if she finds them, really I don't." She whispered, "I told Aunt Mim, honey. Do you mind?"

"Not at all, baby. Will she say anything to your mother?"

"No, she won't. She wants me to tell her, but I think it would just make things worse right now. I'll think about it. I just like thinking about you when I put one in my mouth. I think, someday I'll be close to Rocco," and she pretended to pop a pill into her mouth, grinning.

Oh god, he thought, *there's my opening. I have to say it*. He took a breath, "So how would you like *someday* to be Sunday?"

Time stopped. He felt her stiffen. "What do you mean?"

"I mean, I'll take you back, and . . ."

"Oh, I want you to take me back. Oh, please take me back, it would be so wonderful. I could do it if you took me back."

"Well, like I said, I'll take you back, and we can get close. You know, instead of sleeping on the floor like before, I'll sleep with you," kissing her ear.

"No. No, Rocco, no. I haven't studied. In the future, in the future," pushing away from him.

"Don't pull away, baby, hug me tight. We're just talking. You don't have to study. We'll just kiss, and we won't stop. You like kissing, right? We'll just kiss and kiss."

"I love kissing you, but I'm not ready. I have questions. I thought we had time," whimpering. "You said we have all the time in the world."

"And we do. We do. Let's talk about your questions. Ask me anything you want."

"Would we be in my dorm? Oh, I don't want to be in my dorm, I . . ."

"No, we won't be in your dorm. I made reservations at that Hilton on Sansom. We can drop your things off at your room and walk right over."

"You already made reservations? Oh, Rocco, this isn't right, you said we had time."

"Baby, I didn't make reservations because of that. We haven't had any time together, and I just wanted to take you back and not worry about Megan. We can watch TV and kiss and cuddle. We don't have to do anything else. I told you, you have all the power, remember?"

"We can just watch TV? That would be so nice. I've missed you so much," kissing him softly.

He increased the intensity, making her breathe a little harder. "Just in case we want to go farther, what other questions do you have?"

"It's too embarrassing. I can't."

"We're just talking about information, baby, ask me anything."

She put her head against his chest and pulled his jacket lapel over her face.

"Go ahead," softly.

"Will it hurt?"

He tried to sound calm and clinical, his heart pounding. "Well, I left school before sex ed class, so this is just what I've heard on the street," stroking her back. "There's a membrane I have to get through. Did you learn about it?"

"Ohh," she moaned weakly, "I didn't listen. Oh, I don't want to hear this."

"Shh, sometimes it's not even there because girls are more athletic now, but if it is, it may, well, it probably will, hurt for a couple seconds. And there may be a little blood."

She pulled away with a little cry and put both hands over her face. "Oh, I can't Rocco, I just can't. I'm afraid."

"We're just talking, baby, just talking. But after that part, it's like kissing to the tenth power. We'll be close, so close, and you'll never be afraid again," kissing her hair.

"Tenth power?"

"Yes, you like math, right? And you'll feel so good, I bet you'll feel fireworks in your tummy."

"Fireworks? I like fireworks," she said with wonder, smiling with her eyes down. "But I'm afraid."

"Baby girl, I'm afraid too. I've had sex"—she put her hand over his mouth; he kissed it and moved it away—"but I've never made love. You're my heart and soul. I want to make you feel wonderful."

"And help me find the fireworks?"

"And help you find the fireworks," his eyes stinging, holding her tight.

"But, Rocco, Rocco," tearfully, worried.

"What, baby, what?"

She cupped her hand around his ear and whispered, "We won't have any clothes on." She leaned back, her eyes big.

"Well"—calmly—"let me show you something." He kissed her, starting gently then nibbling, probing, insistent until she cried out, panting. "Were you thinking of what you were wearing just then?"

She looked at him with wonder, shaking her head no, slowly.

"What were you thinking?"

"Get closer," softly.

He gave her a beautiful smile. "That's all it is, baby girl. We kiss and don't stop. Do you think you can do that?" and then laughed out loud, making her laugh, when she said, "Or we can just watch TV."

He nodded seriously. "Or we can just watch TV."

She laid her head on his chest, emotionally exhausted, so he waited a few minutes and said, "Now we need to figure out how I can take you back."

"I'll just tell them you're taking me back, that's all."

"But if they say no, we have no out, baby. I need to bring it up to your dad in a conversation. Could you ask me to supper or something?"

"I'd love to ask you to supper. I can cook you a nice Italian meal. I've wanted to."

"Okay, you tell them you're cooking an Italian meal and you want me to come. I'll tell him I'm going to be going that way, and I'll take you back for them."

The next night at dinner, Blossom put a large salad bowl and garlic bread on the table and said, "I picked lasagna since it's easier to eat. I used turkey, Mom, to be healthier." They ate somewhat comfortably, her dad saying, "Rosalita's cooking is great, kitten, but I've missed your meals just knowing they came from you," smiling at her fondly.

Rocco interjected, "I had to leave the restaurant, but I'd like to have you all over during spring break." Her mother's expression was unreadable. Her father said, "We'd enjoy that, Rocco. And how are things going at the business? Doing okay?"

"On the whole, pretty well, sir. Of course, some of the suppliers are a little nervous. Most we've had a long time, so they knew me as a kid and need reassurance. Actually, I have to be in Lewistown this side of Harrisburg on Monday, so I can take Blossom back tomorrow for you."

Blossom jumped in right on cue, looking completely surprised, clapping, "Oh, that would be so wonderful, Rocco, we can talk the whole ride."

Her mother's mouth opened, but before she could speak, her dad said, "Well, thank you, Rocco. I hate to take more time from the office. You sure it's not an imposition?"

"Not at all, sir. I have to be in the area anyway."

Her mother looked from one to the other with a little frown between her eyes but could see no conspiracy and elected to say nothing.

"I was going to make tiramisu but couldn't find ladyfingers, so cannoli, anyone?" Blossom smiled brightly, her heart pounding, amazed they had managed it so easily.

He knew her mother had been watching when Blossom jumped into his arms Friday so took a little more leeway when he came to pick her up for the ride back. "Is this all you have, baby girl?" She just had one small bag.

She looked startled at the overt endearment but smiled and said, "This is all I brought. I have things here and there." She hugged her parents. He shook hands with her dad and helped Blossom into the truck.

Her dad said, "Thanks again, Rocco, drive carefully."

He drove out of the development and pulled over, just as she said, confused, "Is this a different truck?"

"I wanted to get one with the one-piece seat so you can sit next to me. I didn't want to call attention to it in front of your mother. Slide over, it has a middle seat belt."

She slid over next to him. "This is very nice," kissing him on the cheek.

He winked and smiled, pulling back into traffic. "You can put your head on my shoulder, and I had an extra strap put in so you can lay down and take a nap."

"Lay down?" She looked worried and furrowed her brow.

He rolled his eyes. "Blossom Richards, don't tell me you're thinking what I think you're thinking!"

"Nooo, I wasn't," drawing it out, looking at the length of the seat.

"You were too! Baby, why would you think I'd have that on my mind when I know how you feel about it. I'm not going to seduce you in the truck, for god's sake."

"I'm sorry, I guess I'm just nervous," patting his leg. He didn't let on it felt like an electric shock.

"Let's have a nice ride now. This is so wonderful after I thought you'd be leaving again today. Do you want to lay down," winking and grinning, easing the moment.

"I'll just rest on your shoulder. I didn't sleep much last night," yawning.

As the miles went by, he was completely content, listening to music, kissing her head, all the angst of the last weeks draining away. She whimpered in her sleep, and he was instantly alert, turning down to look in her face to see if she was awake. She wasn't, but she looked worried. Should he wake her? Still so new and wonderful to have someone to worry about. She whimpered again, and her eyes fluttered. "You okay, baby girl?"

"Rocco, Rocco, I have to tell you something. I have to."

"Sweetie, it's okay. You don't have to tell me if it bothers you. We'll deal with it when you want to. Just rest now."

"No, no, I have to tell you something. I thought about it all night. I think it's important to men. I don't want you to be disappointed."

"Oh, Blossom"—looking for a place to pull over—"I've told you not to say that, you could never disappoint me about anything." He unhooked their seatbelts and put her on his lap.

"But Rocco"—hurriedly, burying her face in his chest—"my . . . my breasts are very sensitive, that's why I don't wear bras. I just need to tell you, before, you know, before," crying.

Kissing her hair, "First, precious girl, thank you for telling me. I know it was hard, and I'll remember it all our lives. Second, listen hard, baby, you are not performing for me. *We* are going to make love, *we* are going to be close forever. It's not you or me anymore. We'll be part of each other forever, and I'll love you forever."

"Oh, Rocco"—her deep breath making her shudder—"I love you, but I'm scared."

"I know you are, baby, and I am too. But we're going to be fine. We're going to be great," kissing her nose. "Let's find a place for lunch. We could make it by three, but I'm guessing you didn't eat breakfast, did you?"

She shook her head no and then yes as he said, "We're good, right? We're good? Okay, and let's take that word *disappointed* out of our vocabulary, baby. I can't deal with that, it kills me when you say it."

They had lunch and were still on the road at four when her phone chimed. "My mother." She rolled her eyes. "I didn't think she'd make her Sunday call today. Hi, Mom. No, we had a long lunch, so we're not there yet." With exasperation, "Mom, I know when my first class is. We'll probably have a quick breakfast so Rocco can get on the road for his appointment. Okay, love to Dad and Nixie. Talk to you next week."

They pulled into the parking lot he had used before. The hotel was valet parking, and he wasn't sure how it worked. "This is just fine, honey. It's close, and you won't have to tip." Her nervousness only showing in how tight she clutched his hand as they walked to her dorm. He had her small suitcase and his gym bag over his shoulder, and she carried her computer.

"It's been three weeks, and Megan won't get here until the last minute, so I'll just check things over and get a top for tomorrow."

"And unmentionables." He grinned. "You can say it." He didn't need a stay-over pass, so they checked him in as a temporary visitor and went up to the room. "It's kind of stuffy. I left first, so thank goodness she didn't leave any food laying around," she chattered nervously. "I'll unpack this bag and get a smaller one. You can watch TV."

"Baby, come here."

"I'll just get these put away," picking things up and putting them down, her hands flitting from bag to drawers and back again.

"Blossom, come here."

"I'll just, I'll just . . ."

He went to her, and she hugged him tight around the waist, her head against his chest, whimpering.

He rubbed her back. "We're fine, baby, we're fine. Take some breaths. I love you."

"I'm okay, I'm okay, don't kiss me though," her voice rising as he kissed the top of her head.

"Okay"—patting her butt—"get your things. You wouldn't be more comfortable here, would you?"

"No, oh no. Some of them may come back early. I'd be too worried."

"Okay, let's get organized. A top for tomorrow. Check?"

She smiled. "Check."

"Unmentionables for tomorrow. Check?"

"Check."

"How about sox?"

"Oh yes," getting some from a drawer. "Check."

"A plastic bag for what you have on now?"

"I'm glad you're helping me. Check."

"Why don't you put everything in with your computer and you won't have to carry a suitcase to class—in case we're running late," grinning and giving her his Groucho Marx.

She smiled a little. "That's a good idea. I'll need a little bigger bag." She transferred everything to a Coach tote, and looking worried, "Can I bring my smurfies?"

"Bring your smurfies," smiling. "How about cosmetics and your hairbrush?"

"Oh, I'm not thinking," looking worried again. "Megan will wonder why I'm not here."

"As far as she knows, you've been here and gone, baby. Besides, I'm going to be coming down more often, she's going to know anyway."

She put her fists to her eyes. "You know, because of what she said."

"Sweetie, that was months ago. We're together. We're a couple. People have their own lives to worry about. They don't care what we're doing. Now let's walk over and check in. What do I do, I've never been to a hotel."

"You just walk up to the desk and say, 'You have a reservation for Carnavale,' and you may have to sign in."

Everything went smoothly. He was trying to be cool and hoped Blossom didn't know his heart was thudding like crazy. They just smiled at each other in the elevator, and she blushed when he winked at her.

She looked around the room. "This is really nice, honey, did it cost a fortune?" She tried to avoid looking at the bed even though it dominated the room.

He twirled her around as if they were dancing, pulled her close, and whispered, "Do I need a haircut?"

She whimpered, "Not yet, please not yet."

"Just a kiss, baby girl, just a kiss. It's been rough. Let's celebrate that we're together. That we can be together all night. Remember how lonely you were in Santa Fe? We got through it, and we're together. Aren't you happy?"

"Oh Rocco"—looking into his eyes—"I'm so happy to be with you. I'm sorry to act so scared. I'm so selfish, and you worked so hard so we can be together. Thank you, thank you," nibbling his chin. "If I had to come down with them, I don't think I could have done it. Now it's such a miracle we're here together. I love you, Rocco Carnavale."

He whispered, "Thank you, Blossom Richards. Do you want to go over to the White Dog Cafe or eat downstairs?"

"Let's take a walk and pick one later. We've been sitting a long time."

He laughed, and she said, "What?"

"You just want to get out of this room, don't you?"

"No, but it's only six o'clock. We can take a walk. Please?"

"We can do anything you want, baby girl. You have all the power," winking slowly.

"Let's go toward the White Dog," smiling weakly.

"Good, I'd like a beer."

She looked haughty. "I'm not kissing you if you taste like beer."

He laughed. "Like I said, I'd like a Coke."

Shaking her finger, "No, no, it's too late for caffeine."

"Like I said, I'd like a glass of water."

She laughed and clapped. "I don't care if you have beer," hugging him around the waist.

He whispered into her hair, "I knew you didn't, baby girl, I was just showing you, you have all the power. You do, you know. I'll do anything you want forever."

He had his beer and a philly cheesesteak. She had a cup of barley soup and a toasted whole-grain bagel. She was going to order clam chowder, but he told her never to order fish on a Sunday; it would have been left over from Friday.

"Let's see what they have in chocolate."

"No, I'm full. Let's get a peppermint patty on the way back. We better get a drink for you too. The ones in the room will cost four or five dollars. You didn't tell me how much the room cost."

"It doesn't matter how much it cost, Blossom. It's within walking distance, that makes it worth the cost. You okay to go back now?"

"I'm fine, honey, I'm fine. I love you," kissing him lightly and looking into his eyes, making his sting.

Back at the room, he said, "Why don't you take your shower and put on your smurfies, and we'll watch TV for a while." She nodded yes with big eyes, and he turned down the bed while she showered, taking deep breaths to calm down as he remembered to lay a towel where her hips would be.

He was in the biggest chair in front of the TV when she came out in her smurfies. He held out his arms. She climbed onto his lap, her ear against his chest. "Remember last fall when we did this in your dorm? I loved it, and you smelled so good just like now."

"And your heart was beating hard just like now." She smiled coyly.

"Oh, oh, I'm busted." He grinned.

"I love it that you're nervous. It makes me feel stronger. I don't want to be afraid all by myself."

He cleared his throat. "We don't have to be afraid, we're going to be great. Let's see what movies they have." They started watching *Michael Clayton* until he started rubbing her back and kissing her hair. When she tilted her chin and kissed him, he put his hand under her top and rubbed her bare back.

"Ohh, I've never felt your hand on my skin before. It's so nice."

He said, hoarsely, "I better take a quick shower. Don't go anywhere," kissing her nose.

He brushed his teeth and showered in nine minutes, and his heart thudded when he opened the door and the TV and lights were off and her smurfies folded on the chair. He reached back and flipped the bathroom light off and went to the other side of the bed. He dropped his towel, slid in beside her, crumpling up the sheet between them so he wouldn't be touching her.

She had the sheet up under her chin, clutching it into knots with both hands, her eyes squeezed tight, shaking and shivering.

He didn't mention it, just covered her hands with his left one, and started whispering quietly by her ear, "Remember when you said you wanted God in the equation, baby girl? You sent me that daily prayer book. At least once a month, the subject is 'Let go and let God.' This is the time we do that, baby." He knew she was listening. Her shaking calmed a little. Her eyes relaxed a little. "For the rest of our lives, this is our special time of day. No computer screens, no blueprints, no charts, no graphs. Just us, all alone, doing what we want. No rules, no boundaries, no holding back. All those feelings you have, you just let go and give them to me. I'll be here forever."

He held his breath, waiting, and she turned to him with her lips parted for the first time. He wanted to weep with relief but kissed her gently, waiting for her to take the lead. Soon they were exploring with their tongues, breathing hard. He moved to her throat, inch by inch to her breasts. Her chest was heaving. He nibbled gently around her breasts, lightly licked her nipples, one and then the other as she moaned and moved her hips against him.

He pulled the sheet away. "I'm going to touch you," he whispered, "and see if you're wet. Don't be afraid."

"I feel wet," barely audible. "Is it blood?"

"No, baby, it's just your body getting ready for me to slide in."

"Ohhh"—breathlessly—"that's very clever of God."

"Very clever. Now bend your knees a little. Do you want me to go quick?"

"Yes," whimpering, "yes."

Kissing her face, her throat, "You do anything you want to me. Bite me, scratch me, scream, I don't care. Hang on tight, here we go."

She made a little cry in her throat and dug into his back, her breasts lifting to him.

"I'm in, baby, are you okay?"

"Yes, yes," panting. "I feel full, are we done?"

He smiled tenderly, trying to keep himself in check, overcome with her beauty. "Now we go hunting for the fireworks, are you ready?"

"Yes, yes."

He put a hand behind her head, the other on the small of her back. "Move with me, baby, move with me," slowly starting.

"Like dancing," she said in a tiny, breathless voice, "like dancing."

"That's it, baby, just like dancing. When you feel something happening, you tell me. I'll wait for you."

Panting, using every ounce of control he had, "A little faster now. Wrap your legs around me. You're amazing, Blossom, you're amazing," as she moved and bit and moaned.

"Rocco, Rocco," desperately as she rose against him. He covered her scream with his mouth and felt it to his soul. As she dug into him, he let go and went somewhere he'd never been, waves and waves of release convulsing him.

He intended to keep aware, to do whatever she needed; but when he came to, he was somehow on his knees, she tight against him, her legs around his waist, her arms around his neck gasping for air. Both were slippery with sweat. He laid her gently on the pillow, pulling out sooner than he wanted but worried about his weight against her. He lay beside her, getting air.

"What happened," she panted.

"We made love, baby girl, we made love."

"Ohhh, can we make love forever and ever?"

"Forever and ever," kissing away the tears creeping under her lashes. "Forever and ever."

As he lifted a damp strand of hair from her cheek, she whispered, "You, you didn't tell me there was perspiration involved."

He smiled. "I didn't know, baby, I didn't know." He hadn't known and was too young and callous to care in his teen encounters but desperately cared now. He took a breath and asked, "Did you find the fireworks?"

She sighed sleepily, "Yes, oh yes. And I saw golden sparklies around your head. You're so beautiful."

He kissed her, holding back tears.

"I'm very tired, what do we do now?"

"You go to sleep, my baby. If you feel me get up, I'm just going to the bathroom." She turned on her side and curled her hands beneath her chin. He stroked her back. "Go to sleep, baby, go to sleep."

Just as he thought she was asleep, "Rocco," she whispered, "the towel, don't let them see it."

"Shh, I'll take care of it. Sleep, sleep," He rubbed her back until her breathing was even, the tears freely streaming down his face. *Please, God, let me be worthy of her.*

From far, far away she felt him lift her hips and pull the towel out carefully. Then a warm cloth as he wiped her clean and a kiss on her hip. Then deep into sleep.

He woke at three, never moving, knowing she was there and hardly believing it. He had trained himself from an early age to sleep with as little movement as possible and not call attention to himself. He was surprised it looked as though she hadn't moved. She was still curled up with her back to him, no new indentations in the pillow. Her precious little body so indescribably beautiful; he could hardly swallow. He slid out soundlessly and went to the bathroom.

He was lecturing himself as he came back—let her sleep, she needs to rest—but she was so beautiful. The bed still smelled like love. He was twenty. In a move that would affect them for twenty years, he caressed her hip.

He smiled when she turned so quickly, his desire charging when she put her leg over him and her arms tight around his neck. When she started biting his neck and digging into his back, he said breathlessly, "Baby, are you awake?" She growled in the back of her throat and bit his chin. "Okay, okay, that's a yes, I hear you," and he let himself go. Kissing, licking, moaning, entering her when she cried "Now!" He was wildly with her, barely knowing what was happening, when she screamed, "Rocco. No! Too much, too much, get away, get away!" Digging her heels in, unbelievably bucking him into the air and scrambling backward to the headboard, kicking, crying.

A strangled "Blossom" escaped him as he ejaculated onto the bed. "What, what, are you hurt," panting. "Is there blood? Let me see," moving her legs.

"Get away," kicking his chest. "Too much, too much," worn-out now, crying, breathless.

He jerked the blanket away from the sheets, wrapped her, and crawled to the headboard, leaning against it, exhausted. He held her, panting, reaching for the tissue to wipe her nose. "What, baby, what. Can you tell me?"

She pounded his chest, but her strength was gone. "It wasn't fireworks, it was a freight train. It wouldn't stop. I couldn't stop it," sobbing.

"I've got you, my baby, I've got you. Shh, shh, big breaths now. Don't cry, don't cry," rocking her, soothing her.

Most of the tissue were gone when she finally slept fitfully, but he didn't lay her down until five, keeping her wrapped in the blanket. He was stiff, and cold, and scared as he pulled a sheet up but knew he wouldn't sleep.

He felt her stir, and even after what they'd been through, scared to death of what she would say, he smiled at the wonder of her. He was lying with one arm around her, one over his face. She wriggled up to his ear and whispered, "It's five after six."

"I know," softly. "I was going to wake you at six fifteen."

"I know we need to talk, but I just want to say one thing."

"Okay," reaching back over his shoulder to hold her hand.

She whispered, "I thought I loved you before." His eyes started to sting. "You told me something from the prayer book, and I want to tell you something I remember from it." Still whispering, but saying confidently, "For this I was born, for this I came into the world."

The lack of sleep, the fear, the overwhelming love were too much. He covered his face with his hand and sobbed. "I'll fix it, baby, I'll fix it. I'll see the doctor tomorrow. I told you you'd never be afraid again, I'm so sorry. I did something wrong, I'll fix it."

"Rocco, you didn't do anything wrong. I'm not afraid, I'm not."

"Baby, of course you're afraid. I'm afraid."

"Turn over and kiss me. I'm not afraid."

"Sweetie, I have to talk to the doctor. I can't turn over. We need to get you to your class on time." He was getting calmer now. "It's the principle of the thing, baby, let's do it right."

She sighed deeply. "Is this the way it's going to be for three years then? We make beautiful love and you leave? I hate this, Rocco."

"No, no, it's not going to be like that. I'll come on Saturdays, and we won't have to get up for class." He grinned. "We won't get up until your mother calls at four."

She pulled on his shoulder. "Turn over," insistently, "I want to tell you so many things."

"Baby girl, it's a new semester, new classes, you can't skip the very first one. We have to be responsible. You go in the bathroom first, and I'll straighten things up."

She looked around at the used tissues all over the bed, all over the floor, the covers in disarray. "I'm sorry, honey, I love you so much. I want to tell you how magnificent you are. I want to lay in your arms and talk."

"I know, Blossom, I do too, but I have to be mature and responsible. Here are your smurfies if you want them. Get going now."

Not yet brave enough to walk naked to the bathroom, she turned to the other side of the bed and slipped her smurfies on. She was back in ten minutes, all washed and brushed. "I didn't wash my hair, I'll do it tonight. Can I watch you shave?"

He had put on his jeans, gathered up the tissues, and straightened the bed a little. "I won't bother shaving, baby, I won't get to the shop until three or so. I want to make sure we have time for you to eat breakfast. You didn't eat much yesterday, and you worked hard last night," grinning and winking, trying to lighten things up.

"Rocco!"

"It's okay, baby"—lifting her from behind and swinging her around—"we're allowed to have private jokes. No, no," as she tried to wiggle in front of him. "Let me wash up and brush my teeth."

She was all ready but sitting at the vanity looking at her image when he came out. He had been amazed her talk about the second half of the night had been so casual, and when she was looking so intently, his heart hit his ribcage, fearing a delayed reaction. "You okay, baby girl?"

"I'm wonderful. I was just wondering if I looked different on the outside."

He stood behind her, looking into her eyes through the mirror. "You're more beautiful than ever. Do you feel different on the inside?"

She reached for his hand and kissed it. "I feel wonderful on the inside. I feel strong and safe and pretty."

He pulled her up and put her arms around his neck. "You are such a miracle, Blossom Dove. I love you beyond reason."

In the elevator, she whispered, "The towel. What about the towel?"

"I took it. I want to keep it."

She wrinkled her nose. "No, Rocco."

"I'll wash it, baby, I just want to put it at the bottom of the pile of towels in my closet and see it every now and then. I never wanted to remember anything, baby girl. Now I want to remember everything."

Her face softened as the elevator opened. "You're so sweet."

In the coffee shop, "You need some protein, baby. She'll have a two egg omelet with tomato and ham, easy on the ham. A whole wheat English muffin and what, baby, hot chocolate?"

"No, black coffee, please."

"I'll have a black coffee now, and two breakfast sandwiches to go—one bacon, one ham, and put a Coke in the bag too."

"Why to go, honey?"

"It helps pass the time." His voice changed. "I didn't think ahead on this, Blossom. Leaving you is going to be the hardest thing I've ever done, baby girl."

"Oh, Rocco, you have to be strong. Let's don't think about it yet. Let's talk about last night," smiling and wiggling closer. "When we are dancing, I can feel your muscles through your shirt." She put her lips against his ear. "Your back is so beautiful in bed. More than I could imagine."

"I can't let that go by," chuckling.

"What?"

"Your front is so beautiful in bed. More than I ever imagined."

Her eyes widened, and she blushed bright red. "Rocco," whispering, looking around nervously, "someone might hear."

"I said the exact thing you said, except one word, baby girl." He kissed her cheek as their order came. "No one's listening, I was just teasing."

The separation looming, they got quiet, looking at each other, holding hands tightly. "We better head for your class, Blossom." She swallowed, her eyes getting bigger and darker. He put his breakfast in his gym bag and swung it and her tote over his shoulder and held out his hand to her. She shook her head no, he nodded yes, and the tears started as they left.

"You get a nap as soon as you can. When do you have a break? I'll call."

"I'm done at three today. Usually I work on a project, but I'll sleep today. Be awful careful driving, honey, you didn't get any sleep. I'm so sorry," her voice rising and shaking.

"Baby, we're not going to do this. I'll be back as soon as I can. You know that."

They were in front of her first class. She put her arms around his waist, even though others were arriving. "I'm not embarrassing you, am I?"

"You can't embarrass me, baby girl. Kisses?"

It started as a gentle good-bye kiss but quickly turned into more. He turned her so his back was to the arrivals then picked her up and moved them behind the only tree around.

"I can't do it, Rocco, I can't," desperation creeping in. "I'm tingling all over. I want you to stay."

And then, in one of those "what's the absolutely worst thing I could say here" moments, he said, "You wouldn't satisfy that tingling with anyone else, would you?"

She backed up a step, and for the first and only time in their life, he saw real fury coming from her eyes.

Panic, "I didn't mean that to come out. I didn't mean that, Blossom, I didn't," his voice cracking.

She stared at him, then back at the students milling around, and saw a friend. "Chet, would you record the opening remarks. I'll just be a few minutes," then looked back at Rocco.

"Blossom, I'm going to be sick. I'm sorry, oh god, I'm sorry. I'm going to be sick, baby."

She reached into her tote, handed him a bottle of water, and motioned him behind the tree. She stood stoically as he was sick, waited for him to rinse his mouth, and handed him three Tic Tacs.

When she continued to stare at him, he pleaded, "Don't let me mess this up. Oh god, Blossom, don't let me mess this up. I love you, I love you. I'm sorry."

Finally, after an eternity to him, she stepped close and put her hands around his neck. "I'm going to be the mature and responsible one for a minute. First, you need to know this, Rocco. It felt like you slapped my face when you said that."

He whimpered and started to say again "Please don't . . ." when she put her finger over his lips. "You cannot mess this up. I love you. But that cannot be a part of us. We are going to be apart more than we're together for the next three years. You can't be thinking like that, and I can't be thinking like that. It will destroy us. Let's forget this ever happened and never mention it again."

"Blossom, please—" She put her finger over his lips and shook her head.

"I have to go. I have to go. I love you. Call me around three and drive carefully." She turned and walked into the building, her hair and hips swinging together. He put his head against the tree, the knowledge that he had spoiled their precious night overwhelming him. *Oh god, oh god, help me.* The nausea swept over him again, but he swallowed it back, threw his gym bag over his shoulder, and went to his truck, his legs leaden.

He drove by rote. He couldn't believe he'd said it; he couldn't believe she didn't look back; he couldn't believe the whole night.

An hour into the ride, he started to feel a little better. She had said she loved him. She said to call her. He'd make it up to her. Everything would be all right. At the next rest stop, he checked his phone and was relieved to see Dr. Krienson's number still there. "This is Rocco Carnavale. I was in last fall? As soon as possible, I'd like another last appointment of the day. Wednesday at five-thirty is fine. You have my number? Thank you. See you then."

He used the restroom, got a coffee, opened one of the sandwiches, and headed out, drove too fast, and was in the driveway of the shop at two forty-five. He checked in with Helen, told her to let everyone know to come in early tomorrow for the weekly meeting, and went into his office to call.

"Hi," she said almost shyly. "Where are you?"

"I'm at the shop, baby girl, where are you?"

"I'm lying on my bed thinking of you. I was catching up on reading my daily prayer book. It made my heart jump."

"What did it say?" a knot forming in his stomach.

Softly, "It said, 'I praise my body and give thanks for its reliable functioning. It is God's beautiful expression of life—divine energy flows through me.' Isn't that beautiful, Rocco? I never thanked you for last night. I'm sorry I was so selfish."

Relief and love choked him. "Blossom, you are such a miracle," he said hoarsely. "Baby, I'm so sorry, please forgive me."

Helen saw him through the window, his forehead in his hand, tears running down his face. She shook her head. Poor kid, first his dad and now a girl. So she was surprised when he came out, beaming. "Bob says today's taken care of. See you at the morning meeting. I've got to get to the jewelry store."

Wednesday, five thirty.

"Good afternoon, Rocco, it's nice to see you again. How can I help you today?" She could see he was tense. She hoped it wasn't what she thought.

"Thank you for seeing me on short notice," wringing his hands, clearing his throat. "I came last fall about birth control pills." She nodded, encouraging him to continue. "We had our first, uh, er, encounter, Sunday night." When he saw her eyebrows lift slightly, he added, "We had a lot of postponements. My father died, the holidays, things like that," waving his hand nervously.

She nodded again. He cleared his throat again. "We had talked about it, took things slow." He was taking measured breaths to keep control. "And it was a wonderful experience, I'm pretty sure for both of us." He looked down and started wringing his hands again, looked up, and his eyes were moist. "I can't hurt this girl, doctor, I can't," agony on his face.

She got up, got him a cup of water from her cooler, pulled up a chair next to his. "Go on."

"I woke at three"—starting to talk fast—"the first time was about ten o'clock if that means anything, and . . . and"—he jumped up and started pacing—"I touched her hip. Oh god, I should have let her sleep."

"Sit down, Rocco," calmly. "That was perfectly normal. My goodness, honeymooners seldom get any sleep," patting the chair. "Tell me what happened."

"She was different"—breathing hard, wringing his hands. "Like aggressive. I even asked her if she was awake. It was unbelievable, I mean amazing, I just have to say that, and then she started screaming." He was talking faster, breathing hard, a stricken look on his face. "She was screaming it was too much. I thought I hurt her, I didn't know what to do, and then—I'm not a huge guy, but I'm way bigger than her—she lifted me right off the bed and started kicking and crying. Oh god, she cried a lot. I can't hurt this girl, doctor. I don't want it to happen again, I guess is what I'm saying." He sat down again, worn-out, his head in his hands. "Oh, and when we were talking about it, before, you know, about making love. I don't know what women feel, so I said maybe she'd feel fireworks, and she liked that."

135

He smiled a little. "And she said she did. But the second time"—swallowing hard—"the second time she said it was a freight train, and she couldn't stop it, and did I say how much she cried?" He closed his eyes, exhausted.

"Okay, I think I'm seeing a picture emerging here. First, don't worry about the crying. I'm sure it was a big step for her, and hey, girls cry," smiling at him. "Is she a hyper girl?"

"No, no, she's very brilliant. I mean, I've heard, I don't care. And she likes to know what to expect about everything, and she likes to be in control of her emotions. She has some family issues. I don't think they enter into this, but she likes to be in control."

"All right. From what you've said, she didn't pass out. Did her eyes roll back in her head?"

He almost whimpered, bit his lip, and said, "I don't know, that's why I feel so bad. I should have known something wasn't right, but it had been a long time for me, and it was so unbeliev—Oh god, I . . ."

She patted his hand and continued, "You said she was screaming and kicking, so I think we can rule out a convulsion. Did she go right to sleep? How was she when she woke up?"

"Well, first she cried for a long time, and I held her for a couple hours, and she shivered now and then like kids do when they've been crying. When she woke up, she said she was fine, and she's not afraid, but I don't want her to just say that. I wanted to find out more. She likes to know things."

"I think for now we'll go on the assumption it was a very strong orgasm that she just wasn't prepared for. You said the first time was normal or wonderful as you said, and that was probably what she was expecting, and things just escalated when it wasn't."

"But why not the first time?" He was looking worried again.

"You said you took it slow. Kind of instructional, would you say?" He bit his lip and shook his head yes. "So all the delays and postponements didn't really come into play until the second time. And like you said, she was aggressive. Perhaps she was unconsciously thinking she had it figured out and knew what to do and was in control as you said she likes to be, and we know no one really is at that time," smiling and patting his hand. "Let's do this, I'll look up a few things, and if I find anything we haven't talked about or if it happens again, I'll ask you to bring her in. I'm thinking it won't happen again, but you keep in contact, and I'm sure everything will be fine."

He was looking a little better and actually smiled when she said, "It may help if you can arrange to be together more than one night. It would take that desperation aspect out of it. Trying to do too much in a short amount of time," guiding him to the door.

After he paid and left, the doctor came out and said, "You can close up, Laura. I'm just going to dictate some notes for Melodie and then go. Thank God she's not eighteen and pregnant, but I want to get his concerns down while it's fresh in my mind."

That evening, her heart jumped at his name on her screen. "Hi, baby girl. I'll call again Friday, but I went to the doctor today."

"Oh, Rocco, she's going to think we're crazy people."

"It's her job, sweetie. I've got pretty good news and great news."

"What great news?"

"The pretty good news is it might not happen again. It could have been because we had to put it off so long. And the great news is she thinks I should come for two nights"—she squealed with delight before he could finish—"so we can relax more and not think of me leaving in the morning."

"Oh, Rocco, can you? Can you? Oh please stay two nights, please, please."

"I will, baby, I will. Now, I can't come this weekend, we're starting a big job, but I will next Friday."

"Oh, Rocco"—starting to cry—"I thought it would be a month. I can't believe it, ten days, I can't believe it."

"I have to go. I'll call Friday a little earlier than usual because I have to be at the shop by six. I love you beyond words, Blossom."

Friday at four o'clock.

"Hi, baby girl, where are you?"

"I'm just coming out of the Vagelos Building. The one I showed you on Smith Walk."

"Can you go to that spot you called the Button? Fedex will be there about quarter after four."

"Rocco"—in a chastising voice—"you didn't buy me another gift did you. I told you not to do that."

"I'd like to buy you the moon, Blossom Dove. Are you there yet?"

"Just about there—oh, here comes a Fedex truck."

"Okay, call me back. I love you."

She showed her ID, signed, and smiled at the package, still not used to getting gifts. She remembered she had her Bluetooth so she could call him as she opened it.

"I have the package, honey, I have my Bluetooth, so we can open it together."

"Why do you have a Bluetooth?"

"Sometimes I need both hands when I'm talking to people around the country."

"Jeez, I really should learn more about what you do, baby."

"It's not important, honey. Rocco, another jewelry box, I told . . . oh my god, oh, Rocco," crying openly as she saw two black pearls glistening on gray velvet, then sobbing as she read the note, "Lying with you, I'm born again." She sank to the ground in the busy area, hugging the box to her chest.

"Don't cry, baby, do you like them? I wanted them to stand out so we would always remember."

Still crying but trying to whisper, "But, Rocco, I didn't get you a gift."

"Blossom"—softly—"you gave me the most precious gift there is. I heard that old song a few weeks ago, and it came in my mind while you were sleeping. It's so true, my baby, I feel born again. I'm the luckiest man in the world."

"Rocco," she breathed.

"I'll call back at seven. Get something to eat. I love you."

She sat holding the box to her heart until the cold seeped in then looked around at everyone walking by. One girl saw her tears and looked concerned. She smiled weakly and said, "My boyfriend just sent me an unbelievable gift." The girl smiled, nodded her head in approval, and walked on.

"Hi, baby girl. Are you ready for bed?"

"Umm, I'm all washed and brushed and ready to talk. I put our pearls in the safe with my necklace and just-in-case money. We can add them when you come. They're so beautiful, Rocco."

"I'm glad you like them, little one. It's been a week since we took our walk on Ernst Trail and talked about being together, do you know that?"

"It seems like yesterday, and it seems like a lifetime. You were so wonderful talking to me, honey."

"Thank you, baby. I was scared to death. You know when else I was scared to death?"

"When?" worry creeping in.

"Monday morning when I said that stupid thing. Can we talk about that?"

"No," emphatically.

"Can I try to explain?"

"No. I said we're never going to talk about it again, Rocco."

"But, baby, I wasn't jealous. I was scared."

"And that just makes it worse. Here we are talking about it, and I said I don't want to talk about it. Don't you see what I mean, there's no end to it."

"Blossom, I understand, but if we could just—"

"Rocco, I will close this phone."

"But if I could—" The phone snapped shut. He smiled and waited. Four, three, two, one, and his vibrated.

"Don't you try to control me, Rocco Carnavale."

"Baby girl, I'm not trying to control you. You're getting your two lives mixed up. I love you. Every time we have a rough patch, it's my fault. I'm fighting for my life here."

"Don't be silly. You never have to fight for your life. I love you."

"Seriously, baby, I should have stayed. We never had a chance to talk. What was going on at work wasn't as important as staying."

"What was going on at work, honey?"

"Nothing more important than us."

"Tell me anyway."

"Well, I'm not my father, and at first I thought they'd like a more low-key approach. Now I'm wondering if they think I'm too young and they can walk all over me."

"Not to interfere, honey, but maybe you should remind them you could have closed the business, but you kept it going so they would have their jobs."

"It might come to that, baby, but it's not important right now. You left me standing outside that building," affecting a woebegone voice. "A poor sick guy all alone."

Giggling softly, "I'm so sorry, honey, when you get here, I'll kiss you and make it better."

"I don't know if a kiss is enough, baby girl, I was really, really sad." He knew her suggestive laugh would get him through a couple more days.

"Oh, honey, does coming here add to your problems? What about taking next Friday off? What if you have to cancel? I'm scared."

"No way. No way will I have to cancel. How about our weekend? Do you think there's a western dance place around there?"

"Oh, that would be so wonderful. I'll check online and ask around. I can't believe we can make plans," tearing up.

"Now, baby, it's a big city, so if you see one, we have to be sure it's appropriate. Get all the information you can, and I'll check it out before we go in."

Getting excited again, "And Saturday we could be just like tourists. Would you like to see where that scene in *Rocky* was shot, and the Liberty Bell, and . . . oh, this is so wonderful." Her voice went to a whisper, "And you won't have to take me home."

He heard the nervousness in her voice. "Blossom, it will be fine. We'll go slow. She said it might never happen again, baby."

"I'm not afraid. I just want it to be nice for you."

"Baby, just seeing you is nice for me. Remember, it's us, not me. We're making love together." Pausing a second, "Baby, when I woke you, were you really awake? I didn't force you, did I? I don't want to be that kind a guy."

"Oh, Rocco, no, no. I was awake. The first time was so wonderful," she whispered. "I wanted to contribute. My mother said I don't contribute."

"Oh my god." The wind rushed out of him like someone had kicked him in the stomach. In his mind he said, *What have they done to you?* Out loud, he said, "My precious girl, you contribute by being your own wonderful self. You don't have to do anything that doesn't come natural. Just give me your feelings like we talked about. Sometime we might want to be more aggressive, but that will be later when we know our bodies. We'll know when, baby, we don't force it now because you think you should." He knew she was crying and trying not to let him hear. "You be your own wonderful self. I love you beyond reason, Blossom Dove. Now take some breaths and let's talk about our weekend. I hope I can get started really early, but I'll call you Thursday and give you a rough time. Are you with me, baby?"

She took some shuddering breaths. "Yes."

"The Rocky thing sounds great. Do you know the way?"

"It's right in Fairmont Park. Not far at all. It's at the steps of the Museum of Art. The zoo is right there too, but I don't like zoos, they seem cruel to me. It's a nice place to walk, though, if you'd like to. Oh, and the Rodin Museum. Do you know the sculpture the Kiss? We never talked about art, and oh, wait . . ."

"Blossom, slow down. Any place is fine with me."

"But I just thought of the perfect place. After Rocky, we can go to the Franklin Institute. You can do the climbing wall and ride a bike across a cable if you dare, so bring sneakers. Do you like trains, honey, you can see an actual locomotive. I'm blathering, aren't I? Oh, this is going to be so wonderful, Rocco," and the tears started again.

"Don't cry, sweetie, everything will be great."

"But we won't have time to see the Liberty Bell," her voice rising.

He laughed. "Blossom, it's been there a long time. I'll see it another weekend. You're tired, you always cry when you're tired. You go to bed now, and I'll call on Thursday."

"I don't want to hang up yet. I won't hear your voice until Thursday. I can't do it," wailing now.

"Okay, now you're beyond tired. Lay down and I'll sing to you. What would you like, Elvis?"

"No, Delbert. Not the sad one, the funny one."

He only went through it once before her breathing was steady, so whispered, "Close your phone, baby girl."

His phone chirped. It was her. "Hi, baby girl, everything okay? I'm about forty minutes away."

"Oh, Rocco, I can't find my common sense. I don't know what to do. Should I stay here? Should I go to the parking lot?" Almost whispering, "Should I go to the hotel?"

"Do you want to go to our room, Blossom?"

"Oh yes, please."

"Okay, I'll call them and say you're coming for the key. Are you all packed?"

"Yes, I did that yesterday when I could think. Rocco," crying.

"I'll call you right back, baby, hold on."

"Go ahead over, sweetie, they're expecting you. Don't cry. I'll be there in a half hour. Watch TV or lay down. I'm coming."

"It's me, baby girl." He heard her whimpering trying to open the door. All he saw was a blur of lace ruffles and panties as she jumped into his arms, her legs around his waist. Sobbing outright, she mumbled into his neck, "You can't leave me here, I can't stay here anymore without you."

"Sh, sh, I'm here, baby, I'm here," as he kicked the door shut and dropped his gym bag. He carried her to the biggest chair and arranged her on his lap. She wouldn't let go of his neck. "Can I get freshened up, sweetie?"

"Nooo!"

"Okay, okay, let's just sit here and take some breaths." He rubbed her back under her top. "What's this pretty thing called?"

"It's a camisole."

"It's sure pretty. Big breaths now. How did you get so worked up, baby, you knew I was almost here."

"I can't stay here."

"Now, Blossom, we're not going to use our two nights talking about things we can't change."

Breathing heavily but calming down, "Oh, Rocco, the months and months ahead of us. I just couldn't bear it all of a sudden."

"I'm here now. I'll be here again. We'll make it, baby," turning her face so he could kiss her, moving his hand from her back to her breasts. Her crying turned to little moans. He carried her to the bed and lay her on the pillow, nibbling at her lips. "Let me go to the bathroom, I'll be right back," smiling as she called out, "You're so beautiful." "Looks are an accident of birth." He smiled over his shoulder.

He was back in minutes in his boxers and slipped in beside her, peeling her camisole up over her head. He pulled the sheet up to their chins and said, "Hi."

She put her leg over his hip, and he said, "Go slow now, we don't want Mr. Freight Train to come. Let's explore each other. Maybe we should have done that the first time."

"Oh, I couldn't have done that. It would have been too scary . . . you know," pointing down at his groin.

He laughed out loud. "Run your hands all over me, it won't be scary." She started at his ear and ran her hands down his neck to his nipple. "Do you feel that—you know, down there, like I do?"

"I do," softly.

She nibbled on his other nipple. He sighed. "Isn't that funny," she said. "There's a direct correlation."

"I don't think too many people are saying the term 'direct correlation' while they're making love."

She moved her hand downward exploring his navel as he moaned softly, then a little farther. "You have hair like girls do?"

"Ummm."

"Oh, it's curly," twirling a curl around her finger. "I like it." Another inch lower, she said, "I can't go any farther, it's too scary."

"Give me your hand," he whispered.

"No, no, I can't . . . oh, that's so nice. It's like the muscles in your back. Umm, why is it so hard?"

"I have to be able to slide into you," he whispered.

"But this part is soft," as she caressed the tip.

Breathing hard, "That's so I won't hurt you when it gets in."

"Wasn't that clever of God. Ooh, it's a little wet," sliding her finger along the opening.

Breathing harder, "We better quit exploring now, sweetie."

"But I want to feel this other part."

"Another time, baby, let me catch my breath."

She wiggled closer and whispered in his ear, "I love it when you make noises, it makes me feel powerful."

"I told you, you have all the power, baby girl."

"Are you sure, honey?"

"Oh, I'm very sure," caressing her neck.

Whispering again, "Because after last Sunday, I felt like I would crawl on my hands and knees through broken glass to get to you."

"Oh Blossom, Blossom baby," moving over her and kissing her until they were moaning and moving together. He found his way in. They found their rhythm so new and yet timeless, and then they found that place where the world could never intrude.

She held him when he tried to fall to the side. "You're not heavy," she whispered. "Stay." After breathing hard in time with him, "We fit together so nice."

"My precious baby girl, I had no idea what making love was, no idea," his voice fading with exhaustion, his eyelashes moist, then laughing weakly when she eased him over, crawled up to his ear, and whispered, "And don't you forget it, big boy."

He raised up on his side, caressing her hair, kissing her forehead, "Is my baby girl making sexual jokes?"

She giggled and nodded tiredly. "I need to sleep now. I hope you're not too hungry."

"We're fine, sweetie, go to sleep." She turned her back, wiggled her hips into him, curled her hands under her chin, and promptly fell asleep.

And he, who only slept lightly at night ever on guard and who had never slept in the daytime, kissed her back, succumbed to the delicious exhaustion, and fell asleep.

He woke, oriented himself, smiled in wonder that her body was tucked into his, and opened his eyes. It was six thirty. He couldn't believe they'd slept two hours. He kissed her shoulder and stretched to wake her.

"We didn't sleep all night, did we?"

"No, baby girl, it's a perfect time for supper. Does that place serve food?"

"Yes, it said family-style dinners."

"Do you want me to close my eyes while you run to the bathroom?"

"Yes, please. Don't peek. I'm going to shower, but I won't be long. I'll wash my hair tomorrow."

He turned on some lights, found their underthings, found some music on the TV; and she was out in twelve minutes wrapped in a towel. He headed for her, rubbing his hands together.

"No, no, we're going dancing. Go in the bathroom."

"The tiger's out of the cage now, baby girl."

"Well, I know the tiger hasn't eaten all day, so he better go in the bathroom so we can get going."

"Don't shave, honey," she called after him.

"Why, is it a western thing?"

"No." She peeked in the door. "I want to feel your whiskers on my tummy later." She giggled and pulled the door shut, hearing him laughing.

When he came out of the bathroom, her back was to him. She was sliding on a brown headband. Her dress was tan with Indian print ribbon around the hem. It was a soft material, and when she turned, he saw the ribbons circled under her breasts, emphasizing them. His heart started pounding in his ears. He turned his back to compose himself, saying, "I brought a tan shirt, baby, want me to wear it?"

"Rocco, don't you like my dress? Aunt Mim picked it out."

He kept his eyes averted. "It's beautiful, Blossom, your boots too."

She moved in front of him, puzzled. "Look, honey, see the squash blossoms," as she traced the brown ribbons crisscrossing her breasts.

He cleared his throat. "It's a little tight on top."

"Rocco, there's nothing revealing about this dress. See, it's not tight at all," moving the material. Seeing the agonized look on his face, she put her hands around his neck. "Honey, you're the only person in the world who knows what's under this dress. See my boots go way up to my knees," pulling up her skirt. "They're Minnetonkas, they'll be great for dancing. Everything's fine, right?"

He hugged her and whispered in her ear, "We could stay here and order pizza."

"No, Rocco, we're not staying here. You told me to find a dance place. I did. We're going dancing. You have to get past this, Rocco."

Hoarsely, "It was hard before, baby, it's worse now."

"I know, my darling. Don't you think I feel the same way? You're so beautiful. Remember when you whispered to me bed is our special time? Until then, we have to live in the world." She clapped her hands. "So we're going dancing, we're going to eat, and then we'll come back for our special time. And you know the best part?"

"What?" his tension easing a little.

"We have another whole day and night!" She twirled around the room, making him smile in spite of himself.

The place was called Wild Country, and he saw families going in, so he didn't worry about the atmosphere. The eating area was to the right under a rustic archway. The bar and dance area to the left. The band was setting up, and there was a Gretchen Wilson song on the jukebox. He took it all in as they found one of the smaller tables. He sat with his back to the wall and felt comfortable. Any trouble wouldn't come until later, so he could relax for a while, shifting himself by habit to watch the entrance.

His stomach was empty, so he asked that his beer come with his philly cheesesteak sub and fries. She ordered grilled chicken fingers and applesauce from the kid's section of the menu and was beaming in the friendly atmosphere.

"This looks fine, don't you think, honey?"

"I think it will be great, baby girl. Have a couple fries."

The band members were sitting at the bar when they got up for their first dance at eight thirty. He assumed they would start at nine. A couple was dancing with their children, a gray-haired couple looking pretty good, and then two thirtysomething couples trying to remember how to line dance. They hadn't danced since his father's funeral, but someone had punched a nice tempo Kenny Chesney, and he started slow. She hadn't forgotten a thing and was completely with him from the start, never taking her eyes from his. They danced two numbers and then went to the table while the band got started. Some more couples had come in. Two of the fellows had cowboy hats on.

"I should have worn my hat, but I didn't want to leave it on the table if no one else had one on."

"You have a cowboy hat? Go get it, honey, you would be so handsome!"

"Naw, it's only a $60 Stetson, but I'd hate to lose it. I have it all broken in."

She clapped her hands. "Now I know what I'm getting you for your birthday. When we're at the clinic, we'll go up to Santa Fe and have you fitted for a Resistol. You can meet Aunt Mim, we'll go shopping. Oh, it will be so wonderful, Rocco," squeezing tight against him and kissing his cheek. She whispered, "I never knew what happiness really was until you."

"Don't make me cry in public, baby girl," kissing her forehead.

"Are you happy, Rocco?"

"Blossom, I went from just surviving in my room to being with the girl of my dreams, dancing in Philadelphia, and talking about a trip to New Mexico. I'm past happy, I'm in another universe."

She gave him such a glorious smile, his eyes stung, public or not. "Now let's show these people how to dance."

Their eyes never left each other unless he was making sure they had room for their spins and turns. It was Friday night, and the floor filled up. As the families left, the noise level increased and younger couples filled the floor, alcohol giving them freedom. He no longer needed alcohol. His love of dancing upped his adrenaline, his steps sure, the music flowing through him. She looked more beautiful than ever, her eyes sparkling, her cheeks flushed. He could feel energy emanating from her. She never hesitated when he whispered directions, moved just right at the slightest touch, and he laughed out loud when he held out his arms at the end of a dance and she jumped up, her legs around his waist leaning back as he spun around.

Some groups of noisy singles had started arriving. He heard the guys whooping and was positive it was directed at her and would become more aggressive as the night went on, so he said, "Getting tired, sweetie?"

"A little, but it's so, so fun, Rocco. Are you glad we came?"

"I am, baby, we'll come back next time. This is a great place." A shadow crossed her face. He knew exactly what it was. "Don't think about it, baby girl, we have another night left. One more dance and we better go."

The singer was doing a pretty good version of Brad Paisley's "Then." He lifted her up in his arms again, her legs wrapping around his waist. He sang softly in her ear, nuzzling her neck, loving her mewling noises.

"Rocco, are we being obscene?"

He laughed softly. "Absolutely, baby girl."

She had her face buried in his neck. "Are there children here?"

"No, they left a long time ago. We're fine."

"Am I embarrassing you?"

"Not in a million years, sweetie. All the couples on the floor are doing the same thing we are."

"I'm embarrassed. Can we go?"

"We're dancing that way now. Do you want to get down?"

"No. I'm tingling all over. Everyone will know."

"Nobody knows. You're fine." He shifted her to his hip, picking up their coats. He had seen a doorman/bouncer arrive at ten thirty and smiled at him as they passed. "Sleepy girl?" the guy asked. Rocco nodded. "Great band, we'll come again." The fellow said, "Can I help you with her coat. The wind has kicked up." He whispered to her to hold her arms out. He and the bouncer slipped her coat on, and he thanked him with a smile. He was a little ashamed walking to the truck that he thought the guy was probably helping just to touch her, but hey, you can't be too careful.

The room looked familiar with their things here and there. "I love this room," she said. "Can we get it every time? Is it expensive?"

"We'll get it every time we can, baby. It costs what it costs. It's worth it, why go anyplace else when this is so close."

"I need to take a quick shower, honey, or would you like to go first?"

"Oh, don't take a shower. I want to remember the smell of you and taste of you when I'm home alone."

"Honey, I can't do that. We've been perspiring. I'd be too self-conscious."

"Okay, how about we take a quick shower together?" He gave her his Groucho Marx look.

She looked worried and bit her hands. "We've only been together under the covers. It would be scary."

He tipped her chin up and hugged her. "You've already explored me. You know what I look like. How about you keep your back to me, and we just rinse off real quick and do a whole shower another time?"

She kept biting her lip. "Okay," hesitantly. "I'll try. Will you get out if I can't do it?"

"Sure, I will. You go in and brush your teeth and do your personal things and call me when you're ready."

"I'm coming in," opening the opaque door of the roomy shower. "You wash my back, and I'll wash yours. Is that okay?"

She started at his neck and worked down as he leaned against the wall. "Oh, this is nice. I love your back, and your butt's muscular too. This is fun, Rocco."

"Do you want me to turn around?"

"No!"

"It's okay, I'm not going to. Turn around and I'll do you. Ummm, I thought those were dimples I saw today. Did you know you have two dimples right here?" He put his thumbs on her indentations, working his fingers around her hips.

Her hands were on the wall. She was breathing hard. "Stop, stop. You get out now."

He pulled her back toward him, kissing the back of her neck. "You sure?"

"Rocco, you promised. Maybe tomorrow. Stop that, I'm getting out."

He laughed. "Okay, baby, okay. Holler when you're in bed." He came out with a towel wrapped around his waist. "Am I in the doghouse?"

"No." She smiled. "You're too beautiful to be in the doghouse," marveling at him. His damp curls falling on his forehead. She held her arms out.

He shook his head in wonder. "My god, that has to be the most beautiful sight I've ever seen. Would you like some music on?"

"If you can find something nice."

He fussed with the remote sitting on the edge of the bed but tossed it aside when she started rubbing his back. "I don't have the patience, I have important things to do," dropping the towel and sliding under the covers.

She giggled, and he could see her in the darkness against the pillow. "Baby girl, I've been meaning to tell you. I respect your mother because she made you, but I can't go through our whole life not saying you're beautiful. God, you're beautiful."

"Thank you," snuggling closer.

"Now where were we when the world got in the way. It was my turn to explore you."

"But I wasn't done exploring you. I had another part to do."

"Let's do that another time. I've been waiting for this all night." He started at her ear. "I'll go here next," moving to her breasts, nibbling gently.

Already breathing heavily, "But I didn't explore you with my lips. That's not fair."

"All's fair," laughing softly, moving to her navel, probing with his tongue. "I'm going to kiss you all over. Are you ready?"

"Wait, wait," panting. "What do you mean, all over?"

"I mean all over," moving to her hip bones, "here and . . ."

"Rocco, Rocco"—breathless, incredulous—"you can't do that. Is that even allowed?"

He moved back to her ear, whispering, "Remember, baby girl, no rules, no boundaries."

"But, Rocco"—holding his shoulders, trying to keep him from moving down—"that's, that's . . . it seems so, so decadent," breathing hard.

"What's *decadent* mean?" She arched against him as he nibbled at her breast.

"Like, like, deliciously bad," panting.

"That's exactly right, Blossom Dove, because you're delicious. Put your hands in my hair, push me down."

"No, no," screaming when his tongue reached her. She pulled on his hair. "Come back up. I can't, I can't."

"Is this good," nibbling on her.

"Yes, yes, no, no, come up, I can't, you're crazy," crying, laughing.

He came up, whispering into her mouth, "Let it come if it feels good, let it come."

"Not without you," pushing against him. "I can't breathe, you're a crazy person," gasping.

"I'm right here, I'll catch up after, let's try."

"It's too much, I can't, it's too much. Maybe tomorrow."

He laughed, working the corner of her mouth with his tongue. "We're awfully busy tomorrow. We're taking a shower."

She laughed, trying to get her breath back, until he slid his hand down, inserted his middle finger into her, and rubbed her clitoris gently with his thumb.

She screamed, "Oh god, Rocco, come in, come in, please, please."

He mounted her, groaning at the tightness of her excitement. She moved violently against him. He wanted to go easy, worrying about the freight train; but he couldn't form the words, he couldn't breathe, she was moving him around the bed, he didn't know where he was. Finally, she dug into his back, biting his shoulder to cover her scream; and he let himself go.

They fell back against the pillows. Through a haze, he saw her head lolling from side to side as she fought for breath. Tears were sliding down his face. He was whimpering, "You can't . . . I' can't . . ."

"Shhh," she whispered, "go to sleep." And in one of the few times in their life, she didn't turn her back and go to sleep. She tucked his head under her chin, whispered to him, and rubbed his back until he was asleep. She drifted away with a tiny smile on her face. She wasn't good for nothing. She was good for something.

He woke. They had moved a little. She was in the crook of his arm, and he just looked at her perfection. She had cried out once, and he had made out "good for nothing." What had they done to her? For one of the few times, he let himself think back—the kicks, the punches, the broken arm, the broken collar bone, the fear, the fury, the helplessness. His dad hated him. He hit him. It was simple. It was behind him. What was she dealing with? He could protect her and take care of her, but the feeling of helplessness centered on her now. He didn't know what he was dealing with.

She opened her eyes a little and smiled. He shivered at her sated look. "I should get some Binaca, so I can kiss you in the morning. Why are you looking at me funny?"

"You know why I'm looking at you funny, and I don't want to taste Binaca, I want to taste you."

"But I won't taste good."

"You'll taste delicious. Besides, we'll cancel each other out. Let's try."

"Umm, it works," she said. "You're delicious."

"Not as delicious as you were last night," winking.

"Rocco!" She put her finger over his mouth. "Don't talk about it, it's too private."

"Okay, it will be our little secret," reaching for her.

"No, no, I know you're starving. We have to get going, we have a big day."

His eyes widened as she jumped up and started gathering their things from last night, completely forgetting she was naked. She chattered on about the Franklin Institute, don't forget to wear sneakers, she wished they had a camera . . .

He got out of the bed just as she turned to ask, "Where would you like to go for break—" and her mouth made a perfect *O* as she looked at him and then down at herself.

He took two steps and hugged her. "So can we take that shower now or tonight?"

She giggled. "Tonight."

He slapped her butt lightly, and she wiggled away from him and then wiggled her butt and winked over her shoulder. "I have to wash my hair, so fix some coffee if you like." He shook his head, smiling at the wonder of her.

"Don't you use one of those hair dryers?"

"No, it will dry just as well on its own. You get out of the habit of time-wasting things on the reservation. There's never enough hours in the day."

She had on a light blue turtleneck with her dove necklace, a denim skirt, and matching boots when he came out of the bathroom. He put on sneakers and asked, "Aren't you going to climb the wall with me, baby?"

"No, I'm kind of afraid, and I want to get pictures of you. Honey, there's a place that has a nice brunch near the museum that has Rocky, or up on Fortieth, there's Izzy and Zoe's. I think you'd like it. It has supersized Egg McMuffin thingies that Nixie likes."

"That sounds good. Let's go there." He watched as she put everything they might need for the day in a backpack. "You're very organized, baby girl."

"I like to be prepared."

He hugged her and whispered, "I should have prepared you before I kissed you all over. I'm sorry if I scared you."

She whispered into his mouth, "It was very scary," kissing him thoroughly, then whispered in his ear, "We'll try again."

"Do you want to stay here awhile," huskily.

Laughing, "No, crazy man. I know you're starving, let's go."

The popular spot was busy and noisy, already filled with college students. They found a small booth, sitting on the same side, putting their coats on the other. He had looked the place over in an instant and couldn't admit to himself that the guys made him uncomfortable, her beauty made him uncomfortable, and her sweater made him particularly uncomfortable. He knew better than to say anything and tried to settle in. Maybe as the years went by, it would ease up, but he didn't think so.

He went whole hog and got the bacon-egg-cheese-potato toasted sub, and they laughed as it came hanging over the plate. "You really have to start eating better, honey."

"I know. I will when we're together."

She got a mini ham-and-goat-cheese panini, and they shared a pot of coffee. As close as she was to him, looking at him adoringly, the other customers might be surprised they were talking business.

"This is a great place, baby girl. I don't think Meadville could support something this big though."

"Do you miss the food business, honey?"

"A little. I like the immediate result of making a good meal. In my business, you have to work a long time to get your results. Both businesses have labor issues. There's probably no end of help on the campus, but I'm sure a big turnover. That means they're in a constant state of training. They probably have a hard time finding really good workers, but our service was good."

"I love talking on the phone, Rocco, but it's so nice to talk in person. You know so much, and you're so amazing," kissing his cheek. "You're so wonderful in spite of what you've had to overcome. I love you so much."

It was the opening he wanted. "How about you, little one? You've had a lot to overcome, and it isn't over yet. Have they let up at all?" He tried to keep his voice casual and conversational.

"Oh, Dad's pretty resigned. I think Mom has an underlying fear that I could say I'm not staying, and really, what could they do. We're kind of at an impasse. She keeps on me about how lucky I am, and I guess her method is to degrade me. I recognize it for what it is, honey, it doesn't bother me."

"Sweetie," he said carefully, "you can't hear you're worthless for years and not expect it to have an effect."

"Oh, Rocco, it's so petty compared to you. How did we get on this conversation anyway? We're tourists today."

"Well, let's always talk about it, okay? Remember when you asked me and then said I should talk about it? I can't believe where I am. I never thought I'd tell anyone, never, ever. When it happens, you feel responsible, you feel afraid all the time, you feel embarrassed. You helped me, Blossom, I just want to do it for you."

She wasn't making a sound. No expression on her face. Her big eyes looking at him, tears running down her cheeks. "I'm here, baby, I'll always be here." He took her napkin and dried her face and held her close for a minute. He was about to say let's go to the restroom and start our day when she said so quietly he had to bend his ear to her lips, "It's just that everything I do is wrong."

"Nothing you do is wrong, Blossom," turning so that his back shielded her from the room.

"Yes, it is, Rocco. I wanted to protect Nixie and it just made things at home so bad, it affected him. And then, and then"—shuddering—"I wanted to go far away to school, and look what happened, we're apart all the time, and it's my fault."

"Oh, baby, baby," frantic to find the right thing to say. "Remember what you're always saying from your little prayer book, 'Divine Order'? It may have been worse at home if we tried to see each other every day."

"But Rocco"—in a robotic voice—"my parents are wonderful people. I'm very fortunate to have a comfortable life with material things. I'm the one who has ruined the family."

He just looked at her helplessly for a few seconds, knowing anything he said couldn't wipe away years. Then he said calmly, "This isn't the place, sweetie, let's put this away for another time and go be tourists." He looked in her eyes. "You are a wonderful person, Blossom. I love you with all my heart. Now, stay in the restroom until I call your name. There's a lot of people here." They did the restroom routine and went to the truck.

"We're going to the Philadelphia Museum of Art on Benjamin Franklin Parkway at Twenty-sixth Street, honey," so he could set the GPS. The only residual of their talk was her digging into his leg above his knee. He patted her hand when traffic allowed.

"I kind of expected it to be at the top of the stairs and really big," he said as they viewed the small Rocky statue at the bottom of the stairs.

"The museum's been here since 1876, honey. I imagine the movie will fade away, so they couldn't make it too focal."

They raced to the top. She was surprised he beat her so easily. Track was the only sport she was ever in, and she often beat Nixie running up hills in New Mexico. She took pictures on her phone of him doing Rocky's triumphant arrival. Her heart sang watching him laugh and jump.

"We'll actually do the museum another time, honey. It has marvelous collections, but you have to take two or three hours to do it justice. There are beautiful mansions all along here too. We should pick out a couple next time so you can see the construction."

They headed to the Franklin Institute Science Museum at Twentieth. She made a fuss about him paying the $29 for their admission and again when she had a hot chocolate and he got a pretzel and Coke. They headed to the sports challenge where he did the climbing wall and batting cages and scared her silly doing the sky bike, balancing the two-wheel bicycle on the narrow cable. They did the walk-through heart with some children, and she shook her finger at him, "You pay attention—this is why you should eat better." He loved the train factory, and she had more fun watching the wonder on his face than the things around them.

They were passing the gift shop when he looked in and saw something. "Stay right here, baby, and keep your eyes closed, I'll be right back." He returned with a big bag stapled shut.

"What is it?" She smiled and reached for the bag.

"No, no, show you later."

"This was a great day, baby girl. I've never been a tourist before," as they walked to the truck.

"That doctor was a genius," she whispered, "saying you should stay two nights."

"Was she ever," kissing her head. "Do you know any good places for dinner around here, baby?"

She looked a little shy. "Could we go back to our room awhile before dinner? I have to go to the bathroom," she whispered.

He was immediately concerned. "Should I drive fast, should we find a place around here?"

"No, I like our bathroom. I can make it."

"Okay, I'll pull up front and walk you up."

"Honey, just drop me off. I can go up myself while you park. I'm a grown woman."

"I'll say," winking at her. "People are probably checking in now. I don't want you alone in the hall."

He pulled a little past the door and parked. The doorman came toward them. "I'm sorry, sir, you can't park there."

"I'm just running her up to the room, I'll be right back."

"But, sir . . ."

He gave him a look Blossom had never seen.

"She's not feeling well. I'll be right back."

"Of course, sir."

She had the bathroom door open, brushing her hair when he got back. "Would you like to eat downstairs, honey, it's Italian mostly."

"That's fine, baby. Your tummy okay?"

"I'm fine, honey, I just had to go to the bathroom. You didn't have to scare the doorman."

"Upscale or not, Blossom, they're in the service business. He should have picked up on the situation right away."

She made their reservation on the automated system. "Room 422—two for Penne's at six thirty. Thank you."

He was in the big chair and held out his arms. "Come here, baby girl, I want to ask you something personal."

"Rocco, I don't want to talk about my family anymore."

"No, no. There's something I don't know about, and I think I should."

She climbed onto his lap, looking a little worried. "Okay."

"A fellow at the shop said he was late because it was his wife's period and she was bitchy. You're never bitchy, so I just wondered if you have periods." Her eyes opened wide, but he went on, "I left school too early and never had anyone to ask. I just heard things on the street."

She smiled and patted his cheek. "We wouldn't need birth control if I didn't have periods, honey. It's kind of God's way of telling you that you can have a baby."

He looked puzzled. "How's that work?"

"Well, the short version is my body makes a container every month to hold a baby, and if I don't need it, it breaks up and leaves."

Really looking puzzled now, "I heard it's blood."

"It's mostly blood, and bits and pieces of tissue too."

"But I heard it happens every month."

"That's right. For me, every twenty-eight days. It might be twenty-five to thirty days too. It lasts from five to seven days."

His mouth had dropped open, and he unconsciously held her tighter. "You do that every twenty-eight days?"

"Umm, since I was fourteen."

"No way."

"I was kind of late. Most girls start about twelve. It's usually between eleven and fifteen."

"But that's just little girls," incredulously.

"Honey, what were you doing at fifteen?"

"Oh my god!"

She tipped her head and wagged her finger. "You see how dangerous unprotected sex can be?"

"Holy cow. But, baby, if you have a period every twenty-eight days, why haven't you been bitchy?"

"First"—shaking her finger again—"I don't like that word. Mostly it's just been a coincidence. It affects women in different ways. I'm usually emotional and cry a lot. In fact," she whispered in his ear, "when you came down the first time for my birthday, it was bad enough we talked about important things, scary things, but it was the second day of my period."

"Aw, baby girl"—squeezing her—"but you weren't bi . . . you know."

"I don't usually lose my temper. But, Rocco, if that lady does, she probably has a headache or backache or both. You feel bloated and not pretty. It's only a couple days a month. Maybe he should be nicer."

"But you said it's five days."

"The first couple days are the worst, and then—for me anyway—the last three days are just finishing up."

"So those ads on TV about things you use?"

She jumped up and got a small pink zippered case from her purse. "This is a tampon," giggling when he leaned back. "Here, I'll waste this one so you can see." She pushed it open. "You insert this inside"—his eyes widened—"and it expands as it gets moist. When you go to the bathroom or feel it has absorbed as much as it can, you pull this string and drop it into the bowl," laughing again as his mouth opened. She opened another packet and unfolded a pad. "Overnight or the first couple days, I use this too."

His eyes got big. "You put that inside you?"

"No, no," peeling the covering off the back. "It's sticky, and you put it on your panties for extra protection."

"You carry that with you all the time?"

"It's good to have it. I'm very regular, but they said I might change taking the pills. You've probably heard of this," holding up travel pack of Midol. He shook his head no. "It's like aspirin, but for periods. It helps with the headaches and backaches. It's supposed to help with the bloated feeling, but it doesn't work for me."

He shook his head from side to side. "I'm overwhelmed. I had no idea, Blossom. What can I do for you when you have one?"

"The first couple days I crave chocolate even more than usual."

"You want a box of chocolates? I can do that."

"No, no, honey, not a box. Just four pieces like those tiny boxes. Two for the first day and two for the second," she counted on her finger. "And I don't like caramels, and I don't like truffles, just creamy centers."

He got his phone out, pressed Memo, and wrote 4 pc choc. "Five days every twenty-eight days, umm. So the big question would be, can we make love during your period?"

Her eyes got big; then she looked pensive.

"I love to watch the wheels go round in your brain." He smiled.

"Well, that's not a question you hear every day. I don't think there would be any reason you couldn't. There's probably swelling, but it would be a natural lubricant."

He nuzzled her ear. "Umm, I like that word *lubricant*."

"Stop, crazy man. But . . ."

"I knew there would be a *but*."

155

"My first *but* would be I wouldn't want to offend you. It's not pretty red blood. Like I said, it's bits and pieces. Maybe you wouldn't like me."

"That would never happen. What's the other *but*?"

"Well, the way my birth control pills work is I take twenty-one and then seven that are placebos so to speak, and . . ."

"What's *placebo* mean?"

"It means fake, basically. They're just so you don't forget—like twenty-one are real and seven pretend. So what I'm wondering is during the time I'm taking the placebos, can I get pregnant? I'd have to check on that."

"Can you check on the computer?"

"Honey, I never use my computer for personal things. I know how vulnerable they are, and we're doing sensitive work for Dr. Ng. I'll find out."

"Do you want me to call the doctor?"

"No! She's going to think we're crazy people. I'll do it at the clinic here when I have the courage. Did I explain things okay? Is it all clear?"

"Wow, the more I learn, the more I don't know."

"What did you hear on the street?"

"Baby girl, if you see a bunch of teenage guys standing on a corner talking, 99 percent of the time they're talking about girls, pretending they know things they don't. Let's go eat."

"How about the thing you bought? Is it for me?"

"Later."

"Now, now," jumping up and down.

Shaking his head and getting the bag, "You can talk me into anything."

She opened the bag and squealed, "I love it, I love it," taking a big, soft tiger from the bag and hugging it. "I'm going to sleep with him every night."

"Do you know why I got it?"

"Of course"—softly—"because I let the tiger out of the cage. I don't forget anything you say," winking.

"Let's go eat, or we'll never get there."

He liked the way the restaurant blended modern and Italian and filed away the open kitchen to tell the guys at Mangia's. He took in the room at a glance, okayed the table the hostess showed them to, sitting with his back to the wall.

"I'll have a Bud Light, frozen mug on the side, water with lemon for the lady." After the waiter left, he asked, "Would you like a glass of wine?"

"No. I imagine they ask for identification with students all over." She leaned forward and whispered, "I'm crazy enough with you, I don't need alcohol." He looked a little nervous, but the menus came, and they took a few minutes to decide.

"I'll have a very small portion of the pan-seared red snapper with a little risotto and a small salad with balsamic vinaigrette." He wanted to try their sauce and meatballs and also ordered a hot sausage with his spaghetti.

"I thought you'd like it here. I wasn't just trying to stay close to our room." She grinned.

He smiled but said tentatively, "I have to keep control of myself tonight, baby girl. You drove me out of my mind last night."

She moved closer and said softly, "Isn't that the point, honey, you said no boundaries."

"I have to be ready to protect you, Blossom."

She paused as their salads came, then, "Rocco, the door was locked, the security bar was on, you said we're making love together. You deserve to lose yourself too," picking up his hand and kissing his fingertips. "Wherever we go, we go together, right?"

He stared into her eyes and bit his lip. "I love you beyond words, Blossom Dove."

"I love you to the moon and back, Rocco Anthony."

They ate comfortably, chatting about their day. He thought the waiter hovered a little too much and when their table was cleared couldn't help from saying, "There's so many guys around here, baby."

"And there are so many girls in Meadville, Rocco. Let's don't do this."

"When were you here?" He was trying to be casual and failing.

"Rocco," she said with a cautionary tone.

"Well, I just meant, you seemed to know about the restaurant, and you knew about Izzy and Zoe's way across the campus."

She closed her eyes and sighed heavily. "All right. We stayed here when we looked the school over, and my family stays here when they come. Nixie gets restless after too many fancy restaurants, so we found Izzy and Zoe's. Now do you want me to ask you about every place you've eaten and gone, and we can waste our whole evening like that? I've told you where this can lead, Rocco, please don't do this."

"I'm sorry, I'm sorry. It's our last night, and I get scared."

"Oh, honey, don't remind me it's our last night. I love you so much."

"Oh god, I'm messing up every time I open my mouth. Do you want something chocolate?"

She laughed. "I'm not addicted to chocolate, Rocco"—and gave him her glorious smile, erasing all the tension—"but I think I'm addicted to you." She tipped her head, "Did you ever do any drugs, honey?"

"No, I never did, sweetie. Well, I take that back. Once we were passing around a joint, and I had one hit, and someone yelled 'Cops,' so I dropped it, and we all ran. I was dizzy, but I was drunk already so couldn't see the difference. My dad was a functioning drunk, so drinking he could understand. I just knew if I caused him any trouble with drugs or stealing, he'd kill me for sure. I did steal a pack of cigarettes once though."

She was looking sad, trying to smile. "I'm so sorry, honey."

"All in the past, baby girl, all in the past. Now tell me all the bad things you've done." She wrinkled her brow when he started looking around, under the table, lifted his plate. "I'm looking for a tablet. I know this is going to be a long list!"

Her laugh was so sweet and light, his recurring prayer ran through his head, *God, let me hear that the rest of my life.*

"I guess I just sassed my parents. A lot though."

"What were you sassing them about?"

"Anything and everything. Even before my, ah, situation. I don't like to be told what to do." She lowered her eyes and smiled.

"I've noticed"—he grinned—"and I like it, and I'm scared. You ready to go upstairs and discuss it further"—doing his Groucho Marx eyebrow thing—"in the shower?"

They took their shoes off and folded the bedcovers back, chatting about their day. She looked at him once sadly. He knew she was thinking last night and put his finger over his lips. "Let's brush our teeth, and we won't have to get up if we don't want to." After teeth brushing, he found some music on the TV, unbuttoned his shirt, the zipper on his jeans, and let them slide down. He took a step and lifted her sweater over her head. She was taking deep breaths, and he was too; she had no bra on. "Built in?" nuzzled her neck, her perfection unbelievable.

She made a tiny noise when he pushed his boxers down, stepped out of her skirt and panties, and moved to hug him. "We better get in the shower, or we won't make it," picking her up and sitting her on his hip as he adjusted the temperature. "Let me wash you . . . oh god, you're beautiful." She moaned and leaned against the wall as he soaped her back, her hips, and between her legs.

"Rocco"—breathlessly—"let me do you."

"I don't think I can make it, baby girl," picking her up on his knee to get a position.

She was laughing and panting. "You're too tall, we don't fit in here. Take me to bed."

He grabbed two towels on the way, running, almost tripping, laughing, holding her on his hip, trying to cover the sheet with the towels. He lay her down and grabbed the blankets they had so neatly folded. "Are you cold, are you cold? Do you want to dry off?"

"No. No, you're slippery, I love it. Come in, come in, hurry."

He covered them completely with the blanket, entered her, and groaned as she caught him just right and squeezed. "Bloss . . . ah, Blo . . . it hurts" and growled in his throat as he grabbed her hips and their orgasms shook them. She grabbed Tiger, screamed into him, initiating his new place in their life, her final throe lifting Rocco in the air. The last thing he thought of was the freight train, but he was too far gone to help.

He was gasping for air. "Freight train, freight train?"

"No," she panted, "no. Big, big fireworks," her head drooping, her eyes too heavy to open. "I don't want to sleep yet. Our last night. I don't want to sleep," her voice fading.

"It's okay," still breathing hard. "Sleep awhile, I'll wake you." She rolled on her side, tucked her hands under her chin, and was gone. He rested awhile longer, lifted her to get the towels, dried her hair the best he could, found the extra blanket in a drawer, and tucked it around her.

He picked things up, got in the shower again, then sat, and looked at her. Tears ran down his face—of love, gratitude, disbelief at where his life was. He didn't have the heart to wake her so slid into bed. He had spent at least seventeen years sleeping facing the door, on guard. In just three nights together, he was facing her back, mirroring her curve, not touching her, just protecting her.

She turned and saw him sitting in a chair, his head in his hands. It was two thirty. "You were supposed to wake me in an hour," lifting the blanket for him to slid in.

"I didn't want to wake you. I'm afraid the freight train will come if I wake you in the night."

"We'll deal with it if it comes. What else is bothering you?"

"I don't want to go today. There's no sense pretending I'm strong. I'm not."

She kissed his ear. "You'll be strong by morning. You'll have to be, you know I can't be." She snuggled closer and whispered in his ear, "We've only made love five times. We're really good at it, don't you think?"

"I think we really are, baby girl."

"I like to be good at things. You're a good teacher."

He laughed out loud. "I'm so far out of my depth, it's not even funny. Somewhere along the line, the student became the teacher."

"I love you so much, Rocco. At dinner I wanted to tell you something, but I couldn't get it out."

He turned on his side. "What?"

She held his hand under her chin and looked deep into his eyes. "Rocco, I never knew love like this existed. I had a vague idea where babies came from, but you showed me how to give you my love, and I have no words to tell you how much I love you. I don't know what I did to deserve you, but I'll thank God every day the rest of my life."

She kissed the tears overflowing as he said, "I can't speak, baby girl, I can't speak."

They kissed and caressed slowly as long as they could, joined and moved tenderly as long as they could, and then he held her as she screamed into Tiger and molded herself against him before he let go.

She fell directly to sleep, and as he would always do, he straightened the bedclothes, shielded her, and thanked God for this indescribable gift.

He was in his boxers, shaved, showered, and looking at the paper that had been outside the door when she rolled over at 9:00 a.m. "What are you doing way over there. That's the second time you've been over there when I woke up."

He came over and knelt beside the bed. "I knew what would happen if I were right there, and I need to make sure you're okay. Are you sore? Be honest."

"I'm a little sore, but I don't care," pulling at his shoulders.

"Baby girl, maybe we should get up and have a nice slow breakfast and take your things to your room. We could take a walk."

She was shaking her head no all the while he was talking, put her hand behind his neck and her mouth against his. "Rocco, it's such a long time until spring break. Please get in. We'll just cuddle and talk. Check-out isn't until noon, I checked."

"Aw jeez, woman." He laughed as he nudged his boxers off and climbed in. She started caressing his stomach, and he said, "We're talking, remember?"

She giggled. "Did you figure out how we can make love in the shower? I think we need one with a seat, or a bathtub, don't you?"

"That would help. There's something else we can do, but we'll try it another time. I don't want to scare you."

"What, what? Let's try."

"Another time, baby." He started nibbling on her neck. "You'd be saying no, no, no, just like you'll be saying in a minute when I start kissing you all over," laughing softly.

"No, no, Rocco," trying to hold his head as he moved to her breasts.

"Yes, yes, Blossom, I don't want to come in. You're sore. Put your hands in my hair. Put me where you want me."

"No, no. What about you. I want you to feel good," breathless.

"Making you feel good makes me feel good. Open up for me. I want to eat you up. I want you, I want you."

"I can't, I can't," moving helplessly, arching. "Rocco, ohh ohhh, no."

"Get Tiger. Let it come, I love you, I love you," his tongue probing, his lips pulling.

"Roc . . . ," her scream muffled by Tiger, her nails digging into his shoulders, her wetness released.

He reached for his shorts and let go onto them, licking and kissing her gently as he made his way back up her body. She was gasping and panting and moaned in her throat when he kissed her and probed her mouth with his tongue. He growled in his throat when she sucked it aggressively. He fell back exhausted. He got some air. "Tell me about it," he panted. "The same? Different?"

She lifted her little hands, squeezing them.

"Words, words."

She tried to talk. "It was a clutching, grabbing feeling, with a thrilling edge, I think. I don't know."

"Did you like it?"

"Yes, yes," breathing hard. "But we can only do it when you can come in. I feel selfish."

"Oh, no, baby girl, you made me feel sooo good." He pulled the blanket around them, hugging her tight. "God, you're unbelievable. We'll just rest awhile."

She let her head fall onto his chest, loving the beat of his heart, a smile on her lips. Not a word about her brain, *thank you, God*.

She was brushing her hair, dressed in a pink turtleneck, jean skirt, and pink petticoat when he took the brush and finished for her. "Your hair never gets messed up."

"It's too heavy. It just stays in place."

He leaned down and kissed her neck. "I'm going to mess it up next trip. Get ready," winking at her in the mirror.

They packed her suitcase. "I'm sorry my clothes are so big. I don't care for jeans and T-shirts."

"I love your clothes, and I can't even think of you in a T-shirt around here."

"Rocco . . ."

He lifted his hands in surrender. "Just making conversation."

"Will you be embarrassed to take my suitcase into the restaurant?"

"Heck no. Everyone is coming and going around here, especially on Sundays."

They went downstairs to the Ivy Grille, and he ordered a full breakfast. When she ordered hot chocolate and a bran muffin, he said "Baby girl, eat more" in front of the waitress.

She blushed, kept her eyes on her hands. "I'm fine, I'll have a bite of yours." After the waitress left, she said, "I have to get back on my schedule," her eyes swimming with tears.

"Okay, okay, don't think about it yet, we still have some time." He glanced around the room. "Looks like mostly families in here. A few guys, though. I'll give them the evil eye."

She laughed. "What are you talking about?"

"They know what I mean. I'm saying don't even think about it, she's mine."

"Rocco"—accusingly—"we love each other, we don't own each other."

"Hey"—feigning innocence—"I'm a modern man, I watch movies. I know I don't own you. I just want them to know"—calmly and matter-of-factly, but with narrowed eyes and clenched jaw—"you're mine."

She shook her head but smiled. "What am I going to do with you?"

"I could think of a few things," winking.

"Oh, stop."

They finished, and with big sighs and holding hands, he pulled the suitcase to her dorm, his gym bag over his shoulder. Megan wasn't there, so she put her things away while he watched TV. She got on his lap, and he said, "Why don't you take a nap before your mother calls?"

"No, I want to walk you to your truck."

"Blossom, baby, you have to stay here."

"No, no."

"Sweetheart, I can't look in the rearview mirror and see you standing there. Please, Blossom, do this for me, please."

She closed her eyes, tears coming from under her lashes, but nodded yes.

"Now, are you going to tell your mother I was here two nights?"

"I want to tell her about the dancing place and the Franklin Museum and Rocky. It would be too much for one night, so I'll just tell the truth on that part. I'll leave out dinner at Penne because that would be a funny place to eat unless we were there. I'll just let her assume we were here with Megan. She seemed to accept it last time," big sigh.

"Do you want me to just tell her, baby? I will if it would be easier for you."

"No, not yet, honey, not yet."

"Lay down then. I'll stay awhile and rub your back and you try to sleep. I know you're tired." He sat beside the bed and rubbed her back but could tell from her shuddering breaths she couldn't sleep.

She rolled over. "I can't, Rocco, I can't stay here."

"Shh," picking her up and putting her on his lap. "You said you could finish in three years, right? We've almost got a half year under our belt. We can do this, baby girl."

She put her forehead against his chest, shaking her head no, but he could tell she was tired and resigned.

"Do you want me to sing you to sleep?"

"No. Tell me about our weekend but leave out," whispering, "the private parts."

He smiled. "I was forty-five minutes away, driving faster than I should, when my little girl called all upset. Then I started driving like a madman." She giggled and snuggled closer. "And she threw herself at me, all arms and legs and ruffles."

"Sooo," he whispered, "we had some private time, and then we went dancing. She was gorgeous and beautiful and breathtaking, so we tried to have some private time in the shower, and then we moved to the bed and had some for sure private time," he said pointedly as she giggled. On he went, and somewhere between Rocky and finding Tiger, she fell asleep.

He laid her on her bed, covered her with her quilt, put her phone on her pillow, and forced himself to leave.

Flowers arrived for Dr. Kreinson Monday afternoon. The card said, "Thank You for advice on staying two nights. All good. Rocco C."

Their Friday night call finally came. "Hi, baby girl" set off anguished sobs. He let her go for a while and then said, "How did it go with your mother?" They settled into their previsit routine discussing their days, touching on their fun, but avoiding their private times—teasing, crying, laughing.

The third Friday in, he was about to say he couldn't take it any longer he was coming down when she said, "Honey, I have to go to Baltimore next Friday and Saturday with Dr. Ng and Chet, so I'll call you when I get back to my hotel room on Friday night."

"Who? What are you talking about? You're staying overnight? Can I get there?"

"Honey, it's just as far as here. I'll be in meetings all day, then I'll be back here late Saturday afternoon."

"Blossom?" he said it urgently, hoarsely.

"Rocco, it's nothing, honey. We just have to see one of Dr. Ng's customers in person."

"But, but, who's Chet?"

"You saw him once, he's my lab partner. The Vietnamese fellow, small, looks about twelve, remember?"

"No, I don't remember. You're traveling overnight with two guys? Blossom?"

"Honey, it's going to happen now and then. And they're not two guys, they're Dr. Ng and Chet. They've both heard a lot about you, they both know I love you, they both know you're more important to me than this work. Are you okay now?"

He tried to keep his voice calm, couldn't picture the distance to Baltimore in his head. "It just threw me for a minute, baby. Why do you have to go there?"

"Well, we do video conference calls, and now that Chet and I are featured the most prominently, I guess we look pretty young. Dr. Ng says they act like there's a man behind the curtain. Remember, from the *Wizard of Oz*? So he thinks it's good for the customer to talk to us in person to be sure we actually know what we're doing. It will be fine, honey. We'll talk to a few people Friday, then a bigger group Saturday, then come back. I'll call you at eight, but if it's a little later, you'll know why. Okay?"

He was still breathing hard but said okay; and they went on, a little strained at first, but soon their comfortable talk—she, snuggled into her pillow; he, stretched out on his bed, still dressed, boots off, ankles crossed. Eleven o'clock came. She was yawning every few minutes, so he said, "You go to sleep, baby mine, have a good week. I'll wait for your call."

It took all his strength not to ask what she would be wearing in Baltimore—to ask her, please don't wear a sweater; to ask her, please don't look so beautiful. He hung up almost proud of himself but sick to his stomach. He never knew she cried herself to sleep. Three more weeks until spring break.

He was tense when she called him at eight the next Friday. It had been a rough week. He had wanted to call so many times, but he had set the rule and felt he had to ride it out. He had been naive to think they would make love and things would be so much better, easier. The separation was unbearable. He was out of his mind from wanting her. Bob was watching him like he did when he was a kid, waiting for him to lose it. He was hoping for a job where he could tear down walls—take a sledgehammer to something.

"Hi, honey, I brought a sandwich to my room, I've been waiting to call all day," her sweet voice falling over him like a blanket. He sighed and smiled for the first time since she told him she was going.

"Hey, baby girl, how's your meeting going?"

"It's so wonderful to hear your voice, Rocco, everything's okay here. I had to hold my tongue a couple times, but we handled everything they threw at us. How are you, honey, your voice is a little funny."

"I ache to hold you, Blossom. I'm serious, my arms and chest are aching."

"Oh you. Didn't you tell me you would be taking out a cement slab. That's what it is, silly boy."

"I know that's what it is, but it's really you. Blossom, has your mother talked about spring break. We need to tell her I'll come and get you. Tell her Sunday, okay?"

"Rocco, I have to time it just right, or she'll think up some trip or something."

"Let's be proactive this time. Just tell her Sunday that I'll get you. Like just say it."

"But that gives her two weeks to do something. I think if I wait, it will be better. I have a feeling she'll ask that lady again. That would be good because I have her number, and I'll just say I have a ride."

"God, Blossom, six weeks is too long. We can't do this again."

"I can't even talk about it, Rocco. Let's think about going dancing when I get there."

So on they talked—about her week, his week . . .

"Guess what I did this week, Tuesday it was," he said.

"What, honey."

"I took the deadbolt lock off my bedroom door."

"What's that?"

"It's a super-duper lock no one should be able to get through. I put it on when I was fourteen after I threatened my father."

"Oh, my darling, I'm so sorry. You were afraid and so young. Oh, I'm so sorry. What were you thinking when you took it off?"

"I was just trying to do a nice job. Then I put on a new doorknob with the regular push-button lock. We have to be able to lock it if we're there when we have kids."

"That's all you were thinking? It seems like a big step, honey."

"Blossom, there are things I block out. It's okay, baby, it's over. Besides, I thought it might look a little funny if your parents look around the house. I really want them to come to dinner, baby. Be sure they know."

"I'll remind them the first night I'm home, honey. I'll say it in front of my dad. I know he'd like to come."

"You better go to bed, baby girl. Did you eat all your sandwich? What did you drink?"

"I ate half"—she yawned—"and chocolate milk."

"Go brush your teeth then. I love you beyond reason, Blossom Dove."

"I love you to the moon and back, Rocco Anthony."

They got through another week, their Friday call anxious, tearful. He was sharp when she said she hadn't told her mother yet. "Blossom"—angrily—"they better not take you away."

"Rocco, I don't want to give her time to make plans. I'll take care of it, I will. Don't yell at me, please. You don't know my life, honey," softly, sadly.

"I don't know your life because you won't tell me. I can't help you if you won't let me, Blossom."

"I miss you too much. I can't make sense right now. I won't let them take me anyplace. I'll just say I can't go. I know, I'll say I have to work on your computers. Can I say that?"

"Sure you can. Things are rough at work right now. Maybe it would be a good time to do it, a diversion. If you need to, you can just pretend."

"What's wrong at work, honey?"

"Same old, same old. It's not important. I'm just going to plan on coming to get you, baby. I need to, you have to tell her. I'll go into the shop Friday early and get there at four or five."

"Oh, honey, if things aren't going well, should you wait until Saturday?"

"No way. I have to see you. The hell with the business."

"Oh don't swear, honey. Can I do anything?"

"I'll handle it, honey. It's not important."

"Will you be coming to your dorm soon, baby girl?" It was only noon. He had called Helen at home at six to tell her to handle payroll and then called Bob to handle the day.

"Did you start yet, Rocco?"

"I'm standing in front of your dorm, sweetie."

She cried out as if struck. "Is that a joke, honey?"

"No, I'm here, baby, where are you?"

Whimpering, "I'm right around the corner on Smith Walk. Oh god, I'm coming, I'm coming."

"Close your phone, I see you." She was running, her fist to her mouth, jean skirt and boots, yellow petticoat, yellow jacket. He made it to the nearest bench; then his knees gave out. He stood to catch her as she jumped into his arms, fell back on the bench, kissing her face, her hair, her neck, "My baby, my baby, oh god, oh thank you, God."

She could only sob breathlessly, "Rocco, Rocco, r-r-room, room, go to our room."

"Sh, sh, I'm here, I'm here," breathing her in, squeezing her tight. "Let's put your things in the truck, then we'll go to our room. Big breaths, I love you, I love you."

He rubbed her back. Gradually she calmed. "Is everyone looking? Am I embarrassing you?"

"Yeah, they're all thinking I'm the luckiest guy in the world, and they're right," kissing her some more. Just then two fellows walked by. "Get a room, why don't you?" Her eyes got big, and she blushed bright red. Rocco looked up. "Good idea, we'll do that," picking her up and heading to her dorm.

They went through the procedure to get him into the dorm and got her things—a medium bag since she had clothes at home, her cosmetic bag with fresh underthings. She wrote Megan a note on their dry erase board reminding her not to leave any food around, picked up Tiger, and left. They put her bag into the truck. He put her small one in his gym bag, her computer under the seat, and they walked to the hotel.

Reservations remembered him, had 422 ready as he had requested, and she held his hand so tight going up in the elevator; it actually hurt. They kicked off their boots and turned the bed down. She kept her eyes averted, was having trouble breathing. He said softly, "Would you like lunch, a shower, watch TV?" All the while she was shaking her head no. "That's a pretty top, I haven't seen it before." Up close it was a yellow quilted jacket with tiny blue flowers and a matching long-sleeved jersey tee. "Aunt Mim sent it for spring," her chest heaving.

"You get comfortable, I'm going in the bathroom."

She was in bed with the sheet up to her chin, holding Tiger when he came out in his boxers. She closed her eyes as he pulled them off and slipped in. She dug into his arm and tensed. He just said, "Hi," and stroked her back, kissing her forehead.

"I can't believe you're here. I want to just cuddle for a while, I do, but I'm tingling all over. I feel like I've been underwater trying to breathe. I want you so much, I'm ashamed," moving against him.

"Let's go slow now, it's been a while. We've got to watch for the freight train."

"I can't go slow, I can't. Kiss me, Rocco, please."

She whimpered as he explored her mouth, moving to her chin, her neck, her breasts, moaning and whimpering himself. She clutched Tiger with one hand, her fingers wrapped in his hair with the other, and he cried out as she pushed him down. He devoured her as she screamed into Tiger, entered her as she dug into his back, both of them crying for the weeks they'd been apart, finding solace for the pain and anger they'd been through. She was asleep before he could breathe again. He moved Tiger away from her face, arranged the sheet and blanket over them, and slept the first deep and dreamless sleep he'd had in six weeks.

It was seven forty-five at night when they woke. "We slept for six hours, baby girl, I can't believe it. I never sleep in the daytime."

She turned and snuggled tight against him. "You looked so tired, honey, and you've lost weight," rubbing his stomach. "Aren't you eating?"

"Slipped into the drive-thru habit again. At least I can sit downstairs in front of the TV. But you're not there, and it seems endless, Blossom," burying his face in her hair. "God you smell so good, all warm and soft and smelling like love. Do you want to go dancing?"

"Could we just get room service and stay here, honey? We could cuddle and watch TV."

He reached for the menu on the nightstand and pushed his pillow against the headboard. "Can I get whatever I want?"

"Now be sensible, honey, nothing too greasy this time of night."

"How about philly beef and swiss with french fries and gravy?"

She laughed out loud. "Get whatever you want, crazy man." She looked at the menu and picked oatmeal with a chocolate chip muffin.

"We might as well have drinks from the mini bar. It'll cost a fortune either way."

"Oh, honey, you're spending way too much money."

"Sweetie, if someone said you can see Blossom this weekend but your drink will cost fifty dollars, do you think I would hesitate a tenth of a second?"

They wrapped up in the hotel robes, cuddling and whispering, and she changed to his shirt to eat, her arms lost in the robe. "You should have brought your smurfies," he said.

"You remember my smurfies?"

"Sure I do. I was trying to be on my best behavior, and they were pretty thin. I was nervous," doing his Groucho Marx eyebrows. "My first trip out of town, our first night together. You're such a miracle, Blossom," closing his eyes and holding her close.

She pushed off his lap reluctantly. "I have to wash my hair, honey, my mother will notice if I don't."

"What do you mean? Your hair always looks beautiful."

"Remember I told you she said our job is to be neat and clean. She doesn't think being tired or busy is an excuse to let things go. She'll say something if I let it go two days, and she'll somehow manage to blame you."

He shook his head. "You go first, then, or do you want to wash it in the morning so it will be really clean?"

"Don't tease, honey. I know how to go along to get along."

"Blossom, you shouldn't have to be on pins and needles all the time. Let's just tell them."

"Honey, please, she and I are coming to a crosspoint soon. I haven't wanted anything for a long time. I've had the upper hand with this college thing. I can walk away anytime, and I still can use that, but now she's coming to the realization of how much I love you, and she's trying to figure out how she can use it. I don't know how, I don't know why, but I feel it coming."

She'd never revealed this much before. He talked calmly so she would keep going. "Baby girl, walking a tightrope is a tough way to live. I know. What does she want?"

"I don't think she even knows. She wanted big things from me, and she felt it slipping away when I took a stand. Losing control has made her angry." She sighed heavily. "Let's don't talk about it anymore. I feel disloyal." She closed her eyes and intoned, "My parents are wonderful people, I'm fortun—"

"Blossom, stop!"

She jumped and started to cry.

"Baby, quit trying to brainwash yourself. We're not saying your parents aren't fine people, but something's wrong here."

"Rocco, I don't want to talk about it," her voice rising. "I don't," pounding on his chest.

"We're not talking about it, then," covering her face with kisses. "See, we're not talking about it, all done," smiling. "I'll brush my teeth while you're in the shower."

She dropped the hotel robe below her shoulders as he brushed her hair. He was sure she had no idea how beautiful she looked—dark eyes, dark hair against the white robe. "Your hair is longer than usual."

"I know. I don't seem to be able to do even ordinary things when we're apart so long. Every time I'm heading to my dorm, I think he'll be waiting there. That's why I couldn't believe it today when you said you were there." She suddenly dropped her head on the vanity. "Rocco, Rocco," anguished.

"Baby girl, I'm here, I'm right here," kneeling beside her.

She laid her head against him, "But it seems so temporary. It's always so temporary," tears flowing.

"It's not forever, sweetie. We've got tonight. We have a nice drive tomorrow, and we'll be together as much as we can."

"I'm not allowed at your house. When can we be, you know, together?"

"I'll think of something, Blossom, we'll manage. Now, let's see if we can mess up this nice clean hair," picking her up and carrying her to the bed. "Do you want dark or some music on TV?"

He laid on his back. "Come lay on me. Ummm, heaven," massaging her neck, her back, the rise of her hips. "I love you so much, Blossom, you are an amazing woman."

"Thank you, darling man," knowing he was trying to encourage her. She sucked on his neck and bit his chin until they were breathing heavily.

He whispered against her lips, "Sit up and slide onto me. I'll guide you. Tell me if it hurts."

"Rocco"—achingly—"Rocco." She had her hands on his chest, moving, moving, squeezing, loving his moans, the growl in his throat.

He looked up at her perfection, holding her tiny waist, her breasts unbelievable, her face in beautiful pain, her hair moving with her, falling in her face as she arched her back. It was he who bit Tiger, he who lifted her as she shook silently and dug her nails into his chest, eight tiny half moons above his nipples that he smiled at all week.

She turned to sleep, still panting. He arranged the covers, wiped her and himself with his shorts, and whispered to her, "Your hair was messed up." She smiled as she fell asleep.

Her emotions ran the gamut on the ride home. He smiled inside at each one. She laughed and clapped when he sang, cried when they talked about being together, pounded the dash. "I can't stand this. I need to know what's going to happen."

"Baby girl, I know I'm on dangerous ground here, but wouldn't you know what's going to happen if you had just told your mother not to make any plans for you because we haven't been together for six weeks?"

She narrowed her eyes and her lips and crossed her arms.

"Hey, just putting it out there."

"I told you I have to see her face. I have to gauge which way to go."

"Okay, okay, take a little nap. You didn't get much sleep last night," giving her a look and a wink.

She bit her lip and blushed, laying her head on his shoulder.

He pulled over before turning into Jackson Oaks. It was 5:00 p.m. "Baby girl, do you want to freshen up, we're here."

She gave him a whimpering sigh and a doleful look. "I don't want to be here."

"It will be fine, baby. We probably won't see each other tonight, but we're in the same town. Call me when you go to bed," kissing her softly.

She brushed her hair and put on some lip gloss. "You can just drop me off, honey."

"Blossom, I am not dropping you off. Here we go." He continued into her driveway, got her bag and computer, and they walked to the house, holding hands.

"Blossom," her mother said, managing to look puzzled and annoyed at the same time, "I made arrangements for Dina West to bring you home."

"Yes, Mom, we talked. I told her I had a ride."

Rocco spoke up, "I was in the neighborhood, Mrs. Richards," relieved when her dad walked in.

"Daddy," Blossom said a little too excitedly and hugging him.

"Welcome home, kitten," reaching out to shake Rocco's hand.

Rocco said, "I'll be on my way. Talk to you later, baby." Then he turned, "Oh, we were talking on the way home. Maybe you'd like to come with us dancing in Edinboro tomorrow night." Blossom's mouth had dropped open when he called her baby, and now her eyes were incredulous. He turned slightly and winked at her so they couldn't see. "I'm sure Blossom would like to show you what a great dancer she is."

"Well, Rocco, we'll think about that. Thanks again for driving all that way to get her."

She called at nine. "Am I in the doghouse?" He laughed.

"Are you crazy? They're actually considering it! It will be so uncomfortable."

"Baby, we need some kind of breakthrough. I think we're okay with your dad, but we need to show your mom that we're a couple. Let's go out and act like a couple."

As the hours went by on Sunday, he started to question his quick decision to invite them. Her mom had made up all kinds of reasons why she needed to stay home during the day. Her dad had suggested the four of them have dinner first. Rocco thought it would be too much stress for Blossom so told them a white lie and said he had to make a sales call in Edinboro and would meet them at seven thirty.

He took Delbert's CD in at seven. "Hi, Charlie, Blossom and her parents will be coming in with me. She's a little nervous, so we won't dance until cut 2. Then finish it off and go to the jukebox, but don't forget to skip cut 9."

"No problem, Rocco, it won't be very busy tonight."

When they drove in, he was leaning against the truck—faded jeans, dress boots, western denim shirt with the cuffs rolled up, his Stetson. Blossom had her fist to her mouth, but a little whimper squeaked out. "You okay, kitten?" "Fine, Daddy." Her mother glanced back with a look.

She had on the first outfit she had worn there. It was modest and safe. She had both her mother and Rocco to appease. It tickled her to keep him off kilter, but not when her mother was there.

"I see you play the part, Rocco," her dad said, smiling at his hat and extending his hand. "I hope you had a successful sales call."

"Yes, sir, I did. Getting jobs hasn't been a problem so far. You probably find as well that the help is more of a worry."

As they found a table, Rocco making sure his back was against the wall with a view of the room, her dad continued, "Elaine handles that end, so I'm shielded from those issues."

Blossom nervously chatted, "I want to get Rocco a Resistol for his birthday when we go to the clinic."

"Oh," her mother said, "when is his birthday?"

"June sixth," as her mother nodded.

The waitress arrived and greeted Rocco and Blossom by name, and her mother's eyebrows raised a little. Her dad ordered a Bud Light, and as Rocco said "the same for me," her mother said smoothly, "Would you give us another minute?" As soon as she left, "Rocco, I'm really not comfortable having you drink alcohol when we know you won't be twenty-one until June."

Rocco's face never changed, just motioned the waitress over, and said, "Blossom and I will have ginger ales, and you, Mrs. Richards?"

"I'll have a sloe gin and ginger and some pretzels if you have them," very friendly.

Blossom and Rocco had held hands lightly coming in, but under the table, she was gripping his leg, digging in with her nails.

As the first fast-paced cut was ending, Rocco stood. "Would you folks like to join us?" They said they'd watch for a while, and as he led Blossom to the floor, she whispered, "I feel so self-conscious."

"You'll be fine, baby, we'll start slow. Look at me, not them. You know this music."

She looked into his eyes with a shy smile. He waited a couple beats and started. She was immediately fine, taking a big breath but nodding and smiling as she let it out. He tried not to get too close or suggestive but whispered "I love you" when she was near. Her beautiful smile and sparkling eyes urged him on. "What color unmentionables are you wearing?" She blushed and giggled, and when he started on what he would like to do to her when they could get some private time, she said, "Stop, stop, everyone will know."

He made sure they were at the far end of the floor when the song ended so they could go into the next one before going back to the table. They were comfortable now, oblivious to the surroundings, the music slower, his hand splayed on her lower back, moving her with him.

"Honey, honey, don't hold me there," breathlessly. "That's where you hold me when we make love."

He winked slowly and lifted his hand to her upper back and stepped away a little. As they neared their table, he twirled her with one hand toward her parents then slid her between his legs, back out and up in the air, as she put her legs around his waist, laughing.

Her parents' eyes were wide with surprise. He put his arm under her hips straightening her skirt as he sat her in her chair, gently kissing the top of her head. He didn't realize it appeared more possessive and loving than anything he might have done.

Her dad said, "Why, kitten, I'm dumbfounded. We had no idea."

"Isn't it amazing, Daddy, and I don't even know how to dance!"

"Oh she knows how to dance." Rocco smiled.

"I guess she does," her mother said flatly, looking at Rocco a second too long.

"Have you been taking lessons, kitten?"

"No, I just go where Rocco aims me." She smiled happily.

"And how about you, Rocco, lessons?"

"Well, I just happened to be here a few years ago when line dance lessons were in, and then a regular customer showed me how you can take those basic steps and adapt them to most any music."

"I'm just very impressed. Aren't you, Elaine?"

She smiled tightly and asked, "Is the regular customer here tonight?"

Blossom laughed. "You'd know if she were here, Mom. She's the most unique character I've ever met. I don't like to define someone by their size, but she's huge in both height and width . . . is that being rude, honey," looking at Rocco.

His face never showed he was surprised at her use of "honey," just said, "I think Big Sallie would be the first to say that," smiling.

"She's really nice," Blossom said. And on they chatted, almost companionably, getting second drinks, Blossom and Rocco dancing a couple more numbers, firming up their dinner plans at Rocco's on Friday night.

Her dad said about nine thirty, "Well, we'll run along now," and before her mother could interject, "You staying, Blossom?"

Rocco quickly added, "We'll stay a little longer. I'm really glad you could see Blossom dance."

"Well, it's been a revelation," her mother said. "Don't be too late, Blossom, I'm having some computer problems at the office I'd like you to check out this week."

"Sure, Mom. I'd like to look at Rocco's too," a little warily, trying to read her mother's expression.

After they were out the door, they both let out big sighs, and Blossom laid her face on the table. "I'm exhausted."

"But every now and then, it was okay, don't you think?"

She smiled. "Little minutes here and there. I guess I should be grateful."

He nuzzled her ear. "We have a couple hours, do you want to go to my house and fit in some loving?"

"Oh, honey, then I'd fall asleep, and it would be three or four hours. Besides, I'm not supposed to be at your house."

"Baby girl, where's it going to be—my house, the Holiday Inn . . . or the truck?"

She narrowed her eyes. "Don't you dare say the truck, that's not funny. What if someone we know sees us or your truck at the Holiday Inn? Oh, dear," making a worried face. "I never thought I'd say I wish we were at Penn. I miss room 422."

"I'll take care of it, baby girl. We'll come up here or go to Erie. Let's dance some more and settle for hugs and kisses tonight, no matter how gorgeous you look."

Almost to her house, he said, "How about tomorrow you work at their office and then we go to Erie to find me a sports coat? I don't think I'd fit that one I wore to my father's funeral, so it's a legitimate trip. I've never been to Erie, do you know any stores?"

She kissed his cheek and squeezed his arm. "I love you so much, Rocco. You came all the way to Penn by yourself, and you'd never even been to Erie. You're so wonderful. Daddy and Nixie go to Isaac Baker's in the mall. We can try there first."

"First and last, baby girl. Let's take the first one we see and go find a room."

He walked her to the door, kissed her until they were weak, and said, "Tomorrow night, my baby."

He heard her crying as he opened his phone at ten in the morning, chills running down his spine.

"Rocco," she wailed, "we're going to look at Virginia Tech for Nixie. We won't be back until Friday. I can't stand it, I can't."

"Goddamn it, Blossom, just say you won't go," getting up to close his door, shutting out Helen's startled look.

"Oh, now you're swearing at me," she sobbed. "I can't do this anymore."

A wave of compassion and love flooded him. "I'm sorry, baby girl. Forget I said that. I'm sorry, it's all my fault. Taking them dancing was a bad idea. I was showing off, and now it's hurt you."

"Wha—what do you mean?"

"She was watching us every second, Blossom. A few of those moves were pretty suggestive, and I knew it. She's showing me she's in control. I'm sorry, baby. We'll deal with it. Call me tonight when you can. We'll have Friday, and I'll take you back. It can't last much longer."

"Rocco, Rocco."

"Sh-sh, we'll deal with it, baby girl. Don't show them how upset you are. I love you."

He was at his desk, miserable, when she called Friday. "I'm home," breathlessly. "Can I get into your house to help you with dinner?"

He told her how to put her car in the garage and that he should be there by two-thirty. Her parents said they would come from the office between five thirty and six, the dinner was simple, so they'd have a couple hours.

He'd often said he wanted to see her in his bed, so she went right to the stairs and found his room. She undid the bed, folded her clothes neatly and climbed in to surprise him. Her heart pounded against her chest, up into her throat, when she heard him come in and run up the stairs. He came in, barely glanced at her, and said, "I'll be right with you, baby," glancing at his watch. She was stunned, stared at the bathroom door, fear crawling along her skin. Everything was fine; of course it was; he just wanted to shower. It was hard to breathe.

He came out, breathtakingly beautiful, set his watch on the nightstand, looked at it, and reached for her.

A growing anger replaced the fear. She gave a tiny push against his chest, "I'm not something you cross off your list, Rocco."

He blinked, startled. "No, no, Blossom, I'm sorry. It's been a rough day. I'm right here, baby."

"I don't think you are," covering her breasts with the sheet, lying on her side to face him. "Tell me about your rough day."

"Blossom, that's not important," rubbing his forehead, his eyes narrowing.

"Do you have a headache? Are you okay?"

"Blossom"—sternly—"work problems aren't important. My headache will go away. Let's don't waste time."

"Don't waste time? You mean make love to Blossom, cook the salmon, like that?"

"You know I didn't mean that," exasperated.

She sat up and slid to the other side of the bed. "Let's go downstairs and start over."

"Blossom?"

"It's fine, Rocco," putting her panties on, reaching for her sweater, "maybe I was presumptuous getting into your bed. We'll get together later. I haven't seen the work you've done on the house, let's go downstairs."

"Blossom, please. Please don't go downstairs," but she pulled on her jean tights and left.

"Oh god, oh god"—stumbling to put on clean clothes—"Blossom, don't leave, don't leave."

"I'm not leaving, Rocco, everything's fine. We'll just get dinner organized so you don't have to worry about it." He ran down buttoning his shirt. "Maybe you should have some shoes on. Bare feet look a little personal," she said formally.

"Don't go, Blossom," panic setting in.

"Rocco, I'm not going anyplace. We'll just take a walk around and look at what you've done to the house," her voice strained.

Hoarsely, "I'm going to put a powder room here under the stairs." She smiled and held his hand tightly, both frightened. They walked upstairs silently, and he showed her the door he had put into the wall between Lindsay's room and his parent's bathroom. Stiffly she said it was a good idea and looked very nice. He showed her where he had taken the deadbolt off his door. He looked at her, worried, and then at the bed. She shook her head no. "You go down and start. I'll make the bed in case someone has to go to the bathroom."

His glibness was gone, his suggestive patter lost; it was hard to breathe; his head was pounding.

She came into the kitchen, feigning casualness. "I can be your sous chef. What would you like me to do?"

"You can set the table," he said nervously. "I put everything out to be sure there were enough matching things."

Wordlessly, she set the table for five, coming back in. "Did you have any particular seating in mind? I put my mother across from me. I'd like to see her expressions. That would put Nixie at the end, or I can sit with Nixie and you on the end if you would be uncomfortable facing them."

Not believing they were so tense, he said, "I want to sit by you. We'll use the other end for service, it will be fine." He looked at her in agony.

"Your head aches. Do you have Excedrin?"

"It's not my head, Blossom."

"That's part of it, Rocco. It's only four, and it might get worse. I'll run to Rite-Aid, it's the closest."

"No, don't go, don't go. Please."

She put her arms around his waist, her head against his chest. "We're okay," she said softly. "Are things all set so you can come with me? You need something, honey."

"I can come," he said with relief. They drove to Rite-Aid, and she came out with Excedrin Migraine and a bottle of water.

"This is basically just triple strength, but it's okay if you don't use it too often. You didn't tell me you've been getting headaches, honey."

"Not too often," he said as he downed three capsules. Back in the kitchen, he hugged her and said, "You've been gone all week, and we haven't even kissed hello."

He got a chill as she stepped back and said, "We'll kiss after they're gone, so we can talk. Let's see if we're all ready."

"Please, Blossom, I can do this in my sleep. Can't we sit for a while. I bought this double chair for us." She looked at the brown leather sofa and chair, but it just reminded her that she had gone directly to his room and the changes he had made hadn't registered. She bit her lip and blinked, and he talked faster, "I put the chair my mother always used in their bedroom. Maybe you can help me pick out some tables and lamps, maybe a rug?"

She smiled tentatively. "Are the pills working yet?"

"I think so. I'll put the fries in the oven." She watched him season the sweet potato fries, put miniature spinach soufflés in a cupcake tin, and put the salmon on the broiler pan. "Why don't you put ice in the glasses and put them in the fridge. Put the butter dish on the table so it can get soft and these little croissants on the end. Cover them with a napkin. I got two pies—both pumpkin and pecan match the flavor of the dinner." He put his head in his hand for a second and looked at her. "I'm sorry, baby girl."

"We're okay, Rocco, what else?"

"Put the Cool Whip in a pretty bowl of some kind, look in that cupboard. Get five more matching plates out and five more forks, the smaller ones are okay. Do you think that's it?"

"It's wonderful, Rocco," touching his cheek. "It will be lovely, thank you. I'm sorry this came at the end of a hard week."

He started to say it hadn't been a hard week until they took her away, and the doorbell rang.

"Good evening, Dr. and Mrs. Richards, Nix, come in. I was about to show Blossom a couple projects I did since she was here after my father's funeral."

Before anyone could respond, her mother said, "Blossom, what on earth are you wearing?"

"Oh, Rocco wondered if I had any jeans. I don't, so I wore these denim tights. I wear these in New Mexico, remember?" Rocco cringed inside at her nervousness. "My sweater is long," pulling at the roomy blue cashmere top.

"That is hardly appr . . ." Rocco jumped in, "I'm planning to put a powder room here under the stairs so guests won't have to go upstairs." He led them up to see the new door in the wall.

"You do fine work, Rocco."

"Thank you, Dr. Richards."

"Call me Cal, call me Cal. Something is smelling really good down there."

"It's salmon tonight with a touch of maple and spinach soufflés. I made Nix sweet potato fries. Watch the dip, Nix, it has a kick to it. What would everyone like to drink?"

Dinner went surprisingly well. Her mother watched them closely, sensing something was off but putting it up to nerves. Rocco didn't realize that fixing Blossom's plate for her with half a piece of salmon, half a soufflé, and three of the fries spoke volumes. It was too domestic, and she made a decision.

"How is the business going, Rocco?" Her dad filled in a quiet spot.

"Well, like I said Sunday, plenty of work. I might need some financial advice. Maybe you could suggest someone."

"What type of thing you need?"

"Well, my dad was old-school, and he kept thousands in the checking account to pay suppliers. I put most of it in savings until I get some advice. Then I found some more in a savings account, and the current profits are accumulating too. I admire what you folks do, and I'd like to invest wisely so Blos—er, so I can do something along those lines." He could see his slip including Blossom in his future hadn't escaped her mother by the set of her jaw.

Her dad took a card from his wallet. "Check with this fellow. He's always done well by us. Just listen at first, don't commit. Always go with someone you feel a connection with. They work for you, don't forget, it's your money. I admire you for thinking ahead at twenty. You should be in fine shape for whatever you want to do."

He was starting to feel more comfortable, the headache almost gone; so as he was serving the pie, he said, "You've been traveling this week, so I'll be happy to take Blossom back on Sunday."

Her mother spoke up quickly, "Oh, that won't be necessary. We're going tomorrow to show Nixie Penn State."

Blossom's nails dug into his leg. Nix's brow furrowed as he heaved a sigh, and her dad said, "Did I forget something?"

"You remember, dear, we talked about it before Virginia Tech. Well, this has been lovely, the food was delicious, but we should be going."

With ice in his stomach, Rocco spoke quickly, "We're going to that chick flick at nine, Nix, want to go?"

"No way."

"As long as you're going to the movies, kitten, Mom will drive your car home."

"The key is in it," she said from the kitchen fighting tears.

Rocco walked them out the door, and her mother said, "Please have her home right after the movie, we have a long drive tomorrow."

He shut the door and put his head against it. She came from the kitchen biting her lip, tears streaming down her face. They stood with his chin on her head, swaying. "I'll come down next week, baby girl. We'll figure something out. Let's get everything into the dishwasher. Do you know anything about that movie in case she asks you about it? I don't know what I would have done if Nix said he wanted to go." She was crying too much for small talk.

By the time everything was cleaned up, she was calmer, and he felt brave enough to say hopefully, "Can we sit and cuddle on the chair?" She smiled and nodded, so he forged ahead. "I like your jeans things, what are they again?"

"They're actually tights. I like tight things in New Mexico, there are a lot of creepy-crawlies, and I don't want to give them anyplace to crawl in."

"What should I wear there?"

"We'll bring your work boots, and be sure your jeans are tucked in. That's what Nixie does."

He stroked her leg. "Where will I sleep?"

"Remember I told you it's pretty basic, so don't expect too much. Nixie and I sleep in a room with a bed and a cot, so I imagine we'll get another cot." She touched his cheek, smiling sweetly. "You're a guest, so you can have the bed."

"I'd never take your bed," took a breath and said, "Why don't you take the jeans off." She slipped them off un-self-consciously and climbed back on his lap. His heart was thudding, hoping whatever they'd been through was over. "Will we be able to have any private time?" He wiggled his eyebrows, and she giggled and hugged him around the waist.

"Not at the clinic, but I have a plan."

"Could we go upstairs and talk about your plan?"

"Uh-huh, but remember you said after they left you'd tell me about your rough day."

He stiffened almost imperceptibly, his jaw tightening. "No, you said we'd talk about it, I didn't."

If he'd been prepared, he could have held her, but she jumped up and crossed her arms and narrowed her eyes. "You said we could talk about it. I want to hear about your problems."

"Blossom"—coolly—"I'll take care of work, you take care of school. We don't need to mix them now."

"You won't let me in your life," her voice rising. "I want to be in your life. I mean it!"

In an instant, he was out of the chair, vaulted the sofa, and was standing in front of her, his hands on his hips. Her eyes were round looking from the chair to him but didn't back away, just narrowed her eyes and put her hands on her hips.

"Little girls in blue panties with pink roses shouldn't be giving orders."

"I-want-to-be-in-your-life," loudly, emphatically.

Hollering loudly back, "I don't want you in my life. My life stinks. I want you separate from my life!"

She made her hands into fists, put them tight to her sides, and stamped her foot.

"You're stamping your foot at me? A few months ago, you couldn't even look at me, now you're stamping your foot?"

She shook with fury, screamed in frustration, and ran up the stairs. He fell unto his hands and knees, weak with relief that she hadn't run for the door. "Oh god, oh god, why do I do these things? Why take a stand on a stupid thing and hurt the most precious thing in my life? Help me, help me." He pulled himself up, made sure the door was locked, hoped the neighbors hadn't heard the scream and think his father was back, and went upstairs.

His heart broke when he saw her, on her knees on his bed, crying and pounding the pillow. "Okay, okay, we're done with this," picking her up and putting her on his lap. "Sh-sh, we're going to agree to disagree, baby girl, just for a couple months. I don't know what's going on at work," stroking her hair, kissing her forehead. "Give me a couple months, and we'll see where it stands."

He kept talking softly, laid her on the bed, took off his clothes and her panties, and straddled her. He pulled her sweater over her head, holding her hands in one of his, wiping her tears with his other hand. "I don't want to be like your parents and expect you to solve my problems, baby girl."

"I can't solve your problems, but we can share them," she said through her tears.

"In a couple months, okay?"

"Okay," still shuddering, "in a couple months, or . . ."

"Or what, Blossom? Don't you ever say or to me. There's no or with us."

Whimpering, "But we can't solve everything in bed."

He lay down and whispered in her ear, "Oh yes, we can, my baby. Everything out there is garbage—work is garbage, school is garbage, we're the only important thing. I love you, I love you."

"Oh, Rocco, it's been such an awful day. Such a bad, bad day. I thought you were going to tell me to leave," sobbing.

"Never, never. I thought you were going to leave," kissing her, wild with relief when she responded. "We'll fix it, we'll fix it."

He wanted to make love slowly and tenderly to show her how precious she was, but the awful day overtook them. She winced at his roughness but matched him moan for moan, thrust for thrust, biting, scratching, crying. He felt the top of his head explode with the force of his orgasm and pulled a pillow over for her to scream into without Tiger there.

They fell back drenched and gasping. She turned over to sleep, but she knew she had to go home and turned back to him. "I'm sorry, Rocco, I was very bad."

"It was me, baby. You're my breath, my soul. I don't know what came over me to act so stupid."

She whispered into his neck, "I want to matter to you."

"Blossom, baby, you're the only thing that does matter to me."

"You said we have to live in the world until our private time. I want us to work together and talk things through, and . . ."

"Baby girl, I'm only going to say this once, and please try to understand. I love every inch of you, but your brain is intimidating, sweetie. Let me try to sort things out before I come to you. Let's just call it a man thing, a stupid man thing. Give me the couple months, okay?"

She raised up and smiled, taking his breath away. "I better take a shower. If they hear the shower running so late, they will wonder why."

He looked at his watch. "It's ten-fifteen, you have time."

She cocked an eyebrow at him. "That's the third time today you've looked at that watch. Look at it again and I'm flushing it down the toilet."

He pulled her close, and they laughed out loud—because it was funny, with relief, but mostly with thankfulness they had survived the day.

"What kind of soap do you have, honey?"

"I use Dial," but seeing the worried look, he said, "Hey, there's a couple little bars from our Philly room in that top drawer. What are they?"

"Oh, good, it's Dove. It's not just that Dial is strong for my skin. She might notice the scent."

He hugged her and said, "We don't have time to shower together, so I'll wait till I get back. I think we broke our record for perspiration," winking.

It was after eleven, but they went through McDonald's and got a hot chocolate for her mother to see to account for the extra time. He walked her to her door, and they clung, sighing. Their euphoria was wearing off, resigned to the coming separation. "Don't let her get to you, baby. Keep your chin up, and I'll come as soon as I can."

She nodded, her eyes heavy with exhaustion. "Did we settle anything?"

He whispered against her neck, "Yes, we did, we settled that I love you more than life, that I adore you, that I'm getting myself all worked up again."

She giggled sleepily.

"You didn't get a chance to sleep after. Run upstairs and get in bed. Move the curtain so I know you've set the alarm. I'll call you Sunday night before we go back to our Friday schedule. These breaks are killing me, they're never what we hope." He gave her a sensual but soft kiss and patted her behind.

"I love you, Rocco." She disappeared.

He watched for her signal, went to the truck, and wrote on the dash notepad "buy soap." He should have felt better but was unsettled, the remnants of the headache lingering. He had set things up at work to be gone Sunday and most of Monday. Damn her mother. A germ of an idea formed. He shouldn't do it; things weren't good at work. No, he really shouldn't, but he knew he would.

The Saturday trip with her parents was agonizing. They had no appointments and basically just drove around Penn State for no reason. She felt sorry for Nixie and sorrier for herself. Sunday night she cried herself to sleep. Eight o'clock had come and gone, and he hadn't called. Too much had gone on the last week. The ridiculous trips to colleges, the dinner, the fight. She slept fitfully, whimpering every time she tossed and turned. The phone sounded at 9:50 p.m. She was crying as she opened it. "Are you all right, you didn't call, I'm so scared."

"Sh-sh, it's okay, I'm downstairs.

She let out a strangled sound. "Is this a dream?"

"No, it's not a dream, baby mine. Don't bother to get dressed. Put your tomorrow clothes in a bag and come down. Hang up so you can use two hands. Don't forget shoes and Tiger. Hurry."

She pushed the door open—was barefoot and in her smurfies—and leaped into his arms, wrapping her legs around his waist, sobbing into his neck, "Bad day, such a bad day."

"Bad day all gone, all gone." He was pretty sure the guard hadn't believed him when he said he was waiting for someone so nodded and smiled to him as he put her satchel over his shoulder and started for the hotel. "We're all checked in, baby, go to sleep. I had to work awhile and didn't get on the road until three and I didn't want to call when your parents were here."

Big cities are impersonal and only one eyebrow raised as he walked the couple blocks and into the lobby carrying a barefoot girl in her pajamas.

In room 422, he balanced her on his hip and turned down the bed, laying her down and pulling the covers up. She touched his face. "Is this a dream?"

"No dream, baby girl. Go to sleep. I started driving right from work, and I need a long shower. I'll wake you later." She turned with a big sigh and curled her hands under her chin, safe and content at last. He was exhausted from the last couple weeks and the long ride but stood looking at her, smiling before turning for the shower.

She turned as soon as he touched her. He slipped her smurfies off, and they made love silently and tenderly, their tears mixing. He kissed hers away and rolled her into her position, then, deliciously exhausted, fell asleep.

At 3:00 a.m. her heart stopped as he screamed her name, "Blossom, Blossom, I couldn't find you. I died, and I couldn't find you."

She turned instantly to hold him, his body rigid, his face distorted, his eyes frightened. "I'm here, Rocco, I'm here. It was just a bad dream," putting a hand on each cheek, forcing him to look at her. "It's fine, honey, I'm here."

"I need you, I need you now," breathing raggedly.

"Whatever you need. I love you, I'm here."

He entered her roughly. "I can't . . ."

"It's all right. I'm here," both hands on his neck. "Do whatever you need," moving to help him.

He shuddered and collapsed on her. "I'm sorry, I'm sorry."

"It's all right my darling, go to sleep," as she rubbed his back with both hands.

"My dad died," he mumbled into her neck.

"I know, I know, my darling. I should have been there," she whispered.

"He never liked me."

Her heart ached, but her old soul kicked in. "He didn't know how, honey." She stroked and listened, purred in his ear, saying the things he needed to hear, knowing it was a buildup of months of pressure. She rued any worry she had caused him, caressing and whispering and loving him back to sleep.

When he was deep asleep, she wiggled from under him into the crook of his arm. When she woke, he was looking at her with such adoration she had to close her eyes. He said hoarsely, "You're a miracle." She just smiled and kissed his chin and put her finger over his lips. "I'll always be here. You'll never be alone again."

He wanted to talk about it some more, but her phone chimed. It took her a minute to find it in her bag. She looked at him, worried. "It's my mother." She took a breath, "Hi, Mom."

"Good morning, Blossom. You were so distracted and short tempered this weekend, I thought I'd see if you were all right."

"I'm fine now. Rocco's here." She could sense the disbelief over the phone.

"Rocco's there? Did he follow us?"

"He had to work until three yesterday, so he got here after nine," she said lightly. Then grimacing at him and biting her lip, she lied, "Everyone was coming back, so it was hectic. Megan brought a friend, so he stayed in the common room."

Coolly, "Let me talk to Rocco, please."

"Sure. Here, honey, Mom wants to talk to you," handing him the phone and mouthing "I'm sorry."

In an instant, thoughts flashed through his mind. What if she says are you sleeping with my daughter? I'll just be calm and say yes, we talked it over and discussed birth control—oh god, don't let her ask. What should I call her? He said call him Cal; did she say call her Elaine? Oh god, I can't remember.

His worry was solved when she said, "Rocco, it's Elaine. Could you step out into the hall?"

"Sure," he said casually, "it does get noisy in here." He put his finger to his lips for Blossom to be quiet, then opened and closed the door. Blossom sat in the middle of the bed wrapped in the sheet, looking scared.

"Is she all right? We had a difficult weekend."

"Yes, Elaine, she's fine. We had kind of a bad day Friday, so I wanted to come down and clear the air. We kind of needed that ride here to get ready for the next separation."

"Well"—haughtily—"she should have made that clear to us. We would have understood." Casually, "What was your bad day about?"

He rolled his eyes at Blossom to let her know things were going okay. "Well, she wanted to be more involved with my work problems, and I thought she should concentrate on school. That didn't go too well, and let's just say I had my first experience with the stamping of the foot." He tried to let a smile work into his voice to show he was amused and mature.

"My goodness, we haven't seen that since she was about eight." He could feel her lightening up a bit. "She was so erratic Saturday—worried about you, angry at us."

"I'm sorry if I played any part in spoiling your weekend," surprised they seemed to be talking as equals concerned about Blossom.

"Well, I guess she's made her decisions." And then, poignantly, "We can't control her thoughts."

He wasn't sure what she meant but was pretty sure he had received the only capitulation she would ever give him.

"Take care of her, Rocco, she is a very special girl."

"I'm well aware of that, Elaine"—opening his eyes wide and lifting his shoulders at Blossom—"and I always will take care of her." Anxious to close the conversation while it seemed to be going well, "Did you want to talk to her again?"

"No. Tell her I'll call next Sunday as usual. Good-bye, Rocco," a little curtly.

He collapsed onto the bed, letting out a big breath. "She knows."

Pounding on his back, she cried, "No. No. How do you know, how can you tell?"

"She said, 'Take care of her Rocco.' I'm telling you, Blossom, it's like she was giving up. It's good, isn't it?"

She put the sheet over her head, sitting in the middle of the bed like Casper, making him laugh.

"I don't know what to do."

"You do just as you have been, baby. Or if the time seems right, just say we stay at the hotel. That would just about say it all, wouldn't it? Do you want me to talk to them? I will."

"No, no, oh god, no, not yet. Okay, we'll do it together. No, no, oh, I can't think about it."

He picked her up, sheet and all. "Baby girl, nothing has changed. We carry on, but we won't lie. If she says where did Rocco stay, you just say we went to the Hilton. She hasn't asked lately, has she? Today you just offered the information, right? Maybe she's assumed we were together for a while." He pulled the sheet off her head, raised his eyebrows, and shrugged. They both smiled.

"It's eight forty-five. When's your first class?"

"Eight o'clock." She smiled. "But it was Dr. Ng. I'm okay. I have to make my eleven o'clock, though. We can have breakfast. I bet you didn't eat supper."

Laying her back down and kissing her fingertips, moving up her arms, "Would you like to do anything else besides breakfast?"

Breathing hard, "I can't, I wouldn't have time to sleep. I need to sleep."

"But I don't know when I'll be back," moving across her shoulder and biting her neck. "Sleep in class like every other college kid."

She giggled and slid both hands down his stomach, touching him, moving him. She'd never done it before. He cried out, and she whispered, "Are you ready, crazy man, or are you all talk?"

He wanted to laugh but couldn't breathe. She was kneading him, sliding him. "May I kiss you there?"

"No. No."

"But you kiss me. I want to kiss you."

"No, baby, no. It's hard to talk right now," putting his hands under her arms so she couldn't slide down, working himself in. Her whys were lost as they moved together, moaned together, searching for their special place. She reached for Tiger as the room spun. His neck couldn't hold his head. He fell forward onto her breasts, gasping, "My god, Blossom, you're unbelievable."

Her hands were still entwined in his damp curls, and she giggled weakly. "You need a haircut," remembering his old line. "May I kiss you there now?"

Still breathing hard, "No, baby girl, no."

She put her tongue in his ear. "Why, why, I want to."

"Jesus, woman, you're tough," lifting his head with effort and looking in her eyes.

She gave him a sated, angelic smile. "Why?"

"Blossom, I don't want you to do that," putting his finger over her lips as she started to form why. "Street girls do that, baby, I don't want you to do it." She put her hand over his mouth. "I didn't want to say it, sweetie. Let's talk about it another time."

She whispered close to his ear, "You were just a boy, honey. You kiss me all over, and I want to kiss you all over because I love you."

"You're gonna kill me, you know that? Come on now, you need to get something to eat before class. I'll get something to go."

It was Tuesday. Rocco had only been gone twenty-four hours, and she felt the distance like a pain.

After group, she approached Dr. Ng. She had been thinking about it for weeks, afraid he'd be obligated to report to her parents, but she had to take the chance. "Dr. Ng, may I have about a half hour of your time this week?"

"Would now be convenient, Miss Richards?" She had always appreciated his formality, felt he considered his group adult equals, and hoped it would work for her.

He saw her eyes open slightly with surprise, but a quiet determination replaced it. "I have enjoyed being in your group, the work is interesting."

He nodded and said, "And I hope you will continue," with a slight question in his voice. Despite her calm demeanor, he noticed her hands clasped tightly.

"Yes, I hope to do so, but on an abbreviated basis. By that I mean, I need to leave this area as quickly as possible. I had planned to finish in three years at most, but my personal life is suffering, and I now find it necessary to get your opinion about my thesis so that I can leave in another year." He lifted his brows but said nothing, so she continued. "I've been working on it with the emphasis on the work we're doing. I feel it is time to make a decision if this is the avenue to take and receive your advice and approval to keep going. I guess my first request is that you look at what I've done and tell me if I'm on the right track for my doctorate."

"And your second request?"

"I would always like to work with you, Dr. Ng, but it won't be at this school. I'll be willing and happy to work from a distance, and I know that can be done."

A small smile played at his lips. He made a tent with his fingers. "So I believe we both know what you're saying is if I aid you in pursuing your doctorate, your knowledge will always be available to me?"

She nodded slightly, expressionless. "Exclusively, in this field."

"I'm sure you're aware I have very little to say about the final decision. There are no guarantees."

"All I'm asking is neither my age nor name appear on the initial procedures, so that by the time I'm brought into the equation, my work will have been judged on its merits alone."

"I feel comfortable doing that."

"May we set up a time for you to review what I've done so far?"

They decided on a time schedule, and their mental sparring done, he relaxed in his chair and said, "Have you discussed this with your parents?"

"No, I have not. I'm at this school and in this major at the request and behest of my parents. Out of respect for them, I'd like to finish it, but I intend to leave at the end of the next school year. And out of respect for you and any future endeavors we might pursue, I'll go into medicine at my next school."

"I'm glad to hear you're not concluding your education. That would be tragic, and it is unfortunate if you leave this field."

"I have no particular feeling for it, but I know I have a talent for it."

"Ah, Miss Richards, Schopenhauer comes to mind—talent hits a target no one else can hit; genius hits a target no one else can see. You know you have more than talent."

"I also know of people who pursue their work to the exclusion of all else—love, family, charity. I don't think I'm being selfish to want more than work."

He rose. "Having worked with you, I know mentioning your young age and the vagaries of love would be pointless. You are wise beyond your years. Let us hope it carries over to all aspects of your life."

She was out of the building before she realized she'd been holding her breath. She collapsed onto the nearest bench, her head in her hands, sighing loudly. A student walked by, "Flunking out?" She nodded no to discourage conversation and said to herself, *Step one.*

Her phone sounded once. She didn't pick up. In the middle of the second ring, his brow furrowed, his stomach clenched. At the end of the third ring, before she said, "Hi honey," he was ready to run for his truck.

"It's eight o'clock, baby girl. What were you doing?"

"Just working on a project."

"I thought we talked about you quitting at five so you could eat and recharge."

She sounded so tired. "I just got involved and lost track of time."

"How about I call in a half hour so you can get a sandwich?"

"No, no, don't go. I have a couple PowerBars and some milk I can have."

"Okay, but you sound worn-out. How many nights this week have you done this? It won't do you any good to get sick, little one."

She started crying. "I know, Rocco, but I've got to get out of here."

"Sweetie, you can't do a couple years work in a week. Let me tell you what I did this week while you eat one of those PowerBars."

She wanted to tell him her plan but didn't want both of them to be crushed if she couldn't pull it off. She lay down and inhaled the sound of his voice. "Tell me."

"Remember I told you I didn't think they took me seriously. A couple of them are perpetually late. They always have excuses, and they're good excuses, but it's gone beyond that, and I felt like I was being walked on. So I told Helen to research all the different kinds of time card machines. Then I had a meeting and told them it was coming and rearrange their mornings so they wouldn't be late because there would be no more excuses—if you're not here, you don't get paid. I told them I'd rather not be an SOB like my dad, but I can be if I have to."

"That's a great start, honey. You know the carrot and stick story?"

"I know the general idea."

"Maybe for the carrot you could offer to pay for courses for them. Is there anyone who would be a help to you if they took that management course with you?"

"Well, Bob, of course, but he's never a problem. He's my rock."

"It would be nice to have a second in command who's had that extra education. Are any of the problem fellows talented in any direction?"

"You know, I just got some information on a seminar at the granite supplier. I passed it by because I didn't have time, but Troy's really good at it."

"Maybe it would make him feel more a part of the company. Anybody else?"

"Well, Skip never took any courses like I did, but he's great at blueprints."

On they talked into the night. If he realized they were discussing the very things he had made an issue of not discussing on "the bad day," he never mentioned it, and neither did she. The line between their work was crossed and was never a problem again.

At midnight, she was yawning every other sentence, so he said, "Only a few more weeks until New Mexico, baby girl. Is it really a done deal? Should I call your dad about paying for my ticket?"

"It's definitely a done deal, honey. I'll have him call you next week. It's going to be so wonderful, I love you so much, Rocco."

"I love you, Blossom Dove. Remember to knock off two or three hours before bed. You need some downtime, baby. Next Friday. Go to sleep."

She fell asleep with her clothes on, the phone in her hand. Megan just shook her head when she came in and covered her with her quilt. They were as different as night and day but had grown into a working relationship and had decided to room together again.

After talking with her mother on Sunday, she asked for her dad. "What about, Blossom?"

"I just need to discuss the tickets to New Mexico and give him Rocco's return date."

"Blossom, this whole thing was Mim's idea. I don't think we've discussed it completely. It's really a family trip."

"We've discussed it enough, Mother. Dad was immediately on board. Rocco can be a real help and is interested in seeing what we do."

"Well, I hope he understands this is not a vacation and that you will be busy."

"We know that, Mother. The only free time I plan is going up to Aunt Mim's on Friday and back on Sunday. Then he will leave on Tuesday." She was fully prepared to say he goes or I don't, and she sensed her mother expected it so left it hanging in the air. She firmed up the dates with her father and heaved a sigh of relief. Four more weeks.

"There's a Dr. Richards on one, Rocco."

He picked up. "Cal?"

"Hello, Rocco, I just made the flight reservations and wanted to thank you for taking time from your business to help out."

"It's my pleasure. What's the charge for my ticket. I'll drop that off to you."

"No, no, you're taking your time, and our days are long. We're happy to cover it."

"I insist, sir."

"Very well. Five hundred will be plenty. Maybe one day you can drive out and see the country. Blossom says you haven't had much opportunity to travel."

"I'd really enjoy that. I'll make do with what tools we can scare up, but it would be nice to have my own."

They chatted comfortably about work that needed done there and what might be accomplished in four or five days. Rocco dropped an envelope off at the medical office marked "Dr. Cal Richards" with six hundred dollars in it and a note giving him his cell number.

It had been three weeks, and he was about to say he needed to come down when Blossom said she, Chet, and Dr. Ng were going to Washington DC for a Friday/Saturday trip. "The same deal as before?"

"Yes, honey, I'll call you when I get back to my room on Friday like before."

He bit his tongue and didn't ask what she was wearing. "Do you want to tell me what it's about?"

"It's boring, honey. I'd much rather talk about your week. How about the time clock and the classes?"

They talked until eleven, the separation getting to them, her only animation when she talked about Aunt Mim's and Santa Fe. "Where will we stay there, baby?"

Conspiratorially, "That's my surprise, honey. We'll get a room before we go to her house, then we'll have two nights together."

"As much as that sounds wonderful, it won't get you into trouble, will it?"

"Remember you said if my mom asks where you stay, just say we went to the Hilton? Well, when my aunt says she'll show us our rooms, I'll just say we're at the Adobe House."

"That's pretty brave, Blossom."

"It won't be hard with her. I never told you she asked at Christmas if we were intimate. I told her not yet, so I don't think she'll be surprised."

"Why didn't you ever tell me that?"

"I didn't have a chance. Remember my first day home, you told me you wanted to bring me back so we could be together?"

"I sure do remember," softly. "Are you happy we got together, baby girl?"

"Rocco"—even softer—"that's like asking if I'm happy I can breathe. I love you so much."

"Oh honey," she said so dejectedly when she opened her phone; he got a chill.

"What is it, Blossom? I'll fix it, baby."

"Mom says it's foolish to come home. She says I should go to the Pittsburgh airport and meet you all."

"But that's not terrible, is it? I was hoping to come get you a day early, but at least we'll be together soon."

"I know. I'm just being selfish. I want to be with you so much. Some days I say God, just give me a glimpse of him, just a glimpse, and I'll be all right."

"Ah jeez, baby girl, you're killing me here. You make me want to jump in the truck and forget about everything."

She took a big breath. "Let's go over the trip a little. Bring your toothbrush and cologne if you want your own. We have toothpaste, shaving cream, razors, all that kind of stuff. Just two pair of jeans, one for dress and one for work. I'm hoping to go dancing at Aunt Mim's, so bring either your dress boots or cowboy boots and bring your work boots. Oh, just let me fax you a list. Maybe you should just ship everything like we do . . . am I blathering, honey? I haven't let myself think this would actually happen, it's so unbelievable."

"It's getting close, baby. Where do I park my truck at the airport?"

On they talked about all the details, and the day actually arrived. He met her family at Dairy Queen's parking lot, Nix transferring to his truck. It all seemed surreal even as they got under way. It had been less than a year since he met her.

Nix seemed a little tense. They'd been together four times, so he was a little surprised. "This will be really interesting, seeing what you all do out there."

"Are you sleeping with my sister?"

He wanted to pull over but didn't want to lose sight of her parent's car. "Nix, there's a fine line between being a concerned brother and being a wiseass, and you just crossed it. If you weren't her brother, I'd put your head right through that window. I'm going to be around your whole life, so I'm forgetting you said that. I kind of thought we were getting along. Did I do something to you?"

"No, no. You know, I hear things at home about you interfering with her 'achieving her potential' as they say. She's a genius, you know"—and at Rocco's sideways glance—"really, she's been tested."

"That's nice, Nix, but it's not important to me. I just want to make her happy."

"And she has an I . . . I . . . well, I'm not sure. I think it starts with an E, but it's a photographic memory anyway."

"Again, Nix, not important to me."

Then Nix seemed to relax, like he'd been determined to say something, and now that he had, they could move on. They talked about what Nix liked about New Mexico and the fact he'd be driving before he came back. "How about all the colleges you've been looking at? What do you have in mind?"

"I don't know what that was all about. I don't have a clue where I want to go. Blossom says she thinks the trips are over until I really do have to decide. She is an awful lot happier, if you want to know. Sorry about earlier. No offense."

"None taken, Nix."

They settled into a comfortable silence as he concentrated on keeping up with the other car in the traffic. Dr. Richards turned around and pointed to Long-Term Parking, and they separated until they got to the meeting place. His heart was in his throat. Five weeks. Could he kiss her in front of her parents? Oh god, five weeks.

The situation took care of itself. When he saw her running toward him, everything around him faded away. He ran a few steps, and she was in his arms, her legs around his waist, her face in his neck, crying, making no sense—"You can't not come, I can't stay . . ."

"Sh, sh, your parents are here. I've got you. I'm here, baby girl, I'm here." He kissed her ear, her forehead, set her down, and handed her the handful of tissues he always carried now.

She said to everyone, "I'm sorry if I embarrassed you," blowing her nose. "It's just been so long." She hugged everyone and then came back to Rocco, her arms around his waist, looking up at him. He winked at her and smiled. She said, "You're here, you're really here."

Her mother was looking at them dispassionately; Nix looked away, embarrassed; and her father cleared his throat, saying, "It moves along more quickly if everyone carries their own ticket," passing them out. "Let's move along."

He couldn't believe he, Rocco Carnavale, was on an airplane, let alone on an airplane with her. She wanted him to have the window seat. Nix was with them, her parents across the aisle. She delighted in showing him everything, squeezing his hand, kissing his cheek. "Isn't it fun?"

He lifted his eyebrows and nodded yes, a little nervously. She whispered, "If you take a nap, the time goes quicker."

"You take a nap, baby. I don't want to miss anything."

The flight was direct to Albuquerque International, and someone they evidently knew was waiting. He was introduced to Sam Begay, and they made their way to a beat-up white van. He held Blossom's hand while her dad talked about the area. "Albuquerque has about a half million people, Rocco, and I'm ashamed to say we've never really took advantage of all the interesting things to see. About the only thing we might have time for is the Sandia Peak Transway. It gives you a great overview of the area. So early in the season, though, it's hard to get away from the clinic." He smiled fondly at Blossom. "If this little lady could have waited later in the summer to have you come, things would have quieted down some."

They went west on 40 and came to the compound—a small house past its prime and a little newer building looking more officelike, across a dusty road, a store/coffee shop type thing.

They put their things in the nearest bedroom. Two cots were set up beside a twin bed. The boxes they had mailed ahead were stacked in the room. The closet was tiny, Blossom's skirts and petticoats relegated to a coat rack commandeered from the office. The fellows put their things in Rubbermaid cartons. Blossom cautioned him to keep the lid on tight to keep out creepy-crawlies. Another carton held a variety of unisex cosmetics.

Dr. Richards came in and, for Rocco's benefit, said, "You kids work out your schedules. Blossom will need to be in the office by seven. You fellows report to Sam as soon as you're ready. Rocco, let's do a little walk around. You can get a plan in mind, check the tools, and go into Home Depot for supplies or rentals. Just do what needs to be done. Sam has authority, so your discussions will be with him. I'll be pretty busy the whole week. We usually confer at dinner after the clinic closes, but during the day, patient matters come first."

He was yawning right along with everyone else and couldn't believe they were getting ready for bed at nine. Blossom reminded him it was eleven back east. "You'll feel tired for a day or so, honey, set your watch for this time, it's easier.

Nix told him it was easier to shower in the morning because Blossom and his parents would be gone early, so they got into T-shirts and lounge pants before Blossom came back in her smurfies. "Rocco thinks you should have the bed, so I get it next week."

"I meant she should have it all the time, Nix."

"No way. It's dog-eat-dog around here, Rocco. You'll see. These cots are murder."

He went to the bathroom, kissed her lightly, the first time since seeing her at the airport; and they chatted for a while. "I probably won't see you until dinner, honey."

"What about lunch?"

"We don't leave the office for lunch, especially the first few weeks. Nix, you be sure he gets lunch," but Nix was asleep. She hugged Tiger with one arm and held out her hand. "My dad was right. I should have had you come later in the summer, but I missed you so much," getting teary.

"Everything's great, baby girl. We're in the same place, and that's all I need. Go to sleep now," kissing her fingertips. "I love you beyond words, Blossom Dove."

She stared into his eyes and smiled tenderly. "I love you to the moon and back, Rocco Anthony."

His back was to the door. He felt someone looking in about midnight but didn't turn, by the sound of the footsteps, surmised it was her mother.

He and Nix were ready by seven thirty. They walked from the house, past the clinic toward the coffee shop. He was amazed at the line of people, young and old waiting patiently. "Why do they come so early if they know you'll be here all summer?"

"Unless they had an emergency they went to Albuquerque for, they've been putting things off since last year."

He took Rocco into the odd little coffee shop/variety store. Nix seemed to know the workers, who nodded at him deferentially. "This is Rocco. He'll be helping out this week with repairs. Tell Sam if you need anything done." They nodded some more but kept their eyes down.

"It's easier just to order huevos rancheros or chile rellenos. They're similar to a western omelet and real good. The corn cakes are good too—hot with lots of butter. The coffee is strong. We don't pay, they'll take the slips to Blossom at the end of the day, and she'll pay. I usually leave a dollar too."

"I've never heard of those huevos things, so I'll have the corn cakes and check yours out."

"They seem pretty reserved."

"They'll warm up. Dad says they don't believe we'll be back, and if we come, will it still be free. Even after fifteen years."

They met with Sam Begay at eight, and the day started in earnest. Nix went in another direction. He followed Sam to an old warehouse and was surprised to see a well-arranged work area with basic tools, even carpenter's belts, a power saw, and a router. There were defined plumbing and electrical areas.

He said, "I noticed some little things at the house—dripping faucets, switches loose, like that. Should I start there and work my way out?"

"We'll check with Miss Elaine if there's anything at the clinic first. That house is privately owned, so we wouldn't work there unless she says so. We'll start with this list first."

The day went fast. Sam told him what to do and disappeared and was the kind of guy he liked to work with. Nix had to remind him of lunch. Then he went back to the house, found a container for water and his Stetson. It was unbelievably hot. He dumped water over his head and drank regularly. Nix found him at five, six items already crossed off the list.

"The clinic closes at five thirty, and then we have dinner, so start putting things away at five."

They had both showered and dressed when Blossom and her parents came back to the house. They went toward town to a local pizzeria with a salad bar. The doctor said, "We'll just stop here tonight. The first day everyone is tired."

Rocco was starved but remembered Blossom saying she always got voted down on a veggie pizza so said, "Will you share a small vegetable one with me, Blossom?" From her look, he knew she was aware of what he was doing; and when he ordered the same thing she had at Penn—artichokes, sliced tomatoes, mushrooms, and not too much cheese—she had tears in her eyes. She said a soft thank-you at the salad bar where she got a tiny salad, weeds and seeds he called it, while he and Nix loaded up.

"How did things go today, Rocco?"

"Well, sir, actually it seemed like busy work. I'm happy to do whatever needs done, but I could get a pretty big project done in the four days left."

"Sam's probably just checking you out. Elaine mentioned a counter in the office, and then if you finish the list, we'd be grateful. Come in first thing in the morning and check out the office. Nix, let's hear from you."

Rocco realized they used dinner as their daily meeting, all other hours of the day full. His admiration grew as he watched and listened. Blossom and Nix's comments and opinions considered thoughtfully. As he listened to Nix, he felt ashamed remembering himself at fifteen. His situation aside, he'd wasted four or five years. He held Blossom's hand under the table. She was so amazing. They had failed her in some ways, but their example of service was remarkable.

He came back to the conversation and got a little nervous when her mother said, "I didn't know you had reverted back to sleeping with a stuffed animal, Blossom. I thought I'd gotten rid of those silly things. Is it a tiger?"

"Yes, isn't he darling? Rocco got him for me."

Elaine raised her eyebrows, and he hoped the old adage of "Kitten in the kitchen, tiger in the bedroom" hadn't come to her mind.

After Nix fell asleep, he knelt in front of her bed and kissed her thoroughly. She sighed deeply. "I can't wait until Friday. What do you think so far?"

"I'm overwhelmed, baby girl. This is an amazing thing you all do. I couldn't picture it when you told me, but now I can see how unbelievable it is."

"Would you come back next year?"

"For sure, baby, for sure."

She smiled, hugged Tiger, and drifted off.

In the morning, he checked the office area. "I'm not sure how much money you're thinking, but an easy fix would be a couple of two-drawer filing cabinets with a six-foot preformed counter over them. I could get it and have it in today."

Blossom clapped her hands, and her father said, "Rough number, Rocco?"

"Four hundred, five at the most."

He called Sam and told him he and Rocco were going to Home Depot. Get anything else he needed.

Friday finally came, and they packed lightly for the sixty-mile drive to Aunt Mim's. Her dad gave them the Buick, saying they'd be fine with one of the trucks. Blossom excited about getting him a new hat for his birthday, hopping around to her mother's dismay. She told him to bring his Stetson since he liked the fit and tried to calm down as her mother gave her things to take and admonished her not to let Mim buy her a lot of clothes. Rocco tried not to stare. She was flushed and glowing in a sheer, filmy, ruffled red blouse that moved and floated above her A-line denim skirt and denim moccasins.

As soon as they were out of sight, he pulled to the side of the highway. "I need a kiss."

"Tonight, honey," she said happily.

"Get out, I can't reach you with these bucket seats."

"Rocco!"

"Please, baby girl, just let me hold you for a minute."

So they stood off the highway with traffic whizzing by, swaying with their eyes shut. He kissed her forehead. "I needed that. You've been so close, but so far, this week."

"Rocco, I love you," taking a big breath, finally relaxing from the week.

They switched from Route 25 to 14 and checked into the El Rey Inn. He looked from her to the bed. "Not yet, honey. I want to go get Aunt Mim and order your hat. She'll make sure they have it ready tomorrow. She's very persuasive."

"Aunt Mim, this is Rocco Carnavale. Rocco, my aunt Mimosa Esteban." No apprehension or nervousness. Just happiness that they could actually meet in person.

"Come in, come in," hugging Blossom. "Rocco, it's good to finally meet you. Lourdes"—loudly—"Blossom's here. Bring fruit and muffins. Sit, sit, what to drink? Sparkling water, Blossom? Coffee or something stronger, Rocco?"

They settled at a table by a window and talked comfortably about the first week at the clinic. "Aunt Mim, I'd like to get over town. Remember, I'd like your help in getting him a Resistol for his birthday."

"That won't be a problem, dearie. Rocco, you relax, explore, whatever. I have a couple things I want Blossom to try on."

He didn't feel comfortable wandering too far but followed them a little ways to a powder room near the entrance, hearing them shriek and giggle before the door shut.

"He's gorgeous!"

Blossom clapped her hands. "I know, I know." It lightened her heart to be a silly girl madly in love and have someone to share it with.

Meantime, Rocco circled around a little. The house was traditional Santa Fe styling with unique heavy furnishings. He found pictures of Blossom and Nix in a huge breakfront. She was a few years younger, all in white, sitting and looking down at a white angora cat. It was breathtaking, her dark hair and lashes standing out in the white setting. It made him realize he had never seen a picture of her at her house. On another shelf were three pictures of Mim with three different men. The frames were the same. She aged well progressively in each one, beautifully dressed, maybe ten years younger; it was hard to tell. She looked like Cal, fit yet shapely, her auburn hair like the Dorothy Hamil-cut he'd seen on TV.

He heard them laughing in the other room, and when they came out, his heart started pounding in his ears. He didn't realize he had made a choking sound. She had on a dress similar to the one she had worn to the hot dog stand days after they had met. The top, layers of a sheer material in white with blue flowers; from beneath her breasts to the middle of her hips was a tight, stretchy denim; the skirt the white material again down to below her knees, flowing out as she twirled for him. It was hard to breathe.

"Do you like it?" She smiled radiantly. Then seeing his face, she came and whispered, "Rocco, I'm all covered up. This is a perfectly lovely dress, honey. You'll see when we go shopping, everyone wears sundresses around here."

Mim said, "Don't you love it, Rocco? That designer really suits her. I get one whenever they come in."

He managed to hold himself together, concentrating on taking measured breaths, and they left for the day. Mim and Blossom decided the only thing he absolutely had to see was the famous Miraculous Staircase. As a carpenter, it was bound to intrigue him. But the first stop was for his Resistol hat.

He immediately objected when he saw some prices. "Baby girl, this is too much for a birthday present. You have to let me pay."

"No! I've been planning this for months, honey. It would hurt my feelings if you paid."

"How about half then. I don't think your mother would approve."

"Rocco Anthony, she knows how much these hats cost, and," she said pointedly, "she knows how much pearls cost. She's not going to say anything. You give a gift because it's something you want the person to have. It could be a note or a car, it doesn't matter. Now let's look around."

"Rafael, this is my niece, Blossom, and her friend, Rocco. We'd like him to have a Resistol, ready for tomorrow afternoon. That's no problem, is it?"

"Of course not, Ms. Esteban."

"What do you think with his dark hair, the cream?"

"Well, of course, whatever the gentlemen prefers. Surprisingly, the camel or the mink seem to flatter the dark hair. Let's try a few."

He was right. Rocco turned and looked at Blossom with the mink one on. "What do you think, baby girl?"

"It's perfect"—she clasped her hands under her chin—"just perfect."

Rocco was surprised at the measurements and fittings. He had just walked into the local western wear place in Meadville and bought his

Stetson. This one sure felt good. He was uncomfortable when Blossom paid the $189, but as she kissed his cheek and said "Happy birthday, my darling," a couple customers added their happy birthdays, and it seemed natural.

It was midafternoon. They had decided to do the staircase at the Loretto Chapel on Saturday and were having drinks and snacks at the Anasazi Bar in the Rosewood Inn just off the Plaza before going back to Mim's. Rocco had driven Mim's Mercedes after they strolled around the Plaza shops. He saw a suited fellow in front of the Inn and said, "What do I do here?"

"Just get out and give him the keys," Mim said. And to the valet, "Not too far, hon, we're just having drinks."

Rocco was having the first Corona he had ever tried, Blossom had said no to a white wine spritzer and was having sparkling water, and Mim was on her second margarita. "So tell me all about yourself, Rocco."

Blossom surprised him by interjecting, "Rocco had things decided for him when his father died suddenly, and he had to take over the construction company. I'm so happy he could schedule himself these ten days to come here and maybe more time next year." She skillfully steered the conversation to one of Mim's charities, and Rocco again was struck by the family inclination to help others, especially Indians. He knew the Richards had a comfortable life, and obviously Mim's was even more so, and felt a twinge of guilt that he just assumed such people spent their money on things.

When Mim went to the restroom, he asked Blossom, "What was that about, sweetie?"

"Honey, she delights in putting people on the spot, and I didn't want her to keep prying until you were uncomfortable. Here she comes. Get ready, our sleeping arrangements are going to come up."

"So shall we go back and rest up for dinner, children?"

"We're at the El Rey, Aunt Mim, so we'll go there for a while, Rocco will want a fresh shirt." She hurried on, "I'd love to wear this dress, what are you wearing?"

Aunt Mim never blinked an eye. "Okay, we'll go get your car, and you come get me about six, six thirty. I'll wear dressy casual too. What type of place would you like?"

"I know Rocco's dying for a steak." Blossom smiled.

"Anything's fine with me," he said, ill at ease at the motel discussion and amazed Blossom had handled it so well.

"Honey, Nixie told me the food was a struggle. I want you to have a meal you really like. It's your birthday. What do you think, Aunt Mim, Steaksmith?"

"I think the Railyard would be better. There are more choices for you and I, and the macaroni and cheese is to die for.

They got their car, thanked Mim for the fun day, and pulled away—not seeing the smile on her face. She was barely in the house when her phone chirped. It was Blossom's mother. "Hi, Elaine, how's everyone?"

"Just wondering how the visit is going. I hope you're not going overboard on gifts." Quietly, "Are they right there?"

"No, they're taking a walk. She's showing Rocco the neighborhood," she lied easily.

"So what do you think of Rocco?"

"Elaine, he just seems like a really fine fellow. So old for his age, polite, well-spoken, knowledgeable. I couldn't find a thing wrong with him, kiddo. I hope that doesn't disappoint."

"Oh, I don't know. I just don't want her distracted from her work."

"Maybe her work isn't the most important thing to her, Elaine."

Getting exasperated, "She's too young to know what's important, Mim."

"How's she doing in school, did she end up the year okay?"

"Oh, you know she did. Don't play dumb. She always excels—there's just no passion in it."

Mim laughed. "Well I think she's found someone to be passionate about."

With a worried tone, "You saw something too? God, do you think they're intimate?"

"Of course they're intimate, Elaine. My god, look at her, she's glowing and happy. Remember her at Christmas. She looked like a ghost, dark circles under her eyes, moving her food around her plate, hanging on to that phone like it was a lifeline. She looks at him like he walks on water. I should be so lucky."

"Oh god, I was hoping if I kept them apart . . ."

"I'm afraid that ship has sailed, kiddo, and it's not a bad thing. She's going to do better work if she's happy if that's what you're worried about."

"I wonder if I should tell Cal what you think."

"I'm sure he's already assumed it, Elaine. It's really none of our business, is it. She's legal. She could get married if she wanted to."

"Oh god, don't say that. I'll just file it away, watch her grades, and hope for the best. I mean, we do have some control, we are paying for school."

"Elaine, don't be an idiot. She couldn't care less if you quit paying for school. Probably giving you your money's worth is the only thing keeping her there now. Oh, here they come," she lied. "So you want to talk to her?"

"No, no, we'll see them Sunday. I'll talk to you when I can."

Mim chuckled. She knew she wouldn't want to talk to Blossom and didn't have a qualm about lying to her. Truth was relative to Mim. Not for the first time, she wondered what her children would have been like if she hadn't felt too inconvenienced to have any. "Lourdes," she called, "bring me a Chablis to the bath, dear. I'll wear the navy Donna Karan. Something kicky on the jewelry, I don't want to look too dressed."

Back at the motel, Rocco kicked the door shut, unbuttoning his shirt.

"Honey, I can't," Blossom said, "I'll have to sleep, and it's almost four."

"I'll wake you, baby, please. It's been so long."

She carefully took off her new dress while he folded down the bed, keeping her eyes off his so she could get everything done. Five weeks, six now, her heart banging against her ribs. "I didn't want us to be rushed, honey."

"I'll make it up to you, baby doll, please, please," almost panting.

"Oh stop, crazy man." He was making noises in his throat, his eyes dark. "My crazy, crazy man, I've missed you so much," putting her hands around his neck.

He moaned and carried her to the bed, almost chewing on her lips, and entered quickly. "Sorry, sorry, it's been too long."

Her legs were around him, but she threw herself from side to side, her palms hitting the bed. Fear of the freight train crept up his back. "What is it, baby?"

"I can't get close enough," she cried.

"Blossom," he whispered, "we're very close. What is it?"

She cried in earnest, pounding his chest with her fists, "You never came to see me. You never came after the bad day."

"But I did, I did. The bad day was Friday, and I came Sunday night, baby."

"But you never came again," still pounding, but weaker. "You left me there for five weeks. You never came back, you never came," sobbing.

"I swear to you, Blossom, my mouth was open ready to say I'm coming when you said you were going to Washington. I couldn't tell you, you would have cancelled, and it might have been important. I'm so sorry, baby girl. Why didn't you tell me you needed me?"

"I need you all the time," whimpering.

He had softened from the distraction and pulled out carefully. He carried her to the headboard, pulling up the sheet to cover them.

"I can keep going for you, I can."

"You know what, sweetie, we've never had a chance to cuddle this week. Never even had a chance to take a walk. Let's just get caught up while I look at your beautiful face."

"I'm sorry I made you come when it's so busy. All I could think of was you'd be sleeping right beside me. I forgot we work all the time," smiling a little.

"Boy, I was this close to crawling into that bed with you. I wasn't even going to wake you, I just wanted to be closer. You know, your mother looked in every night about midnight. Wouldn't it have been funny if I was in with you?"

She giggled and moved to get her arms around him. "Do you want to try again?"

He kissed her nose. "We'll wait for tonight, baby mine. I like your aunt by the way. Who are the men in those three pictures?"

"They are her husbands. After the last one died, she got the other pictures out. She said, after all, she loved them each in their own way, and all three were part of her life. She pretty much told me she always married for money. I think it's very sad."

"Did they all die?"

"No, she divorced the first two. I'm pretty sure they were friendly divorces, or I would have heard my parents talking about it."

"Do you think she drinks too much?"

"Oh, probably. I only see her a couple times a year—this year more than ever with that endless visit over Christmas," rolling her eyes. "I know she has faults, but she's basically so kind and generous and funny. Now that I'm older, I almost feel sorry for her. She and Lourdes all alone in that big house. At least Lourdes has a family that she sees now and then."

On they talked until five forty-five, cuddled up in the sheet. He had gathered it around her head to shield her from the air-conditioning, and her dark hair and eyes against the white sheet made him weak. He knew better than to say it out loud but thought, *Mine, mine, mine.* "Are you going to wear that dress tonight?"

"Rocco," threateningly.

"But, baby, it's really thin material," he whispered. "It shows your breasts."

"Honey, there are six or seven layers of material, and it's gathered. No one could possibly see through it."

"But . . ."

"That's all the discussion now. Aunt Mim's feelings would be hurt if I didn't wear it." She freshened up and put on silver sandals with turquoise stones. He narrowed his eyes, but she just shook her head and laughed.

"I changed my mind to the Bull Ring, children. It's in the Wells Fargo building, and the parking is free after the bank is closed." Rocco thought she was kind to think of the free parking. He had gotten a five out for a tip in the afternoon, and she had said "Ten, hon. They expect more for a Mercedes 550."

Blossom made a fuss over Mim's chili pepper earrings and necklace, and Rocco could smell sizzling beef as they exited the car. He mouthed to Blossom, "I'm so hungry," and she said "Now, honey, get a filet mignon. It's still a steak, and it's not so big."

Mim suggested the twin ribeyes as a compromise, and Blossom thought it was a good idea until she saw the size of them swimming in butter. When he passed up their famous potato selections for a traditional baked but loaded with butter, sour cream, and cheese, she just shook her head helplessly. Blossom and Mim ordered salmon, and she ordered three-fourths of hers wrapped for Lourdes to use for a salad. Mim raised her eyebrows when Rocco passed up beer for a Coke. "My limit is one a day, and I had that this afternoon."

The busy, friendly place was comfortable, and the evening passed quickly. "Are there any western dance places nearby? I'd love to show you what a great dancer Blossom is."

"Blossom dances? This I'll have to see. Do you like a small dance area or a big hall?"

"We move around, so a bigger hall would be better."

"I think the Stable would be good then. What's our plan for tomorrow until then?"

Blossom spoke up quickly, "Rocco hasn't been sleeping too well on that cot, so let's pass up breakfast for brunch. Then the Loretto Chapel, and then get the hat, then we freshen up and go dancing," smiling and clapping.

"That's a plan." Mim smiled, loving that Blossom was so happy. "Pick me up elevenish, and we'll have a fun day."

"Baby girl," Rocco said after dropping Mim off, "I should have spoken up. That's the second time you had to handle that situation."

"Honey, they're my family. I know how to deal with them. You have to be direct with Mim, or she'll back you into a corner."

At the motel, Blossom said, "Honey, I'm going to shower in the morning." She whispered, "I don't want Aunt Mim to smell you all over me."

He growled in his throat, "Then come sit a minute. I want to make sure you understand something."

Worried, "What?"

"Baby girl, if you need me, you call me. It breaks my heart you were hurting all those weeks. I'm so low myself, I can't pick up on your signals."

"But, honey, it's so far, and gas is so much. I feel I have to be strong."

"Blossom, I'd die for you. Don't you think I'd buy a tank of gas for you?"

"Don't say that," but smiling.

"Okay, we're clear, right? If it gets really bad, you'll call." She nodded with big eyes. "Let's get ready for bed. Thanks to you being so brave, we don't have to get up early."

He was in bed, music on, when she finished brushing her teeth and came out, naked. "Honey, would you rub lotion on my back, the air is so dry here."

"Baby, I don't want to smell lotion, I want to smell you."

She crawled in and lay on her stomach. "This is a light scent and so silky," handing him the bottle. "Please, please," her lips pouty.

He laughed at his weakness and straddled her, squeezing some on her back. "My god, your back is beautiful. You have no idea—the shape, your spine, these dimples."

"Umm, that feels so good," reaching back and lifting her hair off her neck.

"Wow, baby, I don't think I've ever seen the back of your neck," massaging it then biting it lightly.

She squealed delightedly, "Oohh, I like that. Do it again."

He kissed her shoulder, bit her neck, and whispered in her ear, "Would you like to make love in this position?"

She turned her head, puzzled. "How could we do that?"

Softly, "Just get up on your knees, and I'll be right here."

Her puzzled look became a frown. "But that would be like animals. I don't want to be like animals."

"I'm your tiger, remember."

She smiled. "I don't know, I . . ."

"Raise up, and I'll show you something."

She got on her hands and knees, looking apprehensive. "I don't think . . ."

"If I were back here, I could do this," he said cupping her breasts and squeezing gently.

"Ooh-ooh," breathlessly.

"And I could do this," gently rubbing her clitoris.

She screamed softly and reached for Tiger.

"Do you want to try?" He nibbled at her neck and rubbed his hardness against her.

"Yes, yes," she panted. "Yes, yes."

"Tell me if it hurts," guiding himself in. The afternoon attempt faded away. This was what they needed. This took away the six weeks. This was the strength to keep going. She matched him thrust for thrust. She arched her back; he groaned. She swayed her back; he cried out. She put her head down on Tiger, stiffened her knees, and screamed as her body shook. He felt an electric charge go up his spine, the room spun, as he released and collapsed on her. "Blossom, Blossom," and sobbed.

When they could breathe, she turned over but stayed under him, pulling his head to her chest, kissing his forehead, his tears, his perspiration. "My wonderful, wonderful, crazy man," she whispered. "I love you more than I can say. You are my life." He could still only whimper but helped her into her position and smiled weakly as she put her little hands under her chin.

She woke at four and turned to him. He pulled her close silently, made love to her tenderly, and rolled her over. She sighed deeply and went to sleep.

He knew as soon as her eyes opened and was kneeling by the side of the bed when she turned. He had shaved, showered, and handed her a cup of coffee. "Good morning, Blossom Dove, I love you."

"Good morning, Rocco Anthony, I love you. Don't get too close, I really need a shower."

"I want to get close, I want to talk about last night."

"I can't. You were too wonderful. Let's save it for when I feel fresh and clean."

"Honey," she called from the shower, "remember the first time we made love and you said you didn't know there was perspiration involved? How could you not know? I never knew I could perspire so much."

"Blossom"—exasperated—"I want to talk about how amazing last night was, and you want to talk about that? Now?"

"Well"—innocently—"I wondered, and I keep forgetting to ask. So why?"

"Baby, I don't know. I was a stupid kid, I had no feelings for the person I was with, I had my clothes on . . ."

"You had your clothes on?"

"Sweetie, I was in an alley, I was in the woods, I was in someone's car . . ."

"Oh, Rocco"—wrapping up in a towel and coming to him quickly—"poor baby, poor, sad baby."

Their kisses turned serious. "Do you want to miss brunch," he said huskily.

"No, my darling, Aunt Mim is probably dressing right now. Besides, we're picking your hat up today, and I can hardly wait. I have to wear this dress for a while, honey. My other clothes are at Aunt Mim's house. Do you love it yet?" She twirled in front of him and tipped her head. "Why are you looking at me funny?"

"You know why I'm looking at you funny."

She smiled innocently. "Why?"

He pulled her close and whispered in her hair, "Because you're magnificent, because you make me weak in the knees, because you make me cry, because you love me."

She said against his lips, "I was born to love you."

"Because you say things like that. I know we're not supposed to say this anymore, but I don't deserve you."

"No, we're not saying that anymore."

"But last night I asked you to try something new, and you devastated me. Everything about you is unbelievable."

"Rocco, it's you, honey, you're the one. You thrill me so much I can do anything. It's you. One more kiss now, and we have to go." She found his tongue and whispered, "Tonight, tonight." He shivered and stumbled.

"Good morning, my darlings. Lourdes, coffee for Rocco while Blossom changes." He turned; and Lourdes was already putting a cup of coffee, a carafe, and a plate of tiny muffins on the window table. "Good morning, Lourdes."

"Good morning, Mr. Rocco." She made a tiny bow and left quickly. He wondered about the situation. She was obviously the help, yet Blossom said she and Aunt Mim were close.

Mim and Blossom came back. Blossom dressed again in the filmy ruffled red blouse she had worn before with a denim skirt and moccasins. "Where for brunch, Blossom? We could park and walk to Tia Sophia's and then do our shopping, but they close at two, and we don't want to be rushed."

"I think the Flying Star," Blossom suggested. "They have breakfast all day, and Rocco can find regular eggs, and they have yummy baked things for you and me."

They enjoyed a leisurely brunch, and Rocco hadn't seen any signals, but when he motioned for the check, Mim said, "Just leave the tip, hon, the bill's been paid."

Blossom clapped. "Now we pick up the hat. I'm so excited!"

The hat was amazing. He shook his head, putting it on and off a couple times. Everyone was so complimentary; his self-consciousness passed. They went on to the Loretto Chapel. Rocco was intrigued as he looked and studied, and studied and looked at the 360-degree turns on the staircase with no visible support. Mim watched Blossom smile at him adoringly as if she had built it just for his pleasure. When Blossom took pictures of his face with her phone, Mim said, "You should have a good camera, sweetheart."

"I know, I asked Mom if we had one at the clinic, but"—dropping her eyes—"she said she had given it away since I no longer did anything of note." Then she softened it by smiling and shrugging. "I'm going to get one, though, I love taking pictures of him."

They shopped a little, and seeing Blossom yawning, Mim suggested they go home for a quiet afternoon. "There's so much art and history here, you must come for three or four days so we can cover it properly."

Blossom napped, Mim also after she grilled him a little, softening him up by telling him Blossom was happier than she'd ever seen her. He learned a little too. "I've figured out a few things, but what is her obsession about embarrassing people?"

"Oh Christ, they were realizing she could stop the dog-and-pony show at any time, so they tried to forestall it by saying get out there, and don't you dare embarrass us. She'd wring her little hands and look so worried, it made me sick to my stomach. But you have to realize, even though she was always the youngest one in those things, they were all in the same boat. I don't remember one looking happy. I was so relieved when it was over. I figured it'd take a toll of some kind, but I didn't think it would last this long."

"She sleeps a lot," looking worried.

"I know." Mim shrugged. "I finally decided all that knowledge she carries in her brain just wears her out."

His head was in his hands. She was surprised and touched at how moved he was. "I don't deserve her, but I'll spend my life trying to make it better."

"Hey, lighten up, kiddo. Whatever you're doing, it's working," winking at him. He was surprised to feel himself blushing.

"Hey, Rocco," Mim kidded him, "I think that hat is making you swagger. Remember what he said, treat it rough. It will probably outlive you." They had just arrived at the dance hall. Much to Blossom's dismay, she was outvoted on healthy salads at Vinaigrettes, and they were eating before dancing. She settled on crudités from the starter menu and a baked potato with salsa. Rocco and Mim were sharing a porterhouse for two, and he introduced Mim to french fries with gravy. She tried to introduce him to Rocky Mountain Oysters, but Blossom told him no and whispered to him they were bulls' testicles. His mouth fell open.

It was Saturday night, and the band started at eight. The place was cavernous, and Rocco made sure they had a table so he could sit with his back against the wall with a view of the door and an overview of the room. He saw none of the guys took their hats off to eat, so he didn't either. When the waiter was serving their food, Blossom whispered, "You're impossibly handsome in that hat." He grinned and gave her a slow wink.

Blossom was animated and glowing, so happy Aunt Mim seemed to see how wonderful Rocco was, hoping at Christmas he would be coming with them to Santa Fe. They went to the restrooms after dinner. Mim was puzzled when Blossom stopped her from leaving. "Wait for Rocco." The door opened an inch and a quiet, "Blossom?"

They walked toward their table, and a surprised, "Blossom!" they looked, and a girl from the reservation school got up to hug her. Blossom said, "Go ahead, I'll be right over." Rocco and Mim chatted, but she noticed he turned his chair to keep Blossom in his vision.

A few minutes passed, then he said, "Oh, oh, we're going to have a situation here. Who is that girl again?"

"What do you mean, a situation? She's Naomi Dashee from the reservation school. Blossom worked with her on the computer project."

He nodded. "Well, somehow she's reminded Blossom school's coming fast or that I'm leaving."

Sure enough, Blossom came toward the table, her eyes swimming with tears, oblivious to Mim and everyone else. He tried to forestall it. "Baby girl, I'm right here, I'm right here."

Tender agony on her face, "You can't go back," tears splashing on the table as she put her head on her arms.

"Sweetie, I have a business to run, and you have important work to do."

"No. I have to come with you. I can't go back to school and only see you for a week. I can't."

"They need you here, Blossom."

"No. Nixie can do it." He was rubbing her back, and she looked up. "You don't understand. My heart is breaking. I mean it this time."

"Look up, baby girl." He winked at her. "I'll give you half of mine if you give me half of yours."

She tried to narrow her eyes and pout, but a smile crept in. "That wasn't funny the first time you said it. I'm not staying here."

"Blossom Dove. We can go back to our room and talk about it all night, and I'll do that in a heartbeat if that's what you want. But in the morning, nothing will have changed . . . or"—he made his voice upbeat—"we can stay here and dance and show your aunt how good you are, and things will look better in the morning. How about that?"

She slowly nodded yes and looked around, realizing where they were. "Oh, I've embarrassed you. Oh, I'm so sorry."

Mim realized she'd been holding her breath. "Not in the least, kitten." She reached for her purse to find tissues and saw that Rocco had already passed Blossom a handful.

"So, Mim," he said as though nothing had happened, "you going to be okay here at the table? We'll do two numbers and come back."

"Go, go, I'm fine. I've already seen a couple people I know. I'm dying to see Blossom dance. She didn't even want to do the little classes when she was in kindergarten."

They walked to the edge of the floor. He held her close for a second. "You okay, my baby?"

"I'm fine. I'm sorry. I don't want to spoil our night."

"Can't happen, baby. Listen for a few beats," looking into her eyes. "Feel it?" She nodded yes, smiling, and he said "Here we go." The song was the band's version of "I'm a Cowboy" by the Smokin' Armadillos, a great number for the basic line dance grapevine in all its forms. They moved around the floor smoothly, getting used to the band and the space. Blossom kept her eyes on him as always, but he saw Mim with her mouth open in surprise. The band kicked it up a little, and he spun her in front of him from his right to left hand, making sure they ended up near Mim for their between his legs move at the song's ending.

"I'm seldom at a loss for words, kitten, but I'm speechless, absolutely speechless! How on earth did you learn to dance that well?"

Blossom was luminous at the praise. "I just go where Rocco puts me," smiling shyly.

"She's a natural," Rocco said. "She's so smart, she only needs to see something once, and she has it down. We've only been dancing four or five times," he said proudly.

They got a drink and went back out. It was a fun time, Rocco having Mim join them for Josh Turner's "Why Don't We Just Dance." It had a light and upbeat tempo, and he was able to twirl one in each hand and then putting an arm around each of them showing Mim a basic grapevine step they could do in a line. First one and then more groups in the crowd fell in behind, making lines of six or eight following their movements around the floor.

Rocco and Blossom were inspired by the space and freedom. It was the first time he threw her into the air. She loved it, instinctively assumed a sitting position with her ankles crossed and landed in his arms. They refined and perfected it through the years, and she rewarded him with her glorious smile every time. He lived for that smile. She was careful with her smiles. Generous with small, everyday ones, but cautious with the one that made him feel he was in a force field—as though if anyone knew how happy she was, something would go wrong.

Mim danced with a couple older gentlemen, making Blossom raise her eyebrows, and they never thought of leaving until Rocco saw how often she was yawning. It was a memorable night. Well, there was that one incident . . .

Rocco had gone to the bar to get Mim another Margarita and himself a coke. He had paid and turned when he saw a fellow approach Blossom. He left the drinks and came up behind the guy as Blossom said, "No, thank you, I'm with someone." The guy said, "Oh, he won't mind," just as Rocco moved tight behind him and said, "Actually, he'd mind a great deal," in a steely voice. The guy tried to keep it light saying, "Hey, just asking." Rocco, not smiling, "Just telling," with a penetrating glare.

He went back for the drinks, holding it together, but when he set them down, he was breathing hard. "Can you believe the nerve of that jerk." His jaw clenched, squeezing his glass, his eyes darting around.

Blossom, softly, "Rocco. Rocco."

"Who would do that? I should have put him right through the wall. We've been here over three hours, he knew we're together. I . . ."

She reached over and put her hand over his mouth. "It's over, honey. Everything's fine. Big breaths now, everything's fine," smiling sweetly. "Big breaths," inhaling and breathing with him. "We're fine now, aren't we?"

He looked down. "Sorry," taking her hand. "Sorry."

Mim looked from one to the other, wondering how often this happened.

They did the next dance a little tentatively while he got his breathing regulated and then were surprised when the one after was one of their favorite, Delbert's "Same Kind of Crazy." Rocco had the footwork down to a fine science, and she backed up to join the circle around him, clapping encouragement. She sashayed back, wiggling her hips, and they were back in their zone.

They left reluctantly. Mim saying, "Children, I can't remember when I've had so much fun. Come for breakfast before you start back. I have some things for Nixie. Kiss, kiss."

Rocco headed toward the motel. Neither mentioned the incident. "Baby, you were amazing on that dance floor tonight. Absolutely amazing."

"I love dancing with you so much, Rocco," teary from sleepiness. "I feel I'm a part of you. Like I'm connected to you, like I can read . . ."

"You are a part of me, sweetie. Did you like the toss?"

"Oh, it was so fun! Why did you do that?"

"I was sitting around watching ice skating shows when you were gone at Christmas. I thought we could adapt some of the lifts. We'll try some more. I really like your aunt, baby. She seemed to be having fun. This whole week has been unbelievable," talking a little too fast so she couldn't think too much. "Do people back home know what your family does?"

"Most of their colleagues and friends know they leave for the summer to do charity work, but they don't talk about it that much."

"I know things have been rough, baby, but everything in your life has made you the person you are. I just need to say you are the most wonderful soul. I'm humble that you love me, Blossom."

"Rocco, don't, honey. You're so much better than I am. I'm not a good person. I'm selfish and . . ."

He reached over and took her hand, kissing it. "Stop right there now. We're not going there tonight," pulling into the motel. "Let's go cuddle and enjoy our last night here. It's back to the cots tomorrow," winking.

He made the mistake of telling her to shower first. When he came out from shaving and showering, she had too much time to think. She was sitting naked in bed, uncovered from the waist up, looking at him, her eyes swimming in tears. "I have to go back with you. You'll tell them, won't you? You can make them understand. I just can't stay here. Would you tell them, please?"

He stood in front of the bed. "Baby girl, of course I'll tell them, but you know what they'll think. You do good things here. Try to last a little longer. If you need me, I'll come back."

"I need you all the time," her voice getting angry. "They'll just think I want to go back so we can make love. Is that what you think too?" Her eyes narrowed. "You better not be thinking that," breathing hard. She had Tiger by his tail, and he saw him coming but didn't duck. He hit the side of his face surprisingly hard for a little girl's swing.

"Oh no, now I've hit you just like your father," sobbing and putting her head in her hands.

"Shh, everything's fine, everything's fine," picking her up and holding her on his lap.

"I don't care if we make love. I just want to be near you," plaintive now. "Oh please let me be near you. I just want to hear you talk and see you walk. I want to see your eyes and the curl that falls down and the scar under your ear." He unconsciously touched the scar from the table edge he'd been thrown in to. She hugged Tiger to her chest and crawled into her sleeping position. "I want to see your beautiful back and hear you breathe." He started rubbing her back. She was still murmuring things only she could hear; and he stroked her back, crying too, until she was asleep.

She turned to him at five. He gathered her close, kissed her eyes, her nose, her lips, and loved her back to sleep.

He found Mim's number on Blossom's phone and called at nine. "We had kind of a bad night. I don't want to wake her, so we'll take a rain check on breakfast. It was really a pleasure meeting you."

"Was it more of the same as at the Stable, wanting you to stay?"

"That, and coming with me. We'll work it out."

"Well, it was great meeting you too, Rocco. You've got your hands full there. But let me tell you, last night aside, she's a much happier girl. Like night and day really. I was hoping someday she'd find a balance between her brain and life, and I think you're on the right track. Tell her to call if she needs me."

He remembered later that she nibbled at breakfast, smiled weakly on the ride back, but said little. He was the one who showed her family his hat and told them about Mim dancing. They held hands between her bed and his cot. He spent his last day doing electrical repairs at the house. Her dad agreed it was better not to get into plumbing. It might open a can of worms and be more work for Sam if old pipes gave way.

Her dad suggested at dinner that Sam take Rocco to the airport. "No!" She even startled herself and when everyone looked at her, cleared her throat, and said, "I won't be gone long, and I'll work late," looking at her hands.

Rocco said quietly, "Maybe it would be easier to say good-bye here, baby girl."

She stared hard at him, "What if the plane is late, and you're there, and I'm here? I'll drive you," and her tone told him not to pursue it.

"Tell you what, kitten," her dad said, "I'll have Sam drive you. I don't want you driving back all upset." Her mother just looked annoyed.

At the airport, he knew it would be frustrating to both of them but pulled her behind a pillar, shielded them with his hat, and kissed her passionately—probing, sucking, biting, until their knees buckled. "You call me if it gets too bad. I'll come."

"I can't ask you to spend six hundred dollars. I have to be strong."

"The money doesn't matter. I have money, I'll come. I have to go now, go find Sam."

"No, no, I'll wait. Maybe the plane will have trouble, and everyone will have to get off."

He laughed. "That's not a good thing to tell someone who's only flown once, sweetie. I better go. I'll call when I land."

She sat until the plane was in the air and smiled weakly at Sam when he handed her a latte.

It was July 16, a month since he left New Mexico. He could always tell when someone was in the room with her. "Rocco"—restrained excitement—"Nixie and I are coming home early. Can you pick us up in Pittsburgh tomorrow at three?"

"Absolutely, baby girl. Can you talk?"

"Not right now," softly. "May I call you really late? About midnight, your time?" Her voice was strained, holding back tears.

"Of course, sweetie, are you all right?"

"I am now. I'll call." The phone went off.

It had been a rough four weeks on the phone. They had settled on a Sunday-Wednesday-Friday schedule. He kept the calls short; she needed her sleep. The first week they reminisced about his visit, but she cried a lot and had little interest in telling him what she was doing—the same. Nixie was driving now. Aunt Mim went to Europe. He didn't want to tell her he was almost finished with a closet for her clothes. He knew thinking of how long it would be before she would be using it would make her cry. He had seen the space she needed in New Mexico. Had measured his room, and if they had no larger than a double bed with small nightstands, he could make the closet the length of the room. It had double rods and shelves in the middle. It looked good. He just had to decide on doors.

Quarter to midnight, she called, her voice teary. "What's going on, baby girl?"

"We had a big fight. If it was just me, they wouldn't have agreed, but Nixie wanted to come too. Dad was the most reasonable. He told Mom their dream doesn't have to be our dream, plus Nixie should have a little summer. I'm supposed to work at the office, and Nixie has to get a job, but we can come."

"Who's going to do your work?"

"I have a girl from the high school coming for a talk. I hope she works out. Mom says I'm leaving them in the lurch as usual," crying more.

"I'm sorry you're hurting, Blossom. I love you, and I'm so happy. I hope it doesn't cause you more problems. You better get some sleep now. Three my time, right?"

"Yes, honey. Thank you, I love you so much."

He wore his hat, and she picked him out immediately, dropping her carry-on and running. The familiar kick in the gut to see her—white blouse, denim skirt, white petticoat peeking out. Her hair was longer, flying; she looked tired. And then she was in his arms, so light, too light. She was crying into his neck. He moved her face to look at her. Way too pale, dark circles under her eyes. "Blossom?"

"I can't . . . I need . . . You have to . . ."

"I've got you, baby, I've got you," looking at Nixie over her head, almost angrily.

"She's been crying for the last hour, Rocco. Jeez, Blossom, I told you the plane couldn't go any faster."

"This isn't just the last hour, Nix. Sh, sh, go to sleep, baby, I'm here," tucking her head under his chin, rocking her. "What's been going on, Nix?"

"Well, she wouldn't eat, that's what caused all the trouble. She cried herself to sleep all the time, I didn't know what to do."

"Okay, okay," shifting her to his hip and putting his arm around Nix. "Let's get going." By the time they got to the truck she was fast asleep. He laid her on the crew seat and spent awhile fastening both seatbelts around her. "It's not the best, but I'll drive careful. You sit up here with me and fill me in."

"Nothing more to tell, really. You left, and she quit talking and started eating less and less. Then she almost fainted in the office, and Dad started in on putting her in the hospital, and she said she wanted to come home, and Mom said no, and she told me to say I wanted to come, and then they finally said we could if I get a job. That's about it."

"Did you want to come?"

"I like both places. I was having fun driving 'cause Sam helped me get my license, but Dad said I could use Blossom's car when she doesn't need it. I haven't been in town in the summer, so it should be fun. Jeez, Rocco, I didn't know what to do."

"You did what you could, Nix. I could help you with the job thing if you want to come out to the shop and do gofer work. It would be better than McDonald's."

"Thanks, Rocco. Blossom's got to work at Dad's office."

"She told me. By the looks of her, she better wait a few days, though." He pulled off the road a little. "Here, you drive for a while. This is a nice highway. North on 60, east on 80. I'll show you the GPS later."

"The roads were pretty empty where we were. How fast should I go?"

"Fifty-five, sixty. You're doing fine," turning so he could look at Blossom.

She woke while they were going up 79, looking a little bewildered. "Rocco, Rocco?"

"I'm here, baby girl, I'm right here. We're almost home, do you want to sit up?"

"In a minute. Is Nixie driving?"

"Yes, he's doing fine."

"Was I bad at the airport? Did I embarrass you."

"You can't embarrass me, Blossom. You were fine."

"The last couple days seem like a blur."

"Probably because you haven't eaten. What would you like?"

"Will we be by Casey's? May I have a chocolate milkshake?"

"Of course, baby girl. The exit's coming up, Nix. The second one, take it slow. Okay, check your mirrors and get into the middle lane for a left turn. Good job. I'm going to get a hot dog, want one?"

"Leave the door open, Blossom. Call if you get dizzy or anything. Nix and I are right here on the steps." They were waiting while she took a shower and got ready for bed. "I'll just stay until she's asleep."

"You can stay, Rocco, it doesn't bother me."

"No, I don't want to overstep my boundaries. Your parents are probably doubtful about this whole thing anyway, and I don't want the neighbors to see my truck leaving in the morning."

She came out in her smurfies. "I'm done."

"I'll tuck you in and get going. Rosalita will be here at breakfast time, right?"

She nodded, her hair spread out on the pillow, her skin almost translucent, dark circles under her eyes. "Do you want to talk about it, baby girl?"

She smiled weakly, her eyes closing. "Tomorrow. Can you lay with me?"

"I better not." She was too tired to protest. He kissed her lips gently. "Be sure to eat breakfast. Nixie is taking your car. I'll be here about eleven thirty. I love you beyond words, Blossom Dove." She faded away even before she could roll over.

The first day was quiet. He came at eleven and ate the sub he brought while she had the soup Rosalita had left for her. He went back to work while she napped. He and Nixie brought her favorite pizza at five. She had two-thirds of a piece and seemed to enjoy it. They cuddled and watched TV until she was tired.

She wanted to work the next day against his wishes. They got the car thing arranged, and Nix dropped her at the office. Rocco came at eleven thirty, and she introduced him around. "Do you leave for lunch, baby?"

"No. There's just forty-five minutes, so everyone stays here." They were in the break room.

"I brought you this drink. I hear it's not too bad when it's really cold." He gave her some chocolate Ensure, a third of a turkey sub, and a Hershey bar.

"Oh, honey, that's a lot to eat. I had a big breakfast."

"Oh, yeah, tell me about the big breakfast," grinning, his foot on her chair.

"I had some fruit, a bagel with peanut butter, and coffee. I'm fine, Rocco, really I am." She whispered, "They don't know what to do with me yet. They're not used to us being here in the summer."

"Good. I'll come get you at three thirty today. You can build up to five o'clock. Maybe to get out of their way, you can come next week to the shop and see what we need. Tell your mom when she calls, though."

He cornered one of the girls on his way out. "I'm coming back for her at three thirty. I don't know if her mother told you, but she hasn't been well, and five o'clock is pushing it the first week."

They all looked at each other when he left, shrugging shoulders. They had tremendous admiration and loyalty to Dr. and Mrs. Richards, and a couple of them had known Blossom since she started coming in at ten years old. Rocco had not been mentioned—not once. Mrs. Richards had just said Blossom was coming home early and they could take turns having a couple paid hours off.

"Do you want to go to your house or my house to rest up for dinner?"

"Your house!" It was the first twinkle he had seen in her eyes since Santa Fe.

"Just cuddling, no funny business yet." He shook his finger and grinned.

She pretend pouted but smiled, and the knot in his stomach started to loosen a little.

She twirled and clapped when she saw the closet. "Oh, Rocco, what beautiful work. It's the most beautiful closet I've ever seen." He knew it wasn't true, her closet at home was twice the size, but his heart grew two sizes, and he wanted to build her more things. "You're so wonderful. I can't believe you thought of this for me."

"We can't have a coat rack like at the clinic. I'm still thinking about the doors. We don't have a lot of room."

"Do you want to lay down here or go down and sit in our chair?"

"I don't need a nap today, honey."

"Baby, Nix said you haven't been sleeping, so let's take a nap."

"Okay, let's sit in our chair and watch TV."

As soon as he got her settled in his lap, he said, "Tell me what happened."

"Tomorrow."

"No. You said that yesterday and the day before. Today. Right now."

She took a deep breath. "Well," she whispered, her finger over her lips, "if I was really quiet, they didn't notice me. Then I heard them saying they should send me to Europe to meet Aunt Mim. I started eating a couple bites and leaving the table so they couldn't bring it up, but the food started tasting like sand, and I couldn't get it down, and"—tears started to fall—"and then I got dizzy at work, and Dad said he was going to put an IV in, and Mom said I was just being bad, and I said I wanted to go home, and" sobbing, "I just wanted to fade away."

He had been biting his lip. "But, baby girl," he said softly into her hair, "precious baby girl, didn't you realize you'd fade away from me too?"

"I-I lost my common sense. I just thought I'd float in the air to you, and Nixie said I wouldn't have the strength to come home, and I asked him to say he wanted to come, and then I had a tantrum. Oh, Rocco, I always do everything wrong."

"Sweetie, baby, no, you don't. You were backed into a corner. Oh god, I shouldn't have left you there. You told me. I wasn't listening again," his head in his hand.

"No, no, darling, it wasn't you. It was me, I was the bad one, I—"

"Stop, Blossom, don't say that again. You're here now. We'll get you better. Promise me you won't do that again, please promise me."

"I promise, I promise."

He kissed her and hugged her even closer. "Blossom, I can't lose you. Baby, you have no idea how much I love you. Promise me again—you could be a doctor already. You know how dangerous that was. Oh god . . ."

"I promise, Rocco, I'll be strong, I will."

He leaned his head back, putting her head against his chest, the intense emotion draining them; and they slept.

As usual, he never moved when he woke. He sat listening to her breathe until she woke and stirred. "Sweetie, have you gone to the bathroom yet—number two, I mean?"

"Rocco!"

"I'm serious, baby, it's a good sign your system's working okay."

"I haven't, but I had a lot of fiber today, so I probably will in the morning. Jeez Louise!"

He laughed out loud. "Let's get freshened up for dinner. We better call Nix and see what he's doing."

Between work and Nix's plans, she was home five days before they could schedule being together from four until midnight. He picked her up and brought her to his house. He had made two of her favorites, salad with strawberries and pecans and panko-coated tilapia. He was still pushing the Ensure and thought she had gained a pound or two, and her cheeks were pink, and her eyes were bright.

She flirted outrageously with him during dinner, whispering close, her tongue touching his ear, feeding him, licking her lips. "If this is a contest," he said huskily, "you win."

She clapped. "Where's my prize?"

He winked. "It's upstairs under my pillow."

"Really? I really do get a prize?" She ran for the stairs. He made sure the doors were locked and followed.

She was standing, her mouth agape, two fingers holding her blue panties with pink roses.

"You couldn't find them, so when I did, I kept them under my pillow."

"But that was the bad day. I don't want to remember that." She tossed them and put her hands on her hips.

He winked seductively and said, "Well, it's not a bad day now, and I love them."

"Crazy man," unbuttoning his shirt, her tongue in his mouth.

"Let me fix the bed," breathing hard. "Sweetie, I'm scared, I don't know if you're ready. You're so fragile."

"I'm ready, I'm not scared, and I don't feel fragile. Hurry."

"Baby, baby, easy now," as she wrapped her legs around him, biting his chin.

"No easy. Love me, love me."

He wanted to be careful, had every intention to keep alert, make sure she was okay; but she was biting his neck, digging him with one hand, sliding him with the other, wanting him in, growling, "Blossom, Bloss-ah-ah." The world went away.

This wasn't frustration with the coming school separation. This was fear of a permanent separation. He rolled with her attached, not a scintilla of space between them. Now he on top; now she, "Never leave me, never, never, I love you, I love you." She was beneath him when she came, the force arching her into him as she screamed, biting the side of his hand he offered her with Tiger not there. He groaned and growled as he released, drenched and panting.

When she could lift her head, she licked the side of his face. "Thank you, thank you."

"Don't say that, baby," gasping. "We make love together."

"Thank you for making me feel alive again," rolling to her side, her hands under her chin.

His tears dropped on her shoulder as she slept.

She had been home seven days. His phone said Cal Richards. He held his breath, "Cal?"

"Rocco, how is she?"

"She seems much better, sir. I think she's gained a pound or two. Her color is good, her eyes are bright. I apologize for whatever part I played in this, Cal."

"I'm the one who dropped the ball, Rocco. My god, she was right in front of me. I talked to her, she says she's eating."

"She's never going to be a big eater, but she has part of a sandwich and fruit for lunch and usually fish and a vegetable at dinner. I've been giving her Ensure. I don't know if it's just hype, but it can't hurt, can it?"

"That's fine as long as she'll drink it. I'll check her when we get home. Thanks for using Nix. He working out?"

"No problems at all. He has a great work ethic. I saw that out there. The guys say he'll do anything he's asked."

Clearing his throat, "Well, I thought you'd be the best one to ask about Blossom. We'll be back in about three weeks. Feel free to call with any problems."

The days went by in a surreal, sleepy haze for him. He was leaving at lunch, early at quitting, and getting there at six to make up for it. After a couple weeks, she took a day to come and talk to Helen about the office computers. He left them alone but was within earshot and was impressed with her approach.

"What do you really like about this system? Do you think to yourself, I wish I could do this, or that, or, if only? What do you really hate about it?"

He knew Helen had been expecting her to come in and say here's the way it will be from now on. He was happy to see her softening up. She had been through as much as he had, and he didn't want her to think her opinion didn't count.

After being with Helen forty-five minutes, she came in his office. "Now I have to interview you."

He gave her his Groucho Marx and said "Do you soften me up with a kiss?"

"Oh yes, that's part of the package. What do you want to be able to do with your system?"

"Whatever she's doing. Plus my personal stuff—bank account, investments, like that. We're accumulating a lot of money. I want to be able to transfer it and know it's safe. Know what the inventory is, who uses it, for what, whatever else you think."

"What you have is pretty old. Do you want to spend any money?"

"Whatever you think."

"I'll come Wednesday, Thursday, Friday next week. Some equipment will be coming Fedex, just set it aside."

"Do you need the company credit card number?"

She smiled coyly. "I'll get it."

"What!" He laughed.

"Don't worry, it will be the last time anyone can get it, and if they even try, you'll know about it."

He just shook his head, grinning.

He had never had friends. He had people he met up with to drink, but he never considered them friends. Gradually, Nix was someone he felt really comfortable with, even with the five-years difference. Without being too obvious, he knew Nix was trying to give him and Blossom as much time together as possible. He seemed older than he was.

"Honey, Nixie wants to have a pool party before Dad and Mom get home. Should I just get some trays of pizza?"

"Let me take care of it, baby. I don't want you taking on too much yet."

"Rocco, I'm fine."

"I know. I just don't want to take chances. What day and how many kids?"

"I think Sunday afternoon. He'd probably like it at night, but they might get a little wild. And I think I'll ask Rosalita and her family to keep the group mixed ages."

"Okay, let me know the number. I'll get pizza, salad, and a tub of pop."

That was Monday. On Tuesday at 3:00 a.m., his phone chirped. His feet were immediately on the floor and he breathed a little when the screen said Unavailable. "Yes?"

"Rocco, it's Nix."

"Is she okay. Where are you?"

"She's fine, she's fine. It's just that, well, actually, I'm at the police station. A carful of us got picked up. I wasn't drinking, honest, they checked. A couple were, and they have to stay, but Slim and I are allowed to leave. I told them my parents were out of town. Blossom's too young to come and get me. It has to be someone over twenty-one."

"I'm on my way. Which station?"

"Verner Township."

"Okay, hang tight. I'll be right there."

"I'm here for Phoenix Richards. He came in with some other kids and is allowed to leave." He recognized the desk officer but didn't let on.

"You over twenty-one? A relative?"

"Yes, and no, but will be. I'm with his sister."

He buzzed someone, "Send out Richards," and gave him a paper to sign. He looked at Rocco and winked. "The irony of this striking you, Carnavale?"

"Very much so, sir," grinning.

"Where's your car?"

"It's down at McDonald's. I'm sorry about this, Rocco."

"The only thing bothering me right now, Nix, is she's home alone. I've been counting on you being there by midnight. Most people know your parents are gone all summer. I have her there by eleven, and I don't like to think of her being alone."

"I've been there. I really have. It won't happen again."

Rocco pulled next to Blossom's car in McDonald's lot and turned to him. "I'm glad you weren't drinking, Nix, but it's dangerous being with someone who has been. This is kinda my watch, and I'd sure hate to have to call your parents about an accident. I'm only going to say that I've been in almost every kind of trouble there is, and if I hadn't shaped up, I wouldn't have met your sister. Nothing scares me, but the thought of that scares me more than I can tell you. This is the time in your life to decide what kind of man you want to be, and that feeling you got tonight when you saw the flashing lights and heard the siren isn't the path you want to go down."

He punched him in the arm. "Why didn't Slim's dad sign you out?"

"He said he didn't want to do something behind my dad's back."

"Well, I'm not going to call your dad, but in case he gets anything in the mail from the police, you better tell him. If their paperwork is still slow, you have a week or so, but you never know with computers. I'll follow you home. Check on her and flash the porch light. She's been tired, so maybe she doesn't know you never came home. Don't forget the alarm."

"Thanks again, Rocco."

"Hey, stuff happens. I'll be around."

Nix was at work right on time. Rocco just nodded to him. At eleven, Nix said, "I guess Blossom's eating with the other girls today?"

"Yeah, I'm backing off a little. She's doing fine."

"I don't mean to be a pest, but could I talk to you at lunch or at quitting time?"

"Sure, meet you at the picnic table at noon."

Nix was visibly nervous and eating fast.

"What's up?"

Taking a breath and talking fast, "Uh-h, well, I guess most of my friends are, you know, experienced, so I don't want to ask dumb questions and get razzed." Rocco just nodded and continued eating. "So I was wondering about, you know, protection," coloring and squeezing his Coke can.

Rocco kept his voice casual. "I was in the same spot about your age. What I did was go to the CVS in Edinboro so I wouldn't bump into anybody. I took my time and looked things over. That way you don't just grab something and run. There's lots of brands, types, sizes. If you're not sure, buy a few and try them."

"Try them?"

"Yeah, you know, before you actually need one. How to open it, get it on, like that."

"Jeez, I guess I didn't think that far."

"Let me ask you something, Nix. You asking just for information, or do you have a girl?"

"Well, there is this one girl."

Rocco nodded. "So did they cover in school that anyone under eighteen is off limits? I mean, legally you could get in serious trouble, and it goes the other way too—you being under eighteen." At Nix's crestfallen look, he grinned and punched his arm. "Crappy, huh?"

"But a lot of the guys . . ."

"I'll tell you what. If they are, they're taking an awful chance—legally, if it's girls in your group, or disease-wise, if it's street girls. But I'm thinking a lot of the talk you're hearing is just that, talk."

"But if the girl says it's okay?"

"Doesn't matter, Nix. Her parents wouldn't think it's okay. And I hate to bring this up, but your parents have a little money, and even if the girl's parents didn't want you arrested, they might want to sue."

"Holy sh—cow!"

"Yeah, wouldn't be a call your dad would like to get. Tell you what. This is your first summer being home. Just enjoy driving, hanging out, have fun, but try to avoid the situations where you can't think straight, and hold off as long as you can. If you need me to go with you to Edinboro, I will." Nix still seemed uncomfortable. "Anything else?"

He looked down. "This girl said she knows ways to make me feel good with no danger."

"Aw Christ, Nix, who the hell you hanging out with?"

"Really, Rocco, she's a nice girl. She says it's what everyone in high school does."

Rocco shook his head. "I guess I quit school too soon. Seriously, Nix, now I'm going to come off like an SOB. Back to deciding what kind of man you want to be, I wish someone had told me what a jerk I was sooner than they did. I'm ashamed of things I did, and it doesn't go away, Nix. Just let me tell you this. Until you've been with someone a long time, years, I'm talking, there is absolutely nothing in it for the girl, what you're talking about. Nothing. So you got to ask yourself—why? Do they want paid? Do they want you to be their slave for a few weeks until the novelty wears off? What do they want from you? Hey, I know your hormones are raging, but don't do something you'll regret for a lot of years. It's not the way to go." He stood up and tossed his garbage in the can. "I'm not in a position to preach, Nix. You're a great kid, a smart kid, and in the end, it's up to you."

"I'll just ask you one last time, baby, and then I promise I'll back off. What did you have for lunch?"

"I had half a pita with Rosalita's chicken salad, yogurt, and water. I know how to eat, honey, and I promised you. You don't have to worry."

They were at Mangia's so he could have a steak. He'd been cooking fish for her for days, and she knew he wanted more. "I don't have a bathing suit, baby girl. Should we go to Walmart after?"

"Let's go to Peebles. That's where Mom gets a lot of Nixie's things."

"Am I going to see you in a bikini?"

She smiled. "I don't wear bikinis," and at his questioning look, whispered, "I don't want to shave."

"Women shave!"

"They have to with those tiny suits, or they get waxed."

"Waxed?"

"Uh-huh, at a salon. They put a waxy paste or strip on, and then they pull it off," making a face.

"At a salon? You mean someone else does it?"

She grinned and nodded.

"You'd never do that, would you?"

"Never. I don't like pain. I imagine movie stars and models get laser treatments so it will be permanent."

"So what do you wear, then?"

"I have a suit with a skirt and one with shorts. Which one would you like—the skirt is red, and the shorts are denim."

To him the shorts sounded safer, so he picked them. Then, "You can't ever say I told you or even hint that I told you, but I had the talk with Nix today."

"What do you mean the talk? I'm sure he had that years ago. Well, a few anyway."

"I mean the talk about teenage boys and protection."

"Oh, Rocco"—anguished—"not Nixie. Are you sure it was necessary?"

"He asked me, Blossom. You have to answer the questions if they come up. Do you know who hangs around with his group?"

"I'm ashamed to say I don't. I know Slim better than the rest, but they've always just been Nixie's little friends. Oh dear, oh, I don't like this."

"I'm not sure if it worked, but I discouraged him as much as I could. It's up to him, baby." She just shook her head and looked sad.

The party was at two. Nix said plan for a dozen, his regular buddies and cross-country friends, then Rosalita and her son and daughter. He planned food for twenty and told Nix to let him know right away if some came who weren't invited and don't try to be a nice guy about it. He didn't think there'd be a problem on a Sunday afternoon, but he kept his eyes open.

By one o'clock, he and Nix had the backyard all set up—tables covered with red-checkered vinyl, extra folding chairs they had in storage, aluminum tubs, and a huge salad bowl he had borrowed from Mangia's. He let out an audible oomph from the familiar kick in the gut when Blossom came out in her suit. "Blossom"—carefully—"they aren't shorts."

"Yes, they are, honey, see, there's legs."

"But, sweetie, that's the size of a bikini."

"It's a bikini with legs."

"And the top, it's . . ."

"Rocco, this is a swimming party. Everyone will have suits on."

"But it's a swimming party with teenage boys, baby."

"And teenage girls who'll be wearing smaller suits than this. That's the end of the discussion, honey."

He shivered when she turned, and the tiny suit showed her dimples, her hair still long from New Mexico, her painted toenails. It killed him to think of them looking at her. She turned and saw the torment on his face and came to kiss him. "I'm not going to do this very often, but you've been so wonderful, I'll spoil you this one time and put on a cover-up." He smiled, but his eyes were moist.

He, Blossom, and Rosalita chatted while the younger people swam. He was much more comfortable when she put on a gauzy white dress with denim bows at the shoulders. It looked see-through, but there was so much of it, he could barely make out the suit underneath. He tried to figure out if one of the girls was the one Nix talked about. If she was here, it was probably the one who asked Nix, "Where's that nice car of yours, Nix," and then wandered away to flirt with someone else when he said it was his sister's car. He sighed. He'd done the best he could—hope it was good enough, then laughed inside, an old man at twenty-one.

He realized Blossom had asked Rosalita if she had a free day to come to Rocco's. "You know, laundry, dusting, sweeping?"

"Baby, I can do it. I always have."

"I know, honey, but now you have the house plus the business. It would be one less thing to worry about." She nuzzled his ear, causing all the guys to look at each other. "Please. I don't want coming down to see me to be a burden."

"I have Tuesdays or Thursdays free," Rosalita said.

"Why don't you start the Thursday after Labor Day," Rocco said. "I'll leave the door unlocked and the key in the bowl on the table for you to take. Your money will be there too." Blossom clapped happily.

Her parents came home. Her dad gave her a checkup, blood work, urinalysis, and could find nothing. She looked wonderful, glowing and happy. Her parents' office was running smoothly. At the shop, Rocco and Helen were happy with their new system, and Bob was getting there. The crew was getting larger. If he wanted to, Rocco could see everyone come and go from the cameras in the warehouse. The Monday and Friday morning meetings gave him the pulse of the crew's attitudes, and there was seldom any downtime between jobs.

He had already told Helen and Bob he would be gone every third Friday to Philly, and his holidays would match Blossom's time off. They couldn't live the way they had the year before. The days of "I'll try to get away" were over. He needed to be with her. That's just the way it was going to be.

She stayed home for dinner a couple of days after her parents came home, but on the third day, he picked her up at work and brought her home at eleven as they had been doing. She rode in with her mother since Nix was using her car. It was uncomfortable.

The anniversary of the day they met, two dozen roses came to the office. Everyone made a fuss except her mother. They had dinner at Mangia's. She wore the same outfit she had worn their first date there. He gave her a pearl.

She gave him a Rolex. "Baby girl, I can't wear this. When I measure jobs, people will think we don't need the work."

"Then you'll wear it when we go out. I saw you looking at them. I want you to have it."

"You're unbelievable, Blossom Dove." He lifted his glass. "To the day my life began."

"To the day *our life* began."

"Remember when I asked you if you had a bra on with that top?"

"I do. It was very scary."

"Let's go to the house and check it out."

"That's the worst line I've ever heard."

"How about 'check and see if I need a haircut'?"

"That one I like." She giggled.

They were folding down the bedclothes after taking off their own clothes. "This has been the most wonderful month, Rocco. If I didn't have to go home, it would have been perfection. I thought the summer would be horrible."

He was sitting on the edge of the bed. She was standing in front of him "This is perfection," running his hands over her curves, kissing her lightly. "Are we good for school? I don't have to worry about you eating?"

"I lost my common sense for a while, honey, but you don't have to worry ever again. Now we have to talk about your problem."

"I don't have a problem," his jaw tightening up.

"Rocco"—carefully, tipping her head—"it's happening more and more often, about what I wear or who looks at me."

"Blossom, I'm not one of those men. I'll never tell you what to wear or who to talk to." Then he pulled her close and whispered, "You're the only good thing in my world. I never had anything. I thought buying my first truck was the highlight of my life. How do you think I felt when you said you loved me? I'll try harder, baby girl, I will."

"I know." She cupped his face in her hands and ran her tongue around his lips. "There's entirely too much talking going on here," climbing up and wrapping her legs around him. "Happy one year anniversary, Mr. Carnavale."

He groaned and laid her on the bed, a picture flashing in his mind of that first day—her walking to her car nervously, her hair swinging in time with her hips. Now she was here, and he was going where only she could take him.

It was eleven thirty. Too late, and she'd hear about it, but she'd had to sleep a little. She was sitting on the commode, her arms around her knees.

He had showered for an early meeting, got dressed again, and was running his fingers through his hair. "Honey," she said, "you never look at yourself in the mirror."

"I'm looking at myself right now."

"No. You're looking at your hair. You're looking past yourself. No wonder you don't know how handsome you are. I wonder why that is."

"Baby, I always just made sure I was presentable and got going." Then he looked at her intently, with a strange remembering look. "When you're surprised you lived through the night, you get up and get out."

She put her hands over her mouth, her eyes swimming with tears.

In the truck on the way to her house, "You said you told your father you'd kill him. How were you going to do that?"

"Let's don't talk about this, sweetie."

"Okay." But as usual, she kept going. "I just wondered how, honey. You were only fourteen."

"I bought a gun on the street. Okay? I had a gun."

"Oh, Rocco, no," with disbelief. "You were just a little boy."

"I got it, and I learned how to use it out in the woods. That's it. Now drop it."

"But where did you keep it?"

Big sigh, "I kept it on the nightstand and put it under the bed during the day."

"What did you do with it after, you know, the funeral?"

"It's still under the bed," he said without thinking.

The truck got very quiet. She got very still. "You mean the bed we've been making love on? It's under there?"

"Baby, it's just a piece of machinery. The safety's on. It's nothing. And actually, I didn't know what to do with it and kind of forgot about it."

"Would you take it away tomorrow? Would you not have it there anymore?"

"I will, Blossom, I will."

"I don't want to think it's anywhere around ever again, please."

"It's gone, baby."

Bob and his son were hunters. He tried to make light of it. "Hey, Bob, back in my misspent youth, I bought a gun. Now I don't know how to get rid of it. I can't toss it in French Creek or even Conneaut Lake, or some kids might find it. I could probably take it up to Lake Erie. Any suggestions?"

"Give it to me, I'll take care of it." He didn't ask him why he had it. He was pretty sure he knew.

"Thanks, Bob, it's in the truck wrapped in a towel."

"I took care of that situation, baby girl," when he picked her up at three. They were going to the Erie Mall to get him some clothes, the trip they had planned months before when her mother took her to Virginia Tech.

She kissed his cheek. "Thank you, honey," whispering. "We can't have a home based on love with one of those in it, Rocco. Especially one with that kind of history. It upsets my stomach."

He took her hand and kissed her palm. "All over, my baby."

"Do you need any cargo shorts, honey?"

"I can't imagine needing those, baby." They had picked out two pairs of slacks, one gray, one tan. Two sport coats, one navy, one tan and gray checks. Two turtlenecks, one cream cashmere, one tan silk blend. Four dress shirts, two chambray, two windowpane plaids. "This is more clothes than I'll ever need, baby."

"Your dress boots are still nice, and you have plenty of casual shirts and jeans. I think we've done well. You never know when a measuring job will be important enough to dress for, and now you're prepared." They left his business address for shipment to him after alterations. She made a mental note to get him some business cards. She was so proud of him.

She vetoed Outback Steakhouse and wrinkled her nose at Red Lobster, "too much butter," but relented when he said he would tell them how she wanted hers cooked. He got surf and turf; she, the three-scallop skewer from the appetizer section. The only annoyance a call from her mother. "We're at Red Lobster in Erie, Mom, remember I said we'd be getting Rocco some clothes." Rolling her eyes, "It was only twelve-fifteen, Mom, I'm getting plenty of rest. I have everything ready to go. Can we talk tomorrow? About midnight. Okay, bye, bye." She heaved a big sigh.

"It's so much better than it was, baby girl, cut her some slack." She stuck her tongue out at him.

She got teary and testy, but the day came anyway. There was no question he would be taking her. Her group and Dr. Ng were all arriving early. She wanted them to stay in her room to save money, but he worried about other early arrivals. They checked into room 422 and then went to her dorm. Sprayed Febreze, made the bed, set up her desk, her clothes, water in the fridge, PowerBars in the drawer. "Don't use these for meals, baby."

"I won't," but she was getting quieter and quieter.

They stopped at the hotel dining room. She ordered the red snapper and risotto she usually liked but soon was pushing it around the plate.

"Blossom"—softly but sternly—"I'm not coming down here if you get sick if that's what you're thinking."

Indignantly, "I was not thinking that!" Then whining, "I'm just not hungry. I want to go upstairs."

"You won't have the strength to love me if you don't eat. You promised I wouldn't have to worry about this again. Please Blossom, I'm begging you."

"You don't have to worry, I promise."

He motioned to the waitress. "A chocolate milkshake, please." And then, carefully, "I imagine the clinic here has lots of kinds of doctors, huh?"

"Uh-huh, sure."

"Maybe, if you feel like it, you could talk to someone, you know, about your childhood . . . the competitions, like that."

"The only thing wrong with me is I want to be with you."

"And we're making progress, don't you think? One year under our belt, your parents have to know we're a couple, I'll be here every three weeks, and"—he gave her a lecherous look—"I made you a closet."

She laughed and drank some milkshake. "I love you so much, Rocco, I want to be with you every day, not every three weeks."

"Hey, remember when we thought six weeks was short."

"Oh, my darling, please, please, don't make me do that. I just couldn't do that."

"We don't have to, baby girl. I'll be here before you know it. I'll call Friday. You call if you need me. We can do this, Blossom." She nodded with big eyes and a weak smile.

In the elevator, she was flirting with him with her eyes, backing into him and wiggling. "You're feisty now, but I'm going to have you crying uncle in a few minutes." He laughed.

She giggled and whispered, "We'll see who cries uncle first."

He did. She came out of the bathroom with her lotion and started rubbing it on her tummy, her hips, her breasts. "Uncle, uncle," he cried, reaching for her. She stayed just out of his reach for a few minutes, rolling off the other side of the bed, ducking under his arm, finally letting him catch her. She rubbed his hardness with her hair, bit his nipples, straddled him, and guided him in as he whimpered and moaned. "Three weeks you say, can we make it two?"

"Two, two," he panted.

"Do I still have all the power?" She was moving fast, her hair in his face.

"All the power, all the power, Blossom, oh-my-god, Blossom, Blos-ah-ah-h."

She buried her face in his neck, panting, "Love you, love you," and rolled into her sleeping position.

When he could breathe again and open his eyes, he traced his finger down her spine, still prominent. He read the little book each morning that she had sent him but still didn't feel he knew how to pray, so he just said, *Oh god, oh god, please, please, I'll do anything.*

In the morning, she smiled at him mischievously. "You don't really have to come every two weeks, I just wanted to hear you say it." They were standing at her dorm entrance. It was time to go. "Why have you been looking at me funny this morning?"

"You know why. You're unbelievable, you know that?"

"I don't, but as long as you think so, that's all that's important. I love you, Rocco Anthony, to the moon and back."

"I love you, Blossom Dove, beyond words. Go."

For the first time, she didn't cry. She ran into her dorm, determined not to let him down, ran upstairs, opened a PowerBar to cement her promise, and opened her computer. *Eight months*, she whispered to herself.

He came down every three weeks. They were on a first-name basis with the reception staff at the Hilton. Room 422 was a second home. He got her a pearl for her birthday and silver hair combs with turquoise stones.

Her parents came for Thanksgiving, so he went to his sister's. He promised Madison and Marlee he'd bring Aunt Blossom soon. His mother was failing but seemed content. The new bathroom he'd paid for was a decent job. Lindsay said she was afraid a nursing home, or at least assisted living, was looming. He was unsettled driving home and wondered if his mother should have stayed in Meadville. Blossom told him being with the girls was better than household aides, and he felt a little better.

Christmas was 100 percent different from the year before. He flew to New Mexico with her family. She was coming from Philadelphia the following day. He and Nix were already set up in a room, so there was no awkward who's going to be where from her parents. They stole some kisses, and he wanted to sneak into her room, but she was too nervous.

The Richards' tradition was to open gifts after dinner. Rocco and Blossom had volunteered to cook, but Mim and Lourdes wouldn't hear of it. The prime rib was fabulous. Even Blossom had a palm-sized piece. Everything else had the southwest flavor he wasn't crazy about but was good. The atmosphere was comfortable. He was pretty sure the wines didn't hurt. Even Blossom's mother was relaxed.

He was anxious for Blossom to open her gift and hoped no one would find it inappropriate. He was overwhelmed when Mim gave him the picture of the young Blossom all in white that he had admired. He gave pictures also. One to Mim of her and Blossom at the Stable laughing, heads together. One to her parents of them, Blossom, and Nix looking at a sunset one night at the clinic. When he gave Nix his, he said to Cal and Elaine, "This is a company joke, he could never keep track of his," as Nix opened a DeWalt tape measure.

Blossom gave him a Chief Joseph blanket and said shyly, "I thought it would look nice on your brown leather sofa." Everyone admired it, and she and Rocco smiled at each other knowing it was because their naked bodies had stuck to the leather a time or two.

She opened her box and looked puzzled. "My smurfies?"

"New smurfies." He smiled.

She held the top up. Sure enough, it was her smurfies, but brand-new. "But how?" She was incredulous.

"I found the material online and had that lady on Park Street make them." He laughed. "I think all of us have been holding our breath about the other ones. They are practically transparent."

She shook her head and hugged them and rubbed them against her cheek. "I was afraid they would be gone. Oh, this is the best present ever." He was sitting on the floor and fell over when she jumped into his arms, covering his face with kisses.

Her mother finally said, "We all get the idea you're grateful, Blossom. Let Rocco breathe."

They all went to the airport together. Blossom's plane left first. They walked away a little to kiss good-bye. "I'll be down soon. I'll come for New Year's if you want me to."

"I'll be fine. I'm in the middle of something. What will you do?"

"I volunteered to work at Mangia's so someone else can have some time, but you tell me if you need me. No matter what, baby, promise you'll call if you need me."

"I will. I promise. Thank you for my smurfies. I'll thank you properly when you come."

"Mmm, I like the sound of that."

He came in three weeks. He always stayed two nights now, so they had Saturday afternoons for touristy things, as she called them. It took them two Saturdays to cover the seven historic houses along the Schuylkill River. He loved the architecture and craftsmanship. They were standing on the terrace of the Sweetbriar Mansion, looking at the river.

"Would you like a house like this, baby girl. I'll build it for you."

"Honey, we don't need a big house. Your house is fine. Softly, "Does it feel like your house yet, Rocco? It's hard to believe it's been sixteen months since the funeral."

He smiled with a faraway look. "On good days, it seems like another life, someone else's life. On bad days, it seems like yesterday."

"I don't want you to have any bad days. Why do you have bad days? Are you getting headaches again?"

"Sweetie, any day is a bad day when you're not there. And life gets in the way sometimes. Everybody has bad days." He winked. "When you're finally there, I might have bad days, but there won't be any bad nights."

"Crazy man." She giggled.

Early on, their time together was magical. It was Dr. Ng who told her about the Ninth Street Italian Market downtown after he had asked about Rocco's last name. They spent a couple of Saturdays there. She glowed as he was transfixed by the food, preparations, and displays. One day they strolled and nibbled all afternoon. Another rainy day, they ate at Ralph's and went to Sarcone's Bakery next door.

Gradually, the goal she had set for herself crept into their weekends. She had never had to work hard for anything. Now she was working as hard as she could, wanting it so badly and worried she would fail. When he got to the hotel on Fridays, she was weepy and tense. They started staying in the room on Friday nights, loving, eating, loving again.

"Don't cry when we make love, baby girl. You're breaking my heart."

"You're going to go, you're going to go."

"Baby, I'm here now. It's so much better than it was. What's bothering you?"

"You're going to go."

He tipped her head up with his thumbs so she couldn't turn away. "We're here. We're together. Let's give ourselves something to get us through three more weeks." She finally smiled a little and tightened her legs around him.

They limped into spring. The year they thought would be so much better vacillated between joy and frustration. She was exhausted; he was worried. The third week of April, she had to cancel for a business trip with Dr. Ng and Chet.

"Will you be in Baltimore again? I'll come there."

"No, darling. It's Raleigh, North Carolina. Just in and out, a day and a half."

"I'll fly down there."

"That's foolish, sweetheart."

232

"Why don't you want me to come?" His voice rising, "You never want me around on those trips. What's going on?"

He heard her fist hit the desk. His mouth fell open. "Rocco, don't do this. It's harder on me than it is on you," her voice catching through tears.

"I'm sorry, baby. I'm sorry. I should be thinking of you, and all I can think of is the distance is killing me. I have to move down there, Blossom."

"Oh, darling. We have to be mature and responsible, remember. I'll call Friday night like the other times. I love you so much, Rocco."

It was the middle of May. She would be twenty in October. For the first time that school year, they had been apart five weeks. She had traveled with Dr. Ng two weekends in a row. He was angry when they talked; she was weepy. "You tell him no the next time. I mean it, Blossom, we can't do this anymore."

"I'll tell him, I'll tell him. I love you, I love you."

She had to call him. Goodness, she couldn't wait until the last minute. What if he couldn't get away on Saturday. Why am I so nervous. Just then her phone chimed. She was lucky she heard it. It was six fifteen in the morning. She was just getting into the shower. A stab of fear, "Rocco?"

A hoarse, desperate, "Blossom, I need you."

"Darling, what is it? Is it your head, your head?" her heart pounding.

Gravelly sobs, "Can you get the just-in-case money and come to Pittsburgh? I need you."

"I'll call you right back."

"I took the earliest one. It's at nine fifty-five, gets in at eleven twenty-two. It's US Air 3341. Can you write that down, honey? Can you drive? Should I come all the way. Oh, honey, what is it?"

"I woke up. I hurt. I need you so bad. I'll get there."

"Get a room at the airport Hyatt, honey, and lay down. I'm coming."

She called a cab, washed her face, put a few things in her Coach shoulder bag, and took all the money from the safe. "Can you get me to the airport by eight-fifteen? There's twenty dollars in it for you."

"No problem."

She tried to call him before she got on the plane. No answer. *Oh god, oh god, please let him be all right.*

He was waiting for her, leaning against a wall, his eyes just slits, pain radiating from him. "Oh my darling, you should have gone to a room, I would have found you."

233

"I was there, 512." He handed her a keycard.

"Rocco, you need a doctor, you don't need me."

His eyes closed. "I need you."

She was guiding him down the concourse, saw a newsstand, and stopped. "Excedrin Migraine and a water, please." She gave him three tablets and flagged down a motorized cart with a twenty in her hand. "He's not well, could you take us to the entrance of the hotel."

He had been on the bed, but it wasn't unmade. She sat him in a chair, pulled the drapes shut, darkened the room as much as she could, and helped him get undressed and in bed.

"I need you."

"You need rest, honey, but I'll be right there. Let me go to the bathroom." She freshened up, calmly undressed, folding her clothes neatly, and slid under him as he raised up. He whimpered. "I need to smell you, I need to taste you."

"I'm here, I'm here, whatever you need." She slid her hands down his stomach to massage him to hardness. "Do you need help? I'm here."

"More, more. Put me in. I love you, I'm sorry."

She put her hands around his neck to move with him, wanted to stay detached to be sure he was all right, but it had been five weeks. She was mad at the world that kept them apart. Mad that he'd been in pain and alone. She knew it was like poking a stick into a wounded bear, it was insanity, but she couldn't help it—she bit his neck in anger. He bucked and growled, she bit and clawed, and they screamed together. Her orgasm shook her. She didn't have Tiger, so she bit him some more. He was sobbing as he came, "Blossom, Blossom."

She fought for air, the exertion almost too much for her. Through his pain, he gasped, "Breathe, breathe." And then, "Again, *again*, I need you again."

"No again," she heaved.

"AGAIN!"

"Again after you rest." It mollified him, and his eyes closed. She started to slide away, but he held her wrist like a vise. "I didn't get a shower this morning," she whispered. "Go to sleep."

"Don't go. I need you here."

"I'm right here. I won't leave. Sleep."

They both slept. He was looking at her when she woke. His hair was still damp with perspiration. "Your eyes look a little better. Is the pain easing up?"

"It's better. I have to talk to you about something, baby."

Would the fear never leave her? Just a stab, but still there. "What is it, honey?"

"I can't do this anymore, Blossom. I thought I was going to die this morning without seeing you again. I get up, and you're not there. I come home, and you're not there. Life is too short, we can't be apart. I have to sell the business and come down. I mean it."

"Oh my darling, I have something to tell you."

"No, you can't talk me out of it. It was like I was in a pit this morning. I didn't know if I could climb out."

"Sh-sh. Can you come and get me Saturday. I'm done there."

"I'll come and get you for the summer, but I still have to sell the business, baby."

"No, I mean I'm done, honey. I'm not going back to Penn. I was going to call you tomorrow."

His body was still. He looked at her with cloudy eyes. "What do you mean?" The effects of the migraine bewildering him.

"I mean I'm done, Rocco. I've submitted my thesis for my doctorate. I don't care if I get it or not. I'm transferring to Pitt." She rubbed his back and kissed his cheek. "Do you think you could drive an hour and not sell the business? Some weekends you wouldn't even have to come. I'd come to you."

As it dawned on him, the tears came. "You mean, it's over? But you said three years. How could you be done?" He wiped his nose and eyes with the edge of the sheet.

"It was all because of you, my darling. Back on my eighteenth birthday when my mother asked me what I wanted from life. I just made something up, but when I asked you, you never hesitated. You said you wanted me. I knew I wanted you, and I knew I had to get out of Penn first, so I made a plan, and now I'm done."

"Why didn't you tell me, baby?"

"I couldn't, honey, I couldn't say it out loud in case I couldn't do it. As time went on, I started to think I could. Dr. Ng says he can't guarantee anything, but he says it's good work. It's done. It's printed. I know it's good work, and now I don't care. I contacted Pitt Medical School, and I start in July."

"Oh baby, baby, all by yourself, you carried that. I didn't even help."

"There are a couple ways you can help, my darling."

"What? I'll do anything."

"Well, Dr. Ng and Chet will throw some work my way, but I might need help with my rent now and then. I don't want dorm life again. I wanted you to be able to stay over."

"I'll pay your rent, baby girl, I'll pay it all."

"No, not all. Just sometimes. I want to be self-sufficient."

"Whatever you say. Oh god, whatever you say. What else, sweetie?"

She hesitated and bit her lip. "Honey, I can't come home and go on dates with you. I just can't. We've come too far. So, so, may I live at your house?" She said it hurriedly and chewed on her lip.

His eyes got big and dark. He lost his breath. "Blossom, Blossom?"

She tilted her head and smiled. "Please?"

He sat up and crawled to the headboard. She came to him and put her head on his chest and cried. "My baby, oh my god. I thought I was dying this morning. I can't tell you how bad it was." He started to laugh and cry. "Now I can't tell you how good it is. Oh, Blossom, I have no words to tell you. I love you beyond words. Do you want another house? Is it okay if it's my house? It's not that nice, I'll get you anything you want."

"Oh, sweetheart, don't be silly. I love your house. Now, we have to think a little bit ahead, honey. It's not going to be pleasant when I tell my parents. I think the school change will be difficult, but not too bad. I'll bring my dad a copy of my thesis. Mom won't be happy the doctorate is up in the air, but she'll be able to brag to her friends that I finished early and am going to be a doctor. But living with you . . ."

"I'll tell them, baby."

"No, no, honey, it has to come from me. They have to know it's my idea. I have to be calm and strong. If they're attacking you, I'll fall apart."

"Oh, baby girl, it's too much. I want to take that from you."

She nuzzled his neck. "I know you do. You can do everything else in our life, honey, but this I have to do."

They made their plans. He'd come Saturday and get her things. She could have shipped them, but she wanted to return the chairs to her mother. Maybe Nixie could use them at college. Then they'd travel halfway, getting to town in the middle of Sunday, early enough for a discussion.

They packed the truck, she left Megan a note, and they went up to Route 80 and stayed at the Hampton Inn in Bloomsburg. He wanted to go out for dinner and make an occasion out of her leaving Penn, but she was nervous and just wanted the southwest salad at McDonald's. He loved her to sleep. She whimpered and jumped a couple of times in the night. He rubbed her back until she was calm and breathing steadily.

"Do you want to call and make sure they're home?" They were almost at the Meadville exit. His breakfast was rolling around in his stomach. He could only imagine how she was feeling.

"No. I'm pretty sure they will be there, and I don't want to get into a conversation on the phone."

She dug into his knee every few minutes, but he could feel her determination as they drove into the driveway. "Remember, honey, don't say anything. Just smile your beautiful smile," as she smiled at him bravely.

"Surprise, surprise," she said as they walked into the kitchen. Her parents were sitting at the table with coffee and some papers. Her mother immediately looked at the big appointment calendar on the wall. "I have your return in another two weeks, Blossom. What are you doing here?" She looked at Rocco. She had the knack of making any statement accusatory and somehow indicating Rocco was at fault.

"I'm done and wanted to bring your chairs in case Nixie could use them, so Rocco brought his truck."

"You could have left the chairs. They were fine last summer."

"No, I mean I'm done," taking a book from her bag and handing it to her dad. "Done at Penn. I've submitted my doctoral thesis. I'll probably have to go back and defend it, but I'm already enrolled at Pitt Medical School. I start in July."

Her dad said, "Well, kitten, this is amazing. How are your chances for your doctorate?"

"Dr. Ng thinks good. He's leaving my name and age off it, handpicking the panel, so I think they're good."

"Well, then, Blossom, shouldn't you be seeking a position?"

"Mother, you don't seek a position in that field. I'll do work for Dr. Ng while I'm at Pitt."

"Blossom," in a demanding tone.

"Mother, Daddy wanted me to go to Penn and work with Dr. Ng. I did. You wanted me in medicine, so now I'm doing that. I'm not sure what I want to do, so until I am, I'll do what you want."

"You don't need to be defensive, Blossom. You're fortunate you have the intelligence and family backing to take advantage of these opportunities."

"I'm not defensive, Mother. I just wanted to add that I have been doing what everyone else wants, so for the sake of my soul, I have to do something for myself. When I am in town, I will be living at Rocco's."

"What!" Her mother stood up so suddenly her chair teetered. "Blossom, don't be ridiculous, you are nineteen. You cannot live with Rocco. Cal, do something."

"Elaine, I can see her determination. Numerical age has never applied to Blossom. There's really nothing we can do."

"Cal, are you out of your mind? What is the matter with you?" Her palms hit the table. "This will not happen. I will not fund that lifestyle. Pitt is out, Blossom, until you come to your senses."

"I don't need funding for Pitt, Mother. I'll be on a full scholarship," she said calmly.

"Cal, I can't believe you're just sitting there," her voice rising. "Is this what you want for your daughter—a, a, a carpenter, for god's sake? She has all the promise in the world. I can't believe you're throwing it away, Blossom." She was losing control, flailing her arms around, pacing.

"Mother"—still calm—"I'm not throwing anything away. I've been to Penn, I'm going to Pitt, I'm just living at a different address. Rocco and I need to be together."

"Well, you can just go then. And don't think you're taking that car."

"Elaine!" Her dad spoke sharply, "That car was a gift. It belongs to Blossom."

"We pay the insurance, the upkeep, everything," frustrated, not believing she was losing control of the situation.

Rocco finally spoke, "I'll change all that right away, Elaine."

She spun and looked at him furiously. "You, you," she spit out, "I knew you were trouble." She hit the table again and glared at Blossom. "You are prostituting yourself and ruining your future."

Rocco took Blossom's hand and stood up. "We're done here. You know where we live, and you're always welcome. We'll be back tomorrow for Blossom's clothes."

Her mother started to say, "You're . . ."

"Elaine, enough." Her dad walked them to the door. "We'll talk later. I'm sure things will calm down. It was just a shock. Take your car." He didn't wish them well but patted their backs.

As soon as they were outside, Blossom called Nix. "I saw you at the top of the stairs. I'm sorry you had to hear that last part. They'll probably get you a car for an early birthday present, but you can use mine when I'm not. I love you." She climbed carefully into the truck and looked straight ahead.

"You were wonderful, baby girl."

"Thank you," squeezing her hands tightly. "I didn't say everything I wanted," now wringing her hands. "I wanted to tell them how wonderful you are."

"It wasn't the time, baby, nothing would make them think I'm wonderful. You were magnificent."

"Did she call me a prostitute?"

"No, no, it was just a bad choice of words. She was wound up. Don't think about it."

They pulled into the garage, and she smiled nervously. "You know what, sweetie," he said. "You didn't sleep much last night, and I know that just took a lot out of you. Let's sit in our chair for a while and relax. We can unload later."

She took a big breath and put her head against his chest. "Oh, this is so nice," then laughed and cried as he sang Bobby Darin's "If I Were A Carpenter" to her. She was asleep before the song ended.

He laid her on the sofa and covered her with the Chief Joseph robe, looked at her with tears in his eyes and vowed that would be the last difficult thing she'd ever have to do, lost it again when he put her things from college in his bedroom—their bedroom—and went down to fix supper.

He peeked around the corner just as she was stretching. "Something smells good." She smiled. "We skipped lunch, didn't we?"

"Yes, we did, baby girl. It's scallops, asparagus, and risotto. I cheated and used a mix for the risotto." It had taken him awhile to learn, but he knew now to give her tiny portions. It just turned her off if there was too much food on her plate. She finished it all and had two more asparagus. "These are delicious, what'd you do?"

"Sesame seeds and peanut oil."

"So good," she said, eating them with her fingers.

He said softly, "I know I should be a gentleman and say you can change your mind, but I can't get the words out."

"I don't want to change my mind, Rocco. You're stuck with me." She smiled and patted his hand, "I feel wonderful—like an unbearable weight has been lifted off my back and my heart."

He covered his eyes to hide the tears. She kissed his hand and said, "Let's put things away."

He smiled from ear to ear as she put the clothes away in the new closet. There would be plenty of room. Maybe just her coats would have to go in his parents' old room. "Baby, in the next couple days, just tell me where you want hooks or bars or anything." Talking fast, "And rearrange anything you want, here, in the kitchen. I'll give you my debit card, the PIN is your birthday, buy anything you want, and . . ."

"Rocco, Rocco, it's fine, honey, everything is fine. We'll take our time, we have our whole life," hugging him around the waist.

He put his face in her hair. "It's just that I can't believe it, baby girl, I can't believe it."

"I know what let's do," she said excitedly, clapping. "Let's go to McDonald's and have a sundae and sit where we did on our first almost-date."

So they did. She got the dollar hot fudge and he, the large Oreo McFlurry. "You couldn't look at me."

"It was too much. You were too beautiful."

"I couldn't stop looking at you, you were too beautiful."

So they smiled and laughed. She fed him hot fudge off her finger. He fed her ice cream-softened Oreo pieces. They talked about how she was born to dance and didn't even know it, how he went to Santa Fe before he ever went up the highway to Erie. The scene from her parent's faded away. They mouthed "I love you" in every way. She leaned across the table and whispered, "And you taught me how to make love."

"No way, baby girl, you taught me how to make love." He smiled and said, "Want to go home?"

The glorious smile, "Let's go home."

"Are you still going to take your shower at night?"

"I don't know," tilting her head at him. "Are you going to get me all sweaty and sticky?'

"Absolutely."

He woke at six, sensing her before he opened his eyes, thinking they were at Penn, his eyes stinging when he realized they weren't. He kissed her shoulder, and she said, "We have to have a new rule, honey."

"A rule? We have rules here?"

She giggled. "Our rule is you can't be late for work."

"That's a good rule. But today is a special day, I woke up, and you were here." He kissed her neck. "Can we start tomorrow?"

"We have to be responsible people. Our special time is at night."

"Uh-huh, but I can still be there by seven thirty. The Monday meeting is at eight. And you're warm and soft and here. Wouldn't it feel good if I did this"—nibbling her ear—"and this," sliding his hand between her legs.

"Just this one time, then," turning to him. "Just this one time," breathing hard.

After he shaved and showered, he whispered, "I'll call about ten, and we'll decide when to go to your house and get your things. I love you, baby girl. Sleep."

When he called, she said, "Rosalita is there until noon. She and Mom have coffee when she comes, so I'd rather not run into her today. I don't think Mom would ever bring up the subject, but I don't know." Tears in her voice, "My mother is really a nice person, honey, people like her. It's just me, I—"

"Blossom, stop right there. I know your mother is a nice person, and you're not at fault here. You and she want different things for you, that's all. Things are probably never going to be perfect, baby, but they'll get better. Do you want me to come home now?"

Smiling at the "home" reference, she said, "No, I'm okay. Come at noon, honey. Maybe you better bring a couple boxes."

He was surprised at how little it affected her to get her things and, other than clothes, how few things she had. Her luggage and the painting of the two Indian girls were gifts from Aunt Mim. She had no dolls or toys from her childhood. Left all the books on computers but took a couple of books of poetry, both Emily Dickinson. Most of her clothes fit in the suitcases, her coats he hung in the truck, and put her shoes in the boxes.

Nix came home from school and helped carry things to the truck. Rocco's heart flipped when she said, "Do you want to come to our house and take me on a couple errands and then use the car?"

"Let me see a couple things in the car first, Nix." He checked the registration and was relieved to see it was in her name. No red tape about getting that changed. He made a note of the insurance company to cancel there and add it to his. She could change the address for the license and registration online.

The next morning she heard the door at eight and went to the top of the stairs. "Rosalita, it's me, Blossom."

"Good morning, Miss Blossom. Mr. Rocco called me. He said you were the lady of the house and you'd tell me if you wanted anything different."

"Just do as you've been doing. Start down there, I'm going to take a shower."

After work, he had to stand by the door for a second to compose himself—his hands on his knees, taking deep breaths. She was really there. He could smell sauce cooking and hear music playing. He opened the door, and she was in his arms.

He was good at compartmentalizing; he'd learned hard—his home life from school, his home life from his nightlife, his home life from work. He could put it away until he got in his truck and headed out of the parking lot, gauging how far his father was behind him. Could he make it through a fast-food drive-thru, slink into the house and up to his room before he got there? It had become second nature.

Then Blossom. When she was at Penn, no problem. He couldn't get to her. Had their Friday night call to keep him going—eat, do homework, shower, lie in bed, and let thoughts of her wash over him.

Thinking back, he laughed again at how naive he had been when he thought once they made love, it would be even better. *Better?* Every cell in his body was eaten up with her. Every nerve laid out on top of his skin. Every minute of every day was a struggle to concentrate. And now she was in his house, six minutes twenty seconds away. The struggle was heightened to an unbelievable degree. He'd see Bob watching him. He'd put his hands behind his back and dig into his palms to get back on track.

He was working it out. Doing pretty well, he thought. But once he was in the truck, turned the key, and aimed out of the parking lot, he let himself go. She'd be there, would jump into his arms, warm and soft, her hair smelling like something wonderful, her "oh, I missed you" breathed onto his neck making him dizzy. Gotta watch the speedometer, don't get held up with a ticket, his heart thudding as he made the turn onto Cussewago.

This night she wasn't warm and soft. She was hot and tense, biting his neck, one hand digging into his back, the other frantically pointing to the stairs. He held her tight. "I've got you, baby, I've got you. Let me get my boots off." She fought him, but he cradled her and started up the stairs trying to calm her. "To what do I owe this amazing hello?" She growled, wiggling to hurry him. He laid her on the bed. She pulled at her clothes. "Slow down now. What happened?"

"I thought of you today," clutching at him.

"Don't you think of me every day?" methodically taking their clothes off.

"Yes, but I have rules."

He smiled. "Rules. More rules?"

"Yes. I can only think of you from the neck up. Or if I think of you, you have to have clothes on."

"So what happened to your rules?"

She closed her eyes and breathed deep. "You were sitting on the edge of the bed this morning, and I looked at your back."

"And . . ."

"And I let myself think of it awhile ago, and I couldn't stop," breathing hard, reaching for him, whispering, "and then I thought of other parts, and . . ." And then his lips were on hers, and he took her tension away.

When he came to, he was splayed out on the bed facedown. To the left, his watch said seven thirty; to his right was her adorable butt. He laughed, kissed it, pushed off the bed, and went to the shower. So much for thinking he could ever predict what would be waiting for him when he came home.

He kissed her awake, kneeling beside the bed in his lounge pants, taking her hands, and standing up. "You hungry, baby girl?" She gave him her look and pulled at his waistband. "Whoa, let's get some supper. It smells great."

"Again," she whispered.

He crawled over her, lay down, and pulled her close.

"Don't you want to make love with me?"

"I want to make love with you all day, every day, but let's talk a minute and see if something else is going on here. Tell me some more about your day."

It all came bubbling out. "Oh, Rocco, I don't think I'm allowed to be this happy. I was pounding the steak with my new tenderizer thingy, and I was making you swiss steak, and I thought you would love it, and I wanted to make you mashed potatoes, and it just came over me how much I love you, and it was just waves and waves of love, and I thought how much I love to cook for you." She paused for a big breath. "And then I thought of your back, and I just don't think being this happy is allowed," out of breath. "I really don't," dropping her head to his chest.

His eyes stinging, "Baby girl, you can be as happy as can be. Nobody makes our rules, remember. You can be all the happy you want to be. I'm out-of-my-mind happy. After all those weeks apart, it's a gift, and I'm taking it."

"But you're working hard. I don't contribute, I don't deserve . . ."

"Sh, sh," his finger over her lips. "You just finished four years of work in less than two years, Blossom. What you deserve is to let your brain rest for a couple months and do anything you want to do. Right now, you're making me happy so I can run a business and keep people working, and they can make people happy. You're nineteen, baby girl, there's plenty of time. Just be happy. Everything's good here, baby, everything's good."

"I love you so much, Rocco. You're so wonderful." And they were gone again.

It was ten thirty. He'd been looking at her perfection for a long time. *Christ how can I fix this?* Knew there were no magic words so sighed and rubbed her back to wake her. "You gotta eat, sweetie pie. I'm going to put some of that swiss steak on a sub roll. What can I fix you?"

"May I have oatmeal with half a banana?" He bit his lip as she counted on her fingers and made her little hand motions. "You know, cut up real small, and a couple chocolate chips in it," tipping her head. "Maybe eight or nine?"

He winked at her. "I can do that," and whistled down the stairs. She scooted to the shower.

Two weeks went by. Little changes added up. The chair and sofa were closer together with a rug between, making a cozy area. Her Indian girls painting was in a corner with a rocking chair from his parents' room, a round table covered with a floor-length cloth in an Indian print, and a new lamp with a soft light. The cupboards filled up, the refrigerator too. It had changed from a house to a home. He often had to hide tears in his eyes as they tried to hold back time—she had to find an apartment in Pittsburgh.

The third week, her mother called. She coolly said they were going to cook out with Nix and Slim. Would they like to come for steaks and shrimp? Blossom evenly replied that it would be nice; could they bring anything?

Strained, but not all that bad. Rocco manned the grill and discussed business with her dad. Blossom and her mother tightly discussed apartment locations in Pittsburgh. Blossom wasn't sure they could come to New Mexico with defending her thesis up in the air. Yes, she hoped to come home most weekends. Her mother replying her work should come first. Air kisses all around when they left. He winked at her as they pulled away. Another couple of blocks and they both laughed. "It wasn't that bad," he said.

"It was agony," she said. "I could hardly swallow."

"It's a start, baby girl, it's a start."

He was reading the paper after dinner. She came in and sat at his feet. "What are you doing down there, baby? Come up on my lap."

"I need to talk to you about something, and I don't want you to jump up and drop me."

"I would never drop you. What is it?"

"Honey," she said carefully, "I know your old life is gone." She felt him stiffen but went on, "But in your heart you had to wonder why. Why would a grown man hit a little boy."

He interrupted, "That's in the past, baby, I don't care anymore."

"Just let me ask this. It's been bothering me since the funeral." She paused and said carefully, "You look nothing like your father, Rocco, nothing at all. There's a little of your mother in your mouth and chin. I saw something of your father in Lindsay, but . . ."

"What are you getting at," he interrupted in a monotone.

"Honey"—squeezing his hand tightly—"do, do you think maybe he found out somehow that you weren't his?" the last words in a whisper.

He didn't jump up, and he didn't say anything.

"It would explain a lot, honey. Hitting your mother, hitting you, angry all the time."

"What's the point of talking about it now?" still in the monotone.

"You said your mother is failing. It might be time to ask her somehow. I could do it, honey, if you give me permission. I could ask her as a woman and the mother of your children someday." She felt a reassuring squeeze at the mention of children and forged ahead. "If you gave me permission, I could even ask Gloria about that time in their life. Neighbors know a lot, and maybe Lindsay heard something."

"Blossom, it's in the past. A past I don't care about anymore. I don't want our life to be a daily update on what you've found out or haven't found out. You know how you get."

"But if I promise . . ."

"That's just what I mean, baby."

"Honey, I know you don't think you care now, but one day when you're holding our baby in your arms, it's going to come back—how could a father hit his child? And this is the first time I've ever brought it up since the funeral, isn't it? I won't talk about it all the time. I just want your permission."

"You know what, I don't care. In the end, you're probably going to find out the guy was a miserable and mean SOB, and that's all it was."

She jumped into his lap, kissing his chin, his ear. "Can we go to Lindsay's for Thanksgiving?"

He shook his head, laughing. "Now I'm going to drop you."

He cried out at three in the morning. "He said, he said," an anguished, choking cry.

"I'm here, I'm here," she whispered against his lips. "What did he say, what did he say?"

Breathing hard, raspy voice, "Get him out of my sight," his voice catching, stifling a sob. "I need you baby."

"I'm right here. I'll always be here. Whatever you need." She gave him what he needed, and the bad dream went away.

She rolled over to hug him in the morning. "I'm sorry I made you have a bad dream. I shouldn't have brought it up."

"Baby mine, you didn't cause a bad dream, you were here. They happen less and less now."

On his birthday, she gave him Paul Bond boots. They went dancing. He took his old ones along in case the new ones hurt, but the fit was perfect. He wore his hat. She had on a lightweight denim halter dress with matching boots. The neckline put him a little off kilter, but she wanted to show her doves. They hadn't been to Edinboro in a long time, and it was nice to see all the regulars. Before the band started, the bartender played Delbert's *Room to Breathe* CD, skipping number nine automatically. Someone called Big Sallie, and she rolled into the place like a tsunami. She sat with them, gave them some new ideas, and kept them laughing and dancing until 2:00 a.m.

They had never been out so late, and she promptly fell asleep in the truck. He carried her into the house on his hip, locked up with his free hand,

and took her upstairs. She smiled as he took her boots off. "I'm all hot and sweaty."

"You're going to be hotter and sweatier as soon as I get our clothes off."

She giggled and rolled over for him to unzip her dress and wriggled out. Their lovemaking was usually intense, sometimes desperately so, other times gentle and tender. This night she was so tired; she was silly. She danced around him with his hat on then straddled him with it perched askew. He looked up at her as she laughed, her hair around her shoulders, her breathtaking nakedness. *Don't ever let me forget this, burn it into my mind*, he thought. He rolled her over and put the hat on; then they got busy, and no one had the hat on.

Finally at four o'clock, she lay spent in the crook of his arm and put the hat over his groin. "This is the best hundred and eighty-nine dollars I ever spent."

He laughed with as much strength as he had left. "You are so bad."

"Oh? I thought I was pretty good," batting her eyelashes.

He wanted to tease her some more, but she was fading fast. Her lips moved, and he leaned to hear "Happy Birthday, Rocco Anthony."

He was yawning at supper two days later. "'Scuse me, baby, we're working on an old restaurant and have been carrying marble restroom partitions from the basement upstairs. They want to use them for the bar."

"Ugh. From a restroom?"

"Oh, they'll be fine. We got advice on cleaning them, but I don't know how practical they'll be. They want to keep the history of the place in the remodel. I'm beat, though."

"You're an old man of twenty-two now," she teased. "We'll go upstairs early, I'm tired too. I've been digging out back to make a flower garden. Nixie is going to tell me what will grow good."

"Baby girl, I'll send someone to dig for you."

"No, honey, I really want to do it, and I like it," kissing his cheek as she picked up their plates. "I want it to be something I made for our home." And that was true, but she didn't tell him she was hoping to develop a relationship with Gloria. So far, only "good mornings" and "nice days," but she had hopes.

After she showered, he ran the hot water on the pulsating mode for his sore muscles. She was already asleep in her usual position, and he crawled in to wake her. The next thing he knew it was five thirty in the morning. He couldn't believe it but slid out, brushed his teeth, and dressed, then went to her side of the bed and knelt down. "Baby girl, I have to go. We're going to Mercer, and I told the men to be at the shop by six fifteen."

She didn't open her eyes, just wrinkled her brow. "Is it morning?"

"You go back to sleep, sweetie, I'll call my first break, about ten."

"But is it morning?" Not believing it.

"Yes, baby. I have to go, I need to stop for donuts. I'll call you."

"But . . ."

"I love you, gotta go."

He and the crew were gathered around the tailgate having coffee and donuts when he called at nine forty-five. He took a few steps away and turned his back. "Morning, baby girl."

"Rocco?"

"I'm sorry I didn't wake you, baby," he spoke quietly. "I must have fallen asleep."

"You must have fallen asleep?" Her voice was questioning, teasing.

He took a few more steps away, his face getting warm. "I was really tired, sweetie, I'm only human."

"Oh, now you're only human. So what was it, you fell asleep, or you're only human?"

He took a few more steps away, laughing nervously. The crew couldn't hear, but he felt his manhood was being questioned. "Blossom, I can't come home right now, I'll make it up to you as soon as I get there." He felt himself sweating around his hairline.

"Well, let's hope you don't fall asleep on the way, Mr. Human." She closed her phone, leaving him just looking at his. He shook his head, smiling. Two years and she could bring him to his knees.

She was in his arms as soon as he opened the door. "Do you want to go upstairs, baby girl?"

"I'm not an animal, sir," she said haughtily. "I can keep my feelings under control." She laughed. "Wash up for dinner."

She had fixed him a reuben sandwich, french fries, and gravy. Not a healthy thing on the plate. And a Bud Light with a frozen mug. "Umm, I think someone's after my heart."

She put her chin in her hand, staring into his eyes. "It's not your heart I'm interested in." She fed him french fries, ran her toes up his leg, dabbing an ice cube between her breasts. "It's been so warm today, hasn't it?"

He ate fast, unable to take his eyes off her. Finally, "Race you upstairs."

She was gone in a flash, but he caught her halfway. "I have to brush my teeth," picking her up.

"You're not getting out of my sight. We'll brush together."

After brushing, they started kissing in the bathroom, tearing at each other, but unable to finish, made love half clothed. She got her blouse off, he his jeans. Her panties got in the way, making her howl for him to hurry. Her skirt covered her head; she thrashed around, driving him wild. Tiger got lost in her skirt, and she bit him through his shirt. He released groaning and panting, making whimpering sounds as he got his breath.

He went down and cleaned up the dinner things, showered, put on his lounge pants, and held her as she slept for another hour. She opened her eyes, smiling. "Why do I need you all the time?"

"Baby, we waited weeks and weeks, lots of time. We can copulate like bunnies if we want to. Want some ice cream?"

They sat in bed eating ice cream and watching "Dancing with the Stars" on TV. He made a couple of notes of steps they could try.

She cuddled against him. "We don't have to make love every night you know."

"We don't!" He feigned shock and surprise.

"No, but you can't come out of the shower wrapped in a towel and looking beautiful."

"And you can't be in bed with your hair spread out on the pillow."

"And you can't climb into bed and look at me with those eyes."

"And your breasts can't touch my chest when you kiss me good night."

"And you definitely can't do that," as he stroked the rise of her hip.

"And you definitely can't do that," as she did the same.

And they were off to the races again.

The next day after work, "I have a present for you."

She clapped and jumped up and down. "Give it to me." He took a soft stuffed bunny from the bag. "You can take this to Pittsburgh and leave Tiger here."

She pouted. "I want Tiger with me."

"Baby, this way we'll never forget Tiger, and we can copulate like bunnies down there."

She giggled. "I like that. But you'll have to sleep with Bunny for a while so he'll smell like you."

She had been home a month. It was idyllic, a dream they had both had, a tiny picture of what they hoped the future would hold. She started to get quiet, smiling wistfully when he looked at her. He decided to head off the inevitable and said, "I guess we should head down to Pitt and look at apartments."

"Nooo," she wailed, climbing onto his lap, pounding his chest. "We have time. No, no."

"Baby girl, we don't want to wait until the last minute. Let's go down, take our time, stay overnight, and get a feel for the place. Check online for some options, and we'll go Thursday and get it taken care of."

She put her face in his neck and cried while he rubbed her back. She didn't know how much he felt like crying too.

It was a frustrating and exhausting day, hot and humid as Pittsburgh can be in June. Some buildings he wouldn't even let her go in. She cried off and on, but they finally narrowed it down to two. He liked the one-bedroom on Wilkins Avenue east of the college. It was a professionally managed building and looked safe to him. She didn't like the typical boxy style, the modern furniture, and the year lease. She wanted the attic one on the third floor of an old Victorian house on Evergreen Road in Millvale owned by two elderly sisters. He worried about fire, safety, and outdoor parking. It did have an air conditioner, and he checked the furnace; it was only a few years old. She said it had personality, and she liked the furnishings, but he knew she liked it because it was near Route 279 North.

"Let's get a room and think it over, baby."

"I want to go home," she whined.

"Sweetie, we'll have dinner, get some sleep, and we'll be all fresh in the morning. How about that place we saw, that Inn on Negley?"

She checked it on her phone. "Oh, it's so expensive. Oh, you have to stay two nights in summer."

"We could stay two nights."

She pounded on his knee. "I want to go home!"

"Calm down. We'll go downtown to the Hilton. They must have a Hilton, right?"

"They do," pouting. "There's a Holiday Inn right over on Lytton."

"No, let's go downtown. We can do something after dinner."

"I know where we can go eat, you'll love it," knowing they were staying and making the best of it. "It's in an area called the Strip. They have huge sandwiches, and they put the french fries right in them!"

She showered while he watched TV and peeked around the door, "I'm sorry I was bad, honey."

"We'll see how sorry you are later, Blossom Dove." She giggled and wiggled her butt at him. Her mercurial moods kept him on his toes.

He did love Primanti Brothers and the sandwich, and then they took the Duquesne Incline at nine o'clock. He was quietly on super awareness of the area, and she was afraid to look at the inner operations, but they had a good time, and she admitted there would be a lot to see in the city, but "I'm coming home on the weekends, honey."

"This bed is really comfortable, baby girl."

"Ummm," she said sleepily. "I'll check in the morning, it probably has a down mattress top. We can get one for our bed."

He snuggled closer and whispered, "I love you, Blossom Dove."

She pouted. "If you loved me, you wouldn't let me come here."

"Oh, baby girl, don't put that on me. I'm barely holding on here."

"I'm sorry, I'm sorry, oh my darling, I'm so selfish. I'm sorry." She pulled his head to her chest, moving a nipple to his mouth.

"I don't want to hurt you."

She whispered, "Don't bite, lick. I love you Rocco." She breathed, "I love you so much," arching against him as he licked. She put her hands in his curls and urged him down her stomach, opening her legs for him.

He nibbled and probed until she panted and pulled at his hair. "I can't, I can't, come in, come in."

"A little more, baby, let it come, let it come."

"I can't, I ca—" and screamed as her orgasm shook her.

He entered her quickly, her swollen vulva making him moan. He helped her come again before he let go, kissing her tears and rolling her onto her side, weak with love as she curled her hands under her chin. That little movement touched him more and more. To him it said she felt comfortable, fulfilled, and mostly, safe.

Of course they took the apartment she wanted. It was four hundred eighty a month plus electric. He paid first, last, and deposit; and Blossom transferred the electric into her name on her phone.

Rocco had coffee in the hotel, but they hadn't eaten and stopped at Bob Evans for breakfast. She had a chocolate shake and a bran muffin; and he had three eggs, bacon, and home fries while she shook her head. They were home by noon. She stepped in the door; and suddenly it was so dear to her she turned back to Rocco, put her arms around his waist, and cried.

"We'll be fine, baby girl, we'll be fine," he whispered into her hair. "It will be so much better than it was. So much better."

Time doesn't stop, so the day to leave came as much as she wanted to wish it away.

"Baby, do you want to have Nix follow us in the truck so I can drive you?"

A worried look, a whispered "But what if we want to make love before you leave?"

"Sweetie, tomorrow's Wednesday, you'll be home on Saturday. We'll make up for lost time then. Let's take Nix to Primanti Brothers, he'll love it."

So Nix met the Bauerhoff sisters, Eugenia and Dorothea. They got her room all arranged and went to the Strip for supper. Then it was good-byes all around, Blossom giving him a "how can you leave me here" look, the little ladies waving, "Don't worry we'll take care of her," his heart breaking, he and Nix headed north.

Nix asked, "How long will she be there?"

"That's what's so hard. She did a lot at Penn in a short amount of time, but there's lab work and stuff she'll have to be there for. We'll know more once she's into it." A big sigh, "It's hard."

"Let's face it," Nix said, "she doesn't want to do this."

Rocco smiled at him. "You're pretty observant for seventeen."

"Well, at least I have an idea that I want to go into land management of some kind. She never had a chance to develop a choice. They pushed her where they wanted her to go." He got a stricken look on his face. "Sometimes I feel she sacrificed herself to save me," biting his lip.

"Nix, don't think like that. It doesn't do anyone any good."

"Really, Rocco"—holding back tears—"I don't know what would have happened if she hadn't met you."

Rocco reached over and fist butted him. "You're okay, Nix. Hey, how about that thing we talked about last summer. What'd you decide there?"

A little embarrassed, "I decided to wait. Turns out she wasn't as into me as she let on."

"I'm impressed, Nix, it's a tough road. Another year under your belt can't hurt. It's better to be legal this day and age. How do you like your truck?"

"It's the best. Thanks for backing me up on that. I didn't want a car like Blossom's."

"It wasn't hard. I just told your dad maybe having room for just two friends wasn't a bad idea." He didn't add that he told his dad that with the white flames on the little blue Ford Ranger, he'd always be easy to find.

They chatted comfortably all the way home. Nix had taken an extra class and was leaving for New Mexico late. The fiasco from last year had given him a little more input. Her mother was angry when Blossom said she and Rocco would try, but she wasn't sure they would make it there.

His screen showed her name at four on Thursday. Too early. He steeled himself for tears but got anger instead.

———

251

"I told you this would happen," accusingly. "I knew it would happen. It's all your fault."

"I know it's my fault, baby girl. What's my fault?"

Now the tears, "I can't come home. I have to go to Penn to defend my thesis. The very first weekend! It's a bad sign, a very bad sign," she wailed.

"Blossom, we knew this was coming. We'll just get it over with. You call when you're starting back, and I'll come down and meet you."

"I hate it here. It's all your fault."

He decided to try a different tack. Quietly, "Blossom, your parents aren't paying any more. You don't have to stay there."

Utter silence for fifteen seconds and then a small "I hate it here."

"Baby girl, you've been there one day. Tell me what you've done so far."

They talked as if they'd been apart weeks instead of a day. Her voice softened and calmed. He put his boots up on his desk. Helen saw him smiling and breathed a sigh of relief. Their separation was going to be tough on everyone.

She went to Penn, successfully defended her thesis—Field Programmable Gate Arrays: FPGAs use for Cybersecurity—and received her doctorate in computer sciences.

The months went by. She came Friday night if she could, Saturday morning about seven thirty if she couldn't. She cried when she hugged him hello, cried when she left on Sunday. He wouldn't let her leave any later than seven. She started fussing about it at six. Once a month, they had Sunday dinner at her parents. She gave her mother monosyllabic answers to her questions, eliciting sharp comments about her commitment. Her grades were perfect, her work impeccable, her instructors' comments glowing. She was miserable.

Their lovemaking alternated between poignant and tender to fierce and frenzied. He occasionally showered at work before making a job estimate. He saw Bob looking at his back marked with scratches and scars when he was putting on a fresh shirt. He just shrugged and shook his head. "She doesn't want to be there."

He went down for her twentieth birthday, another pearl, so she wouldn't have to drive. She was working long hours for an extra day at Thanksgiving and a trip to Ohio to Lindsay's.

They arrived Tuesday night before Thanksgiving at Lindsay's. It took Marlee and Madison a couple of minutes to warm up to Blossom. Two years was a long a time for them. She soon had them charmed as Rocco and

Lindsay discussed the menu for Thanksgiving. They went to Olive Garden for dinner on Wednesday, and Blossom made sure she sat beside Rocco's mother. He watched her, but she just chatted and smiled and patted Marie's hand.

Thanksgiving morning she was having coffee with Lindsay while Rocco played outside with the girls. Randy had to work a full day, so Blossom was about to say something when Lindsay, never one for the soft opening, said, "So you're living at the house?"

Blossom smiled. "Yes, I am. It's very wonderful."

"Bet your parents loved that."

"It was rough, but only for a couple weeks."

"You guys use Mom's room? It's the biggest."

It was a good opening. "Oh, no, I don't think he could ever do that. He still has nightmares," she said quietly.

Lindsay shook her head. "The son of a bitch."

"How old was he when it started? Can you remember?"

"Not really. I wasn't in school yet when I knew something was wrong. So if I was four or five, he was two or three. But I think it was before that. I don't know why I have that feeling, but I do. How much did he tell you?"

"He doesn't like to say much. He said he beat him until he was fourteen, but that it was in the past, and it's over. I just thought if he knew why, it would help. I mean, why would a man hit a small child, his child?"

Lindsay shook her head and sighed. "He broke his arm once, you know. They believed Mom's lie at the hospital. I think I was about ten and didn't know about Children's Services, but I remember wishing the police would come. They must have had us on file. Gloria called them once when he was beating Mom. Of course she wouldn't say anything when they came."

"Did he hit you?"

"Never directly. I got in the way sometimes when he was after Mom, but he never came after me."

"Lindsay, this is hard to say, but since it was directed at Rocco and your mother, do you think it might be possible"—she cleared her throat and tightened her hands around her coffee mug—"that, that early on he found out Rocco wasn't his?"

Lindsay stared at her with a surprised, puzzled look and then with a tinge of anger, "Does Rocco know you're asking me this?"

"He didn't know what I was going to talk about, but I asked his permission to start trying to find out why." She touched Lindsay's arm. "We're going to have children someday, Lindsay, and it's going to hit him all over again. You're all used to each other, but I saw at the funeral that Rocco looks nothing like him. Not a single feature."

"Lots of kids don't look like their parents."

"I know, but there's usually something. I can see both your mother and father in you, and yet you're different. There's a little of your mother in Rocco." She could see Lindsay's jaw stiffening so said, "Anyway, I just wondered if you heard or saw anything growing up. I hope your mother's around for a long time, but she is frail, and maybe the opportunity to know will pass us by."

She stood up and looked out the window at Rocco and the girls. "He's such a wonderful person, Lindsay. What he's been through and what he's become. I can't even imagine what it must have been like knowing every day that someone hated you that much. I just think it would help to know why." She turned with tears in her eyes. "If you remember anything, please call me."

Lindsay came over and hugged her, a tenuous bond developing between them. "I can't promise I'll talk to her, but if the time ever seems right, I will."

As they were cuddling in the motel that night, Rocco said "What did you say to Lindsay today? I saw you'd been crying."

Softly caressing his face, "I just opened the subject, honey, just a baby step. I won't push things." She moved her fingers to his mouth, tracing his lips.

He loved watching her desire grow. Her cheeks started to flush, her dark eyes darkening more, her breathing quickening. "I love you, Blossom Dove, nothing will ever change that."

"I know," she breathed, moving against him. The world went away.

Her family was spending two weeks in Santa Fe at Christmas. Since her group was so generous in working every weekend for her, she just took a week for her Christmas break so she could fill in for anyone who needed it. They were at the Pittsburgh airport waiting for their flight to Albuquerque. The times they had to leave each other at the airport seemed to enter their minds at the same time. They smiled and squeezed hands. Her eyes got misty, and he said, "Never again, baby girl."

"I couldn't do it, Rocco, please don't make me do it."

"Sweetie, no one can make you do it anymore. We're never going back to those separations, never. I can barely hold on for five days now. I don't know how we did five weeks."

Nix picked them up at the airport. There was no discussion about sleeping arrangements. Aunt Mim met them at the door and said, "The blue bedroom, hon," before they went in to see her parents.

For him, Christmases now were almost surreal. He numbered this the third Christmas of his life, each one getting better. Her mother marred a few dinner conversations by trying to pin Blossom down on her work at Pitt, but other than that it was a marvelous week.

They went to the Cathedral Basilica on Christmas Eve. He had never been in a church before and whispered to her, "I like the atmosphere here, it's peaceful." While cuddling later, they decided they would check out the three Catholic churches back home and see how they felt. "I've always liked the pomp and circumstance," she said, "if I can get past the scandals."

She got him a buckskin jacket with fringe down the sleeves. He got her a pearl and a first edition *Collected Poems of Emily Dickinson*. She stared at it unbelieving for a few seconds and then looked at him with such a worshiping look her dad cleared his throat. "Where's that pumpkin pie Lourdes promised us?"

They didn't have enough time to do many touristy things. She took him to the Georgia O'Keefe Museum, and the next day it was time to fly back.

She only had a couple of days for New Year's. He drove down as the weather was bad. "Baby girl, can we go to the Hilton? I really miss you, and I'm afraid we might scare the little ladies."

She laughed. "You are missing the whole point of having this apartment, crazy man, but yes, I'll book two nights. Do you want any particular food for New Year's Eve?"

"Whatever you want is fine with me."

"Okay. Bring your hat and jacket. Mim sent me a new dress I'm anxious to show you."

She had made a six o'clock reservation at the LeMont on Mount Washington, early for New Year's Eve, and he was thankful for the few patrons. He was still recovering from her dress—the familiar kick in the gut, pounding in his ears. He didn't know what the material was, but it clung all the way down to the top of her high button shoes. It had the very low neckline Mim favored with gold bands crisscrossing her breasts. The dark wine color reflected in her cheeks, her eyes sparkling. He tried to shield her from the dining room when she took her coat off. He thought he was being unobtrusive, but of course she knew what he was doing. "Rocco, this is a beautiful dress Aunt Mim paid a lot of money for. She'd be hurt if you didn't want anyone to see it." He didn't realize people were looking because they made a striking couple. He would always think someone was trying to take her from him.

She talked him into the crispy duck with cherry sauce. She ordered a shrimp and langostino cocktail with a side salad. He wasn't crazy about the duck, but they had prepared it well, and he loved that she kept pulling off pieces and dipping them into the sauce. Eventually just forgetting the duck and dipping her fingers in the sauce, putting her finger into her mouth, and then into his.

FOUR

They Wed

Her work didn't follow the college calendar, no spring break; but finally, finally, she was home the middle of May for two months. She sat on his lap and cried the first night home, was still quiet and jumpy another couple days, and then started to be herself.

When he came home, smelled dinner cooking and heard music, he had to stay in the garage and compose himself. She would jump into his arms, her legs around his waist. "I hate to be a chauvinist, but this is so nice," he said, his face in her neck.

"My darling," she breathed, "you have no idea what this means to me," leaning back and staring into his eyes. "No idea at all."

Getting advice from Nix, she started the garden, redid the room that had been Lindsay's, puttered, and planned. It was their home, and she loved it. After grocery shopping at Walmart one afternoon, she stopped in at the shop to see how Helen liked the computer system.

He beamed when she was around, finished up with a couple of salesmen, and was walking her to her car when Bob stopped him with a question. She had on moccasins so stood on tiptoe to kiss him good-bye while he finished with Bob. As she got in her car, movement caught his eye. One of the salesmen had the beginnings of a whistle on his lips; the other was shaking his hand in the universal wow signal. He never remembered exactly what happened. An explosion behind his eyes, his pulse pounding in his ears louder than it ever had, he started toward them with a look that made Bob's blood run cold. Bob knew he could never catch him; none of the crew were were out front; calling his name would not deter him; so he just yelled BLOSSOM! as loud as he could, hoping it would penetrate the fury.

His look didn't change, but he turned toward his truck without missing a step, and tires squealed from the lot. Bob collapsed to his knees. The salesmen were looking puzzled about his scream but had no idea how close one of them had come to being dead.

She had just set groceries on the counter when she heard his truck, wondering why, but tickled he had followed her home. She started to turn with a smile when the door flew in and hit the wall. Her mouth fell open, and then he screamed, "This is not working," swinging his arms around wildly, indicating her, the room, everything.

She turned white, a cry escaping her lips—terror, sheer terror, stabbing down her legs like knives, down her arms, circling her stomach. She reached for the table for support, backing into a chair, staring at him, her eyes enormous, her mouth open.

"You see that look on your face," he screamed. "You think I'm going to leave. Why aren't we married? Why didn't you say we could get married?" The fury that had propelled him from the shop to home suddenly exhausted him. He put his head on her lap, sobbing, "Why aren't we married?"

She was gasping for air, the terror subsiding. He wasn't leaving. Anything else she could handle. She rubbed his back while she got her breath, trying to calm him, ease his shivering. "Rocco, Rocco," she whispered, "my darling, I didn't want you to feel trapped."

He jumped up, almost tipping the chair over. Her fist went to her mouth. "Trapped," he screamed, "trapped! I was trapped the first second you looked at me. I was trapped the first time I came to Penn." His voice softened. He knelt in front of her. "I was trapped the first time we made love. Blossom, I want to be trapped. I want to be trapped forever." Agony covered his face. "I need you right now, baby. Now," hoarsely, urgently, picking her up.

"Not here, Rocco, the windows, honey, upstairs."

"I can't make it upstairs. Now!"

"A couple steps, then, a couple steps into the living room."

He made it to the carpet, unzipping his jeans, panting, pulling her panties off, entering her roughly. "Mine, mine. Mine," he growled in his throat, "you're mine." He swallowed a primitive, primal scream as he came and fell against her. "Again," he panted.

"No again, no again." She could barely talk, wincing from his roughness.

"AGAIN!"

"Again after you rest, then again."

He quieted, and when his breathing was even, she said, "Can you sit us up, honey, you're heavy."

He sat them up, his back against the sofa. She was on his lap now, a leg on each side. She put her arms around his neck and looked in his eyes. "Tell me what happened."

"Can we get married?"

"Of course we can get married."

"Tomorrow?"

"I think there's a three-day waiting period, but we'll talk about that after you tell me what happened."

He looked down and swallowed.

"Tell me."

"I wanted to kill a man today," keeping his eyes down.

A sharp intake of breath, "Oh Rocco, Rocco," lifting his chin to look in his eyes. "Didn't I tell you this could destroy us? What if you went to jail.

We would be separated forever." She put her head on his chest and hugged him tight. "Tell me all of it."

"Those salesmen that were there. They were making motions."

"Motions"—incredulously—"motions?"

"Blossom"—trying to justify himself—"you had just kissed me good-bye. They knew you were mine."

She stared at him, her lips clenched. "You jeopardized our life because of some motion?"

"I'm sorry. I'm sorry."

"Did you hit them Rocco?"

"No. Bob yelled at me. It was your name, I came here. I came here," deflated. "I'm sorry. I have a headache."

She couldn't lecture now. He was in pain. "Look at us," shaking her head. "Your jeans around your ankles, your boots still on. What am I going to do with you?"

"Love me again?"

"This isn't a small thing, Rocco. You're going to lay down for a while, and then we're going to talk," getting them untangled. "Go, go," following him upstairs, carrying his jeans. "Take three of those Excedrin Migraine." His phone rang on the waistband of his jeans. It was Bob.

"Is he there, Miss Blossom?"

"He's here. I'm going to have him lay down for a while. Do you need him?"

"No, I just wanted to make sure he was there." He paused, feeling he should say something. "It was close, Miss Blossom."

"I'm sorry, Bob, he told me a little. Something about a motion? Here he is."

"Thanks, Bob," as though nothing had happened. "Sorry I left in a hurry. Do you need me for a couple hours? Blossom and I are going to get married."

"That's wonderful, boss. Things are okay here. Come when you can." The crew was growing, and to avoid any misconceptions because of their ages, he had taken to calling Rocco boss. He hung up and said to Helen, "They're going to get married. God, I hope she knows what she's doing."

She sat beside the bed as he slept. Only forty-five minutes, but the Excedrin had time to work a little. He didn't turn but knew she was there. "We can get married, right?"

"Yes, we can."

He sighed and then, "Do you want one of those big white dresses, baby?"

She smiled. "No, honey, I don't. I'd like to get married in the woods someplace. We'll think about some place we like."

"Can I buy you a diamond ring?"

"No, darling, I don't need diamonds. I was thinking while you were sleeping of silver rings with something written on the inside. Do you like that idea?"

"I like that, baby girl. I'm sorry, Blossom."

"I know, Rocco. We'll talk about it when you feel better."

"I guess you should call your mother."

At first she made a face but then thought of something. "If she acts like she'd like to be there, would you like to get married in New Mexico? Remember that beautiful spot where we watched the sunset?" Talking fast, ignoring the elephant in the room, "And, honey, I'll get married in a few days if you want, but if we have more time, we could plan a little more. Like asking your mother and sister, and even driving home for a little trip?"

He sat up and swung his legs over the side of the bed. "Whatever you want, Blossom. I love you so much. I'm sorry, baby girl."

"People always make jokes about men not remembering their anniversary. Would you like to get married on your birthday so you'd never forget?"

"I'd never forget, baby, but that's a great idea." He put his face in his hands. "That would be the most wonderful gift. I'm sorry, Blossom, god, I'm sorry. I could have ruined everything." She sat beside him on the edge of the bed, put her head on his shoulder, and they cried.

She called her mother at three o'clock New Mexico time. "Rocco and I have decided to get married."

"Well, I suppose that was inevitable," flatly, unemotionally.

She smiled to herself and rolled her eyes to no one. "We just want a simple ceremony and thought his birthday would be a nice date."

"But that's just a few weeks, Blossom, for heaven's sake. We can't get back there right now."

"Well, if you'd like to be with us, we could come there."

Hesitantly, "I guess that would be better. I could call Mim and get Nix here."

Blossom smiled because she seemed to be getting interested. "I've checked New Mexico laws. There's no physical or waiting period, so we just need to show up and get a license. We know where we'd like the ceremony, so I just need to get a justice of the peace to come there."

"Well, Mim knows everyone around here. She could probably do that for you."

"That would be nice. I want to call her about a dress we saw, an Etro. It had all the colors of the sunset in it. Maybe they could send it in my size."

They talked a little more. Her mother made noises like she was disappointed it wouldn't be a traditional ceremony with a wedding dress, but Blossom felt she was relieved. She called Rocco so he could plan time off; and not even knowing why, she twirled around the room, laughing and clapping all by herself.

"Why didn't we get married when you were eighteen?" he asked as they were cuddling that night.

"I was at Penn, honey, and my parents were paying."

"Why didn't you say something when you started at Pitt? I thought you had to be twenty-one, or I would have."

She whispered, "I told you why, honey."

"Blossom, you didn't really think that. You couldn't possibly have thought that."

"Honey, I'm not worth anything, and when you realized it . . ."

"Stop right there. We're not going there, Blossom. That's so ridiculous it's not worth discussing. Baby girl, I'm not smart enough to deal with what they've done to you. You need someone to talk to. Maybe Dr. Krienson could recommend someone."

"Rocco, they didn't do anything to me, they're . . ."

"I know. They're wonderful people, but that doesn't mean you can't talk to someone."

"We're supposed to be talking about what happened today, Rocco. You should be talking to someone."

"Baby, I was raised in a house where hitting was the way it was. My problem isn't hard to figure out. I couldn't see anyone who is smarter than you."

"Honey, my brain goes out the window when it comes to you," caressing his cheek. "You're a wonderful person, but being hit every day had to affect you."

"I'm doing better, Blossom. I really messed up today, but I know it. I'll work on it every day, baby." Then his jaw tightened. His voice got steely. "And they better not send those guys back again." She stared at him as he reached for his phone and found memo. "Tell Helen about salesmen."

"Rocco Anthony Carnavale, this is our precious time when the world goes away. Don't you ever do that again—I'm laying naked in your arms, and you're dictating memos?" She reached for his testicles and squeezed the tiniest bit.

"I won't, never again, never again," laughing. "Is this my precious baby girl? You are so bad."

"Umm, we'll see how bad I can be, Mr. Carnavale."

"Let's just see that, soon-to-be Mrs. Carnavale." And they tried to love away their fear. What they'd been through giving their lovemaking a different edge.

Her parents and Nixie were there, Aunt Mim and Lourdes, and for some reason, Sam Begay. She had set up a webcam at the shop for Helen, Bob, and any of the crew who could be there. She told Rosalita to go to the shop and had Helen call her too to make sure she knew she was welcome.

Blossom didn't care about wedding traditions but loved her dress and didn't want Rocco to see it until the ceremony, so he rode with her parents and Nix and she with Mim and Lourdes.

Of course Mim had found the dress, the Etro they had seen. She was her usual persuasive self. "She wears a two, but I'm concerned about the bodice. She's voluptuous, so overnight me the two and a four. It's easier to tighten than to loosen." She had her seamstress follow her down to Albuquerque. They used the four and adjusted the waist.

It was as pretty as Blossom remembered, more Egyptian than Indian, but the colors were perfect—shades of blue, sunset reds, oranges, purple, the colors all circled and divided by muted gold scrolls. The modest strapless bodice was banded with midnight blue edged with gold, the skirt falling to her ankles in an easy A-line flow. It was highlighted by a choker that matched the neckline band with airy gold threads hanging from it.

Rocco was standing with the justice of the peace at the edge of the canyon wearing jeans, his boots, and the midnight blue shirt she had bought him. His hat was on the rock they had sat on to watch the sunset. A cry escaped him as she came into view, the kick in the gut, tears gathering. She hadn't cut her hair in a while, had just parted it in the middle, tucked it behind her ears, and left it hanging heavy and shiny down her back. The afternoon sun behind her made her glow. She was breathtaking.

The attendees were the witnesses, a few steps back from Rocco and Blossom. Back east, Rosalita said, "Mr. Rocco is crying," and he was. After they exchanged rings, wide silver bands—her's saying "I love you beyond words, R" and his "I love you to the moon and back, B"—even with tears falling, he sang "The First Time Ever I Saw Your Face" in a strong, clear, beautiful voice. She had no idea he was going to do it; but once he started, her eyes never left his face, squeezing his hands to give him confidence. She never shed a tear—unlike Nix, Mim, Lourdes, Helen, and Rosalita who wept openly. Her dad and Bob blinked steadily. Her mother was stoic. Sam took everything in.

As only Mim could do, she had found a justice of the peace whose wife did photography. This was good as Nix was going to take pictures, but once the ceremony started, he was fascinated by the aura around them. He had been with them off and on since they met, but now was of an age where the question of love often occupied him, and he forgot everything he planned to do to watch them.

When the photographer showed them the photos, they chose three—one of them looking at each other holding hands chest high, her hair hanging down her back, he looking at her, mesmerized; the second, they were looking off the cliff, their backs to the camera, his hat on; and the third one of the whole group. Blossom also asked for a small close-up of Rocco looking at her as he put the ring on her finger. The raw emotion was almost palpable. She wanted to see it always, and it later appeared on her nightstand in a silver frame.

She conceded to her mother's wishes to take everyone to dinner—"Really, Blossom, you can't just get married and run off." They went to the Rancher's Club in the Hilton-Albuquerque. She just wanted him to herself, but at least it was right on I-40 heading east. Her mother quietly told the maitre d' there would be eight instead of seven as Sam had followed right along. Rocco said it was the best steak he had ever eaten. He asked her father to please let him pay, or least share, the nine-hundred-dollar tab; but Cal said, "Rocco, nine hundred dollars is pretty reasonable for a wedding," winking at him.

Sam finally cornered him, perhaps the reason he had come, shook his hand, and said, "I've known her since she was seven. She's finally happy." He gave a small bow to Blossom, caught her dad's eye and nodded, and left.

"It's late, you kids should stay right here."

Rocco looked at Blossom, caught the tiny shake of her head, and said, "I think we can make Santa Rosa, Cal. We want to make long stops in Memphis and Nashville, so we better be on our way."

As he pulled on to I-40, he said, "Your dad's right, you know. I can see you're exhausted." Tears started. "No, no. No crying on your wedding day."

She smiled. "You cried."

He winked at her. "Those were tears of joy. They don't count."

"I don't like these bucket seats," reaching for his leg.

"Most cars have them, but we can check in Oklahoma City and see if there's more to choose from. Put your seat back and take a nap. You'll need your strength later, Mrs. Carnavale."

"I love you, Mr. Carnavale," asleep in a few minutes.

He carried her on his left hip into a Hampton Inn off I-40 on Old Route 66. The young fellow at the desk tried not to look surprised and even volunteered to come open the door. Rocco pulled down the spread and blanket with his right hand to lay her on clean sheets. He had gone from never having traveled to wondering how clean the bedspreads and blankets were. He put their toiletries out before undressing her and whispering he was getting in the shower.

When he touched her shoulder, she turned and put her face against his neck. "I thought it didn't matter, a little piece of paper, but it's so wonderful to be your wife. I was born to be your wife."

The kick in his gut, the expulsion of air as though the kick had actually happened. "Go potty, baby girl, you haven't gone since after dinner."

"I will, but that's not very romantic for our first night as married people," smiling.

She freshened up and came back with lotion. "Let me rub your back, you've been driving a long time." She straddled the small of his back and started at his shoulders.

"Heaven, baby girl, that's heaven." She moved down to sit on his thighs, rubbing his butt. "That's not my back, sweetie," laughing at first. Then, "No, baby" as she turned him over and he complied helplessly. "No, Blossom," his voice hoarse as she worked him. "Please, baby, no." She let him pull her up, but not before she sucked once on his tip, making him moan loudly.

His face was in the pillow. He was breathing hard. She whispered in his ear, "Remember our first real date, and you wanted to kiss me? I was scared and kept saying not yet, not yet. And when you kissed me, it was so wonderful and felt so good. I want to kiss you and make you feel good. I'm your wife, honey."

"Can I get used to you being my wife first?"

"Yes, you can. But soon?"

"Soon." He turned and kissed her, and she worked his tongue instead, bringing him back to ecstasy. He held her off nine more months.

She wanted him to drive a little before breakfast. They made it another sixty miles to Tucumcari when he saw a sign for the Kix on 66 Coffee Shop and wanted to try it. He had a huge whole nine-yard breakfast. She had a chocolate shake and a multigrain bagel. He then bemoaned the big breakfast because they went through Amarillo, Texas, too early to try the sixty-four-ounce steak he had seen on the Food Channel.

They made it to Oklahoma City. He wanted to see the Memorial and keep going, but she didn't want to rush it. "It's so profound, honey." They stayed at the Skirvin Hilton and ate there at the Park Avenue Grill. They walked to the Memorial, and the evening hour made it all the more poignant. She cried openly, and his eyes were moist, shaking his head in disbelief.

She surprised him the next morning, taking him to the Cowboy and Western Heritage Museum. She got a picture of him by the End of the Trail statue. She later enlarged it and put it next to the Indian girls painting in the living room. They agreed to come again. There was so much to see, so much Indian history she wanted to study.

They continued east, and he decided not to wake her and passed by the Clinton Library in Little Rock and headed to Memphis. They had decided to splurge on the Peabody Hotel, something about some ducks she wanted to see. He shed tears more than once as he drove—looking at her, his wife, thinking of how he got to where he was. He wanted to give her everything, and the fact she wanted so little brought tears again.

At about five, with the determination of an angry little boy, he had decided never to cry again just to burn up the SOB, and he never had until he met Blossom. He couldn't help but smile to himself—he cried almost as much as she did. What to do with all that emotion—hug, kiss, love, but sometimes it just spilled out of his eyes.

With no examples, what he knew of life and love came from TV and movies. The love stories just hadn't prepared him for what he felt about her. That he wouldn't be able to breathe when he thought of her, that he'd die for her, that he'd kill for her—then he smiled as her hand crept toward his leg, disapproving of his thoughts even in her sleep. Tears again.

She fussed about the price of the room, but the bed was divine. He wanted to eat at Neely's Bar-B-Que. He had watched their show on the Food Channel. After getting a picture of him at Elvis's statue on Beale Street, they turned in. He was anxious to see Graceland the next day.

"Now, honey, this home is very modest compared to the mansions along the Schuylkill. It's kind of like what someone would buy if they suddenly had money."

"I understand, baby, I don't care if it's tacky, I just want to see it."

She had made reservations for the Platinum Tour as soon as they decided to drive home. She just beamed the whole three hours they were there. He enjoyed himself so much; she cried. He got more than a few stares in his jeans, boots, and hat; and she laughed to herself when she made sure her wedding ring was prominent. I mean, really, that blond—you could see the man was married.

She didn't realize he gave his evil eye to a couple of fellows. She had on a white filmy sundress with ruffles from the bodice to her knees. Her hair was pinned back with her silver combs, and she was wearing silver sandals with turquoise stones. It was a magical afternoon.

They went to their room to rest before dinner, and while she was sleeping, he checked with the concierge about any dance clubs around. "Something family friendly. We don't stay out too late." After chatting awhile about where they had been and where they were headed, the fellow encouraged him to try Alfred's on Beale. "Enjoy some good food, watch the people from the second floor patio, and then fit in some dancing. It might be more top forties and rock 'n' roll than country, but you'll find that in Nashville."

He left his hat in the room and asked Charles, "Safe to walk?"

He looked at Rocco pointedly. "The little lady may get tired. I'll have someone take you down." He handed him a card. "Just call when you're ready to come back." The message Rocco got was Blossom was too pretty to be exposed to the nightlife crowds.

They had a wonderful time, easily adapting their dance steps to top-forty tunes. The floor was big, and he had no trouble keeping an eye on everyone. She was always amazed he knew every word to every song and was so proud when his dancing made the others move back to watch. Kris Kristofferson's "Me and Bobby McGee" was a perfect rockabilly style, and his footwork while he twirled her around the floor brought applause.

Back in bed, "I never knew a guy could have a day like this, baby girl. Elvis in the afternoon, dancing at night, and you in my bed. Or," he whispered, "I should have said my wife in bed. I love you, Blossom, beyond words."

"I know," she whispered back, "I have it in writing," spinning her ring.

"Baby girl, I know it's famous, but I don't want to spend our time driving around. Let's just stay at a Hilton. I really like their beds. They have a Hilton, don't they?"

"Yes, honey, they have a Hilton. It's really expensive, though, and all suites. We don't need that much space."

They were discussing the Gaylord Opryland versus a downtown hotel on the ride to Nashville from Memphis. It was just a couple hundred miles and their last stop before heading north to his sister's. She booked the Hilton downtown on her phone, and they let them into their room even though it was only one o'clock.

They freshened up, keeping the clothes they had on, and went downstairs to the Palm for lunch. He had eaten lightly at breakfast, so she didn't frown when he ordered a steak. "Get a lobster tail, baby, it says they're famous for them."

"I'd rather have a salad and have dessert."

"Eat as much as you can, and I'll finish it for you."

The atmosphere was fun and lively. Even at the early hour. He felt right at home in his hat and boots. She had on a halter sundress in a red and blue bandana print, formfitting to her hips and then flowing to the tops of her high blue moccasins. Her hair was in a single loose braid down her back with small blue bows at the beginning and end.

He had chosen a table where he could view the room, and all looked safe. He checked in with Bob at the shop, as he had done every couple days. All was good there. His steak was fabulous. She played with dipping her lobster more than she ate it, but with a couple of bites of his steak, he wasn't concerned. She had a tiny portion of Mississippi mud pie, which he finished. After the close call, he knew he'd always watch but felt the danger was past.

It was a short walk to the Country Music Hall of Fame, and again he couldn't believe the wonderful things he was seeing in the country. It was another city they decided they'd definitely come back to. He was enjoying himself so much, was so animated; she looked at the other visitors as if saying "Isn't he wonderful, isn't he beautiful." They bought Madison and Marlee T-shirts, hats, and glittery belts and headed back to the room to rest for dancing.

"Should we stop at the car for different clothes, honey?" He had been dumbfounded when he saw the box of clothes she had shipped to New Mexico for the ride home, but it fit perfectly in the trunk of the car and allowed them to take a small bag to their rooms.

"Can you put petticoats under that dress, baby? Twirling you in the white one made me nervous."

"This skirt's not full enough." She picked out a flounced denim skirt and peasant blouse, a wide belt and denim boots. It all looked pretty innocent to him, so he smiled his approval.

While she was napping, he checked downstairs for directions to the Wildhorse Saloon. They could walk to it over on Second, but to be careful he arranged for a car to pick them up when he called. Their ad said they had line dance lessons, and he was interested to see how they compared to Big Sallie's. The concierge said the dinners and dessert were great too.

"Blossom?"

She lifted her eyebrows in question as she twirled for him.

"You look beautiful, baby girl. I, um, just wonder a little about that middle thing." He was referring to the cinch belt running from under her breasts to her waist. It was denim and white checks, tied crisscross down the front. It emphasized her breasts and her tiny waist before the skirt flared out over her boots.

"Don't you love it, honey," ignoring his worried look. "It's so comfortable, and I can twirl all I want with these petticoats on." One of the petticoats was red, and she had on a red hair band.

"Do you have a bra on, sweetie?"

"Oh, I can't wear one with this blouse, honey. It comes off the shoulder sometimes. No one will know."

"Blossom?"

"Enough, Rocco. This is fine."

Her tone told him not to press the issue, so he just told himself he'd fight if he had to.

He got a rack of ribs and she, a salad of weeds and seeds as he liked to call it. She ate almost all of it while looking around at the very western decor. Her cheeks were flushed, her eyes sparkling in anticipation of an evening of dancing. What had he done so right that God had given him this beautiful creature? He'd never understand, but he'd be eternally grateful.

They joined the line dance lessons. Blossom didn't know all their steps started with basic moves he had learned. Her delight was contagious as they practiced scuffs, hitches, stomps, into the grapevine, rock step, and jazz box. He could see the wheels turning in her head as she connected steps and turns he had shown her to the basic moves. The footwork he did as he twirled her with one hand down the floor was a quicker, polished version of these same steps.

He found a table against the wall before the evening dances started, had his one beer for the night, and then left a Coke on the table to discourage anyone from buying them a drink. She had a bottle of water as they caught their breath, waving to a girl from the class. It was fun to see faces suddenly familiar so far from home.

Maybe to encourage the class participants, the first number was one they had used, Shania Twain's "Any Man of Mine." The teacher watched for a bit and nodded to Rocco, acknowledging that she knew he hadn't needed any lessons. He surveyed the floor in a glance—it was early and all couples. Only one other girl had a dress on, but he didn't expect any problems until later when singles would no doubt arrive.

The next number was Brooks and Dunn's "Boot Scootin' Boogie," again from the class. You could choose a fast or slow pace depending on which beat you followed. He took the slow route to start and then kicked it up toward the end, giving everyone fair warning they knew what they were doing. Dancing to him was a sport, and no one was going to beat him at it. Blossom clapped at the end of that number, delighted with what he was doing and showing him she was right there with him.

They were inspired all evening. She was ready to try anything he hinted at—through his legs, behind his back, up in the air, smiling gloriously at him, her eyes watching for directions. He snaked through the crowd to avoid one fellow walking their way and gave his evil eye to one heading toward their table.

"One more, baby girl, and we'll call it a night." He smiled and winked when it was "Nothing On But the Radio," smooth and sensual. He put her hands behind his waist, put his hands in the air, and moved her around the floor with his pelvis, staring in her eyes.

"Isn't this awfully suggestive, honey?"

"I hope so. Are you getting my suggestion?"

"I am. Unfortunately a lady across the room is too—I think she just fainted."

He gave one of his out-loud laughs she loved and said, "We better get out of here."

"I don't want to go, it's so much fun," she said even as she yawned. "Who could ever imagine I'd be in Nashville dancing. My life is so wonderful since you."

"Thank you, baby mine, but we better go. It's late, and we have to be on our way back to the real world tomorrow."

The car he had called was waiting, and they were in their room and turning the bed down in fifteen minutes. She took her clothes off, dancing around and humming with each piece she shed until she was naked.

"Dance this way, Mrs. Carnavale."

"Aren't we going to shower?" her eyes big and innocent.

"I don't think I can make it, baby girl," picking her up and twirling to the bed. They melted into each other, caressing, whispering, lost in the night and the moment. He was losing himself to their rhythm when she screamed, "Rocco, Rocco!"

It was panic, not passion, and fear shot up his spine. He had thought about what to do if it happened again. Her hysteria had stopped them the first time, so he said, "Stay with me, baby, stay with me."

Only a second went by, he knew she was trying, but then she started thrashing around, screaming. She pulled away from him; he was amazed at her strength, put her feet against his groin and pushed so hard he almost fell off the bed.

She was curled up with her face in her hands. "I ruined our trip, oh, I ruin everything," panting and sobbing.

"Blossom, baby"—picking her up—"precious baby, you didn't ruin anything." He lay beside her and tucked her into his arm, putting her hair behind her ear and wiping her nose. "Sh, sh, you didn't ruin anything. We know we can get past it, we're not afraid."

"But I ruined our trip. This will be all you think of when you think of our trip, that I did it again."

"Blossom, *you* didn't do anything. *We* will handle this. Big breaths now," breathing with her, smiling at her. "You know what I'll think of when I remember our trip?"

"Wha-wha-t," her voice catching.

"I'll remember you hugging that little chair at the Oklahoma Memorial"—kissing her forehead—"and I'll remember you at Graceland. The wind was blowing your white dress, and the sun touched your silver combs so it looked like a halo around your head. I thought, she's an angel, I married an angel. And tonight when I asked you to try a new step, your eyes said, I know what you mean, and I can do it. That's what I'll remember, that you're amazing and beautiful and my wife."

She touched his face, still trying to breathe normally. "You're so nice. At Graceland, I was thinking if that blonde didn't quit trying to get your attention, I was going to have to hurt her."

They giggled, and she whispered, "Do you want to try again?"

"We'll let your body rest for a while, it's been a busy day." When her hands came up under her chin, he kissed her and rolled her into her sleeping position, filing a thought away to call the doctor.

She turned at 5:00 a.m., clutching at him and whimpering. "Slow and easy, baby, slow and easy," and loved her back to sleep.

He got her going early, telling her she could sleep on the way. "It's over five hundred miles, baby, we'll just drive today and see Lindsay in the morning."

She called Lindsay and said they'd be getting in late and would come over elevenish. The girls were excited and wanted them to go swimming, so they planned a light lunch and swimming after.

He woke her for lunch. She stayed awake a couple hours and napped again. She was sleeping a lot, but every night had been a late one, lovemaking stretching it later, so he wasn't concerned. The miles went by easily for him. He reminisced, starting with the first day he saw her, watched the country go by, and sang. The words reached her now and then, and she leaned over to touch his arm.

They ate supper at a Bob Evans and checked into a Comfort Inn outside Northwood, pretty close to Lindsay's, and got fresh clothes and their swim things.

He was lying on his side holding her, knowing exactly what she was thinking. "Don't look at me like that, we'll have a whole month at home."

"I know. It's just been so wonderful, I don't want it to end."

"It's not the end, Mrs. Carnavale, it's just the beginning," kissing her gently, thinking he should let her sleep.

Then she moved to lie on top of him, slowly kissing his ears, his eyes, his nose, his chin, biting his lips, then probing his mouth. She put a hand on each side of his face, staring into his eyes. "I love you, Rocco Anthony."

"I love you, Blossom Dove," pulling the pillow down under her hips as he lifted her off him and onto the bed. She wrapped her legs around him as they began the search for their special place.

She already had on her suit covered with a terrycloth flounced cover-up with bright blue bows at the shoulders when he came out of the bathroom. "Are you wearing that suit with the jean shorts, baby?"

"No, this is the one with the skirt, honey, the color of these bows. You'll like it."

Lindsay looked thinner since Thanksgiving, with a different hairstyle. The atmosphere in the house felt better to him too. She and Randy apologized again for missing the wedding. Blossom showed pictures, and the girls oohed and aahed over her dress, questioning why it didn't look like a Barbie wedding dress. She explained brides get to pick whatever dress they want, prompting a discussion of what they would wear. His mother just smiled.

Rocco could see why Lindsay was thinner. Lunch was mini creampuffs with chicken salad and platters of fruits and vegetables. Blossom ate two puffs, and he noticed Lindsay poured Ensure into his mother's glass.

The local swimming complex was a nice facility—a splash area and three pools. Other than Nix's pool party, he'd never been swimming. He'd horsed around in French Creek in his jeans with a bunch of guys after drinking but had never learned to swim. They got all set up by the pool the girls liked. He got his mother comfortable in a shady spot and turned just as Blossom slipped out of her cover-up. The kick in the gut, Lindsay turning with the audible expulsion of air. Blossom's suit was brilliant blue with a tiny top and a skirt that started well below her navel. Her perfect little body with her large breasts was unbelievable.

"Aunt Blossom, Aunt Blossom, come with us." The girl were pulling on her even as he started for her with a towel.

"Blossom," controlled, quiet. She turned toward him smiling until she saw his face.

"I'll be right there, girls," and said quietly, "Rocco," and shook her head no.

"Baby, I just think you should cover up more," knowing he wasn't making sense but helpless to stop.

Lindsay called out, "Rocco, don't be a brute."

Blossom had never seen such a look on his face or heard such a tone in his voice. "I am not a brute. I'm protecting her."

"You start telling her how to dress, and you're a brute, and you know what I mean," keeping her voice low so their mother couldn't hear.

Seeing the shattered look on his face, Blossom instinctively went to protect him. "It's okay, Lindsay, we've been talking about it."

"You're just an enabler, Blossom, if you don't put a stop to it. I've been taking classes."

"He's fine, Lindsay, he's fine. Come, honey, we'll get in with the girls," taking his hand and smiling. He went with her with a dazed look and sat on the edge until the girls coaxed him in. He managed to play with them, and Blossom smiled encouragingly whenever he looked from her top to her eyes. There weren't any twentysomethings in their area, but he glared at a couple of teenage boys running through. He had to protect her; anyone could see that. She's tiny and beautiful, and his. Lindsay was wrong about him. He was nothing like him, nothing.

Their mother was in the front seat with Randy, and it looked like she was napping, so Lindsay said, "I won't bring it up again, but I couldn't get past it, and I'm taking a group class. It wouldn't hurt you either. Even in a small town, I bet you could find one."

"What kind of class, Mommy?"

"My weight class, girls."

Rocco was quiet the rest of the afternoon. Blossom held his hand and squeezed his arm reassuringly. After changing from their suits, the girls wanted to wear their new T-shirts and belts to dinner. Blossom let them pick out an outfit for her to wear from the trunk of the car. They picked a flounced denim skirt with pink petticoats and a formfitting pink T-shirt with Nashville in rhinestones across the chest. Rocco looked, looked at Lindsay, and didn't say anything.

They ate at the Maumee Bay Brewing Company. The girls sharing a veggie pizza, Rocco and Randy had the cheddar beer soup before their steaks. While Blossom was telling more about the wedding and their trip, Randy said quietly to Rocco, "Don't mind her. She's like someone who has just quit smoking. She wants to tell everyone what's wrong with them."

After dinner, they were just going to say good-bye in the driveway when Lindsay whispered to Blossom, "Come in, I found something for you." They got the girls into bed. Rocco and Blossom walked his mother to her room and sat awhile. The room was large and pleasant—a dresser from home, her old chair, and a new television. There were pictures of the girls, and Blossom made a mental note to send her one of the wedding.

"You okay here, Mom?"

"Yes, son, I'm very content. I hope you are too. You were very lucky to find Blossom," patting his hand.

Blossom saw his eyes were moist, and he was biting his lip, so she hugged Marie. "I'll come and get you whenever you'd like to stay awhile. You call us anytime," kissing her cheek.

They went back to the kitchen, and Lindsay said, "I haven't made any headway on what we talked about. But to pave the way, one day, I asked if she had any school pictures of me to compare to the girls. She got out a little box I'd never seen and gave me a couple Gloria had paid for, and this." She pushed a small envelope across the table to Blossom. "Gloria said she took it when he was about three. She was going to show the police if anything happened."

And there he was, Rocco, frozen in time, a miniature of himself—a determined, angry little baby. He was standing a little sideways in jeans and a dirty T-shirt, surprised by the camera, holding—and Blossom turned white and started crying—not a ball; it was a rock. She ran to Rocco and climbed on his lap, her head in his neck, sobbing.

"It's okay, baby girl, it's okay. It's the past." Looking at Lindsay with his hands out, "Why show her that, Linds? She's sensitive."

"Rocco, she told me you've talked about things, but no one could know who didn't live through it. It's not only the one picture we have of you, it says it all. You can't deal with things until they're out there."

He stood up, shifting Blossom to his hip, and shook hands with Randy. "I didn't get a chance to ask you. Can we take care of Mom so you can go on a trip? Ours was so great, I'd like you all to take one too. My treat."

Lindsay hugged them both. "We were talking about going to Cedar Point, and I found a lady to stay with Mom. It's just in the talking stage though."

Rocco said, "You and I never got a chance to travel. It would be great for the girls. I'll put a few extra thousand in the account when we get back. Thanks for everything."

Blossom whispered into his neck, "I want the picture, Rocco."

"Baby, you don't need to see that again."

"I want the picture, Rocco," pounding his chest, her voice rising. "I want it."

He shook his head and held out his hand, shooting Lindsay a disgusted look. Lindsay rubbed her back. "I made a couple copies, honey, to bring it up with Mom. I'll keep trying. We love you guys. Thanks for coming."

He was quiet on the ride back to the motel, quiet as they got ready for bed, but she knew it was coming and prayed she could say the right things to help him. They got into their cuddling position—she in the crook of his left arm, he on his left side looking down at her. He put her hair behind her ear. "I'm not a brute, Blossom, I'm not."

"We know you're not, honey. Let's make that one of the words we don't use. It has no part in our life."

"But I never hurt you, did I? Even when I needed you real bad, I didn't hurt you, did I?"

"Never, my darling," she lied, caressing his cheek, "never."

His eyes tearing, "I don't want to be that kind of man, Blossom. I know I get carried away and say stupid things, but I just want to keep you safe. You know that, don't you?"

"Rocco, Lindsay's dealing with it her way, and we'll deal with it our way. You are the most wonderful man in the world. You survived, honey, you survived and saved me. I know it would sound terrible to anyone else, but I love that you love my body. It's so wonderful that you don't say, here's a towel, Blossom, cover your brain. You don't tell me what to wear. You tell me when what I wear bothers you, and I love to bother you because my mind has nothing to do with it. Maybe someday we'll need help, we've talked about it. But tonight I just want to bother you," running her hands down his stomach. "May I bother you, Mr. Carnavale?"

"Yes, Mrs. Carnavale," his body relaxing from the tension, hardening from the pleasure. He kissed her until she was growling for more. "May I kiss you all over, Mrs. Carnavale?"

"Oh yes, oh yes, yes." Her hands were busy, so he put Tiger near her mouth, and they dealt with it their way.

But as he expected, she cried out in the night, thrashing around. "I'm here, baby girl, I'm here."

"A tiny boy. Oh god, a tiny boy. I can't bear it, I can't."

"I'm here, Blossom, I'm here. I made it, baby. Open your eyes." He put her hand on his face. "See, I'm here, baby, I'm right here." He smiled. He held her close, but she still cried herself back to sleep.

"Blossom, I need to talk to you about a couple important things before you fall asleep." They were headed east toward home on I-80/90 after having the continental breakfast at the motel. "First, you know I love you inside and out, don't you. Not just your body?"

"Oh, honey, I was just using that as an analogy. I know you do."

"What's an analogy?"

"Like a little story, comparing things. I was just trying to say you love me for me and not my brain."

"Okay, as long as we understand. Someday we might not look like we do now, and I don't ever want you to think you have to try to stay the same."

She looked at him with a sweet smile. "I promised you what happened last summer won't happen again, honey. It had nothing to do with my appearance. I just wanted to fade away from them. What's the other thing?"

"You cried most of the night, baby."

She laid her head back on the seat. "Oh I can't talk about it right now, Rocco, it's too heartbreaking. The picture made it too real."

"That's exactly what I want to talk about, baby. Just for a minute." She sighed deeply, but he took her hand and went on. "Holding you last night, Blossom, him hurting you from the grave even, it has to stop with us, baby. I know you wanted the picture, but you can't show it to our children. If they see it, don't say what's behind it. Let's just say Grandpa Carnavale died before they were born and leave it at that."

Wiping tears, "What about Lindsay?"

"Well, I noticed she waited until the girls were in bed. Maybe she really doesn't want to say anything when it comes right down to it."

"Honey, sometimes I might have to talk about it with you."

"That's fine, baby girl, we'll always face it when it comes. I just don't want it to go any further."

She laughed a little. "I wonder what Lindsay would say if she knew I'm a mess."

"Blossom! You're not a mess, you're perfect."

"Oh, Rocco, you know better. You have to deal with my mess all the time." Hesitantly, "Honey, they can't hurt us or take me or anything, right? We're safe now, right?"

"We're married, baby. No one can take you now. No one could take you before."

"My common sense knew that, honey, but after I came home to our house, I'd be fixing dinner or doing something that made me so happy, and I'd get a little twinge that she was going to ruin it. Say it again. It can never happen, right?"

"It can never happen, baby. She can't hurt you."

"Oh, she'll try to hurt me, verbally, I know that. I can take that as long as I know that's all she can do."

"She seemed pretty good at the wedding, and your dad was fine. You still think she hasn't accepted us?"

"She'll never be satisfied I didn't do what she wanted way back when, honey. You watch, she'll be calling and asking when I'm leaving for Pitt even though she knows and has it on her calendar. She'll act like the wedding was a little diversion I dreamed up and now I should get serious." She giggled when she said it, but he saw the hurt.

"You can take a nap now, Mrs. Carnavale. I'll wake you when it's time to eat." She smiled contentedly and closed her eyes and was sleeping so soundly, he stopped and got a pizza, quarter veggie, a Coke; and they were home by four o'clock.

She laughed when he carried her over the threshold then cried when she looked around the house. "Our trip was so wonderful, honey, but I love being home. Do you feel better in the house now, Rocco?"

"I love it since you've been here, baby. It's all different, especially with the pictures."

She was glowing and animated as they set up their pizza by the TV. "I'm going to make a memory wall of pictures here, honey. Then if a bad memory sneaks in, you can look at our memory wall and remember our fun times. I want to make all good memories for you," kissing his cheek.

The next fifteen days went blissfully by. She loved running a household—took care of the clothes from the trip, this to the cleaners, that to the washer; restocked the refrigerator; printed their pictures; and started planning her wall, starting with the ones from their weekends at Penn.

"Hi Gloria," she called from the garden. "We went to New Mexico and got married! We stopped to see Marie, come over for coffee." She wanted to ask about the picture of Rocco, but the timing didn't seem right.

She jumped into his arms when he got home. The love in the house surrounded him. As the day loomed for her to go back to Pitt, he knew things would get touchy. He was about to leave one morning when he heard her in the bathroom. He called up from the bottom of the stairs. "It's only seven thirty, baby. Why are you up?"

"I was sick, honey. I'm okay now."

At the word *sick*, he took the stairs three at a time. "What do you mean sick?"

"It's nothing, honey. I'm fine. I've never upchucked before, so it startled me."

It wasn't computing. His voice shaky, "What do you mean sick?"

She patted the bed beside her. "It's okay, darling. It must have been something I ate."

"But we had ham and eggs last night," confused.

"Oh, you never know about eggs. One might have been a little off."

"We better call a doctor."

She laughed. "Honey, I can call Dad. But really, it's nothing. I'm not feverish, I don't ache, and I feel fine now."

"I better stay home."

"Rocco, you have a meeting. Call me later, honey, I'm fine."

He went reluctantly, called her every hour until she said he was bothering her, and was home at four o'clock.

She fixed chicken and dumplings, ate lightly to be on the safe side, and didn't tell him she was sick the next morning after he left. That was it. She felt fine, and it left her mind, her return to Pitt consuming her.

He didn't want her to drive alone, and Nix was still in New Mexico, so Bob followed them down to bring Rocco back. She cried the whole way, blaming him, pounding his knee as they got closer. "You should have told him to come tomorrow so we could be together tonight. You never think ahead. This is all your fault. I hate that room. It's going to be hot . . ."

"Yes, baby, yes, baby. We'll turn the air conditioner on and take Bob to Primanti's so it can get cool . . ."

"I thought I hated Penn. I hate this even more . . ."

"Blossom, enough. You're going to hurt the little ladies' feelings and make Bob uncomfortable. If you can't make it, I'll come down Wednesday. You'll be home Friday afternoon, baby."

She turned to give him her mean look, her eyes narrowed, lips pouting, arms across her chest. He bit his lip but finally had to laugh out loud. "Can I take a picture of you for the memory wall?"

She cried and laughed together. "I'm sorry, I'm sorry."

"I know, baby girl, I know."

She had two extra days for the Labor Day weekend and was home by two o'clock. She called him, "I'm home, and I want to copulate like bunnies."

"I'm on my way." He chuckled. "I'm glad that wasn't on speaker, crazy girl."

He kicked off his boots and bounded up the stairs. "Where are you, crazy girl?"

She put her leg out from behind the door, humming the theme from *The Stripper*.

Shedding clothes as he chased her, he tossed her lightly on the bed. She had never looked more voluptuous and glowing. "God, I love you, woman."

Her back was to him. She was yawning in the afterglow of daytime loving. He cupped a breast in his hand, and his brow wrinkled. He slid his hand down to her tummy and said, "Blossom baby, when was your last period?"

"Why, Mr. Carnavale, what a question to ask a lady."

He kissed the back of her neck and whispered, "I think the lady might be pregnant."

He felt her go still, and then she turned. "No. No. I take pills."

"Did you forget the pills with all the excitement of the wedding?"

"Oh, Rocco, what have I done. Oh dear, oh my, I don't even know where they are," starting to cry.

"Baby girl, it's nothing but wonderful. If we're right, we've made a little person. It's amazing."

"Rocco," whimpering.

"Don't worry, sweetie, I'll help you. Rosalita will help you. It will be wonderful."

"It's not that, honey. It's just . . . two of you? How can my heart take two of you?"

"Don't get ahead of yourself. It might not be a boy."

She stared into his eyes. "It's a boy, and he looks just like you. It's God's little joke. I know it."

"Laura, it's Rocco Carnavale. My wife and I think she's pregnant. We'd like an appointment, please." She smiled at the pride and joy in his voice and couldn't help but be curious about finally meeting the girl he'd been coming in about.

Dr. Krienson recognized Cal Richards' daughter, had heard about her brilliance here and there, but didn't let on. She let Rocco introduce her, beaming, as Blossom shyly said hello. They discussed preliminary things,

Rocco getting a little pale. The doctor told him he could stay for the exam, but as he stood by Blossom's head holding her hand, she saw he was near fainting, and Blossom told him to go get some air. He ran.

He came back in sheepishly as the doctor was saying, "Other than not starting vitamins and folic acid as soon as I prefer, everything's fine. I'd like to see you gain about twenty pounds. Good pounds, not fat and sugar. Eat about six small meals a day. That will help you with morning sickness too. Empty stomachs are more prone. You didn't have any nausea?"

"Well, I guess I did, twice, but I just didn't make the connection."

"Twice, baby?"

"I didn't want to worry you," patting his cheek.

"Go with Melodie, and she'll get your information and give you our information. We don't want to overload you with paperwork. I always tell the girls, any concerns or questions, call me. Your aunt or your neighbor or your girlfriend are all coming from their own places, so I'm the one you want to call.

"Blossom says she's sure it's a boy."

"Well, if you'd like to know, between sixteen and eighteen weeks will give us the best picture. I'm going to say March 10, and we'll adjust that as we get more data.

Rocco cleared his throat. "Umm, how about making love?" Blossom blushed furiously.

"No problems at all. You'll adjust as you go, positions and comfort. We'll be seeing Blossom once a month until her seventh month, so bring any questions, and as I said, don't hesitate to call." She smiled at them and moved toward the door. "Enjoy the ride, you're in for a good time."

They made her next appointment, walked dignified to the elevator, out to the truck, and then looked at each other, and started to laugh. She jumped into his arms, and then they were crying. He covered her face with kisses. "Blossom, Blossom, I love you beyond words."

"Rocco," biting her lip, "I have to call my parents."

"We'll do it later, baby, it's too early anyway." He opened his phone and hit the shop. "Hi, Helen, put me on speaker. Who's there?"

"Just Bob and I right now. Everyone's at the Sandy Lake job."

"Blossom wants to tell you something. Go ahead, baby."

"We just found out we're going to have a baby!"

Helen screamed. Bob hollered into the phone, "Way to go, boss!"

"Bring everyone back a little early and take them to Mangia's for a couple drinks. I'll see you in the morning, we have to make some calls."

He'd never used his mother's number, had always gone through Lindsay. "Rocco?"

"Hi, Mom, I'm impressed you've got that phone figured out. You have my name all programmed in, huh?"

"Maddy did it for me."

"Kids, huh. Well, I called because . . . well, actually, Blossom and I are having a baby. In March. I just wanted you to know so you can tell Lindsay."

A few seconds went by; his jaw was clenched. "I'm very happy for you, son." He could tell she was crying.

"We just wanted you to know." He cleared his throat. "I'm going to get this right, Mom. I am."

"I know you will, son." She hung up abruptly.

"How was she?" Blossom was on his lap in the big chair.

"She was crying."

She hugged him tight. "It's happiness, honey. It has to be like a miracle to her."

"Maybe she's worried."

"No, she's not. She's seen what a wonderful person you are, Rocco. She's not worried."

"Is this so hard for other people, baby? I'm exhausted already."

She kissed him loudly, a hand on each cheek. "In a couple years, we'll be such a normal family, we'll be boring." She took a big breath. "Well, my turn."

"Let me do something before you call them, sweetie." He opened his phone again. "Hey, Nix, how's it going?"

"All good here, Rocco, what's up?"

"Hey, as soon as Blossom gets her nerve up, she's going to call your mom and Dad with some news. Hang around and see what the reaction is so you can tell us sometime, okay?"

"Sure. What's the news? She win the Nobel peace prize or something?"

"No, better than that. We're having a baby, Nix," the grin coming across the phone.

"Holy shit! I mean, holy moley. God, congratulations. That's so totally awesome. How is she?"

"Here she is, ask her yourself."

"Hi, Nixie," shyly.

"You have got to be kidding me. Are you sure?"

"We're sure. We went to the doctor today. About March 10, she thinks. I'm positive it's a boy," her happiness shining through.

"Blossom, that's really great. I can't believe it, my little sister. What will I be?"

"I'm your big sister, and you'll be an uncle. Uncle Nixie."

"I'd like to whoop and holler, but I'd ruin your surprise. You ready to make your call?"

"No, I'm not, but I better do it. It won't get easier."

"Well, I'll wander that way when I hear the phone. Good luck, sis."

"Thanks, Nixie, we'll see you when you get home. I'm so happy, honey. Maybe they will be too . . . someday. We love you."

She took a big breath. "You want me to call your dad, baby girl?"

"No. She'll know I didn't have the courage, and I don't want her to think that." She sat up straight, kissed him on the nose, and pressed Send.

"Hi, Mom."

"Well, hello, Blossom. It's not Sunday, why the call?"

"Do you have a speaker there so I can talk to Dad too?"

"No, that feature is in the office, and we're at the house. I can give him to you or relay information."

"You can tell him then." A tiny pause, "We got some wonderful news today. We're going to have a baby." She winced as though waiting to be struck.

"Oh for god's sake, Blossom"—disgustedly—"you can't remember to take a simple pill? Finishing your work should be foremost in your mind. I can't believe your lackadaisical attitude, young lady." A couple heavy breaths, "How does Rocco feel about this extra responsibility?"

"Actually, he said it was nothing but wonderful." Tears starting, pulling at her dress, "Nothing but wonderful."

"Here's your father." She heard her say in a monotone, "She's pregnant."

"Kitten! This is a surprise. But a nice one. Who are you going to?"

"Thank you, Daddy, we're really excited." Her voice was lightening up again. "We're going to Dr. Krienson in your building. I really like her."

"How are you feeling?"

"I was sick two mornings, but I thought it was something I ate," laughing a little. Rocco's feeling of grabbing the phone and tongue-lashing her mother started to abate.

"She wants me to gain twenty pounds. I don't know how I'll do that."

"You listen to your doctor. We want a nice healthy baby and mama. Your mother can help you with eating advice. She's really good at that." Blossom knew he was trying to include her to pave the way and rolled her eyes at Rocco—he had his ear to the phone.

"It's the same the world over, kitten. Get lots of rest, moderate exercise, eat healthy, and you can't go wrong. We'll be home in about a week. Tell Rocco congratulations from us."

She hung up, let out a big sigh. "I think that will be the hardest part of the whole thing. It will be all downhill from here," hugging him tight.

"We better talk about Pitt now, baby girl."

"Why, honey? Women work right up to eight months, even more."

"But you'll have to leave for a while anyway, Blossom. I'd just soon it be now. I saw something on TV about machines in hospitals being dangerous."

"I'm sure you have to be careful, but I've seen lots of pregnant women there."

"Well, why don't you go find a stopping point. You can always go back in two or three years."

She looked so happy and relieved. And a little guilty. "I do want to help people, Rocco, I do."

"I know you do, baby girl, but you have a little people in your tummy you can help right now. You're young, you have plenty of time."

"Oh, Rocco, I can't believe this. It's so wonderful, you're so wonderful," tears flowing.

"You! You have a baby growing in you that we made. I don't know whether to be happy or terrified."

Blossom finished up at Pitt the next week. She was right. Calling her mother was the hardest part of the whole affair. She was the embodiment of every pregnancy cliché—she glowed, she exuded good health, she was lusty and funny and insatiable in their lovemaking. His love took on a worshipful quality. It was hard to stay at work, and when he was home, his eyes followed her every move. The first time he felt the baby kick, his knees gave way, and he fell to the floor crying. She remembered she had told him when he held his baby in his arms, his past would be magnified. She was just making a point then, but now it worried her.

The sonogram was a week before her birthday. She was already lobbying to go dancing, and he was worried.

"Rocco, we have almost five months. We have to live our lives, honey. A little dancing won't hurt."

"We'll ask the doctor, baby girl. Come sit on my lap, and we'll see if the baby kicks."

Dr. Krienson said, "Wow, there's no question about it, we have a growing boy here."

Blossom squealed, "I told you, I told you. Oh, my darling, he's going to look just like you."

He had to hold on to the exam table, but he remained standing. "He might look like you, baby doll."

"Oh, Rocco," whimpering, and then the tears flowed.

He always got stronger when she faltered. "She'll be fine in a minute," smiling.

"But I want to name him after you, honey." They were curled up on the chair after dinner. He was happy she had eaten a good dinner, had gained two pounds at her checkup, and was nibbling her ear.

"Blossom, baby, anything but that. It's a tough handle to carry around. I know. Let's spare him that."

"Ricardo, then! And we'll call him Ricky when he's little."

"That's almost as bad," but she was clapping and glowing and oozing sex; what was he to do. He changed the nibbling to licking, and she returned the favor, from his ear to his mouth and down his neck. He picked her up and started for the sofa, but she panted, "Bed, bed, I can't move enough there."

After, when he could speak, "Blossom Dove, you are driving me out of my mind."

She whispered, "Welcome to my world, Rocco Anthony."

He laughed disbelievingly, and she said, "What did I do the first five months we knew each other?"

"You cried."

"I wanted you so bad and didn't even know it," her leg creeping over his stomach.

"Baby, give me another half hour."

"Half hour! You're getting old. I'm sure it was only twenty-two minutes before we were married." She giggled. She started drawing circles on his chest. "Why did you follow me out of that class?"

"I told you. I couldn't help it."

"Before that."

"Well, I heard the door open, and Dr. Royce said 'Blossom, come in.' I thought it was an interesting name, so I glanced up. By then you were in front of his desk, and I thought you were just a young girl because you were so small. But I kept looking because I was wondering about your moccasins, and then you turned around, and I saw you weren't a young girl," winking and grinning.

"Don't tell me you were looking at my chest," pulling on his nipple.

"I'm afraid I was, I cannot tell a lie," and his voice softened. "But then you looked in my eyes, and all of a sudden, it was a whole other thing."

She whispered, "The floor moved, Rocco, no one can tell me it didn't."

"I didn't feel that, baby, but something happened. Your eyes looked like they recognized me, and you looked surprised and scared. I had to follow you. What if I hadn't? Would you have done anything? Would you have tried to find out who I was?"

She started to cry. "Oh, I don't know, I don't know. What if you hadn't followed me? I can't even think about it."

"Don't cry, sweetie. I did follow you. I'm pretty sure I would have found you. Even if I had to knock on every door. Blossom's not that common of a name, or I could have gotten it out of Dr. Royce somehow. Don't cry, baby, I followed you. We're good. We're safe. You're just emotional now."

Her eyes were closing. "I know it's only seven thirty, but I have to sleep now." She rolled over and was out.

He covered her and went downstairs to shut things down, got a beer and came back to watch TV in their room. When the weather cooled, she had changed the bedspread to a blue suede-type thing; to match your eyes, she had said. He smiled as he remembered. The room was a haven to him now. A table covered with a cloth of the same material, a lamp with a cowboy boot base, pictures above it—the one of her as a little girl in white, one of them dancing Mim had caught. He had the chair positioned to see her and the TV. She always slept the same, her back to him, seldom moving; and tears ran down his face as he remembered the places he'd looked at her just like this—room 422 in Philly they'd grown to love, Pittsburgh, Santa Fe, Memphis, Nashville. He couldn't believe the changes in his life because of her. "I'll keep them safe, God, please help me."

They were invited to dinner at her parent's house for her twenty-first birthday. Things had been tense, especially when her mother realized she had left Pitt already. She hadn't told him what was said, but she had gone upstairs crying after a couple of phone conversations. He had made the phone call about it being a boy and hoped she got the message he'd be the one she would be talking to. "She's resting right now, but we wanted you to know it's a boy. It's still early, so I don't want her upset until we have a couple more months under our belt."

Blossom was radiant on her birthday. It would be hard for anyone not to be happy for them. She was so little, the baby bump was already noticeable at four months. They were going dancing, and she had on the cream-colored chamois dress with the brown Indian print ribbons crisscrossing her breasts. She was happy to be going to her parents and dancing, so he held his tongue about the ribbons emphasizing her enlarged breasts.

It wasn't hard to see her mother didn't care for the name Ricardo, but Nix made a big fuss over her tummy, and the dinner went fairly smoothly.

They hadn't been to Edinboro for quite a while, so the wedding and coming baby were cause for a grand celebration. He had brought Delbert and told the bartender to skip the first cut, it was too fast, and of course number nine. He was tentative as the second cut began, but when he saw she was moving easily and not winded at all, he relaxed. She knew he didn't forget she was pregnant, but the music and steps got to him, and she was glad she had insisted they come. His eyes were sparkling, his grin easy, and when he put his hands in the air to propel her with his pelvis to Delbert's "Ain't Lost Nothin," raucous "Go, Rocco, go" calls got the crowd stamping.

Late that night when they were cuddling, she said, "I'm so glad you had a good time. It's not too much, is it—a business, a wife, a baby?"

"Are you the wife?"

"I'm the wife."

"Then I can do anything."

In their lovemaking, she could tell he had crossed a line from fear to fun, and he was puffed up with pride and smiled at everyone who looked at her as she grew bigger.

He cooked at their house for Thanksgiving. She and her mother talked about furniture for the baby's room to avoid other subjects. They had finally agreed it would be Lindsay's old room. She wanted it to be his parent's room, it was the one closest to them, but he didn't want the baby in his father's room. "Honey, I'm sorry you have those feelings. I've tried to redecorate everything."

"I know it's silly, baby girl. Just humor me, okay?"

"Of course, darling. Maybe the farthest one will be the best in the long run." Making a mental note to change his parent's room even more but realizing she'd never really know what he'd lived through.

Christmas was quiet. He was afraid to have her fly to Aunt Mim's, and the weather was too iffy to drive to his sister's. They put up their first tree as a married couple. She laughed and cried over everything. "You're killing me here, baby girl." She blamed it on her hormones but knew it was just watching him revel in every part of the holiday.

The tree took awhile to decorate. The first night he put the lights on, they were reflected in her eyes. One thing led to another, and they were in bed by eight o'clock.

He came home the next night and gave her his Groucho Marx eyebrows when he saw his sleeping bag open in front of the tree. "*Miracle on 34th*

Street is on tonight," she said innocently. "I know it's one of your favorites. We can lay here and watch it after dinner." He put the star on the tree, and they did lie there but didn't watch it. She finally put the few ornaments they had bought in Nashville on the next day. She wanted to buy a few every year so they could see their collection grow.

She was almost embarrassed to be so happy, even after her mother's Christmas Day call berating her again for quitting Pitt way too early. He gave her a pearl. She had fourteen now with birthdays, holidays, and the two black ones for their secret remembrance. She gasped when he also gave her a small Georgia O'Keefe print to put near her Indian girls painting.

"We have to take a ride to see your gift, honey. Do you want to go now or after dinner?" She seemed nervous.

"Well, now you have me really curious, so let's go."

"Okay. Let's stop at the shop first. I need something from Helen's desk."

She didn't stop at Helen's desk but went right to the break room door where Helen had left a big red bow and a Merry Christmas, Rocco sign on the door.

"What's all this, sweetie?"

"Rocco"—her arms around his waist, looking up almost shyly—"I'm ashamed to say I'm almost glad for that bad time with those two salesmen because it led to our wedding. But I don't want it to ever happen again. If you feel such anger, honey, come in here. She opened the door on a redone break room with a speed bag hanging from the ceiling and a heavy bag in the corner. "I know it's a funny gift. Is it okay?"

He shook his head. "You are amazing, baby girl. It doesn't happen much anymore, but I'll admit there are days I'd like to put my fist through a wall when an order is late or mixed up. Did Bob help you?"

"He did most everything, honey. He said here would be better so you wouldn't be driving home angry and found the best ones. He was so worried that day, Rocco, he really loves you."

He got out his phone. "Sorry to interrupt your day, Bob. You son of a gun, this is great, man."

"Glad you like it, boss. Miss Blossom had a good idea there." They said Merry Christmas all around, and Blossom gave him the fingerless gloves to use with the bags.

Late January she came out of the kitchen after dinner and found him looking at the drawings in the *What to Expect* booklet the doctor had given them early on. He had an anguished look on his face. "Blossom, I-I," his eyes filling up and pointing to the drawing of the baby's head settling into the birth canal.

"It will be fine, honey. All babies are born the same way. Well, there is Caesarean section, and she is going to explain that the next visit. But we don't want that if we can help it. This way will be the best."

"I don't think we thought this through, baby, this looks really dangerous."

"Let's put the book away, honey," climbing into his lap. "Remember, let go and let God," patting his cheek. But the damage was done. His carefree attitude was gone. Every time she grimaced with a back pain or sighed with tiredness, a little cry escaped him. He carried her upstairs, hovered over her as she showered; lovemaking was out of the question, whispering, "His head's right there, Blossom."

She couldn't move in bed without him knowing, so he knew she was in the bathroom. It was 5:00 a.m., March 10. When he heard a low *ooh*, he was out of bed in a flash. "Blossom?" Another low *ooh* and she was perspiring. His knees gave out.

"I think we should time a couple pains, honey. I might have to call the doctor."

"I'll call her right now, I'll call her right now." He started tossing things around, not seeing the phone right in front of him.

"No, honey. The first thing she'll ask is how far apart the pains are-r-r," panting.

"I'm getting dressed," stumbling, trying to put on two things at once.

She came out for her phone, laughing. "First things first, darling. Let's be organized. You look like that *I Love Lucy* episode." She started getting dressed and then had to lean over on the bed on her hands. "Ooh, ooh, breathe, breathe."

"That's it," he said. "We're going, we're going now."

"Rocco, call the doctor . . . see, right there, press Send. Here, let me have it. You finish getting . . . Dr. Kreinson, it's Blossom . . ."

At the hospital, he went through the motions of putting on all the paraphernalia for staying in the room with her; but as soon as the nurse started to put her feet into the stirrups, he fainted. "Will someone stay with him? Please don't leave him alone out there. Give me a phone, I'll call my brother."

Nix came and paced with Rocco. Her parents figured a first baby would take awhile so missed Ricardo Anthony Carnavale's arrival at 6:48 a.m.—seven pounds, two ounces, nineteen inches long, black curly hair, crystal blue eyes. Blossom was twenty-one; Rocco, twenty-three.

She was energized and wide awake, holding the baby in her left arm, rubbing Rocco's back with her right hand, whispering sweet nothings into his ear as his head lay on her lap, tears running down his face.

"He looks exactly like you, my darling. Wait 'til he he opens his eyes, you'll see. Look at him, look now honey. See, oh I take it back, it's not God's little joke, it's His blessing. Oh, I love you, I love you, Rocco," as her voice faded and her eyes closed.

They brought Ricky in and said the lactation specialist would be right along. Before she got there, Blossom and Ricky had it all figured out. She was happy and confident, so he was too. Rocco's eyes rolled back in his head, and he was gone again. Blossom smiled at the nurse. "He'll be fine, he's sensitive."

Rocco couldn't believe they sent them home with a couple of pieces of paper. "I got a whole book with my Skilsaw and a little human they send you home and say good luck?"

Blossom immersed herself in motherhood with the enthusiasm she had for making love and dancing. Everything was thrilling, nothing too much work. Rosalita stayed three nights, and Blossom sent her home. Ricky was sleeping almost four hours, eating ravenously and sleeping again. Rocco told Rosalita to come at eight each morning to be sure Blossom ate breakfast and lunch and napped when the baby did. He said he'd take care of dinner.

The first night Rosalita was gone and the baby monitor woke them, he followed her into the baby's room. "Honey, go back to bed. I want him to enjoy the quiet of his own room."

"I want to be with you."

"You have to work, honey. I can sleep during the day. I'll be in as soon as he eats." She started to change Ricky. "Go, go, sweetie. He hardly wakes this feeding. I'll wake you when I come in. We'll have almost four hours."

When she came in, she crawled on her hands and knees onto his chest. "He's so beautiful, Rocco, I can't believe it." She slipped her nursing gown off.

"Can I touch you anywhere, baby?"

She was wearing tight panties. "I have stitches and a maxipad, and my breasts are leaking. In a couple days, I'll find a spot for you." She whispered in his ear, "I guess I'll have to make love to you for six weeks."

"Blossom"—sternly—"you need your rest."

"I can rest all day. Just a little nibble? You can be my pacifier."

"Baby, please."

"You've put me off for a month. I can't go another six weeks. One little nibble? We'll work up to it gradually," she whispered, moving down his stomach. "See, this is nice, right? A little bite here, a little bite there. What could be the harm."

"Blossom, baby. No, honey, no," breathing hard.

But she was kneading him like a kitten, biting, sucking. "Blossom," crying out, "the baby, don't swallow, don't swallow, oh god," and he reached for Tiger.

It was hard to take his eyes off her. She winked mischievously when Rosalita came, and he made a herculean effort to give instructions for the day and pretend he was in charge. Every time Rosalita wasn't looking, Blossom stuck out her tongue and licked her lips. His knees gave way, and he reached for a wall. She walked him to the door and whispered, "I'll find a spot for you today, crazy man." A moan escaped him.

Helen saw him with his head in his hands a couple of times, but he was smiling, so she wasn't worried. "Not getting any sleep, boss? You'll get used to it."

"Yeah, yeah, no sleep."

He called Rosalita. "I wanted to call her but thought she might be sleeping. How's everything?"

"Everything is grand, Mr. Rocco. They're both napping. Such a fine little fellow, just sleeps and eats. It's wonderful to watch them. Dinner is in the slow cooker, so don't worry about fixing anything."

"Hi, Daddy," kissing him with her tongue and putting the sleeping Ricky into his arms. "You can put him in the bassinet. He's good until about eight, so we can have supper."

"God, this is unbelievable," as they stood looking at him.

"Don't whisper, honey, I want him to get used to the noises in the house. Let's have supper so we can start a nice routine. Rosalita fixed turkey chili, but it's really just turkey soup 'cause I can't have the spices. Ricky wouldn't like them. You can sprinkle some on yours if you want. She made cornbread too. I had some at lunch." She had a scant ladle of soup but did have a nice-sized piece of cornbread and a Yoo-hoo.

They snuggled on their chair after dinner and had a brownie. "You know what we forgot to talk about?"

"What, baby girl?"

"We'll never test the baby, Rocco."

"Nope, we never will, sweetie."

"Not even if he seems very, very bright."

"Not even, my baby."

She smiled happily and yawned. "You better go to bed after he eats next," he said.

She whispered, "But I had big plans for you now that your bugaboo is gone."

"What's a bugaboo?"

"It's worrying about something for no reason, silly boy."

"Blossom, it was a problem for me. I didn't want to treat you like that."

"I love every inch of you, Rocco, and I want every inch to be mine, mine, mine. You were fifteen and sixteen, honey, a lost little boy." She giggled. "Looking for love in all the wrong places."

"I love you beyond words, Blossom."

"My breasts are tingling. He's waking up. Let's change him."

"Can I take a picture while you feed him, if I can get just his eyes and nose?"

"Not with your phone, honey. I haven't checked yours, and I don't trust them. Use the regular camera. Don't get any private parts."

He didn't. Her hair covered all but Ricky's eyes looking at her, her face in silhouette. "I got it, I got it! Wow, this is the best picture I've ever taken. Will you put it by my side of the bed?" And there it stayed their whole life.

They put him to bed at nine fifteen, and the next thing she knew it was 4:00 a.m. He knew when her eyes opened. "He's fine, sweetie, he slept right through the midnight one."

"Oh my goodness, six days old. Isn't he wonderful, I'm soaked through though. You rest, honey, I'll be back."

She came in at four forty-five and snuggled against him. He held up a finger, winking at her. "Where's that spot you were telling me about."

"What about you," she whispered. "I don't want to be selfish."

"Blossom, how can you say that after last night? Show me where, I want to make you feel good," licking her ear. "Show me."

She guided his finger down her stomach, making squeaky little noises all the way. "Ahh, ooh that's nice. More, more, Roccooo," reaching for Tiger.

She was still in her afterthroes. He was breathing heavily, chattering to calm himself down, "We have to get rid of this bra thingy, baby. I don't like anything between us." Her eyes fluttered; she growled. "I know, I know, you think you need it. We'll talk about it tomorrow. God, isn't this wonderful. You're home, he's here." Her lips moved. He leaned closer.

"Shut up. Now."

He laughed and held her tighter, didn't turn her over and drifted away with her head under his chin.

The six weeks went by dreamlike. Ricky smiled, and Rocco cried. He rolled over, and they thought he was the most clever baby ever. At her checkup, he knew he wouldn't make it, so he stayed out of the exam room. "Come on in, Rocco," Dr. Kreinson said. "She's great, couldn't be better. Now, you won't want to use the birth control pill you have, it can reduce milk production. This prescription is for a progestin-only pill. This plus breast-feeding will reduce the chance of getting pregnant. It's an old wives' tale that breast-feeding alone is birth control. It may reduce the possibility, but it's not dependable. Give yourself a change to rejuvenate, Blossom."

They stopped on the way home and filled the prescription.

"We'll still have to wait, baby girl, they don't work overnight."

"Women used breast-feeding for centuries, honey. I'm sure we'll be fine for a while."

"Blossom, she said give yourself a rest. We better wait."

"We'll see, honey, we'll see," patting his knee.

He went back to work. She fed Ricky. She and Rosalita planned the week's menus. She took a nap. He came home. They had dinner. She winked at him a lot. He shook his head no. She smiled. She fed Ricky at nine. He was sleeping until six in the morning now. They put him to bed. Rocco went in the shower.

She was naked on the bed, her hair spread out on the pillow, another one under her hips. She was holding her arms out to him.

He took a deep breath. "Blossom, we need to talk about this."

"Uh-huh, we'll do that soon. Come here."

"Blossom."

"I just passed my six-week checkup with flying colors, and I want my present."

"Oh, baby, we need to be mature and responsible."

"Come here, and we'll talk about it," motioning with her finger.

She arched her back. She licked her lips. It had been ten weeks. He dropped the towel.

When she could speak, "I was worried it would be different. My body went through so much. Was it the same?"

"Better than ever, baby mine, better than ever."

"I want to please you so much, Rocco."

"Blossom! Baby girl, just breathe in and out, and you please me. You know that by now. I hope everything's okay, I should have more control."

She giggled into his neck. "Your control is just fine, good sir. Could you lose it again in a while? I better put a nursing bra on again, or I'll get milk all over you."

"It's okay, baby, I don't like that thing. I want to be able to see you. Here, use my towel."

He relaxed in a couple weeks when he figured the pills had kicked in. She sensed it and was unrelenting . . . one night demanding, the next kittenish. They were in positions he'd only read about when he was fifteen, hiding in the woods with stolen *Playboy*s and *Penthouse*s. He'd end up gasping for air while she fell asleep looking like half angel, half Cheshire cat as he limped to the bathroom. Life was wonderful.

That fall he started wearing the buckskin jacket she had given him, with his hat and boots. The crew was big enough now that he seldom had to fill in, and he had sales calls or meetings most every day.

She was delighted one day at the supermarket when she overheard two women chatting in the checkout line. "We're finally putting in our two-level deck." "Who's doing the work?" "Carnavale's." "Oh, the cowboy. I hear they do great work."

Blossom smiled at the checkout girl, who said, "Have they done work for you?" "You might say that," laughing, "he's my husband."

When Ricky was seven months, she spent a day patting her chest and saying "Da-Da," until Ricky copied her. When Rocco came home that evening, she handed him the baby and said, "Ricky, who came home to us," patting her chest. Mimicking even better than she hoped, he patted Rocco's chest and said, "Da-Da." Rocco's knees gave out. He just made it to a chair before burying his face in Ricky's hair and crying.

Ricky stood. He walked. He talked. Blossom could be stern with no-no's but couldn't handle his checkups—the poking, the prodding, and absolutely not the shots. She would run into the hall crying, so Rocco took him to his checkups. Talking to him man-to-man in his car seat from the get-go—the message sinking in, we do what we have to do to protect Mommy.

He was almost three, very verbal and serious. Rocco was on his way home when the phone showed Rosalita. A little stab of fear in his stomach, "What?"

"Daddy, it's me, Ricky." He smiled broadly even though Ricky sounded worried. He worried about things.

"Yes, son."

"First, I want to say I didn't do anything."

"Okay, son, go on."

"Mommy is crying. I was playing with my trucks, and I didn't do anything. Rosalita let me use her phone 'cause it's 'portant."

"I'm about to make the turn, so you go hug Mommy, and I'll be right there. It's probably a woman thing, so don't worry."

He came in. She must have been in a state because she didn't come to the door. Ricky was standing by her patting her shoulder, looking frightened. She was sitting on a hassock, her face way over to her knees, her arms covering her head, sobbing hysterically. "You help Rosalita with dinner, son, I'll take over." He picked her up, sat her on his lap, and she grabbed his shirt. "What is it, baby girl, I'm here."

"I can't bear it, I can't bear it."

"Slow down now, tell me."

"Rocco, Rocco, he was playing with his trucks, and you didn't have trucks, and I made a little noise, and he turned and looked just like the picture, and you never had trucks, and you were all alone. Rocco, I can't bear it, you were a baby keeping a rock, oh god, oh god, a baby just like him, I can't . . ."

"Shh, I'm here, baby girl, I'm here." He put her hand on his face. "See, I'm here, I made it," rocking her. "Everything's good. We're all here together, it's all good now." He sensed Ricky at the door, Rosalita trying to hold him back.

"Is it a woman thing, Daddy? Just a woman thing?"

"Yes, it is, that's all it is, son. Women are sensitive sometimes. Hand me the tissues and go with Rosalita. We'll be right in."

He hated it when his abuse reached her—hated it. Maybe he never should have told her, but it was too intertwined in his existence. And he was powerless where she was concerned. She would have wormed it out of him just like she did. He rocked her as he thought; they'd survived their beginnings, and it would end with them. It had to.

He usually knew when it had reached her, but sometimes he didn't.

Before Ricky was born, they had started attending the Catholic Church she had grown up in. She was still reserved about it, but he was very comfortable, even joined the choir and sang at the nine o'clock mass every other week. The nine o'clock was traditionally the student mass, and it tickled her the number of teenage girls who started sitting in front of the choir and the number of twentysomethings who decided to join.

He wanted her and Ricky to sit right behind the row the choir sat so he could join them during the homily. The Sunday after the truck incident, he looked at her holding Ricky on her lap, her chin on his head. Her smile and eyes consumed him, and he sang just for her. She often cried when he sang, so he wasn't worried when tears rolled down her cheeks. He never asked, and she never told that while he sang hallelujah on the altar, she felt the kicks of the steel-toed boots.

When it dawned on her why she had been more emotional than usual, she cried.

A couple of mornings later, he was surprised when he came out of the shower that she was already downstairs. He dressed and went down. "Good mo . . ."

"Mommy's mad," Ricky said, sitting at the table.

"Mommy's not ma . . ."

But Mommy turned from fixing scrambled eggs, a scowl on her face, and stamped her foot.

"Whoa," he said as he took a couple of steps and hugged her close. She tried to wiggle away, but he wouldn't let her. "I bet Mommy needs a bubble bath," and whispered to her as the tears started, "I'll fix it, baby, I'll fix it. Run upstairs, I'll be up as soon as Rosalita comes. There she is, run."

He finished Ricky's egg, sliced a banana, got him some juice, and went upstairs. She hadn't started a bubble bath, was sitting on their chair crying. He picked her up. She pounded on his chest. "Is this my lucky day, you stamp your foot, and now you pound on me?"

"Quit making fun of me."

"I'm not, Blossom Dove. What's going on to get you all upset?"

"We never have time anymore. We make love, and then it's morning, and you leave and don't come back for a long, long time. We never have time, you know, to do things," she whispered. "I'm always afraid he'll hear us now that he's bigger."

"Okay, let me think a minute. How about Rosalita stays and we go to a motel. We'll make love all night long."

Her face brightened, and then, "We can't. What if he wakes up and wants us. It would break my heart."

"Okay, okay, how about in the day? He's used to us being gone then. We'll stay until five o'clock. We can take a picnic and do everything you want. How about that?"

She smiled. "Could we do it Wednesday? Rosalita stays all day Wednesdays. We could have a special day," her voice excited.

"Wednesday it is, baby girl."

She put her head on his chest. "I'm sorry I was bad."

"I'm sorry I messed up, baby. I'm so happy to get home at night, I forget you've been here all day. Now, would you really like a bubble bath, or would you like to fool around," winking at her.

"I'd like to fool around," she said shyly. "I'll be out in a minute."

He called Bob while she was in the bathroom and was taking off his shirt when she came out in a black lacy thing that looked like a one-piece bathing suit. "Wow, what is that," his eyes wide.

"It's called a teddy, you're supposed to like it."

"I love it. Take it off."

She fluttered her eyelashes. "I think you're supposed to do that."

"I can do that," laying her on the bed. "Must be I do this strap and kiss you here, and then this strap and kiss you here." He slipped the rest of the little wispy thing off and, trying to keep the mood playful, said, "I'm taking requests today, what would you like?"

Her eyes were black, penetrating, and closing. She looked out from under her lashes. "Everything," she breathed.

He moaned and shivered and was gone.

He was on his knees, trying to get air. He leaned forward on his knuckles. God, was she okay? Didn't have the strength to open his eyes so tilted his head and looked down. There she was under him, already asleep. Where were they? Philly? Room 422? His eyes snapped open. Ricky? Where was Ricky? His watch said nine fifty. Okay, okay, in preschool. Maybe Rosalita was gone during the loudest part. Had he called Bob? Yeah, yeah, he remembered. Jesus God, he had to get it together. Looked at her full on. Wanted to pick her up and cover her with kisses but covered her with the sheet instead. Stumbled to the shower.

He walked downstairs a little carefully. It had been almost four years, but he was still getting used to having household help. "She's going to sleep a little while. I'll check in with you later." He stepped out into the garage and then stuck his head back in. "Do you think she's pregnant?"

Oh, for sure, Mr. Rocco, for sure."

"You don't have to spoil me because I had a tantrum."

"I'm not spoiling you. I'm feeling guilty because I got preoccupied." He had just asked her if she would like to go dancing Saturday night at a place he had heard about in Cambridge Springs.

"The special day is enough."

"No, we need more nights out. He's old enough now, and I'll ask Rosalita to bring her daughter. One more person to play with. He'll get a kick out of it."

Saturday night she came downstairs. "Blossom," quietly. He couldn't help it and never learned it was dangerous ground. She looked at him with wide eyes. "I've never been to this place, and it is a bar, baby."

"And . . . ?"

"Well, you look beautiful, but I'm just wondering about your top, baby, it's a little low."

She had on a denim skirt, denim boots, and a red scoop-necked blouse showing a bit of cleavage. She gave him a look but said "Would something with a high neck and long sleeves make you happier?"

"Just for tonight, sweetie," pleased he seemed to have handled it well.

She came back a few minutes later with a red turtleneck long-sleeved top, but it was made of a stretchy material that clung to her every curve. The kick in the gut, a little noise escaping, his heart pounding in his ears. "Was there something else you wanted to say, Rocco?"

"No, ma'am."

"I didn't think so. Daddy and Mommy are leaving, Ricky," as she got her jacket. "Bedtime is eight o'clock. You already had a treat with the McDonald's supper, so there's no change in bedtime. Am I clear?"

"Yes, Mommy," as Rocco picked him up to kiss him. "We won't be too late, little guy. We'll see you in the morning."

In the truck, "I'm nervous about leaving him," biting her lip. "We always put him to bed."

"Baby, Rosalita has put him down for his nap a lot of times. It's the same thing."

"Oh, I know. But first preschool and now going out at night. You know, he had a little sniffle. He never did before preschool."

"Blossom . . ."

"Well, he didn't. And the teacher knows he can read. I get scared."

"Baby girl, you're his mother. No one can do anything without your permission. Relax now, we haven't gone dancing in a while. Just enjoy yourself."

The dance club looked promising. It had a coat checkroom, and he didn't see anyone with hats on so checked his and their jackets. He was beyond relieved when Blossom took off her jacket and had added a denim vest over her top. As he looked over the room for a safe table, his eyes paused on a foursome just as one of the fellows looked up. "Rocco?"

"Hey, Jim, long time." They walked over, and his cohort from his crazy days stood up to shake hands. "I knew you made it, Rocco, I've heard about your company. This is my wife, Holly, and our friends, Carl and Marianne."

"Yeah, I'm still standing. This is my wife, Blossom. Nice to see you all. You come here often? We like to dance and usually go to Edinboro." He was glad they were filling up a table for four. He didn't want to get too friendly until he talked to Jim alone. He hadn't seen him in ten years, and they usually had been drunk, so he really didn't know him at all. 'Course he might be thinking the same thing. Rocco at sixteen wasn't someone you'd like to have around. He did notice they all had two bottles in front of them, and it was early. "Great to see you, Jim, stop at the shop and have coffee."

"I will, Rocco. I think you'll enjoy the music here."

He found a table for two against the wall where he had a good view of everything and ordered his beer and her a ginger ale. "And an order of loaded fries," he called after the waitress.

Blossom gave him a look. "We had a perfectly lovely, healthy dinner, honey."

"I know, but, baby, loaded fries. I have to see how they do them. That was the one of my old group I thought had made it."

"We should ask them over. They seem nice."

"I'll ask him to the shop first. It's been a long time, and all we had in common then was trouble."

They chatted as he ate some fries. She took one bite and made a face. "Honey, I saw on TV that husbands like a night out with other men."

He almost spit his beer out.

"What! Baby girl, I'm with men all day long. The last thing I'd want is a night out with them. It's all I can do to take them out for a drink after work on Fridays. What I want is to open that door and smell you and drown in your eyes."

"You're so sweet, honey."

"You need to do something, though, to break up your routine, baby."

A look crossed her face. "I love my routine, Rocco. I love knowing just what each day brings. It's very comforting to me. Every day was always so tense when I was young."

They had a wonderful time dancing, kept it smooth and basic except for a couple intricate moves, which got surprised looks from the crowd and thumbs-up from Jim's table. They left for home at ten-thirty, happy and tired.

On Tuesday, Rocco reminded Rosalita to fix Blossom's favorite chicken salad sandwiches on crunchy bread for their Wednesday picnic and put in a couple of brownies and a couple of waters.

Wednesday they took the short drive to the Holiday Inn Express. Rocco had made arrangements for a room to be ready at 9:00 a.m. and a bouquet of roses on the table. They folded the bedclothes back and undressed each other. After six years together, she couldn't believe how her heart was pounding. "I thought we could talk awhile," she said breathlessly.

"Uh-huh, we'll talk. We'll talk about what I'm going to do to you over and over again." He laid her on the bed and started at her neck right under her ear kissing and biting. "I love you beyond words . . ."

"Ohh, ooh . . ."

"I love you more every day," his tongue in her navel.

"Ahh, ooh . . ."

"You drive me crazy," his tongue in her mound.

She screamed, "Come in, come in!" He entered, and they started their beautiful rhythm. She was panting, arched against him, and then "No, no. Rocco, no. Not on our special day," starting to kick him away.

"Let's try slow. Slow, baby." He kept moving and pushed her stomach slowly, carefully. "Keep moving, slow, breathe, breathe."

She looked at him fearfully—breathing, moving, a tentative smile. "You did it. You did it. Oh, my hero, you did it."

"Okay now, keep moving. Come back to me. That's it, here we go, we can do it."

She was so tight against him, her legs around his waist, her arms around his neck, she couldn't reach for Tiger and screamed against his forehead, digging into his scalp. He shuddered and released, fighting for air as he lowered her with one arm, holding her with the other. His eyes closed, his neck unable to hold his head up. He collapsed.

"We did it, we did it," she panted. "We fought the freight train, and we won." She covered his face with kisses, "My hero, my hero," as she rolled over and slept.

She woke with a smile. "I didn't sleep our special day away, did I?"

"No, it's only lunchtime. Go potty, and I'll set things up." They ate and cuddled and loved and napped. At three thirty, they showered; and as he was washing her enlarged breasts, "So did we do everything you wanted?"

"Oh, yes."

"And did we talk about everything you wanted to?"

"Yes," a little tentatively.

"So when were you going to tell me you're pregnant?"

Her eyes got big and then softly, "Soon. Pretty soon."

"Sweetie, it's wonderful. It couldn't be more wonderful."

"I know. It's just that everything is so perfect now. I have a nice schedule. I was going to do some work for Chet."

299

"Baby, you know how fast the time goes. You'll have another nice schedule before you know it, and we'll have a brother or sister for Ricky. You should be taking those vitamins."

"I have been," she sighed. "I called Dr. Kreinson. We can go in when it's time for the sonogram."

They dried off and dressed. She hugged him tight, and he lifted her up to put her legs around his waist. He whispered into her hair, "Don't scare me, okay?"

"How could I scare a big man like you?"

"If I ever thought you weren't happy, baby girl, I don't know what I'd do."

"Oh, Rocco, don't be silly. I'm bad, and spoiled, and selfish, but I'm never, never unhappy, my darling. Never."

Just then, his phone rang—Rosalita. Fear swept over him. "Daddy, it's me, Ricky."

"Yes, son, everything okay there?"

"I thought I better tell you, Mommy's not here."

"She's with me, son. We're on our way. I needed her help today."

"Oh, okay. I thought you should know so you wouldn't be disappointed when you came."

"Thank you, son, that was thoughtful. We'll be along in about twenty minutes. Bye, bye."

"He's so precious, Rocco. Just like you. Thank you for our special day, my hero," kissing him hungrily.

"Wanna stay a little while longer," lifting his eyebrows, sliding his hand under her skirt.

"You told Ricky twenty minutes."

He whispered into her mouth, "I could introduce you to a quickie."

"I don't even like the sound of that." She fluttered her eyes. "Well, maybe you can tell me more about it tonight."

He laughed. "This has been a wonderful day, Blossom Dove. Let's do it every couple months so things don't get away from us. Is it a date?"

"It's a date, my darling."

And they had their special day every two months after the twins were weaned.

Ricky was in bed. They were in the big chair watching TV. "Have you called your mother yet?"

She shook her head no, wrinkling her nose and making a face.

"Why?"

"Honey, I'm going to be twenty-five my next birthday. I know she's just biding her time ready to say, you're twenty-five now, it's time to get back to work. I just know she is."

"Let me call, baby girl, really. I want to."

"I should do it, Rocco. It's silly to be nervous."

"Blossom, if it makes you uncomfortable, it's not silly. Let me call your dad. Like a man thing."

"Would you, darling, just to break the ice? It'd be so nice."

With Nix in college, Blossom's parents had changed their New Mexico time to the winter months. The next morning at seven, New Mexico time, Rocco called.

"Rocco. Everything okay?" worried at the early hour.

"Everything's great, Cal. I didn't know if Blossom had a chance to call yet, so I wanted you to know we're expecting another baby."

"Elaine, another baby! Blossom's having another baby! When, Rocco? Is she fine?"

"She's wonderful, Cal. Actually we don't know the date yet, but we'll fill you in as we go. You both fine?"

He heard him as he turned from the phone. "You go ahead, Elaine, I'll be right along." He came back. "This is a good opportunity to float something by you, Rocco. Elaine and I have been talking about scaling down now that Nix's gone and maybe getting a place at Conneaut Lake. I've already talked to my money man and wondered if you kids would like to take the Shadow Oaks house. Financially, I think we could make it work for both of us, and now with your family growing . . ."

"Wow, Cal, that's quite an offer. We still have another bedroom for the new baby, but more room would be nice. Let me run it past Blossom and see if it's even a feasibility."

"We've got time, Rocco. I just wanted you to start thinking about it."

Her appointment for a sonogram was the next day. They were spending a quiet evening—he, reading; she, working on pictures. "You seem bigger than last time when we had the sonogram, baby."

"It might be a month later, honey. I wasn't really sure. It was probably silly not to get a diaphragm or IUD when the pills bothered me. We're going to have to decide another way after this one's born."

"I can get fixed, baby. I don't care."

"I don't know why that bothers me, but it does. Let's pray for another healthy baby, and maybe I'll get fixed, or we'll do pills for a few years and then decide. It's more convenient right after birth, but let's don't think about it right now." She climbed on his lap with a contented sigh and curled the hair on the back of his neck with her finger.

Dr. Kreinson said, "We're not doing an exam, Rocco, you can stay for the big reveal. Do we have a brother or a sister?" She wrinkled her brow a little, did some more maneuvers, and smiled. "Well, this is the big reveal. Are you ready for the news?"

They were both smiling and holding hands. "What's the good news?"

"Ricky is going to have—two baby sisters!"

Rocco looked puzzled. Blossom, worried. "Twins?"

The doctor smiled. "Twins. Girls for sure."

It wasn't registering with Rocco. Blossom patted his face. "It's two, honey, two girls."

"Two? You mean two babies?" The doctor nodded and smiled. "But she's too small to have two babies at once." He was losing color and starting to sweat. The doctor propelled him to a chair and gently pushed his head between his knees, calling out, "Melodie, would you clean Blossom up, Rocco and I are going to walk a bit." She got him some water and eased him into the hall.

Blossom called after them, "It's fine, honey, big breaths, big breaths," smiling and shaking her head at Melodie. "He's so sensitive."

After they were settled down, Blossom went to get her vitals recorded while Rocco stayed with the doctor. He still wasn't composed. "She's too small, she's too small."

The doctor sat in front of him, holding his hands. "Rocco, she's healthy, we'll watch her closely, she'll be fine."

He put his head in his hands. "I'm so scared. Oh god, I'm so scared." He looked up at her stricken.

"I will take care of her, Rocco, I promise."

He knew she cared, and he appreciated it, but unlike with Ricky when he enjoyed almost all the pregnancy, he never had a peaceful day the remaining four and a half months.

That night in their chair, she was trying to get something going, and he was resisting. "Rocco, don't get funny on me now. We didn't know last night, and we made love. Just like with Ricky, as long as we're comfortable, it's fine. We can't go four months, honey."

"It's not that, sweetie," he lied. "I have something we need to talk about."

She put her tongue in his ear. "What's that, honey?"

"When I called your dad last week, he mentioned something. I was going to take my time bringing it up, but now with this new situation, we should probably discuss it."

Apprehensive, "What?"

"They're planning on downsizing to something at Conneaut Lake and wondered if we'd like the Shadow Oaks house," saying the last part in a hurry.

She sat up straight, wrinkling her brow, her look growing astonished. "No. No! How could you think I'd want to go back to that house? I hated my life there." He just stared at her for a couple seconds. "Oh, Rocco, oh, I'm so sorry, my darling. Here we are in a house you hated. I'm sorry, honey, that was awful to say."

"Baby girl, that's not important. This house is a different place now. I told him I'd run it by you, so I am. He thought we could use the space, and that's when we thought it was just one baby."

She bit her lip. "We could use more space, but . . ." making a face.

"Blossom, I will build you anything you want. I've always told you that. You can design it, I'll make the blueprints, whatever you want, you can have."

She sighed. "I was brought up not to waste time or money. The landscaping is done, the pool's there, there's plenty of space, I could have an office. Why does it seem awful to me?"

"Sweetie, we'll weigh all the pros and cons. You've changed this house into a home. You could completely change the atmosphere there too."

"Did he say it would be ours to change any way we want?"

"We didn't get that far, but we'll cover all those things. We'll make sure your mind is completely at ease."

Her mind wasn't completely at ease, but she was a product of her upbringing—her fears, her insecurities, her frugality. When the twins were four months old, she moved back to 530 Shadow Oaks and stayed for fifty years.

But prior to that . . .

She was six months along. They were sitting in their chair, and she cringed a little. She laughed at his face. "They're just moving a little. Let's talk about names."

He was looking haggard, was jumpy and nervous. She knew she was fine, and he'd be fine in three more months. "Anything you want, baby, whatever you want."

"I want your help, honey. These are our children."

"Okay, okay. Whatever you say."

She just rolled her eyes, happy to see him smile a little. "Well, my name being Blossom, I thought a flower theme would be nice. I've always liked Lily. Do you like that?"

"I do, sweetie."

"Okay. And there's a little flower in the southwest I just love. It's tough and tenacious, and it's called Coralbell. Do you like that one—like, Coral for the first name and Bell for the middle?"

"I like that too—Lily and Coral. Very nice."

"Now," she said seriously, "I hate myself for doing this, but I thought Lily Elaine goes nice together," raising her eyebrows in question.

"Are you doing it for that reason, baby girl?"

"You know I'm not. But maybe it will help in some way."

"Blossom, you don't even know what you're trying to help. Are you saying that all your mother's disappointments in you will be helped because you name a baby after her?"

"You're mean and awful," pounding his chest and pouting.

"It's a pretty name, baby. Use it because it is, that's all I'm saying."

"How about Coral Marie, instead of Coral Bell? You know, to kind of match."

"*No.*"

"You said anything I wanted."

"No."

"Won't Lindsay think it's funny if we name one with my mother's name and don't use your mother's?"

"First, she probably won't even connect it. Second, she'll know why. She was there, Blossom."

She covered her face with her hands. He hugged her as tight as he dared. "The names are beautiful, Blossom Dove. Lily Elaine and Coral Bell. They feel just right."

She smiled as tears slid under her eyelashes. "You're so wonderful, Rocco. I love you so much."

"It's standard, Rocco. Nothing to worry about." Dr. Kreinson was reacting to his expression when she said Blossom should start coming every two weeks now. "If you get braxton hicks, Blossom, lie down or put your feet up."

"What? What? What was that?"

"It's just a name for contractions that aren't really labor, honey. It's nothing." She tried to hold his hand, but he wanted to pace.

The doctor tried to carry on. "You can start taking it easy. Move around at home, maybe short walks. We want to get you as close to forty weeks as we can without resorting to bed rest."

"Bed! That's what she should do," Rocco said excitedly. "That would be the best, bed!"

The doctor patted his shoulder. "We'll consider that later, Rocco. It's not the best thing now."

The days went by, June 22 getting closer. He hadn't wanted to go out for his birthday even when she said "But it's my anniversary, and I want to go out." Rosalita was staying all day, but he still came home by three. He carried her upstairs to watch from a rocker while Ricky had his bath then hovered over her while she sat in the shower on the plastic chair he put there.

Late on the nineteenth she heard him being sick in the bathroom. "Rocco, sweetie, come here. Let me hold you, you're getting all worked up again." He got into bed, but she couldn't find a way to hold him, so they ended up spooning as best they could. "My darling, you're losing weight. There are dark circles under your eyes. We made it," kissing his hand, "only a couple days to go now."

He was almost whimpering. "Blossom, I can't do this again, baby. I can't. I'm so scared. I'm ashamed to ask, but will you get fixed like you said? Please. I'm so scared. "You're such a great mother, you should have as many babies as you want, but I'm so scared, Blossom. I'm sorry, I'm sorry."

"I'll take care of it, three's a fine family. This will be the last time, honey, you won't have to do it again."

He was talking and crying now. "I thought I was scared hiding under the bed when I was ten. Scared and ashamed to be scared. But that was nothing compared to this, baby. I did this to you. If anything happens . . ."

"Rocco, nothing is going to happen. Millions of people have twins, honey. Everything will be all right. I love you to the moon and back, Rocco Anthony."

He tried to respond, "I love you beyo—I'm going to be sick," running to the bathroom.

It was a few hours later. She moved and stiffened. "Blossom?"

"Ooh, ooh, mmm," panting a little, "better call Rosalita, honey."

He was ashen but amazingly calm. He called Rosalita and the doctor. She slipped on a roomy sundress with tiny roses scattered on it. He brushed her hair, and she smiled at his worried face in the mirror. "You'll tell her, baby?"

"I'll tell her, honey, first thing."

"I'm sorry I can't do it again, baby girl. I just can't."

She was about to respond, but another contraction came. She squeezed his hand, "We b-b-better go."

He picked her up and carried her downstairs just as Rosalita drove in. They got to the hospital at ten minutes after two. After the doctor checked her, he called her mother. "We're at the hospital, Elaine, probably be a couple hours."

So her parents were there this time. Cal pacing with Rocco, Elaine reading, when Coral Bell first, at five pounds eleven ounces, and Lily Elaine, at five pounds ten ounces, arrived at five fifteen and five thirty-nine. They were the image of Blossom—straight dark hair, big brown eyes. Rocco was on his feet when he went in but collapsed across the bed when they put a baby in each of her arms. Her dad took a quick picture with his phone; then she handed the babies back and took care of Rocco. In twenty minutes, they did it all again—she and Rocco smiling, each holding a baby. Her dad sent the official version to Nix, Lindsay, and Mim.

The doctor kept her an extra day and a half in the hospital. Her mother and Rosalita used the twin beds in his parents' old room. They put bassinets in there and a Pack 'n Play downstairs and had two cribs delivered to the Shadow Oaks house. Her mom and Rosalita took turns helping her, first every two hours, and then quickly three, then four, just like Ricky. In six weeks, their schedule was dependable enough; she told her mother she and Rosalita could handle things. Rosalita stayed at night another month and then began a regular workday of seven thirty in the morning until four thirty in the afternoon and continued until the girls were in kindergarten.

They had satisfied each other for four and a half months with their mouths and hands until the doctor gave thumbs-up to marital relations. She was nervous and weepy. He was back to his confident self, so sweet and gentle; it reminded her of their first time. Before he even kissed her, she was crying and digging into his back.

"Easy, baby girl, nice and slow."

"My stomach's not pretty. I have 'twin skin.'"

"Your tummy is beautiful. We had beautiful baby girls, you're beautiful," nibbling and licking her face and her neck.

"I'm leaking all over. It's not pretty."

"I'll skip your nipples. I'll bite right here, and here," sucking and biting the sides of her breasts.

"Oooh, ooh," arching her back. "I'm afraid, I'm afraid. What if I can't satisfy you?"

"Silly girl, silly baby girl," whispering "You ready? Here we go." He entered; and the familiar, full, wonderful feeling brought her hips to him fiercely, her head and arms falling to the bed too overcome to hold him. He put one hand behind her head, the other on the small of her back. "Move with me, my baby, move with me."

Her strength returned, she clawed his back, bit his neck, and met his every thrust moaning, groaning, until it was time to reach for Tiger. His long, continuous orgasm left him dizzy and speechless. They were drenched in perspiration, milk, and tears.

Her eyelids were too heavy to open. She tipped her head and looked under them with a weak smile. He was still getting air but lifted her hand to his lips and returned his own weak smile. "We're back." She nodded. Her chin dropped, asleep. He dragged himself to the bathroom, wiped off, got a warm cloth to wipe her, put a fresh towel over her breasts, and rolled her into her sleeping position. He looked in on Ricky, listened at the door for Rosalita and the girls, then took his position beside her, watching her back. Life was beautiful.

They settled in. She was up when he left for work, feeding one or the other. She had nursing gowns with matching headbands. She was glowing and beautiful. She didn't want to pump milk and have Rosalita feed the girls, so they had her twenty-fifth birthday dinner at her parent's condo. They would be moving in a couple weeks to Shadow Oaks. Her mother got in some pointed remarks—"Well, was this what you were expecting at twenty-five, Blossom?"—things like that. She just smiled.

He had given her two pale pink pearls when the girls were born to join the blue one for Ricky. He gave her a birthday pearl and twenty-five roses and begged her to let him give her diamonds. "I want to give you handfuls of diamonds. I want to give you the moon."

"I have everything I want, my darling. If I think of something, I'll tell you."

They made the move to Shadow Oaks. She had supervised changing the paint colors, changed the family room to complement their leather sofa and double chair and Indian accents. She took a picture of the wall of photos so Rocco's men could duplicate it. They updated the kitchen appliances and added a homey kitchen table. The living room and dining room were empty, but she would think about that. She put the girls in her parent's room since it was the largest and felt guilty, but not very, having the men remove the display case they had built for her trophies. She didn't know where they were and didn't care and didn't want the case around to remind her—even though Rocco said it was fine workmanship. Ricky was in Nix's room, and they were in her room. There was a room between hers and her parents' that had been used once for an office and later as a sewing room. Rocco's men put a door from their room to make a wonderful walk-in closet. She decorated their room with their things from the Cussewago house, leaving his regular-sized bed and using the queen-sized in her room. They had been carrying things back and forth a month or so, making sure Ricky was happy with his room. They all had more space and a wonderful yard to play in, but the actual moving day was hard on her—leaving his bed, the wonderful closet he had made with his own hands. He was busy supervising and making sure everyone was comfortable, but she felt it would affect him at some time.

She looked back and bit her lip. "It's okay, baby girl, wherever we are is home."

"I know, honey. And I know it has ghosts for you, but it's the happiest I've ever been, and I loved it."

"If you can't get past it, Blossom, you tell me. I bet once Ricky is running around and the girls are creeping, you'll forget this house was anything but ours."

She didn't think it would happen, but she smiled because she loved him so.

The move prompted the last time he needed her roughly. He took a long time putting Cussewago on the market, saying he wanted Lindsay to have time to decide if she wanted it. Then, "The market's bad right now," but finally he listed it with RE/MAX.

Blossom thought it would be nice to walk through the house one last time before the sale closed then knew it was a mistake as soon as they stepped in the door. Without their furniture, the music, the laughter, it had reverted back to the house he knew as a boy. She tried to be upbeat as she praised his improvements. "I bet that powder room sealed the deal, honey. Aren't they lucky to have that wonderful closet you made."

But as they walked around, his breathing became labored, his eyes darker, his lips grim. "Get in the truck, baby."

"Rocco, let's go, honey," pulling his arm.

"*Get in the truck.*"

She was biting her lip, whimpering, but went out, and got in, and even with the door closed, heard the scream. She covered her face and then jumped and screamed as his work boot came through the door.

She was sobbing as he got in the truck, her fist to her mouth. His chest was heaving, and he laid his head on the steering wheel for a few seconds. He put his arm around her, pulled her close, took a deep breath, and punched Bob's number. "We'll need a new exterior door at Cussewago, standard size, right facing," he said calmly. "Bring a new deadbolt too. This one might be damaged." He kissed her temple and drove away.

"Rocco."

"All done, baby girl. It's over."

But it wasn't over. He was quiet that evening. The girls were six months old, and he lay on the floor so they could crawl on him, but he was distracted and continued lying there as she put everyone to bed.

She held out her arms when he came out of the shower. "Everything okay, my darling?"

"Everything's perfect, baby girl. I have wonderful wife, three healthy, beautiful children, and a good business. I'm the luckiest guy in the world."

He loved her slowly and tenderly and rolled her over. The scream came at three thirty. "Nooo, you-son-of-a-bitch!" He grabbed Blossom. "Are you okay," panicked, "Are you okay!" Shielding her from something only he could see, his body sweating, his eyes feral.

She held his face with both hands as he twisted. "It's a bad dream, Rocco, a bad dream," shaking his face. "Wake up, honey, it's me, darling," as he started to focus. His eyes black, the skin on his face stretched tight. "I'm here, darling, I'm here."

He moaned, "I need you."

"I'm here, Rocco, whatever you need. I'll always be here," wrapping her legs around him as he moaned hoarsely.

She was cringing from his roughness. He was grunting with effort when she heard the little knock. "Mommy, is Daddy okay? I heard him crying."

Oh god, she thought. She put a hand over his mouth but kept moving and said as calmly as she could, "Daddy had a bad dream, Ricky. He's okay now, you can go back to bed. Thank you for checking, honey."

"Does he need a hug?"

"You can hug him in the morning. Thank you. Night, night.

That was the last time. He was twenty-seven.

He didn't need her roughly, but he needed her often. She knew possessing her was a necessity—his psyche demanded to know she was his. She could have delved into it. Her computer knowledge gave her access to any information and anyone who could understand his needs better than she did. But the truth was, she didn't want to find out. She didn't care. His first twenty years formed him, but she knew they weren't who he was. If he needed her, she would be there—because she often needed him irrationally.

Was she trying to show him that Blossom Richards' brain was not the sum of Blossom Richards's parts? Was she showing him her family demeanor, her public demeanor was one thing, and her wild abandon was their secret? Only they mattered once their door was closed. Just as he had whispered to her their first night together—no rules, no boundaries, no holding back.

Way back the third week she lived at Cussewago, he came out of the shower still amazed she was there. He loved all her little rituals, this night smiling at her concentration in rubbing lotion on her knees and elbows. Then his brow wrinkled, he pointed. "What is that?"

"These are the panties I wear when it's my period, honey. They're nice and snug, and I can wear an extra pad. Remember we talked about it."

"I don't like 'em."

"It's just a couple days, sweetie. I don't want to stain the sheets for Rosalita to have to clean."

"Couldn't we soak the sheets? Couldn't we use a towel? I don't like anything between us. Oh, wait, your period," his face brightened, "I have something for you." He reached in his jeans drawer and brought out a four-piece box of Russell Stover chocolates from his stash. He knelt in front of her "I have some in the truck too," opening them.

"Oh, you're so sweet, Rocco. I wanted a piece of chocolate so bad today. Thank you, thank you," putting one in her mouth and tipping her head back in ecstasy, "Ummm," making little smacking sounds.

He shivered and laid her back and whispered, "Remember when we were talking about it and you said you'd see if we could make love during your period? What about that? Open your eyes."

"I can't think when I look at you. It's safe, but my back aches, honey, and we'd need a big towel and something to soak it in."

"I'll rub your back, and I'll get a pail. Give me a little kiss, I have a surprise for you."

She giggled softly, found his lips and the chocolate he was holding in his teeth. "Oh, you're so bad," pulling some off with her lips. "Ummm," searching his mouth for more. His head was whirling.

"Blossom? I'll clean everything. Please, baby?"

"Okay, darling," she breathed, "let me go to the bathroom, but you have to promise not to look when you wash off. I don't want you not to like me."

He slid in. "Oh my god, oh my god," his breath ragged, "are you all right. Is it okay?" She moved with him. He was gone.

When his heart stopped banging against his chest, when he could breathe again, he washed himself, gently cleaned her, lifted her to slide in a clean towel, found a pail in the garage, got a bottle of bleach from the kitchen, and soaked the towel.

He slipped in behind her and was surprised when she turned and snuggled against him. "Do you still like me?"

"You're a miracle."

She smiled and sighed, wiggling closer, putting her lips to his ear. "My backache's gone."

A sob escaped as a wave of shame came over him. She was excusing his selfishness. He hugged her so hard she squeaked in her sleep as he vowed to be a better man.

She put the snug panties away. He tried to be a better man, but she was there when he needed her, and the pail and bottle of bleach was a fixture in the corner of his closet.

"We're to talk with Dr. Carnavale."

"I'm Dr. Carnavale."

She was in her office at Shadow Oaks. She had contacted Dr. Ng to tell him she was available one day a week; and he, in turn, had told Chet. Chet had proposed she set up a video conferencing capability to help him with potential customers in his cybersecurity business.

She was a little frazzled. The girls had slept longer than usual, had taken longer to eat, and she hadn't been able to change from her pink morning dress. Her hair in braids didn't help age her either.

"You're Dr. Blossom Carnavale with Chang Enterprises?"

The group was from a small fifty-store Ohio chain of fast-food stores. "Gentlemen, I've recently had twins, and my time is limited. I'm Dr. Carnavale, let's move on. You have . . ."

One of the men at the table interrupted, "I think we should check back with Dr. Chang on this."

"Dr. Chang has given me your account, sir. To cut to the chase, employee number 114 or someone using his code in your Delaware, Ohio, store is stealing twenty dollars a day, ten after the breakfast rush and ten after lunch. This in itself might not make it worth your expense of hiring Dr. Chang's firm to update your security system, but said employee has been doing this as long as your present system has been in effect—or eleven years. That location is not the only one with a problem."

A different gentleman asked, "Who are the other problems?"

She did not smile. "This service is only gratis if you sign on with Dr. Chang's firm for a new system. I would suggest you do as your present system is antiquated. If you choose not to, I will give him a breakdown of thefts by employees—times, dates, etc., for two thousand dollars per location, or

$100,000. I realize that seems small in comparison to the $500,000 he will charge you, but you will also be protected from other encroachments besides petty theft. Any questions?"

There were the usual—similar to ones she had encountered on her trips with Dr. Ng. How can you know that, how dare you break into our system, etc., etc. She countered them and then said, "Dr. Chang will have my report today, and you can contact him with your decision. Good morning, gentlemen." She smiled a little. She enjoyed the repartee on a strange level, but it quickly left her mind as Lily started to fuss, and she started leaking.

She had forewarned Dr. Ng and Chet that she would only be checking her office on Wednesdays and to text her if there was something she should see immediately. A message from Chet: They went for the whole package. One hundred thousand coming your way. Account number? She was distracted and just gave him the household account, meaning to tell Rocco later.

A week later Rocco called, "Hi, baby mine, how's your day going?"

"Fine, now that I hear your voice, crazy man," smiling at his antics the night before.

"Sweetie, I was just in the household account to pay some bills, and there was a hundred thousand dollars from Chang Enterprises. You know anything about that?"

"That's Chet, honey, remember from Penn. I did some work for him a week or so ago. I didn't know where to put it so just gave him the household account. Is that okay?"

"I didn't know that had gone beyond the talking stage, Blossom." A little sternly, she thought.

"I thought when we talked about setting up the office, you knew I'd be doing some work, Rocco. It's just one day a week, just to keep in practice. I want to contribute."

"You know I don't like that word. You contribute by running our home, Blossom," cooly. "What were the girls doing when you were working?"

"Rocco Anthony Carnavale, I was in the office all of thirty-five minutes. I don't appreciate your insinuation that I was neglecting our children."

He could almost see her getting ready to stamp her foot, her eyes narrowing. A ball of ice formed in his stomach, but his mouth wouldn't say it's okay. Instead, it said, "We'll talk about it later," and he closed his phone. She gasped audibly, stared at her phone, and started crying.

He was breathing hard, went to the break room and the heavy bag, stubbornly didn't put on his fingerless gloves, and punched until his knuckles bled. *What's wrong with me, what's the matter with me. Six months ago, I thought she'd die, and my life would be over. Now I'm making a thing about her bringing in money. A shrink would have a field day with me.* He ran to his truck. "Call me if you need me," as he went by Helen.

She was nursing Coral and looked up at him, wounded. She'd been crying . . . a lot. "You hung up on me."

"No. No, I didn't. I said we'd talk about it later."

"You-hung-up-on-me."

He fell to his knees and put his head in her lap. She instinctively started stroking his hair. "I'm sorry, I'm sorry, baby girl," his voice muffled in her dress. "Forgive me, I'm sorry. I don't care. Anything you want to do is fine with me."

He was startled when her voice was harsh. "Don't you tell me anything I want to do is fine like you're giving me permission. You don't give me permission. We're equal people here!"

"Baby, I didn't mean it that way," sitting back on his heels. "I just didn't think we talked about it, and it surprised me, that's all. Whatever you—well, jeez, now I don't know how to say it. What should I say?"

Suddenly she was crying so much; Coral's eyes opened in surprise. "I don't know, I don't know. I'm sorry. You sounded like my mother." She detached the baby and handed her to him, "Just burp her for me, please," and went into the powder room. When she didn't come right out, "Blossom, I think she wants more."

She opened the door roughly. "Of course she wants more," taking her and putting her to the other breast, "she wants more, you want more, everybody wants more," turning her back to him.

He crawled on his hands and knees to face her. She turned the swivel rocker the other way. He crawled that way. "No, no, we're not doing this, Blossom Dove. Look at me."

"I can't look at you, you're too beautiful. What did you do to your hands?"

"Nothing."

"You were punching that bag. You were mad at me."

"I would never be mad at you."

"Yes, you were. You were mad, and you hung up on me."

"Baby, I don't know why I hung up. The bag was there, and it served its purpose. Maybe it bothered me you made more money in thirty minutes than I make in three jobs."

"Oh, that's ridiculous. What difference does it make who makes what. It's our money."

"Baby girl, can we put this off until tonight. Ricky will be home soon. You know he'll sense tension." She let him put the baby down on the blanket and hug her. "I know it's too much for you, Blossom. I'd feed them if I could. Think about filling bottles so we can go out. Would that help?"

She stuck her tongue out at him, and even that made him feel better. "Change Lily and bring her here, and don't ever speak to me again." She pouted.

"Okay. Can I kiss you while I'm not speaking to you?"

"Just the little kiss."

He kissed her thoroughly. She swayed against him. "Tonight we'll talk about it, baby. We won't make love, we'll talk all night," nuzzling her neck.

"And then we'll make love."

"And then we'll make love." He smiled.

"And you'll never hang up on me again."

"And I'll never hang up on you again."

"I love you, Rocco Anthony."

"I love you, Blossom Dove. I'll see you again at five."

That night at cuddling time, they were facing each other; but she still managed to get both arms around his neck, his face between her breasts. "Baby, I can't breathe. Back up a little so I can see your eyes."

"I can't get close enough."

"We'll be closer in a minute."

"No, not that way. I want to melt into you. We weren't close today. I hated that feeling. I love you so, Rocco."

"I love you, baby mine. Let's talk about things all the way through next time, that's all. If I hadn't been surprised, maybe I wouldn't have gone off the deep end."

"Rocco," she said primly.

"What, Mrs. Carnavale," just as primly.

"I'm going to work in the office every Wednesday. If Dr. Ng or Chet have jobs I can do in a week or two, there will be a lot of money in the account. Should I start a new one, or can you just transfer it where you want it to go?" She said it seriously without smiling and looked at him with big eyes, waiting for an answer.

Seriously back, "The household account will be fine."

Her glorious smile brought tears to his eyes.

"Baby girl, are things building up too much? Are there things I should be doing?"

"Sometimes it's hard, but six months have gone by already, and I know it will get easier. Other people do it, and most of them aren't fortunate enough to have a Rosalita. I'm sorry I was bad."

"You weren't the one who was bad, Blossom. What can I do for you?"

"If I ask you to get Ricky from school on Wednesdays so Rosalita can watch the girls, would that be okay? Not every Wednesday, just sometimes."

"I'll get him every Wednesday. Give him a little extra attention. Has he acted like the girls get too much attention?"

"Not at all, honey. I've been watching."

They talked into the night, getting caught up on ordinary things that get pushed aside when babies come. When she started yawning, "What did you mean by a lot of money, baby?"

"The next job will be three hundred thousand."

"Holy crap, baby!"

"Rocco, don't be crude," pulling his head to her chest and saying softly, "Honey, the money's out there. We may as well have it. We can build on it to do the things we want to help people. Take over for Dad and Mom, or whatever."

"But I'm going to hate Wednesdays."

"No, you won't. It will be your afternoon with Ricky, and you'll look forward to it."

His voice caught in his throat. "I'm scared, baby. The minute you said I did some work, I got shivers. I'll lose you. I'll lose you to your brain."

"Oh, Rocco, my silly, silly boy," lifting herself to straddle him, kissing his tears, nibbling his neck, his nipples, moving down as he moaned.

She was in his arms after nursing the girls and tucking them in. It was only nine, so they had almost eight hours until 5:00 a.m. when first Lily and then Coral would wake to be fed again. He was waiting for her signal—love or sleep. She had raked him over the coals the night before, so he was guessing sleep when she said, "Rocco?"

It was her worried voice. "Yes, baby girl?"

"I don't think we should make love for a couple years, well maybe one."

He swallowed his laugh. She was worried and serious. "Why is that, sweetie?"

She snuggled in, her lips against his ear. "I didn't know where I was last night. My heart was beating so hard, I couldn't hear anything. What if one of them needed me? I wouldn't have heard." Then cupping her hand around his ear and whispering, "Rocco, I didn't even know we had children. I want to be a good mother, honey. I can't not hear the children."

"Blossom, you usually fall right to sleep. It's just because you stayed awake a little while that you realized you couldn't hear. We're fine, baby, we'll hear the children. See, there's Lily on the monitor sucking her pacifier."

"Are you sure you'll hear them, honey? You were crying last night. Are you sure?"

"Well, for the record, I was not crying, I was just trying to get my breath." She giggled. "I'll hear them, I'm pretty sure. I'm almost pretty, almost sure, baby girl."

"Ohh, that doesn't sound too sure, honey. We better stay alert for a year. At least a few months."

"Baby mine, I will do anything you want, but they've slept through 'til five for a couple months now, and Ricky never wakes up. We're fine. We'll take it easy—go nice and slow."

"But that's how we started last night. Oh, I'm very worried," whimpering as she put her leg over him.

"We'll be fine, we'll be fine," easing her onto his stomach, rubbing her back. "The monitor's on, everything's okay."

"I want to be a good mother, I really do," pulling the towel onto his chest for the seeping milk.

"You're the best mother in the world, Blossom Dove, the very best," sliding the towel away. And then her tongue was in his mouth, and he couldn't breathe, and he couldn't hear, and she was asleep.

When she heard the monitor at five, "Was everything quiet? Could you hear?"

"Didn't hear a peep." He grinned and gave her a slow wink. "And I was on top of the situation." She rolled her eyes and giggled.

The months went by. The girls turned one. Coral quit nursing. They were able to fit in short family suppers at McDonald's or Perkins. Rocco delighted in schlepping all the paraphernalia around. A picture of him walking toward the McDonald's entrance with the supersized diaper bag over his shoulder, a baby carrier in each hand, Ricky holding the door open, a big smile at a customer leaving became one of her favorites. It almost titled itself: I have a family, me, Rocco Carnavale, I have a family. She loved him so.

Nearing Christmas the year the girls were eighteen months and Ricky four and a half, he wanted to make a televised Christmas spot for the business. Lily and Coral wore red velvet dresses with white fur collars and myriads of white lace petticoats. Blossom wore a white cashmere wrap dress that made Rocco very nervous, a red velvet headband, and a necklace of a large ruby surrounded by diamonds Rocco had given her after she thought out loud, "Hmm, I don't have a red necklace." She wanted him to return it, but he wouldn't. Rocco and Ricky wore jeans with red plaid shirts, and Rocco, his trademark hat. He and Ricky had the only speaking parts. Rocco said, "Carnavale Construction would like to thank you for your business this year," as Blossom and the girls walked into the scene. They each picked up a girl as Ricky said, "And Merry Christmas and Happy New Year from our family to yours." The final take was charming and, although too much work to do again, garnered them compliments for months. It was the film of the preparations and outtakes that Blossom loved, however. She made a twelve-inch wallpaper border to go under their memory wall—Lily picking up a piece of lint from the floor, only her ruffled behind showing; Ricky covering Coral's mouth with his hand, afraid she would ruin his line; Rocco throwing his arms up in the air at a third botched scene; and she shaking her finger at the children. The whole afternoon captured. She loved it, and it stayed there in the family room until the children were teenagers and complained. She transferred it to her room-sized closet and smiled at it every day.

Finally, just shy of two, Lily quit nursing; and they were able to go somewhere besides getting groceries or a quiet cup of coffee. The girls' bedtime was before they left, but she was afraid they would be scared if they woke up, so she told them Mommy and Daddy were going dancing. They all practiced dancing. They picked out Mommy's outfit. They heard the story of Mommy's doves when she put them on with her blue chambray peasant blouse and ruffled denim skirt. Coral and Lily each sat on one of Daddy's knees. "Why did you buy Mommy the little birds?"

"Because Mommy's middle name is Dove, and they are baby doves. And I wanted her to love me," winking at Blossom.

"Did you love him, Mommy?"

"Oh, I did. I certainly did."

Ricky was allowed to play chess on the computer for an hour. "One hour, son." They had decided they had to trust Rosalita not to tell Elaine about his abilities just yet.

They took Delbert, and even after almost three years, most of the regulars were at the bar. Hugs all around, pictures out. Most had seen their Christmas TV greeting. Blossom remembered how nervous and scared she was their first time there. Now she looked around and thought, *These dear, dear people.*

They had been dancing in the living and dining rooms. Her mother thought it appalling those rooms never got decorated, just filled with toys they could move aside and practice new steps. With the first beats of the first cut off Delbert, "Same Kind of Crazy," they smiled like crazy at each other—from the freedom of being out and all the room to move. Of course Rocco called Rosalita—once to see if Ricky was in bed, an hour later to see if everything was quiet. He was thrilled Blossom looked so carefree. It had been a consuming two years, and he vacillated between being relieved their family was complete and ashamed he had asked for it.

He never was fully comfortable that she would be in her office on Wednesdays, working in a world he knew nothing about. She sensed his insecurity and loved him intensely on Tuesday nights, letting him know he was the most important thing in her world.

The Tuesday after their wonderful night out dancing, they had joined, and she moved just so, squeezing him, taking his breath away. He opened his eyes to tell her she was hurting him when the look of her stunned him. Her hair spread out on the pillow, her face flushed, her breathing labored, her angelic concentration on trying to please him. He couldn't speak and endured the divine agony as she milked him dry. He hoped he could walk in the morning.

Thinking of it in the shower the next morning made him dizzy. Her face floated in front of him. As he knelt to kiss her good-bye, he said hoarsely, "I could stay home today. We could sneak some time."

She touched his cheek. "That would be lovely, my darling, but you have meetings, and it's my office day."

"Blossom," breathing heavily.

"Go to work, honey, we'll be together tonight," kissing him intensely.

"Blossom?"

"Go now, go."

Helen found Bob in the shop. "He's just sitting in the truck staring. I don't think they had a fight, or he'd be at the bag."

Bob opened the door of the truck. "Boss? Boss?"

His head jerked a little, his eyes focusing. "Working, she's working. It's Wednesday."

Bob nodded. "That's right, boss, it's Wednesday. We better get started. You want coffee?"

It was as if he was trudging through sand, the vision of her face coming to him again and again. He made it until eleven and called.

She saw his name, excused herself from her conference, and turned her back. "Rocco?"

"Can I come home yet?"

"My darling," she whispered, "I'm in a conference call, and you have another meeting. Remember Ricky is off today, so come home after work, sweetie. I'll be here. I love you."

He put his head on his desk, his eyes stinging. "Boss"—Helen came in—"here's some ice water. Can I get you anything?"

"She's working."

"Yes, it's Wednesday, boss. She works on Wednesdays." She called Bob, "Take him out on the job or to lunch or something. He gets obsessed sometimes." She hung up, wringing her hands.

Bob kept him busy. He got through another meeting about a new home, and at four, he couldn't wait any longer.

Blossom was sitting on a footstool supervising toy pickup, singing a song about the planets. The scene was so precious. He was so overcome; he could barely breathe. He knelt in front of her and put his head in her lap. "Is Rosalita here, can we go upstairs?"

The children ran over to pat his back. "Daddy's fine, he just had a hard day working for us. You continue your work." She said softly, "Rosalita just left, darling. Dinner's ready."

"Can you call her to come back?"

"Rocco," she whispered, rubbing his back, "she's had a long day. Play with your children, and I'll put things on the table."

"Blossom," pleading.

"Play with your children, darling. Bedtime is only a couple hours away."

Finally, they tucked Ricky in. The girls were long gone, sleeping sweetly. They went right to their room, closed the door quietly, and she was in his arms. He moaned, "I don't like Wednesdays."

"Shh, do you want to take a shower?"

"No. I want you."

"Let me go potty. I'll be right back." She got in beside him and put a nipple to his mouth. Nursing had toughened her nipples, and it was another avenue for them. She stroked his hair, his neck. "You were my silly boy today."

"You wouldn't let me come home."

"You know I can't resist you. I would have cancelled calls, the children would have been pounding on the bedroom door . . ." He smiled at the thought.

"I get so scared, Blossom. I'm so afraid of losing you."

"Rocco Anthony, you know that's impossible." She put her lips to his ear. "Let me kiss you all over."

"Baby, I have to keep control of myself. I couldn't function today. You're driving me crazy."

She pulled back to look in his eyes. "What do you think I go through every day, Mr. Carnavale? I ache for you. I cry for you. Five o'clock is so far away. Isn't it wonderful we drive each other crazy after ten years?" She slid her hands down his stomach, massaging him. "Drive me crazy, crazy man."

He quickly had her oohing, aahing, and panting with desire. She gave herself completely, and his confidence came back. He'd never say it out loud, was ashamed to even acknowledge it; but as she screamed into Tiger, the twenty-first-century man thought as he had at twenty, *She's mine, mine, mine.*

The summer before her thirtieth birthday, they went to New Mexico for ten days. Her parents were spending June there now, July and August back at Conneaut Lake. The girls would turn four there, and Rocco was worried about the long plane ride. "Let's rent a jet, baby, it'll cut the time, and they won't bother anyone."

"No, honey, they have to understand proper behavior. I drew and read and napped, they can do it too."

Her mother was angry, her dad disappointed, Blossom and the children wouldn't stay the whole month or at least leave Ricky. Rocco tried to take the pressure off Blossom by saying he couldn't bear being away from them that long, that they'd try to stay longer next time. He pitched in and laid concrete sidewalks between the house and office, and the office and parking. Blossom took a picture of him with his foot on a shovel, shirtless, with his hat on. You could see the sheen of perspiration on his chest. She loved it and added it to the wall.

Nix had graduated from the University of New Mexico and was living with Mim in Santa Fe working for New Mexico Water Resources. He told Rocco and Blossom he was going to propose to Nola Begay, one of Sam's granddaughters. On the flight home, Rocco said he wouldn't mind Ricky staying with Nix if he was at the compound and had his own place. Ricky, at seven, had understood the office and helped however he could. Coral wanted to help and ran little errands and emptied wastebaskets and such just as Blossom had done. Lily thought everything was dusty and dirty, so Mim came down and took her shopping in Albuquerque. The girls wore their new fawn-colored dresses with squash blossom trim and their new moccasins on the plane home. Rocco shook his head and winked at Blossom. "Mim strikes again."

Blossom laughed. "Now that she has their sizes and has spent some time with them, they'll be no stopping her."

"She didn't look too good, baby girl."

"I know. I told Nixie to keep me posted."

Book Two

Book Two

Scenes from a Marriage

SCENES FROM A MARRIAGE

Their Thirties

On the eve of her thirtieth birthday, her mother called, and she came out of the office crying. He held out his arms, but she shook her head and started up the stairs, waving him back when he tried to follow.

He was pacing, wondering if they were still going to dinner, when she came downstairs in her new things topping her camel suede skirt and boots, ready for their evening at Mangia's. She had on her pearls and the diamond solitaire necklace that he had given her on their tenth anniversary. She had shaken her head no, but he was prepared and pulled out a little piece of paper from his wallet that listed diamonds as a gift for the tenth anniversary. He had given her the final pearl on her necklace. They thought it was auspicious that it was complete on her thirtieth birthday. He had seen on television that faux furs were in that season so got her a mink vest trimmed in leather with a cashmere sweater in a rich brown.

"I'll have a glass of champagne." She smiled. "I was nursing on my twenty-fifth."

He ordered a split bottle and raised his glass to her. "To the most remarkable woman, wife, and mother in the world."

Her eyes filled. "She said I should be the medical or cybersecurity consultant on CNN by now. That I'm wasting my life and squandering my talent."

"Blossom," softly, "did she add I'm glad you're happy and thank you for the marvelous grandchildren?"

"You know she didn't. She said, she said," trying to laugh, "I'm a total disappointment. I used to be a disappointment," staring into his eyes, breaking his heart. "How about that, a *total* disappointment."

"Blossom," achingly, starting to come over to her chair.

She held up her hand. "Darling, it's all right. When I was young, I didn't know there was such happiness in the world. It grows every day—the thrill of you, the joy of our children, our life. I'm so very happy, Rocco. I love you beyond belief."

Now she was strong, and his eyes were wet. She steered the conversation back to their family. They ate and laughed and flirted and enjoyed their evening. He said, "Everything good, baby girl?"

"Everything's fine." She heaved a sigh. "I guess I just . . . oh, never mind," tossing her hand. "We've spent enough time on this."

"Just a little more, baby, you just what."

"Oh, I don't know. When you're about fifteen, you can't even imagine being thirty. I guess I just thought it would be over by now. That magically somehow we would have come to an understanding or something, and it would be over. Let's don't talk about it anymore."

"We're done, then, my baby." He wiggled his eyebrows. "Would you like some chocolate mousse, little girl?"

"Yes, I would, kind sir, if you won't take advantage of me."

He did take advantage of her later that night, loving her slowly and tenderly from her twenty-ninth year into her thirtieth until she was asleep. At 3:00 a.m. began a three-year period of her assails on him. That night it was whimpering and pounding his chest, escalating over the months to snarling, biting, scratching, loving him ferociously, reaching orgasm, falling back, spent, drenched, and sobbing. He held her through it. "Baby, I'm here, I've got you, I've got you." He wiped her nose, patted her dry, smoothed her hair, and rolled her back into her sleeping position. He never asked her why. He knew she didn't know. It wasn't after every time her mother called but often enough that he saw the pattern and knew what was coming.

One night, he turned on his lamp to wake her. She had a handful of his hair. He couldn't loosen her fingers; they were so rigid, and he was amazed how much it hurt. "Sweetie, you're hurting me."

She startled awake, crying out, "I'm hurting you, what's wrong with me, oh, I'm hurting you."

He put his feet on the floor to go to the bathroom. "It's nothing, baby. You can't hit your mother, so you hit me. It's no big deal."

She cried out and put her pillow over her head, "No. No."

He hurried back. "That was a joke, baby girl. I don't know what I'm talking about. That was my dumb ten-cent analysis. Everything's good, baby, everything's good." He lay down and tucked her against his side. She was rigid, pressing against him, pushing her face into his neck.

"You must get rid of me, you must throw me away, you must. And all my pictures too."

He rubbed her back and gently moved her head so she could look in his eyes . . . grinned and winked. She took a big breath, and her body relaxed. She touched his lips. "You're so beautiful. So indescribably beautiful."

"Thank you, Mrs. Carnavale," arranging her into his arms and flicking the sheet around them. "Can we get back to sleep now?" She sighed and slept.

Finally, when the girls were seven, she buried her face in his neck at cuddling time. "The girls will need me here when they're teenagers, so I guess I should go back to Pitt now," and started crying.

"You know you don't have to do this, Blossom."

"I know, but I can help more if I have my medical degree."

"The money you make is going to fund that foundation for as long as you want it to, baby. You're doing your part."

"She'll never think so, Rocco. I'll just do this one last thing." Both of them knowing there would always be another one last thing.

He held her tight, thinking, not for the first time, which was worse—the fists, boots, broken bones, roaring anger he'd endured but were over or the arsenal of anger she endured, the silent contempt, abusive words, degrading comments that went on and on.

After the initial barrage of tears, decisions, and arrangements, it wasn't horrible. Of course the Bauerhoff sisters were gone, so she took a nondescript apartment in a commercial building. Rocco wanted her to stay in the Holiday Inn right on campus, but she said it was a waste of money. The first trip, Bob drove behind them with the truck. She clung to Rocco when it was time to leave, oblivious to everyone around. "I thought we'd never have to do this again. I can't, I can't."

"Do you want me to come tomorrow? Do you want me to stay until the weekend? I'll call Rosalita."

"No. Just go," pounding his chest, raising her voice. "It's all your fault," sobbing.

"I know, baby girl, I know," holding her until she was quiet. She stamped her foot, turned, and ran into the building, all twirling skirt and swinging hair. The vision of the first day he saw her burning his eyes.

"You okay to go, boss? Should we leave her?"

"Yeah, she'll be okay. Oh god, Bob. Goddamn the world."

"Yeah, boss, yeah."

She was home often. Computers took care of a lot of it. They had her conference call set up for good nights to the children. Really, it wasn't that bad; but when they were together, they held hands and looked at each other wistfully—like, what next.

He expected her the next day, but she called, "I'm home and I want to copulate like bunnies."

He laughed at their old joke. "I'm on my way, baby girl." The three years were over. She had an MD after the PhD at the end of her name. She jumped into his arms, and they cried.

She wanted to help people; she really did. Uninterested in an office setting and unwilling to devote the time her mother wanted, she connected with RMA, Rural Medical Alliance. They spent a week or two in remote, unserviced areas treating low-income, no-income patients.

Her first foray didn't go well. The family discussions were positive, the children's schedules were light, Rosalita could stay until supper, so off she went to West Virginia.

She called Rocco from the airport in White Sulphur Springs, waiting for her ride into the mountains. "Hi," weakly.

"This isn't going to work, baby girl."

"I know. I thought I could do it."

"Make your apologies and come right back."

"Oh, Rocco, it will be so expensive to change my return ticket."

"Blossom."

"I know. I'll do it."

"See where they'll be in a couple weeks. I'll make arrangements at the shop so I can come."

"You don't need to do that, honey," but with excitement in her voice. "I'll just wait a few more years."

"No. This is something you've wanted to do. I'll just have to come too. They must need some grunt work."

She started to cry. "I'm sorry, honey."

"It's not your fault. It's me, baby, it's me. Too many separations. Can't do it anymore."

In a few weeks, they did it together. Rocco became indispensable, erecting tents, finding generators for lights and fans. She laughed in later years—"They really don't care if I come as long as Rocco's there."

Nix and Nola knew they would marry anyway but tried to pacify her parents and relatives. As much as they knew and respected Nix and his parents, Nola marrying "a white man" was an issue. They finally gave their tacit approval and agreed to attend, so the wedding was planned around the Christmas holidays. His parents would already be at the compound, and Rocco and Blossom's children would be on their Christmas break. Blossom was worried about airport delays, so after many years of saying no, she agreed to a private jet. It was a six-passenger, and they took Slim Cousins along as a surprise to Nix. He and Slim had remained friends all through high school, and Nix had been in his wedding. The flight was four hours versus the five plus it usually took and cost eight thousand dollars.

The wedding was December 20 in the tribal meeting house, lovely and simple with Nola in a long white batiste dress and moccasins with feathers intertwined in her loose braid. Nix's shirt was white linen with Indian symbols on the collar and cuffs. They planned their trip for after the New

Year to spend Christmas with the families, so everyone was there when the first tragedy to strike the family hit.

Sam Begay came to get Blossom's dad. A doctor was needed at a truck accident near Grants. The old jeep, not equipped with seat belts, slid off a narrow road off Route 40 and down into a rocky ravine. Both were killed instantly. Her dad was sixty-four.

The days went by in a haze. The girls were ten, Ricky almost fourteen. Blossom was strong during the daytime hours for the children and her mother, devastated and inconsolable in Rocco's arms at night. "I should have done more to make him happy. What could it have hurt to do those stupid competitions."

"Blossom, that hasn't been important to him for years. You gave him three grandchildren he adored. There's no comparison, baby girl."

"A bad daughter, a bad daughter," sobbing.

"I'm here, I've got you, baby. I'm here."

Her parents always knew they would retire in New Mexico and fortunately had discussed their final plans. Her dad's ashes were spread around the clinic that he loved so much. What was disquieting at first became almost comforting to Blossom and Nix as the dust swirled around the buildings. It prompted Rocco to tell Blossom to spread his ashes where they were married, and she said to do the same for her.

They were in the two-bedroom compound house. The girls were in with Grandma. Ricky was with them. He whispered, "You can't go before me, Blossom. You can't, baby, I forbid it."

She kissed his ear. "Shh, my darling, go to sleep. You're only thirty-six and too young to worry about it."

They closed the clinic for the season. Her mother went with Nix and Nola to stay at Mim's. She came back to the Conneaut Lake condo for a couple weeks that summer but skipped the next and finally didn't come back at all. She interviewed a series of doctors, finally settling on a woman from South Dakota who had experience with the Lakotas and was looking for something in a warmer climate during the winters. Of course there had been many pointed comments to Blossom once life got back to something that resembled normal. "You could come for a couple months. The children are old enough to stay with Rocco." "Mother, I couldn't possibly leave him, or them, that long. At their ages, they need me there when they get home every day."

They did go that summer for three weeks. Her mother had bought the house they'd always stayed in, so Rocco assembled a crew and did major renovations. Blossom and her mother handled the clinic, and as she had done at his age, Ricky took over the office computer with Coral doing the other office work. Keeping Lily busy had always been a problem. She couldn't take care of the house because Rocco was working there. While playing with a friend, she stumbled on some Acoma dialect and started keeping a journal of words families would tell her. It fueled an interest in languages she didn't know she had, and it stayed with her throughout her life.

"Come here, baby girl," patting his stomach, "I want to tell you something." He was lying on the bed, a couple of pillows behind him.

She straddled him, her breasts dangerously close to his mouth. "Are you sure you want to tell me something?"

"I really do," kissing a nipple quickly. "God, you're beautiful."

She slapped his hip sharply. "My face is up here, mister."

He laughed and said, "I had the talk with Ricky today."

She looked puzzled. "What do you mean, the ta . . . no!" She pounded his chest. "No, no, no, not my baby!"

He chuckled and kissed her fists. "Baby, he's coming up to fourteen, and he hadn't asked any questions. I thought I'd better bring it up."

"Oh, Rocco, no, honey."

"Everything went fine. He had looked all the information up on the Internet, so we just talked about the mechanics not having anything to do with love. He said he understood that, and we went from there."

She put her head in her hands. "He's just so young, honey, and so sensitive."

"He is, baby, but he's super-intelligent. Don't you wish someone had talked to you?"

She smiled and put her face in his neck. "No. I was waiting for you."

He sat her back up. "You know, you have to talk to the girls soon."

Her eyes got big, and she shook her head no solemnly.

"Do you want me to do it?"

Her eyes got bigger, and she shook her head harder.

"Okay. One more year though. Didn't you tell me periods start about twelve?"

"Oh no. They can't be this old, honey. They were just born."

"I know, baby"—rocking her—"I know."

When the girls were twelve and Ricky fifteen, they drove one way to New Mexico. Rocco scheduled himself a month off so they could stop all along the way. It was going to be a northern route to see Mount Rushmore or a southern route to retrace their honeymoon. The southern route won out—the lure of Nashville too great.

The children had seen their parents dance around the house but had never seen them in a large space. "Mom, how do you do that!"

"I just go where Daddy puts me." She smiled.

"Come on, girls, let's give it a whirl," Rocco said.

Coral, who often answered for both of them, "We can't dance, Dad."

"I can," he said, and tears stung Blossom's eyes. It was the same thing he had said to her so many years ago when he first visited her at Penn.

Blossom's early pictures of Rocco had been on her phone. She had progressed to a Canon EOS, had taken a class on it, and her photos had improved dramatically. Rocco was too tall to put his arms around the girls but took one in each hand and showed them what he was doing with his feet. Blossom got a perfect picture of that and again when he spun them gently around. They were little versions of herself. She had quit asking them to dress alike, but tonight they had on the same sundress in different colors—Lily in pink, Coral in yellow, with cowboy boots, their dark heavy hair swinging, their eyes sparkling.

They all talked Ricky into trying it, and what a sight it was—the five of them, arms intertwined, following Rocco's directions for a simple line dance grapevine. Step right and scuff, left and scuff, hitch your right leg, bend a little forward, right leg down, now the left. It garnered them applause, and being away from their home turf and no need to be cool, the children ate it up. With no friends around, they had no qualms showing their parents how much they loved them. Blossom whispered to Rocco in bed, "It's even better than the first time."

They had time to do things in Nashville they had passed up the first time. They went to Adventure Science Center for Ricky, the Parthenon for Blossom, and the Belle Meade Plantation for Rocco, then on to Memphis to make fun of Dad's obsession with Elvis and more fun dancing. In Oklahoma City, the somber visit to the National Memorial was softened by mindless fun at White Water Bay water park. They took many trips as a family, but this was the one that came up the most during "remember when" times.

Another trip was memorable in other ways. The next year they all went to help after an earthquake near Mexico City. Nix, Nola, and Blossom's mother went too. Busy with the logistics of equipment, supplies, transportation, permits, along with personal safety issues, shots, passports, Rocco and Blossom didn't absorb Ricky's and, to a greater degree, Lily's nervousness. The devastation was upsetting, and the work quickly consumed them—Blossom to the medical group who were sponsoring the trip, Rocco anywhere muscle was needed. At thirteen, Coral's empathy was with the children. She would hunt them out and find what they needed or group them up for games.

After two days, Ricky found Rocco. "Dad, Lily's having a hard time. I'm worried about her." Rocco's first instinct was to say "She'll be all right," but a look in Ricky's eyes told him it was urgent. Lily was under a makeshift table in their tent, rocking back and forth. "I can't be here, Daddy, I can't be here."

"It's okay, Lily," holding her on his lap. "Daddy and Mommy will take care of it. Ricky, find Mom. Tell her I know she doesn't have a stopping point but make one and come back here."

That night they met to decide on a plan. Everyone was tired and said things they shouldn't have. Grandma Elaine, "Give her a lecture and a job to do. You coddle her too much." Blossom, eyes narrowed, "Unlike you, I love my children." "Oh Blossom, quit being a drama queen," Grandma countered.

Rocco quickly intervened, "Let's get to an actual plan. She's hurting, and it's cruel to make her stay twelve more days. Nola, would you take Lily back to Aunt Mim's, and Ricky, would you go along to help?" Ricky knew he was giving him a respectable out and loved him for it.

Back in Santa Fe, Nola or Mim had to be with Lily all the time. A rare summer storm required a doctor and a sedative. Nola slept with her until Blossom got there, and it was another month before she would sleep alone.

Rocco and Blossom beat themselves up about it—"What was I thinking, honey. I did the same thing my parents did to me. Just assumed what I wanted was good for everyone." They made sure from then on to ask each child privately how they felt about any family decision, large or small.

Ricky was pragmatic. "I know what I don't want to do with my life. I'll stick with computers, thank you."

Lily was never able to be blasé about it, even after it receded into memory. Coral, on the other hand, had found her life's calling—go where children needed help.

With the children grown, they danced every chance they had. He lined the walls of the dining room with mirrors for her birthday one year, and they were getting better and better. They were watching television: "Baby, see how she rolled over his back. Think you could do that?"

"Let's try." Over and over, they tried. It looked really good.

"I don't think we can do it, baby girl. I can see your unmentionables."

"I'll put petticoats on and see if that helps."

"No. I'd be too nervous."

"I'll get some knee-length dance tights, and we can check again." She did. They passed muster, so she got them in several colors with lace around her knees. They went dancing every other Saturday, and it was always wonderful. Well, there was the Salsa incident:

Rocco loved the sensuality of the Latin dances, and when Blossom saw a notice in the Erie paper for salsa lessons, she read it to him.

"It's a long drive, honey, but it's only six Mondays. We could go to the Outback Steakhouse a couple times. Wouldn't it be fun?"

"I guess we could do that, baby girl."

"And it says wear your Latin finery. I could get a new dress."

"I don't have any Latin finery, sweetie."

"You could wear a white shirt and black slacks with your black dress boots. Oh, this will be so fun," clapping.

He was about to say "No way" when she came downstairs in a spaghetti strap rust-colored shiny dress fitted tight over her butt before three ruffles started, but then she put on a short matching sweater that toned it down, and he caught himself before he got in trouble.

She had registered, so they stopped at a table in the entrance and paid their two hundred forty dollars—twenty dollars each for six lessons. She smiled at him excitedly as they looked at the large room with one mirrored wall. Some others had already arrived, and they didn't have to worry about being overdressed. The couples, mostly Latinos, were dressed to the nines. It looked like it would be a fun evening until the instructor came over, glanced at the register to see their names, and took Blossom's hand. "Welcome. You come with me, Blossom."

He was about Rocco's height, very slender, in a white satin shirt and formfitting black pants flared at the bottom. He had jet black hair oiled back—Rocco hated him on sight. He reached out and took his wrist in a vise grip, moving in front of Blossom. "She'll only be dancing with me."

The fellow, Eduardo, his name tag said, looked like he was about to say something until he saw the look on Rocco's face. "No problem," he said as he scurried away.

"Oh, honey, now you've scared him."

"He deserves to be scared. I know what he's doing."

"Rocco, we just got here. How could you know he's doing anything."

"Blossom, don't be naive. He's zeroing in on the hottest woman in the room, figuring he'll have a good time for six weeks. Well, it ain't gonna happen."

She shook her head but smiled.

Even though the fellow was afraid to look their way, they did pick up some pointers and had a good time, Rocco ever vigilant. The following

Sunday night, "I don't think we can make that class tomorrow night, baby. Is that okay?"

She bit her lip to keep from laughing. She could have insisted but didn't. "That's okay, honey," smiling and looking at him knowingly. She knew that he knew that she knew, as the saying goes. With the unused lessons, her dress, and shoes, they were out about seven hundred dollars. It was a couple years before she wore the dress again. He was listening to an old *The Best of Dean Martin* CD and called up the stairs, "There's a couple of great Latin-type songs on here. Let's try them." She came down in a couple minutes in the dress, in her bare feet, taking his breath away. He took his shoes off and played "Sway." She was lost in his eyes as he showed her how sensual Latin dancing could be. They made it through that one and half of "Innamorata" before he carried her upstairs.

SCENES FROM A MARRIAGE

Their Forties

Mr. Freight Train came once more under that name and then just became *wow*.

They had been sleeping in group tents in the Appalachian Mountains on a four-day stint with RMA. The children were in New Mexico with Nix, and they would go there after a couple of days' rest to celebrate their anniversary and Rocco's fortieth birthday. He wanted a steak for dinner after camp rations, and she babied him with a New York strip and a loaded baked potato. She put a couple of slices of his steak on a salad for herself, giving him the look, licking her fingers, running her toe up his leg.

He grinned. "Are you insinuating you'd like to go upstairs early, Mrs. Carnavale?"

"Why, it has been a tiring week, Mr. Carnavale, and I have missed you a great deal."

He pretended to yawn and stretch, pushing his chair back, but she knew his signs and was two steps ahead of him when he said, "I'll race you to the shower."

The strain and frustration of the last four days—the poverty, the need, the people they couldn't get to—surprisingly made them silly. They showered, played hide and seek, and tumbled into bed laughing and happy.

They were nicely into their perfect rhythm when she dug into his back and cried, "No, no. Rocco, make it stop. Please, please."

"Try to go with it, baby," panting. "You can do it, baby, keep moving. You can do it."

She was whimpering, shaking her head no, but kept moving, desperate pleading on her face. Her eyes widened—it started as yips, escalated to growls, then she screamed and arched against him, her eyes going back in her head, her nails gouging his back.

An electric charge went up his spine. He felt as if he'd been blown out of a canon as he released, held her tight, and their bodies shuddered. He lowered her to the bed with both hands, laying her down gently, gasping, "Wow." They lay weak and shivering as she gave him a heavy-lidded look of disbelief that thrilled him to his toes.

The next morning, it was she who followed him with her eyes, who asked him to stay home. "I have a meeting first thing, baby mine," he whispered. "Then I have to make sure everything's ready for me to be gone a week. I'll be home as soon as I can." He knew it was juvenile; but he felt bigger, stronger, taller, wiser, and smiled all day.

That night as he slipped into bed, "Why are your eyes closed, baby girl?"

"You're too beautiful," in her worried voice. "Do you think we should rest tonight, Rocco? You know, because, because," keeping her eyes closed, her lips nibbled up his cheek to his ear, and she whispered, "of last night?"

"Last night was amazing, Blossom Dove."

"It was, it was, but"—she opened her eyes, so close to his; he felt a jolt—"I'm scared."

"Don't be scared, you'll break my heart. It only came every few years before. It won't happen every time."

Digging into his shoulder, talking intensely, "The fireworks weren't just in my tummy, they were in my heart and my head, and we were flying above the bed in a tornado or something," her voice rising, tears starting. "I think we should rest, don't you. Don't you?"

"Shh, shh, yes, my baby, we should rest. I'm going to roll you over and rub your back now. You go to sleep. We're all good here, everything's good, baby."

She wiggled back into him, taking a deep breath, "I love you, Rocco," and slept, as he smiled through his tears.

They left the next day for Santa Fe for his birthday and some business with the foundation. Blossom and Nix had generous settlements from their father's estate and planned to realign things to keep the clinic open year-round. It could have been handled online, but they thought it would require delicate conversations with their mother. As it turned out, she was thinking along the same lines and had already been in discussions with a group who funded doctors' educations in exchange for two years' service on reservations. She would spend a couple of years getting it running smoothly and then live with Mim.

They were all at Steaksmith, one of Rocco's favorite restaurants, when Nola asked how far in the future the foundation went. Elaine said, "It's best not to plan too far ahead. Plans have a way of not working out," looking at Blossom. Blossom had a look that said she wasn't going to let that go by, so Rocco jumped in and said, "Hey, guess what I'm thinking of getting myself for my birthday?" When everyone looked his way, he said, "A motorcycle!"

Blossom cried out as if struck from behind, "No, no, noo. Rocco, your beautiful face. You'll fall, a car will hit you. No. No."

Everyone at the table was startled at her outburst. Her mother said, "Blossom," in a tone; so Rocco interrupted, "I've got it, Elaine. Baby, baby"—picking her up and putting her on his lap—"I'm just thinking about it, sweetie, just thinking about it."

"Wow, that'd be so great. It'd be so cool, Mom," Ricky said.

"Oh, no, Rocco. Oh no, not Ricky too," her face in his chest.

"Okay," he laughed, but holding her tight, kissing her hair, "change of subject, everyone."

Nix said, "I can do that, Rocco. We wanted to wait until later, but Nola and I are going to be parents!" It put the festive mood back in the evening. Nix was thirty-five, and they had started to worry.

Later, in bed, "But I got you the Sendra boots for your birthday, honey. I had them made just for you."

"And I love them, baby girl. They're the greatest boots ever. I just thought I could ride to work, that's all. We'll talk about it some more."

She put her fists to her eyes, whimpering, and was so adorable they got sidetracked. Back home she put news stories of motorcycle accidents on his desk and quoted statistics to him. The second Saturday home, "Blossom, you're making way too much of this. Come with me, and we'll go look at a couple bikes. Then we'll stop for frozen custard. How about that?" She just looked at him with her big eyes, shaking her head no.

"Okay, then. I'm going. You're going to miss out on frozen custard." She continued to shake her head.

He wasn't as blasé as he pretended. He forced his feet to move to the truck, squeezed the door handle until his palm hurt, and tried to fill his head with thoughts of riding down a back road. It worked pretty well until he got to the local dealer. He walked around a little looking but not seeing, his head filled with a picture of her crying. *What am I doing? I'd hurt her to feel wind in my hair? Am I nuts?* He waved off a salesman heading his way and got back in the truck.

She threw herself into his arms when he came in the door. "I can't live without you. I can't even think about it. Oh, please, oh please, no motorcycle!"

"It's okay, baby girl. Motorcycle's all gone. We don't need a motorcycle." He carried her to their chair. She was sobbing, trying to get her breath, and covering his face with kisses—"Oh thank you, thank you"—and fell asleep from the release of built-up tension as he rocked her.

Ricky rushed in when he came home. "Dad, did you go look at bikes?"

Rocco smiled and tipped his head at her sleeping in his arms, barefoot in a pink sundress and headband. "I changed my mind, son."

Disappointment flashed briefly across Ricky's face, and then he grinned. "She doesn't look old enough to be anyone's mother, does she?"

"No, son, but she's a good one."

"The best, Dad, the best."

She stirred in his arms and wiggled against him, stretching and yawning, the pleasant warmth spreading in his groin. He kissed her awake.

"I'm sorry I was so bad."

"You weren't bad, baby girl. You were scared, and I wasn't paying attention."

She whispered, "Can we go upstairs?"

"The children are home."

Surprised, "What time is it?"

"Five o'clock."

"Oh, my goodness. Rosalita left pot roast in the slow cooker. I'll make the salad and put some rolls in." She kissed his nose and turned back into being a mother. "Girls, set the table, please," she called up the stairs as she went to the kitchen.

He could feel the house settle back to normal, the built-up tension seeping out through the windows, under the doors. He felt guilty being the cause of it, the children being helplessly drawn in. He smiled recalling the old adage, "If Mama ain't happy, ain't nobody happy."

Without lecturing, Blossom got across that education was important, but not *all*-important. They all excelled—Ricky decidedly so, but she politely refused suggestions of skipping grades or taking advanced courses and encouraged the children to participate in school activities.

She and Rocco reveled in parent-teacher conferences and were always there for any school performances. They drove for field trips, were chaperones at parties then at dances as the children got older. Neither one had ever participated during their own school years and enjoyed every minute of their children's.

Ricky had Blossom's talent for computers and found ways to advance his knowledge online while running track and leading his team in Mathcounts and Scholastic Quiz. The girls worked harder for their grades but made time for cheerleading—Coral only one year, she thought it was silly. She said "Absolutely not" when Lily asked her to run with her for homecoming queen. Blossom took her aside. "It's one of those things that mean so much to Lily, darling. It's just one night for you but everything for her." Coral finally acceded, rolling her eyes at the matching gowns and little fur stoles Aunt Mim sent. Mim flew in for the parade, beaming more than Rocco and Blossom.

Ricky enrolled at Allegheny College in town. He never felt the need to get away like his friends did and was happy to live at home. His interest in computers flourished more in the financial direction than in security like

Blossom. He became fascinated in how Grandpa Richards's modest amount of money continued to fund the clinic and added finance and economics to his computer science major.

The lure of New Mexico permeated through the family. The girls both enrolled in the Santa Fe campus of St John's College. One evening after dinner, Blossom came in from the kitchen and climbed onto Rocco's lap. He held up the book from St John's, wrinkled his brow, and said, "This sounds like a bunch of hokum. No textbooks, no finals, no professors?"

"Darling, Aunt Mim swears by this school. Besides, a curriculum based on the great books of the western world can't hurt anyone." She snuggled closer. "I was pushed into concentrating on one thing in college, honey. I want them to enjoy the whole experience." He hugged her tight and kissed her hair, remembering her misery at college.

The girls lived at Aunt Mim's their first year at St John's. Grandma Elaine was already there. Nix, Nola, and five-year-old Nicole had moved in temporarily when Nix began work with New Mexico Water Resources in town. Mim asked them to make it permanent after Lourdes passed away.

Their second year at St John's, Lily wanted to room on campus. Rocco thought it was nice she was feeling more independent. Blossom just smiled. Soon the name Steven was in every conversation; and at their Christmas visit that year, they met Steven Romero, the son of a political family in Santa Fe. Lily still had a nervous tension about her but was lovely and delicate. She and Coral looked exactly alike from a distance, but Coral was already using school breaks to travel to disaster areas. She was tanned and sinewy from outdoor work in rough areas with few comforts.

That spring, when the girls were twenty, Rocco saw Blossom on her phone walking back and forth outside the family room. She came in, wrinkling her nose in distaste, "Blah, blah, blah," and climbed onto his lap.

"Weren't you talking to Steven's mother?"

"Yes, and I could almost see her looking down her nose at me."

"Blossom, I swear your mother comes out sometimes."

She stuck her tongue out at him. "Humph, I should tell her to deal with my mother. That would serve her right."

"So what happened?"

"Oh, she was saying she knows they're too young, but she understands we were married young, so she hopes we'll understand. Blah, blah. They have to keep Steven's future in mind. They wouldn't want a live-in arrangement in his past to come up when he's running for higher office, blah, blah. And she hopes we don't mind having the wedding there. Lily assured her we were all right with it, blah, blah."

He shook his head and laughed. "You behave."

Suddenly she laughed and clapped her hands, "Oh, this is my best idea. I'll turn everything over to Aunt Mim. She'll love it! Then we can show up a couple days ahead and just enjoy the wedding." She jumped off his lap, punched Mim's button, and walked and talked for a half hour. She told him what dates to tell Helen to clear, and he never heard another word until it was time to leave for the airport.

They had rooms at the Eldorado, and the Romeros hosted the rehearsal dinner at the in-house restaurant there, the Old House. Mim had arranged for the reception to be there also. He thought Steven's family was pleasant, if a little plastic—perfect hair, perfect personalities—but he was off kilter. Blossom was busy and distracted and gone a lot. He spent the days wandering around Nix's house looking out the windows for her.

Even though Mim had the time of her life—no detail too demanding, no meeting too inconvenient—Blossom was worried she had put too much on her. Mim was operating at full throttle, her color was bad, and she had lost weight. At cuddling time, Blossom said, "I insisted she give me the expenses, and she just brushed me off saying 'let me do this one last thing.' She's scaring me, honey."

"What's your mother say?"

"Oh, you know her. She thinks everybody's health is their own business."

"You girls have been gone a lot. If I can corner her, maybe she'll talk to me."

"We'll be gone again right up to the wedding, honey, so I'll see you there. Your tux is fine, right?"

"Perfect fit. First one I've ever worn too. Boy I'm glad we didn't do all this. You're not sorry, are you?"

"Oh, heavens, no. Our wedding was the best day of my life"—snuggling closer—"after meeting you, after loving you." She put her leg over his hip and put his world back in order.

He was dressed and in the anteroom where he was told to be when Lily and Coral came in. They looked adorable, like his little girls playing dress up—Lily in a pretty white gown and Coral in something blue. "Where's your mother? I haven't seen her all day."

"Dad, we had to get our dresses fitted one last time, get our hair done, and have lunch," Lily said with exasperation. "Mom can take care of herself."

"Lily," Coral said, returning her exasperation, "lighten up. They're used to being together. Here she comes, Dad."

He turned, and there she was. His heart stopped. She looked like a spirit floating toward him. Her dress swirled around her like two shades of a blue sky, the top so delicate it looked like a spiderweb of lace, sparkling here and there. Her hair back, her eyes luminous, and diamonds hanging from her ears. He wanted to say she was breathtaking, he wanted to say she had never looked lovelier, but all that came out was a whiny "But I wanted to buy you diamonds."

"Shh, I have to go. Nix and Ricky are ready to walk me down. I love you, darlings. Enjoy every minute of it," her lips brushing his.

When he handed Lily to Steven, he came to sit beside her. "I wanted to buy you diamonds," he whispered.

She put a finger to her lips. "Listen to the service, darling, your daughter is getting married."

He tried, but she was all he felt. He could hear her breathe, her chest rising and falling, a beautiful scent reaching his nose, filling his head. Her hair was on the nape of her neck in some little bundle of curls. She'd done something to her eyes. She sensed him not paying attention and pointed a finger forward, her perfectly oval nail polished in a pale pearly blue. Finally, Lily and Steven turned to the small group as Mr. and Mrs. Some other things took place, and they were dancing. "I wanted . . ."

"Darling, these are not diamonds. I got them at the mall for eleven dollars."

They danced sedately. His heart overflowed when she declined dances, whispering she had to go to the restroom to Steven's father and that her feet hurt to Steven's best man. He knew she had done it for him and was ashamed and grateful at the same time. They excused themselves after the bridal couple left, pleading tiredness from the long trip and all the excitement. They danced in the hall on the way to their room. He spun her away, and she smiled with her arms out as she twirled back. Years after, when talk of Lily's wedding came up, he could close his eyes and see her floating to him.

Five months later, they went back to Santa Fe a week before Aunt Mim died of ovarian cancer. She held his hand tightly on the plane. "At least it's not like Daddy, at least it's not like Daddy." She slept fitfully. Coral picked them up and filled them in.

Blossom ran into Mim's bedroom. She was propped up on her chaise lounge ready for guests. "I'm milking this for all it's worth, kiddo." Blossom fell to her knees beside her. "You should have told me how far along it was. I would have never given you all the work of the wedding. It was exquisite, Aunt Mim."

"It was, wasn't it. Don't ever think it was too much. It was just what I needed then. No sense sitting around all day moping, kitten."

She kissed Rocco and Ricky and waved them from the room. "So I hear I'm just missing Ricky coming here."

"He'll be going to the Albuquerque campus and living at the clinic house, but he would have come up as much as he could, Auntie."

Mim grinned as much as she could. "Who would have dreamed you'd have twins and they'd live with me for college. What a joy it has been, honey. By the way, I'm giving the house to Nix and Nola. Is there anything you want?"

"Oh heavens, no, Auntie. I have everything in the world I want or need."

They both smiled, remembering their girl talks about Rocco. Mim patted her hand. "Someone was looking out for you, kiddo, putting him in your path."

Blossom raised Mim's hand to kiss it, tears flowing. "I always thought it was you, Auntie."

"I worried enough about you and Nixie for eighteen years, so I'll take the credit. Your mom is a great person, honey, but your gift threw her for a loop. How's everything between you two?"

Blossom lifted her shoulders. "Everything's fine, Aunt Mim. I've come to terms with it. You can rest easy."

"You mean, go in peace," laughing.

"Don't say that."

"Sweetheart, it is what it is. I'm happy you got here. It's been a good life. Tell Rocco I love him."

Mim's breathing was labored and her eyes closing, so Blossom arranged her pillows and pulled a chair up. Rocco brought her dinner and wanted to stay too when she said she'd sleep there. "No, honey. Send Nola or Mom up and they can tell me what needs to be done to get her ready for the night, and I can give them a break. I'm sure there are personal things she wouldn't want you here for. Come kiss me before bed. I love you."

He looked in on them through the night and took over the kitchen to relieve Nola. It was only four days before Mim lapsed into a coma, and she was gone two days later.

She was back in bed lying on him, his chest wet with her tears, while he rubbed her back. "You've been magnificent, baby girl," whispering into her hair, rubbing his hands over her, checking her out. She felt like a deflated balloon. He no longer panicked, but the chocolate shakes appeared at meals again.

The following spring, when he was twenty-four, Ricky went to New Mexico to work on his doctorates in computer science and finance. Two doctors were alternating at the clinic, one in summer, one in winter, leaving an extra bedroom in the house. It was a far cry from the cramped space Rocco had first seen. He had completely remodeled it—two bedrooms, two new bathrooms, and a modern kitchen, so Ricky stayed there doing most of his work online and occasionally going the sixty miles over to the University of New Mexico. He helped a nearby hospital with some computer problems and soon was mentioning that he was staying over on campus with the name Angela coming up more and more often.

Ashamed that her hackles went up when Ricky said, "Angela thinks we should give you and Dad a cruise for your twenty-fifth anniversary," she sweetly replied that it wasn't necessary; they would go on a little trip—probably to Nashville.

"No, Mom. It should be something you've never done. Now don't tell Dad. A card from all of us will be coming in the mail."

She waited until Rocco had absorbed the card. First, he fussed about them spending the money then about how they'd rather go to Nashville or maybe explore Chicago instead of lying in the sun—translation, someplace Blossom wouldn't be in a bathing suit—but it was very thoughtful of them. Then Blossom pointed to the signatures: Coral, Lily and Steven, Ricky and Angela. "Who is this person. We don't know this person. Why would her name be on our card?"

"Blossom."

"Really, darling. I mean isn't that some nerve putting your name on a card to people you've never met?"

"Blossom, don't make me say what I'm thinking."

"I do not sound like my mother," pounding his chest.

"Baby girl, these are young people with busy schedules. Write her a note, thank her for the cruise idea, and suggest they all get together and plan to come here."

"Humph," sticking her tongue out. "I suppose I could. Or maybe wait until after the cruise so I can send pictures." She put her finger to her lips, and he smiled as the wheels in her brain started to plan. "It will probably be Christmas before everyone can get away. Thanksgiving breaks aren't that long. That's it, I'll mention Christmas in my note," settling against him and curling the back of his hair with her finger.

Rocco was relaxing on their balcony of the cruise ship. There hadn't been a way out of it. Blossom wouldn't let him cash in the tickets—it would hurt their feelings, she said. She was in the shower preparing for dinner, and he was reminiscing and congratulating himself on his self-restraint in not commenting on her wardrobe so far.

Today had been tough. She wanted to lie by the pool to get a "little pink," she said, for the dress she was wearing this evening. She took off her cover-up, and he could feel every eye on her. The damn pool was centered on the deck, no corners to put her in and stand guard. He tried sitting close and shielding her. "Honey, you're blocking my sun.' She must have felt him looking all over, jumped up saying she'd lie on their balcony, and started walking through the crowd, every head turned her way. He'd almost tripped getting to her with a towel, wrapped her, and picked her up. "I can walk, honey."

"You might trip."

"Aren't you sweet," nuzzling his neck. He thought he was in the clear until she said, "I think I'll lay out with nothing on, honey, no one's around."

"WHAT!"

She grinned mischievously. "Oh I guess not."

God, she kept him on edge. He didn't want to mess up their anniversary. Twenty-five years. Unbelievable. One more day to stay out of trouble. He remembered one of the worst times when he was scared to death.

They were meeting at the shop for their second and last visit to the hot dog stand for that summer. It had remained a rare treat, Blossom always health conscious. With great nieces to buy for, Mim had sent Blossom few outfits the last several years. This summer she had been wearing sheer, flouncy sundresses—worrisome, but they didn't cling or anything; he had come to terms with them.

He was locking up as they pulled into the lot, and he turned and smiled as she got out of the car. They had bought Volvo wagons when the children came. She had read they were the safest. As she stepped from behind the big door, he reached for something to hang on to but was too far away from the building and stumbled before he caught himself. The kick in the gut, blood pounding in his ears, hard to breath. She had on a tiny black skirt, a snug white top with her breasts defined and only one shoulder, and some kind of black and straw shoes laced up her ankles.

At first he thought he handled it well. Quietly, "Blossom."

"Hi, darling, are you ready for supper?"

"Blossom. Where is your dress, baby?"

"What dress, honey?"

"You know, your dress—that covers you up."

A shadow passed over her face, but for the children's sake, her voice upbeat, "The girls and I decided to wear shorts today," smiling.

He looked at the girls, getting out in Meadville Bulldogs T-shirts and black shorts. "But your skirt is very short, sweetie."

"It's not a skirt, it's shorts. See," lifting up the skirt to show him tight shorts, smiling sweetly.

"But you never wear shorts, baby." Ricky now getting out of the car to hear what the conversation was about.

"Rocco"—sternness creeping into her voice—"it's eighty-four degrees. Everyone at the hot dog stand will be dressed like this."

It just came out and loud. "No one at the hot dog stand will be dressed like that!"

Coldly, "Perhaps I'll take the children to supper, and you can run along home."

"Oh no. No way," his voice rising, the children's surprised eyes going from one to the other. "You're not going any place alone dressed like that. I'll drive."

He took perverse pleasure in thinking he was right. He had to glare at several glances her way. It was more than likely it was because they were a beautiful family, but that never entered his mind. He tried to whisper he was sorry several times; but she turned her back, driving him wild, keeping his stomach in knots, the food tasting like sand.

She answered him in monosyllables when they got home, and when the girls went upstairs at eight, she did too. He didn't want to go upstairs until Ricky did, and that was almost ten. He closed the house down and heard her talking to Ricky in his room, the bed not folded back yet.

He got into the shower quickly, sure he could explain at cuddling time. He was rinsing off when the thought hit him—what if she wasn't in bed. Oh god, what if she wasn't there. He felt nauseous; his knees were weak. He stepped out of the shower dripping and pulled the door open. He saw the little mound on the bed, and his legs almost gave out with relief. Thank you, God, thank you God.

He slid into bed. "Thank you for being here."

"I'll always be here, Rocco, but I was very upset."

"I have to protect you, Blossom. You don't understand who might be out there."

"Don't try to rationalize your behavior. You raised your voice at me in front of the children."

"Just open your eyes. I can explain better."

"I'm not opening my eyes."

"Baby, please. It was a shock is all. Your legs were showing. That top was tight. I've never seen those shoes. It just made me a little crazy is all. Please look at me. I won't do it again."

"I was very upset, Rocco. You hurt my feelings."

"If you won't look at me, can I at least give you the little kiss?" He held his breath, feeling sweat around his hairline.

"Well, just the little one. I was very upset."

He felt a wave of relief as she lifted her lips and let him kiss her into submission.

Boy, that was one of the worst. And he certainly wasn't going to fall apart like he did at their anniversary party just ten days ago. Well, that was understandable. Someone should have warned him. She came around the door in her wedding dress. Twenty-five years fell away, and his knees gave out. Nix and Ricky caught him before he fell, but Christ, forty-seven and stumbling around like an old fool. God, she was beautiful, even more beautiful than their wedding day if that was possible. He had gotten himself together after her glorious smile and was able to sing "The First Time Ever I Saw Your Face" just like at their wedding.

Well, he'd better go in and see if she was dressed for dinner. One more dinner to endure and protect her from predators. Actually they had missed three of them. She had looked so beautiful; they'd never made it out of their state room. The Western Night had been fun though. They had brought boots with them when they saw it on the agenda and danced all night. She had on a white dress, ruffles all the way to her boots, with a white ribbon in her hair. Oh god, he loved her.

Rocco was right. Blossom at forty-five was breathtaking. All her edges softened as distance from her mother and her confidence grew. Her softly rounded hips and generous chest, her catlike movements, and glowing skin from years of healthy eating. She was finally secure that to love being a wife and mother was perfectly fine. She felt it her greatest accomplishment that the children were confident in their parents' love and admiration, not frightened and guilty and lonely as she had been. Her contentment gave her a glow and emanated from every pore.

He smelled her after-shower lotion and slid the door open from the balcony. She turned, smiling that smile. All his resolve to be calm disappeared. He grabbed the bureau for balance. "No, absolutely not! No way. I am a reasonable man, Blossom. A reasonable man. You cannot appear in public in that, in that—whatever it is. No, no!"

There she was in a two-piece white outfit—the top a gathered band barely covering her breasts. The bottom a flowing, clingy skirt starting under her navel, and my god, a turquoise stone in her belly button! "That looks like T-shirt material. It doesn't cover anything. No, no, no."

"But, darling," she said innocently, "This is silk jersey. It was very expensive. Don't you love it"—twirling in front of him—"so appropriate for a cruise," looking at him with her big eyes.

"Blossom, you cannot . . ."

She giggled, took out the turquoise gem, and set it on the bureau, gave a tug up on the skirt to cover her navel, a tug down on the bandeau to deemphasize her breasts, pressed against him, and whispered in his ear, "You're so easy."

His look was puzzled and incredulous at the same time. "You did that on purpose?"

"Yes I did"—jumping into his arms, her legs around his waist—"to show you how silly you are."

"Baby girl, I need to protect you."

"Who are you protecting me from—that old gentleman from Des Moines?"

"There are other people in that dining room, Blossom. You are too trusting."

She started nibbling his neck. "Careful now," he said, "or we'll miss dinner again."

"That's my master plan," her tongue in his ear.

He ran his hand up her leg under her skirt. His breath caught. "You have nothing on!"

"All part of my master plan, Mr. Carnavale."

He laid her on the bed, and they missed dinner again.

She woke in an hour. "Let's get a tray of nibbles and find a little place to sit. This is our last night."

"Can the tray have a cut-up steak on it?"

"Yes, it can. Even fries with cheese. Do you want to be on a deck or come back to our balcony?"

"Balcony."

They loaded a tray with goodies, a split of champagne, and a beer. She put a blanket around her shoulders, and they looked at the stars and talked into the night.

Hours later, he said, "I have a little present for you."

"We said no presents!"

"I know, but remember we were busy on our fifteenth and just had a quick dinner?"

"I do. Ricky was fourteen and wanted a swimming party, and then the girls wanted one, and your birthday and our anniversary got lost."

"And you cried and said 'do you love me?' What did I say?"

She got up from her chair, straddled him, and put the blanket around them both. "You said, 'Baby, I passed love years ago. I'm on to worship, heading towards agapé,' and I said you can't say that, that's for the lord."

He laughed and hugged her. "You remembered after ten years."

"I told you, I never forget what you tell me," kissing his nose.

He reached in his pocket and gave her a box. "This is for the ring finger on your right hand to match the one of your left hand. It's dark now, but when we go inside, you can see it says 'I passed love years ago.' Do you like it?"

She gazed in his eyes. "Rocco, Rocco, I love you more every day. I was fussing about the trip, and you were thinking of a gift." She kissed him, kissed him some more, and started moving against him. Again, again.

"Hey, hey, baby, not here. Someone might come out on their balcony."

"No one's out," she whispered, the champagne making her reckless. "Let's make love on the Atlantic Ocean."

"It's not the Atlan . . . aw, jeez, baby, baby, just a second, my zip . . ."

She moved and moaned and giggled until it wasn't funny anymore, and her scream went up into the summer night.

"Oh god, woman, we gotta go inside. I can't move." They heard voices, and she covered their heads, panting and laughing. "Baby, we're not fooling anyone."

"Carry us inside. Do you think they know who we are?"

"Blossom"—laughing—"we've been next to them for a week. Of course they know who we are."

"I think there are four voices."

"Well, it's not like we aren't married. Hold tight, I've got to get the door and keep my pants up." In they went, falling to the bed laughing. "No more champagne for you, little lady."

She sent letters and photos to everyone after the cruise, asking them to clear their schedules for a Christmas visit. As it turned out, Lily had the flu, and Coral was called to a mudslide in Ecuador, but they finally met Angela Cimonelli. She was a registered nurse, twenty-six, small, slender, with long black hair and dark eyes. Blossom whispered to Rocco in bed, as though someone could hear, "Do you think it's funny Ricky picked someone who looks so much like the girls they could all be sisters?"

"No, baby. He's picked someone who reminded him of his mother, and I don't think it's funny at all. It's subconscious, I know, but you're the finest woman he knows, and he wanted someone like you."

"Oh, Rocco, do you think that's good?"

"I think he lucked out. He was attracted to her looks and found out she's a nice person too. Quit looking at her so skeptical. She's fine."

She pretend pouted. "But, my baby."

"I know, sweetie, I know."

"And did you hear her say she wouldn't have to change her monogram—Cimonelli to Carnavale, still AC? I mean, we just met her."

"Blossom."

"Quit laughing. I'm not like my mother."

He laughed from her neck to her navel. "No, no, honey, they'll hear us."

"I'm not going four days without you. Let them hear us."

"Honey, honey," pulling on his hair. It was too late. She put Tiger in her mouth with one hand and pushed him down with the other.

Ricky and Angela were married the following June on Rocco and Blossom's anniversary and Rocco's birthday. It was a large, noisy, and fun affair; and a good time was had by all. They moved into a restored house in the Nob Hill area in Albuquerque so Angela would have a quick commute to the hospital. Ricky completed his doctorate in finance and worked from home on the family's business, gradually helping others hoping to do similar charity work.

A couple more years went blissfully by. Lily and Ricky married, Coral single but busy and seemingly happy, the business growing . . .

He was heading to a job estimate, a good-sized addition farther up Main Street from the turn off to Jackson Oaks. He wasn't going to turn in; he wasn't going to turn in; yet here he was coasting into the driveway, his pulse beating in his ears, barely able to breathe, his nerves strung so tight, they were humming. Christ, how could she still do this to him. Forty-nine and no more control than when he was twenty. What was he thinking—taking her on the floor? God forgive him, that's exactly what he was thinking.

He couldn't believe he hadn't been able to think rationally to the end of the week—there was an end point for heaven's sake. He'd been working nights on a restaurant redo. The owner wanted them there from midnight to noon so he wouldn't have to close. She had been working with hospice and told him she'd volunteered to stay nights with a terminal client as long as he'd be gone. They'd been like ships in the night, apart five days.

He squeezed the steering wheel, his knuckles white. He couldn't burst in like an animal; he couldn't. He took a ragged breath and made it to the door, relieved to see it was locked. She forgot sometimes, but he knew she was there. The client had passed, and she called to tell him she would fix dinner. He got the familiar clutch in his stomach when she wasn't by the door. She was 90 percent of the time when they were first together, but even when she told him he might beat her home by a few minutes, the fear would hit him. When the kids came along, school activities, meetings, and such, he got more used to it; but now that they were gone, back came that stab of fear when she didn't meet him at the door. He was just about to holler when he saw the back door was open, took a deep breath, and stepped onto the deck. There she was, a little down the hill, on her knees planting flowers. He started to sweat, gripped the railing—she felt him and looked up, the glorious smile. "Darling, you stopped to see me."

"I did," talking carefully. "What are you doing, baby girl? We have a gardener."

Sitting back on her heels, "I know, sweetie, I just wanted to dig in the dirt and plant something living—you know, Betty and all. Look at the faces on these pansies," holding one up to her cheek. "Aren't they adorable? Isn't God wonderful?"

"Very wonderful," he said with effort, trying to be casual. "Will there be a service we can go to?"

"They'll let me know. She only had a niece left. So sad."

He started down the steps, her little hand motion stopping his heart, as she said, "You stay over there now, I'm all hot and sweaty." He remembered the same motion from their first date when she directed him not to sit beside her.

"I like you hot and sweaty. I bet you're salty too."

"Now, now. Our special time is tonight. What are you doing in this neighborhood anyway?"

Easing himself to the ground, "Can I sit over here? I stopped to say hi to my wife, I was . . . what are you wearing, little one?"

"Overalls," a big smile. "These are overalls. I got them to work in the dirt. I'm going to put all these pansies in this little corner. Won't they be pretty?"

"Very pretty. You know what I always wondered about overalls?"

Giggling, "I didn't know you wondered anything about overalls."

"Oh yeah. I always wondered how those straps came undone, that funny hook thing."

"Now, Rocco, you stay over there. I want to plant these."

"Okay. I'll lay here and look at the clouds," stretching out, crossing his ankles. He let a couple minutes go by, the nearness of her pounding in his ears. "Why don't you come over and look at the clouds too."

"Well, just for a minute. I want to finish and fix dinner." He held his breath as she lay beside him. "Oh, look"—she pointed up—"that one looks like a little piggy."

He reached for her finger and kissed it as he turned on his side, staring into her eyes.

"Honey," she whispered, "I'm all dirty."

"Please. It's been five days."

"But I wanted to come to you tonight after a bubble bath, all fresh and clean. We used to wait five weeks, remember?"

"A drink of water, then," breathing hard. "Let me carry you inside for a drink of water."

"Just a drink of water, then," her breath coming faster.

He scooped her up, nuzzling her neck, pushing the door shut with his foot. "I like the water upstairs better, don't you?"

"Oh, yes"—trembling—"I've always liked the water upstairs. I have, I really have."

He stood her on the floor, undid the metal hooks, the overalls sliding to the floor. She had something over her breasts. He made a choking sound as he slid it over her head. "Go potty, hurry."

"Can I shower?"

"No!" too loudly. "No, baby, no." As she ran into the bathroom, he punched Bob on his phone. Helen was training a new girl, and he didn't want to get into a discussion. To Bob, roughly, "Move everything up two hours," stripped, and slid into the middle of the bed before she could see his hardness.

She ran to the bed, climbing in on his side, laughing, "We're backwards," before she saw his eyes, the crystal blue dark and dangerous. She pressed against him. "Do you need me, my darling."

"I can go slow," almost gasping. "We'll go slow."

She put her leg over his hip. "I can be anything you need, anything."

He lost all resolve, growled, and covered her roughly with his body. "No, no, I can . . ." and cried out as she bit his neck.

"Yes, yes, anything," pulling him in, pushing him away. He was always the dominant one, but she knew when he needed even more. She moved around the bed, fighting him until he was screaming with need, finally letting him enter and begin their perfect rhythm as he sobbed. Tiger had fallen off the bed in their frenzy. She bit his chest to muffle her cries, and they collapsed gasping.

He let himself rest for twenty minutes, wiped her face with the edge of the sheet, and whispered, "You rest, I have a call to make. I'll be back about five." He didn't see her worried look as he went to the shower.

He drove back in at five, smiling at the thought of her jumping into his arms. The door opened before he could unlock it. She was all in white, her hair damp, held back with a white ribbon, a shy smile. No jump. She stood on tiptoe to kiss him, lips closed. She took his hand and walked to the table. "I made your favorite meatloaf, the one covered with bacon. Dinner's all ready," eyes down.

Okay, something a little off, but she's smiling. Everything's fine. "This is delicious, baby. I love your scalloped potatoes."

She put her fork across her plate—she had only eaten a couple bites—her hands on her lap, eyes down. "Rocco, I can't make you late for appointments, darling, it's not right. I . . ."

"Blossom, you did not make me miss an appointment. I did. Everything is fine. I got the job, no harm, no foul."

"But . . ."

"No buts. The business is way down the list, baby girl. You're the most important thing in my life . . ."

"And the children," she said worriedly.

"Of course, and the children. There's a long list before we get to the business, baby." He winked at her. "My world rocked once today, and it wasn't when I got that job," winking again. She blushed. Forty-seven and she blushed. God he loved her.

"Love you beyond words, Blossom Dove. Now eat a little more, this meatloaf is great."

"I've had enough."

"No, you've had two bites. Come sit on my lap, and we'll do bite for me bite for you," holding out his arms.

She climbed onto his lap happily, and they ate and talked. He felt her tension ebb away, and his worry with it. By the time she pushed the fork away, she'd finished a small piece of meatloaf, two bites of scalloped potatoes, and three of peas and carrots. He was satisfied and hugged her. "Will you tell those people not to make you work nights anymore?"

"You just stop. They're not 'those people,' it's Jean and Diane, and you agreed I could do it."

"But it was so long," he whined, nuzzling her ear.

"I know. I won't do nights again."

"You don't hurt anywhere, do you?"

"Not a single place," she lied.

"Good. Maybe you can help me heal this hole in my chest then."

She giggled. "I'm sorry. I couldn't find Tiger."

They snuggled and kissed, getting as close as they could. "Do you want me to call the gardener to finish your pansies?"

She sat back and said proudly, "I finished."

He opened his eyes wide. "You did that and fixed dinner too?

"Yes," fluttering her eyelashes. "I had renewed vigor."

"Ooh, renewed vigor. I like the sound of that." He did his Groucho Marx and slid his hand under her skirt and up her leg. "How's that renewed vigor holding up, little lady?"

"My renewed vigor is just fine, kind sir, but don't you want dessert?"

"Dessert is just what I'm thinking about," exploring with his hand.

"Oh, you're so bad," giggling and jumping down. "We're having peach cobbler. I worked hard on it, and that's your dessert, crazy man."

It was heaven feeding each other, cleaning up, dance stepping around, loading the dishwasher. Home was home again.

In bed at cuddling time, nose to nose, "I have to sell the business." She put her finger over his lips. "I do. I have to be with you every minute, or you'll do things like buy overalls." He got his giggle. "Will you wear them for me with nothing on under?"

"I can't for very long. The material is a little rough, you know . . ."

"You mean here," circling a nipple lightly.

"Yes"—shivering, tipping her head back—"there, there."

He caressed her there and everywhere and loved her tenderly to sleep.

SCENES FROM A MARRIAGE

Their Fifties

She should have connected it for heaven's sake. She was thinking of something special for his fiftieth birthday coming up in June. A trip? No, he didn't enjoy them as much as she did. What he loved to do was dance, so maybe she'd have Ricky check around Albuquerque for a new place. He loved the Stable in Santa Fe but also loved new bands and new floors. She was about to talk to him when he came out of the bathroom, his eyes already dark, dropping his towel. No cuddling, no sweet nothings. An almost rough push back onto the pillow, a strangled "I can't go," her "what" lost in his rough kisses. Her heart was pounding, she had a fleeting thought she'd ask him later what was wrong, but by then she was caught up in it with him, spent and exhausted and asleep after.

He was gone in the morning, and she thought during the day he'd tell her later, but she needed to give him the freedom he had always given her when she was troubled. That night the same, even more so. Whimpering, not yet, not yet, frenetic, rough, insatiable. She met him, matched him, even surpassed him. He woke her at five but seemed to relax, just pulled her close. She whispered, "Again."

"No again, baby, go to sleep," kissing her forehead.

"Again," softly, pleading.

He could have distracted her, but her eyelashes were brushing his cheek, her breath warm on his neck, her hand reaching down. He opened his phone, punched Bob, and croaked, "I'll be late," as she squeezed him. He started to recharge as he moved down her body, still moist and warm, her musky smell making him dizzy. He wasn't just recharged; he was supercharged. She felt his exuberance had a desperate edge to it, that this was the culmination of what had been bothering him. She wrapped her legs around him, hugged him tight around his neck, and held on as he bucked and rolled, cried out, and finally collapsed, asleep. They ended up with her on top, but her worry wouldn't let her sleep. For the first time in their life, she was up before him. She covered him and went to the girls' old room for a shower.

At Bob's house, he closed his phone, chuckling. His wife asked, "Who, honey?"

"Rocco. Sounds like Blossom's got him over a barrel."

"Aww. Are they fighting?"

"Not hardly, Marie," laughing. "Not hardly."

"Robert! Don't talk about people's personal lives."

"Hey, sometimes the poor kid can hardly walk."

"Robert!" And then giggling, "Little Blossom?"

"Yeah, little Blossom." Then seriously, "I don't know what would have become of him without her, Marie," reaching for her, so happy she was still there after all her illnesses.

Blossom tried puttering around the house but was too worried and ended up sitting beside him. She saw his eyes move under his lids and was kneeling beside the bed when he opened them. "Hi."

"Did I hurt you?"

"Never," her ribs rebelling, her vagina stinging.

"What time is it?"

"Eleven thirty. Bob said call about one, he just needs to check something with you."

"I'll get going."

"Darling, just rest. They're fine."

He closed his eyes. "Blossom, my dad died at fifty-two. I'm going to be fifty. I can't leave you yet," his voice catching.

"Oh, sweetheart. You're healthy as a horse."

"But he was healthy."

"No, honey. Something was wrong. Remember, he had started making plans. Let me do a few tests. You'll see you're fine."

"No. No. I don't want to know."

"Shh, shh, you're fine, my darling boy, you're fine."

"Can we have everybody here for my birthday. I want to see everybody in the house again."

"Of course, darling, but it's so much easier to go to them. Lily's pregnant, Nixie's girls have so many activities."

"But I want to see them around the house again. Would you ask them, baby?"

"I'll do it tonight, honey."

"And don't tell them I'm crazy, will you."

"I won't," winking. "You're only my crazy man."

"I love you beyond words, Blossom. It just came over me that I can't leave you."

"You're not going anywhere. I forbid it. I'll get everyone here. We'll have a wonderful three or four days, and everything will be fine."

"Do we have everything in order? Like our will and stuff?"

"Everything's in order. You're the picture of health," pulling the sheet back and squeezing his butt. "Up and at 'em now. Call Bob, and if it's something you can handle on the phone, we'll go to lunch."

That evening after dinner, "Everyone's all set, honey. Lily said she has to discuss it with Steven, but that's just her. It looks like it will be hot. You get the pool ready, and Cassie and I will get all the rooms ready. Did you like the last caterer we used?"

"I can do the cooking, baby."

"No. I don't want you cooking the whole time. We'll do steaks one night, and you can do that, but I'll order some side dishes, breakfasts, and lunches." She put her finger to her lips, counting items on her fingers. He smiled, loving to watch her brain turn. "Maybe Italian one night . . . hmmm, Ricky and Angela can have his room. Lily and Steven like bed-and-breakfasts, Nixie and Nola can use the girls' room, and their girls and Coral can camp out in the family room. Isn't it funny, when they're all here, the house isn't big enough. She clapped and hugged him. "Grandchildren are starting to come. Isn't this unbelievable." She snuggled closer. "Why didn't you tell me why you were worried?"

"You couldn't stop me turning fifty, baby girl."

"So you were going to ravage me until you expired?"

"First, let's get it straight who ravaged who," getting the giggle he was hoping for.

She sat up, a hand on each of his cheeks. "Tonight you rest."

"I rested all day."

"That's not enough. Tonight we sleep," kissing his nose.

She was already turned into her sleeping position when he got into bed. He lifted her hair and kissed her neck. "Sleeping only," she cautioned.

"Did I ever tell you how beautiful your neck is?"

She turned over, smiling and shaking her head, "You need to rest, honey." But she put her hand on the back of his neck. He was encouraged.

"I feel good. Do you feel good?"

"I feel wonderful, but we decided to rest."

"We could just go slow. Nice and easy. It would be just like resting."

"Sweetheart."

"Tomorrow's Saturday. I have one couple to meet with, and that's not until eleven," little kisses on her nose, her eyes, her lips. "What harm would it be. Nice and slow." Back to her lips, lingering, "No harm at all," his tongue exploring.

"Ooh, ooh," her lips parting.

He didn't wake her until ten, had shaved, showered, and eaten, and was feeling great. "I gotta go, baby. Take your time. I'll be back in a couple hours." He put her hand to his lips. "You were right. I'll have a wonderful birthday, and we'll have a wonderful anniversary with Ricky and Angela."

And they did. The house was filled with music, love, laughter, great conversations, and great food for three days. He turned white when Lily and Steven announced they were having twins, his fear when Blossom had the girls wafting over him, but they seemed calm and happy about it, so he sought out Blossom's eyes and breathed deep with her.

When the last car drove away, they sat with their feet up listening to her gift to him—the complete collection of Delbert McClinton's music—holding hands and yawning. Of course, as fifty-two approached he thought of his mortality again, but she kept him busy, and it passed, until . . .

"It will be fun." She smiled tremulously. "Like a guy thing," her little hand creeping into his.

"Sure. It will be nice." He smiled, his forehead wrinkled in worry. "The three of us. Nice."

Ricky and Nix had called on her conference setup. Nix was going to Winnipeg, Canada, for a conference. He and Ricky thought it would be great if they and Rocco went on a camping trip after. "Sleeping under the stars, Dad, cooking over a campfire. How about it? Make him do it, Mom."

"It's kind of sudden, honey."

"We didn't want to give him time to make excuses. Call me tomorrow. Talk him into it."

They just looked at each other for a minute. She had always been the one to go away. First Penn, then Pitt, the short times in the hospital with the babies. She was a little short of breath with the thought of it but still trying to be upbeat. "Three men out in the wild," then worried. "You don't think it will be dangerous, do you?"

"Nah, Nix is out in the mountains all the time. But I won't even consider it unless Cassie's free to stay nights."

"I'll be fine, honey."

"No. Call her, and then we'll consider it."

"I'll call her right now." She didn't move, though, her hand squeezing his. "This is fine. It's wonderful they thought of you," her eyes welling up. "The world's always trying to separate us. I can't do it again, Rocco, I can't."

"Baby girl"—picking her up—"no one can separate us. I'll do this little thing for Ricky. He never asks anything of us, and then we'll just say no. No matter who asks, we'll just say no. Would you rather go see the girls?"

"Oh, I can't get on another plane so soon. We just got home. I need to nest for a while."

They had gone to Paris for Blossom's fiftieth birthday. She had studied basic phrases and reveled in the culture, the food, the art. He had tried to get involved but quietly thought the food portions small, the men aggressive, the people pretentious, and for the most part rude. There had been some memorable moments, but even she had seemed glad to start home.

So the plan went forward. Nix had made arrangements for all the equipment and told him what to pack—a hooded sweatshirt for bugs, a couple of long-sleeved flannel shirts, his shearling coat, and work boots. Seven days—a day and a half to travel, four days there, a day and a half to get back.

At cuddling time the night before he left, they were nose to nose; he was stroking her back and hip. He made a mental note to call Cassie and tell her to make a couple of hearty soups and have chocolate shakes a few times. She had lost a couple of pounds on their trip and since Ricky called had been pushing her food around her plate.

He traced her eyebrows with his finger. "You're very beautiful."

"You're just trying to soften me up."

"I am. How am I doing?"

She lifted her eyebrows and smiled. "Very, very well."

He laughed and lifted her onto him, hugging her tight. "It will be fine, baby girl. I'll call whenever I can and be back before you know it." She buried her face in his neck, and he could feel her tears.

She fussed about not driving him to the airport, close to stamping her foot. "No, Blossom. It's final, and I mean it. I don't want you driving back alone." He flew into the airport in Winnipeg and met Ricky and Nix. They drove about 150 miles east on Sixteen and then up Ten into Riding Mountain National Park. The first night was good. They sat around the campfire and talked. Rocco was amazed how much Nix knew about camping, and it was great hearing them talk about their work and families.

He knew Ricky had Blossom's brilliance, and it was nice to see him enjoy it instead of it being a burden. The foundation was flourishing under his guidance. Ricky said, "Don't tell anyone. Not even Mom, Dad. Angela wants to tell everyone." He got a big, proud grin. "We're finally expecting!" High fives and hugs and then stories of Nix's three girls. Nicole was six when Mim died, but then Nadine and Nancy had come a year apart. Elaine still lived at the house. She was well and busy. Didn't go down to their clinic much—there was a free clinic in Santa Fe she helped at two days a week.

She and Nola got along fine. Rocco thought silently, *It seemed to be only her disappointment in not being able to direct Blossom's life that caused the hurt that never went away.*

On the second night, Ricky woke; and for a couple of seconds, his stomach clenched at the figure out in the clearing, until he realized it was Rocco. He walked toward him. "Dad, what are you doing up. Come get some sleep."

Rocco lifted his phone skyward. "I was just wondering if I could get a signal from a satellite going by."

"It doesn't work like that, Dad." He smiled. "Come on, we'll be back in range in a couple days."

He was in good shape. They had added treadmills and weight machines to the punching bags at the shop, but he had a twinge in his chest as they were hiking that scared him. He had never mentioned to the children that his dad died at fifty-two, his age now. Try as he might to get into the trip, all he could think of was what if he died and never saw Blossom again.

At the crest of the mountain when Ricky and Nix were exclaiming over the view, he was someplace else staring at something only he could see. Nix told Ricky, "We're going to have to go back."

"No, no. He'll be fine."

"Rick, they went through a lot before you came along. I've seen that look before, it's not fair. He's not enjoying this, and that was the whole point."

That night Ricky looked over at him lying on his back in his sleeping bag, looking straight up. A tear came out of the corner of his eye. Ricky looked away, embarrassed.

The next morning he said, "God, Nix, I forgot that meeting with the Albuquerque hospital. We better start back." Rocco was so relieved. He didn't stop to think that Ricky would never forget a meeting.

"I've got a signal here, could you pull over for a minute," Rocco asked Nix. He got out and walked away, his foot on a boulder, his body tense. Soon he was laughing, wiping his nose with his sleeve, his body relaxed, standing tall. He came back to the truck smiling.

"She okay, Dad?"

"She'll be fine. You know your mother, separations upset her." He missed the rolled eyes between Ricky and Nix.

Finally they were at Winnipeg International waiting for his flight. He was loose and happy, checking his watch when he saw a startled look on Nix's face, turned, and there she was. He was back at Penn, back in Pittsburgh, back everywhere she had run to him, knees pumping, all skirt and petticoats and hair flying, her large tote over her shoulder, Tiger's head peeking out. He moaned, he hoped it was in his mind, but Ricky's look told him it wasn't, and then she was in his arms, sobbing, "You can't . . . I can't," covering his face with kisses. They moved away. "Sh-sh, I've got you, I've got you."

At twenty-nine, Ricky was young enough to be embarrassed. At forty-seven, Nix just thought it was funny. "Jeez, Blossom, you couldn't wait a few more hours? Give the guy a break."

Rocco changed their flight to the next day. They all went to the Delta Winnipeg, had lunch at the Blaze Bistro, then Nix and Ricky started back. Rocco and Blossom checked in. She blushed when he asked for a room with a whirlpool. "You didn't have to be embarrassed. I've used muscles I didn't know I had. It sounded relaxing."

"He looked at me funny."

"He looked at you because you're beautiful."

"Oh, silly, I'm old enough to be his mother. Don't shave until morning," rubbing his whiskers. "I want to feel you all over me."

"Fill the whirlpool, baby, while I get a couple layers off in the shower."

"Ahh," sitting her on his lap in the hot water. "Don't tell anyone, but camping is for the birds. This is nice. We should get one of these." They sat silently, breathing deeply, her head on his chest, the water lapping around them. "How's my baby girl?"

"Good now. Wonderful now," she whispered.

They dried each other off, the hot water making her yawn after five sleepless nights. She stared into his eyes. "Never again, never again."

"Never again, baby. Where you go, I go. Where I go, you go. Go to sleep for a while, I'll wake you."

She cried out as she drifted off. "No, no."

His eyes stung. She still carried the scars, still didn't feel in control of her life.

She turned to him in the night, a sob catching in her throat. "I'm here, baby girl, I'm here."

"Hurt me so I know you're not a dream."

"No. No, baby. I have whiskers, and we're in Canada. It's not a dream. I don't want to hurt you." But she knew him too well; and at his point of no return, she turned onto her knees, pushed roughly back against him as he groaned, unable to stop. She cried out when his thrusts were too much for her, crying into Tiger, shuddered with him, and collapsed with tears running down her face.

He fell to his side, still holding her to him, gasping for breath. "We can't, I don't . . . ," crying into her neck. She lifted his hand from her stomach to her lips to kiss it and fell asleep. After he could move, he cleaned them both, biting his lip and shaking his head at the trace of blood, and went in to shave.

She woke in the morning, turned, and pouted when she patted his shaved face. "But I wanted to watch."

"Blossom"—softly—"we can't do that anymore. There was blood, baby, you might be hurt."

"Okay," coyly.

"I mean it, Blossom. No more now," knowing he was so totally not in control of anything.

"I said okay," kissing his cheeks.

"Please, baby," whispering against her hair. "If something happened to you, and it was my fault . . ."

"Shh, I'll be good." And when he smiled, "For a while." He groaned.

On the plane home, he squeezed her hand. "Thank you for coming to meet me. Are there going to be two cars at the airport now?"

"No. Bob took me to Erie. I rented a jet"—and winced—"but I made a lot of money on that last job, honey," she said, talking fast. "I know it was silly, Rocco, but after the thought came into my mind, I couldn't stop. I just couldn't stop. It was so awful trying to sleep without you and waking up and you weren't there. Worse than college. Way worse. I can't do it, honey. I know we have years and years left, but what if we don't. Look what happened to Daddy, I . . ."

"It's okay, baby, it's okay. We agree, we're a package deal from now on."

Time flew by. Back to New Mexico for two weeks when Ricky's son was born. Anthony Rocco Carnavale was the picture of Rocco and Ricky and joined Lily's twins, Sage Elaine and Steven Allen. Birthdays, anniversaries, holidays, trips for fun, and trips to work with RMA. Some trips were inevitable. Blossom's mother died of a brain aneurysm at seventy-nine. She was active right up until her death. Blossom was calm when she got Nix's call. *Too calm*, Rocco thought. She was unnaturally quiet throughout. She had called him at work. "Honey, could you make arrangements to be away a few days. Mother died."

"I'll be right home, baby."

"That's not necessary. I'll get things ready here."

Nix asked if she'd like to do the eulogy since she was the oldest. She demurred saying he'd been with their mother more the last thirty years. "It hasn't been bad, sis."

"I know, Nixie, it was just me."

"Oh, don't say that. She's had a sharp tongue around Nola and the girls, but they just chalk it up to that's the way she is. I haven't had to think about it for a long time, but you protected me during the rough years. I know that, Blossom."

It was a lovely eulogy, extolling her tireless work for over fifty years at their clinic and others. He made no mention of her as a mother. After the funeral, the luncheon, the socializing, she lay in Rocco's arms that night. "I had to do it," she said softly.

"I know that, baby. No one can live being a puppet. You did all you could."

"I hope God doesn't hold it against me."

He kissed her forehead. "God was saying, 'Way to go, Blossom.'"

She stared in his eyes. "You saved me, Rocco."

"You saved me, baby. We saved each other."

She gave him a wistful smile, closed her eyes, and slept in his arms that night.

Rocco's mother, always frail, outlasted all the parents. She died at eighty-four in the nursing home she'd been in for three years. Blossom held Rocco's hand at the small service. She knew he had made his peace with her, but his body was tense with memory.

In and around all their trips, they always found time to dance, taking lessons when they could.

"Honey, isn't that *enganche* a little too suggestive?"

He chuckled. "Isn't that the whole point of the tango, baby girl?"

They were driving back from a tango weekend at an Arthur Murray studio outside Pittsburgh.

"And you know how she kept turning my head over my shoulder. *Bien Parado*, Blossom, *Bien Parado*. I can't do that. I need to look at you when we're dancing, honey."

"You can look anywhere you want, sweetie. We're doing this for fun. We're not interested in competitions. You were amazing. Did you have a good time?

"Oh, I did. A couple times when we were really moving well, I felt you were making love to me," looking at him from under her lashes.

He kissed her fingers. "I was."

"But, honey, I don't think you liked my dress, the Saturday one."

"I loved your dress." He put his arm around her shoulder. "I wanted to stay out of trouble this weekend," kissing her temple. "You didn't have anything on under the top."

"The bra was built in." She lifted one finger.

"There were no petticoats or anything to hide your bottom."

She lifted the next finger. "I had on dance panties. They're very snug and went way up to my waist."

"It was open way up to your waist."

"No, it wasn't," lifting another finger. "It had a slit on my right hip so I could wrap my leg around yours. I bought it on a dance site, honey. It even said perfect for the tango."

"I liked the color, though. It seemed like everyone else had on black."

"I got it to match your eyes."

"You win."

She laughed out loud. He loved it.

"I had to glare at a couple guys. You were wiggling your butt."

"Rocco, I'm fifty-five. No one is looking at my butt. There was only one other couple about as old as us. They were good, weren't they?"

"They were okay. And he was one of the ones I glared at."

She laughed. "I confess, I glared a couple times too." He lifted his eyebrows in surprise. "I did. That red-haired instructor. She wanted to dance with you so bad. I could tell. I gave her a 'don't even think about it' look."

He laughed and shook his head. "I love you, Blossom Dove." Keeping his eyes on the highway, he bent to kiss her ear. "You have the best butt in the universe."

She snuggled in and nibbled his neck right under his ear. "We'll discuss later how you would know that, Rocco Anthony."

SCENES FROM A MARRIAGE

Their Sixties

The spring Rocco was sixty-one, Coral sent him a blueprint for a log cabin she wanted to build herself. The last few years they had been back to New Mexico every couple of months—three weeks when the twins were born, two more when Ricky's son arrived. As the family grew, time away from the business was growing.

"Baby girl, I think it's time to start the ball rolling on selling the business." They were sitting on their chair talking about Coral's log cabin plans. "I'm starting to sound like a worried dad when she and I talk. I think we should go out there for a few months."

"I'll do whatever you want, honey, but you know she can do most anything when she puts her mind to it."

"I know she'll do it, but she's just stubborn enough to make mistakes and not ask for help. She wants it to be real rustic with an outhouse, for Christ's sake. What's she going to do in the winter when she's our age?"

"Don't swear, darling," she said automatically. "You're right, it would sound better if you were right there. Not so preachy."

"I could ease her through the permits and stuff. I'm sure their inspectors are picky. Those historical areas are nightmares to work in."

"But why sell the company, honey. Just leave for a couple months."

"I've been thinking about it anyway. Bob Two and Three"—the names they called Bob's son and grandson—"cornered me awhile back. They have three other guys interested in a group thing. Bob and I think it would be a mess—he and I don't agree on things, and there's only two of us. How are five guys going to make decisions. But if we're gone for a few months, it might be a chance for a dry run. Let them see how they'd do."

She clapped. "Oh, this could be fun. So close to the babies. It could be a dry run for us too. In case we want to move there. I haven't been there for three months in a row since the summer we met."

"I'll talk to Bob Two about a plan and call Coral about an apartment. Her place is too small, and it's too long to stay at Nix's."

The preparations at the shop took a few weeks, and Coral called every few days about apartments. Her first choice was a furnished one two blocks from the plaza for 850 a month. "She would love it, Dad. She could walk all over."

"No, that's not good. I don't want your mother living on used furniture. How about a suite at a hotel?"

"Dad, even if we could make a deal at 150 a night—that's over thirteen thousand for three months. Mom would never agree to that."

"Well, look at unfurnished apartments, and we can rent some furniture. All we need is a big chair and a TV."

They finally decided to stay at the Hampton Inn on Route 68 three miles south of Taos and check out vacation condos and unfurnished apartments when they got there. They decided against driving. He would have liked to take his truck and big saws, but Coral wanted to buy some tools for herself, and Nix said he would use a company truck, and Rocco could use his.

Rocco had a final meeting with Bob Two and Three and the three other fellows. One was a CPA, and the two others were familiar with construction. He liked them all. "This business has my name on it, guys, so I'll try to give you as much slack as possible, but I'll be sticking my nose in."

She still remembered how her parents got the house ready for their summers away so had that taken care of. "Honey, I'm only taking my doves, so I'm putting everything else in a safety deposit box. Do you want one of your watches?"

"I probably won't need one, but take the Breitling just in case." He smiled to himself about the Breitling. On his sixtieth birthday, he finally had to tell her no more watches. She was spending more and more. "Sweetie-baby-darling mine, I love it. It's the most amazing watch I've ever seen, but could it be my last one. That would make it even more special."

"You don't like it." She had pouted.

"Baby girl, I love it, but who am I going to leave these watches to? I know I'll give them to Ricky, but he's really not a watch person."

"Oh, you don't like it. I've spoiled your birthday." She had climbed onto his lap, her lower lip sticking out. He had nibbled on it, and they fixed everything like they always did. It worked for them.

Too well. "Baby girl, I've been thinking about looking at apartments. You know we've never had an apartment. First our house on Cussewago and then here. No close neighbors on the other side of the wall," raising his eyebrows. Her brow wrinkled, and then her eyes got big. "Yes, baby, we tend to make noise. A lot of noise, even with Tiger."

Her eyes stayed big. "But, Rocco, hotels, what about hotels? Oh dear, oh dear."

"Baby, it's nothing. I just didn't want to bring it up out there. Coral might wonder."

"But hotels, Rocco. We've been in so many hotels," wringing her hands.

"Sweetie, quit worrying about the hotels. They're people we would never see again. Apartments and condos usually don't have the best insulation, that's all I'm saying. Wouldn't you like a little house?" trying to distract her.

"Oh, Rocco, I've embarrassed you all these years. Oh my, oh dear," burying her face in her hands.

"Now just stop. You're getting carried away over nothing." He nuzzled her neck up to her ear and whispered, "I'm right there with you, baby. You make me make noises I didn't know I could. Your screams drive me wild. I wouldn't change them for the world."

She lifted her head, tears on her cheeks, but smiling, "I could try not to make noises in Taos. But when we're close I can't think."

"I don't want you to think, and I don't want to think. Can we tell Coral we've decided on a house?"

She looked down and smiled, shaking her head yes. "I love you so much." Then her mood changed, she clapped. "Let's find a tiny little place and play house."

And they did, settling happily on one listed as "Authentic charming adobe. Great views, large living area/skylights. One bed, one bath, garden, parking. 675+elec." It was in Talpa, four miles south of the center of Taos. Rocco had hoped for one in town so she could walk to galleries and shopping. She said she couldn't do that for three months and would go over to the University of New Mexico/Taos and see if she could help out there. It was just west of their little house, off Route 68, not far at all.

She spent the first week shopping for furniture, taking a sketch of Coral's cabin layout with her so anything she bought Coral could use later. Her first priority was to make Rocco feel comfortable as soon as he walked in after work. She chose a brown leather sofa and oversized chair, an Indian print carpet and a couple of tables and lamps. The kitchen would only hold a table for two, but that was okay; they would be having family dinners at Nixie's. She got a queen-sized mattress set and a sturdy frame, one chest, and one nightstand and lamp. She had shipped their clothes ahead as her family had always done and included their bedside photos and a couple for the living area. She knew the closet space would be limited, and it was, but she had only brought three denim outfits with petticoats and boots for every day and two nice dresses in case she needed them. Rocco's jeans and shirts could go in the chest. She spent twenty dollars on a service for four of plates, fifteen on silverware, and twelve for glasses, fussed about a hundred for pots and pans; but he would like to cook at some point and liked good pans. Finally she was done.

It was six thirty on a Tuesday night. Rocco had just come in from the job site. "The house is all ready, my darling. You can come there after work tomorrow."

He flopped into the nearest chair. "Sorry you had to do that all by yourself baby. Did the deliveries go all right?"

"It was fun, and everything went fine. Take a quick shower, and we'll go eat. What would you like tonight?"

"Can we just walk over to Los Vaqueros again? I'm beat. It will be nice to eat at home tomorrow."

She looked at his exhaustion and said, "May I bring lunch out to you two tomorrow? I'll tell Coral not to pack anything."

He was ready to go again in the morning. She knew he was fit, but it had been years since he'd worked nine-hour days. She brought three folding chairs to the job site at eleven thirty, figuring they were just sitting on whatever was handy, if they were sitting at all. Putting the tail of his truck down, she spread a cloth and a bowl of halfed subs, a couple turkey a couple Italian, and bottles of water. Nibbling on some turkey from a sub, "You know, it doesn't matter how long we're here. Three months, five months, what's the difference. I insist you two drive out of here by four thirty."

"Baby, we're doing fine. The first few weeks are always hectic, but it will level off."

Staring at him intently, "Rocco, I said I insist." Looking at Coral, "This is important to me, honey. I don't want to look back on this time as a blur of work and sleep. I want to remember it as a wonderful time when we were all together. We can accomplish your goals and still have weekends together and enjoy our evenings."

"I understand, Mom. Really, I haven't been pushing him. He never stops, and I lose track of time. We'll be more aware now, I promise."

Blossom got up and gathered the lunch debris and kissed Coral. "Walk me to the car, darling? I'll leave the chairs here." She circled his waist with her arms and tipped her face up for a kiss.

He grinned. "Is this little lecture because I fell asleep last night?"

"Absolutely." She laughed.

"Does the new bed have a down mattress pad?"

"Absolutely." She winked.

"I love you, Blossom Dove."

"I love you, Rocco Anthony. Dinner's at six, and I want you home and showered so I can have my way with you."

Coral looked on from a distance. She didn't know what they were talking about, but their body language was pretty easy to read. They had an aura about them, always had. She was sure not finding it with someone accounted for her still being alone. There was a doctor she was always happy

371

to see when they both ended up helping in the same crisis area, but the fact he didn't look her up between times wasn't lost on her.

Later that afternoon. Coral laughed. "Dad, you're such a wuss."

"What? Why?"

"You've been checking your watch since quarter to four. You're worried we won't be out of here by four thirty. You're afraid of her."

"I'm not afraid of her. I just don't like to disappoint her," smiling sheepishly.

"Well, I'm not afraid to admit it. We were scared to death of her in high school."

"No way. Not Mom."

"Way. I remember one time you called us to set the table, and I can't remember why, but being fifteen, we were just puttering around and didn't come right away. We heard our bedroom door close and looked up. Mom was standing in front of it with such a look. Lily turned white, and I probably did too 'cause I could feel the blood draining from my face. She said, and her voice was really low, 'Your father called you three minutes ago.' We stammered and stuttered something about putting things away, and she just held up a finger. We shut up with our mouths open. She mimicked Blossom, standing stiff and intoning, "Your father is the most wonderful person in the world. It is a form of disrespect to ignore his call without telling him you'll be a few minutes. This will never happen again. Go down and apologize, and if you ever show any sign of disrespect to your father again, the punishment will be immediate, and it will be severe." We were already and inch taller than her, but we went by her holding our breaths. I don't know what we thought she was going to do to us." She laughed. "Believe me, we toed the mark from then on."

Rocco just shook his head and smiled. "I never knew that. She never said a thing." He turned and blinked rapidly, smiling and shaking his head again. Coral blinked too. She loved them so much.

Blossom and Coral were right. He had started out obsessively. First, he almost lost it when Coral told him she had paid thirty-nine thousand for her eight acre lot. Sure it was a beautiful spot, overlooking the Rio Grande Gorge, but even at thirty-five, she was his little girl, and he worried about the responsibility she was taking on.

"Dad," she had said, "I have money. I give all my money to Ricky to invest and live in that tiny apartment. I'm ready to do this."

Carnavale Construction had built a huge log home, so he was familiar with the procedure. Their name was acting as the builder, and she having the same last name helped. She had wisely situated the foundation slab to accommodate the wind and sun, and faced the back deck toward the gorge to take advantage of the view from the kitchen or for outdoor meals. She picked a seventeen-hundred-square-foot style from Log Homes of America, an A-frame with a wing on each side. Thank goodness she had backed off from the outhouse idea. The master bedroom was in one wing with a bath. Two more bedrooms shared a bath in the other wing. A great room was in the center. He was proud of the preliminary work she had done. She was a funny mix of compassion in her disaster aid work coupled with Elaine's no-nonsense approach to life.

He tried to remember he was the hired help and only contradicted her when necessary. She had done her homework, and he let her lead the way, suggesting instead of telling about subcontractors for plumbing, electric, insulation. They had some ground to cover before the manufacturer's rep came to be sure the home was erected according to their system. He'd come to the job site a number of hours for technical questions. Rocco listened to Coral discussing things on the phone and was amazed at her poise and knowledge. All of the children, Ricky mostly, had a share of Blossom's brilliance; and it made him feel good that Coral seemed to have his building gene, if he had one.

He let his mind wander as he worked. Lily had Grandma Elaine's obsession about appearances, always worried about how things looked. She had Blossom's love of being a wife and mother, though, and he hoped that would be her strong trait when the twins became their own persons. Ricky had been a concerned and worried little boy, but now that he was confident in his life and work, he was cool and calm. Rocco knew the girls could always turn to him for anything.

"Huh?" He realized Coral had said something to him, so concentrated on the job at hand. They chatted when possible. "Do you have anyone special in your life?"

She laughed at his way of prying. "Not too many out there like you, Dad."

"That's nice, honey, but I married way up when I got your mother. I just meant this is a pretty big lot for just you."

A little exasperated, "Dad, I'm only a few years out of school. That degree in International Studies, finishing up my doctorate in child psychology, fitting in my trips, I'm just enjoying this process now. Maybe I'll get a horse. Maybe I'll adopt a baby. Who knows. Let me get in here and nest as Mom says. Ricky wants me to come down and meet the new doctor at the clinic. That seems a little obvious, though. Here's my single sister."

"Well, let's all go down then. It would be natural since we're in town. Besides, you're part of the foundation. You can look things over anytime."

The first full week of work wound down. They got a little flack from Blossom about a long half day on Saturday; but he was home, showered, and at her disposal by three o'clock.

"We don't have that many Sundays, darling, so the girls and I have decided we'll have Sunday dinners at Nixie's. Ricky and Angela will come up from Albuquerque, and we'll meet in Santa Fe. Aunt Mim's house is the biggest anyway."

"Baby, don't call it Aunt Mim's house. You'll hurt Nola's feelings."

"I'll remember, honey. Until we get a chance to plan a little, you and I can do the cooking. What should we get for this week? I was thinking spaghetti and meatballs."

"How about a cookout with steaks?"

"Nixie's girls are big, honey. That would be a dozen steaks. Isn't that a lot of work for you?"

"No way. We'll get four T-bones for the guys and small steaks for you girls. What for the kids, hot dogs?"

"I'll call Lily on the way to the store. I doubt she lets the twins have hot dogs. So meat, salad things, garlic toast, and what, oven fries?"

So that's how their Sundays went. They had spent time with Angela and Steven at weddings, funerals, births of babies; but this was real family time. They were happy to see that Steven unabashedly adored Lily and the twins and actually was a warm and funny fellow when he wasn't politickin'. Angela started coming into the kitchen while Rocco and Blossom were working together. Gradually Blossom asked her to do some things, and in a couple weeks it was Rocco and Angela working while Ricky and Blossom chatted at the table.

Ricky's son, Anthony Rocco, was almost nine and headstrong. When Angela called out, "Tony Carnavale, stop that right now." Blossom saw Rocco turn in slow motion, looking for a ghost. She went to him quickly, a hand on each cheek staring into his frightened eyes. "Everything's fine, darling. Everything's wonderful. It's your grandson. See, Anthony, Tony, see. It's your grandson, Rocco." He came back and smiled. She breathed again.

Ricky asked later, "What was wrong with Dad earlier?"

"Daddy just gets overcome sometimes seeing his wonderful family," she lied. "We all haven't been together for a while, and it was too much for a second."

Rocco was a little distant getting ready for bed. When they were nose to nose, she said, "It's a common name, honey, I'm sure you've known people named Tony."

"Not Tonys with our last name. It just threw me for a second. It was nothing."

"Say his name for me."

"Tony."

"No. Say his whole name."

"I don't need to say his whole name, Blossom. I'm fine."

She dropped it for a minute. "Wasn't that cute, Nixie had Lincoln Logs for the children so they can see what you and Coral are doing." She got a smile. "Say his whole name for me."

"Anthony Rocco Carnavale."

"And what is he called?" He didn't respond, just took a deep breath. "Rocco, he's a little boy. He needs to feel love from all of us. You know that better than anyone." She kissed him, lifting her eyebrows.

"Tony Carnavale."

She kissed his wet eyelashes and put his mouth to her breast. "You're a magnificent husband, father, and grandfather. It's over. You made it all go away. I love you, Rocco."

He couldn't answer without crying, so they did what they did best, loved their past away.

They settled in to dinners at their little house Monday through Friday. She knew he would never admit he was tired. On Saturdays they tried all the restaurants. Most of the menu items were too froufrou for Rocco, but he tolerated Lamberts so she could have the chocolate mousse with raspberry sauce. She tolerated going again and again to Los Vaqueros so he could have a steak. On Thursdays they ate lightly and went to the Plaza for the music and a gooey dessert. She was looking forward to the Taos Pueblo Pow Wow in July.

They hadn't found a dance place, but Nix told him the Stable in Santa Fe where Mim had taken them was still going strong. One Sunday during dinner, Rocco said, "How about Nix's girls watch the young ones, and we all go dancing."

"Oh, honey, you've got to see this." Ricky laughed at Angela. "You'll never believe it."

"See what?"

"Dad and Mom dancing."

"I saw them dancing at our wedding."

"No, you didn't. Not even."

"Well, I'm not sure how much dancing I can do, but we better go see them." After eight years and a rough time, Ricky and Angela were expecting a girl in six weeks.

So off they went—Rocco and Blossom, Nix and Nola, Ricky and Angela, Lily and Steven, and Coral. Lily was concerned it didn't look right for Coral to be alone, but Rocco said we'll take turns, and Angela said, "She won't be alone for long."

The place hadn't changed all that much in thirty-some years, and group tables were plentiful. Rocco was observant but not as paranoid as the old days, and everyone was upbeat about being out together. Steven was relieved he hadn't been recognized. Lily a little annoyed he hadn't. Ricky and Angela were homebodies, so a night out was exciting. Blossom and Lily had on dresses—Blossom, a chambray halter style with a dropped waist flaring over her petticoat; Lily, a pretty summer voile scattered with violets. Coral and Nola were in blue jeans and summer tops. Angela, blue jeans too, but maternity style with a voluminous top.

The house band didn't start until nine, but Rocco checked the jukebox, and the selections were great. He smiled when he saw one of them but pushed two ahead of it, hoping Blossom would be warmed up when it came around.

He whispered to her, "Are you ready for 'Mama's Little Girl'? They have a whole section of Delbert."

She cupped her hand over his ear. "Rocco! I can't dance to that in front of the children."

Ricky called from across the table. "What are you two whispering about?"

"There's a song I want your mother to dance to, and she says it's inappropriate for you children," laughing.

"Come on, Mom. We're adults. You're supposed to be giving us a demonstration. We haven't seen you in a long time, and Angela and Steven have never seen you."

"Come on, Mrs. C," from Steven, and "Go, Mom, go," from Ricky and Coral. Lily was looking worried. Blossom gave Rocco a little glare and said, "We'll see when it comes up."

They got up, and Rocco winked at her, grinning, "Hey, they want a demonstration, let's give it to them."

She shook her head. "Not too crazy now, I don't want them to be embarrassed."

"Just pretend we're home. Remember this floor?" She started smiling as he nodded his head to the beat, a nice up-tempo old Willie Nelson, "If You've Got the Money, I've Got the Time" that someone else had chosen. They hadn't danced in a couple of months. It was something they loved, something they almost needed to do. It showed their joy in each other, their love, their trust, and the ever-present sexual tension. As always, she looked in his eyes and everything else fell away. He was doing simple steps and turns, passing her from hand to hand and behind his back, twirling around the perimeter of the floor in basic steps. Still, Angela and Steven's mouths were open in utter surprise. They went right into the next two numbers he had chosen. Delbert McClinton's "Won't Be Me" to get their feet warmed up and Elvis's "Loving You" to let her catch her breath. He tried to propel her with his pelvis to that one, but she said, "You stop that right now, or I'm walking off this floor." He laughed and held out his arms, and she jumped into them, her legs around his waist. They were at the opposite end of the cavernous club from the children, so he was nuzzling her neck, keeping her interested as he moved toward their table. He put her down as the first beat of "Mama's Little Girl" started. They had developed a dance story to the rockabilly-style tune. She lured him on then pushed him away, shimmying toward him, turning, and sashaying away with exaggerated hip wiggles. He pleading, circling her, tossing her up and then between his legs, ending with him on the floor, her foot on his chest.

The crowd had stopped dancing and moved back. They erupted into cheers and applause as Rocco bowed toward Blossom, and she shyly curtsied. Their table had stood and were clapping wildly, dumbstruck. He was so proud of her, held her on his lap for a while dabbing at her perspiration.

The evening progressed in lively spirits. Rocco and Blossom talking everyone into a basic line dance. He and she danced in front of the others, slowly going through the steps as Rocco called them out. Several other couples joined, and soon three lines of ten each were moving around the floor doing the grapevine to Brooks and Dunn's "Boot Scootin' Boogie." Blossom noticed a couple of fellows hovering around Coral and caught Rocco's eye as they appeared to be exchanging phone numbers.

It was one of the most memorable nights of their stay. Steven said, "That was the most fun we've had in I don't know when."

Lily chastised, "But, dear, we've had lovely evenings at the country club."

"Yeah, lovely, honey, but this was downright fun."

"Well, you have to remember your station in life."

Rocco and Blossom looked at each other with raised eyebrows and hidden grins. Was Elaine in the room?

Ricky and Angela stayed at Nix and Nola's to avoid the long drive down to Albuquerque. Nix said, "Come on, sis, you guys stay too. Coral is."

Rocco had been getting the look from Blossom so said, "It's only sixty-five miles to our place, and it goes fast. Sleep in, Coral, we'll meet at the job site at noon tomorrow."

In the truck, he said, "Stop looking at me like that. We'll be home in an hour and a half."

"I can't wait an hour and a half," whimpering, shaking her hands. "There, there!" She pounded his knee and pointed.

So he risked life and limb crossing the highway median, screeching the tires, and pulled into the Days Inn in Espanola. He checked in as quick as he could, running back to the truck, his own urgency mounting as she mouthed *Hurry, hurry*. They made it through the door as she climbed him, biting his neck, "Quickie, quickie," breathlessly.

"We could have had a quickie in the truck," kicking his boots off. She bit into his neck, ready to take a chunk out. "I was joking, I was joking," trying to get out of his shirt. She growled; he grabbed the middle of the bedspread and pulled everything off with his right hand, holding her squirming body with his left. He got his jeans down and one leg out, had to help her with her panties as she cried in frustration, entered her, thrust four times; and she screamed and dug in. He let himself go, fell to his side, his chest heaving, "Woman, woman," closing his eyes to catch his breath. She would sleep awhile.

Thirty seconds later, "Darling, we have to wear these clothes tomorrow, look at the mess you've made." He opened his eyes with disbelief, and there it was, her glorious smile. He just shook his head as she jumped up, finished taking his jeans off and hung up his shirt. She took off her dress and petticoat, hung them up, "Up, up, we have to take a shower. I don't know what you were thinking, all that dancing and having your way with me before we showered. Tsk, tsk, tsk, and now, look, you're running down my leg, crazy man."

He staggered to the bathroom, holding himself up, clutching the doorjamb as she adjusted the shower and checked the complimentary cosmetics, chatting all the while. "We'll just have a teeny taste of mouthwash tonight and save the rest for morning. I'm going to have to carry a few things with us if you're going to be making these unexpected stops." His mouth fell open; then she winked at him.

"You straighten up the bed while I dry my hair." He was stretched out, checking the TV channels when she came out. She twirled with her arms out. "I feel so refreshed," going to the bottom of the bed, flipping the sheet away, and crawling in on her hands and knees.

"Blossom . . ."

"Now, I'm going to start at your toes and kiss every part of you. Like this," sucking on his big toe.

"Sweetie . . ."

"And up here behind your knee,"

"Let's sleep, baby girl," his voice starting to crack.

"And here. Ohh, this is nice, I think I'll stay here awhile," her face in his groin, kissing, kissing.

"No, no. Baby," but her little hands were turning him sideways, those tiny hands, no pressure at all; but he always did whatever they said. "Baby. Baby, oh god . . ."

She woke him again clutching and whimpering at four o'clock. He loved her back to sleep.

"Wake up, crazy lady, I have to go to work," nuzzling her neck, patting her bottom."

She turned, groaning, sleepy. "You're working with your daughter, you can be late. Oh, you're dressed already," trying to unbutton his shirt.

"No, no. Come on now, I have to get home and change and get my work boots on. I'll go get some coffee, you get dressed. There's a half bottle of mouthwash, your hair's fine." Still she pulled at him. "No, you don't. I'm whipped. What got into you last night?"

"You," she said haughtily, "several times as I recall."

His laugh filled the room. He picked her up in the sheet and sat on the bed with her on his lap. "I love you like crazy, little girl. You're amazing." He whispered in her ear, "I know I've been tired a lot lately, am I giving you everything you need? You were wild last night."

"Don't be silly, honey. It was just the whole night. It was so wonderful, and you're so sexy when you dance, you have no idea. By the time we got here, I guess I was a little crazy."

"You want to stay longer? I can call Coral." He laughed. "I can hardly walk now, but we can stay."

"No. I have to go to the college at one. Go get your coffee and me a hot chocolate, and you better get a sandwich for on the way."

"You sure."

"I'm sure"—coyly—"until tonight."

He shook his head. "You are sixty you know," winking. "Chain the door, I'll be back in a few minutes."

She chained the door and called out through the space, "Rocco, darling." He turned and looked in around the chain. She had narrowed eyes and a grimace. "I won't be sixty until October, Mr. Almost-Sixty-Two who kept me awake all night!" stuck out her tongue and slammed the door. He laughed all the way to the lobby.

They were driving north, almost to the little house. "Wouldn't it be embarrassing if Coral passed us?"

He laughed. "It would be kind of funny, but it wouldn't be embarrassing. We're married, baby girl. Do you think they figured we stopped making love after the girls were born?"

He got changed and was on his way to the cabin, still smiling at her whispered "Don't work too hard" as she bit his earlobe. God he loved her. He beat Coral by twenty minutes and laughed to himself that he was glad.

"That was a great night, Dad. You and Mom are amazing."
"Thanks, kiddo. I saw you made a couple new acquaintances."
"Yeah, nice guys, but you know Santa Fe is seventy miles from me. Not exactly handy dating distance. Whoa, speak of the devil," as she looked at a text. She laughed, "See what I mean about not many out there like you. Remember when you told us you used to drive six hours one way to see Mom?"
"I sure did. And couldn't wait to do it."
"Well, the cute one says, 'Last night sure fun. Call when in SFe & will do again.'"
"Mark him off the list, he's lazy."
She cocked her head. "He was cute."
Rocco's laugh rang through the trees.
They spent the day getting ready for the manufacturer's rep. He would be there Tuesday through Friday. Coral looked as her text chimed and said "And the second contingent is heard from." She raised her eyebrows and read, "Will be in Taos Thurs. Dinner?'
Rocco said, "Well, well, dinner can't hurt. What do young people do nowdays—will you phone or just keep texting?"
Her fingers flew over the keypad. "I just said dinner sounds nice. Call tonight about eight."
He knew she was pleased. Her work probably didn't allow much social life, and she'd been really busy getting degrees the last few years. "So you'll see him, and then we'll go down to the clinic and meet the doctor and see how that goes."
"Dad, the clinic is 120 miles!"
He smiled. "As a dad, distance is good. Besides, he won't be there much longer, and Taos has a nice hospital your mom tells me."

He relayed the story to Blossom over dinner.
"Do we know what the one in Santa Fe does, how old he is, things like that?"

He smiled. "He looked about her age, don't you think? She'll fill us in on Friday. Besides, baby, we weren't around when Lily and Ricky were meeting people, and they did just fine. We can't start micromanaging just because we're here. She's very intelligent, she'll be fine."

"I know. But a doctor would complement her work so well."

"Baby girl, what did we have in common? Movie trivia? We know now, but we didn't know when we met."

"What we had in common was I couldn't breathe when I looked at you, that the world tipped." She shook her finger. "Don't you smile. I know it did. I felt it."

"I know it did, sweetie. What I meant was don't get upset now, I know you hate to think of it, we were both abused. In different ways, in different ways," quickly, seeing the angst on her face.

"I don't want to talk about that. Let's talk about how wonderful you were Sunday night dancing. You could have been a teacher. You had everyone lined up and dancing in no time."

"That was nothing, baby. Big Sallie did that with a bunch of drunks. I was just copying her."

"She was special, wasn't she?" They had mourned when Sallie died suddenly at forty-eight. Blossom wasn't terribly surprised, given her weight. Rocco took it hard, though. He had formed a quasi-family in his mind without even realizing it, and Sallie was the matriarch. Blossom was glad the bar had a surprise forty-fifth birthday party for her. Rocco remembered an old June Haver musical from the 1940s, and the song "Oh You Beautiful Doll, You Great Big Beautiful Doll," sat her on a bar stool in the middle of the floor, and sang it to her. Sallie had tried to laugh it off, but Blossom could see it was one of the best times she'd ever had. They were chagrined they never knew her last name until they read it in her obituary, Johannsen, and that she had gone to Erie Business Center and had been the office manager at a car dealership since she graduated.

Rocco was looking sad thinking about it, so she gave him a little kiss. It turned into a big kiss, and that turned into let's call it a night. She got through the teeth brushing, got a little lotion on her knees and elbows, but was breathless and flushed and clutching at him.

"Slow down, slow down, we have all night," pulling her close.

"Do you think there's something wrong with me? I don't want to hurt you, but I want you all the time."

"You can't hurt me, sweetie, it's nothing but wonderful."

"Remember what you said our first night together?"

"Baby girl, I was so scared that night, I don't know what I said."

"You said, 'Bite me, scratch me, scream, I don't care.' You were so wonderful. I've done all those things. I don't want to hurt you, I really don't," putting her leg over his hip.

"Blossom, something's bothering you. You'll come to it soon. In the meantime, I'm here, I love you, and you're amazing."

They explored each other with their mouths; and when they paused for air, she said, "I think I know what's bothering me," starting to whimper.

"Tell me."

Softly, "I feel like we're running out of time. I looked at the children when we were dancing. Ricky's thirty-eight, I'm almost sixty. I can't lose you yet. I'm scared."

He stroked her hair and looked in her eyes. "Precious baby girl, don't live afraid. We're not running out of time. We've got fifteen or twenty years easy. I'll be right here, and you can hurt me all you want. How about it? Best two out of three?" He got the giggle he wanted, and knew she'd be okay for a while.

The cabin came together—house, really. Rocco hoped Coral didn't regret that it wasn't the rustic place she had first envisioned, but it sure was a pleasure to see as he drove in. The center A-frame held the great room. They had added a deck on the back and a porch running along the whole front. The occupancy permit was waiting for her to cut back the trees for forest fire protection. It did have a rustic feeling inside, and he was happy the plumbing and electric were state of the art.

There had been a few holdups. Ricky and Angela had their baby girl, Alyssa Rose—Alyssa for Angela's mother, Alice; Rose in deference to Blossom. They had gone down to Albuquerque for a week until Angela's mother could get there. Coral thought he was going to take Blossom down and come back, but he said "Mom and I don't separate, kiddo." It had been a long time between babies for Ricky and Angela, and it called for a celebration when she arrived healthy and beautiful—the first girl to look like Rocco, black curls and blue eyes.

Then Coral got called away to a mine cave-in in Chile. She had passed on a couple of requests but felt this one needed her. The length of uncertainty in cave-ins was particularly hard on children. She didn't want Rocco to work without her, so he and Blossom took Tony and the twins to the Grand Canyon and then stayed at Ricky's and helped at the clinic.

So it wasn't three months, not even five months. Just shy of nine months, he had to bring up going back home. She had been weepy over silly things, and he knew it was on her mind. "Let's have Christmas, baby girl, and then head for home."

"No. No. We have babies here, and I love our little house."

"Blossom, we'll finish selling the business, get the house sold, and come back. It's always been on the horizon, but this time we'll really work towards it. We'll have Christmas here, we'll be back for Ricky's birthday in March, we'll be back for all the important things."

"But it's not like having Sunday dinner together."

He laughed. "Sweetie, they've never had so many dinners together. Everyone would probably like their lives back."

"Could we at least keep the little house? It's not that much a month."

"No, we can't keep the house." At her pout, he said, "Baby, we might not want to live in this area. Somebody might move, there might be a better central location."

She climbed on his lap. "You're just mean."

"I know, baby girl, I know."

"Well, I want a picture of all of us. I've got some great ones, but I want a professional one. I'll see if Nixie knows someone who can come to the house." He smiled as she put her fingers to her lips and started planning. "Not at Christmas, the children will be too wound up. Next Sunday is too soon, but maybe the next one. Umm, everyone should have white tops on, the girls can wear white dresses if they like . . ." On she went, and he knew she would be fine up until leaving day.

She loved the girl who did the pictures. She ordered three big ones—them with the children and grandchildren, and them with just the grandchildren. Her heart stopped when Tony maneuvered himself beside Rocco. He was a little perturbed that someone else might take his place and for a second had a look on his face like the picture of Rocco holding the rock. But her favorite was all their children, grandchildren, and Nix's family. As the photographer was showing her the shot, she hugged Rocco around the waist. "This one for the mantle? Everyone we love all together. Our family."

"Perfect, baby girl, perfect."

And perfect it was—Rocco and Blossom in the center, sitting on stools that didn't show; Coral on one just a little higher behind them; Ricky and his family on the left, six-month-old Alyssa in white ruffles down to her white patent shoes; Nix, their girls, and Nola across the top; Steven, Lily, and the twins, Sage and Steven, on the right—the girls all in white dresses; the fellows in white shirts with the cuffs rolled twice. Blossom had on a beautiful high-necked white dress with her pearls. Rocco gently touched the two black ones and winked at her. She blushed. The photographer said it had never been so easy to get sixteen smiling faces all looking in the same direction at the same time.

The day came for their last Sunday dinner. Rocco and Blossom had moved back to the Hampton Inn a few days earlier and had the furniture they bought moved to the cabin. They were leaving in the morning. When they drove into Nix's driveway, the children had gathered on the porch and saw Rocco go to Blossom's side and lift her into his arms. Her legs were around his waist, her face in his neck. "You're the mother, baby girl," he whispered. "You have to be strong. They're going to take their cue from you, okay? Now let's go have a wonderful day. Can you do that?" She nodded yes. He kissed her and put her down.

"Grandpa christened Coral's new stove. We have lasagna and sausage and peppers. Come help carry," she called out, smiling.

They got home, settled back in. She spent evenings with all the pictures she had taken spread out on the floor, got three boxes, and added her old ones too, then added a fourth and explained to him she planned to make a book for each of them and Nixie too. "Not a photo album," she explained to him earnestly, "but an actual bound book with stories of the pictures interspersed." He nodded knowingly, even though he didn't know what *interspersed* meant.

He couldn't get involved in a book because she kept showing him pictures and reminding him of this occasion or that trip. He didn't mind. She was having a good time.

She showed him one of her and the children he had taken—she in full Indian regalia, dancing. He remembered it well. The girls were four, Ricky seven. She seldom just answered their questions but made it something they'd never forget. One of them had evidently asked about rain dancing, and when he got home, he heard the drums from the garage and came in quietly. There she was, in a buckskin dress, high moccasins, a feather in her hair, twirling and stomping. The children were sitting Indian fashion among the posters and books she had shown them, transfixed, staring, their mouths open. He took a picture with his phone, joined the children on the floor, and led the applause when she finished. No wonder it was taking so long to get through the pictures. Every one brought on another story, smiles, memories.

The Indian rain dance evening continued with a memory he wanted to both forget and remember. There wasn't a picture for what happened later that night. It was one of those storms when the thunder rumbled and growled all night, the lightning never letting up. He was listening for the children, but all was surprisingly quiet. About 1:00 a.m. in a lousy choice of words, he said, "We're awake. We might as well make love."

He knew her so well, the tenth of a second she paused took the air from the room. His stomach flip-flopped; nausea wafted over him. "Might as well," she said flatly but didn't move.

His throat felt closed, but he got it out. "That didn't come out right, did it?"

"No. It did not."

"What I mean to say was when the lightning flashed, I saw your shoulder—just a little bit by your hair. It was so beautiful, I wanted to reach for you, but I thought I should see if you were awake first." He took a big breath. "That's what I meant to say." He tentatively touched her shoulder, his pulse pounding in his throat.

She turned, and he saw her smile in the lightning. "Nice save, Mr. Carnavale."

Just as he expelled air in relief, Ricky tapped at the door. "I think Mommy's rain dance worked too good. Can I sleep in your bed?"

"Better get your sleeping bag, son. The girls will probably wake up too." While Ricky went for his sleeping bag, Rocco reached for his lounge pants on the chair by the bed and brought her nightgown over to her, sliding it over her head, whispering, "Damn, I was about to get lucky."

She giggled. "When did you ever need to get lucky? You touch me, and I'm all over you."

"I'm lucky every single time, lovely lady, every single time."

Ricky had no sooner settled himself on the floor beside Rocco when Coral padded down the hall. "Come here, princess, get in the middle."

And then shortly, "Mommy"—plaintively from Lily—"there's boomers, and I can't see Coral."

Blossom pressed a button on the monitor. "Come in our room, darling, Coral's here."

"Will you walk me?"

"You're a big girl. Just run down the hall."

"Daddy?"

"I'm coming, angel," getting her and putting her in the middle with Coral. He and Blossom smiled over the heads of their little girls, mouthing "I love you."

She continued working on the pictures almost every night. One evening there wasn't much on TV, so while she worked, he put on headphones and listened to Sinatra instead of Elvis. The beginning strains of "One for My Baby and One More for the Road" took him back. Ricky had just joined the girls in New Mexico. The house empty. He was reading the paper after dinner when he heard Sinatra all through the house. He looked up to ask why she had flipped the speaker switch on, and his heart stopped then pounded in his ears. She danced toward him in her bare feet, wearing a maroon satiny thing with tiny straps barely covering her nipples, the shadow of her navel hinted at, the material slipping over her hips to her ankles, her hands joined over her head, her hips swaying. "Wha . . ."

"Isn't this pretty, honey. It's the slip to the dress Aunt Mim sent me." She undulated slowly in front of him. "We don't dance enough to Frank Sinatra."

It was getting hard to breathe. "May I dance with you?"

Twirling away, "Oh, you have too many clothes on to dance to Sinatra."

He was just remembering how fast he tried to get his clothes off, tripping over his jeans, when his conscious self realized she hadn't said anything for a while. He opened his eyes, and she was looking at him in agony, tears running down her face. He whipped the headset off and dove across the room. "Baby girl, what is it, what is it? I'll fix it, sweetie, tell me."

She held up a photo of them at a park where she had asked a passerby to take their picture. Ricky was eighteen months, sitting at the top of a sliding board. Blossom was on the ladder behind him, Rocco at the bottom to catch him. "I remember, baby, I told him I'd catch him. What's wrong, I'll fix it."

"You can't fix it," she said in despair. "Don't you see? This was just a little while ago. It seems like yesterday. Time is running out. You said we had plenty of time. Time is running out," her voice rising. "I never did anything right, she—"

He put a finger over her lips. "No 'she,' Blossom. This is your life, and you did everything right. We just left our three remarkable, amazing children, you've made me happier than I have a right to be, you've helped thousands of people. You've done nothing but good, baby girl."

"But the most important thing, the most important thing—" covering her face with her hands.

"What is it, baby, what?"

"I thought I had time to-to find the right words, the perfect words, to tell you how much I love you, how much we all love you. You never felt love, you were all alone, oh, I can't bear it," sobbing.

"Blossom, my precious baby girl. You tell me every day in every way. It's how I live, how I breathe, how I exist because I know you love me."

"But time," she said, spreading the pictures.

"Okay, little lady, we're going to put this project away for a few days."

"No"—her voice rising again—"I have to organize, I have to categorize."

"And we'll do that, but not tonight," putting them back in the boxes. "Is this Ricky's pile? See, they're all organized in the boxes. We're just going to take a little break." He put the boxes on the bottom shelf of the wall-length bookcase way at the end. And there they stayed for thirteen years.

He picked her up to rock her, shushing her as she whimpered, "No time, no time." She finally slept, and he thanked God for the millionth time that he had followed her out of that class. She reminded him of an old thermometer he found when he was little. He broke it and chased the little beads of mercury around the floor trying to catch them. Just when he thought he had one, it escaped. Who was he waking up to each morning? Would she be Dr. Carnavale, brilliant, in charge, unflappable. Mrs. Carnavale, funny, earthy, so sexy she had kept him weak and reeling for forty years. Or little Blossom Richards, worried, frightened, insecure. He had to think of her as Blossom Richards then, so he could blame her mother. He couldn't bear it if it was him who caused those moments.

He carried her upstairs and laid her on the bed, arranging her clothes to make her comfortable, and looked down at her, shaking his head. He didn't care which Blossom she'd be as long as she was there.

The importance of Rocco's birth father had faded over the years. She gave it only a passing thought now and then. When they lived on Cussewago, she and the neighbor, Gloria, had become friends; and she finally felt comfortable bringing it up.

"Marie and I were close in the early days," she had said, "but I don't know if she would have told me something like that." She patted Blossom's hand. "Lovey, it was a very violent household. I don't know if it was nature or nurture. As he got older, I could hear some nights he gave as good as he got. Then it got quiet, and for a while that was almost more frightening. When the quiet became normal, I jumped when a door slammed. I started seeing Rocco in his own truck, and when he started to come home and stay home in the evenings, I didn't know what to think. Marie would come for coffee when she knew for sure Tony was on a job or away. She would show me pictures of Lindsay's girls, and one day she whispered as she was leaving, 'I think Rocco is going to college.' Then she ran as if saying it out loud would get her into trouble."

They made it a point to spend every Thanksgiving at Lindsay's and brought his mother there from the assisted living facility. When she declined and was in the nursing home wing, Blossom often visited her alone. One year, she seemed especially alert. They were chatting lovingly, so Blossom had the courage to ask her if there was anything she would like them to know about Rocco's birth.

"So many years have gone by, Mother Carnavale. He's such a wonderful person and has been since I've known him. Could you tell me what it was about him that upset Tony so?"

Marie just looked at her with tears running down her face. "It wasn't his fault. He's a good boy. He protected me."

Blossom hugged her. "He's a very good boy." And it just didn't matter anymore if Tony was his father. She felt it was dawning on him too. And if he wasn't, someone had missed out on knowing a wonderful son.

Blossom didn't worry too much about him over the sale of the business. First, it had taken a few years. It wasn't an established entity buying it, but five disparate fellows. The bank was nervous even after several meetings. Because of his confidence in Bobs Two and Three, Rocco advanced them the down payment and carried the paper for four years. Second, it was vastly different from the family business he had inherited forty-six years before—millions of dollars in inventory, bulldozers, cranes, graders, two locations, and three different crews with different areas of expertise.

To be cautious, she planned a long trip to Italy. They had toured the major cities over the years, but she wanted something quiet and secluded. Her Internet search found that the Molise region seemed to have the most surnames Carnavale.

They were sitting in their big chair. "Baby girl, we're going to have quite a chunk of money soon. I'll keep a couple million in some accounts here and give the rest to Ricky. You tell him about any places you want to help and let him check them out."

"Okay, darling. And I'd like to take a nice long trip to Italy. Maybe a villa in a smaller village instead of the big cities. A month or so?" A grin played around his mouth. "Why are you smiling like that?"

"Blossom, remember your mother taking you on trips to keep us apart? It just reminded me of that for a second. Selling the business doesn't bother me, baby. It's time. I'm satisfied with the outcome. You don't have to get me out of the country to keep my mind off it."

She pouted. "I'm not thinking of that. When we move to New Mexico, we'll want to take grandchildren when we travel. I just want you all to myself for a nice long trip."

"We could go to Nashville and Memphis. You like that."

"No, I want you farther away. And not so much like a touristy thing. Like a month where we can settle in and grocery shop and cook." She tipped her head. "Don't you want to go?"

"I'd love to go, baby girl. I love you in Italy. You're very sultry."

She smiled. "Where'd you hear that word?"

"I saw it on TV, and it reminded me of you. We were in Palermo. You were perspiring here"—running his finger between her breasts—"and you were in your bare feet."

She gave him the glorious smile. "I'll find a place, then. I think we'll go to the Molise region. There's a town there called Campobasso I'd like to see."

He laughed out loud. "You are so transparent, Blossom Dove."

"What?" Innocently.

"Are you thinking we'll be walking down the street and we'll see someone who looks just like me? I thought you quit worrying about that years ago."

"I did. But it's nice to know your heritage, honey."

"I noticed we never searched out yours."

"We went to England. Anyway, mine's boring. Yours is in Italy. It's more fun."

When he was sixty-eight, the closing of the business sale finally took place, and off they went to Italy for a month. She had worked her computer magic and found a little house in Larino on the inland east coast of the Molise region, about halfway between the coastal town of Tremoli and Campobasso, the town she was most interested in. She had shipped their clothes ahead, and they were able to fly with just a couple of carry-ons into Rome and then a commuter Ryanair flight to Pescara.

He had long ago given up the appearance of being in charge during foreign travel. She scanned information quickly and committed it to memory, leading them easily from place to place, planes to trains. She changed a few thousand dollars into euros, and they boarded their train headed for Tremoli. It made a stop in Vasto. "I don't want to do touristy things, honey, but as long as we're here, I thought you'd like to see these wooden fishing platforms. Supposedly they've been here six hundred years, so I knew you'd appreciate the construction." They had a little while before reboarding the train and walked around the area. He passed by guides giving information and seemed drawn to an older man looking at them. She stepped away as they started communicating—neither one knowing the other's language but somehow getting across questions and answers with eyes and gestures. She thought no wonder he had been so successful in business. His intense concentration, his desire to know what the other person was trying to get across showed in his look and posture. She was almost dizzy with love as she looked at him—his black dress boots, well-worn jeans, blue chambray shirt, his hair almost all white now but still lush and wavy, so tall and lean. She started to sway, and he instinctively reached for her hand, pulled her to his side, as he shook the old fellow's hand. "We better get back on the train, honey," she said, smiling up at him. They continued on to Tremoli, picked up the rental car she had reserved, and drove to Larino. He was relieved he could drive on the right. England had been crazy for him.

Blossom and Gemma fell into each other's arms like long-lost cousins. They had been on the computer and phone for weeks working out every detail, and still Gemma fluttered about as she showed them around. "Will you stay, will you stay?"

"Of course, we'll stay," Blossom gushed. "It's perfect."

He smiled. A villa, it sure wasn't. To say it was rustic was upgrading it somewhat, but as he had marveled at the first time he saw the clinic accommodations so many years ago, Blossom was just as comfortable in simplicity as luxury. He had to hand it to her parents. Blossom and Nix were adaptable to any inconvenience, and it hadn't changed through the years.

The cottage had one main room with two new-looking comfortable chairs. The kitchen area antiquated with what was a dorm fridge in the States, the bedroom big enough for a double bed and dresser, the bathroom an afterthought—basically a shed on the back of the cottage with a small metal shower. Blossom had seen all the rooms on the Internet and didn't bat an eye.

She and Gemma had worked out a price. It had been Gemma's grandfather's cottage and had never been rented before. It certainly couldn't be called a villa, and there was no pool anywhere near, so Blossom had suggested $2500 US for the month. She had already sent Gemma half, gave her the rest, and they were on their own—thankfully with a lamb stew, loaf of bread, and bottle of wine Gemma had left for them.

"You take a shower first, baby. I'm not sure how long the hot water will last. I'll look things over tomorrow." She was almost asleep, smelling warm and like her lotion when he slid in after showering and securing the doors as best he could. The bedcovers were all new, but the mattress was old and slanted, and they giggled as they both ended up in the center. He kissed her ready to christen the bed, but the long day and time change caught up. The next thing he knew, the dual watch she had given him for the trip said it was 5:30 a.m. in Italy. He went to the bathroom, looked out the windows—all hazy and quiet—wondered if they had coffee things, but decided against making any noise so she could sleep. He slid back into bed intending to just watch her but was gone again.

He woke puzzled and then smiled and shook his head. He lifted the sheet. She was sucking on him with her hands under her chin. He reached down, held her up with his hands around her waist. "Come up here, you crazy lady."

Her eyes stayed closed tight, her fists trying to pound his chest. "I want my pacifier back." He offered her his tongue, and she latched on to it happily until he started working it and they were both moaning. They caught up on all the love they had missed, initiating all the spots on the bed until it was theirs.

"I gotta have some coffee, baby girl." He was looking through the cupboards, and they weren't bare, but no coffee.

"I didn't have her get coffee, honey. I thought we could have a nice routine of going into the village for breakfast. Everything's later here, so eleven o'clock is still okay."

They walked to the village and sat at the first place with outdoor tables. He wore his standard jeans with denim shirt out. Blossom had on her blue chambray halter dress with white petticoats and sandals. She had cut her hair to above her shoulders for convenience in traveling and had a blue headband to match her dress. She felt it only polite to learn a few local phrases when they traveled. "Buon giorno," smiling, touching her chest. "Una cioccolata caldo and brioche." Touched Rocco's arm, "Cappuccino," and with a tilt of her head and a questioning look, "Fritatta? Oh grazie," as he nodded and smiled. "Pancetta, formaggio? Grazie, grazie." Despite her salt and pepper hair, he was smitten. He couldn't do enough for her.

They lingered over breakfast and eventually got across that they were at Gemma's cottage for a month. He brought the other waiter over, and soon a woman came from inside who spoke a few words in English. They all had a good laugh when she asked if they were newlyweds and Blossom said, "Yes, forty-six years ago." They stumbled over her name, but they slapped Rocco on the back upon hearing Carnavale, pronouncing the *e* on the end. Blossom asked, "L'alimintare?" They pointed the way to get groceries, Rocco and Blossom headed in that direction.

He reminded her of the size of the refrigerator when she saw the fresh meat and produce. They were going to take turns cooking, she one night and he the next, and walked back to the cottage. "I don't think we've ever walked home from grocery shopping," smiling at him. She spent the rest of the day unpacking and puttering—putting a board on bricks in the bathroom, covering it with a towel for their cosmetics. He got his old CD player out, and they had Elvis for dinner. Gemma stopped to see if they needed anything, and he asked for some basic tools and did she mind if he fixed a couple of things and where was a hardware-type store.

Blossom startled him when she said, "Tomorrow we have to go to the police station and tell them we're here."

"What!"

"You have three days to tell them you're in the country and how long you'll be here."

"We've never done that before." Police still made him nervous, even after fifty-odd years.

"In the big cities, the hotel takes care of it. Not too many people do it, but this is a small town, and we'll be noticed, so I just want to go by the rules to be polite."

They settled into a comfortable routine, brunch in the village, marketing, home to putter, cooking dinner. He put heavier chain locks on the doors, fixed leaky pipes, cleared the patio area, and bought a couple of chairs and a Coleman-like grill. At night, he whispered to her, "This is the best vacation we've ever had." She patted his cheek because she knew he had needed it.

She waited for it, and soon it came. It was her turn to cook. She had a leg of lamb in the oven all day, cooking to the fall-apart stage, seasoned the Molise way with red wine, rosemary, sage, bay leaves, and spicy red peppers. The aroma filled the little house. She was making gnocchi. The fact that she had never done it before didn't deter her. She was happily rolling them, cutting them, and proudly showing him as she rolled them off the fork to make the little grooves.

"You should have been born a hundred years ago." He laughed.

"If you were there too, it would be divine."

He looked at her with wonder. She had on a white ruffled top that fell off one shoulder, a red printed skirt with a towel tucked into her waist. Her hair was swinging as she turned, the sides pinned up with barrettes, flour on her hands and cheeks, humming as she worked. He was just thinking how adorable she was when a ray of sunlight hit her just right. He smiled as she seemed to glow, but in an instant, she was fading away. A bolt of fear hit him as if his whole life had been a dream. The air was sucked out of the room. He couldn't breathe. He shot up, screaming, "Blossom!" She walked over calmly, put her arms around his waist, her head on his chest. He expelled air, breathing hard. "I couldn't see you for a second, I couldn't see you."

She could feel his heart pounding. "It was probably just the sun moving, darling."

"I need you, baby, I need you now." She covered the gnocchi with a towel, took his hand and moved to the bedroom. "I'm too old to do this to you. You've worked so hard on dinner."

"The dinner is fine. Come, I'm right here." She helped him undress, tears running down his face.

"I can't live without you, baby girl."

"Shh, you don't have to. I'm here, I'll always be here."

"But you won't. Oh god, Blossom, I can't live without you."

She slid under him, kissing his tears, hugging him right. "Tell me."

"I was so scared. I'm okay now, baby, I was just so scared," trying to smile.

"Tell me more." When he only whimpered, she whispered, "The shop's been a part of you since you were fourteen, darling. It's only normal to feel a little lost."

"No. No."

"Darling, you told me when I was eighteen that it's okay to feel. Remember? It's okay, Rocco, I'm here," rubbing his back, kissing his neck.

A cry escaped him, and real tears came. "He never saw what I did. I made it better. It was a good business. He said I was good for nothing, but I made it better. Blossom"—achingly—"I think he's in hell. He was bad, awful bad."

In her mind, she thought he should be in hell, hitting a little boy; but she said what he needed to hear. "We don't know that, darling. He didn't kill you. He tried to kill your spirit, but he couldn't. Maybe he's in purgatory, that in-between place. Maybe God's working on him. Maybe he does know what you did," she whispered and rubbed until his breathing evened.

"I'm sorry, baby girl."

She put a hand on each cheek and looked into his eyes, smiling. "We're a team, remember."

Hoarsely, "Blossom, you have no idea how much I love you."

She gave him the look and moved her pelvis against him. "Why don't you show me?"

Smiling weakly, "I can do that."

Later, much, much later, "This is the best meal I ever ate, baby." The lamb fell apart with a fork, the drippings with a little red wine made the gravy, and the bread, oh, the bread. They were sitting as close as they could on two chairs at the old metal table, her legs over his thigh, eating, feeding each other, kissing between bites.

"You're just saying that so you can have your way with me later."

He laughed. "I used to be ready again in twenty minutes. Now it takes me twenty hours."

She winked at him coyly. "We'll see. Oh, good thing we got dressed, here comes Gemma." She got up for another plate. "Come in, come in, try my gnocchi. It's so wonderful to have a neighbor we know."

They talked about ways to fix gnocchi, and then Blossom said, "We want to take a ride to Campobasso. How is the Vecchia Trattoria?"

"Oh, it wonderful," Gemma said. "Expensive, of course, and you'll need a booking. Tuesdays or Wednesdays should be okay. Call now, and I'll help you if you need me."

Blossom used the number from her tourist book and slowly said, "Vorrei reservare un tavola" (I'd like to book a table). "Grazie, due, Martedi, quattro. Carnavale. Grazie, A presto." (Two on Tuesday at four. Carnavale—pronouncing the *e*, making Rocco raise his eyebrows.)

Tuesday they were on their way—he in his jeans, blue shirt tucked in this time with a belt, riding easily on his hips, dress boots; she in her dark blue silk jersey wrap dress she always wore on planes. It was an expensive Diane von Furstenberg she'd had for years, and it wasn't her nature to get rid of it. There was something about it that he didn't like. It wasn't low cut; it wasn't tight, just the way it crossed her breasts and slid over her hips. He didn't want to get into trouble, so he didn't even raise an eyebrow. And the high heels—she seldom wore them, and they gave her a different stance and posture, emphasizing her breasts and tiny waist. He was a little off kilter when they were in other countries. Unsure of what to expect, he was on alert and ready to fight if necessary. It left him slightly uncomfortable, his stomach muscles knotted.

"Now, darling, I should tell you Campobasso has a big prison and police training school, so don't be alarmed if we see more police than usual."

"Blossom! I have a record."

"Oh, sweetie, stop. No one cares about a record from your childhood. Besides, I just wanted to bring it up so you'd know. Gemma gave us directions right to the restaurant. Everything will be fine."

"Honestly, Blossom"—slightly irked—"this is so unnecessary."

"Rocco, you're missing the whole point. Breathe in the history, darling, your ancestors might have been born in this area. Isn't it wonderful?"

In his heart, he knew it was, but he was just enough unsettled to wish the day over.

They were a little concerned because they were eating so early, but the trattoria had a welcoming family atmosphere, and they could pretend it was a late lunch. As in Larino, she charmed their waiter with her careful, respectful attempts at the language. Touching her chest, "Acqua minerale gasata," and touching Rocco's hand, "Una birra" (fizzy mineral water and beer). Then smiling sweetly, "Il pane and caponata?" (Bread and mixed vegetables to start?)

He started to relax and was tickled when she ordered him a steak and fries (la bistecca al ferre, le potatine fritte). Her sweet questioning look made the waiter smile and nod in approval. "Insalata di mare" for herself. Even Rocco could recognize the *insalata* part. "You came all this way to have a salad?"

"We've been eating so much, honey. And they have osso buco too"—wiggling her tongue—"but I want the bread." She barely made a dent in her seafood salad and had them wrap the rest.

They loved eating out. There were conversations they saved just for then. They reverted back to their long conversations when she was in college. They teased. They flirted. They whispered, lost in each other. "We're in Italy, we really should have the tiramisu. Would you like wine too?"

"No wine. I don't want to get stopped with wine on my breath."

Her laugh made the waiters smile. "No one would get picked up in Italy for drinking wine. Not Italy!"

They sat on a bench near their car, cuddling and kissing, oblivious to people looking and smiling as they went by. Rocco saw one couple and, despite her graying and his nearly white hair, lifted his shoulders saying "Momento sposato," hoping he was saying just married. "This was really nice, baby girl."

"Did you think I was going to knock on doors?"

"I never know what to expect with you, Blossom Dove. You're my crazy lady. I know you're trying to replace my childhood with something else. You don't have to. As far as I'm concerned, I was born at twenty when we met."

She patted his cheek. "You're so sweet. But do you feel a connection, darling? Breathe deep now. I feel it, and I'm not even Italian. Isn't it marvelous?"

"Yes, it's marvelous"—standing up and taking her hands—"but you're more marvelous. We better start back, the road is curvy."

"You must let me pay you for the work and the chairs," Gemma was saying.

"No, no," Blossom said. "We didn't pay you enough as it is." It was two days to leaving. Gemma stopped in to say she was taking the next day off and could she meet them at Valaro's for their morning coffee. "You have to come back, you just have to."

"We'll try, we'll certainly try. This is the longest trip we've ever had for ourselves. If you don't sell it, we'll tell our children. It would be wonderful for them too. Ciao, see you tomorrow."

"Let's pack our clothes, baby. We can ship them tomorrow after coffee."

She'd been weepy for a couple days, and now the tears started in earnest. "Oh, Rocco." She wasn't to be put off. She needed to cry it out. He picked her up and sat with her on his lap, caressing her back while she cried.

"We have a life, baby girl. This was a wonderful interlude, but you'd be missing the children soon. We knew it had to end." Her head was on his chest looking up at him smiling down at her. He whispered against her lips, "Cara Mia Te Amo."

Her eyes got big, darker, darker. "I felt a shiver in my soul when you said that," breathlessly. She put a hand on the back of his neck.

"Oh, oh, I got myself in trouble." He smiled.

She tipped her head, questioning, even as she pressed closer.

"When you hug me around my waist, I'm okay. If you put your hands on my neck, you want to get serious." He winked.

The glorious smile as she pulled him down for a deep kiss, heat already rising from her body. "Baby, we're kind of exposed here," looking out the window, the door, the chain not on. "Slow down now, let me get us to the bedroom." His breath coming faster, her tongue probing, insisting. "Blossom, baby . . ." It was too late. She was gone—climbing him, biting his neck, pulling on his shirt, transferring her sadness in leaving to her need. She was wrapped around him, scratching, biting. He held her with one arm, pushed out of the chair, put the chain on the door and stumbled to the bed, kicking the door shut. He laid her on the bed. "I'm here, I'm here," trying to get his jeans and shirt off as she clawed the air. He pulled at her skirt, but she screamed in frustration, so he threw her panties aside entering carefully to slow her down. She was too far gone. It wasn't a joining; it was a collision. She flung herself against him, the nails she had let grow for the trip ripping into his neck, his shoulders, his back. She came in a growl and a scream. He struggled to stay with her; but the freight train got him, sweeping him away with it, then riding up his back. His chest was heaving, he couldn't get enough air, there wasn't enough air in the room. The way the slant of the bed forced them into the middle, he was afraid she wasn't getting any air at all, forced himself to crawl up against the headboard, lifting her onto his lap, pulling the sheets around them, trying to get his breath to even out.

He put his ear down to listen for her breathing, was relieved when she whispered, "There's something wrong with me, isn't there?"

"There's nothing wrong with you, baby girl, nothing at all. Go to sleep."

"Did I hurt you?"

"Not a bit. Sleep now."

He thought about packing but couldn't leave her alone yet. It hadn't been this violent since she knew she should go to Pitt. He wished Dr. Krienson was still alive. He stayed away from doctors for the most part and hadn't developed a relationship with one since her. The scratches and bites on his neck were starting to sting. His back too. Should take a shower, but she might wake. She seemed a little too warm, her cheeks pink. Too pink? He put her down and took her skirt off. He'd leave her blouse; she might wake if he pulled it over her head. He lay beside her, felt her forehead. Thought it was okay. She used to kiss the kids' foreheads. Christ, married forty-six years and he didn't know anything. She'd know. She could take care of herself and anyone else. It was only when he or the children were involved that she fell apart.

Too worried to leave her, he drifted in and out of sleep, memories coming and going.

Ricky was three. She was six months pregnant with the twins. He opened his phone, she said calmly, "Ricky fell and broke his wrist, meet me at the Liberty Street ER."

He ran to his truck, his phone at his ear. "How did it happen? You didn't pick him up, did you? Blossom, did you?"

"Close your phone, darling, I'm fine. Concentrate on driving."

He didn't close his phone, found Dr. Krienson's number, and pressed. "Laura, Rocco. Have the doctor meet us at the Liberty Street ER. Ricky fell, and I think she carried him, running." He rushed into the ER. She was talking with a couple nurses completely composed. When he was two steps away, she fainted into his arms, shocked expressions on the nurses' faces. Dr. Krienson arrived, checked Blossom, and told them what to watch for. He breathed again.

Ricky had twin beds in his room, and she insisted Rocco push them together so she could sleep beside him. In two nights, Ricky told her she had to leave. "It's just a broked wrist, Mama, I'm a big boy." She paced around his bed after he was asleep until Rocco picked her up, rocked her to sleep, and put her to bed.

Then the time he had a twenty-four hour bug.

He was throwing up in their bathroom. "Open the door, Rocco, I need to be with you."

"Blossom, there's a bug going around the shop. Go downstairs so you don't get it."

"No. No. Let me in," rattling the knob. "I need to be with you."

"Baby, I want to lay down. I'm begging you, go downstairs."

He could tell her voice was at the keyhole. "Let me check you, darling. I better call a doctor."

"Baby girl, you are a doctor. Please go downstairs." Now she was jumping on the bed. "I'm a doctor. I'm a doctor. Weak tea and dry toast. Weak tea and dry toast."

"That's it, baby. Go get me that but stay far away. Just put it on the nightstand. You go get it, and I'll come out." He fell asleep immediately; and of course she was sleeping on the chair beside the bed when he woke, still dressed, covered with the Chief Joseph robe.

Finally at four in the morning, he got up and started packing. He hadn't seen her pack but had helped unpack so reversed it. They'd get everything done, still had most of the day. It was slowgoing—every time she made a sound, he'd watch her for a while. So beautiful. So beautiful.

It was foggy, and early—six a.m., and it would be a long day back to Rome, drop the car, get the train, reversing the trip they had made thirty days earlier. She was making polite conversation, trying to hold it together. "That was very nice of Gemma, wasn't it?"

"Very nice, baby. They were all great people." Gemma had walked with them to breakfast the previous morning, and when they were all settled at their table, all the shopkeepers in the area came for a surprise good-bye party.

"Thank you for packing and finishing the cleaning," twisting her hands in her lap.

"It was my pleasure," talking as formally as she, reaching over to cover her hands with his right one.

"I'm sorry about my behavior, I'm sorry about the scratches, I, I . . . I don't want to leave, Rocco," her voice rising.

"We can always come back, baby girl."

"I just don't think it could ever be the same, Rocco. It was so perfect. So perfect," biting her lip. "It was the shopping for your food and fixing it for you and washing your clothes with my own hands." The tears started. "I love you so much, and I can't explain it. I could show you better here. It just seemed like it was better," covering her face with her hands.

He pulled over smoothly. She looked up startled when she realized they weren't moving. He was turned facing her, an arm on the steering wheel, the other on the seat back. "Blossom, we're not doing this anymore. It's upsetting you too much. I know you love me. I feel it in my soul, I feel it all around me."

"It seems so trite when people say 'I love you.'"

"It's not trite when we say it. You know that. When I say I love you, I'm saying I miss you when you're in the next room. I'm saying I can't breathe when you walk back in. I'm saying thank-you for our incredible family, thank you for whispering me through my bad times." His voice softened even more. "I'm saying thank-you for answering the phone that first night I called."

"But . . ."

"No buts. We both know a word doesn't seem enough, but it is when we say it."

"Your neck . . ."

"My neck is fine. Badges of honor, baby, badges of honor."

"Everyone will know. They were looking yesterday. I embarrassed you."

"If anyone was looking like that, they were thinking I'm a lucky guy. But they weren't. I could have gotten these from a kitten." He smiled and winked. "And I did." Then he smiled more. "I could have fallen into a thornbush. And I did. It was covered with Blossoms."

He finally got a smile. "How long have you been waiting to use that line?"

He pulled back onto the road. "Just thought of it, swear to God."

They checked back into the Cavalieri Hilton in Rome. She would have liked to try a small boutique hotel, but she knew he liked Hiltons. Just the familiar name made him more comfortable. It was one in the afternoon in Meadville, ten in the morning at Ricky's in Albuquerque; he called while she was in the bathroom. "We're done being peasants, son, we'll fly out in the morning."

"That was a long time to be out of touch, Dad. How's Mom?"

"She's a little sad to be leaving. You know Mom. She'll just need a couple days. Pass the word we're on our way, and we'll talk to you all later. Love you, Ricky."

"Love you, Dad."

"Would you like to walk around, baby?"

"Could we just eat downstairs, honey, that LaPergola place?"

After dinner, he came out of the bathroom wrapped in a huge towel. "What a great shower."

"You didn't like the cottage." She made her pouty lips.

"Babykins, I loved the cottage. It was heaven. But you have to admit the shower was close quarters," as he slid in beside her. He caressed her hip.

"Just hold me tonight."

"I just held you last night, Blossom. Tell me."

She whispered, "I don't want to hurt you," touching his neck.

"You can't hurt me, baby girl. You've never hurt me."

"They seem worse this time. The scratches, the bites."

"I love the scratches, I love the bites. I'll be anything you need, anytime, any way. It's nothing sweetie."

"But just hold me, please."

"Of course I will. All I'm saying is this bed is really big and comfortable, and these sheets feel like silk. He was whispering into her neck now, "They have to change the sheets anyway, we might as well get them dirty."

"Rocco!"

"Well, I'm just saying. May I have a little kiss while I'm just holding you," nibbling on her ear.

She shivered, moving closer. "Just the little one."

"Let me look in your eyes. Let me drown in your eyes."

"Oh Rocco, I love you. How can I love you so much," putting her leg over his hip. They dirtied the sheets and slept peacefully.

They had flown first class for years. He didn't want anyone beside her or crawling over her. Her head was leaning into him ready to sleep. He was still trying to struggle through Ken Follett's *Pillars of the Earth*. She had given it to him after a Paris trip when he was fascinated by the construction of the old cathedrals. "Baby, this sure has some rough spots. Did you read this at Penn?"

"No, at Pitt. The girls were eight. And don't mention Penn, I hated Penn." She was still looking for reasons to cry, and this was as good as any. "It was awful, awful," crying and pounding his arm.

He whispered into her hair, "What about room 422?"

"Oh, I loved room 422. I loved it so much, Rocco," kissing his neck.

He bit his lip to keep from smiling. He prided himself on keeping his equilibrium as her moods changed at a dizzying pace. He remembered when it scared him, and now it just made her more precious.

"I couldn't have lived without room 422. How did we do it, how did we do it?" She buried her face in her hands. "Five weeks apart, six weeks sometimes. Oh, Rocco, it was so hard. So hard, honey."

"Shh, go to sleep now. That was fifty years ago. It'll never happen again."

"It seems like yesterday." She pouted, lifting his arm and putting it around her, getting comfortable against him. She lifted her face for a kiss and whispered against his lips, "Don't ever mention Penn again, or I'll have to hurt you." His laugh filled the cabin.

———

It was wonderful to be home; of course it was—their own bed, their favorite chair, their beautiful kitchen and baths. She had left Cassie a list of basic groceries to get. Two days home, they went to Walmart to restock the meats and other perishables. She looked at Rocco as they started up the aisle. The ridiculous amount of choices brought tears to her eyes, and not in a good way. It comforted her to know that he knew exactly what she was thinking.

Things settled back to normal. The days filled up; and at night, nose to nose, they talked about Larino. "Remember," she'd whisper. "Remember, remember?"

They were cuddling when she said, "Tell me some more about what you're saying when you say I love you, like you did on the way to Tremoli."

"Okay, I'll do one, and then you do one. But we have rules here."

She giggled. "George Kennedy, *Cool Hand Luke*."

"The rule is, no body parts below the neck."

"Ohh, can't I talk about your back? I love your back."

"No," he said, "or I'd have to talk about your front," winking.

He started right out, never at a loss. Still thinking she needed perfect words to get it right, she said, tentatively and softly, "When I say I love you, I'm saying your eyes are so blue they're like the sky and I can see heaven."

As the nights went on, their life unfolded little memory by little memory. It soothed her and consoled her. She lost the anxious look she'd had when she told him she loved him during the day. She didn't need a perfect word. She had gotten it right. It had been right from the very start.

Another little gift from Larino. With the slant in the bed, he couldn't lie three or four inches behind her as he always had. A couple nights home, he rolled her into her sleeping position, and she wiggled back against him. "Do you mind? Now I'm used to touching you."

"I love it, baby girl." He smiled, her head was against his chest, so he put his chin on the top of her head. She put her chin on the top of Tiger's head, and they slept. As they drifted off, he thought he'd never been more content.

The cartons with their clothes arrived. Everything got cleaned and put away. She helped at the local free clinic. He went to the shop daily for coffee with Bob and to use the heavy bag or Nautilus, listen to what was going on, help when asked. Bob was eleven years older, almost eighty now. He really was the father Rocco never had. Just as the children started in again on the "When are you selling the house and coming to New Mexico" comments, Bob had a stroke.

His wife had passed a few years earlier. Bob Two and Three were busy at the shop, so Rocco put him into an assisted living apartment in the retirement community across the road from their house. He went over every morning to have coffee and read the paper to him, shaved him, and helped with his shower every other day. As he weakened, had him transferred to the nursing home section.

"Baby, I don't want to be in a nursing home."

"You'll never be in a nursing home, darling."

"But you couldn't do it, Blossom, it's really hard."

"Rocco, sweetie, we would have someone come here. If the money is good for something, it's good for that. Put it out of your mind now." She put a hand on each cheek and kissed him. "You'll never be in a nursing home. I promise you."

SCENES FROM A MARRIAGE

Their Seventies

They flew to New Mexico for birthdays and holidays, did some trips for RMA; and before they could believe it, he was seventy-three, she seventy-one, and the children were talking about their fiftieth wedding anniversary.

He stuck his head in the shower. "Baby girl, are you going to wear your wedding dress this time? It shook me up last time, I just want to know ahead."

"Yes I am darling, but I'm wearing my pearls and doves instead of the choker," smiling through the shampoo suds.

His voice went down a couple of tones, and he did his Groucho Marx. "Do you want me to come in and wash your back?"

"I'd love you to, but I'm afraid we'd be late."

"Aw fudge."

The children thought it wasn't fair for them to travel for their own party, so everyone came east. Ricky and Angela in his old bedroom. Lily and Steven in the girls' old room. All the rest at the Holiday Inn, taking over one floor with the grandchildren, Nix and his family, Lindsay, her girls and their families. At Lily's insistence, they were having the dinner at the country club. Rocco thought there were a couple of other spots with bigger dance floors, but Lily felt they were too plebeian. "Really, Dad, think of your position in the community." It wasn't worth an argument, so he acquiesced, smiling to himself at her Elaine traits.

Blossom called from her dressing room. "Are you going to sing to me this time? This is such a big group, I think I'll be self-conscious."

"Just look at me, baby. I'm going to sing something different. I like to shake things up every twenty-five years." He laughed.

She came out in her panties, carrying her dress, as he picked up the shirt she had laid out for him. His wedding shirt hadn't made it through the years, but this one was similar to the blue in her dress. He was wearing jeans and his favorite Sendra boots, his body lean and rangy, tight and taut from workouts.

She laid her dress on the bed and sat down at her dressing table, her hair wrapped in a towel, rubbing on her lotion. Her petite body barely changed in their years together. Her skin healthy and amazingly supple, her generous breasts heavy with age but still constricting his breathing. She started brushing her hair, more gray than dark now, and he took the brush and winked at her in the mirror. "Your hair's longer."

"I let it grow for you, but I have to cut it the next few days. Old ladies in long gray hair look a little silly."

"I love it. You're very beautiful, Mrs. Carnavale."

"Why thank you, Mr. Carnavale, you're very beautiful too," reaching up to tousle his hair, beautiful white waves.

"You finish up, baby. I'll go down and double-check the music." The children had asked them what kind of party they wanted, and their wishes were simple—room to dance and a good sound system.

Even forewarned, he got the kick in the gut when she came down the stairs—the beautiful dress, a headband to match his shirt. "Oh, Mother C," Angela cried out, "imagine wearing the same dress after fifty years. You look unbelievable. I hope my gown lasts long enough for Alyssa."

Lily added, "It's beautiful, Mom, really beautiful." But being Lily, "I don't know about the pearls and the locket together, though." Her brow wrinkled. "They don't really match."

"I know, honey, but I love them. They'll be fine."

"Mom, why is there a cut up the side? That wasn't there."

"I had it slit for dancing. Daddy wants to show you all how we've progressed at the tango." Lily looked worried.

It was a wonderful group gathered at the club when they arrived—Nix and Nola, and their girls all married with families; Ricky and Angela with Tony and Alyssa. Tony going into graduate school, not serious about anyone yet; Lily, Steven, and the twins—Steven III in broadcasting, Sage flirting with medicine; Coral with Neil McAllister, the doctor who started at their clinic. Ricky had introduced them way back when, and they'd been a couple since. After two years at the clinic, he'd gone to Holy Cross Hospital in Taos to be closer to Coral but no marriage. Coral used the "I'm always traveling" to forestall it. She had her home, he had his, but they'd been together almost twelve years.

Lindsay came with her girls and their families, a little frail at seventy-five, looking so much like their mother now. Randy couldn't make it. She had gotten a sitter for him. Even a six-hour ride at seventy-eight wasn't possible with his heart condition. Of course, Bob couldn't make it, but Bob Two and Three were there with their families and some other old-timers from the shop. Helen had retired from the shop twenty years earlier but was still their dear friend and getting around fine with just a cane at eighty-four.

Before dinner, Rocco and Blossom made sure to circle around and thank everyone for coming. After the dinner, steak for who wanted it, lobster tail for who didn't, after the wedding cake and the toasts, Rocco pulled a high bar stool to the center of the floor. Blossom was shaking her head no worriedly. He was smiling yes. Completely at ease, he lifted her onto the stool. "I want to sing to Mom before we start dancing. It's an old song I heard Kenny Rogers sing a few weeks ago." Clear and strong he sang "Through the Years." Those that knew him well smiled, not surprised. Others were incredulous. She clenched her hands tightly, only looking into his eyes, and didn't cry until the end when he lifted her hand and kissed it. He carried her back to the table during the applause. "We'd like to show you a couple Latin type numbers we enjoy dancing to, and then please get up and join us. Dancing is our passion, and let's all enjoy it tonight."

He led Blossom to the center of the floor as Lily called out, "Don't throw her in the air, Dad. Ricky, tell him." Rocco just smiled. "No throwing going on in these numbers, honey." They saw him whisper to her as the opening bars of "Sway" began. Rocco, who prided himself on always knowing what was going on around them, heard a collective gasp from the guests, saw the waitresses gather by the service area, a couple with their hands over their mouths; but then he was lost in her eyes and the tango.

Angela whispered to Ricky, "I don't think they even know we're here." When Blossom snaked around him and put her leg over his thigh, he looked at her with such passionate intensity, Lily whispered loudly, "Oh my god. Ricky, tell them there are children here. Ricky!"

"It's okay, Lil, it's okay. They're married." But when the music went right into "Innamorata," even he hoped twelve-year-old Alyssa had her hands over her mouth because Grandpa and Grandma looked so wonderful and not because she was picking up on the sensuality of the dance.

Rocco had taped all the music, alternating fast and slow. After their opening dance, everyone breathed again. There was a five-minute break, and all their favorites followed until midnight. Rocco never missed a dance. When Blossom was tired, he danced with Alyssa, Sage, Madison's girls, or all of them together.

He and Blossom were dancing to "Willie," one of their favorite Delbert's, a nice medium tempo to catch their breaths. Her back was to him, his right arm around her waist, their left arms out. She was keeping an eye out for children and rubbing against him at every opportunity. He whispered to her, "I want you so bad. Where can we go?"

She did a half step to twirl and face him, looking at him innocently. "Why, darling, we're the guests of honor, we can't leave."

He grinned and gave her a mischievous look. "How about we sneak out to the truck for a little bit?"

They had made love all over the house except the children's rooms, in the pool, in the gazebo, at his office, in the mountains, on what they hoped was a secluded beach on Amelia Island off the coast of Florida—but never, ever, in the truck.

She stopped, smiled sweetly, lifted her gown up a fraction with her dainty hands, and kicked him smartly in the chin. He howled and hopped after her as she turned and ran, laughing as he caught her and swung her around. She wiggled away and ran again, Lily calling out, "Daddy! All these children and you two are the only ones misbehaving."

"She started it." He laughed, chasing her again, inciting twenty minutes of bedlam as all the children followed suit. Back at the table, his lips to her ear, "I'm going to get you for that."

"I know." She smiled. "That was my master plan."

He laughed out loud. Coral and Ricky caught each other's eyes, shook their heads, and smiled in shared remembrances of home.

Back home, he carried her upstairs and tucked her in at one thirty. "I can't go to bed without a shower," she yawned. "We've been dancing for hours."

He tucked the covers under her chin. "It won't hurt this one time. Besides"—he winked—"I'm going to get you all dirty in a little while."

"Rocco!"

He went back down to talk with the guys, Ricky, Nix, and Steven. He figured something was up because Nola had dropped Nix there and went on to the motel. Thought it might be a group talk about them moving to New Mexico, and he was right. "Really, Dad," Ricky started, "it's time. Way past time."

"I know, son, I know. I think we need more work done to put the house on the market."

"Not that much, Dad. The kitchen redo wasn't that long ago. The baths are old, but the marble is neutral, and people won't mind. You gotta do something about the dining room, though. The chances of someone wanting a dance studio smack in the middle of the house are zero to none." They all laughed.

"You guys are unbelievable, Mr. C," Steven said.

"Thanks. We really enjoy it. It keeps us young."

Nix said, "I tried to get into Blossom's computer while you were upstairs. Nothing doing. She's got it locked up. Is she still working?"

"Oh yeah," Rocco said, "keeping her hand in as she says. Well, you know that, Ricky, the money comes to you, right?"

"Yeah. Wow"—shaking his head—"amazing amounts of money. And still from Chet's company."

"It's his son and grandson now mostly, but Chet's still involved. I think it's addictive. They're all a little crazy," he laughed. "But only Wednesdays, just like she started out."

"Well, anyway," Nix added, "I'll send you some diagrams for the landscaping. It could use some updating, and pavers for the driveway will give it a more modern look. You could have everything done by fall and put it on the market."

"Fall's not too good a time, is it?"

"Dad! Quit procrastinating."

"Okay. Okay," throwing up his arms.

"It's almost three, baby girl, why are you still awake?"

"I've just been catnapping, waiting for you," holding her arms out. "What took you so long?"

"You know, the usual. Why haven't we sold the house yet, etc., etc.?"

She smiled. "Why haven't we sold the house yet?"

He shrugged. "It needs updating, change is hard at our age. What do you think?"

"I know one reason," giving him the look.

"What?"

"Because right now I want to love you fifty different ways for our anniversary and we can't make any noise," pouting.

He laughed. "I know. I love them more than life, but not in the house. Did you like your song tonight?"

"I loved it. It was beautiful. I missed my other song, though."

Just then, Ricky and Steven got to the top of the stairs. Steven, heading to the right to the girls' old room and Lily; Ricky, to the left to his old room and Angela. They heard him begin "The First Time Ever I Saw Your Face." They raised their eyebrows and smiled, but as Ricky turned, tears filled his eyes. He loved them so much. He crawled in beside Angela, and she smiled in her sleep as he whispered, "I love you."

After her song, they giggled lips to lips. "Maybe you can love me twenty-five quiet ways and save twenty-five noisy ways for when everyone's gone," he whispered.

"Did you tell anyone we'd be up early?"

"Nope. We're good."

"Then get on your knees, Mister."

"Blossom! That's not quiet."

"It's quiet for me, my mouth will be busy. You'll have to use Tiger."

"You're a crazy woman," trying to crawl away. "Ow"—laughing—"you're hurting me." And they tickled and laughed and kissed and loved, waking entangled at nine. He hugged her tight and kissed her nose, shivering at the heavy-lidded, sated look she gave him. "Stay put, I want to run Nix out to the motel so Nola doesn't have to come back here." She held on. "Tonight, baby girl, tonight. Go back to sleep." He took a quick shower and was tempted to get back in when he looked at her in the swirl of sheets.

Good-byes, kisses, and hugs for the next two days as everyone left. They promised to start on the house, and trying not to nag, everyone left it to Ricky for the final "Really, Dad please, it's time. We want you closer."

The day came as they all must. It wasn't the day they met, but close. In her mind, she called it the day her life ended. She wasn't being melodramatic; it made perfect sense to her. When Rocco came, her life began. When Rocco left, her life ended. She learned not to say it out loud when she saw the expression on Cassie's face and knew she would call Ricky first chance she got.

It started like any other day. Rocco was seventy-five, she almost seventy three. She woke smiling. He was nibbling her neck right below her ear. "Hey, you."

"I'm just kissing you good morning."

"That doesn't seem like a good morning kiss," as she rolled over to him. "That seems like a let's continue last night kiss."

"Well, there's that," smoothing her hair behind her ears. He whispered, "Is that cream still good?"

"Will you stop obsessing about the cream. I'll take care of it."

She had scared him to death a few years before when she said he was hurting her. Usually she was blasé about her health, but this involved him, so she couldn't think straight. She panicked and cried and scared him more. "Think, baby, think now. If someone came to you and told you that, what would you say?"

"Men, men, menopausal dryness probably," still sobbing.

"Okay, okay. Where can you check, what can we do?"

So they got themselves straightened around, and she solved the problem.

"I have to tinkle. I'll be right back."

He patted his stomach and held out his arms. "What's on tap for today?"

She laid on him, kissing his neck while he rubbed her back. "After you take care of Bob, you're going to RE/MAX and list the house for sure today."

She raised herself up to see his face. "Ricky said you're to the point now of overimproving, and you're supposed to call a halt."

"I know, I know. I'll do it today."

They had spent the last couple of years getting the house updated to sell. The hardest part for her was taking the mirrors off the walls and changing their dance area back to a dining room. She cried when he took the mats they used to practice lifts to Goodwill and cried again at how beautiful the room was with the new dining room set.

"I'm going to the free clinic, and I have a conference call with Chet's grandson. Chet told me he thinks he can talk me into doing some work for the government. I told him he's wasting his time."

"Okay, after Bob and RE/MAX, I'll stop at the shop for some exercise and then check and see where you are so we can plan the rest of the day. But first"—kissing her seriously and moving her against him—"ummm, love you, love you, love you."

She heard a vehicle and looked out to see Bobs Two and Three. At first, she smiled and shook her head. He must have thought of something else he wanted them to do. When they looked to the door and she saw their faces, she could feel the blood in her veins turning to ice.

She opened the door. "What happened? Where is he?"

Bob Two made sure he didn't answer until he was beside her. "It was a heart attack, Miss Blossom, they took him to the hospital." At the flash of hope, he had to quell it. "I'm sorry, Miss Blossom, he's gone," guiding her to the nearest chair.

She started shivering, bit her lip, breathed deeply, her eyes shut. Her mind was saying, *No. No. Please no.* Her voice said, "Where?"

"He was just done exercising. They said it was probably instantaneous. We didn't want you to hear it on the phone."

She kept her eyes shut, handed him the phone from her pocket. "Would you get Ricky for me?"

He handed the phone to Bob Three so he could keep watching her. She was still taking in breaths with her eyes closed, grasping the edge of the table. "Ricky, it's Bob Petillo. I'm with your mother. I had to bring her some very hard news, son. Yes, he had a fatal heart attack at the shop today. I'm very sorry. Here's your mother."

Her voice was wavering, very quiet, very calm. "Hello, darling. Yes, I'm fine. Would you get everyone together and bring them here? Yes, I'll be going to the hospital now. I love you too. Call me before you start."

"Would you ride with us, Miss Blossom? You probably shouldn't be driving. Do you have anything you'd like to take?"

"Oh, oh. Yes." She calmly put things into her briefcase—things for herself, his health care directive, her power of attorney. He felt funny following her around, but she didn't seem to notice. Her eyes were getting glazed, and he hoped the nurses could see she wasn't as calm as she pretended.

A doctor she seemed to know met them, and she told him he could go back to the shop. Ricky would keep them up to date.

She wasn't aware of the passage of time, and then, "Dr. Carnavale, we have him all comfortable now."

The nurses heard her talking, crying some, laughing some. When Linda went by and saw her sleeping beside him, she covered her. About 6:00 a.m., she came out and asked where a shower was she could use. Then she stopped at the desk and said, "Please leave a message downstairs that none of our family is to come up until I give the word."

Ricky called her at twenty past eleven. "I used a private jet. We're all here except Coral. She's driving from West Virginia, should be here by noon. Yes, Neil's with us."

"I'll call you in a few minutes, honey." She motioned to the nurse that she was ready. They took the machines away and did their necessary paperwork. She kissed him and tousled his hair to look like himself, pulled her favorite curl down his forehead, and called Ricky.

The visitation was difficult. The children protected her as much as they could, whispering among themselves that the one-night three-hour session probably hadn't been a good idea in retrospect. She looked exhausted after one hour. Rocco had told her that he hated the idea of an open casket like his father had. Since they both wanted cremation, she had the florist arrange the flowers around a vignette of his boots, hat, and folded buckskin jacket, along with a picture she had taken of him in them looking over the Rio Grande Gorge at Coral's cabin.

She had wanted to put them in with him at the cremation, but Ricky was elected to talk to her.

"Mom, we really think you don't want to do this. Maybe Tony would like them."

"Honey, if they're passed down through the family at some point, they'll lose their meaning and be sold at a garage sale. I just don't want that."

"How about this, then, while you think it over. In the future when you go, we'll put them in with you?"

Her face softened, and she smiled. "That's good. I like that."

"Okay." Holding her hands, he said softly, "Now how about his wedding ring?"

"Oh, his ring has to be with him," tearing up. "It has to be with him," shuddering.

"Mom, wouldn't it be nice if you maybe wear it around your neck . . ."

She was openly crying now, and he gave her his handkerchief. "See, Angela put it on a silver chain—and then when your time comes, all three rings will be together. We just don't want you to be sorry later when you think about it, Mom. Wouldn't it be nice to have it with you until you go?"

She smiled through her tears. "Thank you, honey," putting the chain over her head. "So, so"—trying to get her crying under control—"I'll add it to my papers," counting off on her fingers. "I want to wear my wedding dress with my doves and pearls and his ring around my neck, and I'll have my rings on. And you'll put in his hat and boots and jacket."

"We'll do exactly that, Mom."

"And Tiger too?"

"And Tiger too."

"Ricky."

"What is it, Mom."

"I don't think I can do this."

He took her hands in his again. "Mom, you're the strongest person I know. You can do this. I know you can. And more importantly, he knows you can."

"Thank you, honey."

They hugged and went out to the others. Him thinking how frail she was under his hug. What to do, what to do? Talk to Cassie and see if she knew.

She couldn't wear black to the funeral, picked a dark wine silk jersey that he loved. It had a jewel neckline and long sleeves, the skirt flaring softly to her ankles, matching pumps. She tucked his ring on the chain under her dress and wore her pearls and doves. Ricky and Nixie walked her down the church aisle. She stumbled a little when they entered and she saw the church full to overflowing, thinking back to the five people at his dad's funeral. She sat between Lily and Coral, Steven, Angela, and Neil with her, the grandchildren in the second row. She whispered to Coral, "Where's Ricky?"

"He's giving the eulogy, remember, Mom?"

"Oh." She didn't remember, didn't remember much of the last few days, had talked little, ate less, but tried hard. She smiled when Ricky got up to the podium. He looked so handsome, so much like Rocco; but when he said, "My father, Rocco Carnavale, was the finest man I ever knew," she fainted.

Neil changed places with Lily, unobtrusively checked her pulse, and gave her a few minutes before using the smelling salts he had brought along. Her eyes fluttered when the service was almost over. Only the family had noticed, and they didn't think she even realized what happened.

She started talking a little again at the country club where they were having an informal luncheon. Ricky slid a comfortable-looking chair from the foyer beside their table, and Alyssa sat with her, coaxing her to eat a little finger food. She got through it.

Neil gave her a sedative that night, and she slept twelve hours. After ten hours, Ricky said he didn't think she should wake up alone. Lily said, "You shouldn't be there, Ricky. You look just like Daddy." Coral took the first hour, and Lily was napping for the second, so it was Ricky there when she woke up.

"It's me, Mom, Ricky."

"I know it's you, silly. Daddy is Daddy."

They all thought she should have a couple weeks to rest and recoup before spreading his ashes, so Coral stayed with her. "You should plan to stay the winter when we go, Mom."

"Oh, no, honey. I know they say you shouldn't make any big decisions for a year, but we were already planning to sell the house, so I'll do that. I'll come out for a week, but then I'll come back for a couple months before the holidays to get some things done. Did I ever tell you about my book?"

"No. What book?"

"Well, not an actual book, but a booklike picture album of our life. I started and then got busy." She didn't tell her she had fallen apart thinking of their mortality, and Rocco made her put it away. "My goodness, it's been thirteen years ago. So I want to do that. If I get busy, I could have it done for Christmas gifts."

"Now, Mom, don't push yourself."

"I won't, but that might not be a bad thing. I'd like to leave everything spread out, but if they start showing the house, it would look messy." She was starting to wring her hands, so Coral jumped in.

"You know what. We have eight days until our flight, and they're not going to show it until you get back. Let's look things over. It'll be fun."

They spent hours going through the pictures, laughing, crying. It was good for both of them, and Blossom started to see the design in her mind.

Blossom came down to breakfast. Her morning routine had already changed from luxuriating after his morning sweet nothings and dozing a little more to a quick shower. "Coral, darling, you decorate a lot like we do, is there anything here you want?"

"No thanks, Mom. I've accumulated my own things. Do you want to ship anything when you come?"

"I would like our chair. It's a great curl-up chair for television."

"How about your bed?" She was sorry she said it as soon as it was out. The raw agony on her mother's face was palpable. Blossom's eyes were closed, her hand clutched her stomach, but she breathed deeply and said, "No, I think a small one would be less lonely." That was as close as she came to breaking down. She knew if she went there, she'd never come back.

Coral carefully brought up the subject of where Blossom would live when she came for good.

"We had pretty much decided on Santa Fe just to be central to everyone."

"Maybe you should stay with me for a while. It'd be silly to live all by yourself and have to travel to everyone. Think about it, and we'll talk about it at the ash ceremony."

"Now, honey, I hope you all haven't been talking about a formal thing. Daddy and I just wanted to toss our ashes into the wind. That's all I want to do."

"It's totally up to you, Mom. We'll meet at Ricky's, and you tell everyone what you want."

They flew into Albuquerque with Rocco's ashes. Blossom wanted them to be with her. She wouldn't put them with her checked luggage, and she wouldn't Fedex them. Coral was relieved to learn from a funeral director that her mom could carry them on with the proper paperwork. The box fit in a cosmetic bag she had and the prominent words "Human Remains" on the box didn't seem to affect her.

Blossom said, "Lily, don't call it the ash ceremony. Daddy wanted his ashes to be scattered where we were married. That's all." Then she softened. "It's very nice of you, honey, but I don't want a service. I don't even want music. If you want to do that with my ashes, be my guest, but really, I just want the same. Please."

"Fine, Mother, fine. It just seems a little too simple to me."

"We had a lovely service back home, honey. It couldn't have been nicer. I could never have done it without you children, but this is between Daddy and me."

It was a small group. She actually wanted to be alone, but she knew they'd never permit it. They were all at Ricky's, and when she came downstairs in her wedding dress, Lily gasped. She had lost weight and pinned the dress in the back, and it was showing its age. Before Lily could say anything, Ricky and Coral said simultaneously, "Mother, you look beautiful."

They took two seven-passenger vans—Blossom, Ricky, Angela, Tony, Alyssa, Coral, and Neil in one; Lily, Steven, young Steven, Sage, Nix, Nola, and Nicole, the only one of Nix's three girls who could make it, in the other. Blossom and Ricky had gone to a local funeral director and had the ashes transferred from the traveling box to an urn with a stem she could hold on to. It was circled with a southwestern sunset and the image of Kocopelli. Blossom liked the eternal sunset and music symbolism.

She held him on her lap during the ride with her eyes closed. She knew they were all watching her, but she was strangely peaceful. It had only been fifteen days, but time was irrelevant now. He was gone. Fifteen days or fifteen years. She would finish things up so he would be proud of her.

Ricky and Nix walked her around the bend. There was the rock. She closed her eyes and smiled. She could still see them standing there, his hat on the rock. "I'll just go sit a minute," she said softly. She sat on the rock and held him. She felt a strength she hadn't felt at home. He was in the air, the wind, the setting sun. "I'll never forgive you, you know, for going first." She heard him, *You know I couldn't have made it without you. If we couldn't go together, this was the best way.* They saw her smile and nod, her lips moving.

"I love you to the moon and back, Rocco Anthony."

I passed love years ago, Blossom Dove, she heard.

"Come, children, come see Daddy become part of the wind." Ricky held her lightly around her waist as she swung the urn from right to left, and the wind picked up the ashes. They all stood quietly; then she wanted to sit on the rock a few more minutes. She sat with her knees bent, her arms around them, the setting sun picking up the gold threads in her dress, the wind blowing her hair back. Coral took a picture with her phone. She knew Blossom was planning the last page of her book to be her favorite one of them from their fiftieth anniversary, but Coral knew she would put this one in her book at the end.

She stayed a few more days. They had discussions around Ricky's kitchen table, and she finally agreed to live with Coral when she returned for good. Rocco's spirit was in the cabin he had helped build. She'd have her solitude when Coral traveled, but she said no to taking Coral's master suite. "But, Mom, it's a nice big room. You could have some of your things."

"No, Coral, that's your room. I can fit everything I want into one of the other bedrooms. I like small spaces."

So it was settled. She'd go home until Thanksgiving and come back to New Mexico until after the first of the year. Ricky called Cassie and asked her to stay every day until Blossom was in bed.

When Blossom heard the plan, she told Cassie, "That's ridiculous. You have a life. You come eight to five every other day. That's plenty."

"Well, I'll come eight to five, Miss Blossom, but Ricky said every day, so I better come every day."

It worked out fine. Cassie made sure she ate, and she could show Cassie the pictures. Rosalita had been with them when the children were little; so it was fun for Cassie to see them grow.

She worked almost all day every day on her project, and by her birthday, she had a decision to make. They might ask, "Where are pictures of you and daddy before you met," and she felt the title of the book took care of that. But she had to keep her promise to Rocco and still not destroy *the picture*.

When everything was ready to assemble, she went upstairs, picked up her precious picture of Rocco sliding her wedding ring on her finger, took the backing off, and slid out the picture of three-year-old Rocco with the rock. He had wanted the violence to end with him, and she would honor that, but she couldn't bring herself to destroy it and couldn't leave it hidden to be found and wondered about later. She studied it and decided.

She used the website www.Blurb.com to assemble the books, and when she left for New Mexico for the holidays, her Christmas gifts were finished. She was pleased, and she knew Rocco would approve.

They all gathered at Nix's house in Santa Fe. It was the largest, and everyone could stay over. To the young ones, it had always been Uncle Nix's, and Blossom was the only one who occasionally slipped and called it Aunt Mim's. Christmas morning she smiled, contentedly looking at the large group. When she was young, it had only been she and Nixie, her parents and Aunt Mim. A quick count now came to twenty-two, and she may have missed a couple. The young ones opened their gifts first, then a cleanup and a break with coffee and pastries. When they were all back around the tree, she passed out the boxes to each couple. Coral looked amazed. "You finished?" Blossom nodded happily.

Lily was the first to get her box open. She clutched it to her chest, "Ohh, oh," peeked at some pages, clutched it again, and burst into tears. Ricky looked at it, looked at his mother, looked at Angela, smiling and blinking rapidly. Coral said, "It's great, Mom. I knew it would be." Nix was flipping pages. "Wow! This is really something, sis."

It was a twelve-by-twelve-inch bound book. The burgundy cover inscribed in gold:

Rocco and Blossom
A Love Story

On the first page, upper left, was the picture of three-year-old Rocco holding the stone with the caption "Daddy was always determined to be a builder," and lower right, the only picture she had found of herself. True to her words, her disappointed mother had destroyed every one. Mim had unearthed this one. Blossom was four, sitting primly on a footstool in a black dress with a white lace collar, her ankles crossed, her hands folded, a nonexpression on her face. The inscription was "Mommy waits patiently for Daddy to find her."

And then the pages followed as she started documenting their life: Rocco at the Rocky Balboa statue, all the things they had done around Philadelphia; their wedding, their honeymoon, their home on Cussewago; the births of the children, the move to Shadow Oaks, the TV spot; the girls in tumbling and dance class, cheerleading, homecoming; Ricky at the computer at three, in track, Mathcounts and Scholastic Quiz; swimming in the backyard, holidays, trips for fun and trips to help others, birthdays, graduations, weddings, anniversaries. They were usually alone dancing; but Mim had snapped a great one at the Stable, the ship's photographer one on their twenty-fifth anniversary cruise, and a breathtaking one at their fiftieth anniversary with her lying over his knee and looking into his eyes at the end of "Innamorata." Some captions in print, some with her beautiful handwriting meandering around the photos.

Rocco had survived and saved her, and they had made a family. This was her gift to the children and her homage to him. She napped on and off through the lovely day and smiled as they picked it up and she heard, "Look at this one, Daddy and Elvis. Oh, oh, look at this one."

Ricky took her to the airport on January 15. "Now, Mom, you don't have to stay until the house is sold. Bob Two can follow up with the realtor, and Cassie can keep things dusted. Just do the things you want to do and come back."

"I'll see how I feel, darling. I'm sure it will be just a couple months."

And that's all it was, a family with boys eight and ten bought the house in March, along with the furniture Cassie didn't want. Bob Two and Three picked up Rocco's chair to ship to Coral's. She and Cassie packed her clothes, his music, her Emily Dickinson books, her favorite picture of him putting her wedding ring on, his favorite picture of her discreetly breastfeeding Ricky. She had all the pictures from the *wall* shipped to Ricky to distribute.

Coral wanted the big one over the mantle of the whole family. She added a few kitchen things she liked to use, and it was done.

She had left Shadow Oaks at nineteen to be with Rocco, and she was leaving to be with him again.

She was very comfortable at Coral's. Alyssa and Sage visited Aunt Coral often and had some of their things in the two rooms at the east wing of the cabin. Sage quietly moved her things from the room Blossom would be using, and the girls took turns coming. She had a twin bed, a nightstand, a dresser, leaving plenty of room for their chair. It had arrived before she did, and it made the room cozy, especially when she put her favorite pictures on the nightstand. She fought tears when she saw their Chief Joseph robe folded on the back of the chair. She had given it to Rocco their second Christmas together. Cassie must have had Bob pack it with the chair.

Sage lived in Santa Fe and was familiar with the sights; but when Alyssa came up from Albuquerque, Blossom took her to the art galleries, lunch, and shopping just as Aunt Mim had done with her.

By summer, she felt it was time to be productive. She helped Neil at his office and went on trips with Coral that weren't too dangerous. In the fall, she worked a couple of days a week at the Taos branch of the University of New Mexico as an adjunct professor in the advanced computer sciences classes. Ricky and Coral laughed about it. "I would have loved being a fly on the wall for that," Ricky said. "Imagine what the kids thought when this little-bitty gray-haired lady was introduced as an expert."

"Well, they wouldn't have thought it for long. God, what she can see on those screens that nobody else can."

They were all nervous the first year Rocco's birthday and their anniversary approached. Ricky said, "It's Angela's and my anniversary too, and she'll know we're worried if we don't celebrate. Let's just carry on as normal."

"You ready, Mom?" Coral came into Blossom's bedroom, and her heart jumped seeing her standing by their wedding picture caressing Rocco's face.

But she turned, smiling. "So beautiful. He was so beautiful and so wonderful. Did I tell you when we met that second day at McDonald's, I thought he looked like a movie star?" Coral smiled and nodded, fighting tears. "And so very wonderful. I was such a frightened girl, and he made the world wonderful." She picked up the sweater she needed even in the New Mexico June weather. "Come along, honey, we don't want to be late for Ricky and Angela's party." Coral swallowed hard and sent Ricky a text. "She's fine, I'm not."

Five years passed, not unpleasantly. She was seventy-eight. Along with her work, it was nice to drive with Coral or Lily to holidays, birthdays, and anniversaries. A hundred twenty miles to Albuquerque was just a nice Sunday drive compared to the twenty-five-hundred-mile flight from Meadville. This occasion was Alyssa's nineteenth birthday. Blossom had given Sage the diamond pendant Rocco had given her on their tenth anniversary. She gave Alyssa the ruby circled with diamonds he had given her to wear in the Christmas TV spot. "Mother C," Angela said, "that's way too expensive for a girl her age."

"She can save it for special occasions. She has Rocco's coloring and looks, so pretty in red. I've never been a collector of things, so I don't have much to give the children. They can go through my clothes when the time comes."

"Mom," Lily called from the other room, "don't be morbid, this is a party." Blossom, Coral, and Angela rolled their eyes. She always enjoyed the festivities but didn't take pictures anymore.

Ricky was fifty-seven, Coral and Lily fifty-four. Melancholy years for memories. Ricky had been calling Coral each week to see how their mom was doing, and the conversations usually turned to remember whens.

"What's she wearing to bed? They didn't used to wear anything."

"Ricky!"

"No, I'm not being perverse or anything. Remember the 'knock on our door' speech."

Coral laughed. "Oh my god, that was so funny. I thought he was going to have apoplexy."

Ricky went on. "It was my fault. I was talking to Tim Watson that night, and he said they were getting rid of their truck. I was going to be sixteen the next week and ran into their room to see if I could have it. They were just lying on a couple pillows watching TV. I could tell she didn't have anything on but really never gave it a thought. The sheet was way up her chest under her arms, but he had such a shocked look on his face and pulled a blanket right over her head. He almost looked scared. I could never figure that out, he wasn't afraid of anything. Just as she said, 'It's just Ricky, darling,' he yelled, 'Ricky, don't ever come in our room without knocking!'

"I told him about the truck real quick, and he said we'd discuss it at the appropriate time, go to my room. I felt really bad, mostly about the truck actually, and then Mom came in and said, 'Darling, Daddy considers our room sacrosanct. Just be sure you knock is all he was saying.' When I asked her what *sacrosanct* meant, she told me to look it up like she always did. So

I thought it was over, but he started in again at breakfast and you guys got involved."

"Yeah"—Coral laughed—"me and my big mouth. When he said 'You other two should understand this,' I said, as sarcastic as I could, 'You other two? We have names, Dad.' Then he said 'Don't be smart' and hit the table. 'I will not have your mother's dignity compromised' just as she came running in. 'I think everyone understands, darling.' He started waving his arms around, 'Blossom, they have the run of this whole place. We should have one place that's ours. One place!' She sat him down and got on his lap. 'Big breaths, darling, big breaths.'"

Ricky and Coral were laughing. "And then you had to ask if he was going to knock on our doors. Mom was mouthing 'big breaths, big breaths,' patting his cheeks. God they were cute."

"He calmed down and sounded like himself, so I asked again if he was going to knock on our doors." Laughing, talking like her father, "'Do you pay the gas and electric? No? How about the garbage? Water? Sewer? Not them either?' I was trying to look as disgusted as I could, but he just went on, 'Taxes, insurance, phones, cable, gardener? None of those, huh? Well, until you do, we can go in any room at any time. But because we want to teach you how to be ladies and gentlemen, out of respect, yes, we will knock on your doors.' Mom was looking at him like he was an oracle or something. Then he said, 'Have we all learned something?' I just stamped out of the room." Then giggling, "He didn't know that what we learned was to ask him things when she was on his lap."

"Yeah," Ricky said, "he was always so mellow then. I better get some work done, sis. I'll call you next week. Love you."

There was one memory Ricky didn't share, had never shared, and never would. He was eleven; the girls were eight. Blossom was on a short break from Pitt. The girls were at the last day of a church camp, staying late for a cookout. He had eaten supper at a friend's up the street, planning to stay and play basketball, but one of the guys had come down hard on his foot, and he limped home early.

He was walking gingerly, concentrating on placing his foot just so and didn't announce himself. He heard their low voices, a hum of tension in the house. It was so unnatural he moved quietly toward them and stopped to the right of the kitchen. She was on his lap but leaning back, both profiles tight, a few things still on the table from their dinner.

"But I know something's bothering you. I saw it when I stopped in today, and it's still there."

"Nothing's bothering me, Blossom, everything's fine," but his fingers were drumming on the table.

"Rocco, we hardly talked during dinner. You're very tense, honey, please tell me."

"Blossom, for god's sake, leave it alone, okay. Let me enjoy my evening home."

Her voice quieter, but sterner, "Darling, I thought after our bad day, we agreed we're a team. Remember?"

"Oh, for Christ's sake. Someone's stealing from the warehouse, okay. It's not only driving me crazy that I can't spot it on the tapes, but that means it's an old-timer who knows where the cameras are. And that means it's someone I consider a friend."

"Oh, darling, I'm so sorry," her sweet voice back to normal. "Let me look at the tapes. Maybe I can spot something."

He put his hands around her waist, stood up rigidly, and set her firmly on the floor. Her eyes widened, her mouth open. "See that's just why I didn't tell you. You always want to fix everything. This is my problem, and I'll take care of it."

"But . . ."

"No buts. It's business. Don't bother your pretty head about it," knowing it was the worst thing to say as soon as it was out.

She turned white but tried to keep her voice level. "My pretty head? That was very demeaning, Rocco. Insulting even."

He couldn't stop. "Yeah, well, how do you think I feel when you want to fix everything? I don't come into your office and tell you how to use that damn computer, do I?"

A sharp intake of breath, "Rocco . . ."

"Don't 'Rocco' me. It's my business. Mine."

Her mouth opened wider, her eyes bigger.

"Go ahead, stamp your foot. See if I care," his voice rising.

Her eyes narrowed, she was breathing hard, her hand reached out and slapped his face. She screamed and ran for the stairs.

It stung, but it was the shock that left him glued to the spot, giving her a few seconds to make it to their bedroom.

When she passed, Ricky sank to the floor, clearly visible behind a chair but not to them. It hit Rocco what he had started, and he flew past Ricky up the stairs. "Blossom, baby, baby, oh god I'm sorry. Baby!" He shrieked as his hand hit the locked door.

"Open the door, baby. It was me. It's all my fault. Please, baby, open the door," jiggling the knob, slapping his palm against the door. "Please, Blossom. I love you, baby. Please open the door, I love you. I'll break it down. You know I *will. Don't make me, baby, I love you, I love you," pounding with his fist now, crying uncontrollably. In agony, "Bloss . . ."*

The door opened. She threw herself into his arms with such force he was knocked back against the wall. They were both sobbing, both trying to cover faces with kisses, his knees so weak he slid down the wall. "I hit you. I hit you like your father. Oh no, oh no, I love you, I love you."

"It's nothing, nothing. I'm sorry, oh my god, I'm so sorry. I don't know what happens. I can't shut up. Dumb words keep coming out of my mouth. Baby, I love you, please, I love you."

They were still in a heap on the floor, still crying, gasping, kissing when Ricky limped out, his tears and nose running over the hand covering his mouth. He made it to some bushes out back before he threw up and collapsed on the ground.

Rocco didn't know how long they were on the floor. When she was whimpering less and the suppressed sobs had lessened, he pushed them up the wall. He couldn't believe how exhausted he was, went to their bathroom, wrung out a cold washcloth with one hand, still cradling her with the other, wiped their faces, and went down to their chair. They still couldn't speak of it. She sat with her head on his chest, patting him when he took ragged breaths. He circled her with both arms, kissing the top of her head, grasping at things that always brought them closer. "We'll go dancing. Want to go dancing? Want to go to dinner? We never get a chance with you at Pitt." He rubbed her back when she muffled a sob.

And that's the way Ricky found them when he limped in an hour later. He listened, felt the usual comfort of the house, so called out to them. Mama took care of his foot, Dad fixed him a philly cheesesteak sub, the girls came home, all was normal and comfortable . . . but he always counted it as the worst day of his life.

Someday he would have a love of his own, but then he was too young to know that deep love can be a gut-wrenching experience. He never knew the aftermath.

She was looking at him with her big beautiful eyes when he slid into bed. "Don't ever lock the door between us, baby. We can't have anything between us."

"What happened," she whispered against his lips," what happened?"

"I'm stupid, that's what happened. That's all that happened, baby girl. I'm stupid and stubborn. I don't know what comes over me sometimes."

"But I hit you, Rocco"—caressing his cheek—"I hit your beautiful face."

"It was nothing, my baby. You were trying to get through to me. Don't even think about it," kissing her hand.

"I'm afraid."

"No. We're not afraid. We're fine, baby girl, we're fine. I love you," kissing her gently, tentatively, rewarded with her hand reaching behind his neck, pulling him closer, the tip of her tongue gently probing. His low moan brought her leg over his hip, and they loved their worries away.

The next morning, shaved, showered, dressed, "Can you stop out to the shop and show me what I'm not seeing, baby?"

"Of course, darling," spreading warmth through him as she stretched under the sheet. "I can do it from here if you like."

"No, come and walk me through it, and I'll buy you lunch. Will the kids be okay?"

"The girls have been getting up early all week for camp, so they'll probably just laze around, and I want Ricky to stay off his foot as much as he can. They'll be fine, and Rosalita will be here in a little while."

He knelt by the side of the bed. "I love you, Blossom Dove," rubbing the little worry frown between her eyebrows. "Open your eyes now and give me a kiss good-bye."

Eyes still closed, she whispered, "We didn't talk enough last night. I think we should talk some more."

"We can talk all you want. Do you want me to stay?"

"No, the children will be knocking on the door if they know you're still here. Tonight."

"Okay. We'll talk all night if you want. But you know, baby doll, it's just going to boil down to I'm a jerk. That's all it is."

"Don't say that! You're not a jerk. I'm a jerk, I hit you. Why are you laughing," indignantly.

"Sweetheart, that coming out of your mouth is just funny." He kissed her forehead. "That's all for now. We'll talk tonight. See you in a while?"

She nodded yes. He stood, winked at her, and whistled down the stairs. The tears poured out so fast; she couldn't wipe them away, so she got up to shower before the kids came in.

They met for lunch at a new steakhouse by the shop. "That's not a lunch," she chided when he ordered a steak.

"It's a filet mignon, it probably won't even be as big as your palm."

She shook her head. "You're getting a salad for supper," smiling a little.

It was inane married couples talk, but he loved it. A little stilted, but he'd take it. He got a little giggle when he fed her a bite of steak and reminded her of their second date. By the end of lunch, he felt they were okay.

They went to the shop. She solved his problem. Reminding him every key had a code and showing him how to bring up the user. She enlarged a faint view *she saw on the tape of a truck at the side door to reinforce the key user's identity and didn't make any suggestions as to what he should do.*

That night he tucked her into his left arm, put her hair behind her ear, "Blossom, my soul, I know you don't like to even think about this, but I am my father's son . . ."

"No. No"—starting to cry—"we don't know that."

"Sweetie, I know what you want to believe in your heart, but you know I have some bad times. You know I do. Because of you, they're few and far between, but let's face it, I do dumb things, and I say dumb things. Saying I'm sorry for last night is just not enough, I know, but I'm so sorry. I don't deserve you, I never have . . ."

"No," strong and firm. "We don't say that. You're the most wonderful person in the world."

"Blossom . . ."

"I mean it. Don't you ever say that. I was the one who was wrong. I hit you."

"That was nothing, baby, and you know it. You're not going to take the blame for this. You always try to do too much. You're at Pitt to please your mother, you don't want to go out when you're home because you think you're neglecting the kids." She opened her mouth, and he put his finger over it. "You say we're partners, but you try to do everything."

"I don't want to talk about this anymore," her pouty lips.

He chuckled. "That's what I figured."

"You're mean and awful," her eyes narrowing.

"I know," kissing her eyes, her nose, rubbing her back, moving down to her hips. "May I have a little kiss?"

"Just a little one"—breathing against his mouth—"'cause we really didn't solve anything."

"Tomorrow," nibbling on her lips. "Tomorrow we'll solve everything," moving his tongue in.

"Everything," she moaned and moved against him.

That story wasn't shared, but others were as the weeks went by. Lily joining in occasionally. They all knew they had had a charmed childhood.

Summer came, college classes were over for Blossom, and she told Neil she wouldn't be coming into the office until fall either. Chet's grandson was moving his company more toward work for the government, so she declined jobs from him as well. Coral found her sleeping all night in Rocco's chair, not for the first time, and suggested they move it out to the great room. "You'll be all stiff in the morning, Mom, curled up like that. It can't be good for you."

"Of course, honey."

"She's too compliant, Ricky." Coral was giving him an update on their weekly call. "She has no requests, no opinions. She's always been sweet about everything, but you knew what she felt."

"How's she eating?"

"Oh, you know. A tablespoon of this, a tablespoon of that. We both started laughing last night when I gave her another chocolate shake at supper. I mean, how many of those things can a person drink."

"How's she sleeping?"

"That's the other thing. Remember when you asked what she wears to bed, and then we got sidetracked. Well, she had been wearing white cotton nightgowns with long sleeves. The other night I went to check on her, and she had on these old blue pajamas with some weird cartoon character on them and hugging that ratty old tiger, and . . ."

He started laughing.

"What?"

"Those are her smurfies. Nix told me about them years ago, and I remember seeing her in them when I was little. She had a pair when she was a teenager that were worn-out, so Dad found the material and had another pair made for her one Christmas. It was before they were married, and I guess Grandma had a bird. She was desperate to keep them apart. She's probably just cold. She's pretty frail. Has Neil looked at her?"

"I don't really like to act as if something's wrong with her."

"Hey, next time he's over, leave the room for something so he can talk to her doctor to doctor. I don't think she'd object to that."

Neil didn't have a chance for the chat.

The weight of carrying on without Rocco lay heavy on her. Two nights later, she went to bed cozy in her smurfies. She turned on her right side like always. She hadn't had any trouble sleeping since Rocco left, after the first couple of horrible nights. She'd conjure up two images to comfort her—the first him behind her watching her back, the second she wrapped in his arms. This night she was especially tired, so very, very tired. She hugged Tiger close, put her chin on his head, and sighed deeply. Drifted far, far away, her eyes filled with light and love, and she heard him. "Blossom? I'm Rocco Carnavale. You were looking at me. Have we met before?"

This time she didn't cry. This time she smiled.

Coral found her in the morning, the smile still there. "Aw, Mom. Aw, jeez . . ." She knew death when she saw it. Had dealt with it hundreds of times in her work. She kissed her forehead, tucked her hair behind her ear, and made her calls.

They carried out all her wishes—dressed her in her wedding dress, around her neck her pearls, her doves, and Rocco's ring; put in his boots, jacket, hat, Tiger, and Coral added her smurfies, lovingly washed and folded. On a beautiful, sunny day, her ashes joined Rocco's at their wedding spot.

Two Saturdays later, Coral took a ride south. She stopped first at Lily's in Santa Fe and then on down to Ricky's in Albuquerque to give them each a stepping stone for their gardens, one of the three she'd had made. They were engraved "If love could have saved you, you would have lived forever," with a small plaque on the bottom: In memory of our beloved parents, Rocco and Blossom Carnavale.

*

*

*

"The Lovers"

The rose did caper on her cheek,
Her bodice rose and fell,
Her pretty speech, like drunken men,
Did stagger pitiful.

Her fingers fumbled at her work,—
Her needle would not go;
What ailed so smart a little maid
It puzzled me to know,

Till opposite I spied a cheek
That bore another rose;
Just opposite, another speech
That like the drunkard goes;

A vest that, like the bodice, danced
To the immortal tune,—
Till those two troubled little clocks
Ticked softly into one.

—Emily Dickinson

Edwards Brothers Malloy
Thorofare, NJ USA
February 11, 2013